The Book of the Year!
COAST-TO-COAST RAVES!

"Good, exciting reading. Once you get into it you are drawn on and on . . . breathtakingly exciting stuff." *Newsday*

"An excellent novel . . . more than entertainment." *Chicago Sun-Times*

"Keeps you up tight, right down to the last paragraph. It's a super reading experience."
The Hartford Courant

"A towering novel . . . powerful and haunting, with mounting, tautening suspense."
Charleston Evening Post

"No doubt this will hit the bookstalls with the same impact as THE GODFATHER."
Cleveland Plain Dealer

"As well written as anything anyone ever committed to paper . . . one of the best detective stories ever written. Profound philosophy and thrill-packed reading marks the skill of a writer who has matured into one of our great ones."
The Pittsburgh Press

"A superlatively readable novel."
Omaha World-Herald

"Unbearable suspense . . . hard to put down."
Fort Worth Press

"An unparalleled time passer." *Time Magazine*

If there was no God, how
could I be a captain?

The Possessed

THE FIRST DEADLY SIN

Lawrence Sanders

A BERKLEY MEDALLION BOOK
PUBLISHED BY G. P. PUTNAM'S SONS
DISTRIBUTED BY BERKLEY PUBLISHING CORPORATION

PART I

1

There was quiet. He lay on his back atop a shaft of stone called Devil's Needle, and felt he was lost, floating in air. Above him, all about him stretched a thin blue sac. Through it he could see scribbles of clouds, a lemon sun.

He heard nothing but his own strong heart, the slowly quieting of his breath as he recovered from his climb. He could believe he was alone in the universe.

Finally he stood and looked around him. Waves of foliage lapped at the base of his stone; it was a dark green ocean with a froth of autumn's russet. He could see the highway, the tarred roofs of Chilton, a steel ribbon of river uncoiling southward to the sea.

The air had the bite of Fall; it moved on a breeze that knifed lungs and tingled bare skin. He gulped this stern air like a drink; there was nothing he might not do.

He moved over to the cleft in the edge of the stone and began hauling up the nylon line clipped to his belt. At the end of the rope was his rucksack. In it were sandwiches, a thermos of black coffee, a first aid kit, spiked clamps for his climbing boots, pitons, an extra sweater and, buckled to the outside, his ice ax.

He had made the sandwiches himself, of stone-ground whole wheat said to be organically grown. The filling of one was sliced onions, of the other white radishes and plum tomatoes.

He sat on the smooth granite and ate slowly. The coffee was still warm, the sandwich bread fresh with a crunchy crust. Out of nowhere a blue jay appeared and greeted him with its two-note whistle. It landed on the stone, stared at him fearlessly. He laughed, tossed a crust. The bird took it up, then dropped it immediately and was gone in an azure flash.

Finished, he replaced sandwich wrappings and thermos in his rucksack. He lay back, using it as a pillow. He turned onto his side, bowing his spine, drawing up his knees. He determined to awake in half an hour. He was asleep almost instantly and dreamed of a woman hairless as a man's palm.

He awoke in half an hour and lighted a cigarette. The day was drawing on; he must be down and out of the park before dark. But there was time to smoke, time for silence, a final coffee, cold now and gritty with dregs.

He had been recently divorced. That was of no concern; it had happened to a stranger. But he was perplexed by what was happening to *him* since he and Gilda had parted. He was assembling a jigsaw puzzle. But he didn't have all the pieces, had no conception of what the completed picture might be.

He pulled off his knitted watch cap, exposing his shaven skull to watery sunlight. He pressed fingers to the smooth, soft skin slid on hard bone.

The divorce had just been obtained (in Mexico) but he had been separated from his wife for almost two years. Shortly after they agreed to live apart, he had shaved his head completely and purchased two wigs. One ("Ivy League") he wore to the office and on formal occasions. The other ("Via Veneto") was crisp curls and ringlets. He wore it to parties or when entertaining at home. Both wigs were in the dark brown shade of his own hair.

It was true his hair had been thinning since he was 24. At the time of his separation from Gilda, when he was 33, the front hairline had receded into a "widow's peak" and there was a small tonsure at the back of his head. But he was far from bald. His remaining hair had gloss and weight.

Nevertheless, he had shaved his entire skull when he purchased the wigs, though the coiffeur assured him it was not necessary; the artificial hair could be blended ("Absolutely undetectable, sir") with his natural hair.

When climbing, or swimming, or simply alone in his apartment, he preferred the shaven pate. He had developed a habit—almost a nervous tic—of caressing it with his fingertips, probing the frail cranium and that perilous stuff that lay beneath.

He pulled on his cap, tugging it down over his ears. He prepared for the descent by donning horsehide gloves, rough side out. He then lowered his rucksack to the boulders below. The end of the line was still clipped to his belt, a wide canvas band similar to that used by professional window washers.

The cleft, by which ascents to and descents from the flat top of Devil's Needle were made, was a chimney. It was a vertical crack in the granite shaft, four feet across at the base. It narrowed as it rose until, at the top, it was barely wide enough for a climber to scrape through to the summit.

The climber braced shoulders and back against one wall of the chimney. He bent his knees, placing the soles of his boots against the opposite wall. He then, literally, walked up the cleft, depending upon the strength of buttocks, thighs and calves to maintain sufficient pressure to keep from falling.

As he took small steps, not relaxing one foot to scrape it upward until the other was firmly planted, he "walked his shoulders" slowly higher—right, left, right, left. He continued tension in his bent legs to keep himself jammed between opposing walls of the chimney.

As the cleft narrowed toward the top of the 65-foot shaft, the climber's legs became increasingly bent until his knees were almost touching his chin and gains upward were measured in inches. At the top, it was necessary to apply pressure with knees instead of feet. The climber then reached up and grabbed two heavy pitons a previous conqueror of Devil's Needle had thoughtfully left embedded in the stone. With their aid, the man ascending could pull himself out of the narrow chimney, over the lip, onto the flat top. It was a bedsheet of stone.

The descent, though more difficult, was not excessively dangerous for an experienced climber. Gripping the pitons, he allowed his body to slide down into the cleft. He started by bracing his knees against one granite wall, his back against the other. Releasing the pitons, he then slowly "walked" downward, until the crack widened sufficiently so he could put the rubber-ridged soles of his boots against the opposing wall.

At this time of day, in September, as he began the descent, the top of Devil's Needle was washed with pale sunshine. But the slit into which he lowered himself was shaded and smelled rankly.

He braced his knees, took a deep breath, released the pitons. He was suspended in gloom, emptiness below. He hung a moment in blemished light, then placed flat hands against the facing wall to take some of the tension off his knees. He started the slow wiggle downward and out.

The cleft spread until it was wide enough to press his feet against the wall. Moving faster now, he twisted, struggled, writhed, his entire body in a steady left-right rhythm, shifting from foot to foot, shoulder to shoulder, until the stretched stone thighs popped him out and he was in murk.

He rested five minutes while his breathing eased. He coiled his nylon line, slung his rucksack. He hiked across boulders, through a meadow, along a dirt road to the ranger's cabin.

The park guardian was an older man, made surly by this visitor's refusal to heed his warning about climbing alone. He shoved the register angrily across the wooden counter. The climber signed in the Out column and noted the time.

His name was Daniel Blank.

2

Under the terms of the separation agreement, Gilda Blank had retained possession of their car: a four-door Buick sedan. Daniel thereupon purchased for himself a Chevrolet Corvette, a powerful machine of racy design. Since buying the sports car he had twice been arrested for speeding. He paid a fine in each case. One more similar violation would result in suspension of his license.

Now, standing beside his car to strip off canvas jacket, wool sweater and cotton T-shirt, he admired the car's clean feminine lines. He toweled off bare skull, face neck shoulders, arms, upper torso. The evening air was astringent as alcohol. He had a sense of healthy well-being. The hard climb, sculpted day, simple food all had left him with the exhilaration of a new start. He was beginning.

Daniel Blank was a tall man, slightly over six feet, and was now slender. In high school and college he had competed in swimming track (220 high hurdles), and tennis individual sports that required no teamwork. These physical activities had given his body a firm sheath of long muscle. His shoulders, pectorals and thighs were well-developed. Hands and feet were narrow fingernails and toenails long. He kept them shaped and buffed.

Shortly after his separation, he had taken a "physical inventory," inspecting his naked body minutely in the full-length mirror on the inside of his bathroom door. He saw at once that deterioration had begun the flesh beneath his jaw had started to sag his shoulders slumped, the lower abdomen protruded it was soft and without tone.

He had at once begun a strict regimen of diet and exercise. In his methodical way he bought several books on nutrition and systems of physical training. He read them all carefully, making notes and devised for himself a program that appealed to him and that he felt would show almost immediate improvement in his physical appearance.

He was not a fanatic. he did not swear off drinking and smoking. But he cut his alcohol intake by half and switched to non-nicotine cigarettes made of dried lettuce leaves. He tried to avoid starches, carbohydrates, dairy products, eggs, blood meats. He ate fresh fruits, vegetables, broiled fish, salads with a dressing of fresh lemon juice Within three months he had lost 20 pounds, his ribs and hip bones showed.

Meanwhile he had started a program of daily exercise, 30 minutes in the morning upon rising, 30 minutes in the evening before retiring.

The exercises Daniel Blank selected for himself came from a manual based on the training of Finnish gymnasts. All the movements were illustrated with photographs of young blonde women in white leotards. But Blank felt this was of no import; only the exercises counted, and these promised increased agility, pliancy, and grace.

The exercises had proved efficacious. His waist was now down to almost 32 inches. Since his hips were wide (though his buttocks were flat) and his chest enlarged from his youthful interest in running and swimming, he had developed a feminine "hourglass" figure All his muscles regained their youthful firmness. His skin was smooth and blood-flushed. Age seemed stayed.

But the diet and exercise had also resulted in several curious side effects His nipples had become permanently engorged and, since he ordinarily wore no undershirt, were obvious beneath the stuff of thin dress shirts or lisle pullovers. He did not find this displeasing. A heavier garment, such as a wool turtleneck sweater worn next to the skin, sometimes resulted in a not unpleasant irritation.

Another unexpected development was the change in appearance of his genitals. The testicles had become somewhat flaccid and hung lower than previously. The penis, while not growing in size (which he knew to be impossible at his age), had altered in color and elasticity. It now seemed to be slightly empurpled in a constant state of mild excitation. This also was not disagreeable It might be caused by agitation against the cloth of the tighter trousers he had purchased.

Finally he found himself free of the diarrhea that had frequently plagued him during his marriage. He ascribed this to his new diet, exercise, or both Whatever the reason, his bowel movements were now regular, without pain, and satisfying. His stool was firm.

He drove toward Manhattan. He had pulled on a fresh velour shirt. The radio was no more than a lulling hum. He followed an unlighted two-laner that led into the Thruway.

9

The speedometer climbed slowly: 50, 60, 70, 80. The car roared to catch the headlight glare. Trees flung backward; billboards and ghost houses grew out of darkness, blazed, flicked back into dark.

He loved speed, not so much for the sensual satisfaction of power as for the sense of lonely dislocation.

It was Saturday night; the Thruway was heavy with traffic pouring into the city. Now he drove with brutal hostility, switching lanes, cutting in and out. He hunched over the wheel, searching for openings to plunge through, for sudden breaks in the pattern enabling him to skin by more cautious drivers.

He came over the bridge; there were the hard edges, sharp corners, cheap lights of Manhattan. Slowed by signals, by trucks and buses, he was forced to move southward at moderate speed. He turned eastward on 96th Street; his city closed in.

It was a city sprung and lurching. It throbbed to a crippled rhythm, celebrated death with insensate glee. Filth pimpled its nightmare streets. The air smelled of ashes. In the schools young children craftily slid heroin into their veins.

A luncheonette owner was shot dead when he could not supply apple pie to a demanding customer. A French tourist was robbed in daylight, then shot and paralyzed. A pregnant woman was raped by three men in a subway station at 10:30 in the morning. Bombs were set. Acid was thrown. Explosions destroyed embassies, banks, and churches. Infants were beaten to death. Glass was shattered, leather slashed, plants uprooted, obscene slogans sprayed on marble monuments. Zoo' ere invaded and small animals torn apart.

His poisoned city staggered in a mad plague dance. A tarnished sun glared down on an unmeaning world. Each man, at night, locked himself within bars, hoping for survival in his iron cage. He huddled in upon himself, hoarding his sanity, and moved through crowded streets glancing over his shoulder, alert to parry the first blow with his own oiled blade.

The apartment house in which Daniel Blank lived was a raw building of glass and enameled steel. It was 34 stories high and occupied an entire city block on East 83rd Street. It was built in a U-shape; a black-topped driveway curved in front of the entrance. A stainless steel portico protruded so that tenants alighting from cars were protected from rain. The entrance step was covered with green outdoor carpeting.

Inside, a desk faced plate glass doors. Doormen were on

duty 24 hours a day. They were able to inspect the underground garage, service entrances, hallways and elevators by closed-circuit TV. Behind them was a wide lobby with chairs and sofas of chrome and black plastic. There were abstract paintings on the walls and, in the center, a heavy bronze sculpture, non-representational, entitled "Birth."

Daniel Blank pulled into an alley alongside the curved driveway. It led down to the garage where tenants, for an additional rental, could park their cars, have them washed, serviced, and delivered to the main entrance when required.

He turned the Corvette over to the attendant on duty. He took his rucksack and outdoor clothes from the car, and rode the escalator to the main lobby. He went to the desk where tenants' mail was distributed, deliveries accepted, messages held.

It was almost 10:00 p.m.; no one was on duty at the mail desk. But one of the doormen went behind the counter. There was no mail in Blank's cubbyhole, but there was a small sheet of paper folded once. It said: "Brunch Sunday (tomorrow) at 11:30. Don't miss. Come early. Thousands of fantastic pipple. Love and kisses. Flo and Sam." He read the note, then tucked it into his shirt pocket.

The doorman, who had not spoken to him nor raised his eyes to Daniel's, went back behind his desk. His name was Charles Lipsky, and he had been involved with Blank in an incident that had occurred about a year previously.

Daniel had been waiting under the portico for a taxi to take him to work. He rarely drove his own car to the office since parking space near Ninth Avenue and 46th Street was almost non-existent. Doorman Lipsky had gone down to the street to whistle up a cab. He halted one and rode it up the driveway. He opened the door for Blank and held out his hand for the usual 25-cent tip.

As Daniel was about to pay him, a man he recognized as a tenant of the building came up the entrance step hauling a German shepherd pup on a long leather leash.

"Heel!" the man was shouting. "Heel!"

But the young dog hung back. Then he lay on the driveway, muzzle down between his paws, and refused to budge.

"Heel, you bastard!" the man screamed. He then struck the dog twice on the head with a folded newspaper he had been carrying under his arm. The dog cringed away. Whereupon the man kicked him heavily in the ribs.

Daniel Blank and Charles Lipsky saw all this clearly. Blank leaped forward. He could not endure the sight of an animal

11

being mistreated; he couldn't even *think* of a horse pulling a load.

"Stop that!" he cried furiously.

The tenant turned on him in outrage. "Mind your own goddamned business!"

He then struck Daniel on the head with his folded newspaper. Blank pushed him angrily. The man staggered back, became entangled in the leather leash, stumbled off the step onto the driveway, fell awkwardly, and broke his left arm. Police were called, and the tenant insisted on charging Daniel Blank with assault.

In time, Blank and Lipsky were summoned to the 251st Precinct house to give sworn statements. Daniel said the tenant had abused his dog, and when he, Daniel, objected, the man had struck him with a folded newspaper. He had not pushed the man until after that first blow. Charles Lipsky corroborated this testimony.

The charge was eventually withdrawn, the case dropped. The dog owner moved from the building. Blank gave Lipsky five dollars for his trouble and thought no more of the matter.

But about six months after this incident, something of a more serious nature happened.

On a Saturday night, lonely and jangling, Daniel Blank put on his "Via Veneto" wig and strolled out into midnight Manhattan. He wore a Swedish blazer of black wool and a French "body shirt" in a lacy polyester weave, cut to cling to the torso. It was a style called *"Chemise de gigolo"* and had a front that opened halfway to the waist. An ornate Maltese cross hung from a silver chain about his neck.

On impulse, nothing else, he stopped at a Third Avenue tavern he had seen before but never entered. It was called "The Parrot." There were two couples at the bar and two single men. No one sat at the tiny tables. The lone waiter was reading a religious tract.

Blank ordered a brandy and lighted a lettuce cigarette. He looked up and, unexpectedly, caught the eye of one of the single men in the mirror behind the bar. Blank shifted his gaze immediately. The man was three seats away. He was about 45, short, soft, with the meaty nose and ruddy face of a bourbon drinker.

The bartender had his radio tuned to WQXR. They were playing Smetana's "The Moldau." The bartender was reading a scratch sheet, marking his choices. The couples had their heads together and were murmuring.

"You have beautiful hair."

Daniel Blank looked up from his drink. "What?"

The porky man had moved onto the barstool next to his.

"Your hair. It's beautiful. Is it a rug?"

His first instinct was to drain his drink, pay, and leave. But why should he? The dim loneliness of The Parrot was a comfort. People together and yet apart: that was the secret.

He ordered another brandy. He turned a shoulder to the man who was hunching closer. The bartender poured the drink, then went back to his handicapping.

"Well?" the man asked.

Blank turned to look at him. "Well what?"

"How about it?"

"How about what?"

Up to now they had been speaking in conversational tones: not loud, but understandable if anyone was interested in listening. No one was.

But suddenly the man leaned forward. He thrust his flabby face close: watery eyes, trembling lips: hopeful and doomed.

"I love you," he whispered with an anxious smile.

Blank hit him in the mouth and toppled him off the stool onto the floor. When the man got up, Blank hit him again, breaking his jaw. He fell again. Blank was frantically kicking him in the groin when the bartender finally came alive and rushed around the bar to pinion his arms and drag him away.

Once again the police were summoned. This time Blank thought it best to call his lawyer, Russell Tamblyn. He came to the 251st Precinct house and, shortly before dawn, the incident was closed.

The injured man who, it was learned, had a sad record of offenses including attempts to molest a child and to proposition a plain-clothed patrolman in a subway toilet—refused to sign a complaint. He said he had been drunk, knew nothing of what had happened, and accepted responsibility for the "unfortunate accident."

The detective who took Daniel Blank's statement was the same man who had taken his testimony in the incident involving the tenant who kicked his dog.

"You again?" the detective asked curiously.

The attorney brought the signed waiver to Daniel Blank, saying, "It's all squared away. He's not making a charge. You're free to go."

"Russ, I told you it wasn't my fault."

"Oh sure. But the man has a broken jaw and possible

internal injuries. Dan, you've got to learn to control yourself."

But that wasn't the end of it. Because the doorman, Charles Lipsky, found out, even though nothing had been published in the newspapers. The bartender at The Parrot was Lipsky's brother-in-law.

A week later the doorman rang the bell of Blank's apartment. After inspection through the peephole, he was admitted. Lipsky immediately launched into a long, jumbled chronicle of his troubles. His wife needed a hernia operation; his daughter needed expensive treatment for an occluded bite; he himself was heavily in debt to loansharks who threatened to break his legs, and he needed five hundred dollars at once.

Blank was bewildered by this recital. He asked what it had to do with him. Lipsky then stammered that he knew what had happened at The Parrot. It wasn't Mr. Blank's fault, certainly, but if other tenants . . . If it became known . . . If people started talking . . .

And then he winked at Daniel Blank.

That knowing wink, that smirky wink, was worse than the victim's whispered, "I love you." Daniel Blank felt attacked by a beast whose bite excited and inflamed. Violence bubbled.

Lipsky must have seen something in his eyes, for he turned suddenly, ran out, slammed the door behind him. Since then they had hardly spoken. When necessary, Blank ordered and the doorman obeyed, never raising his eyes. At Christmas, Daniel distributed the usual amounts: ten dollars to each doorman. He received the usual thank-you card from Charles Lipsky.

Blank pushed the button; the door of the automatic elevator slid silently open. He stepped inside, pushed button C (for Close door), button 21 (for his floor), and button M (for Music desired). He rode upward to the muted strains of "I Got Rhythm."

He lived at the front end of one leg of the building's U. It was an exceptionally large four-room apartment with living room windows facing north, bedroom windows east, and kitchen and bathroom windows west, or really down into the apartment house courtyard. The walk to his door from the elevator was along a carpeted tunnel. The corridor was softly lighted, the many doors blind, air refrigerated and dead.

He unlocked his door, reached in and switched on the foyer light. Then he stepped inside, looked about. He closed the door, double-locked it, put on the chain, adjusted the Police Bar, a burglar-proof device consisting of a heavy steel rod that

14

fitted into a slot in the floor and was propped into a recess bolted to the door.

Mildly hungry, Blank dropped clothing and gear on a foyer chair and went directly to the kitchen. He switched on the blued fluorescent light. He inspected the contents of his refrigerator, selected a small cantaloupe and sliced it in half, at right angles to the stem line. He wrapped half in wax paper and returned it to the refrigerator. He scooped seeds and soft pulp from the other half, then filled the cavity with Familia, a Swiss organic cereal. He squeezed a slice of fresh lemon over all. He ate it steadily, standing, staring at his reflection in the mirror over the kitchen sink.

Finished, he dumped melon rind into the garbage can and rinsed his fingers. Then he moved from room to room, turning the light on in the next before turning it off in the last. Undressing in his bedroom he found the note in his shirt pocket: ". . . Thousands of fantastic pipple . . ." He placed it on his bedside table where he'd see it upon awakening.

He closed the bathroom door tightly before taking a shower so hot it filled the air with heavy steam, clouding the mirrors and sweating the tiles. He lathered with an emollient soap of cocoa butter that slicked his skin. After rinsing in cool water and turning off the shower, he rubbed his wet body with a cosmetically treated tissue claiming to "restore natural oils to dry skin" and "smooth, soften, and lubricate the epidermis."

His twice-a-week maid had been in during the afternoon. His bed was made with fresh sheets and pillowcases. The top sheet and sateen comforter were turned down. It was hardly 11:00 p.m., but he was pleasantly weary and wanted sleep.

Naked, allowing water and tiny oil globules to dry on his exposed body, he moved about the apartment, drawing drapes, checking window latches and door locks. He stepped into the bathroom again to swallow a mild sleeping pill. He felt sure he would not need it, but he didn't want to think in bed.

The long living room was dimly lit by light from the bedroom. The end of the living room faced north, with drapes over wide plate glass windows that could not be opened. The east wall, abutting the bedroom, was almost 25 feet long and nine feet high.

This expanse, painted a flat white, Daniel Blank had decorated with mirrors. He had allowed a space four feet from the floor to accommodate a couch, chairs, end tables, lamps, a bookcase, a wheeled cart of hi-fi equipment. But above the four-foot level, the wall was covered with mirrors.

Not one mirror or fitted tiles of mirrors, but more than fifty individual mirrors adorned that wall; tiny mirrors and large mirrors, flat and beveled, true and exaggerative, round and square, oval and rectangular. The wall quivered with silver reflections.

Each mirror was framed and hung separately: frames of wood and metal, painted and bare, plain and ornate, modern and rococo, carved wood and bland plastic. Some were fogged antiques; one was a 3X4-inch sheet of polished metal: the mirror issued to Marines in World War II.

The mirrors were not arranged in a planned pattern on this nervous wall; they had been hung as they were purchased. But somehow, haphazardly, as the wall filled, frames and reflections had grown an asymmetrical composition. His city was there, sprung and lurching.

Padding back to the bedroom, naked, scented, oiled, Daniel Blank looked to his mirrored wall. He was chopped and fragmented. As he moved, his image jumped, glass to glass. A nose there. Ear. Knee. Chest. Navel. Foot. Elbow. All leaped, were held, disappeared to be born again in something new.

He stopped, fascinated. But even motionless he was minced and snapped, all of him divided by silvered glass that tilted this way and that. He felt himself and saw twenty hands moving, a hundred fingers probing: wonder and delight.

He went into the bedroom, adjusted the air-conditioner thermostat, slid into bed. He fell asleep seeing in the dim glow of the nightlight those myriad eyes reflecting him in framed detail. Waist in steel. Shoulder in carved oak. Neck in plastic. Knee in copper. Penis in worm-eaten walnut.

Art.

3

She had been one of the first women in Manhattan to leave off her brassiere. He had been one of the first men in Manhattan to use a necktie as a belt. She had been one of the first to adopt a workman's lunch pail as a purse. He had been one of the first to wear loafers without socks. The first! A zeal for the new bedeviled them, drove them.

No notice of Florence and Samuel Morton was made in the long, detailed separation agreement signed by the Blanks.

Gilda took the Buick sedan, the Waterford crystal, the Picasso print. Daniel took the apartment lease, 100 shares of U.S. Steel, and the Waring blender. No one mentioned the Mortons. It was tacitly assumed they were Daniel's "best friends," and he was to have them. So he did.

They contradicted the folk saying, "Opposites attract." Husband and wife, they were obverse and reverse of the same coin. Where did Samuel leave off and Florence begin? No one could determine. They were a bifocal image. No. They were a doubled image, both in focus simultaneously.

Physically they were so alike that strangers took them for brother and sister. Short, bony-thin, with helmets of black, oily hair, both had ferrety features, the quick, sharp movements of creatures assailed.

He, married, had been a converter of synthetic textiles. She, married, had been a fabric designer. They met on a picket line protesting a performance of "The Merchant of Venice," and discovered they had the same psychoanalyst. A year later they were divorced, married to each other, and had agreed to have no children because of the population explosion. Both gladly, cheerfully, joyfully, submitted to operations.

Their marriage was two magnets clicking together. They had identical loves, fears, hopes, prejudices, ambitions, tastes, moods, dislikes, despairs. They were one person multiplied by two. They slept together in a king-sized bed, entwined.

They changed their life styles as often as their underwear. They were ahead of everyone. Before it was fashionable, they bought pop art, op-art, and then switched back to realism sooner than art critics. They went through marijuana, amphetamines, barbiturates, speed, and a single, shaking trial of heroin, before returning to dry vermouth on the rocks. They were first to try new restaurants, first to wear Mickey Mouse watches, first to discover new tenors, first to see new movies, plays, ballets, first to wear their sunglasses pushed atop their heads. They explored all New York and spread the word: "This incredible little restaurant in Chinatown . . . The best belly-dancer on the West Side . . . That crazy junk shop on Canal Street . . ."

Born Jews, they found their way to Catholicism via Unitarianism, Methodism, and Episcopalianism (with a brief dabble in Marxism). After converting and confessing once, they found this groovy Evangelical church in Harlem where everyone clapped hands and shouted. Nothing lasted. Everything started. They plunged into Yoga, Zen, and Hare Krishna.

They turned to astrology, took high colonics, and had a whiskered guru to dinner.

They threw themselves in the anti-Vietnam War movement and went to Washington to carry placards, parade and shout slogans. Once Sam was hit on the head by a construction worker. Once Flo was spat upon by a Wall Street executive. Then they spent three weeks in a New Hampshire commune where 21 people slept in one room.

"They did nothing but verbalize!" said Sam.

"No depth, no significance!" said Flo.

"A bad scene!" they said together.

What drove them, what sparked their search for "relevance," their hunger to "communicate," to have a "meaningful dialogue," to find the "cosmic flash," to uncover "universal contact," to, in fact, refashion the universe, was guilt.

Their great talent, the gift they denied because it was so vulgar, was simply this: both had a marvelous ability to make money. The psychedelic designs of Florence sold like mad. Samuel was one of the first men on Seventh Avenue to foresee the potential of the "youth market." They started their own factory. Money poured in.

Both, now in their middle 30's, had been the first with the new. They leeched onto the social chaos of the 1960's: the hippies, flower children, the crazy demand for denim jeans and fringed leather jackets and pioneer skirts and necklaces for men and Indian beads and granny glasses and all the other paraphernalia of the young, taken up so soon by their elders.

The Mortons profited mightily from their perspicacity, but it seemed to them a cheesy kind of talent Without acknowledging it both knew they were growing wealthy from what had begun as a sincere and touching crusade Hence their frantic rushing about from picket line to demonstration, from parade to confrontation They wanted to pay their dues.

In further expiation, they sold the factory (at an enormous profit) and opened a boutique on Madison Avenue, an investment they were happily convinced would be a disaster. It was called "Erotica," based on a unique concept for a store. The idea had come to them while attending religious services of a small Scandinavian sect in Brooklyn which worshipped Thor.

"I'm bored with idleness," he murmured.

"So am I," she murmured.

"A store?" he suggested. "Just to keep busy."

"A shop?" she suggested. "A fun thing."

"A boutique," he said.

"Elegant and expensive," she said. "We'll lose a mint."

"Something different," he mused. "Not hotpants and paper dresses, miniskirts and skinny sweaters, army jackets and newsboy caps. Something really *different*. What do people want?"

"Love?" she mused.

"Oh yes," he nodded. "That's it."

Their boutique, Erotica, sold only items related, however distantly, to love and sex. It sold satin sheets in 14 colors (including black), and a "buttock pillow" advertised merely "for added comfort and convenience." It carried Valentines and books of love poetry; perfumes and incense; phonograph records that established a mood; scented creams and lotions; phallic candles; amorous prints, paintings, etchings and posters; unisex lingerie; lace pajamas for men, leather nightgowns for women; and whips for both. An armed guard had to be hired to eject certain obviously disturbed customers.

Erotica was an instant success. Florence and Samuel Morton became wealthier. Depressed, they turned to blackstrap molasses and acupuncture. Making money was their tragic talent. Their blessing was that they were without malice.

And the first thing Daniel Blank saw upon awaking Sunday morning was the note on his bedside table, the invitation to brunch from Flo and Sam. They would, he remembered fondly, serve things like hot Syrian bread, iced lumpfish, smoked carp, six kinds of herring. Champagne, even.

He padded naked to the front door, unlocked chains and bars, took in his New York *Times*. He went through the ritual of relocking, carried the newspaper to the kitchen, returned to the bedroom, began his 30 minutes of exercise in front of the mirror on the closet door.

It was the quiet Sunday routine he had grown to cherish since living alone. The day and its lazy possibilities stretched ahead in a golden glow. His extensions and sit-ups and bends brought him warm and tingling into a new world; anything was possible.

He showered quickly, gloating to see his dried skin had softened and smoothed. He stood before the medicine cabinet mirror to shave, and wondered once again if he should grow a mustache. Once again he decided against it. It would, he felt, make him look older, although a drooping Fu-Manchu mustache with his glabrous skull might be interesting. Exciting?

His face was coffin-shaped and elegant, small ears set close to the bone. The jaw was slightly aggressive, lips sculpted, freshly colored. The nose was long, somewhat pinched, with elliptic

19

nostrils. His eyes were his best feature: large, widely spaced, with a brown iris. Brows were thick, sharply delineated.

Curiously, he appeared older full-face than in profile. From the front he seemed brooding. Lines were discernible from nose creases to the corners of his mouth. The halves of his face were identical; the effect was that of a religious mask. He rarely blinked and smiled infrequently.

But in profile he looked more alert. His face came alive. There was young expectation there: noble brow, clear eye, straight nose, carved and mildly pouting lips, strong chin. You could see the good bones of cheek and jaw.

He completed shaving, applied "Faun" after-shave lotion, powdered his jaw lightly, sprayed his armpits with a scented antiperspirant. He went back into the bedroom and considered how to dress.

The Mortons with their ". . . Thousands of fantastic pipple . . ." were sure to have a motley selection of the bizarre friends and acquaintances they collected: artists and designers; actors and writers; dancers and directors; with a spicy sprinkling of addicts, whores and arsonists. All, on a Sunday morning, would be informally and wildly costumed.

To be different—aloof from the mob, above the throng—he pulled on his conservative "Ivy League" wig, grey flannel slacks, Gucci loafers, a white cashmere turtleneck sweater, a jacket of suede in a reddish brown. He stuffed a yellow-patterned foulard kerchief in his breast pocket.

He went into the kitchen and brewed a small pot of coffee. He drank two cups black, sitting at the kitchen table and leafing through the magazine section of the Sunday *Times*. The ads proved that current male fashions had become more creative, colorful, and exciting than female.

At precisely 11:30, he locked his front door and took the elevator up to the Mortons' penthouse apartment on the 34th floor.

He was alone in the elevator, there was no one waiting for entrance at the Mortons' door and, when he listened, he could hear no sounds of revelry inside. Perplexed, he rang the bell, expecting the door to be answered by Blanche, the Mortons' live-in maid, or perhaps by a butler hired for the occasion.

But Samuel Morton himself opened the door, stepped quickly out into the corridor, closed but did not latch the door behind him.

He was a vigorous, elfin man, clad in black leather shirt and jeans studded with steel nailheads. He twinkled when he moved. His eyes, shining with glee, were two more nailheads. He put a hand on Daniel Blank's arm.

"Dan," he pleaded, "don't be sore."

Blank groaned theatrically. "Sam, not again? You promised not to. What's *with* you and Flo? Are you professional matchmakers? I told you I can find my own women."

"Look, Dan, is it so terrible? We want you to be happy! Is that so terrible? Your happiness—that's all! All right, blame us. But we're so happy together we want everyone to be happy like us!"

"You promised," Blank accused. "Sam, your cuffs are about a half-inch too long. After that disaster with the jewelry designer, you *promised*. Who's this one?"

Morton stepped closer, whispering . . .

"You won't believe. An original! I swear to God . . ." Here he held up his right hand. ". . . an *original*! She comes into the store last week. She's wearing a sable coat down to her ankles! It's a warm day, but she's wearing an ankle-length fur. And sable! Not mink, Dan—*sable*! And she's beautiful in an off-beat, kinky way. Marilyn Monroe she's not, but she's got this thing. She scares you! Yes. Maybe not beautiful. But something else. Something better! So in she comes wearing this long sable coat. Fifty thousand that coat—at least! And with her is this kid, a boy, maybe eleven, twelve, around there. And he *is* beautiful! The most beautiful boy I've ever seen—and you know I don't swing that way! But she's not married. The kid's her brother. Anyhow, we get to talking, and Flo admires her coat, and it turns out she bought it in Russia. Russia! And she lives in a townhouse on East End Avenue. Can you imagine? East End Avenue! A townhouse! She's got to be loaded. So one thing leads to another, and we invited her up for brunch. So what's so terrible?"

"Did you also tell her you were inviting a friend—male and divorced—who is living in lonely anguish and seeking the companionship of a good woman?"

"No. I swear!"

"Sam, I don't believe you."

"Dan, would I lie to you?"

"Of course. Like your 'thousands of fantastic pipple'."

"Well . . . Flo may have casually mentioned a few neighbors might stop by."

Daniel laughed. Sam grabbed his arm, pulled him close.

"Just take a look, a quick look. Like no woman you've ever met! I swear to you, Dan—an *original*. You have simply got to meet this woman! Even if nothing comes of it—naturally Flo and I are hoping—but even if nothing happens, believe me it will be an experience for you. Here is a new human being! You'll see. You'll see. Her name is Celia Montfort. My name is Sam and her name is Celia. Right away that tells a lot—no?"

The Mortons' apartment was a shambles, thrift shop, rats' nest, charity bazaar, gypsy camp: as incoherent as their lives. They redecorated at least twice a year, and these upheavals had left a squabble of detritus: chairs in Swedish modern, a Victorian love seat, a Sheraton lowboy, a wooden Indian, Chinese vases, chromium lamps, Persian rugs, a barber pole, a Plexiglas table, ormolu ashtrays, Tiffany glass, and paintings in a dozen trendy styles, framed and unframed, hung and propped against the wall.

And everywhere, books, magazines, prints, photographs, newspapers, posters, swatches of cloth, smoking incense, boxes of chocolates, fresh flowers, fashion sketches, broken cigarettes, a bronze screw propeller and a blue bedpan: all mixed, helter-skelter, as if giant salad forks had dug into the furnishings of the apartment, tossed them to the ceiling, allowed them to flutter down as they would, pile up, tilt, overlap, and create a setting of frenzied disorder that stunned visitors but proved marvelously comfortable and relaxing.

Sam Morton led Daniel to the entrance of the living room, tugging him along by the arm, fearful of his escaping. Blank waved a hand at Blanche, working in the kitchen, as he passed.

In the living room, Flo Morton smiled and blew a kiss to Dan. He turned from her to look at the woman who had been speaking when they entered, and who would not stop to acknowledge their presence.

"It is bad logic and worse semantics," she was saying in a voice curiously devoid of tone and inflection. " 'Black is beautiful'? It's like saying 'Down is up.' I know they mean to affirm their existence and assert their pride. But they have chosen a battlecry no one, not even themselves, can believe. Because words have more than meaning, you see. The meaning of words is merely the skeleton, almost as basic as the spelling. But words also have emotional weight. The simplest, most innocent words—as far as definition is concerned—can be an absolute horror emotionally. A word that looks plain and unassuming when written or printed can stir us to murder or delight. 'Black is beautiful'? To the human race, to whites, blacks, yellows, reds, black can *never* be beautiful. Black is evil and will always seem so. For black is darkness, and that is where fears lie and nightmares are born. Blackhearted. Black sheep of the family. Black art: the magic practised by witches. Black mass. These are not racial slurs. They spring from man's primitive fear of the dark. Black is the time or place without light, where dangers lurk, and death. Children are naturally afraid of the dark. It is not taught them; they are born with it. And even some adults sleep with a nightlight. 'Behave yourself or the boogie man will get you.' I imagine even Negro children are told that. The 'boogie'—a black monster who comes out of the dark, the perilous dark. Black is the unknowable. Black is danger. Black is evil. Black is death. But 'Black is beautiful'? Never. They'll never get anyone to believe that. We are all animals. I don't believe we've been introduced."

She raised her eyes to look directly at Daniel Blank. He was startled. He had been so engrossed with her lecture, so intent on following her thought, that he had no clear idea of what she looked like. Now, as Florence Morton hastily introduced them, as he crossed the room to take Celia Montfort's proffered hand, he inspected her closely.

She sat curled up in the softness of a big armchair that was all foam, red velvet and cigarette burns. Strangely, for a Sunday morning, she was wearing an elegant evening shift of black satin. The neckline was straight across, the dress suspended from bare shoulders by "spaghetti straps." She wore a thin choker of diamonds, and on the wrist of the hand she held out to Blank was a matching bracelet. He wondered if perhaps she had been to an all-night party and had been unable to go home to change. He thought so when he saw the silk evening slippers.

Her hair was so black it was almost purple, parted in the middle, and fell loosely below her shoulders without wave or curl. It gave her thin face a witch-like appearance, enhanced by long, slender hands, tapering fingers with stiletto nails.

Her bare arms, shoulders, the tops of her small breasts revealed by the low-cut gown: all gleamed against the red velvet. There was a peculiar, limpid *nakedness* to her flesh. The arms were particularly sensual: smooth, hairless, as seemingly boneless as tentacles: arms squeezed from tubes.

It was difficult to estimate her height or appreciate her figure while she was coiled into the armchair. Blank judged her a tall woman, perhaps five foot six or more, with a good waist, flat hips, hard thighs. But at the moment all that was of little importance to him; her face bewitched him, her eyes locked with his.

23

They were grey eyes, or were they a light blue? Her thin brows were arched, or were they straight? Her nose was— what? An Egyptian nose? A nose from a sarcophagus or bas-relief? And those parted lips: were they full and dry, or flat and moist? The long chin, like the toe of her silk slipper—was that enchanting or perhaps too masculine? As Sam Morton had said, not beautiful. But something there. Something better? It needed study.

He had the impression that at this time, noon on a bright Sunday, wearing Saturday night's stale finery, her face and body were smudged with weariness. There was a languor in her posture, her skin was pallid, and faint violet shadows were beneath her eyes. She had the scent of debauchery, and her toneless voice came from senses punished beyond feeling and passions spent.

Florence and Samuel immediately launched into a violent denunciation of her "Black is beautiful" comments. Daniel watched to see how she reacted to this assault. He saw at once she had the gift of repose: no twistings there, no squirmings, no fiddling with bracelet, fluffing hair, touching ears. She sat quietly, composed, and Daniel suddenly realized she was not listening to her critics. She was withdrawn from all of them.

She was gone but not, he guessed, day-dreaming. She was not floating; she had pulled back within herself, sinking deeper into her own thoughts, hungers, hopes. Those eyes, indecipherable as water, attended them, but he had a sense of her estrangement. He wanted to be in her country, if only for a visit, to look around and see what the place was like.

Flo paused for an answer to a question. But there was no answer. Celia Montfort merely regarded her with a somewhat glassy stare, her face expressionless. The moment was saved by the entrance of Blanche, pushing a big-three-shelved cart laden with hot and cold dishes, a pitcher of Bloody Marys, an iced bottle of sparkling rosé.

The food was less unconventional than Blank had hoped, but still the poached eggs were sherried, the ham was in burgundy sauce, the mushroom omelette brandied, the walnut waffles swimming in rum-flavored maple syrup.

"Eat!" commanded Flo.

"Enjoy!" commanded Sam.

Daniel had a single poached egg, a strip of bacon, a glass of wine. Then he settled back with a bunch of chilled Concord grapes, listening to the Mortons' chatter, watching Celia Montfort silently and intently devour an immense amount of food.

Afterward they had small, warmed Portuguese brandies. Daniel and the Mortons carried on a desultory conversation about Art Deco, a current fad. Celia's opinion was asked, but she shook her head. "I know nothing about it." After that she sat quietly, brandy glass clasped in both hands, eyes brooding. She had no talent for small talk. Complain of bad weather and she might he thought, deliver you a sermon on humility. Strange woman. What was it Sam had said— "She scares you." Why on earth should he have said that—unless he was referring to her disturbing silences, her alienation: which might be nothing more than egoism and bad manners.

She rose suddenly to her feet and, for the first time, Blank saw her body clearly. As he had guessed, she was tall, but thinner and harder than he had suspected. She carried herself well, moved with a sinuous grace, and her infrequent gestures were small and controlled.

She said she must go, giving Flo and Sam a bleak smile. She thanked them politely for their hospitality. Flo brought her coat: a cape of weighted silk brocade, as dazzling as a matador's jacket. Blank was now convinced she had not been home to that East End Avenue townhouse since Saturday evening, nor slept at all the previous night.

She moved to the door. Flo and Sam looked at him expectantly.

"May I see you home?" he asked.

She looked at him thoughtfully.

"Yes," she said finally. "You may."

The Mortons exchanged a rapid glance of triumph. They waited in the hallway, in their studded jumpsuits, grinning like idiots, until the elevator door shut them away.

In the elevator, unexpectedly, she asked: "You live in this building, don't you?"

"Yes. The twenty-first floor."

"Let's go there."

Ten minutes later she was in his bedroom, brocaded cape dropped to the floor, and fast asleep atop the covers of his bed, fully clothed. He picked up her cape, hung it away, slipped off her shoes and placed them neatly alongside the bed. Then he closed the door softly, went back into the living room to read the Sunday New York *Times,* and tried not to think of the strange woman sleeping in his bed.

At 4:30, finished with his paper, he looked in upon her. She was lying face up on the pillows, her great mass of black hair fanned out. He was stirred. From the shoulders down she had turned onto her side and slept holding her bare arms. He took a light wool blanket from the linen closet and covered her gently. Then he went into the kitchen to eat a peeled apple and swallow a yeast tablet.

An hour later he was seated in the dim living room, trying to recall her features and understand why he was so intrigued by her sufficiency. The look of the sorceress, the mysterious wizard, could be due, he decided, to the way she wore her long, straight hair and the fact, as he suddenly realized, that she wore no make-up at all: no powder, no lipstick, no eyeshadow. Her face was naked.

He heard her moving about. The bathroom door closed; the toilet was flushed. He switched on lamps. When she came into the living room he noted that she had put on her shoes and combed her hair smooth.

"Don't you ever wear any make-up?" he asked her.

She stared at him a long moment.

"Occasionally I rouge my nipples."

He gave her a sardonic smile. "Isn't that in poor taste?"

She caught his lewd meaning at once. "Witty man," she said in her toneless voice. "Might I have a vodka? Straight. Lots of ice, please. And a wedge of lime, if you have it."

When he came back with identical drinks for both, she was curled up on his Tobia Scarpa sofa, her face softly illuminated by a Marc Lepage inflatable lamp. He saw at once her weariness had vanished with sleep; she was serene. But with a shock he saw something he had not noticed before: a fist-sized bruise on the bicep of her left arm: purple and angry.

She took the drink from his hand. Her fingers were cool, bloodless as plastic.

"I like your apartment," she said.

Under the terms of the separation agreement, Gilda Blank had taken most of the antiques, the overstuffed furniture, the velvet drapes, the shag rugs. Daniel was happy to see it all go. The apartment had come to stifle him. He felt muffled by all that carved wood and heavy cloth: soft things that burdened, then swaddled him.

He had redecorated the almost empty apartment in severe modern, most of the things from Knoll. There was chrome and glass, black leather and plastic, stainless steel and white enamel. The apartment was now open, airy, almost spidery in its delicacy. He kept furniture to a minimum, leaving the good proportions of the living room to make their own statement.

The mirrored wall was cluttered wit, but otherwise the room was clean, precise, and exalting as a museum gallery.

"A room like this proves you don't require roots," she told him. "You have destroyed the past by ignoring it. Most people have a need for history, to live in a setting that constantly reminds of past generations. They take comfort and meaning from feeling themselves part of the flow, what was, is, will be. I think that is a weak, shameful emotion. It takes strength to break free, forget the past and deny the future. That's what this room does. Here you can exist by yourself, in yourself, with no crutches. The room is without sentiment. Are you without sentiment?"

"Oh," he said, "I don't think so. Without emotion perhaps. Is your apartment in modern? As austere as this?"

"It is not an apartment. It's a townhouse. It belongs to my parents."

"Ah. They are still living then?"

"Yes," she said. "They are still living."

"I understand you live with your brother."

"His name is Anthony. Tony. He's twenty years younger than I. Mother had him late in life. It was an embarrassment to her. She and my father prefer him to live with me."

"And where do they live?"

"Oh, here and there," she said vaguely. "There is one thing I don't like about this room."

"What is that?"

She pointed to a black cast iron candelabrum with twelve contorted arms. Fitted to each was a white taper.

"I don't like unburned candles," she said tonelessly. "They seem to me as dishonest as plastic flowers and wallpaper printed to look like brick."

"Easily remedied," he said, rose and slowly lighted the candles.

"Yes," she said. "That's better."

"Are you ready for another drink?"

"Bring the vodka and a bucket of ice out here. Then you won't have to run back and forth."

"Yes," he said, "I will."

When he returned, she had snuffed three of the tapers. She added ice and vodka to her glass.

"We'll snuff them at intervals. So they will be in various lengths. I'm glad you have the dripless kind. I like candles, but I don't like leavings of dead wax."

"Memories of past pleasures?"

"Something like that. But also too reminiscent of bad Italian restaurants with candles in empty Chianti bottles and too much powdered garlic in the sauce. I hate fakery. Rhinestones and padded brassieres."

"My wife—" he started. "My ex-wife—" he amended, "wore a padded bra. The strange thing was that she didn't need it. She was very well endowed. Is."

"Tell me about her."

"Gilda? A very pleasant woman. We're both from Indiana. We met at the University. A blind date. I was a year ahead of her. We went together occasionally. Nothing serious. I came to New York. Then she came here, a year later, and we started seeing each other again. Serious, this time."

"What was she like? Physically, I mean."

"A large woman, with a tendency to put on weight. She loved rich food. Her mother is enormous. Gilda is blonde. What you'd call a 'handsome woman.' A good athlete. Swimming, tennis, golf, skiing—all that. Very active in charities, social organizations. Took lessons in bridge, Chinese cooking, and music appreciation. Things like that."

"No children?"

"No."

"How long were you married?"

"Ahh . . ." He stared at her. "My God, I can't remember. Of course. Seven years. Almost eight. Yes, that's right. Almost eight years."

"You didn't want children?"

"I didn't—no."

"She?"

"Yes."

"Is that why you divorced?"

"Oh no. No, that had nothing to do with it. We divorced because—well, why did we divorce? Incompatibility, I guess. We just grew apart. She went her way and I went mine."

"What was her way?"

"You're very personal."

"Yes. You can always refuse to answer."

"Well, Gilda is a very healthy, well-adjusted, out-going woman. She likes people, likes children, parties, picnics, the theatre, church. Whenever we went to the theatre or a movie where the audience was asked to sing along with the entertainer or music, she would sing along. That's the kind of woman she was."

"A sing-alonger with a padded brassiere."

"And plastic flowers," he added. "Well, not plastic. But she did buy a dozen roses made of silk. I couldn't convince her they were wrong."

He rose to blow out another three candles. He came back to sit in his Eames chair. Suddenly she came over to sit on the hassock in front of him. She put a light hand on his knee.

"What happened?" she whispered.

"You guessed?" he said, not surprised. "A strange story. I don't understand it myself."

"Have you told the Mortons?"

"My God, no. I've told no one."

"But you want to tell me?"

"Yes. I want to tell you. And I want you to explain it to me. Well, Gilda is a normal, healthy woman who enjoys sex. I do too. Our sex was very good. It really was. At the start anyway. But you know, you get older and it doesn't seem so important. To her, anyway. But I don't mean to put her down. She was good and enthusiastic in bed. Perhaps unimaginative. Sometimes she'd laugh at me. But a normal, healthy woman."

"You keep saying healthy, healthy, healthy."

"Well, she was. Is. A big, healthy woman. Big legs. Big breasts. A glow to her skin. Rubens would have loved her. Well . . . about three years ago we took a summer place for the season on Barnegat Bay. You know where that is?"

"No."

"The Jersey shore. South of Bay Head. It was beautiful. Fine beach, white sand, not too crowded. One afternoon we had some neighbors over for a cook-out. We all had a lot to drink. It was fun. We were all in bathing suits, and we'd drink, get a little buzz on, and then go into the ocean to swim and sober up, and then eat and drink some more. It was a wonderful afternoon. Eventually everyone went home. Gilda and I were alone. Maybe a little drunk, hot from the sun and food and laughing. We went back into our cottage and decided to have sex. So we took off our bathing suits. But we kept our sunglasses on."

"Oh."

"I don't know why we did it, but we did. Maybe we thought it was funny. Anyway, we made love wearing those dark, blank glasses so we couldn't see each other's eyes."

"Did you like it?"

"The sex? For me it was a revelation, a door opening. I guess Gilda thought it was funny and forgot it. I can never forget it. It was the most sexually exciting thing I've ever done in my life. There was something primitive and frightening about it. It's hard to explain. But it shook me. I wanted to do it again."

"But she didn't?"

"That's right. Even after we came back to New York and it was winter, I suggested we wear sunglasses in bed, but she wouldn't. I suppose you think I'm crazy?"

"Is that the end of the story?"

"No. There's more. Wait until I blow out more candles."

"I'll get them."

She snuffed out three more tapers. Only three were left burning, getting down close to the iron sockets. She came back to sit on the ottoman again.

"Go on."

"Well, I was browsing around Brentano's—this was the winter right after Barnegat Bay—and Brentano's, you know, carries a lot of museum-type things: antique jewelry and semi-precious stones, coral and native handicrafts. Stuff like that. Well, they had a collection of African masks they were selling. Very primitive. Strong and somehow frightening. You know the effect primitive African art has. It touches something very deep, very mysterious. Well, I wanted to have sex with Gilda while we both wore those masks. An irrational feeling, I know. I knew it at the time, but I couldn't resist. So I bought two masks—they weren't cheap—and brought them home. Gilda didn't like them and didn't dislike them. But she let me hang them in the hallway out there. A few weeks later we had a lot to drink—"

"You got her drunk."

"I guess. But she wouldn't do it. She wouldn't wear one of those masks in bed. She said I was crazy. Anyway, the next day she threw the masks away. Or burned them, or gave them away, or something. They were gone when I got home."

"And then you were divorced?"

"Well, not just because of the sunglasses and the African masks. There were other things. We had been growing apart for some time. But the business with the masks was certainly a contributing factor. Strange story—no?"

She got up to extinguish the three remaining candles. They smoked a bit, and she licked her fingers, then damped the wicks. She poured both of them a little more vodka, then regarded the candelabrum, head cocked to one side.

"That's better."

"Yes," he agreed. "It is."

"Do you have a cigarette?"

"I smoke a kind made from dried lettuce leaves. Non-nicotine. But I have the regular kind too. Which would you like?"

"The poisonous variety."

He lighted it for her, and she strolled up and down before the mirrored wall, holding her elbows. Her head was bent forward; long hair hid her face.

"No," she said, "I don't believe it was irrational. And I don't believe you're crazy. I'm talking now about the sunglasses and the masks. You see, there was a time when sex itself, by itself, had a power, a mystery, an awe it no longer has. Today it's 'Shall we have another martini or shall we fuck?' The act itself has no more meaning than a second dessert. In an effort to restore the meaning, people try to increase the pleasure. They use all kinds of gadgets, but all they do is add to the mechanization of sex. It's the wrong remedy. Sex is not solely, or even mainly, physical pleasure. Sex is a rite. And the only way to restore its meaning is to bring to it the trappings of a ceremony. That's why I was so delighted to discover the Mortons' shop. Probably without realizing it, they sensed that today the psychic satisfactions of sex have become more important than physical gratification. Sex has become, or should become, a dramatic art. It was once, in several cultures. And the Mortons have made a start in providing the make-up, costumes, and scenery for the play. It is only a start, but it is a good one. Now about you . . . I think you became, if not bored then at least dissatisfied with sex with your 'healthy, normal' wife. 'Is this all there is?' you asked. 'Is there nothing more?' Of course there is more. Much, much more. And you were on the right track when you spoke about 'a revelation . . . a door opening' when you made love wearing sunglasses. And when you said the African masks were 'primitive' and 'somehow frightening.' You have, in effect, discovered the unknown or disregarded side of sex: its psychic fulfillment. Having become aware of it, you suspect—rightly so—that its spiritual satisfactions can far surpass physical pleasure. After all, there are a limited number of orifices and mucous membranes in the human body. In other words, you are beginning to see sex as a religious rite and a dramatic ceremony. The masks were merely the first step in this direction. Too bad your wife couldn't see it that way."

"Yes," he said. "Too bad."

"I must be going," she said abruptly, and marched into the bedroom to retrieve her cape.

"I'll see you home," he said eagerly.

"No. That won't be necessary. I'll take a cab."

"At least let me come down to call a cab for you."

"Please don't."

"I want to see you again. May I call you?"

"Yes."

She was out the door and gone almost before he was aware of it. The smell of snuffed candles and old smoke lingered in the room.

He turned out the lights and sat a long time in darkness, pondering what she had said. Something in him responded to it. He began to glimpse the final picture that might be assembled from the bits and pieces of his thought and behavior that had, until now, puzzled him so. That final picture shocked him, but he was neither frightened nor dismayed.

Once, late in the previous summer, he had been admiring his naked, newly slender and tanned body in the bedroom mirror. Only the nightlight was on. His flesh was sheened with its dim, rosy glow.

He noted how strange and somehow exciting the gold chain of his wrist watch looked against his skin. There was something there . . . A week later he purchased a woman's belt, made of heavy, gold-plated links. He specified a chain adjustable to all sizes, and then had it gift-wrapped for reasons he could not comprehend.

Now, only hours after he had first met Celia Montfort, after she had slept in his bed, after she had listened to him and spoken to him, he stood naked again before the bedroom mirror, the room illuminated only by the caressing nightlight. About his wrist was the gold chain of his watch, and around his slim waist was the linked belt.

He stared, fascinated. Chained, he touched himself.

4

Javis-Bircham Publications, Inc. owned the office building, and occupied the top fifteen floors, on 46th Street west of Ninth Avenue. The building had been erected in the late 1930s, and was designed in the massive, pyramidal style of the period, with trim and decoration modeled after that of Rockefeller Center.

Javis-Bircham published trade magazines, textbooks, and technical journals. When Daniel Blank was hired, six years previously, the company was publishing 129 different periodicals relating to the chemical industry, oil and petroleum, engineering, business management, automotive, machine tools, and aviation. In recent years magazines had been added on automation, computer technology, industrial pollution, oceanography, space exploration, and a consumer monthly on research and development. Also, a technical book club had been started, and the corporation was currently exploring the possibilities of short, weekly newsletters in fields covered by its monthly and bi-monthly trade magazines. Javis-Bircham had been listed as number 216 in Fortune Magazine's most recent list of America's 500 largest corporations. It had gone public in 1951 and its stock, after a 3-1 split in 1962, showed a 20-fold increase in its Big Board price.

Daniel Blank had been hired as Assistant Circulation Manager. His previous jobs had been as Subscription Fulfillment Manager and Circulation Manager on consumer periodicals. The three magazines on which he had worked prior to his employment at Javis-Bircham had since died. Blank, who saw what was happening, had survived, in a better job, at a salary he would have considered a hopeless dream ten years ago.

His first reaction to the circulation set-up at Javis-Bircham was unequivocal. "It's a fucked-up mess," he told his wife.

Blank's immediate superior was the Circulation Manager, a beefy, genial man named Robert White, called "Bob" by everyone, including secretaries and mailroom boys. This was, Blank thought, a measure of the man.

White had been at Javis-Bircham for 25 years and had surrounded himself with a staff of more than 50 males and females who seemed, to Blank, all "old women" who smelled of lavender and whiskey sours, arrived late for work, and were continually taking up office collections for birthdays, deaths, marriages, and retirements.

The main duty of the Circulation Department was to supply to the Production Department "print-run estimates": the number of copies of each magazine that should be printed to insure maximum profit for Javis-Bircham. The magazines might be weeklies, semi-monthlies, monthlies, quarterlies, semi-annuals or annuals. They might be given away to a managerial-level readership or sold by subscription. Some were even available to the general public on newsstands. Most of the magazines earned their way by advertising revenue. Some carried no advertising at all, but were of such a specialized nature that they sold solely on the value of their editorial content.

Estimating the "press run" of each magazine for maximum profitability was an incredibly complex task. Past and potential circulation of each periodical had to be considered, current and projected advertising revenue, share of general overhead, costs of actual printing—quality of paper, desired process, four-color plates, etc.—costs of mailing and distributing, editorial budget (including personnel), publicity and public relations campaigns, etc., etc.

At the time Daniel Blank joined the organization, this bewildering job of "print-run estimation" seemed to be done "by guess and by God." Happy Bob White's staff of "old women" fed him information, laughing a great deal during their conversations with him. Then, when a recommendation was due, White would sit at his desk, humming, with an ancient slide rule in his hands, and within an hour or so would send his estimate to the Production Department.

Daniel Blank saw immediately that there were so many variables involved that the system screamed for computerization. His experience with computers was minimal; on previous jobs he had been involved mostly with relatively simple data-processing machines.

He therefore enrolled for a six months' night course in "The Triumph of the Computer." Two years after starting work at Javis-Bircham, he presented to Bob White a 30-page carefully organized and cogently reasoned prospectus on the advantages of a computerized Circulation Department.

White took it home over the weekend to read. He returned it to Blank on Monday morning. Pages were marked with brown rings from coffee cups, and one page had been crinkled and almost obliterated by a spilled drink.

White took Daniel to lunch and, smiling, explained why Blank's plan wouldn't do. It wouldn't do at all.

"You obviously put a lot of work and thought into it," White said, "but you're forgetting the personalities involved. The people. My God, Dan, I have lunch with the editors and advertising managers of those magazines almost every day. They're my friends. They all have plans for their books: an article that might get a lot of publicity and boost circulation, a new hot-shot advertising salesman who might boost revenue way over the same month last year. I've got to consider all those personal things. The human factors involved. You can't feed that into a computer."

Daniel Blank nodded understandingly. An hour after they returned from lunch he had a clean copy of his prospectus on the desk of the Executive Vice President.

A month later the Circulation Department was shocked to learn that laughing Bob White had retired. Daniel Blank was appointed Circulation *Director*, a title he chose himself, and given a free hand.

Within a year all the "old women" were gone, Blank had surrounded himself with a young staff of pale technicians, and the cabinets of AMROK II occupied half the 30th floor of the Javis-Bircham Building. As Blank had predicted, not only did the computer and auxiliary data-processing machines handle all the problems of circulation—subscription fulfillment and print-run estimation—but they performed these tasks so swiftly that they could also be used for salary checks, personnel records, and pension programs. As a result, Javis-Bircham was able to dismiss more than 500 employees and, as Blank had carefully pointed out in his original prospectus, the annual leasing of the extremely expensive AMROK II resulted in an appreciable tax deduction.

Daniel Blank was currently earning $55,000 a year and had an unlimited expense account, a very advantageous pension and stock option plan. He was 36.

About a month after he took over, he received a very strange postcard from Bob White. It said merely: "What are you feeding the computer? Ha-ha."

Blank puzzled over this. What had been fed the computer, of course, were the past circulation and advertising revenue figures and profit or loss totals of all the magazines Javis-Bircham published. Admittedly, White had been working his worn slide rule during most of the years from which those figures were taken, and it was possible to say that, in a sense, White had programmed the computer. But still, the postcard made little sense, and Daniel Blank wondered why his former boss had bothered to send it.

It was gratifying to hear the uniformed starter say, "Good morning, Mr. Blank," and it was gratifying to ride the Executive Elevator in solitary comfort to the 30th floor. His personal office was a corner suite with wall-to-wall carpeting, a private lavatory and, not a desk, but a table: a tremendous slab of distressed walnut on a wrought-iron base. These things counted.

He had deliberately chosen for his personal secretary a bony,

28-year-old widow, Mrs. Cleek, who needed the job badly and would be grateful. She had proved as efficient and colorless as he had hoped. She had a few odd habits: she insisted on latching all doors and cabinets that were slightly ajar, and she was continually lining up the edges of ashtrays and papers with the edges of tables and desks, putting everything parallel or at precise right angles. A picture hanging askew drove her mad. But these were minor tics.

When he entered his office, she was ready to hang away his coat and hat in the small closet. His black coffee was waiting for him, steaming, on a small plastic tray on the table, having been delivered by the commissary on the 20th floor.

"Good morning, Mr Blank," she said in her watery voice, consulting a stenographer's pad she held. "You have a meeting at ten-thirty with the Pension Board. Lunch at twelve-thirty at the Plaza with Acme. regarding the servicing contract. I tried to confirm, but no one's in yet. I'll try again."

"Thank you," he said. "I like your dress. Is it new?"

"No," she said.

"I'll be in the Computer Room until the Pension Board meeting, in case you need me."

"Yes, Mr Blank."

The embarrassing truth was that, as Mrs. Cleek was probably aware, he had nothing to do. It was true he was overseer of an extremely important department—perhaps *the* most important department- of a large corporation. But, literally, he found it difficult to fill his working day.

He could have given the impression of working. Many executives in similar circumstances did exactly that. He could accept invitations to luncheons easily avoided. He could stalk corridors carrying papers over which he could frown and shake his head. He could request technical literature on supplies and computer systems utterly inadequate or too sophisticated for Javis-Bircham's needs, with a heavy increase of unnecessary correspondence He could take senseless business trips to inspect the operations of magazine wholesalers and printing plants. He could attend dozens of conventions and trade meetings, give speeches and buy the bodies of hat-check girls.

But none of that was his style. He needed work; he could not endure inaction for long. And so he turned to "empire building," plotting how he might enlarge the size of the Circulation Department and increase his own influence and power.

And in his personal life he felt the same need for action

after the brief hibernation following his divorce (during which period he vowed, inexplicably, to remain continent). This desire to "do" dated from his meeting with Celia Montfort. He punched his phone for an outside line, then dialed her number. Again.

He had not seen her nor had he spoken to her since that Sunday he was introduced at the Mortons' and she had napped on his bed. He had looked her up in the Manhattan directory. There it was: "Montfort, C." at an East End address. But each time he called, a male voice answered, lisping: "Mith Montforth rethidenth."

Blank assumed it was a butler or houseman. The voice, in spite of its flutiness, was too mature to be that of the 12-year-old brother. Each time he was informed that Mith Montfort was out of town and, no, the speaker did not know when she might return.

But this time the reply was different. It was "Mith Montforth rethidenth" again, but additional information was offered: Miss Montfort had arrived, had called from the airport, and if Mr. Blank cared to phone later in the day, Mith Montforth would undoubtedly be at home.

He hung up, feeling a steaming hope. He trusted his instincts, though he could not always say *why* he acted as he did. He was convinced there was something there for him with that strange, disturbing woman: something significant. If he had energy and the courage to act . . .

Daniel Blank stepped into the open lobby of the Computer Room and nodded to the receptionist. He went directly to the large white enameled cabinet to the right of the inner doors and drew out a sterile duster and skull cap hermetically sealed in a clear plastic bag.

He donned white cap and duster, went through the first pair of swinging glass doors. Six feet away was the second pair, and the space between was called the "air lock," although it was not sealed. It was illuminated by cold blue fluorescent lights said to have a germicidal effect. He paused a moment to watch the ordered activity in the Computer Room.

AMROK II worked 24 hours a day and was cared for by three shifts of acolytes, 20 in each shift. Blank was gratified to note that all on the morning shift were wearing the required disposable paper caps and dusters. Four men sat at a stainless steel table; the others, young men and women, sexless in their white paper costumes, attended the computer and auxiliary data-processing machines, one of which was presently chatter-

37

ing softly and spewing out an endless record that folded up neatly into partly serrated sheets in a wire basket. It was, Blank knew, a compilation of state unemployment insurance taxes.

The mutter of this machine and the soft start-stop whir of tape reels on another were the only sounds heard when Blank pushed through the second pair of swinging glass doors. The prohibition against unnecessary noise was rigidly enforced. And this glaring, open room was not only silent, it was dust-proof, with temperature and humidity rigidly controlled and monitored. An automatic alarm would be triggered by any unusual source of magnetic radiation. Fire was unthinkable. Not only was smoking prohibited but even the mere possession of matches or cigarette lighters was grounds for instant dismissal. The walls were unpainted stainless steel, the lamps fluorescent. The Computer Room was an unadorned vault, an operating theatre, floating on rubber mountings within the supporting body of the Javis-Bircham Building.

And 90 percent of this was sheer nonsense, humbuggery. This was not an atomic research facility, nor a laboratory dealing with deadly viruses. The business activities of AMROK II did not demand these absurd precautions—the sterile caps and gowns, the "air lock," the prohibition against normal conversation.

Daniel Blank had decreed all this, deliberately. Even before it was installed and operating, he realized the functioning of AMROK II would be an awesome mystery to most of the employees of Javis-Bircham, including Blank's superiors: vice presidents, the president, the board of directors. Blank intended to keep the activities of the Computer Room an enigma. Not only did it insure his importance to the firm, but it made his task much easier when the annual "budget day" rolled around and he requested consistently rising amounts for his department's operating expenses.

Blank went immediately to the stainless steel table where the four young men were deep in whispered conversation. This was his Task Force X-1, the best technicians of the morning shift. Blank had set them a problem that was still "Top Secret" within this room.

From his boredom, in his desire to extend the importance of the Circulation Department and increase his personal power and influence, Blank had decided he should have the responsibility of deciding for each magazine the proportion between editorial pages and advertising pages. Years ago this ratio was

38

dictated in a rough fashion by the limitations of printing presses, which could produce a magazine only in multiples of eight or 16 pages.

But improvements in printing techniques now permitted production of magazines of any number of pages—15, 47, 76, 103, 241: whatever might be desired, with a varied mix of paper quality. Magazine editors constantly fought for more editorial pages, arguing (sometimes correctly, sometimes not) that sheer quantity attracted readers.

But there was obviously a limit to this: paper cost money, and so did press time. Editors were continually wrangling with the Production Department about the thickness of their magazines. Daniel Blank saw a juicy opportunity to step into the fray and supersede both sides by suggesting AMROK II be given the assignment of determining the most profitable proportion between editorial and advertising pages.

He would, he knew, face strong and vociferous opposition. Editors would claim an infringement of their creative responsibilities; production men would see a curtailment of their power. But if Blank could present a feasible program, he was certain he could win over the shrewd men who floated through the paneled suites on the 31st floor. Then he—and AMROK II, of course—would determine the extent of the editorial content of each magazine. It seemed to him but a short step from that to allowing AMROK II to dictate the most profitable subject matter of the editorial content. It was possible.

But all that was in the future. Right now Task Force X-1 was discussing the programming that would be necessary before the computer could make wise decisions on the most profitable ratio between editorial and advertising pages in every issue of every Javis-Bircham magazine. Blank listened closely to their whispered conversation, turning his eyes from speaker to speaker, and wondering if it was true, as she had said, that she occasionally rouged her nipples.

He waited, with conscious control, until 3:00 p.m. before calling. The lisping houseman asked him to hang on a moment, then came back on the phone to tell him, "Mith Montfort requeth you call again in a half hour." Puzzled, Blank hung up, paced his office for precisely 30 minutes, ate a chilled pear from his small refrigerator, and called again. This time he was put through to her.

"Hello," he said. "How are you?" (Should he call her "Celia" or "Miss Montfort"?)

"Well. And you?"

"Fine. You said I could call."

"Yes."

"You've been out of town?"

"Out of the country. To Samarra."

"Oh?" he said, hoping she might think him clever, "you had an appointment?"

"Something like that."

"Where exactly is Samarra?"

"Iraq. I was there for only a day. Actually I went over to see my parents. They're currently in Marrakech."

"How are they?" he asked politely.

"The same," she said in her toneless voice. "They haven't changed in thirty years. Ever since . . ." Her voice trailed off.

"Ever since what?" he asked.

"Ever since World War Two. It upset their plans."

She spoke in riddles, and he didn't want to pry.

"Marrakech isn't near Samarra, is it?"

"Oh no. Marrakech is in Morocco."

"Geography isn't my strong point. I get lost every time I go south of 23rd Street."

He thought she might laugh, but she didn't.

"Tomorrow night," he said desperately, "tomorrow night the Mortons are having a cocktail party. We're invited. I'd like to take you to dinner before the party. It starts about ten."

"Yes," she said immediately. "Be here at eight. We'll have a drink, then go to dinner. Then we'll go to the Mortons' party."

He started to say "Thank you" or "Fine" or "I'm looking forward to it" or "See you then," but she had already hung up. He stared at the dead receiver in his hand.

The next day, Friday, he left work early to go home to prepare for the evening. He debated with himself whether or not to send flowers. He decided against it. He had a feeling she loved flowers but never wore them. His best course, he felt, was to circle about her softly, slowly, until he could determine her tastes and prejudices.

He groomed himself carefully, shaving although he had shaved that morning. He used a women's cologne, *Je Reviens*, a scent that stirred him. He wore French underwear—white nylon bikini briefs—and a silk shirt in a geometric pattern of white and blue squares. His wide necktie was a subtly patterned maroon. The suit was navy knit, single breasted. In addition to wrist watch, cufflinks, and a heavy gold ring on his right forefinger, he wore a gold-link identification bracelet loose about his right wrist. And the "Via Veneto" wig.

He left early to walk over to her apartment. It wasn't far, and it was a pleasant evening.

His loose topcoat was a black lightweight British gabardine, styled with raglan sleeves, a fly front, and slash pockets. The pockets, in the British fashion, had an additional opening through the coat fabric so that the wearer did not have to un-button his coat to reach his trouser or jacket pockets but could shove his hand inside the concealed coat openings for tickets, wallet, keys, change, or whatever.

Now, strolling toward Celia Montfort's apartment through the sulfur-laden night, Daniel Blank reached inside his coat pocket to feel himself. To the passer-by, he was an elegant gen-tleman, hand thrust casually into coat pocket. But beneath the coat . . .

Once, shortly after he was separated from Gilda, he had worn the same coat and walked through Times Square on a Saturday night. He had slipped his hand into the pocket open-ing, unzipped his fly, and held himself exposed beneath the loose coat as he moved through the throng, looking into the faces of passersby.

Celia Montfort lived in a five-story greystone townhouse. The door bell was of a type he had read about but never en-countered before. It was a bell-pull, a brass knob that is drawn out, then released. The bell is sounded as the knob is pulled and as it is released to return to its socket. Daniel Blank ad-mired its polish and the teak door it ornamented . . .

. . . A teak door that was opened by a surprisingly tall man, pale, thin, wearing striped trousers and a shiny black alpaca jacket. A pink sweetheart rose was in his lapel. Daniel was conscious of a scent: not his own, but something heavier and fruitier.

"My name is Daniel Blank," he said. "I believe Miss Montfort is expecting me."

"Yeth, thir," the man said, holding wide the door. "I am Valenter. Do come in."

It was an impressive entrance: marble-floored with a hand-some staircase curving away. On a slender pedestal was a crys-tal vase of cherry-colored mums. He had been right: she did like long-stemmed flowers.

"Pleath wait in the thtudy. Mith Montfort will be down thoon."

His coat and hat were taken and put away somewhere. The tall, skinny man came back to usher him into a room paneled with oak and leather-bound books.

"Would you care for a drink, thir?"

Soft flames flickering in a tiled fireplace. Reflections on the polished leather of a tufted couch. On the mantel, unexpectedly, a beautifully detailed model of a Yankee whaler. Andirons and fireplace tools of black iron with brass handles.

"Please. A vodka martini on the rocks."

Drapes of heavy brocade. Rugs of—what? Not Oriental. Greek perhaps? Or Turkish? Chinese vases filled with blooms. An Indian paneled screen, all scrolled with odd, disturbing figures. A silvered cocktail shaker of the Prohibition Era. The room had frozen in 1927 or 1931.

"Olive, thir, or a twitht of lemon?"

Hint of incense in the air. High ceiling and, between the darkened beams, painted cherubs with dimpled asses. Oak doors and window mouldings. A bronze statuette of a naked nymph pulling a bow. The "string" was a twisted wire.

"Lemon, please."

An art nouveau mirror on the papered wall. A small oil nude of a middle-aged brunette holding her chin and glancing downward at sagging breasts with bleared nipples. A tin container of dusty rhododendron leaves. A small table inlaid as a chessboard with pieces swept and toppled. And in a black leather armchair, with high, embracing wings, the most beautiful boy Daniel Blank had ever seen.

"Hello," the boy said.

"Hello," he smiled stiffly. "My name is Daniel Blank. You must be Anthony."

"Tony."

"Tony."

"May I call you Dan?"

"Sure."

"Can you lend me ten dollars, Dan?"

Blank, startled, looked at him more closely. The lad had his knees drawn up, was hugging them, his head tilted to one side.

His beauty was so unearthly it was frightening. Clear, guileless blue eyes, carved lips, a bloom of youth and wanting, sculpted ears, a smile that tugged, those crisp golden curls long enough to frame face and chiselled neck. And an aura as rosy as the cherubs that floated overhead.

"It's awful, isn't it," the boy said, "to ask ten dollars from a complete stranger, but to tell you the truth—"

Blank was instantly alert, listening now and not just looking. It was his experience that when someone said "To tell the truth—" or "Would I lie to you?" the man was either a liar, a cheat, or both.

"You see," Tony said with an audacious smile, "I saw this absolutely marvelous jade pin. I know Celia would love it."

"Of course," Blank said. He took a ten dollar bill from his wallet. The boy made no move toward him. Daniel was forced to walk across the room to hand it to him.

"Thanks so much," the youth said languidly. "I get my allowance the first of the month. I'll pay you back."

He paid then. Blank knew, all he was ever going to pay: a dazzling smile of such beauty and young promise that Daniel was fuddled by longing. The moment was saved of souring by the entrance of Valenter, carrying the martini not on a tray but in his hand. When Blank took it, his fingers touched Valenter's. The evening began to spin out of control.

She came in a few moments later, wearing an evening shift styled exactly like the black satin she had been wearing when he first met her. But this one was in a dark bottle green, glimmering. About her neck was a heavy silver chain, tarnished, supporting a pendant: the image of a beast-god. Mexican, Blank guessed.

"I went to Samarra to meet a poet," she said, speaking as she came through the door and walked steadily toward him. "I once wrote poetry. Did I tell you? No. But I don't anymore. I have talent, but not enough. The blind poet in Samarra is a genius. A poem is a condensed novel. I imagine a novelist must increase the significance of what he writes by one-third to one-half to communicate all of his meaning. You understand? But the poet, so condensed, must double or triple what he wants to convey, hoping the reader will extract from this his full meaning."

Suddenly she leaned forward and kissed him on the lips while Valenter and the boy looked on gravely.

"How are you?" she asked.

Valenter brought her a glass of red wine. She was seated next to Blank on the leather sofa. Valenter stirred up the fire, added another small log, went to stand behind the armchair where Anthony coiled in flickering shadow.

"I think the Mortons' party will be amusing." he offered. "A lot of people. Noisy and crowded. But we don't have to stay long."

"Have you ever smoked hashish?" she asked.

43

He looked nervously toward the young boy.

"I tried it once," he said in a low voice. "It didn't do anything for me. I prefer alcohol."

"Do you drink a lot?"

"No."

The boy was wearing white flannel bags, white leather loafers, a white knitted singlet that left his slim arms bare. He moved slowly, crossing his legs, stretching, pouting. Celia Montfort turned her head to look at him. Did a signal pass?

"Tony," she said.

Immediately Valenter put a hand tenderly on the boy's shoulder.

"Time for your lethon, Mathter Montfort," he said.

"Oh, pooh," Tony said.

They walked from the room side by side. The lad stopped at the door, turned back, made a solemn bow in Blank's direction.

"I am very happy to have met you, sir," he said formally.

Then he was gone. Valenter closed the door softly behind them.

"A handsome boy," Daniel said. "What school does he go to?"

She didn't answer. He turned to look at her. She was peering into her wine glass, twirling the stem slowly in her long fingers. The straight black hair fell about her face: the long face, broody and purposeful.

She put her wine glass aside and rose suddenly. She moved casually about the room, and he swiveled his head to keep her in view. She touched things, picked them up and put them down. He was certain she was naked beneath the satin shift. Cloth touched her and flew away. It clung, and whispered off.

As she moved about, she began to intone another of what was apparently an inexhaustible repertoire of monologues. He was conscious of planned performance. But it was not a play; it was a ballet, as formalized and obscure. Above all, he felt *intent*: motive and plan.

"My parents are such sad creatures," she was saying. "Living in history. But that's not living at all, is it? It's an entombing. Mother's silk chiffon and father's plus-fours. They could be breathing mannequins at the Costume Institute. I look for dignity and all I find is . . . What is it I want? Grandeur, I suppose. Yes. I've thought of it. But is it impossible to be grand in life? What we consider grandeur is always connected with defeat and death. The Greek plays. Napoleon's return from Moscow. Lincoln. Superhuman dignity there. Nobility, if you like. But always rounded with death. The living, no matter how noble they may be, never quite make it, do they? But death rounds them out. What if John Kennedy had lived? No one has ever written of his life as a work of art, but it was. Beginning, middle, and end. Grandeur. And death made it. Are you ready? Shall we go?"

"I hope you like French cooking," he muttered. "I called for a reservation."

"It doesn't matter," she said.

The dance continued during dinner. She requested a banquette: they sat side by side. They ate and drank with little conversation. Once she picked up a thin sliver of tender veal and fed it into his mouth. But her free hand was on his arm, or in his lap, or pushing her long hair back so that the bottle green satin was brought tight across button nipples. Once, while they were having coffee and brandy, she crossed her knees. Her dress hiked up; the flesh of her thighs was perfectly white, smooth, glistening. He thought of good sea scallops and Dover sole.

"Do you like opera?" she asked in her abrupt way.

"No," he said truthfully. "Not much. It's so—so made up."

"Yes," she agreed, "it is. Artificial. But it's just a device: a flimsy wire coat hanger, and they hang the voices on that."

He was not a stupid man, and while they were seated at the banquette he became aware that her subtle movements—the touchings, the leanings, the sudden, unexpected caress of her hair against his cheek—these things were directorial suggestions, parts of her balletic performance. She was rehearsed. He wasn't certain of his role, but wanted to play it well.

"The voices," she went on, "the mighty voices that give me the feeling of suppressed power. With some singers I get the impression that there is art and strength there that hasn't been tapped. I get the feeling that, if they really let themselves go, they could crush eardrums and shatter stained glass windows. Perhaps the best of them, throwing off all restraint, could crush the world. Break it up into brittle pieces and send all the chunks whirling off into space."

He was made inferior by her soliloquies and made brave by wine and brandy.

"Why the hell are you telling me all this?" he demanded.

She leaned closer, pressed a satin-slicked breast against his arm.

"It's the same feeling I get from you," she whispered. "That

45

you have a strength and resolve that could shatter the world."

He looked at her, beginning to glimpse her intent and his future. He wanted to ask, "Why me?" but found, to his surprise, it wasn't important.

The Mortons' party leavened their heavy evening. Florence and Samuel, wearing identical red velvet jumpsuits, met them at the door with the knowing smirks of successful matchmakers.

"Come in!" Flo cried.

"It's a marvelous party!" Sam cried.

"Two fights already!" Flo laughed.

"And one crying jag!" Sam laughed.

The party had a determined frenzy. He lost Celia in the swirl, and in the next few hours met and listened to a dozen disoriented men and women who floated, bumped against him, drifted away. He had a horrible vision of harbor trash, bobbing and nuzzling, coming in and going out.

Suddenly she was behind him, hand up under his jacket, nails digging into his shirted back.

"Do you know what happens at midnight?" she whispered.

"What?"

"They take off their faces—just like masks. And do you know what's underneath?"

"What?"

"Their faces. Again. And again."

She slipped away; he was too confused to hold her. He wanted to be naked in front of a mirror, making sure.

Finally, finally, she reappeared and drew him away. They flapped hands at host and hostess and stepped into the quiet corridor, panting. In the elevator she came into his arms and bit the lobe of his left ear as he said, "Oh," and the music from wherever was playing "My Old Kentucky Home." He was sick with lust and conscious that his life was dangerous and absurd. He was teetering, and pitons were not driven nor ice ax in.

There was Valenter to open the door for them, the sweetheart rose wilted. His face had the sheen of a scoured iron pot, and his lips seemed bruised. He served black coffee in front of the tiled fireplace. They sat on the leather couch and stared at blue embers.

"Will that be all, Mith Montfort?"

She nodded; he drifted away. Daniel Blank wouldn't look at him. What if the man should wink?

46

Celia went out of the room, came back with two pony glasses and a half-full bottle of marc.

"What is that?" he asked.

"A kind of brandy," she said. "Burgundian, I think. From the dregs. Very strong."

She filled a glass, and before handing it to him ran a long, red tongue around the rim, looking at him. He took it, sipped gratefully.

"Yes," he nodded. "Strong."

"Those people tonight," she said. "So inconsequential. Most of them are intelligent, alert, talented. But they don't have the opportunity. To surrender, I mean. To something important and shaking. They desire it more than they know. To give themselves. To what? Ecology or day-care centers or racial equality? They sense the need for something more, and God is dead. So . . . the noise and hysteria. If they could find . . ."

Her voice trailed off. He looked up.

"Find what?" he asked.

"Oh," she said, her eyes vague, "you know."

She rose from the couch. When he rose to stand alongside her, she unexpectedly stepped close, reached out, gently drew down the lower lid of his right eye. She stared intently at the exposed eyeball.

"What?" he said, confused.

"You're not inconsequential," she said, took him by the hand and led him upward. "Not at all."

Dazed by drink and wonder, he followed docilely. They climbed the handsome marble staircase to the third floor. There they passed through a tawdry wooden door and climbed two more flights up a splintered wooden stairway flecked with cobwebs that kissed his mouth.

"What *is* this?" he asked once.

"I *live* up here," she answered, turned suddenly and, being above him, reached down, pulled his head forward and pressed his face into the cool satin between belly and thighs.

It was a gesture that transcended obscenity and brought him trembling to his knees there on the dusty stairs.

"Rest a moment," she said.

"I'm a mountain climber," he said, and their whispered exchange seemed to him so inane that he gave a short bark of laughter that banged off dull walls and echoed.

"What?" he said again, and all the time he knew.

It was a small room of unpainted plank walls, rough-finished and scarred with white streaks as if some frantic beast had clawed to escape. There was a single metal cot with a flat spring of woven tin straps. On this was thrown a thin mattress, uncovered, the striped grey ticking soiled and burned.

There was one kitchen chair that had been painted fifty times and was now so dented and nicked that a dozen colors showed in bruised blotches. A bare light bulb, orange and dim, hung from a dusty cord.

The floor was patched with linoleum so worn the pattern had disappeared and brown backing showed through. The unframed mirror on the inside of the closed door was tarnished and cracked. The iron ashtray on the floor near the cot overflowed with cold cigarette butts. The room smelled of must, mildew, and old love.

"Beautiful," Daniel Blank said wonderingly, staring about. "It's a stage set. Any moment now a wall swings away, and there will be the audience applauding politely. What are my lines?"

"Take off your wig," she said.

He did, standing by the cot with the hair held foolishly in his two hands, offering her a small, dead animal.

She came close and caressed his shaven skull with both hands. "Do you like this room?" she asked.

"Well . . . it's not exactly my idea of a love nest."

"Oh it's more than that. Much more. Lie down."

Gingerly, with some distaste, he sat on the stained mattress. She softly pressed him back. He stared up at the naked bulb, and there seemed to be a nimbus about it, a glow composed of a million shining particles that pulsed, contracted, expanded until they filled the room.

And then, almost before he knew it had started, she was doing things to him. He could not believe this intelligent, somber, reserved woman was doing those things. He felt a shock of fear, made a few muttered protests. But her voice was soft, soothing. After awhile he just lay there, his eyes closed now, and let her do what she would.

"Scream if you like," she said. "No one can hear."

But he clenched his jaws and thought he might die of pleasure.

He opened his eyes and saw her lying naked beside him, her long, white body as limp as a fileted fish. She began undressing him with practiced fingers . . . opening buttons . . . sliding down zippers . . . tugging things away gently, so gently he hardly had to move at all . . .

48

Then she was using him, *using* him, and he began to understand what his fate might be. Fear dissolved in a kind of sexual faint he had never experienced before as her strong hands pulled, her dry tongue rasped over his fevered skin.

"Soon," she promised. "Soon."

Once he felt a pain so sharp and sweet he thought she had murdered him. Once he heard her laughing: a thick, burbling sound. Once she wound him about with her smooth, black hair, fashioned a small noose and pulled it tight.

It went on and on, his will dissolving, a great weight lifting, and he would pay any price. It was climbing: mission, danger, sublimity. Finally, the summit.

Later, he was exploring her body and saw, for the first time, her armpits were unshaved. He discovered, hidden in the damp, scented hairs under her left arm, a small tattoo in a curious design.

Still later they were drowsing in each other's sweated arms, the light turned off, when he half-awoke and became conscious of a presence in the room. The door to the corridor was partly open. Through sticky eyes he saw someone standing silently at the foot of the cot, staring down at their linked bodies.

In the dim light Daniel Blank had a smeary impression of a naked figure or someone dressed in white. Blank raised his head and made a hissing sound. The wraith withdrew. The door closed softly. He was left alone with her in that dreadful room.

5

One night, lying naked and alone between his sateen sheets, Daniel Blank wondered if this world might not be another world's dream. It was conceivable: somewhere another planet populated by a sentient people of superior intelligence who shared a communal dream as a method of play. And Earth was their dream, filled with fantasies, grotesqueries, evil—all the irrationalities they themselves rejected in their daily lives but turned to in sleep for relaxation. For fun.

Then we are all smoke and drifting. We are creatures of another world's midnight visions, moving through a life as illogical as any dream, and as realistic. We exist only in a stranger's slumber, and our death is his awaking, smiling at the mad, tangled plot his sleep conceived.

It seemed to Blank that since meeting Celia Montfort his

existence had taken on the quality of a dream, the vaporous quality of a dream shot through with wild, bright flashes. His life had become all variables and, just before falling asleep to his own disordered dream, he wondered if AMROK II, properly programmed, might print out the meaning in a microsecond, as something of enormous consequence.

"No, no," Celia Montfort said intently, leaning forward into the candlelight. "Evil isn't just an absence of good. It's not just omission; it's commission, an action. You can't call that man evil just because he lets people starve to put his country's meager resources into heavy industry. That was a political and economic decision. Perhaps he is right, perhaps not. Those things don't interest me. But I think you're wrong to call him evil. Evil is really a kind of religion. I think he's just a well-meaning fool. But evil he's not. Evil implies intelligence and a deliberate intent. Don't you agree, Daniel?"

She turned suddenly to him. His hand shook, and he spilled a few drops of red wine. They dripped onto the unpressed linen tablecloth, spreading out like clots of thick blood.

"Well . . ." he said slowly.

She was having a dinner party: Blank, the Mortons, and Anthony Montfort seated around an enormous, candle-lighted dining table that could easily have accommodated twice their number in a chilly and cavernous dining hall. The meal, bland and without surprises, had been served by Valenter and a heavy, middle-aged woman with a perceptible black mustache.

The dishes were being removed, they were finishing a dusty beaujolais, and their conversation had turned to the current visit to Washington of the dictator of a new African nation, a man who wore white-piped vests and a shoulder holster.

"No, Samuel," Celia shook her head, "he is not an evil man. You use that word loosely. He's just a bungler. Greedy perhaps. Or out for revenge on his enemies. But greed and revenge are grubby motives. True evil has a kind of nobility, as all faiths do. Faith implies total surrender, a giving up of reason."

"Who was evil?" Florence Morton asked.

"Hitler?" Samuel Morton asked.

Celia Montfort looked slowly around the table. "You don't understand," she said softly. "I'm not talking about evil for the sake of ambition. I'm talking about evil for the sake of evil. Not Hitler—no. I mean saints of evil—men and women who see a vision and follow it. Just as Christian saints perceived a vision of good and followed that. I don't believe there have been any modern saints, of good *or* evil. But the possibility exists. In all of us."

"I understand," Anthony Montfort said loudly, and they all turned in surprise to look at him.

"To do evil because it's fun," the boy said.

"Yes, Tony," his sister said gently, smiling at him. "Because it's fun. Let's have coffee in the study. There's a fire there."

In the upstairs room the naked bulb burned in the air: a dusty moon. There was a smell of low tide and crawling things. Once he heard a faint shout of laughter, and Daniel Blank wondered if it was Tony laughing, and why he laughed.

They lay unclothed and stared at each other through the dark sunglasses she had provided. He stared—but did she? He could not tell. But blind eyes faced his blind eyes, discs of black against white skin. He felt the shivery bliss again. It was the mystery.

Her mouth opened slowly. Her long tongue slid out, lay flaccid between dry lips. Were her eyes closed? Was she looking at the wall? He peered closer, and behind the dark glass saw a far-off gleam. One of her hands wormed between her thighs, and a tiny bubble of spittle appeared in the corner of her mouth. He heard her breathing.

He pressed to her. She moved away and began to murmur. He understood some of what she said, but much was riddled. "What is it? What is it?" he wanted to cry, but did not because he feared it might be less than he hoped. So he was silent, listened to her murmur, felt her fingertips pluck at his quick skin.

The black covers over her eyes became holes, pits that went through flesh, bone, cot, floor, building, earth, and finally out into the far, dark reaches. He floated down those empty corridors, her naked hands pulling him along.

Her murmur never ceased. She circled and circled, spiraling in, but never named what she wanted. He wondered if there was a word for it, for then he could believe it existed. If it had no name, no word to label it, then it was an absolute reality beyond his apprehension, as infinite as the darkness through which he sped, tugged along by her hungry hands.

"We've found out all about her!" Florence Morton laughed.

"Well . . . not all, but some!" Samuel Morton laughed.

They had appeared at Daniel's door, late at night, wearing matching costumes of blue suede jeans and fringed jackets. It was difficult to believe them husband and wife; they were sexless twins, with their bony bodies, bird features, helmets of oiled hair.

He invited them in for a drink. The Mortons sat on the couch close together and held hands.

"How did you find out?" he asked curiously.

"We know everything!" Florence said.

"Our spies were everywhere!" Samuel said.

Daniel Blank smiled. It was almost true.

"Lots of money there," Flo said. "Her grandfather on her mother's side. Oil and steel. Plenty of loot. But her father had the family. He didn't inherit much but good looks. They said he was the handsomest man of his generation in America. They called him 'Beau Montfort' at Princeton. But he never did graduate. Kicked out for knocking up—someone. Who was it, Samovel?"

"A dean's wife or a scullery maid—someone like that. Anyway, this was in the late Twenties. Then he married all that oil and steel. He made a big contribution to Roosevelt's campaign fund and thought he might be ambassador to London, Paris or Rome. But FDR had more sense than that. He named Montfort a 'roving representative' and got him away from Washington. That was smart. The Montforts loved it. They drank and fucked up a storm. The talk of Europe. Celia was born in Lausanne. But then things went sour. Her parents got in with the Nazis, and daddy sent home glowing reports about what a splendid, kindly gentleman Hitler was. Naturally, Roosevelt dumped him. Then, from what we can learn, they just bummed around in high style."

"What about Celia?" Daniel asked. "Is Tony really her brother?"

They looked at him in astonishment.

"You wondered?" Flo asked.

"You guessed?" Sam asked.

"We didn't get it straight," she acknowledged. "No one really knows."

"Everyone guesses," Sam offered. "But it's just gossip. No one *knows*."

"But Tony could be her son," Flo nodded.

"The ages are right," Sam nodded. "But she's never been married. That anyone knows about."

"There are rumors."

"She's a strange woman."

"And who is Valenter?"

"What's his relationship to her?"

"And to Tony?"

"And where does she go when she goes away?"

"And comes back bruised? What is she *doing*?"

"Why don't her parents want her in Europe?"

"What's *with* her?"

"Who *is* she?"

"I don't care," Daniel Blank whispered. "I love her."

He worked late in his office on Halloween night. He had a salad and black coffee sent up from the commissary. As he ate, he went over the final draft of the prospectus he was scheduled to present to the Production Board on the following day: his plan to have AMROK II determine the ratio between advertising and editorial pages in every Javis-Bircham magazine.

The prospectus seemed to him temperate, logical, and convincing. But he recognized that it lacked enthusiasm. It was as stirring as an insurance policy, as inspirational as a corporate law brief; he poked it across the table and sat staring at it.

The fault, he knew, was his; he had lost interest. Oh the plan was valid, it made sense, but it no longer seemed to him of much import.

And he knew the reason for his indifference: Celia Montfort. Compared to her, to his relations with her, his job at Javis-Bircham was a game played by a grown boy, no worse and no better than Chinese Checkers or Monopoly. He went through the motions, he followed the rules, but he was not touched.

He sat brooding, wondering where she might lead him. Finally he rose, took his trench coat and hat. He left the prospectus draft on the table, with the garbage of his dinner and the dregs of cold coffee in the plastic cup. On his way to the executive elevator he glanced through the window of the Computer Room. The night shift, white-clad, floated slowly on their crepe soles over the cork floor, drifting through a sterile dream.

The rain came in spits and gusts, driven by a hacking wind. There were no cabs in sight. Blank turned up his coat collar, pulled down the brim of his hat. He dug toward Eighth Avenue. If he didn't find a cab, he'd take a crosstown bus on 42nd Street to First Avenue, and then change to an uptown bus.

Neon signs glimmered. Porno shops offered rubdowns and

body painting. From a record shop, hustling the season, came a novelty recording of a dog barking "Adeste Fidelis." An acned prostitute, booted and spurred, murmured, "Fun?" as he passed. He knew this scruffy section well and paid no heed. It had nothing to do with him.

As he approached the subway kiosk at 42nd Street, a band of young girls came giggling up, flashing in red yellow green blue party dresses, coats swinging open, long hair ripped back by the wind. Blank stared, wondering why such beauties were on such a horrid street.

He saw then. They were all boys and young men, transvestites, on their way to a Halloween drag. In their satins and laces. In evening slippers and swirling wigs. Carmined lips and shadowed eyes. Shaved legs in nylon pantyhose. Padded chests. Hands flying and throaty laughs.

Soft fingers were on his arm. A mocking voice: "Dan!"

It was Anthony Montfort, looking back to flirt a wave, golden hair gleaming in the rain like flame. And then, following, a few paces back, the tall, skinny Valenter, wrapped in a black raincoat.

Daniel Blank stood and watched that mad procession dwindle up the avenue. He heard shouts, raucous cries. Then they were all gone, and he was staring after.

She went away for a day, two days, a week. Or, if she really didn't go away, he could not talk to her. He heard only Valenter's "Mith Montforth rethidenth," and then the news that she was not at home.

He became aware that these unexplained absences invariably followed their erotic ceremonies in the upstairs room. The following day, shattered with love and the memory of pleasure, he would call and discover she was gone, or would not talk to him.

He thought she was manipulating him, dancing out her meaningful ballet. She approached, touched, withdrew. He followed, she laughed, he touched, she caressed, he reached, she pulled back, fingers beckoning. The dance inflamed him.

Once, after four days' absence, he found her weary, drained, with yellow bruises on arms and legs, and purple loops beneath her eyes. She would not say where she had been or what she had done. She lay limp, without resistance, and insisted he abuse her. Infuriated, he did, and she thanked him. Was that, too, part of her plan?

She was a tangle of oddities. Usually she was well-groomed, bathed and scented, long hair brushed gleaming, nails trimmed and painted. But one night she came to his apartment a harridan. She had not bathed, as he discovered, and played the frumpish wanton, looking at him with derisive eyes and using foul language. He could not resist her.

She played strange games. One night she donned a child's jumper, sat on his lap and called him "Daddy." Another time —and how had she guessed *that?*—she bought him a gold chain and insisted he link it about his slim waist. She bit him. He thought her mad with love for him, but when he reached for her, she was not there.

He knew what was happening and did not care. Only she had meaning. She recited a poem to him in a language he could not identify, then licked his eyes. One night he tried to kiss her—an innocent kiss on the cheek, a kiss of greeting— and she struck his jaw with her clenched fist. The next instant she was on her knees, fumbling for him.

And her monologues never ended. She could be silent for hours, then suddenly speak to him of sin and love and evil and gods and why sex should transcend the sexual. Was she training him? He thought so, and studied.

She was gone for almost a week. He took her to dinner when she returned, but it was not a comfortable evening. She was silent and withdrawn. Only once did she look directly at him. Then she looked down, and with the middle finger of her right hand lightly touched, stroked, caressed the white tablecloth.

She took him immediately home, and he followed obediently up that cobwebbed staircase. In the upstairs room, standing naked beneath the blaring orange light, she showed him the African masks.

And she told him what she wanted him to do.

6

Daniel Blank inched his way up the chimney of Devil's Needle. He could feel the cold of the stone against his shoulders, against his gloved palms and heavy boots. It was dark inside the cleft; the cold was damp and smelled of death.

He wormed his way carefully onto the flat top. There had been light snow flurries the day before, and he expected ice. It was there, in thin patches, and after he hauled up the rucksack he used his ice ax to chip it away, shoving splinters over the side. Then he could stand on cleated soles and search around.

It was a lowery sky, with a look of more snow to the west. Dirty clouds scummed the sun; the wind knifed steadily. This would, he knew, be his last climb until Spring. The park closed on Thanksgiving; there were no ski trails, and the rocks were too dangerous in winter.

He sat on the stone, ate an onion sandwich, drank a cup of coffee that seemed to chill as it was poured. He had brought a little flask of brandy and took small sips. Warmth went through him like new blood, and he thought of Celia.

She went through him like new blood, too; a thaw he knew in heart, gut, loins. She melted him, and not only his flesh. He felt her heat in every waking thought, in his clotted dreams. His love for her had brought him aware, had made him sensible of a world that existed for others but which he had never glimpsed.

He had been an only child, raised in a large house filled with the odors of disinfectant and his mother's gin. His father was moderately wealthy, having inherited from an aunt. He worked in a bank. His mother drank and collected Lalique glass. This was in Indiana.

It was a silent house and in later years, when Daniel tried to recall it, he had an absurd memory of the entire place being tiled: walls, floors, ceilings plated with white tile, enamel on steel, exactly like a gleaming subway tunnel that went on forever to nowhere. Perhaps it was just a remembered dream.

He had always been a loner; his mother and father never kissed him on the lips, but offered their cheeks. White tiles. The happiest memory of his boyhood was when their colored maid gave him a birthday present; it was a display box for his rock collection. Her husband had made it from an old orange crate, carefully sanding the rough wood and lining it with sleazy black cloth. It was beautiful, just what he wanted. That year his mother gave him handkerchiefs and underwear, and his father gave him a savings bond.

He was a loner in college, too. But in his sophomore year he lost his virginity at the one whore house in the college town. In his last two years he had a comforting affair with a Jewish girl from Boston. She was ugly but had mad eyes and a body that didn't end. All she wanted to do was screw. That was all right with him.

He found a piece of chalcedony and polished it in his rock

tumbler and on the buffing wheel. It wasn't a priceless stone, but he thought it pretty. The Jewish girl laughed when he gave it to her on graduation day. "Fucking *goy*," she said.

His graduation present from his parents was a summer in Europe, a grand tour of a dozen countries with enough time for climbing in Switzerland and visiting archeological digs in the south of France. He was waiting for his plane in New York, in a hotel bed with the Jewish girl who had flown down from Boston for a last bang, when a lawyer called to tell him his mother and father, driving home from his graduation, had gone off the highway, had been trapped in their car, and burned to death.

Daniel Blank thought less than a minute. Then he told the lawyer to sell the house, settle the estate, and bury his parents. Daniel himself would be home after his trip to Europe. The Boston girl heard him say all this on the phone. By the time he hung up, she was dressed and marching out of there, carrying her Louis Vuitton bag. He never saw her again. But it was a wonderful summer.

When he returned to his hometown late in August, no one would talk to him but the lawyer—and he as little as possible. Daniel Blank couldn't care less. He flew to New York, opened a bank account with his inheritance, then flew back to Bloomington and was finally accepted at the University of Indiana, going for an M.S. with emphasis on geology and archeology. During his second year he met Gilda, the woman he later married.

Two months before he was to get his degree, he decided it was all a lot of shit; he didn't want to spend the rest of his life shoveling dirt. He gave the best stone in his collection (a nice piece of jade) to Gilda, donated the remaining rocks to the University, and flew to New York. He played the part of a modestly moneyed bachelor in Manhattan for about six months. Then most of the cash was gone, but he hadn't sold off any of the stocks or bonds. He got a silly job in the circulation department of a national magazine. He found, to his amusement, that he was good at it. And he discovered he had an ambition unhampered by conscience. Gilda came to New York, and they were married.

He was not a stupid man; he knew the tiled emotions of his boyhood and youth had deadened him. And that house that smelled of CN and gin . . . those cheek-kisses . . . the Lalique glass. Other people fell in love and wept; he collected stones and scorned his parents' funeral.

What Celia Montfort had done for him, he decided, was to peel clean what had always been in him but had never been revealed. Now he could feel, deeply, and react to her. He could love her. He could sacrifice for her. It was *passion*, as warming as brandy on a bleak November afternoon. It was a fire in the veins, a heightened awareness, a need compounded of wild hope and fearful dread. He sought it, following the same instinct that had led him to discard his rock collection, those mementoes of dead history.

He started the climb down, still thinking of his love for Celia, of her naked and masked in the upstairs room, and of how quickly she had learned to slide her hand into his slitted pocket and fondle him as they walked in public.

Descending, he moved one boot too quickly. The heel hit the toe of the other boot, pressed against the opposite chimney wall. Then both legs dangled. For a long, stomach-turning moment he was suspended only by the pressure of his arms, clamped by shoulders and palms shoving against opposing walls. He forced himself to take a deep breath, eyes closed in the cold darkness. He would not think of the fast fall to the boulders below.

Slowly, smiling, he drew up one knee and planted a sole carefully against the opposite wall. His elbows were trembling with strain. He lifted the other boot into position and pressed. Now he could take the load off shoulders, arms, wrists, hands.

He looked up at the little patch of murky sky above the black hole he was in, and laughed with delight. He would descend safely. He could do anything. He had the strength to resist common sense.

PART II

1

Captain Edward X. Delaney, Commanding Officer of the 251st Precinct, New York Police Department, wearing civilian clothes, pushed open the door of the doctor's office, removed his Homburg (stiff as wood), and gave his name to the receptionist.

He planted himself solidly into an armchair, glanced swiftly around the room, then stared down at the hat balanced precisely on his knees. It was the "Observation Game": originally a self-imposed duty but now a diversion he had enjoyed for almost thirty years, since he had been a patrolman. If, for any reason, he was called upon to describe the patients in the waiting room . . .

"Left: male, Negro, dark brown, about 35, approximately 5 feet 10 inches, 160 pounds. Kinky black hair cut short; no part. Wearing plaid sports jacket, fawn-colored slacks, cordovan loafers. Necktie looped but not knotted. Heavy ring on right hand. Slight white scar on neck. Smoking cork-tip cigarette held between thumb and forefinger of left hand.

"Center: female, white, about 60-65; short, plump, motherly type. Uncontrollable tremor of right hand. Wearing black coat, soiled; elastic stockings, hole in left knee; old-fashioned hat with single cloth flower. Dark reddish hair may be wig. Approximately 5 feet 1 inch, 140 pounds. Fiddles with wen on chin.

"Right: male, white, about 50, 6 feet 2 inches. Extremely thin and emaciated. Loose collar and suit jacket show recent weight loss. Sallow complexion. Fidgety. Right eye may be glass. Nicotine-stained fingers indicate heavy smoker. Gnaws on lower lip. Blinks frequently."

He raised his eyes, inspected them again. He was close. The Negro's ring was on the left hand. The old woman's hair (or wig) was more brown than reddish. The thin man wasn't quite as tall as he had estimated. But Captain Delaney could provide a reasonably accurate description and/or identify these strangers in a line-up or courtroom if needed.

He was not, he acknowledged, as exact as some men in his

judgment of physical characteristics. There was, for instance, a detective second grade attached to the 251st Precinct who could glance at a man for a few seconds and estimate his height within an inch and his weight within five pounds. That was a special gift.

But Captain Delaney also had an eye. That was for the Negro's necktie that was looped but not knotted, the old woman's wen, the thin man's continual blinking. Small things. Significant things.

He saw and remembered habits, tastes, the way a man dressed, moved, grimaced, walked, spoke, lighted a cigarette or spat into the gutter. Most important, Captain Delaney—the cop—was interested in what a man did when he was alone, or thought he was alone. Did he masturbate, pick his nose, listen to recordings of Gilbert & Sullivan, shuffle pornographic photos, work out chess problems? Or did he read Nietzsche?

There was a case—Delaney remembered it well; he had been a detective in the Chelsea precinct where it happened—three young girls raped and murdered within a period of 18 months, all on the roofs of tenements. The police thought they had their man. They carefully charted his daily movements. They brought him in for questioning and got nowhere. Then they established very close surveillance. Detective Delaney watched the suspect through binoculars from an apartment across the courtyard. Delaney saw this man, who had never been known to go to church, this man who thought he was alone and unobserved, this man went each night onto his knees and prayed before a reproduction of the face of Jesus Christ—one of those monstrous prints in which the eyes seem to open, close, or wink, depending upon the angle of view.

So they took the suspect in again, but this time, on Delaney's urging, they brought in a priest to talk to him. Within an hour they had a complete confession. Well . . . that was what one man did when he thought he was alone and unobserved.

It was the spastic twitch, the uncontrollable tic that Captain Delaney had an eye for. He wanted to know what tunes the suspect whistled, the foods he ate, how his home was decorated. Was he married, unmarried, thrice-married? Did he beat his dog or beat his wife? All these things told. And, of course, what he did when he thought he was alone.

The "big things" Captain Delaney told his men—things like a man's job, religion, politics, and the way he talked at cocktail parties—these were a facade he created to hold back a hostile world. Hidden were the vital things. The duty of the cop, when necessary, was to peek around the front at the secret urges and driven acts.

"Doctor will see you now," the receptionist smiled at him.

Delaney nodded, gripped his hat, marched into the doctor's office. He ignored the hostile stares of the patients who had, obviously, been waiting longer than he.

Dr. Louis Bernardi rose from behind his desk, holding out a plump, ringed hand.

"Captain," he said. "Always a pleasure."

"Doctor," Delaney said. "Good to see you again. You're looking well."

Bernardi caressed the bulged grey flannel waistcoat, straining at its tarnished silver buttons which, Barbara Delaney had told her husband, the doctor had revealed to her were antique Roman coins.

"It's my wife's cooking," Bernardi shrugged, smiling. "What can I do? He-he! Sit down, sit down. Mrs. Delaney is dressing. She will be ready to leave soon. But we shall have time for a little chat."

A chat? Delaney assumed men had a talk or a discussion. That "chat" was Bernardi. The Captain consulted a police surgeon; Bernardi was his wife's physician, had been for thirty years. He had seen her through two successful pregnancies, nursed her through a bad bout of hepatitis, and had recommended and seen to her recovery from a hysterectomy only two months previously.

He was a round man, beautifully shaved. He was soft and, if not unctuous, he was at least a smooth article. The black silk suit put forth a sheen; the shoes bore a dulled gleam. He was not perfumed, but he exuded an odor of self-satisfaction.

Contradicting all this were the man's eyes: hard, bright. They were shrewd little chips of quartz. His glance never wavered; his toneless stare could bring a nurse to tears.

Delaney did not like the man. He did not, for a moment, doubt Bernardi's professional competence. But he mistrusted the tailored plumpness, the secret smile, the long strands of oily hair slicked across a balding pate. He was particularly incensed by the doctor's mustache: a thin, carefully clipped line of black imprinted on the upper lip as if marked by a felt-tipped pen.

The Captain knew he amused Bernardi. That did not bother him. He knew he amused many people: superiors in the Department, peers, the uniformed men of his command. Newspapermen. Investigators. Doctors of sociology and criminal pathology. He amused them all. His wife and children. He knew. But on occasion Dr. Bernardi had made no effort to conceal his amusement. Delaney could not forgive him that.

"I hope you have good news for me, doctor."

Bernardi spread his hands in a bland gesture: the dealer who has just been detected selling a ruptured camel.

"Regrettably, I do not. Captain, your wife has not responded to the antibiotics. As I told her, my first instinctive impression was of a low-grade infection. Persistent and of some duration. It accounts for the temperature."

"What kind of infection?"

Again the gesture: hands spread wide and lifted, palms outward.

"That I do not know. Tests show nothing. Nothing on X-rays. No tumor, so far as I am able to determine. But still, apparently, an infection. What do you think of that?"

"I don't like it," Delaney said stonily.

"Nor do I," Bernardi nodded. "First of all, your wife is ill. That is of most importance. Second, it is a defeat for me. What is this infection? I do not know. It is an embarrassment."

An "embarrassment," Delaney thought angrily. What kind of a thing was that to say? The man didn't know how to use the king's English. Was he an Italian, a Lebanese, a Greek, a Syrian, an Arabian? What the hell *was* he?

"Finally," Dr. Bernardi said, consulting the file open on his desk, "let us consider the fever. It has been approximately six weeks since your wife's first visit complaining of, quote, 'Fever and sudden chills.' Unquote. On that first visit, a temperature a bit above normal. Nothing unusual. Pills for a cold, the flu, a virus—whatever you want to call it. No effect. Another visit. Temperature up. Not a great increase, but appreciable. Then antibiotics. Now, third visit and temperature is up again. The sudden chills continue. It worries me."

"Well, it worries her and it worries me," Delaney said stoutly.

"Of course," Bernardi soothed. "And now she finds many loose hairs in her comb. This is undoubtedly the result of the fever. Nothing serious, but still . . . And you are aware of the rash on the insides of her thighs and forearms?"

"Yes."

"Again, undoubtedly the result of the fever stemming from the infection. I have prescribed an ointment. Not a cure, but it will take the itch away."

"She looks so healthy."

"You are seeing the fever, Captain! Don't believe the blush of health. Those bright eyes and rosy cheeks. Ha! It is the infection."

"What infection?" Delaney cried furiously. "What the hell *is* it? Is it cancer?"

Bernardi's eyes glittered.

"At this stage, I would guess no. Have you ever heard of a Proteus infection, Captain?"

"No. I never have. What is it?"

"I will not speak of it now. I must do some reading on it. You think we doctors know everything? But there is too much. There are young physicians today who cannot recognize (because they have never treated) typhus, small pox or poliomyelitis. But that is by the by."

"Doctor." Delaney said, wearied by all this lubricous talk, "let's get down to it. What do we do now. What are our options?"

Dr. Bernardi leaned back in his swivel chair, placed his two forefingers together, pressed them against his plump lips. He regarded Delaney for a long moment.

"You know, Captain," he said with some malevolence, "I admire you. Your wife is obviously ill, and yet you say, 'What do *we* do' and 'What are *our* options'. That is admirable."

"Doctor . . ."

"Very well." Bernardi sat forward sharply and slapped the file on his desk. "You have three options. One: I can attempt to reduce the fever, to overcome this mysterious infection, by heavier doses of antibiotics or with drugs I have not yet tried. I do not recommend this out of the hospital; the side effects can be alarming. Two: Your wife can enter a hospital for five days to a week for a series of tests much more thorough than I can possibly administer in this office. I would call in other men. Specialists. Neurologists. Gynecologists. Even dermatologists. This would be expensive."

He paused, looking at the Captain expectantly.

"All right, doctor," Delaney said patiently. "What's the third choice?"

Bernardi looked at him tenderly.

"Perhaps you would prefer another physician," he said softly. "Since I have failed."

Delaney sighed, knowing his wife's faith in this oleaginous man.

"We'll go for the tests. In the hospital. You'll arrange it?"

"Of course."

"A private room."

"That will not be necessary, Captain. It is only for tests."

"My wife would prefer a private room. She's a very modest woman. Very shy."

"I know, Captain," the doctor murmured, "I know. Shall you tell her or shall I?"

"I'll tell her."

"Yes," Dr. Bernardi said. "I believe that would be best."

The Captain went back to the reception room to wait for her, and practiced smiling.

It was a doxy of a day, merry and flirting. There was a hug of sun, a kiss of breeze. Walking north on Fifth Avenue, they heard the snap of flags, saw the glister of an early September sky. Captain Delaney, who knew his city in all its moods and tempers, was conscious of a hastened rhythm. Summer over, vacation done, Manhattan rushed to Christmas and the New Year.

His wife's hand was in his arm. When he glanced sideways at her, she had never seemed to him so beautiful. The blonde hair, now silvered and fined, was drawn up from her brow and pinned in a loose chignon. The features, once precise, had been softened by time. The lips were limpid, the line of chin and throat something. Oh she was something! And the glow (that damned fever!) gave her skin a grapy youthfulness.

She was almost as tall as he, walked erect and alert, her hand lightly on his arm. Men looked at her with longing, and Delaney was proud. How she strode, laughing at things! Her head turned this way and that, as if she was seeing everything for the first time. The last time? A cold finger touched.

She caught his stare and winked solemnly. He could not smile, but pressed her arm close to his body. The important thing, he thought—the most important thing—was that . . . was that she should out-live him. Because if not . . . if not . . . he thought of other things.

She was almost five years older than he, but she was the warmth, humor, and heart of their marriage. He was born old, with hope, a secret love of beauty, and a taste for melancholy. But she had brought to their home a recipe for lentil soup, thin nightgowns with pink ribbons, and laughter. He was bad enough; without her he would have been a grotesque.

They strolled north on Fifth Avenue, on the west side. As they approached the curb at 56th Street, the traffic light was about to change. They could have made it across safely, but he halted her.

"Wait a minute," he said. "I want to catch this."

His quick eye had seen a car—a station wagon with Illinois license plates—coming southward on Fifth Avenue. It attempted to turn westward onto 56th Street, going the wrong way on a one-way street. Immediately there was a great blaring of horns. A dozen pedestrians shouted, "One-way!" The car came to a shuddering halt, nosing into approaching traffic. The driver bent over the wheel, shaken. The woman beside him, apparently his wife, grabbed his arm. In the seat behind them two little boys jumped about excitedly, going from window to window.

A young uniformed patrolman had been standing on the northwest corner of the intersection, his back against a plate glass window. Now, smiling, he sauntered slowly toward the stalled car.

"Midtown Squad," Captain Delaney muttered to his wife. "They pick the big, handsome ones."

The officer wandered around to the driver's side, leaned down, and there was a brief conversation. The couple in the out-of-state car laughed with relief. The policeman cocked thumb and forefinger at the two kids in the back and clicked his tongue. They giggled delightedly.

"He's not going to ticket them?" Delaney said indignantly. "He's going to let them go?"

The patrolman moved back onto Fifth Avenue and halted traffic. He waved the Illinois car to back up. He got it straightened out and heading safely downtown again.

"I'm going to—" Captain Delaney started.

"Edward," his wife said. "Please."

He hesitated. The car moved away, the boys in the back waving frantically at the policeman who waved back.

Delaney looked sternly at his wife. "I'm going to get his name and tin number," he said. "Those one-way signs are plain. He should have—"

"Edward," she repeated patiently, "they're obviously on vacation. Did you see the luggage in the back? They don't know our system of one-way streets. Why spoil their holiday? With two little boys? I think the patrolman handled it beautifully. Perhaps that will be the nicest thing that happens to them in New York, and they'll want to come back again. Edward?"

He looked at her. ("Your wife is obviously ill . . . the fever

. . . hair in her comb . . . you have three options . . . infection that . . .") He took her arm, led her carefully across the street. They walked the next block in silence.

"Well, anyway," he grumbled, "his sideburns were too long. You won't find sideburns like that in *my* precinct."

"I wonder why?" she said innocently, then laughed and leaned sideways to touch her head against his shoulder.

He had plans for lunch at the Plaza, window-shopping, visiting the antique shops on Third Avenue—things she enjoyed doing together on his day off. It was important that she should be happy for a time before he told her. But when she suggested a walk through the Park and lunch on the terrace at the zoo, he agreed instantly. It would be better; he would find a bench where they could be alone.

As they crossed 59th Street into the Park, he looked about with wonder. Now what had been there before the General Motors Building?

"The Savoy-Plaza," she said.

"Mind-reader," he said.

So she was—where he was concerned.

The city changed overnight. Tenements became parking lots became excavations became stabbing office buildings while your head was turned. Neighborhoods disappeared, new restaurants opened, brick changed to glass, three stories sprouted to thirty, streets bloomed with thin trees, a little park grew where you remembered an old Irish bar had been forever.

It was his city, where he was born and grew up. It was home. Who could know its cankers better than he? But he refused to despair. His city would endure and grow more beautiful.

Part of his faith was based on knowledge of its past sins: all history now. He knew the time when the Five Points Gang bit off enemies' ears and noses in tavern brawls, when farm lads were drugged and shanghaied from the Swamp, when children's bordellos flourished in the Tenderloin, when Chinese hatchetmen blasted away with heavy pistols (and closed eyes) in the Bloody Triangle.

All this was gone now and romanticized, for old crime, war, and evil enter books and are leached of blood and pain. Now his city was undergoing new agonies. These too, he was convinced would pass if men of good will would not deny the future.

His city was an affirmation of life: its beauty, harshness, sorrow, humor, horror, and ecstasy. In the pushing and shoving, in the brutality and violence, he saw striving, the never-ending flux of life, and would not trade it for any place on earth. It could grind a man to litter, or raise him to the highest coppered roof, glinting in benignant sunlight.

They entered the Park at 60th Street, walking between the facing rows of benches toward the zoo. They stopped before the yak's cage and looked at the great, brooding beast, his head lowered, eyes staring at a foreign world with dull wonder.

"You," Barbara Delaney said to her husband.

He laughed, turned her around by the elbow, pointed to the cage across the way where a graceful Sika deer stood poised and alert, head proud on slim neck, eyes gleaming.

"You," Edward Delaney said to his wife.

They lunched lightly. He fretted with his emptied coffee cup: peering into it, turning it over, revolving it in his blunt fingers.

"All right," she sighed in mock weariness, "go make your phone call."

He glanced at her gratefully. "It'll just take a minute."

"I know. Just to make sure the Precinct is still there."

The thick voice said, "Two hundred and fifty-first Precinct. Officer Curdy. May I help you?"

"This is Captain Edward X. Delaney," he said in his leaden voice. "Connect me with Lieutenant Dorfman, please."

"Oh. Yes, Captain. I think he's upstairs. Just a minute; I'll find him."

Dorfman came on almost immediately. " 'Lo, Captain. Enjoying your day off? Beautiful day."

"Yes. What's happening?"

"Nothing unusual, sir. The usual. A small demonstration at the Embassy again, but we moved them along. No charges. No injuries."

"Damage?"

"One broken window, sir."

"All right. Have Donaldson type up the usual letter of apology, and I'll sign it tomorrow."

"It's done, Captain. It's on your desk."

"Oh. Well . . . fine. Nothing else?"

"No, sir. Everything under control."

"All right. Switch me back to the man on the board, will you?"

"Yes, sir. I'll buzz him."

The uniformed operator came back on.

"Captain?"

67

"Is this Officer Curdy?"

"Yes, sir."

"Curdy, you answered my original call with: 'Two hundred and fifty-first Precinct.' In my memo number six three one, dated fourteen July of this year, I gave very explicit orders governing the procedure of uniformed telephone operators on duty. I stated in that memorandum that incoming calls were to be answered: 'Precinct two five one.' It is shorter and much more understandable than 'Two hundred and fifty-first Precinct.' Did you read that memo?"

"Yes, sir. Yes, Captain, I did read it. It just slipped my mind, sir. I'm so used to doing it the old way . . ."

"Curdy, there is no 'old way.' There is a right way and a wrong way of doing things. And 'Two five one' is the right way in my precinct. Is that clear?"

"Yes, sir."

He hung up and went back to his wife. In the New York Police Department he was known as "Iron Balls" Delaney. He knew it and didn't mind. There were worse names.

"Everything all right?" she asked.

He nodded.

"Who has the duty?"

"Dorfman."

"Oh? How is his father?"

He stared at her, eyes widening. Then he lowered his head and groaned. "Oh God. Barbara, I forgot to tell you. Dorfman's father died last week. On Friday."

"Oh Edward." She looked at him reproachfully. "Why on earth didn't you tell me?"

"Well, I meant to but—but it slipped my mind."

"Slipped your mind? How could a thing like that slip your mind? Well, I'll write a letter of condolence as soon as we get home."

"Yes, do that. They took up a collection for flowers. I gave twenty dollars."

"Poor Dorfman."

"Yes."

"You don't like him, do you?"

"Of course I like him. As a man, a person. But he's really not a good cop."

"He's not? I thought you told me he does his job very well."

"He does. He's a good administrator, keeps up on his paperwork. He's one of the best lawyers in the Department. But he's not a good cop. He's a reasonable facsimile. He goes through all the motions, but he lacks the instinct."

"And tell me, oh wise one," she said, "what is this great cop's instinct?"

He was glad to have someone to talk to about such things.

"Well," he said, "laugh if you like, but it does exist. What drove me to become a cop? My father wasn't. No one in my family was. I could have gone on to law school; my marks were good enough. But all I ever wanted was to be a cop. As long as I can remember. And I'll tell you why: because when the laundry comes back from the Chinaman—as you well know, my dear, after thirty years—I insist on—"

"Thirty-one years, brute."

"All right, thirty-one years. But the first year we lived in sin."

"You *are* a brute," she laughed.

"Well, we did: the most marvelous year of my life."

She put a hand over his. "And everything since then has been anti-climax?"

"You know better than that. All right, now let me get back to the instinct of a true cop."

"And the Chinaman's laundry."

"Yes. Well, as you know, I insist on putting my own clean clothes away in the bureau and dresser. Socks are folded once and piled with the fold forward. Handkerchiefs are stacked with the open edges to the right. Shirts are stacked alternately, collar to the rear, collar to the front—so the stack won't topple, you understand. And a similar system for underwear, pajamas, and so forth. And always, of course, the freshly laundered clothes go on the bottom of each pile so everything is worn evenly and in order. That's the word: 'order.' That's the way I am. You know it. I want everything in order."

"And that's why you became a cop? To make the world neat and tidy?"

"Yes."

She moved her head back slowly and laughed. How he loved to see her laugh. If only he could laugh like that! It was such a whole-hearted expression of pure joy: her eyes squinched shut, her mouth open, shoulders shaking, and a surprisingly full, deep guffaw that was neither feminine nor masculine but sexless and primitive as all genuine laughter.

"Edward, Edward," she said, spluttering a little, taking a lace-edged hanky from her purse to wipe her eyes. "You have a marvelous capacity for deluding yourself. I guess that's why I love you so."

"All right," he said, miffed. "You tell me. Why did I become a cop?"

Again she covered his hand with hers. She looked into his eyes, suddenly serious.

"Don't you know?" she asked gently. "Don't you *really* know? Because you love beauty. Oh, I know law and order and justice are important to you. But what you really want is a beautiful world where everything is true and nothing is false. You dreamer!"

He thought about that a long time. Then they rose, and hand in hand they strolled into the park.

In Central Park, there is an inclosed carrousel that has been a delight to generations of youngsters. Some days, when the wind is right, you can hear its musical tinkle from a distance; the air seems to dance.

The animals—marvelously carved and painted horses— chase each other in a gay whirl that excites children and hypnotizes their parents. On a bench near this merry-go-round, Barbara and Edward Delaney sat to rest, shoulders touching. They could hear the music, see the giddy gyrations through trees still wearing summer's green.

They sat awhile in silence. Then she said, not looking at him, "Can you tell me now?"

He nodded miserably. As rapidly as he could, he delivered a concise report of what Dr. Bernardi had told him. He omitted only the physician's fleeting reference to a "Proteus infection."

"I see no choice," he said, and gripped her hand harder. "Do you? We've got to get this cleared up. I'll feel better if Bernardi brings in other men. I think you will, too. It only means five days to a week in the hospital. Then they'll decide what must be done. I told Bernardi to go ahead, get the room. A private room. Barbara? Is that all right?"

He wondered if she heard him. Or if she understood. Her eyes were far away, and he did not know the smile on her soft lips.

"Barbara?" he asked again.

"During the war," she said, "when you were in France, I brought the children here when the weather was nice. Eddie could walk then but Elizabeth was still in the carriage. Sometimes Eddie would get tired on the way home, and I'd put him in the carriage with Liza. How he hated it!"

"I know. You wrote me."

"Did I? Sometimes we'd sit on this very bench where we're sitting now. Eddie would ride the merry-go-round all day if I let him."

"He always rode a white horse."

"You do remember," she smiled. "Yes, he always rode a white horse, and every time he came around he'd wave at us, sitting up straight. He was so proud."

"Yes."

"They're good children, aren't they, Edward?"

"Yes."

"Happy children."

"Well, I wish Eddie would get married, but there's no use nagging him."

"No. He's stubborn. Like his father."

"Am I stubborn?"

"Sometimes. About some things. When you've made up your mind. Like my going into the hospital for tests."

"You will go, won't you?"

She gave him a dazzling smile, then unexpectedly leaned forward to kiss him on the lips. It was a soft, youthful, lingering kiss that shocked him with its longing.

And late that night she still burned with that longing, her body kindled with lust and fever. She came naked into his arms and seemed intent on draining him, exhausting him, taking all for herself and leaving nothing.

He tried to contain her fury—so unlike her; she was usually languorous and teasing—but her rage defeated him. Once, thrashing about in a sweated paroxysm, she called him "Ted," which she had not done since their life together was born.

He did what he could to satisfy and soothe, wretchedly conscious that his words were not heard nor his caresses felt; the most he could do was be. Her storm passed, leaving him riven. He gnawed a knuckle and fell asleep.

He awoke a few hours later, and she was gone from the bed. He was instantly alert, pulled on his old patterned robe with its frazzled cord. Barefoot, he went padding downstairs, searching all the empty rooms.

He found her in what they still called the "parlor" of their converted brownstone, next door to the 251st Precinct house. She was on the window seat, clad in a white cotton nightgown. Her knees were drawn up, clasped. In the light from the hallway he could see her head bent forward. Her hair was down, hiding her face, drifting shoulders and knees.

"Barbara," he called.

Her head came up. Hair fell back. She gave him a smile that twisted his heart.

"I'm dying," she said.

2

Barbara Delaney's stay in the hospital for tests was longer than the five days predicted by Dr. Louis Bernardi. It became a weekend and five days, then two weekends and five days, and finally a total of fifteen days. To every inquiry by Captain Edward X. Delaney, the doctor answered only, "More tests."

From his daily—sometimes twice-daily—visits to his wife's private room, Delaney came away with the frightening impression that things were not going well at all. The fever persisted, up one day, down slightly the next. But the course was steadily upward. Once it hit almost 103; the woman was burning up.

He himself had been witness to the sudden chills that racked her body, set teeth chattering and limbs trembling. Nurses came hurrying with extra blankets and hot water bottles. Five minutes later she was burning again; blankets were tossed aside, her face was rosy, she gasped for breath.

New symptoms developed during those fifteen days: headaches, urination so difficult she had to be catheterized, severe pain in the lumbar region, sudden attacks of nausea that left her limp. Once she vomited into a basin he held for her. She looked up at him meekly; he turned away to stare out the window, his eyes bleary.

On the morning he finally decided, against his wife's wishes, to dismiss Bernardi and bring in a new man, he was called at his Precinct office and summoned to an early afternoon meeting with Bernardi in his wife's hospital room. Lieutenant Dorfman saw him off with anguished eyes.

"Please, Captain," he said, "try not to worry. She's going to be all right."

Marty Dorfman was an extraordinarily tall (6'4") Jew with light blue eyes and red hair that spiked up from a squeezed skull. He wore size 14 shoes and couldn't find gloves to fit. He seemed constantly to be dribbled with crumbs, and had never been known to swear.

Nothing fitted; his oversize uniform squirmed on thin shoulders, trousers bagged like a Dutch boy's bloomers. Cigarette ashes smudged his cuffs. Occasionally his socks didn't match, and he had lost the clasp on the choker collar of his jacket. His shoes were unshined, and he reported for duty with a dried froth of shaving cream beneath his ears.

Once, when a patrolman, he had been forced to kill a knife-wielding burglar. Since then he carried an unloaded gun. He thought no one knew, but everyone did. As Captain Delaney had told his wife, Dorfman's paperwork was impeccable and he had one of the finest legal minds in the Department. He was a sloven, but when men of the 251st Precinct had personal problems, they went to him. He had never been known to miss the funeral of a policeman killed in line of duty. Then he wore a clean uniform and wept.

"Thank you, lieutenant," Delaney said stiffly. "I will call as soon as possible. I fully expect to return before you go off. If not, don't wait for me. Is that clear?"

"Yes, Captain."

Dr. Louis Bernardi, Delaney decided, was perfectly capable of holding the hand of a dying man and saying, "There there." Now he was displaying the X-rays proudly, as if they were his own Rembrandt prints.

"The shadows!" he cried. "See the shadows!"

He had drawn a chair up close to the bedside of Barbara Delaney. The Captain stood stolidly on the other side, hands clasped behind him so their tremble might not reveal him.

"What are they?" he asked in his iron voice.

"What is it?" his wife murmured.

"Kidney stones!" Bernardi cried happily. "Yes, dear lady," he continued, addressing the woman on the bed who stared at him sleepily, her head wavering slightly, "the possibility was there: a stubborn fever and chills. And more recently the headaches, nausea, difficulty in passing water, pain in the lower back. This morning, after more than ten days of exhaustive tests—which I am certain, he-he, you found exhausting as well as exhaustive—we held a conference—all the professional men who have been concerned with your condition—and the consensus is that you are, unhappily, suffering from a kidney calculus."

His tone was so triumphant that Delaney couldn't trust himself to speak. His wife turned her head on the pillow to look warningly at him. When he nodded, she turned back to Bernardi to ask weakly:

"How did I get kidney stones?"

The doctor leaned back in his chair, made his usual gesture of placing his two index fingers together and pressing them against his pouting lips.

"Who can say?" he asked softly. "Diet, stress, perhaps a predisposition, heredity. There is so much we don't know. If we knew everything, life would be a bore, would it not? He!"

Delaney grunted disgustedly. Bernardi paid no heed.

"In any event, that is our diagnosis. Kidney stones. A concretion frequently found in the bladder or kidneys. A hard, inorganic stone. Some no larger than a pinhead. Some quite large. They are foreign matter lodged in living tissue. The body, the living tissue, cannot endure this invasion. Hence, the fever, the chills, the pain. And, of course, the difficulty in urinating. Oh yes, that above all."

Once again Delaney was infuriated by the man's self-satisfaction. To Bernardi, it was all a crossword puzzle from the *Times*.

"How serious is it?" Barbara asked faintly.

A glaze seemed to come down over Bernardi's swimming eyes, a milky, translucent film. He could see out but no one could see in.

"We needed the blood tests and these sensitive plates. And then, since you have been here, the symptoms that developed gave us added indications. Now we know what we are facing."

"How serious is it?" Barbara asked again, more determinedly.

"We feel," Bernardi went on, not listening, "we feel that in your case, dear lady, surgery is indicated. Oh yes. Definitely. I am sorry to say. Surgery."

"Wait," Delaney held up his hand. "Wait just a minute. Before we start talking about surgery. I know a man who had kidney stones. They gave him a liquid, something, and he passed them and was all right. Can't my wife do the same?"

"Quite impossible," Bernardi said shortly. "When the stones are tiny, that procedure is sometimes effective. These X-rays show a large area of inflammation. Surgery is indicated."

"Who decided that?" Delaney demanded.

"We did."

" 'We'?" Delaney asked. "Who is 'we'?"

Bernardi looked at him coldly. He sat back, pulled up one trouser leg, carefully crossed his knees. "Myself and the specialists I called in," he said. "I have their professional opinions here, Captain—their written and signed opinions—and I have prepared a duplicate set for your use."

Captain Edward X. Delaney had interrogated enough witnesses and suspects in his long career to know when a man or woman was lying. The tip-off could come in a variety of ways. With the stupid or inexperienced it came with a physical gesture: a shifting away of the eyes, a nervous movement, blinking, perhaps a slight skim of sweat or a sudden deep breath. The intelligent and experienced revealed their falsehood in different ways: a too deliberate nonchalance, or an "honest" stare, eyeball to eyeball, or by a serious, intent fretting of the brows. Sometimes they leaned forward and smiled candidly.

But this man was not lying; the Captain was convinced of that. He was also convinced Bernardi was not telling the whole truth. He was holding something back, something distasteful to him.

"All right," Delaney grated, "we have their signed opinions. I assume they all agree?"

Bernardi's eyes glittered with malice. He leaned forward to pat Barbara's hand, lying limply atop the thin blue blanket. "There there," he said.

"It is not a very serious operation," he continued. "It is performed frequently in every hospital in the country. But all surgery entails risk. Even lancing a boil. I am certain you understand this. No surgery should ever be taken lightly."

"We don't take it lightly," Delaney said angrily, thinking this man—this "foreigner"—just didn't know how to talk.

During this exchange Barbara Delaney's head moved side to side, back and forth between husband and doctor.

"Very well," Delaney went on, holding himself in control, "you recommend surgery. You remove those kidney stones, and my wife regains her health. Is that it? There's nothing more you're not telling us?"

"Edward," she said. "Please."

"I want to know," he said stubbornly. "I want you to know."

Bernardi sighed. He seemed about to mediate between them, then thought better of it.

"That is our opinion," he nodded. "I cannot give you an iron-clad one hundred percent guarantee. No physician or surgeon can. You must know that. This, admittedly, will be an ordeal for Mrs. Delaney. Normal recuperation from this type of surgery demands a week to ten days in the hospital, and several weeks in bed at home. I don't wish to imply that this is of little importance. It is a serious situation, and I take it seriously, as I am certain you do also. But you are essentially a healthy woman, dear lady, and I see nothing in your medical record that would indicate anything but a normal recovery."

"And there's no choice but surgery?" Delaney demanded again.

"No. You have no choice."

A small cry came from Barbara Delaney, no louder than a kitten's mew. She reached out a pale hand to her husband; he grasped it firmly in his big paw.

"But we have no assurance?" he asked, realizing he was again repeating himself, and that his voice was desperate.

The translucent film over Bernardi's eyes seemed to become more opaque. Now it was the pearly cover on the eyes of a blind dog.

"No assurance," he said shortly. "None whatsoever."

Silence fell into the pastel room like a gentle rain. They looked at each other, all three, heads going back and forth, eyes flickering. They could hear the noises of the hospital: loudspeakers squawking, carts creaking by, murmured voices, and somewhere a radio playing dance music. But in this room the three looked into each others' eyes and were alone, swaddled in silence.

"Thank you, doctor," Delaney said harshly. "We will discuss it."

Bernardi nodded, rose swiftly. "I will leave you these documents," he said, placing a file on the bedside table. "I suggest you read them carefully. Please do not delay your decision more than twenty-four hours. We must not let this go on, and plans must be made."

He bounced from the room, light on his feet for such a stout man.

Edward X. Delaney had been born a Catholic and raised a Catholic. Communion and confession were as much a part of his life as love and work. He was married in the Church, and his children attended parochial schools. His faith was monolithic. Until 1945 . . .

On a late afternoon in 1945, the sun hidden behind a sky black with oily smoke, Captain Delaney led his company of Military Police to the liberation of a concentration camp in north Germany. The barbed wire gate was swinging wide. There was no sign of activity. The Captain deployed his armed men. He himself, pistol drawn, strode up to an unpainted barracks and threw open the door.

The things stared at him.

A moan came up from his bowels. This single moan, passing

76

his lips, took with it Church and faith, prayer and confidence, ceremony, panoply, habit and trust. He never thought of such things again. He was a cop and had his own reasons.

Now, sensing what lay ahead, he yearned for the Church as a voluntary exile might yearn for his own native land. But to return in time of need was a baseness his pride could not endure. They would see it through together, the two of them, her strength added to his. The aggregate—by the peculiar alchemy of their love—was greater than the sum of the parts.

He sat on the edge of her bed, smiled, smoothed her hair with his heavy hand. A nurses' aide had brushed her hair smooth and tied it back with a length of thick blue knitting wool.

"I know you don't like him," she said.

"That's not important," he shook his great head. "What is important is that you trust him. Do you?"

"Yes."

"Good. But I still want to talk to Ferguson."

"You don't want to decide now?"

"No. Let me take the papers and try to understand them. Then I'll show them to Ferguson and get his opinion. Tonight, if possible. Then I'll come back tomorrow and we'll discuss it. Will that be all right?"

"Yes," she said. "Did Mary do the curtains?" She was referring to their Monday-to-Friday, 8-to-4 maid.

"Yes, she did. And she brushed and aired the living room drapes in the backyard. Tomorrow she'll do the parlor drapes if the weather holds. She wants so much to visit you but I said you weren't up to it. I've told all your friends that. Are you sure it's what you want?"

"Yes. I don't want anyone to see me like this. Maybe later I'll feel up to it. What did you have for breakfast?"

"Let's see . . ." he said, trying to remember. "A small orange juice. Cereal, no sugar. Dry toast and black coffee."

"Very good," she nodded approvingly. "You're sticking to your diet. What did you have for lunch?"

"Well, things piled up, and we had to send out for sandwiches. I had roast beef on whole wheat and a large tomato juice."

"Oh Edward," she said, "that's not enough. You must promise that tonight you'll—" Suddenly she stopped; tears flooded up to her eyes and out, down her cheeks. "Oh Jesus," she cried. "Why me?"

She lurched up to embrace him. He held her close, her wet face against his. His blunt fingers stroked her back, and he kept repeating, "I love you, I love you, I love you," over and over. It didn't seem enough.

He went back to the Precinct carrying her medical file. The moment he was at his desk he called Dr. Sanford Ferguson, but couldn't reach him. He tried the Medical Examiner's office, the morgue, and Ferguson's private office. No one knew where he was. Delaney left messages everywhere.

Then he put the medical file aside and went to work. Dorfman and two Precinct detectives were waiting to see him, on separate cases. There was a deputation of local businessmen to demand more foot patrolmen. There was a group of black militants to protest "police brutality" in breaking up a recent march. There was a committee of Jewish leaders to discuss police action against demonstrations held almost daily in front of an Egyptian embassy located in the Precinct. There was an influential old woman with an "amazing new idea" for combatting drug addiction (put sneezing powder in cocaine). And there was a wealthy old man charged (for the second time) with exhibiting himself to toddlers.

Captain Delaney listened to all of them, nodding gravely. Occasionally he spoke in a voice so deliberately low his listeners had to crane forward to hear. He had learned from experience that nothing worked so well as quiet, measured tones to calm anger and bring people, if not to reason then to what was possible and practical.

It was 8:00 p.m. before his outer office had emptied. He rose and forced back his massive shoulders, stretching wide. This kind of work, he had discovered, was a hundred times more wearying than walking a beat or riding a squad. It was the constant, controlled exercise of judgment and will, of convincing, persuading, soothing, dictating and, when necessary, surrendering for a time, to take up the fight another day.

He cleaned up his desk, taking a regretful look at the paperwork that had piled up in one day and must wait for tomorrow. Before leaving, he looked in at lockups and squad rooms, at interrogation rooms and the detectives' cubbyholes. The 251st Precinct house was almost 90 years old. It was cramped, it creaked, and it smelled like all antique precinct houses in the city. A new building had been promised by three different city administrations. Captain Delaney made do. He took a final look at the Duty Sergeant's blotter before he walked next door to his home.

Even older than the Precinct house, it had been built originally as a merchant's townhouse. It had deteriorated over the years until, when Delaney bought it with the inheritance from his father's estate ($28,000), it had become a rooming house, chopped up into rat- and roach-infested one-room apartments. But Delaney had satisfied himself that the building was structurally sound, and Barbara's quick eye had seen the original marble fireplaces and walnut paneling (painted over but capable of being restored), the rooms for the children, the little paved areaway and overgrown garden. So they had bought it, never dreaming he would one day be commanding officer of the Precinct house next door.

Mary had left the hall light burning. There was a note Scotch-taped to the handsome pier glass. She had left slices of cold lamb and potato salad in the refrigerator. There was lentil soup he could heat up if he wanted it, and an apple tart for dessert. It all seemed good to him, but he had to watch his weight. He decided to skip the soup.

First he called the hospital. Barbara sounded sleepy and didn't make much sense; he wondered if they had given her a sedative. He spoke to her for only a few moments and thought she was relieved when he said good-night.

He went into the kitchen, took off his uniform jacket and gun belt and hung them on the back of a chair. First he mixed a rye highball, his first drink of the day. He sipped it slowly, smoked a cigarette (his third of the day), and wondered why Dr. Ferguson hadn't returned his calls. Suddenly he realized it might be Ferguson's day off, in which case he had probably been out playing golf.

Carrying the drink, he went into the study and rummaged through the desk for his address book. He found Ferguson's home number and dialed. Almost immediately a jaunty voice answered:

"Doctor Ferguson."

"Captain Edward X. Delaney here."

"Hello, Captain Edward X. Delaney there," the voice laughed. "What the hell's wrong with you—got a dose of clap from a fifteen-year-old bimbo?"

"No. It's about my wife. Barbara."

The tone changed immediately.

"Oh. What's the problem, Edward?"

"Doctor, would it be possible to see you tonight?"

"Both of you or just you?"

"Just me. She's in the hospital."

"I'm sorry to hear that. Edward, you caught me on the way out. They've dragged me into an emergency cut-'em-up." *(The doctor's slang for an autopsy.*) "I won't be home much before midnight. Too late?"

"No. I can be at your home at midnight. Will that be all right?"

"Sure. What's this all about?"

"I'd rather tell you in person. And there are papers. Documents. Some X-rays."

"I see. All right, Edward. Be here at twelve."

"Thank you, doctor."

He went back into the kitchen to eat his cold lamb and potato salad. It all tasted like straw. He put on his heavy, black-rimmed glasses, and as he ate slowly, he methodically read every paper in Barbara's medical file, and even held the X-rays up to the overhead light, although they meant nothing to him. There she was, in shadows: the woman who meant everything to him.

He finished eating and reading at the same time. All the doctors seemed to agree. He decided to skip the apple tart and black coffee. But he mixed another rye highball and, in his skivvie shirt, went wandering through the empty house.

It was the first time since World War II he and his wife had slept under separate roofs. He was bereft, and in all those darkened rooms he felt her presence and wanted her: sight, voice, smell, laugh, slap of slippered feet, touch . . . *her*.

The children were there, too, in the echoing rooms. Cries and shouts, quarrels and stumblings. Eager questions. Wailing tears. Their life had soaked into the old walls. Holiday meals. Triumphs and defeats. The fabric of a family. All silent now, and dark as the shadows on an X-ray film.

He climbed stairs slowly to vacant bedrooms and attic. The house was too big for the two of them: no doubt about it. But still . . . There was the door jamb where Liza's growth had been marked with pencil ticks. There was the flight of stairs Eddie had tumbled down and cut his chin and never cried. There was the very spot where one of their many dogs had coughed up his life in bright blood, and Barbara had become hysterical.

It wasn't much, he supposed. It was neither high tragedy nor low comedy. No great heights or depths. But a steady wearing away of the years. Time evened whatever drama there may have been. Time dimmed the colors; the shouting died. But the golden monochrome, the soft tarnish that was left had meaning for him. He wandered through the dim corridors of his life, thinking deep thoughts and making foolish wishes.

Dr. Sanford Ferguson, a bachelor, was a big man, made bigger by creaseless tweed suits worn with chain-looped vests. He was broad through the shoulders and broad through the chest. He was not corpulent but his thighs were as big around as another man's waist, and his arms were meaty and strong.

No one doubted his cleverness. At parties he could relate endless jokes that had the company helpless with laughter. He knew many dialects perfectly and, in his cups, could do an admirable soft-shoe clog. He was much in demand as an after-dinner speaker at meetings of professional associations. He was an ineffectual but enthusiastic golfer. He sang a sweet baritone. He could make a soufflé. And, unknown to everyone (including his older spinster sister), he kept a mistress: a middle-aged colored lady he loved and by whom he had fathered three sons.

He was also, Delaney knew, an experienced and cynical police surgeon. Violent death did not dismay him, and he was not often fooled by the obvious. In "natural deaths" he sniffed out arsenic. In "accidental deaths" he would pry out the fatal wound in a corpus of splinters.

"Here's your rye," he said, handing the highball to Delaney. "Now sit there and keep your mouth shut, and let me read and digest."

It was after midnight. They were in the living room of Ferguson's apartment on Murray Hill. The spinster sister had greeted Delaney and then disappeared, presumably to bed. The doctor had mixed a rye highball for his guest and poured a hefty brandy for himself in a water tumbler.

Delaney sat quietly in an armchair pinned with an antimacassar. Dr. Ferguson sat on a spindly chair at a fine Queen Anne lowboy. His bulk threatened to crush chair and table. His wool tie was pulled wide, shirt collar open: wiry hair sprang free.

"That was a nice cut-'em-up tonight," he remarked, peering at the documents in the file Delaney had handed over. "A truck driver comes home from work. Greenwich Village. He finds his wife, he says, on the kitchen floor. Her head's in the oven. The room's full of gas. He opens the window. She's dead. I can attest to that. She was depressed, the truck driver says. She often threatened suicide, he says. Well . . . maybe. We'll see. We'll see."

"Who's handling it?" Delaney asked.

"Sam Rosoff. Assault and Homicide South. You know him?"

"Yes. An old-timer. Good man."

"He surely is, Edward. He spotted the cigar stub in the ashtray on the kitchen table. A cold butt, but the saliva still wet. What would you have done?"

"Ask you to search for a skull contusion beneath the dead woman's hair and start looking for the truck driver's girl friend."

Dr. Ferguson laughed. "Edward, you're wonderful! That's exactly what Rosoff suggested. I found the contusion. Right now he's out looking for the girlfriend. Do you miss detective work?"

"Yes."

"You were the best," Ferguson said, "until you decided to become Commissioner. Now shut up, lad, and let me read."

Silence.

"Oh-ho," Ferguson said. "My old friend Bernardi."

"You know him?" Delaney asked, surprised.

"I do indeed."

"What do you think of him?"

"As a physician? Excellent. As a man? A prick. No more talk."

Silence.

"Do you know any of the others?" Delaney asked finally. "The specialists he brought in?"

"I know two of the five—the neurologist and the radiologist. They're among the best in the city. This must be costing you a fortune. If the other three are as talented, your wife is in good hands. I can check. Now be quiet."

Silence.

"Oh well," Ferguson shrugged, still reading, "kidney stones. That's not so bad."

"You've had cases?"

"All the time. Mostly men, of course. You know who get 'em? Cab drivers. They're bouncing around on their ass all day."

"What about my wife?"

"Well, listen, Edward, it could be diet, it could be stress. There's so much we don't know."

"My wife eats sensibly, rarely takes a drink, and she's the most—most serene woman I've ever met."

"Is she? Let me finish reading."

He went through all the reports intently, going back occasionally to check reports he had already finished. He didn't even glance at the X-rays. Finally he shoved back from the table, poured himself another huge brandy, freshened the Captain's highball.

"Well?" Delaney asked.

"Edward," Ferguson said, frowning, "don't bring me in. Or anyone else. Bernardi is a bombastic, opinionated, egotistical shit. But as I said, he's a good sawbones. On your wife's case he's done everything exactly right. He's tried everything except surgery—correct?"

"Well, he tried antibiotics. They didn't work."

"No, they wouldn't on kidney stones. But they didn't locate *that* until they got her in the hospital for sensitive plates, and then the trouble passing urine started. That's recent, isn't it?"

"Yes. Only in the last four or five days."

"Well, then . . ."

"You recommend surgery?" Delaney asked in a dead voice.

Ferguson whirled on him. "I recommend nothing," he said sharply. "It's not my case. But you've got no choice."

"That's what he said."

"He was right. Bite the bullet, m'lad."

"What are her chances?"

"You want betting odds, do you? With surgery, very good indeed."

"And without?"

"Forget it."

"It's not fair," Delaney cried furiously.

Ferguson looked at him strangely. "What the fuck is?" he asked.

They stared at each other a long moment. Then Ferguson went back to the table. flipped through the X-rays, selected one and held it up to the light of a tilted desk lamp. "Kidney," he muttered. "Yes, yes."

"What is it, doctor?"

"He told you and I told you: calculus in the kidneys, commonly known as stones."

"That's not what I meant. Something's bothering you."

Ferguson looked at him. "You son of a bitch," he said softly. "You should never have left the detective division. I've never met anyone as—as *attuned* to people as you are."

"What is it?" Delaney repeated.

"It's nothing. Nothing I can explain. A hunch. You have them, don't you?"

"All the time."

"It's little things that don't quite add up. Maybe there's a rational explanation. The recent hysterectomy. The fever and chills that have been going on since then. But only recently the headaches, nausea, lumbar pain, and now the difficulty passing urine. It all adds up to kidney stones, but the *sequence* of symptoms is wrong. With kidney stones, pain at pissing usually comes from the start. And sometimes it's bad enough to drive you right up a wall. No record of that here. Yet the plates show . . . You tell me she's not under stress?"

"She is not."

"Every case I've had is driven, trying to do too much, bedeviled by time, rushing around, biting fingernails and screaming at the waitress when the coffee is cold. Is that Barbara?"

"No. She's totally opposite. Calm."

"You can't tell. We never know. Still . . ." He sighed. "Edward, have you ever heard of Proteus infection?"

"Bernardi mentioned it to me."

Ferguson actually staggered back a step, as if he had been struck a blow on the chest. "He *mentioned* it to you?" he demanded. "When was this?"

"About three weeks ago, when he first told me Barbara should go into the hospital for tests. He just mentioned it and said he wanted to do some reading on it. But he didn't say anything about it today. Should I have asked him?"

"Jesus Christ," Ferguson said bitterly. "No, you shouldn't have asked him. If he wanted to tell you, he would have."

"You've treated cases?"

"Proteus? Oh yes, I have indeed. Three in twenty years. Mr. Proteus is a devil."

"What happened to them?"

"The three? Two responded to antibiotics and were smoking and drinking themselves to death within forty-eight hours."

"And the third?"

Ferguson came over, gripped Delaney by the right arm, and almost lifted him to his feet. The Captain had forgotten how strong he was.

"Go have your wife's kidney stones cut out," the doctor said brutally. "She'll either live or die. Which is true for all of us. No way out, m'lad."

Delaney took a deep breath.

"All right, doctor," he said. "Thank you for your time and your—your patience. I'm sorry to have bothered you."

"Bother?" Ferguson said gruffly. "Idiot."

He walked Delaney to the door. "I might just stop by to see Barbara," he said casually. "Just as a friend of the family."

"Yes," Delaney nodded dumbly. "Please do that. She doesn't want any visitors, but I know she'll be glad to see you."

In the foyer Ferguson took Delaney by the shoulders and turned him to the light.

"Have you been sleeping okay, Edward?" he demanded.

"Not too well."

"Don't take pills. Take a stiff shot. Brandy is best. Or a glass of port. Or a bottle of stout just before you get into bed."

"Yes. All right. Thank you. I will."

They shook hands.

"Oh wait," Ferguson said. "You forgot your papers. I'll get the file for you."

But when he returned, Delaney had gone.

He stopped at his home to put on a heavy wool sweater under his uniform jacket. Then he walked next door to the Precinct house. There was a civilian car parked directly in front of the entrance. Inside the windshield, on the passenger's side, a large card was displayed: PRESS.

Delaney stalked inside. There was a civilian talking to the Desk Sergeant. Both men broke off their conversation and turned when he tramped in.

"Is that your car?" he asked the man. "In front of the station?"

"Yes, that's mine. I was—"

"You a reporter?"

"Yes. I was just—"

"Move it. You're parked in a zone reserved for official cars only. It's clearly marked."

"I just wanted—"

"Sergeant," Delaney said, "if that car isn't moved within two minutes, issue this man a summons. If it's still there after five minutes, call a truck and have it towed away. Is that clear?"

"Yes, sir."

"Now look here—" the man started.

Delaney walked by him and went up to his office. He took a black-painted three-cell flashlight from the top drawer of his file cabinet. He also slipped a short, hard rubber truncheon into his jacket pocket and hung a steel "come-along" on his gun belt.

When he came out into the chilly night again, the Press car had been reparked across the street. But the reporter was standing on the sidewalk in front of the Precinct house.

"What's your name?" he asked angrily.

"Captain Edward X. Delaney. You want my shield number?"

"Oh . . . Delaney. I've heard about you."

"Have you?"

" 'Iron Balls.' Isn't that what they call you?"

"Yes."

The reporter stared, then suddenly laughed and held out his hand.

"The name's Handry, Captain. Thomas Handry. Sorry about the car. You were entirely right and I was entirely wrong."

Delaney shook his hand.

"Where you going with the flashlight, Captain?"

"Just taking a look around."

"Mind if I tag along?"

Delaney shrugged. "If you like."

They walked over to First Avenue, then turned north. The street was lined with stores, supermarkets, banks. Most of them had locked gates across doors and windows. All had a light burning within.

"See that?" Delaney gestured. "I sent a letter to every commercial establishment in my precinct requesting they keep at least a hundred-watt bulb burning all night. I kept after them. Now I have ninety-eight-point-two percent compliance. A simple thing, but it reduced breaking-and-entering of commercial establishments in this precinct by fourteen-point-seven percent."

He stopped in front of a shoe repair shop that had no iron gates. Delaney tried the door. It was securely locked.

"A little unusual, isn't it?" Handry asked, amused. "A captain making the rounds? Don't you have foot patrolmen for that?"

"Of course. When I first took over the 251st, discipline was extremely lax. So I started unscheduled inspections, on foot, mostly at night. It worked. The men never know when or where I may turn up. They stay alert."

"You do it every night?"

"Yes. Of course, I can't cover the entire Precinct, but I do a different five or six blocks every night. I don't *have* to do it anymore, you understand; my men are on their toes. But it's become a habit. I think I enjoy it. As a matter of fact, I can't get to sleep until I've made my rounds. My wife says I'm like a householder who has to go around trying all the windows and doors before he goes to bed."

A two-man squad car came purring by. The passenger officer inspected them, recognized the Captain and threw him a salute, which he returned.

Delaney tried a few more un-gated doors and then, flashlight burning, went prowling up an alleyway, the beam flickering over garbage cans and refuse heaps. Handry stayed close behind him.

They walked a few more blocks, then turned eastward toward York Avenue.

"What were you doing in my Precinct house, Handry?" the Captain asked suddenly.

"Nosing around," the reporter said. "I'm working on an article. Or rather a series of articles.

"On what?"

"Why a man wants to become a policeman, and what happens to him after he does."

"Again?" Delaney sighed. "It's been done a dozen times."

"I know. And it's going to be done again, by me. The first piece is on requirements, screening, examinations, and all that. The second will be on the Academy and probationary training. Now I'm trying to find out what happens to a man after he's assigned, and all the different directions he can go. You were originally in the detective division, weren't you?"

"That's right."

"Homicide, wasn't it?"

"For a while."

"They still talk about you, about some of your cases."

"Do they?"

"Why did you switch to patrol, Captain?"

"I wanted administrative experience," Delaney said shortly.

This time Handry sighed. He was a slender, dapper young man who looked more like an insurance salesman than a reporter. His suit was carefully pressed, shoes shined, narrow-brim hat exactly squared on his head. He wore a vest. He moved with a light-footed eagerness.

His face betrayed a certain tension, a secret passion held rigidly under control. Lips were pressed, forehead bland, eyes deliberately expressionless. Delaney had noted the bitten fingernails and a habit of stroking the upper lip downward with the second joint of his index finger.

"When did you shave your mustache?" he asked.

"You should have stayed in the detective division," Handry said. "I know I can't stop stroking my lip. Tell me, Captain— why won't policemen talk to me? Oh, they'll talk, but they won't really open up. I can't get into them. If I'm going to be a writer, that's what I've got to learn to do—how to get into people. Is it me, or are they afraid to talk for publication, or what the hell is it?"

"It isn't you—not you personally. It's just that you're not a cop. You don't belong. There's a gulf."

"But I'm trying to understand—really I am. This series is going to be very sympathetic to the police. I want it to be. I'm not out to do a hatchet job."

"I'm glad you're not. We get enough of that."

"All right, then you tell me: why *does* a man become a policeman? Who the hell in his right mind would want a job like that in this city? The pay is miserable, the hours are miserable, everyone thinks you're on the take, snot-nosed kids call you 'pig' and throw sacks of shit at you. So what the hell is the *point?*"

They were passing a private driveway alongside a luxury apartment house. Delaney heard something.

"Stay here," he whispered to Handry.

He went moving quietly up the driveway, the flashlight dark. His right hand was beneath his jacket flap, fingers on the butt of his gun.

He was back in a minute, smiling.

"A cat," he said, "in the garbage cans."

"It could have been a drug addict with a knife," Handry said.

"Yes," Delaney agreed, "it could have been."

"Well then, *why?*" Handry asked angrily.

They were strolling slowly southward on York Avenue heading back toward the Precinct house. Traffic was light at that hour, and the few pedestrians scurried along, glancing nervously over their shoulders.

"My wife and I were talking about that a few weeks ago," Delaney mused, remembering that bright afternoon in the Park. "I said I had become a cop because, essentially, I am a very orderly man. I like everything neat and tidy, and crime offends my sense of order. My wife laughed. She said I became a policeman because at heart I am an artist and want a world of beauty where everything is true and nothing is false. Since that conversation—partly because of what has happened since then—I have been thinking of what I said and what she said. And I have decided we are not so far apart—two sides of the same coin actually. You see, I became a policeman, I think, because there is, or should be, a logic to life. And this logic is both orderly and beautiful, as all good logic is. So I was right and my wife was right. I want this logic to endure. It is a simple logic of natural birth, natural living, and natural death. It is the mortality of one of us and the immortality of all of us. It is the on-going. This logic is the life of the individual, the family, the nation, and finally all people everywhere, and all things animate and inanimate. And anything that interrupts the rhythm of this logic—for all good logic does have a beautiful rhythm, you know—well, anything that interrupts that rhythm is evil. That includes cruelty, crime, and war. I can't do much about cruelty in other people; much of it is immoral but not illegal. I can guard against cruelty in myself, of course. And I can't do a great deal about war. I *can* do something about crime. Not a lot, I admit, but *something*. Because crime, *all* crime, is irrational. It is opposed to the logic of life, and so it is evil. And that is why *I* became a cop. I think."

"My God!" Handry cried. "That's great! I've got to use that. But I promise I won't mention your name."

"Please don't," Delaney said ruefully. "I'd never live it down."

Handry left him at the Precinct house. Delaney climbed slowly to his office to put away his "beat" equipment. Then he slumped in the worn swivel chair behind his desk. He wondered if he would ever sleep again.

He was ashamed of himself, as he always was when he talked too much. And what nonsense he had talked! "Logic . . . rhythm . . . immortality . . . evil." Just to tickle his vanity, of course, and give him the glow of voicing "deep thoughts" to a young reporter. But what did all that blathering have to do with the price of beans?

It was all pretty poetry, but reality was a frightened woman who had never done an unkind thing in her life now lying in a hospital bed nerving herself for what might come. There were animals you couldn't see gnawing away deep inside her, and her world would soon be blood, vomit, pus, and feces. Don't you ever forget it, m'lad. And tears.

"Rather her than me" suddenly popped into his brain, and he was so disgusted with himself, so furious at having this indecent thought of the woman he loved, that he groaned aloud and struck a clenched fist on the desk. Oh, life wasn't all that much of a joy; it was a job you worked at, and didn't often succeed.

He sat there in the gloom, hunched, thinking of all the things he must now do and the order in which he must do them. Brooding, he glowered, frowned, occasionally drew lips back to show large, yellowed teeth. He looked like some great beast brought to bay.

3

In the Metropolitan Museum of Art there is a gallery of Roman heads. Stone faces are chipped and worn. But they have a quality. Staring into those socket eyes, at those broken noses, crushed ears, splintered lips, still one feels the power of men long dead. Kill the slave who betrayed you or, if your dreams have perished, a short sword in your own gut. Edward Delaney had that kind of face; crumbling majesty.

He was seated now in his wife's hospital room, the hard sunlight profiling him. Barbara Delaney stared through a drugged dimness and saw for the first time how his features had been harshened by violence and the responsibilities of command. She remembered the young, nervy patrolman who had courted her with violets and, once, a dreadful poem.

The years and duty had not destroyed him, but they had pressed him in upon himself, condensing him. Each year he spoke less and less, laughed infrequently, and withdrew to some iron core that was his alone; she was not allowed there.

He was still a handsome man, she thought approvingly, and carried himself well and watched his weight and didn't smoke or drink too much. But now there was a somber solidity to him, and too often he sat brooding. "What is it?" she would ask. And slowly his eyes would come up from that inward stare, focus on her and life, and he would say, "Nothing." Did he think himself Nemesis for the entire world?

He had not aged so much as weathered. Seeing him now, seated heavily in sharp sunlight, she could not understand why she had never called him 'Father." It was incredible that he should be younger than she. With a prescience of doom, she wondered if he could exist without her. She decided he would. He would grieve, certainly. He would be numb and rocked. But he would survive. He was complete.

In his methodical way, he had made notes of the things he felt they should discuss. He took his little leather-bound notebook from his inside pocket and flipped the pages, then put on his heavy glasses.

"I called the children last night," he said, not looking up.

"I know, dear. I wish you hadn't. Liza called this morning. She wanted to come, but I told her absolutely not. She's almost in her eighth month now, and I don't want her traveling. Do you want a boy or girl?"

"Boy."

"Beast. Well, I told her you'd call as soon as it's over; there was no need for her to come."

"Very good," he nodded. "Eddie was planning to come up in two weeks anyway, and I told him that would be fine, not to change his plans. He's thinking of getting into politics down there. They want him to run for district attorney. I think they call it 'public prosecutor' in that state. What do you think?"

"What does Eddie want to do?"

"He's not sure. That's why he wants to come up, to discuss it with us."

"How do you feel about it, Edward?"

"I want to know more about it. Who'll be putting up the campaign funds. What he'll owe. I don't want him getting into a mess."

"Eddie wouldn't do that."

"Not deliberately. Maybe from inexperience. He's still a young man, Barbara. Politics is new to him. He must be careful. Those men who want him to run have their own ambitions. Well . . . we'll talk about it when he comes up. He promised not to make any decision until he talks to us. Now then . . ." He consulted his notes. ". . . how do you feel about Spencer?"

He was referring to the surgeon introduced by Dr. Bernardi. He was a brusque, no-nonsense man without warmth, but he had impressed Delaney with his direct questions, quick decisions, his sharp interruptions of Bernardi's effusions. The operation was scheduled for late in the afternoon of the following day. Delaney had followed the surgeon out into the hall.

"Do you anticipate any trouble, doctor?" he asked.

The surgeon, Dr. K. B. Spencer, looked at him coldly.

"No," he said.

"Oh, I suppose he's all right," Barbara Delaney said vaguely. "What do you think of him, dear?"

"I trust him," Delaney said promptly. "He's a professional. I asked Ferguson to check him out, and he says Spencer is a fine surgeon and a wealthy man."

"Good," Barbara smiled faintly. "I wouldn't want a *poor* surgeon."

She seemed to be tiring, and there was a hectic flush in her cheeks. Delaney put his notebook aside for a moment to wring out a cloth in a basin of cold water and lay it tenderly across her brow. She was already on intravenous feeding and had been instructed to move as little as possible.

"Thank you, dear," she said in a voice so low he could hardly hear her. He hurried through the remainder of his notes.

"Now then," he said, "what shall I bring tomorrow? You wanted the blue quilted robe?"

"Yes," she whispered. And the fluffy mules. The pink ones. They're in the righthand corner of my closet. My feet are swollen so badly I can't get into my slippers."

"All right," he said briskly, making a note. "Anything else? Clothes, makeup, books, fruit . . . anything?"

"No."

"Should I rent a TV set?"

She didn't answer, and when he raised his head to look at her, she seemed asleep. He took off his glasses, replaced his notebook in his pocket, began to tiptoe from the room.

"Please," she said in a weak voice, "don't go yet. Sit with me for a few minutes."

"As long as you want me," he said. He pulled a chair up to the bedside and sat hunched over, holding her hand. They sat in silence for almost five minutes.

"Edward," she breathed, her eyes closed.

"Yes. I'm here."

"Edward."

"Yes," he repeated. "I'm here."

"I want you to promise me something."

"Anything," he vowed.

"If anything should happen to me—"

"Barbara."

"If anything should—"

"Dear."

"I want you to marry again. If you meet a woman . . . Someone . . . I want you to. Will you promise?"

He couldn't breathe. Something was caught in his chest. He bowed his head, made a small noise, gripped her fingers tighter.

"Promise?" she demanded.

"Yes."

She smiled, nodded, slept.

Captain Delaney was detained by another demonstration at the embassy. By the time he got it squared away and the chanting marchers shunted off into side streets, it was late afternoon and almost time for Barbara's operation. He had one of the precinct squad cars rush him over to the hospital. He knew it was a breach of regulations, but he determined to make a full report on it, explaining the circumstances, and if they wanted to discipline him, they could.

He hurried up to her room, sweating under his longjohns and uniform jacket. They were wheeling her out as he arrived; he could only kiss her pale cheek and smile at her. She was on a cart, bundled up in blankets, the tube still attached to her arm, the jar of feeding fluid high on a rod clamped to the cart.

He left her on the second floor where the operating rooms were located. There was also a recovery ward, offices of physicians and surgeons, a small dispensary, and a large waiting room painted a bilious green and furnished with orange plastic couches and chairs. This brutal chamber was presided over by a handsome nurse, a woman of about 40, buxom, a blonde who kept poking tendrils of hair back under her starched cap.

Delaney gave his name, and she checked a frighteningly long list on her desk.

"Mrs. Barbara Delaney?"

"Yes."

"Captain, it will be another half-hour until the operation. Then Mrs. Delaney will go to the recovery ward. You won't be allowed to see her until she's returned to her room, and then only if her doctor approves."

"That's all right. I'll wait. I want to talk to the surgeon after the operation is finished."

"Well . . . " she said doubtfully, consulting her list, "I'm not sure you'll be able to. Dr. Spencer has two more scheduled after your wife. Captain, if you're hungry or want a cup of coffee, why don't you go downstairs to the cafeteria? Our paging system is connected there, and I can always call if you're needed."

"A good idea," he nodded approvingly. "Thank you. I'll do that. Do you happen to know if Dr. Bernardi is in the hospital?"

"I don't know, sir, but I'll try to find out."

"Thank you," he said again.

The food in the hospital cafeteria was, as he expected, wretched. He wondered how long they had to steam it to achieve that spongy texture and uniform color; the string beans were almost the same shiny hue as the mashed potatoes. And it all tasted as bad as it looked. Even liberal sprinklings of salt and pepper couldn't make the meat loaf taste like anything but wet wallboard. He thought of his wife's Italian stew, scented and spiced with rosemary, and he groaned.

He finally shoved the dishes away, hardly touched, and had a cup of black coffee and half a dish of chocolate pudding. Then he had another cup of coffee and smoked a cigarette. He was sweltering in the overheated cafeteria, but he never considered unhooking his choker collar. It wouldn't look right in public. He reflected on how you could always spot old cops, even in a roomful of naked men. The cops had a ring of blue dye around their necks: a lifetime of wearing that damned choker collar.

He returned to the waiting room on the second floor. The nurse told him she had located Dr. Bernardi; he was gowned and observing the kidney operation on Mrs. Delaney. The Captain thanked her and went out to the public telephone in the hall. He called the precinct. Lieutenant Rizzo had the duty and reported nothing unusual, nothing that required the Captain's attention. Delaney left the extension number of the waiting room in case he was needed.

He went back in, sat down, and looked around. There was an elderly Italian couple sitting on a couch in a corner, holding hands and looking scared. There was a young man standing propped against a wall, his face vacant. He was smoking a cigarette that threatened to burn his fingers. Seated on a plastic chair was a mink-clad matron, face raddled, showing good legs and a wattled neck. She seemed to be making an inventory of the contents of her alligator handbag.

Delaney was next to an end table scattered with magazines. He picked up a six-months-old copy of "Medical Progress," flipped through it, saw he could never understand it, put it aside. Then he sat solidly, silently, and waited. It was the detectives' art. Once, on a stake-out, he had sat in a parked car for 14 hours, relieving himself in an empty milk carton. You learned to wait. You never got to like it, but you learned how to do it.

A few things happened. The big, buxom nurse went off duty

and was replaced by a woman half her size: a tough, dark, surprisingly young Puerto Rican girl with glowing eyes, a brisk way of moving, a sharp way of talking. She took all their names and why they were there. She straightened magazines on the tables. She emptied ashtrays. Then, unexpectedly, she sprayed the room with a can of deodorant and opened a window. The room began to cool; Delaney could have kissed her.

The vacant-faced young man was called and slouched out, staring at the ceiling. The mink-clad matron suddenly stood, wrapped her coat tightly about her, and pushed through the door without speaking to the nurse. The elderly Italian couple still sat patiently in the corner, weeping quietly.

New arrivals included a stiff, white-haired gentleman leaning on a cane. He gave his name to the nurse, lowered himself into a chair, and immediately fell asleep. Then there was a pair of hippie types in faded jeans, fringed jackets, beaded headbands. They sat cross-legged on the floor and began to play some game with oversize cards whose design Delaney could not fathom.

Finally he let himself glance at the wall clock. He was shocked to see it so late. He hurried to the desk and asked the nurse about his wife. She dialed, asked, listened, hung up.

"Your wife is in the recovery ward."

"Thank you. Can you tell me where Dr. Spencer is, so I can talk to him?"

"You should have asked before. Now I have to call again."

He let her bully him. "I'm sorry," he said.

She called, asked, hung up.

"Dr. Spencer is operating and not available."

"What about Dr. Bernardi?" he said doggedly, not at all fazed by her furious glare.

Again she called, asked, spoke sharply to the person on the other end, then punched the phone down.

"Dr. Bernardi has left the hospital."

"What? What?"

"Dr. Bernardi has left the hospital."

"But he—"

At that moment the door to the waiting room slammed back. It hit the wall with the sound of a pistol shot. Thinking of it later, Delaney decided that from that moment on, the night simply exploded and went whirling away.

It was the mink-clad matron, her wrinkled face crimson.

"They're killing him!" she screamed. "They're killing him!"

The little nurse came from behind her desk. She reached for the distraught woman. The matron raised one fur-covered arm and clubbed her down.

The others in the room looked up. Dazed. Bewildered. Frightened. Delaney rose lightly to his feet.

"They're killing him!" the woman screamed.

The nurse scrambled up, rushed out the door.

Delaney moved very slowly toward the hysterical woman.

"Oh yes," he said in a voice deliberately dulled, slowed. "They're killing him. Oh yes," he nodded.

The woman turned to him. "They're killing him," she repeated, not yelling now but pulling at the loose skin beneath her chin.

"Oh yes," Delaney kept nodding. "Oh yes."

He, to whom touching a stranger was anathema, knew from experience how important physical contact was in dealing with irrational or maddened people.

"Oh yes," he kept repeating, nodding his head but never smiling. "I understand. Oh yes."

He put a hand lightly, tentatively, on her furred arm.

"Oh yes," he kept nodding. "Oh yes."

She looked down at the hand on her arm, but she didn't throw him off.

"Oh yes," he nodded. "Tell me about it. I want to know all about it. Oh yes. Tell me from the beginning. I want to hear all about it."

Now he had his arm about her shoulders; she was leaning into him. Then an interne and attendant, white-clad, came flinging in, followed by the furious nurse. Delaney, leading the matron slowly toward a couch, waved them away with his free hand. The interne had enough sense to stop in his tracks and halt the others. The old Italian couple, open-mouthed, and the hippie couple watched in silence. The white-haired gentleman slept on.

"They're killing him!" she screamed once more.

"Oh yes," he nodded, hugging her closer. "Tell me all about it. I want to know all about it."

He got her seated on a plastic couch, his arm still about her shoulders. The interne and his aides watched nervously but didn't approach.

"Tell me," Delaney soothed. "Tell me everything. Start from the beginning. I want to know."

"Shit," the woman said suddenly, and fumbled in her alligator bag for a handkerchief. She blew her nose with a tremendous fluttering blast that startled everyone in the room. "You're a beautiful man, you know that? You're not like those other mother-fuckers in this butcher shop."

"Tell me," he droned on, "tell me all about it."

"Well," she said, dabbing at her nose, "it began about six months ago. Irving came home early from the office and complained about—"

Delaney heard a scuffling of feet and looked up. The room seemed filled with police uniforms. Oh God, he thought despairingly, don't tell me that stupid nurse called the cops because of one poor, sad, frightened, hysterical woman.

But it couldn't be. There was Captain Richard Boznanski of the 188th Precinct, just north of his. And he recognized a detective lieutenant and a man from the public relations section. A sergeant had his arm around Boznanski's waist and was half-supporting him.

Delaney pulled apart from the matron.

"Don't go away," she pleaded. "Please don't go away."

"Just for a minute," he whispered. "I'll be back. I promise I'll be back."

The loudspeaker was shouting: "Dr. Spencer, report to 201, please. Dr. Ingram, report to 201, please. Dr. Gomez, report to 201, please. Drs. Spencer, Ingram and Gomez, report to 201, please."

Delaney stalked over to Boznanski. He didn't like the way the man looked. His face was waxy white and covered with a sheen of sweat. His eyes seemed to move uncontrollably, and there was a tremor to his chin: his lips met and drew apart every second.

"Dick," Delaney urged, "what is it? What is it?"

Boznanski stared at him with dazed eyes. "Edward?" he said. "What are you doing here? Edward? How did you hear so soon?"

Delaney felt a hand on his arm and turned. It was Ivar Thorsen, Deputy Inspector, in charge of personnel in the patrol division. He drew Delaney to one side. He began to speak in a low voice, his light blue eyes never moving from Delaney's.

"It was an ambush, Edward. A call came in about a prowler. A two-man car checked it out. Jameson was black, Richmond white. It was a false alarm. At a housing project on 110th Street. They were returning to their car. Shotguns from the bushes. Jameson got his head blown off. Richmond took it in the chest and belly."

"Any chance?" Delaney asked, stone-faced.

"Well . . . no, I'd guess. I saw him. I'd guess no. But they're rounding up this team of surgeons to work on him. Listen, Edward, if Richmond dies, it'll be the fourth man Boznanski's lost this year. He's shook."

"I saw."

"Will you stay with him? The corridor's full of reporters, and they're moving in TV cameras. The Mayor and Commissioner are on their way. I've got a lot of crap to do—you know?"

"Yes."

"Just sit by him—you know."

"Sure."

Thorsen looked at him curiously, his ice eyes narrowing.

"What are you doing here, Edward?"

"My wife was operated on tonight. For kidney stones. I'm waiting to hear how she made out."

"Jesus," Thorsen breathed. "I'm sorry, Edward. I didn't know. How is she?"

"I'm trying to find out."

"Forget about Boznanski. The sergeant will stand by."

"No," Delaney said. "That's all right. I'll be here."

"They're killing him!" the matron cried, grabbing his arm. "They told me it was just a simple operation, and now they say there are complications. They're killing him!"

"Oh yes," Delaney murmured, leading her back to the couch. "I want to hear. I want to know all about it."

He lighted a cigarette for her, then started out into the hall. He fumbled in his pocket and found he had only a quarter. He was about to ask someone for change, then realized how stupid that was. He called Dr. Bernardi's office. He got an answering service. They told him they'd give the doctor his message.

He came back into the waiting room. The shaken nurse was behind her desk. He asked if Dr. Spencer was still in surgery. She said she'd check and also check on his wife in the recovery ward. He thanked her. She thanked him, softened and human.

He went back to Captain Richard Boznanski, seated now, his head thrown back, gasping for breath. He didn't look good. The sergeant was standing by, worried.

"Captain," he said, "is there any booze . . . ?"

Delaney looked at the man in the chair. "I'll try," he said.

"He came home early from work about six months ago," the mink-clad matron said at his elbow, "and he complained of this pain in his chest. He's always been a heavy smoker, and I thought—"

"Oh yes," Delaney said, holding her by the arm. "And what did they say it was?"

"Well, they weren't sure, and they wanted to do this exploratory."

"Oh yes," Delaney nodded. "Just a minute now, and I'll be right back."

He asked the nurse if she had any or could find any whiskey. She explained that regulations prohibited her from giving anything like that to patients or visitors. Delaney nodded and asked if she could find Dr. Bernardi's home phone number. She said she'd try. He asked if she could change a dollar. She couldn't, but she gave him what change she had and refused to accept the dollar he offered. He gave her a grateful smile.

He called Ferguson, who wasn't home. Delaney realized he had awakened the spinster sister. He explained the situation and asked, if Ferguson returned, if he would try to reach Bernardi and find out about Mrs. Delaney's condition. Then Ferguson could call Delaney in the waiting room.

The Captain stalked to the end of the second floor corridor. The swinging doors to the elevators were guarded by two patrolmen. They drew back to let him through.

The moment he stepped out he was surrounded by reporters, all shouting at once. Delaney held up a hand until the newsmen quieted.

"Any statements will have to come from Deputy Inspector Thorsen or others. Not from me."

"Is Richmond still alive?"

"As far as I know. A team of surgeons is working. That's all I know. Now if you'll . . ."

He pushed through the crush. They were setting up small TV cameras on tripods near the elevators. Then Delaney saw Thomas Handry leaning against a wall. He was the reporter who had accompanied Delaney on his midnight rounds. He pulled Handry aside. The man's eyes seemed huge and feverish.

"I told you, I told you," he said to Delaney.

"Do you have any whiskey?" the Captain asked.

Handry looked at him, bewildered.

"Take off your hat," Delaney commanded.

Handry snatched his hat away.

"Do you have any whiskey?" Delaney repeated.

"No, I don't, Captain."

"All I need is a shot. Ask around, will you? See if any of your boys is carrying a flask. Maybe one of the TV men has a pint. I'll pay for it."

"I'll ask, Captain."

"Thank you. Tell one of the men on the door to call me. I'll be in the waiting room."

"If no one's got anything, I'll go out for it."

"Thank you."

"Is Richmond dead?"

"I don't know."

He went back into the waiting room.

"Dr. Spencer is still in surgery," the nurse told him.

"Thank you. Did Dr. Ferguson call?"

"No. But I checked recovery. Your wife is sleeping peacefully."

"Thank you."

"An exploratory," the matron said, holding onto his elbow. "They said it would just be an exploratory. Now they won't tell me anything."

"What's his name?" Delaney asked. "Maybe I can find out what's going on."

"Modell," she said. "Irving Modell. And my name is Rhoda Modell. We have four children and six grandchildren."

"I'll try to find out," Delaney nodded.

He went back to the nurse. But she had heard his conversation with the woman.

"Not a chance," she said softly. "A few hours. Before morning. They took one look and sewed him up."

He nodded and glanced at the clock. Had time speeded up? It was past midnight.

"What I'd like—" he started, but then there was a patrolman next to him.

"Captain Delaney?"

"Yes."

"There's a reporter at the door. Guy named Handry. Says you—"

"Yes, yes."

Delaney walked back with him. The door was opened wide enough for Handry to give him a wrinkled brown paper bag.

"Thank you," Delaney said, and reached for his wallet. But Handry shook his head angrily and turned away.

He peeked into the bag. It was an almost full pint bottle of bourbon. He took several paper cups from the water cooler in the hallway and went back into the waiting room. Boznanski was still lolling in the chair, his head thrown back. Delaney filled a cup with bourbon.

"Dick," he said.

Boznanski opened his eyes.

"A sip," Delaney said. "Dick, just take a little sip."

He held the cup to the policeman's lips. Boznanski tasted, coughed, bent forward in dry heaves, then leaned back. Delaney fed him slowly, sip by sip. Color began to come back into the captain's face. He straightened in his chair. Delaney poured a cup for the sergeant who drained it gratefully, in one gulp.

"Oh my," he said.

"May I, sir?" a voice asked. And there was the white-haired gentleman, finally awake and holding out a quivering hand that seemed skinned with tissue paper. And the two hippies. And the old Italian couple. Just a taste for all: the sacramental cup.

"He's not going to make it, is he?" the matron asked suddenly, looking at Delaney. "I know you wouldn't lie to me."

"I wouldn't lie to you," Delaney nodded, pouring her the few drops remaining in the bottle. "He's not going to make it."

"Ah Jesus," she sighed, rolling a pale tongue around the inside of the waxed paper cup. "What a miserable marriage that was. But aren't they all?"

There was noise outside in the corridor. Deputy Inspector Thorsen came in, composed as ever. He stalked directly to the seated Captain Boznanski and stared at him. Then he turned to Delaney.

"Thanks, Edward."

"What about Richmond?"

"Richmond? Oh. He's gone. They tried, but it was hopeless. Everyone knew it. Five surgeons working four hours."

Delaney looked up at the clock. It couldn't be two in the morning, it *couldn't* be. What had happened to time?

"The Mayor and Commissioner are out there now," Thorsen said in a toneless voice, "giving statements about the need for gun control laws and a new moral climate."

"Yes," Delaney said. He strode over to the nurse's desk. "Where can I find Dr. Spencer?" he asked harshly.

She looked at him with tired eyes. "Try the lounge. Turn right as you go out. Then, after you go through the swinging doors, there's a narrow door on the left that says 'No Admittance.' That's the surgeons' lounge."

"Thank you," Captain Delaney said precisely.

He followed her directions. When he pushed back the narrow door without knocking, he saw a small room, one couch and two armchairs, a TV set, a card table and four folding chairs. There were five men in the room wearing surgical gowns, skull caps, and masks pulled down onto their chests. Three were dressed in light green, two in white.

One man was standing, staring out a window. One was fiddling with the knobs on the TV set, trying to bring in a clear picture. One was trimming his fingernails with a small pocket knife. One was seated at the card table, carefully building an improbable house of leaned cards. One was stretched out on the floor, raising and lowering his legs, doing some kind of exercise.

"Dr. Spencer?" Delaney said sharply.

The man at the window turned slowly, glanced at the uniform, turned back to the window.

"He's dead," he said tonelessly. "I told them that."

"I know he's dead," the Captain said. "My name is Delaney. You operated on my wife earlier this evening. Kidney stones. I want to know how she is."

Spencer turned again to look at him. The other men didn't pause in their activities.

"Delaney," Spencer repeated. "Kidney stones. Well, I had to remove the kidney."

"What?"

"I had to take out one of your wife's kidneys."

"Why?"

"It was infected, diseased, rotted."

"Infected with what?"

"It's down in the lab. We'll know tomorrow."

The man building a house of cards looked up. "You can live with one kidney," he said mildly to Delaney.

"Listen," Delaney said, choking, "listen, you said there'd be no trouble."

"So?" Spencer asked. "What do you want from me? I'm not God."

"Well, if you're not," Delaney cried furiously, "who the hell is?"

There was a knock on the door. The man on the floor, the one lifting and lowering his legs, gasped, "Come in, come in, whoever you are."

A colored nurses' aide stuck her capped head through the opened door and looked about boldly.

102

"Any of you gentlemen a certain Captain Delaney?" she asked saucily.

"I'm Delaney."

"You have a call, Captain. In the waiting room. They say it's very, very, very important."

Delaney took a last look around. Spencer was staring out the window again, and the others were trying to stay busy. He stalked down the hall, pushed angrily through the swinging doors, slammed back into the waiting room. The little nurse handed him the phone, not looking up.

"Captain Edward X. Delaney here."

"Captain, this is Dorfman."

"Yes, lieutenant. What is it?"

"Sorry to bother you, Captain. At this hour."

"What is it?"

"Captain, there's been a murder."

PART III

1

The street was blocked off with sawhorses: raw yellow wood with "New York Police Department" stencilled on the sides. Below the barricades were oil lanterns, black globes with smoking wicks. They looked like 19th century anarchists' bombs.

The patrolman on duty saluted and pulled one sawhorse aside to let Delaney through. The Captain walked slowly down the center of the street, toward the river. He knew this block well; three years previously he had led a team of officers and Technical Patrol Force specialists in the liberation of a big townhouse that had been taken over by a gang of thugs and was being systematically looted. The house was near the middle of the block. A few lights were on; in one apartment the tenants were standing at the window, staring down into the street.

Delaney paused to survey the silent scene ahead of him. Understanding what was happening, he removed his cap, made the sign of the cross, bowed his head.

There were a dozen vehicles drawn up in a rough semicircle: squad cars, ambulance, searchlight truck, laboratory van, three unmarked sedans, a black limousine. Thirty men were standing motionless, uncovered heads down.

This city block had been equipped with the new street lights that cast an orange, shadowless glow. It filled doorways, alleys, corners like a thin liquid, and if there were no shadows, there was no brightness either, but a kind of strident light without warmth.

Into this brassy haze a morning mist seeped gently and collected in tears on hoods and roofs of cars and on black asphalt. It damped the hair and faces of the silent watchers. It fell as a shroud on the bundle crumpled on the sidewalk. The kneeling priest completed extreme unction and rose from his knees. The waiting men replaced their hats; there was a subdued murmur of voices.

Delaney stared at this night lithograph, then walked forward slowly. He came into a hard white beam from the searchlight truck; men turned to look at him. Lieutenant Dorfman came hurrying up, face twisted.

"It's Lombard, Captain," he gasped. "Frank Lombard, the Brooklyn councilman. You know—the one who's always talking about 'crime on the streets' and writing the newspapers what a lousy job the police are doing."

Delaney nodded. He looked around at the assembled men: patrolmen, precinct and Homicide North detectives, laboratory specialists, an inspector from the Detective Division. And a deputy commissioner with one of the Mayor's personal aides.

Now there was another figure kneeling alongside the corpse. Captain Delaney recognized the massive bulk of Dr. Sanford Ferguson. Despite the harsh glare of the searchlights, the Police Surgeon was using a penlight to examine the skull of the dead man. He stood away a moment while photographers placed a ruler near the corpse and took more flash photos. Then he kneeled again on the wet sidewalk. Delaney walked over to stand next to him. Ferguson looked up.

"Hullo, Edward," he smiled. "Wondering where you were. Take a look at this."

Before kneeling, Delaney stared down a moment at the victim. It was not difficult to visualize what had happened. The man had been struck down from behind. The back of his skull appeared crushed; thick black hair was bloodied and matted. He had fallen forward, sprawling heavily. As he fell, the left femur had snapped; the leg was now flung out at an awkward angle. He had fallen with such force that the splintered end of the bone had thrust out through his trouser leg.

As he fell, presumably his face smacked the sidewalk, for blood had flowed from a mashed nose, perhaps from a crushed mouth and facial abrasions. The pool of blood, not yet congealed, bloomed from his head in a small puddle, down into a plot of cracked earth about a scrawny plane tree at the curb.

Delaney kneeled carefully, avoiding a leather wallet lying alongside the body. The Captain turned to squint into the searchlight glare.

"The wallet dusted?" he called to men he couldn't see.

"No sir," someone called back. "Not yet."

Delaney looked down at the wallet.

"Alligator," he said. "They won't get much from that." He took a ballpoint pen from the inside pocket of his uniform jacket and gently prized open the wallet, touching only one edge. Dr. Ferguson put the beam of his penlight on it. They both saw the thick sheaf of green bills.

Delaney let the wallet fall closed, then turned back to the body. Ferguson put his light on the skull. Three men in civilian clothes came up to kneel around the corpse. The five bent over closely, heads almost touching.

"Club?" one of the detectives asked. "A pipe maybe?"

"I don't think so," Ferguson said, without looking up. "There's no crushing or depression. That's blood and matting you see. But there's a penetration. Like a puncture. A hole about an inch in diameter. It looks round. I could put my finger in it."

"Hammer?" Delaney asked.

Ferguson sat back on his heels. "A hammer? Yes, it could be. Depends on how deep the penetration goes."

"What about time, doc?" one of the other detectives asked.

"Looks to be within three hours tops. No, call it two hours. Around midnight. Just a guess."

"Who found him?"

"A cabby spotted him first but thought he was a drunk and didn't stop. The cabby caught up with one of your precinct squads on York Avenue, Captain, and they came back."

"Who were they?"

"McCabe and Mowery."

"Did they move the body or the wallet?"

"McCabe says they didn't touch the body. He says the wallet was lying open, face up, with ID card and credit cards showing in plastic pockets. That's how they knew it was Lombard."

"Who closed the wallet?"

"Mowery did that."

"Why?"

"He says it was beginning to drizzle, and they were afraid it might rain harder and ruin any latent prints on the plastic windows in the wallet. He says they could see it was a rough leather wallet and chances are there'd be a better chance of prints on the plastic than on the leather. So they closed the wallet, using a pencil. He says they didn't touch it. McCabe backs him up. McCabe says the wallet is within a quarter-inch at most from where they found it."

"When did the cabby stop them on York Avenue and tell them there was someone lying here?"

"About an hour ago. Closer to fifty minutes maybe."

"Doctor," Delaney asked, "can we roll him over now?"

"You got your pictures?" a detective roared into the darkness.

"We need the front," the reply came back.

"Careful of that leg," Ferguson said. "One of you hold it together while we roll him over."

Five pairs of hands took hold of the corpse gently and turned it face up. The five kneeling men drew back as two photographers came up for long shots and closeups of the victim. Then the circle closed again.

"No front wounds that I can see," Ferguson reported, his little flashlight beam zigzagging down the dead body. "The broken leg and facial injuries are from the fall. At least the abraded skin indicates that. I'll know better when I get him downtown. It was the skull penetration that did it."

"Dead before he hit the ground?"

"Could be if that puncture is deep enough. He's a—he was a heavy man. Maybe two twenty-five. He fell heavily." He felt the dead man's arms, shoulders, legs. "Solid. Not too much fat. Good muscle layer. He could have put up a fight. If he had a chance."

They were silent, staring down at the body. He had not been a handsome man, but his features were rugged and not unpleasant: strong jaw, full lips, a meaty nose (now crushed), thick black brows and walrus mustache. The teeth still unbroken were big, white, square—little tombstones. Blank eyes stared at the weeping sky.

Delaney leaned forward suddenly and pressed his face close to the dead man's. Dr. Ferguson grabbed him by the shoulder and pulled him back.

"What the hell are you doing, Edward?" he cried. "Kissing the poor bastard?"

"Smell him," Delaney said. "Smell the mustache. Garlic, wine, and something else."

Ferguson leaned forward cautiously, and sniffed at the thick mustache.

"Anise," he said. "Wine, garlic, and anise."

"That's an Italian dinner," one of the detectives said. "Maybe he stiffed the waiter and the guy followed him down here and offed him."

No one laughed.

"He is Italian," someone said. "His name isn't Lombard, it's Lombardo. He dropped the 'o' when he went into politics. His district in Brooklyn is mostly Jewish."

They looked up. It was Lieutenant Rizzo from the 251st.

"How do you know, lieutenant?"

"He's—was my wife's cousin. He was at our wedding. His

mother lives around here somewhere. I called my wife. She's calling relatives, trying to find out the mother's address. My wife says Lombard came over from Brooklyn occasionally to have dinner with his mother. She's supposed to be a good cook."

The five men climbed shakily to their feet and brushed their damp knees. Dr. Ferguson signaled toward the ambulance, and two men came forward lugging a canvas body bag. A man came from the laboratory van with a plastic bag and a small pair of tongs to retrieve the wallet.

"Edward," Ferguson said, "I forgot to ask. How is your wife getting along?"

"She was operated on tonight. Or rather yesterday afternoon."

"And . . . ?"

"They had to take out one of her kidneys."

Ferguson was silent a moment, then . . . "Infected?"

"That's what Spencer told me. Bernardi observed the operation but I can't get hold of him."

"The prick. As soon as I get to a phone I'll try to find out what the hell is going on. Where can I reach you?"

"The precinct house probably. We'll have to re-shuffle schedules and figure out how many uniformed men we can spare for door-to-door questioning. They're taking our detectives away."

"I heard. Edward, I'll call if I learn anything. If I don't call, it means I haven't been able to reach Spencer or Bernardi."

Delaney nodded. Dr. Ferguson climbed into the back of the ambulance, and it went whining away. Lt. Dorfman was moving toward him, but the deputy commissioner came out of the darkness and clamped a hand on Delaney's elbow. The Captain didn't like to be touched; he tugged his arm gently away.

"Delaney?"

"Yes sir."

"My name's Broughton. B-r-o-u-g-h-t-o-n. I guess we never met.

They had, but Delaney didn't mention it. The two officers shook hands. Broughton, a thick, shapeless man, motioned Delaney toward the black limousine. He opened the back door, waved Delaney in, climbed in beside him.

"Go get a coffee, Jack," he commanded the uniformed driver.

Then they were alone. Broughton offered a cigar but Delaney shook his head. The deputy lighted up furiously, the end of the cigar flaring, the car filling with harsh smoke.

"It's a piece of shit," he said angrily. "Why the hell can't we get Havana cigars? We're defeating Communism by smoking horse shit? What kind of insanity is that?"

He sat back, staring out the window at the sidewalk where someone had chalked an outline around the corpse before it was removed.

"A lot of flak on this one, Captain," Broughton said loudly. "A *lot* of flak. The Commissioner cancelled a speech in Kansas City—Kansas *City,* for Chrissakes—and is flying back. You probably saw the Mayor's aide. His Honor is on our ass already. And don't think the fucking governor won't get in the act. You know this Lombard—the guy who got hisself killed?"

"I read his statements in the newspapers and I saw him on television."

"Yeah, he got the publicity. So you know what we're up against. 'Crime in the streets . . . no law and order . . . hoodlums and muggers running wild . . . shake up the police department . . . the Commissioner should resign . . .' You know. The shithead was running for Mayor. Now he's knocked off, and if we don't pull someone in, it proves he was right. You understand how serious this is, Captain?"

"I consider every homicide serious."

"Well . . . yeah . . . sure. But the politics involved. You understand that?"

"Yes sir."

"All right. That's one thing. Now the other thing . . . This killing couldn't have happened at a worst time. You get the Commissioner's memo about precinct detectives?"

"Memorandum four six seven dash B dated eight October; subject: Detective division, reorganization of? Yes sir, I received it."

Broughton laughed shortly. "I heard about you, Delaney. Yeah, that's the memo." He belched suddenly, a ripe, liquid sound. He didn't excuse himself, but scratched in his crotch. "All right, we're pulling all the detectives out of the precinct houses. You're next on the list. You got the notification?"

"Yes."

"Starts on Monday. All detectives will be organized in special units—homicide, burglary and larceny, truck thefts, hotel thefts, and so on. Uniformed officers will make the first investigation of a crime. You're going to give your cops a crash course on what to look for. It's all spelled out in a manual you'll be getting. The investigating officers file a report. If it's a major theft, say, involving more than $1,500 in money or goods, the detective unit takes over. If it's a minor crime, say b-and-e or a mugging, the patrolman does what he can or reports it unsolvable. We tried it out in two test precincts, and we think it's going to work. What do you think?"

"I don't like it," Delaney said promptly. "It takes detectives out of the precincts and out of the neighborhoods. Sometimes they make their best busts just by knowing the neighborhood —who's missing, new hoods who have shown up, who's been flashing a roll. And of course they all have their neighborhood informers. Now, as I understand it, one specialized detective unit might be covering as many as four or five precincts. I like the idea of uniformed men getting experience in investigation work. They'll like that. They'll be functioning like detectives —which is what most of them thought police work was all about, instead of taking old people to hospitals and settling family squabbles. But while they're investigating and making out that preliminary report, they're off the beat, and I'll have less men on patrol and visible. I don't like that."

Broughton pried a fingertip roughly into one nostril, dug out some matter, rolled it into a ball between thumb and forefinger. He opened the car window and flicked it outside.

"Well, you're going to have to live with it," he said coldly. "At least for a year until we get some numbers and see what's happening to our solution rates. But now this son of a bitch Lombard gets hit right in the middle of the change-over. So we have Homicide North still in existence, the new homicide unit covering your precinct, and you still got your precinct detectives. Jesus Christ, all those guys will be walking up each other's heels, covering the same ground—and whose responsibility is it? It's going to be as fucked up as a Chinese fire drill. It is already. You got any ideas how to straighten it out?"

Delaney looked up in surprise. The final question had come so suddenly, so unexpectedly, that even though he had wondered about the reason for this private talk, he wasn't prepared for the demand.

"Can you give me twenty-four hours to think it over? Maybe I can come up with something."

"No good," Broughton said impatiently. "Right now I got to go out to the airport to pick up the Commissioner, and I got to have some suggestions on how to straighten out this mess. He'll want action. The Mayor and every councilman will be leaning

110

on him. And if he don't produce, it's probably his ass. And if it's his ass, it's my ass too. You understand?"

"Yes."

"You agree that right now it's screwed up as far as organization goes?"

"Yes."

"Christ, you're a regular chatterbox, ain't you?" Broughton farted audibly and squirmed his buttocks on the car seat. "I been hearing how smart you are, Captain. Okay, here's your chance; give me a for-instance right now."

Delaney looked at him with distaste, recognizing the man's crude energy but angered by his bullying, disgusted by his personal habits, sensing a personality that reeked of the jungle.

"Try a temporary horizontal organization," he said tonelessly. "The Department, just like the army and most business corporations, is organized vertically. Responsibility and authority are vested in the man at the top. Orders come down the chain of command. Each division, precinct, unit, or whatever, has a definite assignment. But sometimes problems come up that can't be solved by this type of organization. It's usually a problem of limited duration that might never occur again. The Lombard homicide comes right in the middle of the reorganization of the detective division. All right, do what the army and most corporations do when they're faced with a unique situation that doesn't require a permanent organization. Set up a temporary task force. Call it 'Operation Lombard,' if you like. Appoint an overall commander. Give him full responsibility and authority to draw on any unit for personnel and equipment he needs. Detectives, patrolmen, specialists anyone who'll help him do the job. The men are detached on a temporary basis. The whole operation is temporary. When and if Lombard's killer is found, the task force is disbanded, and the men go back to their regular units."

A light came into Broughton's muddy eyes. He laughed with glee and rubbed his palms together between his knees.

"They weren't kidding; you're a smart son of a bitch, Delaney. I like it. And I think the Commissioner will like it. A special task force: 'Operation Lombard.' It'll show we're doing something—right? That should satisfy the Mayor and the newspapers. How long do you think it'll take to break the Lombard thing?"

Delaney looked at him in astonishment.

"How would I know? How would anyone know? Maybe

111

someone's confessing right now. Maybe it'll never be solved."

"Jesus, don't say that."

"Did you ever read solution statistics on homicides? If they're not solved within the first forty-eight hours, the solution probability drops off steeply and continues to plunge as time passes. After a month or two, solution probability is practically nil."

Broughton nodded glumly, got out of the car, spat his cold cigar into the gutter. Delaney got out too and stood there as the uniformed driver came running up. Broughton got in the front seat alongside the driver. As the limousine pulled away, the Captain saluted gravely, but it was not returned.

Delaney stood a moment, inspecting the street. The first contingent of uniformed patrolmen from his precinct came straggling up in twos and threes, to gather about the chalked outline on the sidewalk. The Captain moved over to listen to a sergeant giving them orders.

"Everyone got a flashlight?" he asked. "Okay, we spread out from here. We move slowly. Got that? Slowly. We check every garbage can—" There was a groan from the massed men. "There was a pickup on this street yesterday afternoon so most of the cans should be empty. But even if they're full, spill them out. Every can has got to be searched. After you're through, try to kick most of the shit back in. We're calling for another sanitation pickup today, and the cans will be clawed through again when they're spilled into the garbage truck. Also, every area and alley, and put your light in every sewer and catch basin. This is a preliminary search. By tomorrow we'll have some sewer and street men here to take off the manhole covers and gratings and probe the sludge. Now, what we're looking for is anything that looks like a weapon. It could be a gun or a knife. But especially look for a club, a piece of pipe, an iron rod, a hammer, or maybe a rock with blood and matted hair on it. Anything with blood on it. And that includes a hat, clothing, a handkerchief, maybe a rag. If you're not sure, call me. Don't pass up anything. We do this block first. Then we cross York to the next block. Then we come back and do one block south and one block north. Got it? All right, get moving."

Delaney watched the searchlights spread out from where the dark blood still glistened in the morning mist. He knew it had to be done, but he didn't envy the men their task. It was possible they might find something. Possible. They would, he knew,

112

also find gut-wrenching garbage, vomit, a dead cat, and perhaps the bloody body of an aborted baby.

By morning there would be more men doing the same thing, and more, and more. The search would spread farther and farther until it covered all his precinct and, finally, most of Manhattan.

Now he watched carefully as the men started their search. Then, suddenly, he realized his weariness had dropped away, or perhaps he was so exhausted he was numb. He clasped his hands behind his back and strolled down to the river fence. There he turned, faced toward York Avenue, and began to consider how the murder might have happened.

Lombard's body had been found on the sidewalk almost half-way between the river and York Avenue. If indeed he had dinner with his mother, it was reasonable to assume she lived between the river and the point where the victim was found. Lombard had fallen forward toward York. Had he, about midnight, been walking toward a bus line, a subway station, or perhaps his parked car for the trip home to Brooklyn?

Pacing slowly, Delaney inspected the buildings between the river and the spot where the body was found. They were all converted brownstones and townhouses. Fronts of the townhouses were flush; there were no areas where a killer might lurk, although it was conceivable he might have been in a lobby, ostensibly inspecting bells, his back turned to passersby. Delaney doubted that. Too much chance of being spotted by a tenant.

But the entrances to the converted brownstones were three or four steps down from the sidewalk. There were high bushes and boxes of ivy, still green, that offered some concealment for a crouching assassin. Delaney could not believe it. No killer, even if trained and wearing crepe-soled shoes, could leap from concealment, charge up three or four steps, and rush his victim from behind without making *some* noise. And Lombard would have turned to face his attacker, perhaps throw up an arm to protect himself, or make some movement to escape. Yet apparently he was struck down suddenly and without warning.

Barely moving, Delaney stared at the building fronts across the street. It was possible, he acknowledged, that the killer had waited in an outside lobby until Lombard passed on his way to York Avenue, had then come out on the sidewalk and followed him. But again, Lombard would surely have heard him or sensed his presence. And on this block at midnight, would a man as aware of street crime as Lombard allow a man to stalk him? The councilman could have run toward the traffic on York Avenue, or even dashed across the street to seek refuge in the big townhouse lobby with the doorman.

All this theorizing, of course, assumed that Lombard was a marked target, that the killer had followed him or at least been aware that he would be on this particular street at this particular time. But the suddenness and complete success of the attack were the points that interested Delaney at the moment. He retraced his steps to the river fence, turned around, and began again a slow walk toward York.

"What's Iron Balls up to, sarge?" a uniformed patrolman asked. He was stationed at the chalked outline on the sidewalk to shoo away the curious.

The sergeant stared across the street at the slowly pacing Captain.

"Why, he's looking for clues," he explained blandly. "He's sure to find a cancelled French postage stamp, or a lefthand glove with the little finger missing, or maybe a single turkey feather. Then he'll solve the murder and make deputy inspector. What the fuck do you think he's doing?"

The patrolman didn't know, and the sergeant didn't either.

Another possibility, Delaney was thinking, was that the killer was walking along with Lombard, the two were friends. But could the killer pull out a weapon, get behind his victim, and strike him directly from the rear without Lombard turning in alarm, dodging, or trying to ward off the blow?

The sticking point was still the suddenness of the attack and the fact that Lombard, a big, muscular man, had apparently offered no resistance, had allowed the killer to come up on him from behind.

Delaney stopped a moment and reflected; he was racing ahead too fast. Perhaps the killer didn't approach from the rear. Perhaps he came directly toward Lombard from York Avenue. If he was well-dressed, walking swiftly like a resident of the block anxious to get home at midnight, chances are Lombard would have inspected him as he approached. And if the man looked all right, Lombard might have moved aside slightly to let him pass.

The weapon, of course, would have to be concealed. But if it was a pipe or a hammer, there were a number of ways that could be done—in a folded newspaper, under a coat carried on the arm, even in a trick package. Then, the instant after passing Lombard, the victim's attention now on the area in front of him, the killer could bare his weapon, whirl, crush

Lombard's skull. All in an instant. Lombard would have no warning. He would topple forward, already dead. The assassin would return his weapon to its cover, and retrace his steps to York Avenue or even continue on to his own apartment, if he was a resident of the block, or to the apartment of a friend, or to a car parked for a convenient getaway.

Delaney ran through it again. The more he inspected it, the stronger it looked. It *felt* right. It assumed the killer approaching Lombard was a stranger to him. But if he was well-dressed, "legitimate" looking, and apparently hurrying home, it was doubtful if Lombard or anyone else would cross the street to escape attack. The Captain discarded the notion that after the murder the killer went on to his own apartment or that of a friend; he would surely guess that every resident of the block would be questioned and his whereabouts checked at the time of the slaying. No, the killer either went back toward York or escaped in a car parked nearby.

Delaney returned to the fence blocking off East River Drive, crossed the street, and started down the sidewalk where the body had been found, heading in the direction the victim had been walking.

Now I am Frank Lombard, soon to be dead. I have just had dinner with my mother, I have come out of her apartment house at midnight, I am in a hurry to get home to Brooklyn. I walk quickly, and I look about constantly. I even look down into the bush-surrounded entrances to the brownstones. I am acutely aware of the incidence of street assaults, and I make certain no one is lurking, waiting to bash me on the head or mug me.

I look up ahead. There is a man coming toward me from York Avenue. In the shadowless glare of the new street lights I can see that the man is well-dressed, carrying a coat over his arm. He too is hurrying, anxious to get home. I can understand that. As he approaches, our eyes lock. We both nod and smile reassuringly. "It's all right," the smile says. "We're both well-dressed. We look okay. We're not muggers." I draw aside a little to give the man room to pass. The next instant I am dead.

Delaney stopped at the chalked outline on the sidewalk. It began to seem real to him. It explained why Lombard apparently made no move to defend himself, didn't have time to make a move. The Captain walked slowly down to York Avenue. He turned, started back toward the river.

Now I am the killer, carrying a coat across my arm. Under the coat, hidden, I am grasping the handle of a hammer. I am walking quickly, with purposeful strides. Ahead of me, in the orange glare, I see the man I am to kill. I walk toward him briskly. As I come up, I nod, smile, and move to pass him. Now he is looking straight ahead. I pass, lift the hammer free, whirl, raise it high and strike. He goes down, sprawling forward. I cover the hammer again, walk quickly back to York Avenue again and escape.

Captain Delaney paused again at the chalked diagram. Yes, it could have happened that way. If the killer had nerve and resolution—and luck, of course. Always luck. No one looking out a window. No one else on the street at that hour. No cab suddenly coming down from York, its headlights picking him up the instant he struck. But assuming the killer's luck, it all— ah, Jesus! The wallet! He had forgotten that damned wallet completely!

The wallet was the folding type, the kind a man customarily carries in a hip pocket. Indeed, Delaney had noted it had acquired a slight curve, taking its shape from the buttock. He carried the same type of wallet himself, and it began to curve after several months of use.

Lombard had been wearing a three-quarter "car coat" fastened in front with wooden toggles. In back, the coat and suit jacket beneath it had been pulled up high enough to expose his hip pockets. Now why had the killer paused long enough to frisk his victim for his wallet and then leave it open beside the body, even though it was stuffed with money? Every moment he tarried, every second, the killer was in deadly peril. Yet he took the time to search the corpse and remove the wallet. And then he left it open beside the body.

Why didn't he take the money—or the entire wallet? Not because he was frightened away by someone's appearance at a window or on the street. A man with nerve enough to approach his victim from the front would have nerve enough to take his loot, even if emperiled. A man can run just as fast with a wallet as without it. No, he just didn't want the money. What did he want? To check the identification of his victim—or did he take something from the wallet, something they didn't know about yet?

Delaney went back to York Avenue, turned, started back, and ran through it again.

Now I am the killer, carrying a coat across my arm. Under the coat . . .

Delaney knew as well as any man in the Department what

116

the chances were of solving this particular homicide. He knew that in 1971 New York City had more murders than American combat deaths in Vietnam during the same period. In New York, almost five victims a day were shot, knifed, strangled, bludgeoned, set on fire or thrown from roofs. In such a horrific bloodbath, what was one more?

But if that became the general attitude, the *accepted* attitude, society's attitude—"What's one more?"—then the murder of Frank Lombard was an incident of no significance. When plague strikes, who cares enough to mourn a single soul?

When Captain Edward X. Delaney explained to the newspaperman why he had become a cop, he said what he thought: that he believed there was an eternal harmony in the universe, in all things animate and inanimate, and that crime was a dissonance in the chiming of the spheres. That is what Delaney thought.

But now, playing his victim-killer game in the first raw attempt to understand what had happened and to begin a possible solution of this crime, he was sadly aware that he had a deeper motive, more felt than thought. He had never spoken of it to anyone, not even Barbara, although he suspected she guessed.

It was perhaps due to his Catholic nurture that he sought to set the world aright. He wanted to be God's surrogate on earth. It was, he knew, a shameful want. He recognized the sin. It was pride.

2

What was it? He could not decipher its form or meaning. A frail thing there under white sheet and blue blanket, thin arms arranged outside. Heavy eyelids more stuck than shut, cheek bones poking, pale lips drawn back in a death's head grin, a body so frail it seemed even the blanket pressed it flat. And tubes, bandages, steel and plastic—new organs these—jars and drainage bags. He looked frantically for signs of life, stared, stared, saw finally a slow wearied rise and fall of breast no plumper than a boy's. He thought of the body of Frank Lombard and wondered, Where is the connection? Then realized he saw both through mist, his eyes damped and heavy.

"She's under heavy sedation," the nurse whispered, "but

she's coming along just fine. Dr. Bernardi is waiting for you in the Surgeons' Lounge."

He searched for something he could kiss, a naked patch of skin free of tubes, needles, straps, bandages. All he wanted was to make a signal, just a signal. He bent to kiss her hair, but it was wire beneath his lips.

"I mentioned it," Bernardi said, inspecting his fingernails. Then he looked up at Delaney accusingly, daring him to deny it. "You'll remember I mentioned Proteus infection."

The Captain sat stolidly, craving sleep like an addict. They were at opposite sides of the card table in the Surgeons' Lounge. Cards were scattered across the surface, most of them face down but a queen of hearts showing, and a nine of spades.

"Proteus infection," Delaney repeated heavily. "How do you know?"

"That's what the lab tells us."

"And you think your lab is more knowledgeable than you and your associates who diagnosed my wife's illness as kidney stones?"

Again the opaque film coated the doctor's glistening eyes. His body stiffened, and he made a gesture Delaney had never seen him use before: he put the tip of his right forefinger in his right ear with the thumb stuck up in the air, exactly like a man blowing his brains out.

"Captain," he purred in his unctuous voice, "I assure you—"

"All right, all right," Delaney waved the apology away. "Let's not waste time. What is Proteus infection?"

Bernardi brightened, as he always did at an opportunity to display his erudition. Now he made his usual gesture of placing his index fingers together and pressing them against pouting lips.

"Proteus," he sang happily. "A Greek sea-god who could change his appearance at will. You should be interested in that, Captain. A million different shapes and disguises at will. That would complicate a policeman's task, would it not? He!"

Delaney grunted disgustedly. Bernardi paid no heed.

"And so the name was given to this particular infection. An infection is not an illness—but we needn't go into that. Suffice to say that Proteus infection frequently takes on the shape, appearance, form, and symptoms of a dozen other infections and illnesses. Very difficult to diagnose."

"Rare?" Delaney asked.

"Proteus rare?" the doctor said, eyebrows rising. "I would say no. But not too common. The literature is not extensive. That is what I was researching this morning, and why I did not return your calls. I was reading everything I could find on Proteus."

"What causes it?" Delaney asked, trying to keep the hatred out of his voice, to be as clinical and unemotional as this macaroni.

"I told you. Bacillus Proteus. B. Proteus. It exists in all of us. Usually in the intestinal tract. We have all kinds of good and bad little animalcules squiggling around inside us, you know. Sometimes, usually following an abdominal operation, b. Proteus goes on a rampage. Breaks loose. Sometimes in the urinary tract or in a specific organ. Rarely in the blood stream itself. The usual symptoms are high fever, chills, headaches, sometimes nausea. Which are—as I am certain you are aware —the symptoms of a dozen other infections. Proteus also causes certain changes in the blood, difficult to determine definitely. The recommended treatment for this infection is the employment of antibiotics."

"You tried that."

"True. But I assure you, Captain, I did not go through the entire spectrum. These so-called 'wonder drugs' are not all that wonderful. One of them may stifle a particular bacillus. At the same time it encourages the growth of another, more virulent bacillus. The antibiotics are not to be used lightly. In your wife's case, I believe the Proteus infection was triggered by her hysterectomy. But all the symptoms pointed to kidney stones, and there was nothing in the tests or plates to discourage that diagnosis. When Dr. Spencer got in there, we realized one kidney had to be removed. *Had* to. You understand?"

Delaney didn't answer.

"We saw there were still pockets of infection, small and scattered, that could not be removed by surgery. Now we must start again, hoping the main source of infection has been eliminated and we can clear up the remaining pockets with antibiotics."

"Hoping, doctor?"

"Yes. Hoping, Captain."

The two men stared at each other.

"She's dying, isn't she, doctor?"

"I wouldn't say that."

"No. You wouldn't."

He dragged to his feet, stumbled from the room.

Now I am the killer, Bacillus Proteus. I am in my wife's kidneys. I am . . .

He went back to the precinct house in hard afternoon sunlight. He thought he would be with her. He did not think he ought or should be with her, but that he would. He knew he could not attend her, for as long as it took, and still function efficiently as Captain Edward X. Delaney, New York Police Department. On his old portable he typed out a letter to Deputy Inspector Ivar Thorsen, Patrol Division, asking immediate retirement. He filled out the "Request for Retirement" form and told Thorsen, in a personal note, that the request was due to his wife's illness. He asked his old friend to expedite the retirement papers. He sealed, stamped the envelope, walked down to the corner postbox and mailed it. Then he returned to his home and rolled onto his bed without undressing.

He slept for perhaps three minutes or eight hours. The brilliant ringing of the bedside phone brought him instantly awake.

"Captain Edward X. Delaney here."

"Edward, this is Ferguson. Did you talk to Bernardi?"

"Yes."

"I'm sorry, Edward."

"Thank you."

"The antibiotics might work. The main source of the infection is gone."

"I know."

"Edward, I woke you up."

"That's all right."

"I thought you might want to know."

"Know what?"

"The Lombard homicide. It wasn't a hammer."

"What was it?"

"I don't know. The skull penetration was about three to four inches deep. It was like a tapered cone. The outside hole, the entrance, was about an inch in diameter. Then it tapered down to a sharp point. Like a spike. Do you want a copy of my report?"

"No. I've retired."

"What?"

"It's not my concern. I filed my retirement papers."

"Oh, Jesus. Edward, you can't. It's your life."

"I know."

Delaney hung up. Then he lay wake.

Three days later Captain Delaney received the telephone call he had been expecting: the assistant to Deputy Inspector Thorsen asked if he could meet with Thorsen that afternoon at four o'clock. Delaney went downtown via subway, wearing his uniform.

"Go right in, Captain," Thorsen's pretty secretary said when he gave his name. "They're expecting you."

Wondering who "they" might be, Delaney knocked once and pushed open the heavy oak door to Thorsen's office. The two men seated in leather club chairs rose to their feet, and the Deputy Inspector came forward smiling.

Ivar Thorsen was Delaney's "rabbi" in the Department. The term was current police slang for a superior officer or high official in city government who liked an officer personally, took an interest in his career, and generally guided and eased his advancement in rank. When a "rabbi" moved upward in the hierarchy, sooner or later his protege moved upward also.

Deputy Inspector Ivar Thorsen, a man in his late 50s, was called "The Admiral" by his subordinates, and it was easy to see why. Of relatively short stature, his body was slender and stringy, but all muscle and tendon; he bounced as he walked. His skin was fair and unblemished, features classically Nordic but without softness. His pale blue eyes could be distressingly piercing. The white hair seemed never combed but rigorously brushed until it hugged tightly the shape of his head from a leftside part that showed pink scalp.

He shook Delaney's hand, then turned to the other man in the room.

"Edward, I think you know Inspector Johnson."

"I surely do. Good to see you, inspector."

"Likewise, Edward," the grinning black Buddha said. He extended a huge hand. "How you been?"

"Can't complain. Well . . . I can, but no one will listen."

"I know, I know," the big man chuckled, and his heavy belly moved up and down. "Wish we could get together more often, but they keep me chained to those damned computers, and I don't get uptown as often as I'd like."

"I read your analysis of arrest and conviction percentages."

"You did?" Johnson exclaimed with genuine pleasure. "You must be the only cop in town who did."

"Wait a minute, Ben," Thorsen protested. "I read it."

"The hell," the black scoffed. "You started it maybe, and read the last paragraph."

"I swear I read every word."

"I give you five-to-one you didn't—and I can ask questions to prove it."

"I'll take that bet."

"Misdemeanor," Delaney said promptly. "I can place you both under arrest. Gambling laws."

"Not so," Johnson shook his great head. "The courts have held a private wager between two gentlemen cannot be prosecuted under anti-gambling statutes. See *Harbiner v. the City of New York.*"

"See *Plessy v. Novick*," Delaney retorted. "The court held a private unpaid wager between two persons cannot be a matter for judicial decision only because the wager itself was illegal."

"Come on," Thorsen groaned. "I didn't ask you here to argue law. Sit down." He waved them to the club chairs, then took the upholstered swivel chair behind his glass-topped desk. He flicked on his intercom. "Alice, please hold all incoming calls except emergency."

Inspector Johnson turned toward Delaney and regarded him curiously.

"What did you think of my report, Edward?"

"The numbers were a shock, inspector. And the—"

"You know, Edward, if you called me Ben I really don't think I'd have you up for insolence and insubordination."

"All right, Ben. Well . . . the numbers were a shock, your analysis was brilliant, but I can't agree with your conclusion."

"What can't you agree with?"

"Suppose only five percent of felony arrests eventually produce convictions. From that you argue that we—the men on the beat—should make fewer arrests but better ones—arrests that will stand up in court. But aren't you disregarding the deterrent effect of mass arrests, even if we know the evidence will never stand up? The suspect may never be convicted, but after he goes through booking, a time in jail until he can raise bail —if he can—and the expense of a lawyer for his day in court, maybe he'll think twice before he strays again."

"Maybe, maybe not," Johnson rumbled. "I was aware of the deterrent angle when I wrote the report. As a matter of fact, I agree with it. But if I had come out recommending more arrests—whether or not they stood up in court—if I had recommended dragnet operations on prostitutes, drifters, homosexuals, gamblers—you know what would have happened? Some radical in the Department would have leaked that report to the press, and every civil liberties group would be down on our necks, and we'd be 'fascist pigs' all over again."

"You mean you tailored your convictions for the sake of public relations?"

"That's right," Johnson agreed blandly.

"Are public relations that important?"

"Got to be. For the Department. Your world is your own Precinct. My world is the Commissioner's office and, by extension, the Mayor's."

Delaney stared at the big black. Inspector Benjamin Johnson was on the Commissioner's staff, in charge of statistics and production analysis. He was an enormous man, a former All-American guard from Rutgers. He had gone to fat, but the result wasn't unpleasant; he still carried himself well, and his bulk gave him added dignity. His smile was appealing, almost childlike—a perfect disguise for what Delaney knew was a hard, complex, perceptive intelligence. A black didn't attain Johnson's rank and reputation by virtue of a hearty laugh and a mouthful of splendid teeth.

"Please," Thorsen raised a palm. ."The two of you get together some night and fight it out over a beefsteak or soul food."

"Steak for me," Johnson said.

"I'll take the soul food," Delaney smiled.

"Let's get on with it," Thorsen said in his no-nonsense way. "First of all, Edward, how is Barbara feeling?"

Delaney came back to realities. He enjoyed "police talk" and could sit up all night arguing crime and punishment. But only with other cops. Civilians simply didn't *know*. Or perhaps it was like atheists arguing with priests. They were talking about different things, or in different languages. The atheist argued reason; the priest argued faith. In this case, the policeman was the atheist, the civilian the priest. Both were right and both were wrong.

"Barbara is not so good," he said steadily. 'She hasn't snapped back from the operation the way she should—or at least the way I hoped she would. They've started her on antibiotics. The first didn't do a thing. They're trying another. They'll go on trying."

"I was sorry to hear your wife was ill, Edward," Johnson said quietly. "What exactly is it?"

"It's called Proteus infection. In her case it's an infection of the urinary tract. But the doctors wouldn't tell me a damned thing about how really ill she is and what her chances are."

"I know," Johnson nodded sympathetically. "The thing I hate most about doctors is when I go to one with a pain in my gut and explain exactly what the symptoms are, and the doctor says, 'That doesn't worry me.' Then I say, 'I know, goddamn it, it's *my* pain; why should it worry you'?"

Delaney smiled wanly, knowing Johnson was trying to cheer him up.

"I hate to hear about illnesses I never heard of before," Thorsen said. "There are so many things that can go wrong with the human body, it's a wonder any of us get through this life alive." Then, realizing what he had said and seeing the others' sad smiles, he added. "That's right—we don't, do we? Well, Edward, I have your application for retirement here. First if all, let me confess, I haven't done a thing with it yet. It's perfectly in order. You have every right to retire if you wish. But we wanted to talk to you first. Ben, you want to take it from here?"

"No." Johnson shook his massive head. "You carry the ball."

"Edward, this concerns the Lombard homicide in your precinct. I know you know the man's reputation and the publicity he got and how important it is to the Department to come up with a quick solution and arrest. And, of course, it came in the middle of the reorganization of the Detective Division. Did you get the memo on the special task force Operation Lombard headed by Deputy Commissioner Broughton?"

Delaney paused before answering, wondering how much he should say. But Broughton was a slob—and what could the man do to him since he was retiring?

"Yes, I know," he nodded. "As a matter of fact, I suggested Operation Lombard to Broughton the morning of the murder. We had a private talk in his car."

Thorsen turned his head swiftly to look at Johnson. The two men stared at one another a moment. Then the inspector slammed a heavy palm down onto the arm of his leather chair.

"I told you," he said angrily. "I told you that stupid, racist son of a bitch didn't have the brains to come up with that idea himself. So it was you, Edward?"

"Yes."

"Well, don't expect a thank-you from brother Broughton. That bastard is strictly 'Hurray for me, fuck you.' He's flying mighty high right now."

"That's why we asked you here today, Edward," Thorsen said softly. "Broughton is flying high, and we'd like to bring him down."

Delaney looked from man to man, realizing he was getting involved in something he had vowed to avoid: the cliques and cabals that flourished in the upper echelons of the Department —and in all levels of government, and in the military, and in corporations, and in every human organization that had more than two members.

"Who is 'we'?" he asked cautiously.

"Inspector Johnson and myself, of course. And about ten or a dozen others, all of superior rank to us, who don't, for obvious reasons, want their names used at this time."

"What ranks?"

"Up to Commissioner."

"What are you trying to do?"

"First of all, we don't like Broughton. We believe he's a disgrace—hell, he's a catastrophe!—to the Department. He's amassing power, building a machine. This Operation Lombard is just another step up for him. If he can solve the murder."

"What motivates Broughton?" Delaney asked. "Ambition? What does he want? Commissioner? Mayor?"

Delaney looked at him, ready to laugh if Johnson was smiling. But he was not.

"Ben's not kidding, Edward. It's not impossible. Broughton is a relatively young man. He has an ego and hunger for power you wouldn't believe. Theodore Roosevelt went from the Commissioner's office to the White House. Why not Broughton? But even if he never gets to be President, or governor, or mayor, or even commissioner, we still want him out."

"Fascist bastard," Johnson grumbled.

"So . . . ?" Delaney said.

"We have a plan. Will you listen to it?"

"I'll listen."

"I'm not even going to talk about discretion and all this being in strict confidence, etcetera. I know you too well for that. Edward, even if you retired today, you couldn't spend every waking hour with your wife. She's going to be in the hospital for the foreseeable future, isn't she?"

"Yes."

"If you retired today, you'd still have plenty of time on your hands. And I know you; after almost thirty years in the Department, you'd go nuts. All right . . . Now it's been three —no, almost four days since the Lombard homicide. It's been almost three days since the formation of Operation Lombard. Since then, Broughton has been drawing men and equipment from all over the city. He's built up a big organization, and it's still growing. I told you, the man's power-hungry. And I can also tell you that Broughton and Operation Lombard haven't come up with a thing. Not a lead, not a clue, not a single idea of how it was done, why it was done, and who did it. Believe me, Edward, they're no farther ahead at this moment than when you saw Lombard on the sidewalk."

"That doesn't mean they might not solve it tomorrow, tonight, or right now, while we're talking."

"True. And if Broughton brings it off, he'll crucify us. I mean Ben here and me and our friends. Broughton may be stupid, but he's shrewd. He knows who his enemies are. I tell you this man is capable of farming you out just because you suggested Operation Lombard from which he profited. He's the kind of man who can't stand to feel gratitude. He'll cut you down . . . somehow."

"He can't touch me. I'm retiring."

"Edward," Inspector Johnson said in a deep, throbbing voice, "suppose you didn't retire. Suppose you requested an indefinite leave of absence. We could swing it."

"Why should I do that?"

"It would relieve you of the responsibility of the Two-five-one. We'd put in an Acting Captain. An *Acting* Captain. You wouldn't be replaced. You agree it's possible your wife may recover faster than anyone expects, and then you'd want back to active duty? That's possible, isn't it?"

"Yes. It's possible."

"All right," Johnson said, seeming to look for words, to feel his way. "Now, say you're on leave of absence. You're relieved of responsibility. Now what we want you to do—" Then it all came out in rush: "WhatwewantyoutodoisfindLombard'skiller."

"What?"

"You heard me. We want you to solve the Lombard homicide before Broughton and his Operation Lombard do it."

Delaney looked from man to man, astonished.

"Are you insane?" he finally demanded. "You want me, a single cop not even on active duty, working outside the Department like some kind of—some kind of private detective, you expect me to bring in Lombard's killer before five hundred or a thousand detectives and uniformed men and specialists with all the resources of the Department behind them? Impossible."

"Edward," Thorsen said patiently. "We think there's a chance. A small chance, true, but it's worth taking. Yes, you'd have to work in civilian clothes. Yes, you'd be by yourself; you couldn't request personnel from the Department, or equipment. But we'll set up a contact, and through the contact we'll make certain you got anything you'd need: print identification, evidence analysis, lab work, criminal records. Whatever you need, you'll get. We'll cover it somehow so Broughton doesn't get wind of it. If he does, we're all down the drain."

"Listen," Delaney said desperately, "is it only you two out to get Broughton or are there really a dozen others all the way up to the Commissioner?"

"There are others," Thorsen said gravely, and Johnson nodded just as solemnly.

"It won't work," Delaney said definitely. He stood and began to pace back and forth, hands clasped behind him. "You know how many men you need for a homicide investigation like this? Men to search sewers. Men to dig in garbage cans. Men to ring doorbells and ask questions. Men to investigate Lombard's private life, his business life, his political life. Men to trace him back to the day he was born, trying to find an enemy. How in God's name could I—or any one man—do all that?"

"Edward," Johnson said softly, "you wouldn't have to do all that. That's what Operation Lombard is doing right now, and I swear to you, you'd get a Xerox copy of every report filed. Anytime a patrolman or detective or specialist puts anything down on paper about the Lombard off, you'll see a copy within twenty-four hours."

"That's a promise," Thorsen nodded. "Just don't ask how we'll do it."

"I won't, I won't," Delaney said hastily. "But just what more do you think I could do than Operation Lombard is doing right now?"

"Edward," Thorsen sighed, "don't put yourself down. I remember once I had dinner at your house, and we were talking about something you had done and let your division commander take the credit for—you were a lieutenant then—and Barbara got angry and told you that you should assert yourself

127

more. She was right. Edward, you have a talent, a drive, a genius—call it whatever the hell you like—for investigative work. You know it but won't admit it. I know it and shout it every chance I get. It was my idea to bring you in on this, this way. If you say yes, fine. Then we'll go to work. If you say no, and want to go through with your retirement, okay and no hard feelings."

Delaney walked over to one of the windows and stared down into the crowded street. People were scurrying between honking cars in a traffic jam. There was bright movement, surge and thrust. He heard the horns, a siren, the far-off hoot of a liner putting to sea, the drone overhead of a plane slanting down to Kennedy Airport.

"No leads at all?" he asked, without turning around.

"None whatsoever," Thorsen said. "Not a thing. Not even a theory that makes sense. A blank. A complete blank. Broughton is beginning to show the strain."

Delaney turned around with a bleak smile. He looked at Inspector Johnson and spoke to him.

"Ben, I gave him the solution probability figures on homicide. You know how they drop off after forty-eight hours?"

"Yes," Johnson nodded. "It's been almost four days now, with probability dropping every minute for Broughton."

"For me too," Delaney said ruefully. "If I took this on," he added hastily.

He turned back to the window, his hands jammed into his pockets now. He wished with all his heart he could discuss this with Barbara, as he had discussed every important decision in his career. He needed her sharp, practical, aggressive, *female* intelligence to probe motives, choices, possibilities, safeguards. He tried, he strained to put himself in her place, to think as she might think and decide as she might decide.

"I'd be in civilian clothes," he said, his back to them. "Could I use my tin?"

"Yes," Johnson said immediately. "But as little as possible."

Delaney began to realize how completely they had thought this out, planned it, worried it for flaws, before they approached him.

"How often would I report?"

"As often as possible. Once a day or, if not, whenever you have something or a request for something."

"Who would I report to?"

"Me," Thorsen said promptly. "I'll give you a clean number."

"Don't tell me you think your home phone is tapped?"

"I'll give you a clean number," Thorsen repeated.

Delaney made up his mind and said what he thought Barbara would want him to say.

"If I'm on leave of absence but not retired, I can still be racked up on Departmental charges. If Broughton finds out about this, he'll fix me good. I met the man. I know what he is. I'll do what you want if I get a signed letter from either of you, or both of you, authorizing this investigation."

He turned to face them. They looked at him, then at each other.

"Edward . . ." Thorsen started, then stopped.

"Yes?"

"It's our ass."

"I know it. Without the letter, it's my ass. Mine alone. If Broughton discovers what's going on."

"Don't you trust—" Thorsen began.

"Now wait just one fat minute," Johnson held up his ham-hand. "Let's not get all riled here and start talking about trust and friendship and saying things we might be sorry for later. Just let me think a minute. Edward has a very good point, Ivar. It's something we didn't consider. Now just let me think and see if I can come up with something that will satisfy all the parties concerned."

He stared off into the middle distance, while the other two watched him expectantly. Finally Johnson grunted and heaved himself to his feet. He scrubbed his curly grey hair with knuckles, then motioned toward Thorsen. The two men went over to one corner and began to speak in low voices, Johnson doing most of the talking and gesturing frequently. Delaney took his seat again in the club chair and wished he was with his wife.

Finally the whispering ceased. The two men came over to stand before his chair.

"Edward," Johnson rumbled, "if we got a letter addressed to you personally, authorizing your unofficial or semi-official investigation into the death of Frank Lombard, and if this letter was signed by the Commissioner, would that satisfy you?"

Delaney looked up in amazement.

"The Commissioner? Why on earth would he sign a letter like that? He just appointed Broughton commander of Operation Lombard."

Inspector Johnson sighed heavily. "Edward, the Commish is a man of some ability. About a middleweight, I'd guess. And he's well-meaning and kind. All to the good. But this is the first time he's operated in New York. He's never had to keep afloat in a school of barracudas. Not the kind we got. He's learning—but the question is, will they give him time to learn? He's just beginning to realize a good executive has got to spend as much time protecting his ass as he does coping with the problems in front of him. Nine times out of ten, it's those strong, efficient executive assistants with the long knives who do a top man in. I think the Commissioner may just be starting to realize what Broughton is doing between those farts and belches. Broughton has some palsy-walsys on the Mayor's staff, you know. There's also another factor. This is something never talked about in business management manuals, but it exists in the Department, in federal, state and local government, in business, and in the military. I think the Commissioner is physically frightened of Broughton. I can't give you any evidence, but that's what I feel. It was the source of a lot of Joe McCarthy's power. Plenty of those old, frail Senators were physically afraid of Joe. Well, we've got a man, a friend —real Machiavelli type—a Deputy the Commissioner trusts who could maybe put a bug in his ear. 'Look, Commissioner, Broughton is a fine fellow—a little crude for my taste but he gets things done—and maybe he'll bring off this Operation Lombard thing and find the killer. But look, Commissioner, wouldn't it be wise to have an ace in the hole? I mean if Broughton falls on his face, you really should have a back-up plan in the works. Now it just so happens I've got this smart-ass Captain who right now is on leave of absence, and this smart-ass Captain is the best detective this town ever saw, and if you ask him nice, Commissioner, and write him a po-lite letter, this smart-ass Captain just might be willing to smell around and find Frank Lombard's killer for you. Without Broughton knowing a thing about it, of course.' "

Delaney laughed. "Do you think he'll go for that? Do you really think he'll give me a letter of authorization?"

"If we get it, will you do it?"

"Yes."

4

The following evening, as he was preparing to leave for the hospital, an envelope was delivered to his home by commercial messanger. The envelope contained a letter signed by the Commissioner, authorizing Captain Edward X. Delaney to undertake a "discreet inquiry" into the homicide of Frank Lombard. There was also a letter signed by the Chief of Patrol granting Captain Delaney an indefinite leave of absence "for personal reasons." Delaney began to appreciate the clout swung by Thorsen, Johnson, and their friends.

He was about to call Ivar Thorsen from his home, but after dialing two digits he hung up and sat a moment, staring at the phone. He remembered the Deputy Inspector had stressed that the number he had been given was "clean." He pulled on his overcoat, walked two blocks to a public phone booth and called from there? The "clean" number proved to be an answering service. He gave only his last name and the number of the phone he was calling from. Then he hung up and waited patiently. Thorsen was back to him within three minutes.

"I got the papers," Delaney said. "Quick work."

"Yes. Where are you calling from."

"A public phone booth two blocks from my house."

"Good. Keep doing that. Use different booths."

"All right. Have you made any decision on an Acting Captain?"

"Not yet. Any suggestions?"

"I have a lieutenant. Dorfman. Know him?"

"No. But a *lieutenant?* I'm not sure we can swing it. That's a boss precinct, Edward. It should have a captain or deputy inspector. I don't believe there's any precedent for a lieutenant commanding a precinct."

"Consider it, will you? Look up Dorfman's file. Four commendations. A good administrator. A fine lawyer."

"Can he hack it?"

"We'll never know until he gets the chance, will we? There's another thing."

"What's that?"

"He trusts me. More than that, he likes me. He'd make a perfect contact. The man to handle the requests I'll have for records, print identification, research, lab analysis, things like that. It could be shuffled in with the usual precinct paper. No one could spot it."

"How much would you tell him?"

"As little as possible."

There was a silence.

"There's another factor," Delaney said quickly. "I gave Broughton the idea for Operation Lombard and the homicide was in my precinct. It would be natural for him to think I was pissed off and jealous. He'll be suspicious of any possible inter-

131

ference from me. I'm guessing how this mind works from what you and Johnson told me about him."

"You guess right."

"Well, he'll hear I've gone on leave of absence, and he'll relax. He'll relax even more if he hears Dorfman has been appointed Acting Captain. A *lieutenant?* And a man with no detective experience? Broughton will cross off my old Precinct as a potential trouble spot, and I'll be able to use Dorfman as a contact with little possibility of discovery."

"It's a thought," Thorsen said. "And a good one. Let me discuss it with—with others. Maybe we can swing it. I'll get back to you. Anything else?"

"Yes. I know Broughton came out of patrol. Who's strawboss of his detectives on Operation Lombard?"

"Chief Pauley."

"Oh God. He's good."

"You're better."

"Keep telling me that. I need all the reassurance I can get."

"When are you starting?"

"As of now."

"Good. You'll have the Xerox tomorrow. You understand?"

"Yes."

"Keep me informed."

The two men hung up without saying goodby.

Delaney took a cab to the hospital, pressed back into a corner of the rear seat, biting at his thumbnail. He was beginning to feel the old, familiar excitement. Forget his reasoning and emotions about police work. His gut reaction was obvious: the chase was on and he was the hunter.

He came into her room smiling determinedly, taking from his pocket a silly little thing he had bought her: a cheap, brilliant brooch, a rhinestoned penguin she could pin to her hospital gown. She held her arms out to him; he bent to embrace her.

"I was hoping you'd come."

"I told you I would. Better?"

She smiled brightly and nodded.

"Here." He handed her the penguin. "From Tiffany's. A little over a hundred thousand."

"Beautiful," she laughed. "What I've always wanted."

He helped her pin it to the shoulder of her gown. Then he took off his overcoat, pulled a chair over to the bed, sat down and took one of her hands in his.

"Truly better?"

"Truly. I think I should start seeing people. Some close friends."

"Good," he said, being careful to avoid false heartiness. "Eddie will be up next week. What about Liza?"

"No, Edward. Not in her condition. Not yet."

"All right. Shall I call your friends?"

"I'll do it. Most of them I want to see call me every day. I'll tell them I'd like to see them. You know—two or three a day. Not everyone at once."

He nodded approvingly and looked down at her smiling. But her appearance shocked him. She was so thin! The tubes and jars were gone, her face was flushed with the familiar fever, but the frailty was what tore his heart. She who had always been so active, strong, vibrant . . . Now she lay flaccid and seemed to strain for breath. The hand he was not holding picked weakly at blanket fluff.

"Edward, are you eating all right?"

"Fine."

"Sticking to your diet?"

"I swear."

"What about sleep?"

He held out a hand, palm down, then turned it over, then flipped it back and forth a few times.

"So-so. Listen, Barbara, there's something I must tell you. I want to—"

"Has something happened? Are the children all right?"

"The children are fine. This doesn't concern them. But I want to talk to you for about an hour. Maybe more. It won't tire you, will it?"

"Of course not, silly. I've been sleeping all day. I can tell you're excited. What is it?"

"Well . . . four days ago—actually early in the morning following your operation—there was a homicide in my precinct."

He described to her, as concisely and completely as he could, the discovery and appearance of Frank Lombard's body. Then he went on to tell her how important it was to solve Lombard's murder in view of the man's public criticism of the Department, and how the current reorganization of the Detective Division hampered efficient handling of the case. Then he described his private talk with Deputy Commissioner Broughton.

"He sounds like a horrible man!" she interrupted.

"Yes . . . Anyway, the next day I filed for retirement."

She came up from the bed in shock, then fell back, her eyes filling with tears.

"Edward! You didn't?"

"Yes. I wanted to spend more time with you. I thought it was the right decision at the time. But it didn't go through. This is what happened . . ."

He recounted his meeting with Deputy Inspector Thorsen and Inspector Johnson. He detailed their plan for Delaney to make an independent investigation of the Lombard homicide, in an effort to humiliate Broughton. As he spoke, he could see Barbara come alive. She propped herself on one elbow and leaned forward, eyes shining. She was the politician of the family and dearly loved hearing accounts and gossip of intra-Departmental feuding, the intrigues and squabbles of ambitious men and factions.

Delaney told her how he had demanded a letter of authorization from a superior officer before he would agree to the Lombard investigation.

"Barbara, do you think I did the wise thing?"

"You did exactly right," she said promptly. "I'm proud of you. In that jungle, the first law is 'Save yourself'."

Then he told her about receiving the Commissioner's letter, the authorization of indefinite leave of absence, and his most recent conversation with Thorsen.

"I'm glad you recommended Dorfman," she nodded happily. "I like him. And I think he deserves a chance."

"Yes. The problem is making a lieutenant even an *acting* commander of a precinct. And of course they can't suddenly promote him without possibly alerting Broughton. Well . . . we'll see what happens. Meanwhile, I'll be getting copies of all the Operation Lombard reports tomorrow."

"Edward, it doesn't sound like you have much to go on."

"No, not much. Thorsen says that so far Operation Lombard has drawn a blank. They don't have any description of a possible suspect, how he killed, or why he killed."

"You say 'he'. Couldn't it have been a woman?"

"Possibly, but the probability percentages are against it. Women murder with gun, knife, and poison. They rarely bludgeon. And when they do, it's usually when the victim is asleep."

"Then you're really starting from scratch?"

"Well . . . I have two things. They don't amount to much and I expect Chief Pauley has them too. Lombard was a tall man. I'd guess about six feet. Now look . . ." Delaney rose to his feet and looked around the hospital room. He found a magazine, rolled it up tightly, and gripped one end. "Now I'm the killer with a hammer, a pipe, or maybe a long spike. I'm striking down at the victim's skull." He raised the magazine above his head and brought it down viciously. "See that? I'll do it again. Watch the position of my right arm." Again he raised the magazine and brought it down in a feigned crushing blow. "What did you see?"

"Your arm wasn't extended. Your right arm was bent. The top of the magazine was only about six inches above your head."

"Correct. That's the way a man would normally strike. When you're hammering in a nail, you don't raise your arm to its full length above your head; you keep your elbow bent the better to control the accuracy of the blow. You raise your arm just high enough to provide what you estimate to be sufficient force. It's an unconscious skill, based on experience. To drive a carpet tack, you might raise a hammer only an inch or two. To drive a spike, you'd raise the hammer to your head level or higher."

"Was Lombard killed with a hammer?"

"Ferguson says no. But it was obviously something swung with sufficient force to penetrate his brain to a depth of three to four inches. I haven't seen Ferguson's report yet."

"Could the killer be lefthanded?"

"Could be. But probability is against it, unless the nature and position of the wound indicate otherwise, and then it might be due to the position of the victim at the moment of impact."

"There are so many possibilities."

"There surely are. Barbara, are you getting tired?"

"Oh no. You can't stop now. Edward, I don't understand the significance of what you just showed me—how a man strikes with his elbow bent."

"Just that Lombard was about six feet tall. If the killer raised the weapon about six inches above his own head— which is about the limit any man would raise a tool or weapon before striking downward—and the puncture was low on Lombard's skull (not so far down as to be in that hollow where the spine joins the skull, but up from that toward the crown of the skull), then I'd guess the killer to be approximately of Lombard's height or maybe a few inches taller. Yes, it's a guess. But based, it seems to me, on what little physical evidence is available. And I've got to start guessing *somewhere*."

"You said you had two things, Edward. What's the other?"

"Well . . . I worked this out the morning of the murder. While I was on the scene. Just to satisfy my own curiosity, I guess. What bothered me most about the murder was why a man of Lombard's size and strength, with his awareness of street crime, alone on a deserted street at midnight, why he would let an assailant come up behind him and chop him down without making any apparent effort to defend himself. Here's how I think it was done . . ."

He acted it out for her. First he was Lombard, in his overcoat, walking briskly around the hospital room, head turning side to side as he inspected entrances and outside lobbies. "Then I see a man coming toward me from York Avenue. Coming *toward* me." Delaney-Lombard, explaining as he performed, peered ahead, watching the approaching figure. He slowed his steps, ready to defend himself or run to safety if danger threatened. But then he smiled, reassured by the stranger's appearance. He moved aside to let the smiling stranger pass, and then . . .

"Now I'm the killer," Delaney told a wide-eyed Barbara. He took off his overcoat and folded it over his left arm. Beneath the coat, hidden, the rolled up magazine was grasped in his left hand. His right arm swung free as he marched briskly around the hospital room. "I see the man I want to kill. I smile and continue to walk quickly like a resident of the block anxious to get home."

Delaney-killer turned his head as he passed Lombard. Then his right hand swooped under the coat. The rolled-up magazine was transferred. At the same time Delaney-killer whirled and went up on his toes. Now he was behind the victim. The magazine whistled down. The entire action took a few seconds, no longer.

"Then I bend over—"

"Get him!" Barbara cried. "Edward, get him! Get him!"

He straightened in astonishment, riven by the hatred and venom in her voice. He rushed to the bed, tried to take her in his arms, but she would not be comforted.

"Get him!" she repeated, and it was a curse. "You can do it, Edward. You're the only one who can do it. Get him! Promise me? It's not right. Life is too precious. Get him! Get him!"

And even after he calmed her, a nurse had been summoned, a sedative had been administered, Barbara was sleeping, and he left the hospital, still he heard that virulent "Get him! Get him!" and vowed he would.

Xerox copies of the Operation Lombard reports constituted a bundle of almost 500 sheets of typed papers, official forms, photostats, transcriptions of tape recordings, signed statements, etc. In addition, there was a separate envelope of more than 30 photo copies: Lombard in death and in life, his wife, mother, two brothers, political and business associates, and close friends. The dead man and his wife had been childless.

Captain Delaney, impressed with this mass of material spread out on the desk in his study, and realizing the urgency with which Operation Lombard was working, set out to organize the documents into manila folders marked Physical Evidence, Personal History, Family, Business (Lombard had been an active partner in a Brooklyn law firm), Politics, and Miscellaneous.

It took him almost two hours to get the material filed in some kind of rough order. Then he mixed a rye highball, put his feet up on the desk, and began reading. By two in the morning he had read every report and stared at every photo in every file. He was doubly impressed with the thoroughness of Broughton's investigation, but as far as first impressions went, Ivar Thorsen was right: there was nothing—no leads, no hints, no mysteries at all—except who killed Frank Lombard.

He started his second reading, going slower this time and making notes on a pad of long yellow legal notepaper. He also set aside a few documents for a third reading and study. Dawn was lightening the study windows when he closed the final folder. He rose to his feet, stretched and yawned, put his hands on his hips and bent his torso backward until his spine cracked.

Then he went into the kitchen and drank a large glass of tomato juice with a lemon wedge squeezed into it. He made a carafe of three cups of instant coffee, black, and carried that into the study along with a dry and stale bagel.

He consulted his notes and, sipping coffee, read for the third time Dr. Sanford Ferguson's medical report. It was one of Ferguson's usual meticulous autopsies; the eight-page statement included two sketches showing the outside wound in actual size and a profile outline of the human skull showing the location and shape of the penetration. It looked like an elongated isosceles triangle. The outside wound was roughly circular in shape, slightly larger than a quarter.

The essential paragraph of the report was as follows:

"The blow caused a penetrating wound, fracturing the right occipital bone, lacerating the dura, piercing the right occipital lobe. Laceration of the cerebellum caused hemorrhaging with resultant rupture into the posterior fossa and 4th ventrical causing acute compression of the brain stem with subsequent death."

Delaney made several additional notes on the autopsy report. He had questions he knew could only be answered in a personal interview with Ferguson. How he would explain to the doctor his interest in the Lombard homicide was a problem he'd face when he came to it.

His other notes concerned the interviews with the widow, Mrs. Clara Lombard. She had been interviewed five times by three different detectives. Delaney nodded approvingly at Chief Pauley's professionalism. It was standard detective procedure: you send three different detectives for the first three interviews. Then the three get together with their chief, discuss the subject's personality, and select the detective who has established the closest rapport with her, the one she feels most *simpatico* with. He returns for the two final interviews.

Delaney began to get a picture of the widow from the typed reports. (The first three were transcriptions made from tape recordings.) Mrs. Clara Lombard seemed to be a flighty, feather-brained woman, trying hard to appear devastated by the tragedy of her husband's violent death, but still capable of infantile laughter, jokes of a dubious nature, sudden inquiries about insurance money, questions about probating the will, illogical threats of legal action against New York City, and statements that could only be construed as outright flirtation.

Delaney wasn't interested in all that; careful investigation showed that although Clara was a very social woman—a happy party-goer with or without her husband—she had no boyfriend, and no one, not even her women friends, even hinted she might have been unfaithful.

The portion of her testimony that interested Delaney most was concerned with Frank Lombard's wallet. That damned wallet irritated the Captain . . . its position near the body . . . the fact that it had been deliberately removed from the hip pocket . . . it was lying open . . . it was still full of money . . .

To Delaney's surprise, in only one interview had Mrs. Lombard been handed a detailed inventory of the wallet. This document was included in the Physical Evidence file. Clara had been asked if, to her knowledge, anything was missing. She had replied no, she thought all her late husband's identification and credit cards were there, and the sum of money—over two hundred dollars—was what he customarily carried. Even two keys, one to his home, one to his office—in a "secret pocket" in the wallet—were there.

Delaney didn't accept her statement. How many wives could tell you exactly what their husbands carried in their wallets? How many husbands could list exactly what their wife's purse contained? As a matter of fact, how many men knew exactly how much money they had in their own wallets? To test this, Delaney thought a moment and guessed he had fifty-six dollars in the wallet on his hip. Then he took it out and counted. He had forty-two—and wondered where his money was going.

The only other Operation Lombard report that interested him was an interview with the victim's grieving mother. Delaney read this transcription again. As he had suspected, Mrs. Sophia Lombard lived in a converted brownstone between the East River and the point where her son's body had been found.

Mrs. Lombard had been questioned—and very adroitly, Delancy acknowledged; that was Chief Pauley's doing—on the circumstances of her son's visits to her. Did he come every week? The same night every week? The same time every night? In other words, was it a regular, established routine? Did he call beforehand? How did he travel over from Brooklyn?

The answers were disappointing and perplexing. Frank Lombard had no regular schedule for dining with his mother. He came to see her when he could. Sometimes two weeks, sometimes a month would elapse before he could make it. But he was a good boy, Mrs. Sophia Lombard assured her interrogator; he called every day. On the day he could come to dinner, he would call before noon so Mrs. Lombard could go out and shop in the markets along First Avenue for the things he liked.

Lombard didn't drive his car over from Brooklyn because parking space was hard to find near his mother's apartment. He would take the subway, and a bus or taxi from the subway station. He didn't like to walk on the streets at nights. He always left for his Brooklyn home before midnight.

Did Mrs. Clara Lombard ever accompany her husband to his mother's home for dinner?

"No," Mrs. Sophia Lombard said shortly. And reading that reply, Delaney smiled, understanding the discords that must have existed in *that* family.

Delaney replaced the reports in their folders, and put all the Operation Lombard file in a small safe in the corner of his study. As he well knew, an experienced "can man" could be into that in one minute flat. And two inexperienced thieves could carry it out between them to sledge it open later.

His eyes were sandy and his bones ached. It was almost seven a.m. He dumped the cold coffee, went upstairs, undressed and rolled into bed. Something was nagging at his mind, something he had read in the Operation Lombard reports. But that had happened to him frequently: a lead sensed but not recognized. It didn't worry him; he tried not to think about it. He knew from experience that it would come to him eventually, sliding into his mind like a remembered name or a tune recalled. He set the alarm for eighty-thirty, closed his eyes and was instantly asleep.

He arrived at the precinct house a little after nine a.m. The Desk Sergeant was a policewoman, the second of her rank in New York to be assigned to such duty. He went over the log with her, and asked questions. She was a tall, powerfully built woman with what he termed to himself, without knowing why, a *thunderous* body. In truth, he was intimidated by her, but could not deny her efficiency. The book was in order; nothing had been neglected that could have been done—a sad, sad list of drunks, missing persons, beaten wives, stolen welfare checks, mistreated children, burglaries, Peeping Toms, prostitutes, dying oldsters, homosexuals, breaking-and-entering, exhibitionists . . . People. But the moon was full, and Delaney knew what that meant.

He climbed the creaking wooden steps to his office and, on the landing, met Detective Lieutenant Jeri Fernandez who was, or had been, in command of detectives assigned to the 251st.

"Morning, Captain," Fernandez said glumly.

"Good morning, lieutenant," Delaney said. He looked at the man sympathetically. "Having a rough time, aren't you?"

"Oh shit!" Fernandez burst out. "Half my men are gone already. The others will be gone within a week. Okay, that's one thing. But the paper work! All our open cases have to be transferred to the proper unit covering this precinct. Jesus, it's a mess."

"What did you get?"

"I drew a Safe, Loft and Truck Division in midtown," Fernandez said disgustedly. "It covers four precincts including the Garment Center. How does that grab you? I'm second in command, and we'll be getting dicks from all over Manhattan. It'll take us at least a year to set up our snitches. What great brain dreamed up this idea?"

Delaney knew how Fernandez felt. The man was a conscientious, efficient, but unimaginative detective. He had done a good job in the 251st, training his men, being hard when he had to be hard and soft when he had to be soft. Now they were breaking up his crew and farming them out to specialized divisions. And Fernandez himself would now be number two man under a detective captain. He had a right to his anger.

"I would have guessed Broughton would have grabbed you for Operation Lombard," Delaney said.

"Not me," Fernandez said with a sour grin. "I ain't white enough."

They nodded and separated. Delaney went on to his office, marveling how quickly a man's prejudices and record spread throughout the Department. More fool Broughton, he thought; Fernandez could have been a big help. Unimaginative he might have been, but when it came to dull, foot-flattening routine, he was excellent. The important thing was to know how to use men, to take advantage of their particular talents and the best in them.

The moment he was at his desk he called the hospital. The head floor nurse told him his wife was down in the lab, having more X-ray plates taken, but she was doing "as well as can be expected." Trying to conceal his distaste for that particular phrase, Delaney thanked her and said he'd call later.

Then he called Dr. Sanford Ferguson and, unexpectedly, was put through to him immediately at his office.

"That you, Edward?"

"Yes. Can we get together?"

"How's Barbara?"

"Doing as well as can be expected."

"I seem to recognize the words. Is it about Barbara you want to see me?"

"No. The Lombard homicide."

"Oh? I was glad to hear you hadn't retired. Now it's an indefinite leave of absence."

"News travels fast."

"It was on the Telex about ten minutes ago. Edward, what's this about Lombard? I thought Broughton was handling it."

"He is. But I want to see you, to talk to you. Can you make it?"

"Well . . ." Ferguson was cautious, and Delaney didn't blame him. "Look, I've got to go up to 34th Street today. It's my sister's birthday, and I want to get her something. At Macy's. Any suggestions?"

"When in doubt, a gift certificate."

"Won't work. I know her. She wants something personal."

"A silk scarf. That's what I always buy for Barbara. She's got enough silk scarves to make a parachute."

"Good idea. Well then, how about lunch?"

"Fine."

"I know a good chop house near Macy's. Do you like mutton chops?"

"Hate them."

"Idiot. That heavy, gamy taste . . . nothing like it."

"Can I get a broiled kidney?"

"Of course."

"Then let's have lunch at your chop house."

"Good. You get there at twelve-thirty. I'll be finished shopping by then and will be there before you. Ask the head waiter for my table. He knows me. It will be in the bar, not the main dining room. All right?"

"Of course. Thank you."

"For what? I haven't done anything for you yet."

"You will."

"Will I? In that case you're paying for the lunch."

"Done," Captain Edward X. Delaney said.

Ferguson gave him the address of the chop house and they hung up.

"Oysters!" Ferguson boomed happily. "I definitely recommend the oysters. The horse-radish is freshly ground. Then I'll have the mutton chop."

"Very good, sir," the waiter said.

"Oysters for me also," Delaney nodded. "Then I'll have the broiled kidney. What comes with that?"

"Home-fries and salad, sir."

"Skip the potatoes, please. Just the salad. Oil and vinegar."

"I'll have everything," Ferguson cried, and drained half his martini.

"What did you buy your sister?" Delaney asked.

"A silk scarf. What else? Come on, Edward, what's this all about? You're on leave of absence."

"Do you really want to know?"

Dr. Sanford Ferguson was suddenly sober and quiet. He stared at Delaney a long moment. "No," he said finally. "I really don't want to know. Except . . . will my name be brought into it?"

"I swear to you—no."

"That's good enough for me."

Their oysters were brought, and they looked down at them, beaming. They went through the business with the horse-radish sauce and the hot stuff. They swallowed, looked at each other, groaned with pleasure.

"All right," Ferguson said. "What do you want?"

"About your report on the Lombard—"

"How did you get my report?"

Delaney looked at him steadily. "You said you didn't want to know."

"That's right; I don't. All right, what about the report?"

"I have a few questions." Delaney took a short list out of his side pocket, put it on the cloth before him, donned his heavy glasses, consulted it, then leaned toward Ferguson.

"Doctor," he said earnestly, "your official reports are most complete. I don't deny it. But they're couched in medical language. As they should be, of course," he added hastily.

"So?"

"I have some questions about what your medical terms mean."

"Edward, you're jiving me."

"Well . . . really what the significance is."

"That's better," Ferguson smiled. "You can read a PM as well as a third-year medical student."

"Yes. Also, I happen to know, doctor, that you include in your official reports only that which you objectively observe and which could be substantiated by any other capable surgeon doing the identical post-mortem. I also know that in an autopsy—in *any* investigation—there are impressions, feelings, hunches—call them what you like—that can never be part of an official report because the physical evidence doesn't exist. And its those impressions, feelings and hunches that I want from you."

Ferguson slipped a dipped oyster into his mouth, swallowed, rolled his eyes.

"You're a bastard, Edward," he said amiably. "You really are a bastard. You'll use anyone, won't you?"

"Yes," Delaney nodded. "I'll use anyone. Any time."

"Let's start from word one," Ferguson said, busily stirring his oyster sauce. "Let's start with head wounds. Much experience?"

"No. Not much."

"Edward, the human skull and the human brain are tougher beyond your comprehension. Ever read a detective novel or see a movie where a man has a single bullet fired into his head and dies instantly? Practically impossible. I've had cases of victims with five bullets in their heads who lived. They were vegetables, true, but they lived. Three years ago I had a would-be suicide who fired a bullet at his head with a low calibre revolver. Twenty-two, I think. The slug bounced off his skull and hit the ceiling. Literally. Commit suicide by firing a bullet into your temple? Forget it. The slug could pass completely through, come out the other side, and you still wouldn't be dead. You might live hours, weeks, or years. Maybe you couldn't talk, or move, or control your bowels, but you'd be alive. How are your oysters, Edward?"

"Very good. Yours?"

"Marvelous. There's only one way of committing sure suicide—instantaneous suicide—by a gunshot to the head. That's by using a pistol or revolver of reasonably heavy calibre, say a thirty-eight at least—a rifle or shotgun would do as well, of course—put the muzzle deep into your mouth aimed at the back of your head, close your lips and teeth firmly about the barrel, pull the trigger, and splatter your brains onto the opposing wall. Some of these little oysterettes, Edward?"

"Yes, thank you."

"Now about the Lombard homicide. The entry was made from the back, low on the crown. About halfway to where the spine joins the skull. The only other spot where death might be instantaneous."

"You think the killer had a surgeon's knowledge?"

"Oh God, no," Ferguson said, signaling the waiter to remove their emptied oyster plates. "Yes, to hit that spot deliberately would require a surgeon's experience. But the victim would have to be on an operating table. No killer swinging a weapon violently could hope to hit it. It was luck. The killer's luck, not Lombard's luck."

"Was death instantaneous?" Delaney asked.

"Close to it. If not instant, then within a few seconds. A half-inch to the right or left and the man might have lived for hours or weeks."

"It was that close?"

144

"I told you the human skull and brain are much tougher than most people realize. Do you know how many ex-soldiers are walking around today with hunks of shrapnel in their brains? They live normally, except for occasional crushing headaches, but we can't operate. And they'll live out their normal lives and die from smoking too many cigarettes or eating too much cheese."

The mutton chop, broiled kidney, and salads were served. Ferguson got his home-fries, a big plate with plenty of onions. After consultation with the head waiter, who was 343 years old, they ordered a bottle of heavy burgundy.

"To get back to Lombard," Delaney said, digging into his broiled kidney, "was it really a circular wound?"

"Oh you're so smart," Ferguson said without rancor. "You're so fucking smart. My report stated it *appeared* to be a circular penetration. But I had the impression it could have been triangular. Or even square. Look, Edward, you've never probed a brain penetration. You think it's like pounding a spike into modeling clay, and then you pull out the spike and you've got a nice, clean perfect cavity? It's nothing like that. The wound fills up. Brain matter presses in. There is blood. Bits of bone. Hair. All kinds of crap. And you expect me to— How's the kidney?"

"Delicious," Delaney said. "I've been here before, but I forgot how much bacon they give you."

"The mutton chop is fine," Ferguson said, dipping into his little dish of applesauce. "I'm really enjoying this. But about that Lombard wound . . . In addition to the impression I had that the opening was not necessarily circular in shape, I also had the feeling that the penetration curved downward."

"Curved?"

"Yes. Like a limp cone. The tip of the weapon lower than the shaft. A curve. Like a hard-on just beginning to go soft. You understand?"

"Yes. But why are you so uncertain about the shape of the wound and the shape of the penetration? I know what you wrote, but what do you guess?"

"I think, I *guess* that Lombard fell forward with such force that it wrenched the weapon out of the killer's hand. And that the killer then bent forward and twisted his tool or weapon to remove it from Lombard's skull. If the spike was triangular or square, the twisting would result in a roughly circular shape."

"And it would mean the weapon was valuable to the killer," Delaney said. "He took the time to recover it. It was valuable intrinsically, or valuable because it might be traced to the killer. Murderers who use a hammer or pipe or rock usually wear gloves and leave the weapon behind."

"Beautiful," Dr. Ferguson said, draining his wine. "I love to listen to you think."

"I'm glad it wasn't a hammer," Delaney said. "I never really believed it was."

"Why not?"

"I've handled three hammer cases. In two of them the handle broke. In the third, the head snapped off."

"So you knew how tough the human skull is? But you let me talk."

"That's the name of the game. Anything else?"

"What else? Nothing else. It's all smoke. On the evidence, the penetration was circular, but it might have been triangular. It might have been square. It hit the one spot that killed the man instantly. Do I think the killer has surgical knowledge? No. It was a lucky hit."

"Dessert?" Delaney asked.

"Just coffee for me, thanks."

"Two coffees, please," Delaney ordered. "Any ideas, any guesses, any wild suggestions at all as to what the weapon might have been?"

"None whatsoever."

"Was there anything inside the wound you didn't expect to find? Anything that wasn't in your report?"

Ferguson looked at him sternly a moment, then relaxed and laughed. "You never give up, do you? There were traces of oil."

"Oil? What kind of oil?"

"Not enough for analysis. But undoubtedly hair oil. The rest of his hair was heavily oiled, so I assume the oil in the wound came from the hair driven into it."

"Anything else?"

"Yes. Since you're paying, I'll have a brandy."

After Ferguson took a cab back to his office, Delaney walked slowly toward Sixth Avenue. He realized he was only a few blocks from the flower market and sauntered down there. He was in no hurry. He knew from experience that each investigation had a pace of its own. Some shouted of a quick solution and were wrapped-up in hours. Others had the feel of slow growth and the need for time. The Lombard homicide was one of those. He consoled himself that Broughton, who *was* in a hurry, was getting nowhere. But was he doing any better? As Dr. Ferguson had said, it was all smoke.

He found what he was looking for in the third flower shop he visited: violets, out of season. They were the flowers with which he had courted Barbara. They were sold by street vendors in those days, old ladies with baskets next to old men selling chestnuts. He would buy a bunch for Barbara and ask, "Fresh roasted violets, lady?" She was always kind enough to laugh. Now he bought the last two bunches the store had and took a cab to the hospital.

But when he tiptoed into her room she was sleeping peacefully and he didn't have the heart to awaken her. He unwrapped the violets and looked around the room for something to put them in, but there was nothing. Finally he sat in the straight chair, his uniformed bulk overflowing it. He grasped the tender violets in his big fist and waited quietly, watching his wife sleep. He glanced once at the dusty windows. The sharp November sunlight was diluted and softened.

Perhaps, the sad, hunkering man wondered, a marriage was like one of those stained glass windows he had seen in a modest village church in France. From the outside, the windows were almost opaque with the dirt and grime of centuries. But when you went inside, and saw the sunlight leaping through, diffused by the dust, the colors struck into your eye and heart with their boldness and purity, their youth and liveliness.

His marriage to Barbara, he supposed, must seem dull and dusty to an outsider. But seen from within, as father of a family, it was all bright and beguiling, touching and, finally, holy and mysterious. He watched his wife sleep and *willed* his strength to her, making her whole and laughing again. Then, unable to endure his thoughts, he stood and placed the violets on her bedside table with a scribbled note: "Fresh roasted violets, lady?"

When he got back to his office, Dorfman was waiting for him with a sheet of paper torn from the Telex.

"Captain," he said in a choked voice, and Delaney was afraid he might weep, "is this—"

"Yes, lieutenant, it's correct. As of now, I'm on leave of absence. Come on in and let's talk about it."

Dorfman followed him inside and took the scarred chair next to Delaney's desk.

"Captain, I had no idea your wife was so ill."

"Well, as far as I can guess, it's going to be a long haul, and I wanted to spend as much time with her as possible."

"Is there anything I can do?"

"Thank you, no. Well, perhaps there is something. You might call her. I have a feeling she'd like to see you. Whenever you can spare the time."

"I'll call her right away," Dorfman cried.

"Wait a few hours. I've just come from there, and she's sleeping."

"I'll call just before my watch ends. Then if she wants to see me, I can go right over. What can I bring—flowers, candy, what?"

"Oh nothing, thanks. She has everything she needs."

"Maybe a cake?" Dorfman said. "A nice cake. She can share it with the nurses. Nurses love cake."

"Fine," Delaney smiled. "I think she'd like a cake from you."

"Captain," Dorfman mourned, his long horse-face sagging again, "I suppose this means we'll be getting an Acting Captain?"

"Yes."

"Do you have any idea who it will be, sir?"

Delaney debated a moment, briefly ashamed of manipulating a man so honest and sincere. But it was the sensible thing to do, to cement Dorfman's trust and affection.

"I recommended you for the job, lieutenant," he said quietly.

Dorfman's pale blue eyes widened in shock.

"Me?" he gasped. Then, "Me?" he repeated with real pleasure.

"Wait a minute," Delaney held up his hand. "I recommended you, but I don't think you'll get it. Not because your file isn't good enough or you couldn't handle the job, but your rank is against you. This precinct calls for a captain or deputy inspector. You understand that?"

"Oh sure, Captain. But I certainly do appreciate your recommending me."

"Well, as I said, I don't think you're going to get it. So if I were you, I wouldn't mention it to a soul. Particularly your wife. Then, if they turn you down, it'll just be your disappointment, and no one will think they considered you and passed you over, for one reason or another."

"I won't mention it, sir."

Delaney considered whether or not to hint to Dorfman the services as a contact he might be asked to provide in the Captain's investigation of the Lombard homicide. Then he de-

148

cided against it. This wasn't the right time, and he had given the man enough to think about.

"In any event," Delaney said, "if you get the job or don't get it, remember I'm still living next door and if there is ever anything I can help you with, don't hesitate to give me a call or ring my bell. I mean that. Don't get the idea you'll be bothering me or annoying me. You won't. As a matter of fact, I'd appreciate knowing what's going on over here. This is my precinct and, with luck, I hope to be back in command some day."

"I hope so too, Captain," Dorfman said fervently. "I really do hope so." He rose and stuck out a hand. "Best of luck, sir, and I hope Mrs. Delaney is feeling better real soon."

"Thank you, lieutenant."

After Dorfman left, Delaney sat swinging back and forth slowly in his swivel chair. Was a man as gentle and sensitive as the lieutenant capable of administering a busy precinct in the New York Police Department? It was a job that occasionally demanded ruthlessness, a certain amount of Broughton-type insensibility. But then, Delaney reflected, ruthlessness could be an acquired trait. Even an assumed trait. He certainly hoped *he* had not been born with it. Dorfman could learn to be ruthless when necessary, just as he, Delaney, had learned. He did it, but he didn't enjoy it. Perhaps that was the essential difference between Broughton and him: he didn't enjoy it.

Then he slammed his swivel chair level and reached into his bottom desk drawer to haul out a long card file. The grey metal box was dented and battered. Delancy opened it and began searching for what he wanted. The cards were filed by subject matter.

Soon after Patrolman Edward X. Delaney was promoted to detective third grade—more years ago than he cared to remember—he became aware that despite the enormous resources of the New York Police Department, he frequently came up against problems that could only be solved, or moved toward solution, by civilian experts.

There was, for instance, a retired detective, delighted to cooperate with his former colleagues, who had established and maintained what was probably the world's largest collection of laundry marks. There was an 84-year-old spinster who still operated a shop on Madison Avenue. She could glance at an unusual button you showed her, and name the material, age, and source. There was a Columbia University professor whose specialty was crickets and grasshoppers. There was an amateur archeologist, all of whose "digs" had been made within city limits. He could examine rocks and soil and place them within a few blocks of their origin. A Bronx recluse was one of the world's foremost authorities on ancient writing, and could read hieroglyphics as quickly as Delaney read English.

All these experts were willing—nay, *eager* to cooperate with police investigations. It was a welcome interruption of their routine, gave them a chance to exhibit their expertise in a good cause. The only problem was shutting them up; they all did seem to talk excessively, like anyone whose hobby is his vocation. But eventually they divulged the information required.

Delaney had them all in his card file, carefully added to and maintained for almost twenty years. Now he flipped through the cards until he found the one he was looking for. It was headed: "Weapons, antique and unusual." The man's name was Christopher Langley, an assistant curator of the Arms and Armor Collection of the Metropolitan Museum of Art. (The card following his was "Weapons, modern," and that man was a retired colonel of Marines.)

Delaney called the Metropolitan (the number on the card), asked for the Arms and Armor Section, and then asked for Christopher Langley.

"I'm sorry, sir," a young, feminine voice replied. "Mr. Langley is no longer with us. He retired about three years ago."

"Oh. I'm sorry to hear that. Do you happen to know if he's living in New York?"

"Yes sir, I believe he is."

"Then he'll be in the phone book?"

There was a moment's silence.

"Well . . . no sir. I believe Mr. Langley has an unlisted number."

"Could you tell me what it is? I'm a personal friend."

"I'm sorry, sir. We cannot reveal that information."

He was tempted to say, "This is Captain Edward X. Delaney, New York Police Department, and this is official business." Or, he could easily get the number from the phone company, as an official police inquiry. But then he thought better of it. The fewer people who knew of his activities, the better.

"My name is Edward Delaney," he said. "I wonder if you'd be kind enough to call Mr. Langley at the number you have, tell him I called, and if he wishes to contact me, he can reach me at this number." He then gave her the phone number of the 251st Precinct.

"Yes sir," she said. "I can do that."

"Thank you."

He hung up, wondering what percentage of his waking hours was spent on the telephone, trying to complete a call, or waiting for a call. He sat patiently, hoping Langley was in. He was: Delaney's desk phone rang within five minutes.

"Delaney!" Christopher Langley cried in his remarkably boyish voice (the man was pushing 70). "Gosh, I asked for *Lieutenant* Delaney and your operator said it was *Captain* Delaney now. Congratulations! When did that happen?"

"Oh, a few years ago. How are you, sir?"

"Physically I'm fine but, gee, I'm bored."

"I heard you had retired."

"Had to do it, you know. Give the young men a chance—eh? The first year I dabbled around with silly things. I've become a marvelous gourmet cook. But my gosh, how many *Caneton à l'Orange* can you make? Now I'm bored, bored, bored. That's why I was so delighted to hear from you."

"Well, I need your help, sir, and was wondering if you could spare me a few hours?"

"As long as you like, dear boy, as long as you like. Is it a big caper?"

Delaney laughed, knowing Langley's fondness for detective fiction.

"Yes sir. A very big caper. The biggest. Murder most foul."

"Oh gosh," Langley gasped. "That's marvelous! Captain, can you join me for dinner tonight? Then afterwards we can have brandy and talk and you can tell me all about it and how I can help."

"Oh I couldn't put you to that—"

"No trouble at all!" Langley cried. "Gee, it'll be wonderful seeing you again, and I can demonstrate my culinary skills for you."

"Well . . . " Delaney said, thinking of his evening visit to Barbara, "it will have to be a little later. Is nine o'clock too late?"

"Not at all, not at all! I much prefer dining at a late hour. As soon as I hang up, I'll dash out and do some shopping." He gave Delaney his home address.

"Fine," the Captain said. "See you at nine, sir."

"Gosh, this is keen!" Langley said. "We'll have frogs' legs sauteed in butter and garlic, *petite pois* with just a hint of bacon and onion, and *gratin de pommes de terre aux anchois*. And for dessert, perhaps a *crème plombières pralinée*. How does that sound to you?"

"Fine," Delaney repeated faintly. "Just fine."

He hung up. Oh God, he thought, there goes my diet, and wondered what happened when sauteed frogs' legs met broiled kidney.

A young woman was walking toward Central Park, between Madison and Fifth Avenues, pushing a baby carriage. Suddenly a wooden rod, about nine inches long, was projecting from her breast. She slumped to her knees, falling forward, and only the fast scramble of a passerby prevented the baby carriage from bouncing into Fifth Avenue traffic.

Delaney, who was then a detective lieutenant working out of Homicide East (as it was then called) arrived on the scene shortly after the woman died. He joined the circle of patrolmen and ambulance attendants staring down incredulously at the woman with the wooden spike driven through her heart, like some modern vampire.

Within an hour they had the missile identified as a quarrel from a crossbow. Delaney went up to the Arms and Armor Department of the Metropolitan Museum of Art, seeking to learn more about crossbows, their operation, range, and velocity of the bolts. That was how he met Christopher Langley.

From the information supplied by the assistant curator, Delaney was able to solve the case, to his satisfaction at least, but it was never prosecuted. The boy responsible, who had shot the bolt at a stranger from a townhouse window across the street, was the son of a wealthy family. They got him out of the country and into a school in Switzerland. He had never returned to the United States. The District Attorney did not feel Delaney's circumstantial evidence was sufficiently strong to warrant extradition proceedings. The case was still carried as open.

But Delaney had never forgotten Christopher Langley's enthusiastic cooperation, and his name was added to the detective's "expert file." Delaney frequently recalled a special memory of the skinny little man. Langley was showing him through a Museum gallery, deserted except for a grinning guard who evidently knew what to expect.

Suddenly the assistant curator plucked a two-handed sword from the wall, a XVI Century German sword as long as he was tall, and fell into a fighting stance. The blade whirled about his head in circles of flashing steel. He chopped, slashed, parried, thrust.

152

"That's how they did it," he said calmly, and handed the long sword to Delaney.

The detective took it, and it almost clattered to the floor. Delaney estimated its weight as thirty pounds. The wiry Christopher Langley had spun it like a feather.

When he opened the door to his apartment on the fifth floor of a converted brownstone on East 89th Street, he was exactly as Delaney remembered him. In another age he would have been called a fop or dandy. Now he was a well-preserved, alert, exquisitely dressed 70-year-old bachelor with the complexion of a maiden and a small yellow daisy in the lapel of his grey flannel Norfolk jacket.

"Captain!" he said with pleasure, holding out both hands. "Gosh, this *is* nice!"

It was a small, comfortable apartment the ex-curator had retired to. He occupied the entire top floor: living room, bedroom, bath, and a remarkably large kitchen. There was a glass skylight over the living room which, Delaney was glad to see, had been fitted with a guard of iron bars.

Langley took his hat and overcoat and hung them away.

"Not in uniform tonight, Captain?"

"No. As a matter of fact, I am not on active duty. I'm on leave of absence."

"Oh?" Langley asked curiously. "For long?"

"I don't know."

"Well . . . do sit down. There—that's a comfortable chair. Now what can I bring you? Cocktail? Highball?"

"Oh, I don't—"

"I have a new Italian aperitif I'm trying for the first time. It's quite dry. Very good on the rocks with a twist of lemon."

"Sounds fine. Are you having one?"

"Of course. Just take me a minute."

Langley bustled into the kitchen, and the Captain looked around. The walls of the living room were almost solid bookcases with deep, high shelves to accommodate volumes on antique weaponry, most of them out-size "art books" illustrated with color plates.

Only two actual weapons were on display: an Italian arquebus of the 17th century with exquisitely detailed silver-chasing, and an African warclub. The head was intricately carved stone. Delaney rose to his feet and went over to inspect it. He was turning it in his hands when Langley came back with their drinks.

153

"Mongo tribe," he said. "The Congo. A ceremonial ax never used in combat. The balance is bad but I like the carving."

"It's beautiful."

"Isn't it? Dinner in about ten minutes. Meanwhile, let's relax. Would you like a cigarette?"

"No, thank you."

"Good. Smoking dulls the palate. Do you know what the secret of good French cooking is?"

"What?"

"A clear palate and butter. Not oil, but butter. The richest, creamiest butter you can find."

Delaney's heart sank. The old man caught his look of dismay and laughed.

"Don't worry, Captain. I've never believed you had to eat a lot of one dish to enjoy it. Small portions and several dishes—that's best."

He was as good as his word; the portions were small. But Delaney decided it was one of the best dinners he had ever eaten and told the host so. Langley beamed with pleasure.

"A little more dessert? There is more, you know."

"Not for me. But I'll have another cup of coffee, if you have it."

"Of course."

They had dined at a plain oak table covered with a black burlap cloth, a table Delaney was sure, doubled as Langley's desk. Now they both pushed back far enough to cross their legs, have a cigarette, drink coffee, sip the strong Portuguese brandy Langley had served.

"About this—" Delaney had started, but just then the apartment doorbell rang, in the familiar "shave and a haircut, two bits" rhythm, and the Captain was surprised to see Langley's face go white.

"Oh gracious," the old man whispered. "It's her again. The Widow Zimmerman! She lives right below me."

He bounced to his feet, trotted across the room, looked through the peephole, then unlocked and opened the door.

"Ahh," he said. "Good evening, Mrs. Zimmerman."

Delaney had a clear view of her from where he sat. She was perhaps 60, taller than Langley by about six inches, certainly heavier than he by fifty pounds. She balanced a beehive of teased brassy hair above her plump face, and her bare arms looked like something you might see on a butcher's block. She was so heavily girdled that her body seemed hewn from a single chunk of wood; when she walked, her legs appeared to move only from the knees down.

"Oh, I do hope I'm not disturbing you," she simpered, looking at the Captain boldly over Langley's shoulder. "I know you've got company. I heard you go out to shop and then come back. I heard your bell ring and your guest arrive. One of your fantastic foreign dinners, I'm sure. Now I just happened to bake a fresh prune strudel today, and I thought you and your guest might enjoy a nice piece for dessert, and here it is."

She held out the napkin-covered dish to Langley; he took it with the tips of his fingers.

"That's very kind of you, Mrs. Zimmerman. Won't you come—"

"Oh, I won't interrupt. I wouldn't think of it."

She waited expectantly, but Langley did not repeat his invitation.

"I'll just run along," the Widow Zimmerman said, pouting at Delaney.

"Thank you for the strudel."

"My pleasure. Enjoy."

She gave him a little-girl smile. He closed the door firmly behind her, bolted and chained it, then put his ear to the panel and listened as her steps receded down the stairs. He came back to the table and whispered to Delaney . . .

"A dreadful woman! Continually bringing me food. I've asked her not to, but she does. I'm perfectly capable of cooking for myself. Been doing it for fifty years. And the food she brings! Strudel and chopped liver and stuffed derma and pickled herring. Gracious! I can't throw it away because she might see it in the garbage cans and be insulted. So I have to wrap it like a gift package and carry it three or four blocks away and dump it into a litter basket. She's such a problem."

"I think she's after you," Delaney said solemnly.

"Oh my!" Christopher Langley said, blushing. "Her husband—her late husband—was such a nice, quiet man. A retired furrier. Well, let me put this in the kitchen, and then please go on with what you were saying."

"Did you read in the papers about the murder of Frank Lombard?" the Captain asked when Langley had rejoined him.

"Goodness, I certainly did. Everything I could find. A fascinating case. You know, whenever I read about a real-life murder or assault, I always look for a description of the weapon.

After all, that was my life for so many years, and I'm still interested. But in all the accounts of the Lombard killing, the description of the weapon was very vague. Hasn't it been identified yet?"

"No. It hasn't. That's why I'm here. To ask your help."

"And as you know, I'll be delighted to give you every assistance I can, dear boy."

Delaney held up his hand like a traffic cop.

"Just a minute, sir. I want to be honest with you. As I told you, I am not on active duty. I am on leave of absence. I am not part of the official investigation into the death of Frank Lombard."

Christopher Langley looked at him narrowly a moment, then sat back and began to drum his dainty fingers against the table top.

"Then what is your interest in the Lombard case?"

"I am conducting a—a private investigation into the homicide."

"I see. Can you tell me more?"

"I would prefer not to."

"May I ask the purpose of this—ah—private investigation?"

"The main purpose is to find the killer of Frank Lombard as quickly as possible."

Langley stared at him a long, additional moment, then left off his finger drumming and slapped the table top with an open palm.

"All right," he said briskly. "Was it a striking weapon or a swinging weapon? That is: do you visualize it as a knife, a dagger, a dirk, a poniard—something of that sort—or was it a sword, pole, battleax, club, mace—something of that sort?"

"I'd say the percentages would be in favor of the swinging weapon."

"The percentages!" Langley laughed. "I had forgotten you and your percentages. This is a business to you, isn't it?"

"Yes. It's a business. And sometimes the only things you have to work with are the percentages. But what you said about a striking weapon—a knife or dagger—surely a blade couldn't penetrate a man's skull?"

"It could. And has. If blade and handle are heavy enough. The Marines' combat knife in World War Two could split a man's skull. But most blades would glance off, causing only superficial wounds. Besides, Lombard was struck on the head from behind, was he not?"

"That's correct."

"Then that would probably rule out a striking weapon. An assailant using a blade and coming from behind would almost certainly go in between the shoulder blades, into the ribs, sever the spine, or try for the kidneys."

Delaney nodded, marveling at the gusto with which this impish man ticked off these points on his fingers, an enthusiasm made all the more incredible by his age, diminutive physique, elegant appearance.

"All right," Langley went on, "let's assume a swinging weapon. One-hand or two-hand?"

"I'd guess one-hand. I think the killer approached Lombard from the front. Then, as he passed, he turned and struck him down. During the approach the weapon could have been concealed beneath a coat on the killer's arm or in a newspaper folded under his arm."

"Yes, that certainly rules out a halberd! You're talking about something about the size of a hatchet?"

"About that."

"Captain, do you believe it was an antique weapon?"

"I doubt that very much. Once again, the percentages are against it. In my lifetime I've investigated only two homicides in which antique weapons were used. One was the crossbow case in which you were involved. The other was a death caused by a ball fired from an antique duelling pistol."

"Then we'll assume a modern weapon?"

"Yes."

"Or a modern tool. You must realize that many modern tools have evolved from antique weapons. The reverse is also true, of course. During hand-to-hand combat in Korea and Vietnam, there were several cases of American soldiers using their Entrenching tool, shovel, or Entrenching tool, pick-mattock, as a weapon both for offense and defense. Now let's get to the wound itself. Was it a crushing, cutting, or piercing blow?"

"Piercing. It was a penetration, about three to four inches long."

"Oh my, that *is* interesting! And what was the shape of the penetration?"

"Here I'm going to get a little vague," Delaney warned. "The official autopsy of the examining surgeon states that the outside wound was roughly circular in shape, about one inch in diameter. The penetration dwindled rapidly to a sharp point, the entire penetration being round and, as I said, about three or four inches deep."

"Round?" Langley cried, and the Captain was surprised at the little man's expression.

"Yes, round," he repeated. "Why—is anything wrong?"

"Is the surgeon certain of this? The roundness, I mean?"

"No, he is not. But the wound was of such a nature that precise measurements and analysis were impossible. The surgeon had a feeling—just a guess on his part—that the spike that penetrated was triangular or square, and that the weapon became stuck in the wound, or the victim in falling forward, wrenched the weapon out of the killer's hand, and that the killer then had to twist the weapon back and forth to free it. And this twisting motion, with a square or triangular spike, would result in—"

"Ah-ha!" Langley shouted, slapping his thigh. "That's exactly what happened! And the surgeon believes the spike could have been triangular or square?"

"Believes it *could* have been—yes."

"*Was*," Langley said definitely. "It was. Believe me, Captain. Do you know how many weapons there are with tapering *round* spikes that could cause the kind of wound you describe? I could name them on the fingers of one hand. You will find round spikes on the warclubs of certain Northwest Coast Indian tribes. There is a Tlingit warclub with a jade head that tapers to a point. It is not perfectly round, however. Thompson Indians used a warclub with a head of wood that was round and tapered: a perfect cone. The Tsimshian Indians used horn and bone, again round and tapered. Esquimo tribes used clubs with spikes of bone or narwhale or walrus tusks. Do you understand the significance of what I am saying, Captain?"

"I'm afraid not."

"The materials used in weapons that had a cone spike were almost always *natural* materials that tapered naturally—such as teeth or tusks—or were soft materials, such as wood, that could be tapered to a cone shape easily. But now let's move on to iron and steel. Early metal weapons were made by armorers and blacksmiths working with a hammer on a hot slug held on an anvil. It was infinitely easier and faster to fashion a flat spike, a triangular spike, or a square spike, than a perfect cone that tapered to a sharp point. I can't recall a single halberd, partison or *couteaux de brèche* in the Metropolitan that has a round spike. Or any war hammer or war hatchet. I seem to remember a mace in the Rotterdam museum that had a round spike, but I'd have to look it up. In any event, early weapons almost invariably were fashioned with flat sides, usually triangular or square, or even hexagonal. A perfectly proportioned round spike was simply too difficult to make. And even after dies and stamping of iron and steel came into existence, the same held true. It is cheaper, faster, and easier to make blades and spikes with flat sides than round ones that taper to a point. I think your surgeon's 'guesses' are correct. Using your famous 'percentages'."

"Interesting," Delaney nodded, "and exactly what I came to you for. But there's another thing I should tell you. I don't know what it means, if anything, but perhaps you will. The surgeon has a feeling that the sharp tip of the penetration was lower than the opening wound. You understand? It was not a straight, tapered penetration, but it curved gently downward. Maybe I should make a little drawing."

"Oh gosh," Langley chortled, "that's not necessary. I know exactly what you mean." He leaped to his feet, rushed to a bookcase, ran his fingers over the bindings, grabbed out a big book, and hustled it back to the table. He turned to the List of Illustrations, ran his finger down, found what he was looking for, and flipped pages. "There," he said. "Take a look at that, Captain."

Delaney stared. It was a one-handed club. The head had a hatchet blade on one side, a spike on the other. The spike was about an inch across at the head, tapered to a sharp point and, as it tapered, curved downward.

"What is it?" he asked.

"Iroquois tomahawk. Handle of ash. Those are feathers tied to the butt. The head is iron, probably cut out of a sheet of hot metal with shears or hammered out with a chisel and then filed sharp. White traders carried them and sold them for pelts."

"Are you suggesting . . . ?"

"Heavens, no. But note how that flat spike curves downward? I could show you that same curve in warclubs and war-axes and halberds of practically every nation, tribe, and race on earth. Very effective; very efficient. When you hack down on a man, you don't want to hit his skull with a horizontal spike that might glance off. You want a spike that curves downward, pierces, penetrates, and kills."

"Yes," Delaney said. "I suppose you do."

The two men sat in silence a few moments, staring at the color photo of the Iroquois tomahawk. How many had *that* killed, Delaney wondered, and then, leafing slowly through the book, was suddenly saddened by the effort, art, and genius that the human race had expended on killing tools, on powder and shot, sword and stiletto, bayonet and bludgeon, crossbow and Centurion tank, blowpipe and cannon, spear and hydrogen bomb. There was, he supposed, no end to it.

But what was the need, or lust, behind all this interest, ingenuity, and vitality in the design and manufacture of killing tools? The lad with his slingshot and the man with his gun: both showing a dark atavism. Was killing then a passion, from the primeval slime, as valid an expression of the human soul as love and sacrifice?

Suddenly depressed, Delaney rose to his feet and tried to smile at his host.

"Mr. Langley," he said brightly, "I thank you for a pleasant evening, a wonderful dinner, and for your kind cooperation. You've given me a lot to think about."

Christopher Langley seemed as depressed as his guest. He looked up listlessly.

"I haven't helped, Captain, and you know it. You're no closer to identifying the weapon that killed Frank Lombard than you were three hours ago."

"You *have* helped, sir," Delaney insisted. "You've substantiated the surgeon's impressions. You've given me a clearer idea of what to look for. In a case like this, every little bit helps."

"Captain . . ."

"Yes, Mr. Langley?"

"In this 'private investigation' of yours, the weapon isn't the only thing. I know that. You're going to interview people and check into past records and things like that. Isn't that true?"

"Yes."

"Well, gosh, then you can only spend so much time trying to identify the weapon. Isn't that so?"

"Yes."

"Captain, let me do it. Please. Let me *try*."

"Mr. Langley, I can't—"

"I know you're not on active duty. I know it's a private investigation. You told me. But still . . . you're trying. Let me help. Please. Look at me. I'm seventy. I'm retired. To tell you the truth, Captain, I'm sick of gourmet cooking. My whole life was . . . Oh God, what am I supposed to do—sit up here and wait to die? Captain, please, let me *do* something, something important. This man Lombard was murdered. That's not right. Life is too precious."

"That's what my wife said," Delaney said wonderingly.

160

"She knew," Langley nodded, his eyes glistening now. "Let me do some work, some *important* work. I know weapons. You know that. I might be a help to you. Truly. Let me try."

"I don't have any funds," Delaney started. "I can't—"

"Forget it," the old man waved him away. "This will cost nothing. I can pay for cabs and books, or whatever. But let me work. At an important job. You understand, Captain? I don't want to just drift away."

The Captain stared, wondering if the ex-curator was prey to his own gloomy thoughts. Langley was far from being stupid, and how did an intelligent man justify a lifetime devoted to killing tools? Perhaps it was true, as he had said, that he was simply bored with retirement and wanted to work again. But his insistence on something "important," "important" work, an "important" job led Delaney to wonder if the old man, his life drawing to a close, was not, in a sense, seeking a kind of expiation, or at least hungering to make a sunny, affirmative gesture after a career celebrating shadows and the bog.

"Yes," Captain Delaney said, clearing his throat. "I understand. All right. Fine. I appreciate that, sir. If I find out anything more relating to the weapon, I'll make sure you know of it. Meanwhile, see what you can come up with."

"Oh!" Langley cried, effervescent again, "I'll get on it right away. There are some things I want to check in my books tonight, and tomorrow I'll go to the museums. Maybe I'll get some ideas there. And to hardware stores. To look at tools. Captain, am I a detective now?"

"Yes," Delaney smiled. "You're a detective."

He moved toward the door, and Langley scampered to get his coat and hat from the closet. He gave his unlisted phone number to the Captain, and Delaney carefully copied it into his pocket notebook. Langley unlocked the door, then leaned close.

"Captain," he whispered, "one final favor . . . When you go down the stairs, please try to tiptoe past the Widow Zimmerman's door. I don't want her to know I'm alone."

6

The home of the late Frank Lombard was on a surprisingly pastoral street in the Flatbush section of Brooklyn. There were trees, lawns, barking dogs, shrieking children. The house itself was red brick, two stories high, its ugliness hidden in a tight cloak of ivy that was still green and creeped to the eaves.

There was an asphalt driveway leading to a two-car garage. There were four cars, bumper to bumper, on the driveway, and more in front of the house, two double-parked. Captain Delaney observed all this from across the street. He also observed that one of the double-parked cars was a three-year-old, four-door Plymouth, and had the slightly rusted, slightly dusty, nondescript appearance of an unmarked police car. Two men in civilian clothes were in the front seat.

Delaney approved of a guard being stationed for the protection of the widow, Mrs. Clara Lombard. It was very possible, he thought, there was also a personal guard inside the house; Chief Pauley would see to that. Now the problem was, if Delaney went through with his intention to interview the widow, would one of the cops recognize him and report to Broughton that Captain Delaney had been a visitor.

The Captain pondered this problem a few minutes on the next corner, still watching the Lombard home. While he stood, hands shoved deep in his civilian overcoat pockets, he saw two couples leave the house, laughing, and another car double-park to disgorge two women and a man, also laughing.

Delaney devised a cover story. If the guards made him, and he was eventually braced by Broughton, he would explain that because the homicide occurred in his precinct, he felt duty-bound to express his condolences to the widow. Broughton wouldn't buy it completely; he'd be suspicious and have the widow checked. But that would be all right; Delaney did feel duty-bound to express his condolences, and would.

As he headed up the brick-paved walk to the door, he heard loud rock music, screams of laughter, the sound of shattering glass. It was a party, and a wild one.

A man answered his ring, a flush-faced, too-handsome man wearing not one, but two pinkie rings.

"Come in come in come in," he burbled, flourishing his highball glass and slopping half of it down the front of his hand-tailored, sky-blue silk suit. "Always room for one more."

"Thank you," Delaney said. "I'm not a guest. I just wanted to speak to Mrs. Lombard for a moment."

"Hey, Clara!" the man screamed over his shoulder. "Get your gorgeous ass out here. Your lover is waiting."

The man leered at Delaney, then plunged back into the dancing, drinking, laughing, yelling mob. The Captain stood patiently. Eventually she came weaving toward him.

A *zoftig* blonde who reminded him of Oscar Wilde's comment about the widow "whose hair turned quite gold from grief." She overflowed an off-the-shoulder cocktail dress that seemed capable of standing by itself, so heavily encrusted was it with sequins, rhinestones, braid, a jeweled peacock brooch and, unaccountably, a cheap tin badge, star-shaped, that said "Garter Inspector." She looked down at him from bleary eyes.

"Yeah?"

"Mrs. Clara Lombard?"

"Yeah."

"My name is Delaney, Captain Edward X. Delaney. I am the former commanding officer of the—"

"Jesus," she breathed. "Another cop. Haven't I had enough cops?"

"I would like to express my condolences on the death—"

"Five," she said. "Or six times. I lost count. What the hell is it now? Can't you see I've got a houseful of people? Will you stop bugging me?"

"I just wanted to tell you how sorry I—"

"Thanks a whole hell of a lot," she said disgustedly. "Well, screw all of you. This is a going-away party. I'm shaking New York, and the whole lot of you can go screw."

"You're leaving New York?" he asked, amazed that Broughton would let her go.

"That's right, buster. I've sold the house, the cars, the furniture—everything. By Saturday I'll be in sunny, funny Miami and starting a new life. A brand new life. And then you can all go screw yourselves."

She turned away and went rushing back to her party. Delaney replaced his hat, walked slowly down to the corner. He watched the traffic, waiting for the light to change. Cars went rushing by, and the odd thing that had nagged him since his reading of the Operation Lombard reports whisked into his mind, as he knew it would. Eventually.

In the interview with the victim's mother, Mrs. Sophia Lombard, she had stated he never drove over from Brooklyn because he couldn't find parking space near her apartment; he took the subway.

Delaney retraced his steps, and this time the outside guards stared at him. He rang the bell of the Lombard home again. The widow herself threw open the door, a welcoming smile on her puffy face—a smile that oozed away as she recognized Delaney.

"Jesus Christ, you again?"

"Yes. You said you're selling your car?"

"Not car—cars. We had two of them. And forget about getting a bargain; they're both sold."

"Your husband—your late husband drove a car?"

"Of course he drove a car. What do you think?"

"Where did he usually carry his driver's license, Mrs. Lombard?"

"Oh God," she shouted, and immediately the pinkie-ringed man was at her shoulder.

"Wassamatta, honey?" he inquired. "Having trouble?"

"No trouble, Manny. Just some more police shit. In his wallet," she said to Delaney. "He carried his driver's license in his wallet. Okay?"

"Thank you," Delaney said humbly. "I'm sorry to bother you. It's just that the license wasn't in his wallet when we found him." He refrained from mentioning that she had stated nothing was missing from the wallet. "It's probably around the house somewhere."

"Yeah, yeah," she said impatiently.

"If you come across it while you're packing, will you let us know? We've got to cancel it with the State."

"Sure, sure. I'll look, I'll look."

He knew she wouldn't. But it didn't make any difference; she'd never find it.

"Anything else?" she demanded.

"No, nothing. Thank you very much, Mrs. Lombard, for your kind cooperation."

"Go screw yourself," she said, and slammed the door in his face.

He went back to his home and methodically checked the inventory of personal effects taken from the body of Frank Lombard, and Mrs. Sophia Lombard's statement about her son's visiting habits. Then he sat a long time in the growing darkness. Once he rose to mix a weak rye highball and sat nursing that, sipping slowly and still thinking.

Finally he pulled on his overcoat and hat again and went out to find a different phone booth. He had to wait almost fifteen minutes before Deputy Inspector Ivar Thorsen got back to him, a period during which three would-be phone users turned away in disgust. One of them kicked the phone booth in anger before he left.

"Edward?" Thorsen asked.

"Yes. I've got something. Something I don't think Broughton has."

He heard Thorsen's swift intake of breath.

"What?"

"Lombard was a licensed driver. He owned two cars. His wife has sold them, incidentally. She's leaving town."

"So?"

"She says he carried his driver's license in his wallet. That makes sense. The percentages are for it. The license wasn't in the wallet when it was found. I checked the inventory."

There was a moment's silence.

"No one would kill for a driver's license," Thorsen said finally. "You can buy a good counterfeit for fifty bucks."

"I know."

"Identification?" Thorsen suggested. "A hired killer. He takes the license to prove to his employer he really did hit Lombard."

"What for? It was in all the papers the next day. The employer would know the job had been done."

"Jesus, that's right. What do you think? Why the driver's license?"

"Identification maybe."

"But you just said—"

"Not a hired killer. I have two ideas. One, the killer took the license as a souvenir, a trophy."

"That's nuts, Edward."

"Maybe. The other idea is that he took the license to prove to a third party that he had killed. Not killed *Lombard*, but killed someone, *anyone*. If the stories were in the papers, and the killer could present the victim's driver's license, that would prove *he* was the killer."

The silence was longer this time.

"Jesus, Edward," Thorsen said finally. "That's wild."

"Yes. Wild." (And suddenly he remembered a sex killing he had investigated. The victim's eyelids had been stitched together with her own hairpins.)

Thorsen came on again: "Edward, are you trying to tell me we're dealing with a crazy?"

"Yes. I think so. Someone like Whitman, Speck, Unruh, the Boston Strangler, Panzram, Manson. Someone like that."

"Oh God."

"If I'm right, we'll know soon enough."

"How will we know?"

"He'll do it again."

PART IV

1

He thought she was wearing a loose-fitting dress of black crepe with white cuffs. Then he saw the cuffs were actually bandages about both wrists. But he was so inflamed with what he wanted to tell her that he didn't question the bandages, knowing. Instead, he merely held up before her eyes Frank Lombard's driver's license. She would not look at it, but took him by the arm and drew him slowly, step by step, to the upstairs room. Where he was impotent.

"It's all right," she soothed. "I understand. Believe me, I understand and love you for it. I told you sex should be a ritual, a ceremony. But a rite has no consummation. It's a celebration of a consummation. Do you understand? The ritual celebrates the climax but does not encompass it. It's all right, my darling. Don't think you've failed. This is best. That you and I worship the fulfillment—a continuing celebration of an unknowable finality. Isn't that what prayer is all about?"

But he was not listening to her, so livid was he with the need to talk. He snapped on that cruel overhead light and showed her the driver's license and newspaper headlines, proving himself.

"For you," he said. "I did it for you." Then they both laughed, knowing it was a lie.

"Tell me everything," she said. "Every detail. I want to know everything that happened."

His soft scrotum huddled in her hand, a dead bird.

He told her, with pride, of the careful planning, the long hours of slow thought. His first concern, he said, had been the weapon.

"Did I want a weapon that could be discarded?" he asked rhetorically. "I decided not, not to leave a weapon that might be traced to me. So I chose a weapon I would take with me when I left."

"To be used again," she murmured.

"Yes. Perhaps. Well . . . I told you I'm a climber. I'm not an expert; just an amateur. But I have this ice ax. It's a tool of course, but also a very wicked weapon. All tempered steel. A hammer on one side of the head for pitons, and a tapered steel pick on the other. There are hundreds just like it. Also, it has a leather-wrapped handle and a rawhide thong hanging from the butt. Heavy enough to kill, but small and light enough to carry concealed. You know that coat I have with slits in the pockets, so that I can reach inside?"

"Do I not!" she smiled.

"Yes," he smiled in reply. "I figured I could wear that coat, the front unbuttoned and hanging loose. My left hand would be through the slit, and I could carry the ice ax by the leather thong, dangling from my fingers but completely concealed. When the time came to use it, I could reach inside the unbuttoned coat with my right hand and take the ax by the handle."

"Brilliant," she said.

"A problem," he shrugged. "I tried it, I practised. It worked perfectly. If I was calm and cool, unhurried, I could transfer the ax to my right hand in seconds. *Seconds!* One or two. No more. Then, after, the ax would disappear beneath my coat again. Held by my left hand through the pocket slit."

"Did you see his eyes?" she asked.

"His eyes?" he said vaguely. "No. I must tell you this in my own way."

She leaned forward to put her lips on his left nipple; his eyes closed with pleasure.

"I didn't want to travel too far," he said. "The farther I went, carrying the concealed ice ax, the greater the danger. It had to be in my own neighborhood. Near. Why not? The murder of a stranger. A crime without motive. What difference if it was next door or a hundred miles away? Who could connect me?"

"Yes," she breathed. "Oh yes."

He told her how he had walked the streets for three nights, seeking the lonely blocks, noting the lighting, remembering bus stops and subway stations, lobbies with doormen, deserted stretches of unattended stores and garages.

"I couldn't plan it. I decided it would have to be chance. Pure chance. 'Pure.' That's a funny word, Celia. But it was pure. I swear to you. I mean, there was no sex connected with it. I mean, I didn't walk around with an erection. I didn't have an orgasm when I did it. Nothing like that. Do you believe me?"

"Yes."

"It really was pure. I swear it. It was religious. I was God's will. I know that sounds insane. But that's how I felt. Maybe it is mad. A sweet madness. I was God on earth. When I looked at people on shadowed streets . . . Is *he* the one? Is *he* the one? My God, the *power!*"

"Oh yes. Darling, oh yes."

He was so tender with her in that awful room . . . so tender. And then, the memory of the two times he had been unfaithful to his wife . . . He had enjoyed both adventures; both women had been his wife's superior in bed. But he had not loved her the less for that. Instead, unaccountably, his infidelity had increased his affection for and kindness toward his wife. He touched her, kissed her, listened to her.

And now, telling this woman of murder, he felt the same thaw: not increased sexuality but heightened sweetness because he had a new mistress. He touched Celia's cheek, kissed her fingertips, murmured, saw to her comfort, and in all things acted the gentle and *parfait* lover, loving her the more because he loved another most.

"It was not someone else doing it," he assured her. "You've read these stories where the killer blames it on someone else. Another *him*. Someone who took over, controlled his mind and guided his hand. It was nothing like that. Celia, I have never had such a feeling of being myself. You know? It was a sense of *oneness*, of *me*. Do you understand?"

"Oh yes. And then?"

"I hit him. We smiled. We nodded. We passed, and I transferred the ax to my right hand. Just as I had rehearsed. And I hit him. It made a sound. I can't describe it. A sound. And he fell forward so heavily that it pulled the ax out of my hand. I didn't know that might happen. But I didn't panic. Jesus, I was cool. Cold! I bent down and twisted the ax to pull it free. Tough. I had to put my foot on the back of his neck and pull up on the ax with both hands to free it. I did that. I did it! And then I found his wallet and took his driver's license. To prove to you."

"You didn't have to do that."

"Didn't I?"

"Yes. You did."

They both laughed then, and rolled on the soiled bed, holding.

He tried, again, to enter into her and did not succeed, not caring, for he had already surpassed her. But he would not tell her that since she knew. She took his penis into her mouth, not licking or biting, but just in her mouth: a warm communion. He was hardly conscious of it; it did not excite him. He was a god; she was worshipping.

"One other thing," he said dreamily. "When, finally, on the night, I looked down the street and saw him walking toward me through that orange glow, and I thought yes, now, he is the one, I loved him so much then, *loved* him."

"Loved him? Why?"

"I don't know. But I did. And respected him. Oh yes. And had such a sense of gratitude toward him. That he was giving. So much. To me. Then I killed him."

2

"Good-morning, Charles," Daniel called, and the doorman whirled around, shocked by the friendly voice and pleasant smile. "Looks like a sunny day today."

"Oh. Yes sir," Lipsky said, confused. "Sunny day. That's what the paper said. Cab, Mr. Blank?"

"Please."

The doorman went down to the street, whistled up a taxi, rode it back to the apartment house entrance. He got out and held the door open for Daniel.

"Have a good day, Mr. Blank."

"You too, Charles," and handed him the usual quarter. He gave the driver the address of the Javis-Bircham Building.

"Go through the park, please. I know it's longer but I've got time."

"Sure."

"Looks like a nice sunny day today."

"That's what the radio just said," the driver nodded. "You sound like you feel good today."

"Yes," Blank smiled. "I do."

"Morning, Harry," he said to the elevator starter. "A nice sunny morning."

"Sure is, Mr. Blank. Hope it stays like this."

"Good-morning, Mrs. Cleek," Blank said to his secretary as he hung away his hat and coat. "Looks like it's going to be a beautiful day."

"Yes sir. I hope it lasts."

"It will." He looked at her closely a moment. "Mrs. Cleek, you seem a bit pale. Are you feeling all right?"

She blushed with pleasure at his concern. "Oh yes, Mr. Blank, I feel fine."

"How's that boy of yours?"

"I got a letter from him yesterday. He's doing very well. He's in a military academy, you know."

Blank didn't, but nodded. "Well, you do look a bit weary. Why don't you plan on taking a few Fridays off? It's going to be a long winter. We all need relaxation."

"Why . . thank you very much, Mr. Blank. That's very kind of you."

"Just let me know in advance and arrange for someone from the pool to fill in. That's a pretty dress."

"Thank you very much, Mr. Blank," she repeated, dazed. "Your coffee is on your desk, and a report came down from upstairs. I put it next to your coffee."

"What's it about?"

"Oh, I didn't read it, sir. It's sealed and confidential."

"Thank you, Mrs. Cleek. I'll buzz when I want to do letters."

"Thank you again, Mr. Blank. For the days off, I mean."

He smiled and made a gesture. He sat down at his bare table and sipped coffee, staring at the heavy manila envelope from the president's office, stamped CONFIDENTIAL. He didn't open it, but taking his plastic container of coffee walked to the plate glass windows facing west.

It was an extraordinarily clear day, the smog mercifully lifted. He could see tugboats on the Hudson, a cruise liner putting out to sea, traffic on the Jersey shore, and blue hills far away. Everything was bright and glittering, a new world. He could almost peer into a distant future.

He drained his coffee and looked into the plastic cup. It was white foam, stained now, and of the consistency of cottage cheese. It bulged in his grip and felt of soap. He flicked on his intercom.

"Sir?" Mrs. Cleek asked.

"Would you do me a favor?"

"Of course, sir."

"On your lunch hour—well, take your usual hour, of course, but then take some more time—grab a cab over to Tiffany's or Jensen's—someplace like that—and buy me a coffee cup and saucer. Something good in bone China, thin and white. You can buy singles from open stock. If it's patterned, pick out something attractive, something you like. Don't be afraid to spend money."

"A coffee cup and saucer, sir?"

"Yes, and see if you can find a spoon, one of those small silver French spoons. Sometimes they're enameled in blue patterns, flowered patterns. That would be fine."

"One coffee cup, one saucer, and one spoon. Will that be all, sir?"

"Yes—no. Get the same thing for yourself. Get two sets."

"Oh, Mr. Blank, I couldn't—"

"Two sets," he said firmly. "And Mrs. Cleek, from now on when the commissary delivers my coffee, will you pour it into my new cup and leave it on my desk that way?"

"Yes, Mr. Blank."

"Keep track of what you spend, including cab fares there and back. I'll pay you personally. This is not petty cash."

"Yes, Mr. Blank."

He clicked off and picked up the president's envelope, having no great curiosity to open it. He searched the outside. Finally, sighing, he tore open the flap and scanned the two-sheet memo swiftly. It was about what he had expected, considering the lack of zeal in his prospectus. His suggestion of having AMROK II compute the ratio between editorial and advertising in all Javis-Bircham magazines was approved to this extent: it would be tried on an experimental basis on the ten magazines listed on the attached page, and would be limited to a period of six months, after which time a production management consultant would be called in to make an independent evaluation of the results.

Blank tossed the memo aside, stretched, yawned. He couldn't, he realized, care less. It was a crock of shit. Then he picked up the memo again and wandered out of the office.

"I'll be in the Computer Room," he said as he passed Mrs. Cleek's desk. She gave him a bright, hopeful smile.

He went through the nonsense of donning the sterile white skull cap and duster, then assembled Task Force X-1 about the stainless steel table. He passed around the second sheet of the president's memo, deeming it wise, at this time, not to tell them of the experimental nature and limited duration of the project.

"We've got the go-ahead," he said, with what he hoped they would think was enthusiasm. "These are the magazines we start with. I want to draw up a schedule of priorities for programming. Any ideas?"

The discussion started at his left and went around the table. He listened to all of them, watching their pale, sexless faces, not hearing a word that was said.

"Excellent," he said occasionally. Or, "Very good." Or, "I'll take a raincheck on that." Or, "Well . . . I don't want to

171

say no, but . . ." It didn't make any difference: what they said or what he said. It had no significance.

Significance began, I suppose, when my wife and I separated. Or when she wouldn't wear the sunglasses to bed. Oh, it probably began much sooner, but I wasn't aware of it. I was aware of the glasses, the masks. And then, later, the wigs, the exercises, the clothes, the apartment . . . the mirrors. And standing naked in chains. I was aware of all that. I mean, I was conscious of it.

What was happening to me—is happening to me—is that I am feeling my way—feeling: that's a good word—feeling in the sense of emotion rather than the tactile sense—feeling my way to a new perception of reality. Before that, before the sunglasses, I perceived and reasoned in a masculine, in-line way, vertical, just like AMROK II. And now . . . and now I am discovering and exploring a feminine, horizontal perception of reality.

And what that requires is to deny cold order—logical, intellectual order, that is—and perceive a deeper order, glimpsing it dimly now, somewhere, an order much deeper and broader because . . . The order I have known up to now has been narrow and restricted, tight and disciplined. But it cannot account for . . . for all.

This feminine, horizontal perception applies to breadth, explaining the apparent illogic and seeming madness of the universe—well, this perception does not deny science and logic but offers something more—an emotional consciousness of people and of life.

But is it only emotional? Or is it spiritual? At least it demands a need to accept chaos—a chaos outside the tight, disciplined logic of men and AMROK II, and seeks a deeper, more fundamental order and logic and significance within that chaos. It means a new way of life: the truth of lies and the reality of myths. It demands a whole new way to perceive a—

No, that's not right. Perception implies a standing aside and observing. But this new world I am now in requires participation and sharing. I must strip myself naked and plunge—if I hope to know the final logic. If I have the courage . . .

Courage . . . When I told Celia of the power I felt when selecting my victim, and the love I had for him when he was selected—all that was true. But I didn't mention the fear—fear so intense it was all I could do to control my bladder. But isn't that part of it? I mean emotion—feeling. And from emotion to a spiritual exaltation, just as Celia is always speaking of ceremony and ritual and the beauty of evil. That is *her* final logic. But is it mine? We shall see. We shall see.

I must open myself, to everything. I grew in a tiled house of Lalique glass and rock collections. Now I must become warm and tender and accept everything. I must be open to everything in the universe, good and evil, the spread and the cramped. But not just accepting. Because then I'd be a victim. I must plunge to the heart of life and let its heat sear me. I must be moved.

To *experience* reality, not merely to perceive it: that is the way. And the final answer may be dreadful to divine. But if I can conquer fear, and kill, and feel, and learn, I will bring a meaning out of the chaos of my new world, give it a logic few have ever glimpsed before, and then I'll know.

Is there God?

3

He pulled that brass plunger, standing at her teak door, grasping the bundle of long-stemmed roses, blood-colored, and feeling as idiotic and ineffectual as any wooer come to call upon his lady-love with posies, vague hope, a vapid smile.

"Good-afternoon, Valenter."

"Good-afternoon, thir. Do come in."

He was inside, the door closed behind him, when the tall, pale houseman spoke in tones Daniel was certain were a burlesque, a spoof of sadness. That long face fell, the muddy eyes seemed about to leak, the voice was suited for a funeral chapel.

"Mithter Blank, I am thorry to report Mith Montfort hath gone."

"Gone? Gone where?"

"Called away unexthpectedly. She athked me to prethent her regreth."

"Oh shit."

"Yeth thir."

"When will she be back? Today?"

"I do not know, thir. But I thuthpect it may be a few dayth."

"Shit," Blank repeated. He thrust the flowers at Valenter. "Put these in some water, will you? Maybe they'll last long enough for her to see them."

"Of courth, thir. Mathter Tony ith in the thtudy and would like you to join him, thir."

"What? Oh. All right."

It was a Saturday noon. He had imagined a leisurely lunch, perhaps some shopping, a visit to the Mortons' Erotica, which was always crowded and entertaining on a Saturday afternoon. And then, perhaps, a movie, a dinner, and then . . . Well, anything. Things went best, he decided, when they weren't too rigidly programmed.

The boy languished on the tufted couch—a beauty!

"Dan!" he cried, holding out a hand.

But Blank would not cross the room to touch that languid palm. He sat in the winged armchair and regarded the youth with what he believed was amused irony. The roses had cost twenty dollars.

"About Celia," Tony said, looking down at his fingernails. "She wanted me to make her apologies."

"Valenter already has."

"Valenter? Oh pooh! Have a drink."

And suddenly, Valenter was there, leaning forward slightly from the waist.

"No, thank you," Blank said. "It's a little early for me."

"Oh come," Tony said. "Vodka martini on the rocks with a twist of lemon. Right?"

Daniel considered a moment. "Right," he smiled.

"What will your son have?" the waiter asked, and they both laughed.

"My son?" Blank said. He looked to Tony. "What will my son have?"

They were in a French restaurant, not bad and not good. They didn't care.

Tony ordered oysters and frogs' legs, a salad doused with a cheese dressing. Blank had a small steak and endives with oil and vinegar. They smiled at each other. Tony reached forward to touch his hand. "Thank you," he said humbly.

Daniel had two glasses of a thick burgundy, and Tony had something called a "Shirley Temple." The boy's knee was against his. He didn't object, wanting to follow this plot to its denouement.

"Do you drink coffee?" he asked. They flirted.

"How is school?" he asked, and Tony made a gesture, infinitely weary.

They were strolling then, hands brushing occasionally, up Madison Avenue, and stopped to smile at a display of men's clothing in a boutique.

"Oh," Tony said.

Daniel Blank glanced at him. The lad was in sunlight, brazen. He gleamed, a gorgeous being.

"Let's look," Blank said. They went inside.

"Ooh, thank you," Tony said later, giving him a dazzling smile. "You spent so much money on me."

"Didn't I though?"

"Are you rich, Dan?"

"No, I'm not rich. But not hurting."

"Do you think the pink pullover was right for me?"

"Oh yes. Your coloring."

"I would have loved those fishnet briefs, but I knew even the small size would be too large for me. Celia buys all my underwear in a women's lingerie shop."

"Does she?"

They sat on a park bench unaccountably planted in the middle of a small meadow. Tony fingered the lobe of Dan's left ear; they watched an old black man stolidly fly a kite.

"Do you like me?" Tony asked.

Daniel Blank would not give himself time to fear, but twisted around and kissed the boy's soft lips.

"Of course I like you."

Tony held his hand and made quiet circles on the palm with a forefinger.

"You've changed, Dan."

"Have I?"

"Oh yes. When you first started seeing Celia, you were so tight, so locked up inside yourself. Now I feel you're breaking out. You smile more. Sometimes you laugh. You never did that before. You wouldn't have kissed me three months ago, would you?"

"No, I wouldn't have. Tony, perhaps we should get back. Valenter is probably—"

"Valenter," Tony said in a tone of great disgust. "Pooh! Just because he—" Then he stopped.

But Valenter was nowhere about, and Tony used his own key to let them in. Daniel's roses were arranged in a Chinese vase on the foyer table. And in addition to the roses' sweet musk, he caught another odor: Celia's perfume, a thin, smoky scent, Oriental. He thought it odd he had not smelled it in this hallway at noon.

And the scent was there in the upstairs room to which Tony led him by the hand, resolute and humming.

He had vowed not only to perceive but to experience, to strip himself bare and plunge to the hot heart of life. The killing of Frank Lombard had been a cataclysm that left him riven, just as an earthquake leaves the tight, solid earth split, stretched open to the blue sky.

Now, alone and naked with this beautiful, rosy lad, the emotions he sought came more quickly, easily, and fear of his own feelings was already turning to curiosity and hunger. He sought new corners of himself, great sweetness and great tenderness, a need to sacrifice and a want to love. Whatever his life had lacked to now, he resolved to find, supply, to fill himself up with things hot and scented, all the emotions and sentiments which might illume life and show its mystery and purpose.

The boy's body was all warm fabric: velvet eyelids, silken buttocks, the insides of his thighs a sheeny satin. Slowly, with a deliberate thoughtfulness, Daniel Blank put mouth and tongue to those cloths, all with the fragrance of youth, sweet and moving. To use youth, to pleasure it and take pleasure from it, seemed to him now as important as murder, another act of conscious will to spread himself wide to sentient life.

The infant moved moaning beneath his caresses, and that incandescent flesh heated him and brought him erect. When he entered into Tony, penetrating his rectum, the boy cried out with pain and delight. Dimly, far off, Blank thought he heard a single tinkle of feminine laughter, and smelled again her scent clinging to the soiled mattress.

Later, when he held the lad in his arms and kissed his tears away—new wine, those tears—he thought it possible, probable even, that they were manipulating him, for what reason he could not imagine. But it was of no importance. Because whatever the reason, it must certainly be a selfish one.

Suddenly he *knew;* her slick words, her lectures on ritual, her love of ceremony and apotheosis of evil—all had the stench of egotism; there was no other explanation. She sought, somehow, to set herself apart. Apart and above. She wanted to conquer the world and, perhaps, had enlisted him in her mandarin scheme.

But, enlisted or not, she had unlocked him, and would find he was moving beyond her. Whatever her selfish motive, he would complete his own task: not to conquer life, but to become one with it, to hug it close, to feel it and love it and, finally, to know its beautiful enigma. Not as AMROK II might know it, but in his heart and gut and gonads, to become a secret sharer, one with the universe.

4

After wrenching his ice ax from the skull of Frank Lombard, he had walked steadily homeward, looking neither to the right nor to the left, his mind resolutely thoughtless. He had nodded in a friendly fashion to the doorman on duty, then ascended to his apartment. Only after he was inside, the battery of chains and locks in place, did he lean against the wall, still coated, close his eyes, draw a deep breath.

But there was still work to be done. He put the ax aside for the moment. Then he stripped naked. He examined coat and suit for stains, of any kind. He could see none. But he placed coat and suit in a bundle for the drycleaner, and shirt, socks and underclothing in the laundry hamper.

Then he went into the bathroom and held the ice ax so that the head was under water in the toilet bowl. He flushed the toilet three times. Practically all the solid matter—caked blood and some grey stuff caught in the saw-tooth serrations on the bottom point of the pick—was washed away.

Then, still naked, he went into the kitchen and put a large pot of water on to boil. It was the pot he customarily used for spaghetti and stew. He waited patiently until the water boiled, still not reflecting on what he had done. He wanted to finish the job, then sit down, relax, and savor his reactions.

When the water came to a rolling boil he immersed the ice ax head and shaft up to the leather around the handle. The tempered steel boiled clean. He dunked it three times, swirling it about, then turned the flame off under the pot, and held the ax head under the cold water tap to cool it.

When he could handle it, he inspected the ax carefully. He even took a small paring knife and gently pried up the top edge of the blue leather-covered handle. He could see no stains that might have leaked beneath. The ax smelled of steel and leather. It shone.

He took the little can of sewing machine oil from his kitchen closet and, with his bare hands, rubbed oil into the exposed steel surfaces of the ax. He applied a lot of oil, rubbing strongly, then wiped off the excess with a paper towel. He started to discard the towel in his garbage can, then thought better of it and flushed it down the toilet. The ice ax was left with a thin film of oil. He hung it away in the hall closet with his rucksack and crampons.

Then he showered thoroughly under very hot water, using a small brush on hands and fingernails. After he dried, he used cologne and powder, then donned a short cotton kimono. It was patterned with light blue cranes stalking across a dark blue background. Then he poured himself a small brandy, went into the living room, sat on the couch before the mirrored wall, and laughed.

Now he allowed himself to remember, and it was a beloved dream. He saw himself walking down that oranged street toward his victim. He was smiling, coat rakishly open, left hand inside the slit pocket, right arm swinging free. Was he snapping the fingers of his right hand? He might have been.

The smile. The nod. The hot surge of furious blood when he whirled and struck. The sound. He remembered the sound. Then the victim's incredible plunge forward that pulled the ice ax from his grasp, toppled him forward. Then, quickly pulling the ax free, search, wallet, and the steady walk homeward.

Well then . . . what did he feel? He felt, he decided, first of all an enormous sense of pride. That was basic. It was, after all, an extremely difficult and dangerous job of work, and he had brought it off. It was not too unlike a difficult and dangerous rock climb, a technical assignment that demanded skill, muscular strength and, of course, absolute resolve.

But what amazed him, what completely amazed him, was the *intimacy!* When he spoke to Celia about his love for the victim, he only hinted. For how could she understand? How could anyone understand that with one stroke of an ice ax he had *plundered* another human being, knowing him in one crushing blow, his loves, hates, fears, hopes—his *soul*.

Oh! It was something. To come so close to another. No, not close, but *in* another. Merged. Two made one. Once, he had suggested in a very vague, laughing, roundabout fashion to his wife that it might be fun if they sought out another woman, and the three might be naked together. In his own mind he had visualized the other woman as thin and dark, with enough sense to keep her mouth shut. But his wife didn't understand, didn't pick up on what he was suggesting. And if she had, she would have attributed it to his depraved appetites—a man naked in bed with two women.

But sex had nothing to do with it. That was the whole point! He wanted another woman both he and his wife could love because that would be a new, infinitely sweet intimacy between them. If he and his wife had gone to bed with a second woman, simultaneously sucked her hard nipples, caressed her, and their lips—his and his wife's—perhaps meeting on foreign flesh, well then . . . well then that would be an intimacy so sharp, so affecting, that he could hardly dream of it without tears coming to his eyes.

But now. Now! Recalling what he had done, he felt that sense of heightened intimacy, of entering into another, merging, so far beyond love that there was no comparison. When he killed Frank Lombard, he had become Frank Lombard, and the victim had become Daniel Blank. Linked, swooning, they swam through the endless corridors of the universe like two coupling astronauts cast adrift. Slowly tumbling. Turning. Drifting. Throughout all eternity. Never decaying. Never stopping. But caught in passion. Forever.

5

Whenever Daniel Blank saw Florence and Samuel together, he remembered a film he had once seen on the life of sea otters. The pups! They nuzzled each other, touched, frolicked and frisked. And the Mortons' close-fitting helmets of black, oily hair were exactly like pelts. He could not watch them without amused indulgence.

Now, seated in the couch in his apartment, they insisted on sharing one Scotch-on-the-rocks—which he had replenished four times. They were clad in their black leather jumpsuits, sleek as hides, and their bright eyes and ferrety features were alive and curious.

Since they were so ready—ready? eager!—to reveal intimate details of their private lives, they assumed all their friends felt the same. They wanted to know how his affair with Celia Montfort was coming along. Had they been physically intimate? Was it a satisfying sex relationship? Had he discovered anything more about her they should know? What was Anthony's role in her household? And Valenter's?

He answered in generalities and tried to smile mysteriously. After awhile, balked by his reticence, they turned to each other and began to discuss him as if they were alone in their own apartment. He had endured this treatment before (as had all their silent friends), and sometimes he found it entertaining. But now he felt uncomfortable and, he thought, perhaps fearful. What might they not stumble on?

"Usually," Sam said, speaking directly to Flo, "when a man like Dan is asked point-blank if his sex relations with a particular woman are satisfactory, he will say something like, 'How on earth would I know? I haven't been to bed with her.' That means, A, he is telling the truth and has not been to bed with her. Or B, he has been to bed with her and is lying to protect the lady's reputation."

"True," Flo nodded solemnly. "Or C, it was so bad he doesn't want to mention it because he has failed or the lady has failed. Or D, it was absolutely marvelous, so incredible he doesn't want to talk about it; he wants to keep this wonderful memory for himself."

"Hey, come on," Dan laughed. "I'm not—"

"Ah yes," Sam interrupted. "But when a man like Dan replies to the question, 'How was sex with this particular woman?' by answering, 'It was all right,' what are we to understand from that? That he has been to bed with the lady but the experience was so-so?"

"I think that is what Dan would like us to believe," Flo said thoughtfully. "I think he is concealing something from us, Samovel."

"I agree," he nodded. "What could it be? That he has not yet made the attempt?"

"Yes," Flo said. "That makes psychological sense. Dan is a man who was married several years to a woman his physical and mental inferior. Correct?"

"Correct. And during that time sex became a routine, a habit. Suddenly separated and divorced, he looks around for a new woman. But he feels uncertain. He has forgotten how to operate."

"Exactly," Flo approved. "He is unsure of himself. He fears he may be rejected. After all, the boy isn't a mad rapist. And if he is rejected, then he will think the failure of his marriage was his fault. And his ego can't accept that. So in Dan's approach to this new woman, he is careful. He is wary. Did you ever know a wary lover to succeed?"

"Never," Sam said definitely. "Successful sex always demands aggression, either attack on the man or surrender on the part of the woman."

"And surrender on the part of the woman is as valid a method of aggression as attack on the part of the man."

"Of course. You remember reading—"

But at this point, tiring of their game, Daniel Blank went into the kitchen to pour himself a fresh vodka. When he returned to the living room, they were still at it, their voices louder now, when the bell of the hall door rang so stridently they were shocked to silence. Daniel Blank, to whom an unexpected knock or ring now came as a heart flutter or spasm of the bowels, behaved, he assured himself later, with nonchalant coolness.

"Now who on earth can that be?" he inquired of no one.

He rose and moved to the hallway door. Through the peephole he caught a glimpse of a woman's hair—long, blonde hair —and a padded coat shoulder. Oh my God, he thought, it's Gilda. What's she doing here?

But when he unhooked the chain and opened the door, it wasn't Gilda. It was and it wasn't. He stared, trying to understand. She stared back just as steadily. It wasn't until his mouth opened in astonishment that she broke into a laugh, and then he saw it was Celia Montfort.

But what a Celia! Wearing a blonde wig down to her shoulders, with the tips curled upward. Thick makeup including scarlet lip rouge. A tacky tweed suit with a ruffled blouse. A necklace of oversize pearls. Crimson nail polish. And, obviously, a padded brassiere.

She had never seen his ex-wife, never seen a photo of her, but the resemblance was startling. The physical bulk was there, the gross good health, high color, muscular swagger, a tossing about of elbows and shoulders.

"My God," Daniel said admiringly, "you're marvelous."

"Am I like her?"

"You wouldn't believe. But why?"

"Oh . . . just for fun, as Tony wou'd say. I thought you'd like it."

"I do, I really do. My God, you're so like her. You really should have been an actress."

"I am," she said. "All the time. Aren't you going to ask me in?"

"Oh, of course. Listen, the Mortons are here. I'll announce you as Gilda. I want to see their reactions."

He preceded her to the doorway of the living room.

"It's Gilda," he called brightly, then stepped aside.

Celia came to the doorway and stood posed, sweeping the Mortons with a beaming smile.

"Gilda!" Sam cried, bouncing to his feet. "This is—" He stopped.

"Gilda!" Florence cried, waving. "How nice that—" She stopped.

Then Celia and Daniel burst out laughing, and within a moment the Mortons were laughing too.

Flo came over to embrace Celia, then patted the padded shoulders of her suit and the tweed behind.

"A padded ass," she reported to the men. "And sponge rubber tits. My God, sweetie, you thought of everything."

"Do you think I'm like?"

"Like?" Sam said. "A dead ringer. Even the makeup."

"Perfect," Flo nodded. "Even to the fingernails. How did you do it?"

"Guessed," Celia said.

"You guessed right," Daniel said. "Now would you like to take off your jacket and get comfortable?"

"Oh no. I'm enjoying this."

"All right. Vodka?"

"Please."

He went into the kitchen to prepare new drinks for all of them. When he came back, Celia had turned off all the lights except for one standing lamp, and in the gloom she looked even more like his ex-wife. The resemblance was shattering, even to the way she sat upright in the Eames chair, her back straight, feet firmly planted on the floor, knees slightly spread as if the thickness of her thighs prevented a more modest pose. He felt . . . something.

"Why the disguise?" Flo asked.

"What's the point?" Sam asked.

Celia Montfort fluffed her blonde wig, smiled her secret smile.

"Haven't you ever wanted to?" she asked them all. "Everyone wants to. Walk away from yourself. Quit your job, desert wife or husband and family, leave your home and all your possessions, strip naked if that is possible, and move to another street, city, country, world, and become someone else. New name, new personality, new needs and tastes and dreams. Become someone entirely different, entirely new. It might be better or it might be worse, but it would be *different*. And you might have a chance, just a chance, in your new skin. Like being born again. Don't you agree, Daniel?"

"Oh yes," he nodded eagerly. "I do agree."

"I don't." Sam said "I like who I am."

"And I like who I am," Flo said. "Besides, you can never change. really."

"Can't you?" Celia asked lazily. "What a drag."

They argued the possibility of personal change, *essential* change. Blank listened to the Mortons' hooted denials and sensed the presence of an obscene danger: he was tempted to refute them, calmly, a cool, sardonic smile on his lips, by saying, "I have changed. I killed Frank Lombard." He resisted the temptation, but toyed with the risk a moment, enjoying it. Then he contented himself with an unspoken, "I know something you don't know," and this childish thought, for reasons he could not comprehend, made them immeasurably dear to him.

Eventually, of course, they were all talked out. Daniel served coffee, which they drank mostly in silence. At an unseen signal, Flo and Sam Morton rose to their feet, thanked Daniel for a pleasant evening, congratulated Celia Montfort on her impersonation, and departed. Blank locked and chained his door behind them.

When he returned to the living room, Celia was standing. They embraced and kissed, his mouth sticking to the thick rouge on her lips. He felt her padded ass.

"Shall I take it off?" she asked.

"Oh no. I like it."

They emptied ashtrays, carried glasses to the kitchen sink.

"Can you stay?" he asked.

"Of course."

"Good."

She went into the bathroom. He moved around the apartment, checking windows, turning off lights, putting the iron bar on the hallway door. When he walked across the living room he saw his ghostly reflection jump from mirror to mirror, bits and pieces.

When he came back into the bedroom she was sitting quietly on the bed, staring.

"What do you want?" she asked, looking up at him.

"Oh, leave the wig on," he said quickly. "And the brassiere and girdle. Or whatever it is. You'll want to take off the suit and blouse."

"And slip? And stockings?"

"Yes."

"The pearls?"

183

"No, leave them on. Would you like a robe? I have a silk robe."

"All right."

"Is it too warm in here?"

"A little."

"I'll turn down the heat. Are you sleepy?"

"More tired than sleepy. The Mortons tire me. They never stop moving."

"I know. I showered this morning. Shall I shower now?"

"No. Let me hold you."

"Naked?"

"Yes."

Later, under a single light blanket, she held him, and through her silk robe he felt padded brassiere and girdle.

"Mommy," he said.

"I know," she murmured. "I know."

He curled up in her arms, began weeping quietly.

"I'm trying," he gasped. "I really am trying."

"I know," she repeated. "I know."

The thought of fucking her, or attempting it, offended him, but he could not sleep.

"Mommy," he said again.

"Turn over," she commanded, and so he did.

"Ahh," she said. "There."

"Oh. Oh."

"Am I hurting you?"

"Oh yes! Yes."

"Am I Gilda now?"

"Yes. But she never would."

"More?"

"Slowly. Please."

"What is my name?"

"Celia."

"What?"

"Gilda."

"What?"

"Mommy."

"That's better. Isn't that better?"

He slept, finally. It seemed to him he was awake a moment later.

"What?" he said. "What is it?"

"You were having a nightmare. You screamed. What was it?"

"A dream," he said, snuggling into her. "I had a bad dream."

"What did you dream?"

"All confused."

He moved closer to her, his hands on cotton batting and sponge rubber.

"Do you want me to do it again?" she asked.

"Oh yes," he said thankfully. "Please."

In the morning when he awoke, she was lying beside him, sleeping naked, having sometime during the night taken off her wig, robe, costume. But she still wore the pearls. He touched them. Then he moved stealthily down beneath the blanket until he was crouched, completely covered, and smelled her sweet warmth. He spread her gently. Then he drank from her, gulping from the fountain, greedy he, until he felt her come awake. Still he persisted, and she moved, reaching down under the blanket to press the back of his head. He groaned, almost swooning, fevered with the covered heat. He could not stop. Afterwards she licked his mouth.

And still later, when they were dressed and at the kitchen table, she said, "You'll do it again?"—more of a statement than a question.

He nodded wordlessly, knowing what she meant, and beginning to comprehend the danger she represented.

"From the front?" she asked. "Will you? And look into his eyes, and tell me."

"Difficult," he said.

"You can do it," she said. "I know you can."

"Well . . ." He glowed. "It needs planning. And luck, of course."

"You make your own luck."

"Do I? Well, I'll think about it. It's an interesting problem."

"Will you do something for me?"

"Of course. What?"

"Come to me immediately afterwards."

He thought a moment.

"Perhaps not immediately afterwards. But soon. That night. Will that do?"

"I may not be home."

He was instantly suspicious. "Do you want to know the night? I don't know that myself. And won't."

"No, I don't want to know the night, or the place. Just the week. Then I'll stay home every night, waiting for you. Can you tell me the week?"

"Yes. I'll tell you that. When I'm ready."

"My love," she said. "The eyes," she said.

Bernard Gilbert took life seriously—and he had a right to be mournful. Orphaned at an early age he had been *schlepped* around from uncle to aunt, cousin to cousin, six months at each, and always assured that the food he was eating, his bed, his clothes—all this came from the labor of his benefactors, at their expense.

At the age of eight he was shining shoes on the street, then delivering for a delly, then waiting on table, then selling little pieces of cloth, then bookkeeper in a third-rate novelty store. And all the time going to school, studying, reading books. All joylessly. Sometimes, when he had saved enough money, he went to a woman. That, too, was joyless. What could he do?

Through high school, two miserable years in the army, City College, always working, sleeping four or five hours a night, studying, reading, making loans and paying them back, not really thinking of *why?* but obeying an instinct he could not deny. And suddenly, there he was, Bernard Gilbert, C.P.A., in a new black suit, a hard worker who was good with numbers. This was a life?

There was a spine in him. Hard work didn't daunt him, and when he had to, he grovelled and shrugged it away. Much man. Not a swaggering, hairy-chested conqueror, but a survivor. A special kind of bravery; hope never died.

It came in his 32nd year when a distant cousin unexpectedly invited him for dinner. And there was Monica. "Monica, I'd like you to make the acquaintance of Bernard Gilbert. He's a C.P.A."

And so they were married, and his life began. Happy? You wouldn't believe! God said, "Bernie, I've been shitting on you for 32 years. You can take it, and it's time you deserve a break. Enjoy, kid, enjoy!"

First of all, there was Monica. Not beautiful, but handsome and strong. Another hard worker. They laughed in bed. Then came the two children, Mary and Sylvia. Beautiful girls! And healthy, thank God. The apartment wasn't much, but it was home. *Home!* His home, with wife and children. They all laughed.

The bad memories faded. It all went away: the cruelties, the hand-me-down clothes, the insults and crawling. He began, just began, to understand joy. It was a gift, and he cherished it. Bernard Gilbert: a melancholy man with sunken cheeks always in need of a shave, stooped shoulders, puzzled eyes, thinning hair, a scrawny frame: a man who, if he had his life to live over again, woud have been a violinist. Well . . .

He had this good job with a large firm of accountants where his worth was recognized. In the last few years he had started to moon-light, doing the tax returns of self-employed people like doctors, dentists, architects, artists, writers. He made certain his employers knew about it; they didn't object, since he was doing it on his own time and it didn't conflict with their own commercial accounts.

His private business grew. It was hard, putting in an eight-hour day and then coming home for another two- to four-hours' work. But he talked it over with Monica—he talked *everything* over with Monica—and they agreed that if he stuck to it, maybe within five to ten years he might be able to cut loose and start his own business. It was possible. So Monica took a course in accounting, studied at home, and after awhile she could help him at night, in addition to cooking and cleaning and taking care of Mary and Sylvia. They were both hard workers, but they never thought of it, would have been surprised if someone had told them they worked hard. What else?

So there they were in a third-floor walk-up on East 84th Street. It wasn't a fancy apartment, but Monica had painted it nice, and there were two bedrooms and a big kitchen where Monica made matzoh brie like he couldn't believe, it was so good, and a record player with all of Isaac Stern's recordings, and a card table where he could work. It wasn't luxury, he acknowledged, but he wasn't ashamed of it, and sometimes they had friends or neighbors in and laughed. Sometimes they even went out to eat, with the children, at an expensive restaurant, and were very solemn, giggling inside.

But the best times were when he and Monica would finish their night's work, and would sit on the couch, after midnight, the children asleep, and they just were there, listening to Vivaldi turned down low, just together. He would have worked his ass off for the rest of his life for moments like that. And when Monica brushed her lips across his sunken cheek . . . Oh!

He was thinking of moments like that when he got off the First Avenue bus. It wasn't even midnight. Well, maybe a little later. He had been downtown, working on the books of a medical clinic. It was a possible new account, a good one and a big one. The meeting with the doctors had taken longer than he had expected. Patiently he explained to them what the tax laws said they could do and what they could not do. He felt he had impressed them. They said they'd discuss it and let him know within a week. He felt good about it, but resolved not to be too optimistic when he discussed it with Monica. In case . . .

He turned into his own block. It had not yet been equipped with the new street lights, and far ahead, in the gloom, he saw a man walking toward him. Naturally, he was alerted—at that hour, in this city. But as they drew closer he saw the other man was about his age, well-dressed, coat flapping wide. He was striding along jauntily, left hand in his pocket, right arm swinging free.

They came closer. Bernard Gilbert saw the other man was staring at him. But he was smiling. Gilbert smiled in return. Obviously the man lived in the neighborhood and wanted to be friendly. Gilbert decided he would say, "Good-evening."

They were two steps apart, and he had said, "Good—" when the man's right hand darted beneath the open flap of his coat and came out with something with a handle, something with a point, something that gleamed even in the dull street light.

Bernard Gilbert never did say, "—evening." He knew he halted and drew back. But the thing was in the air, swinging down. He tried to lift a defending arm, but it was too heavy. He saw the man's face, handsome and tender, and there was no hate there, nor madness, but a kind of ardor. Something struck high on Bernard Gilbert's forehead, slamming him down, and he knew he was falling, felt the crash of sidewalk against his back, wondered what had happened to his new-found joy, and heard God say, "Okay, Bernie, enough's enough."

PART V

1

Three times a week a commercial messenger arrived at Captain Delaney's home with copies of the most recent Operation Lombard reports. Delaney noted they were becoming fewer and shorter, and Chief Pauley was sending his detectives back to recheck matters already covered: Lombard's private life and political career; possible links with organized crime; any similar assaults or homicides in the 251st Precinct, neighboring precincts, and eventually all of Manhattan, then all of New York; and then queries to the FBI and the police departments of large cities asking for reports of homicides of a similar nature.

Delaney admired Chief Pauley's professional competence. The Chief had assembled a force of almost 500 detectives brought in from all over the city. Many of these men Delaney knew personally or by reputation, and they included assault specialists, weapons technicians, men familiar with the political jungle, and detectives whose success was based on their interrogative techniques.

The result was nil: no angle, no handle, no apparent motive. Chief Pauley, in a confidential memo to Deputy Commissioner Broughton, had even suggested a possibility that Delaney himself had considered: the snuff had been committed by a policeman angered by Lombard's public attacks on the efficiency of the Department. Pauley didn't believe it.

Captain Delaney didn't either. A policeman would probably kill with a gun. But most career cops, who had seen mayors, commissioners, and politicians of all ranks come and go, would shrug off Lombard's criticism as just some more publicity bullshit, and go about their jobs.

The more Delaney pondered the killing, the more Operation Lombard reports he studied, the more firmly he became convinced that it was a motiveless crime. Not motiveless to the killer, of course, but motiveless to any rational man. Lombard had been a chance victim.

Delaney tried to fill up his hours. He visited his wife in the hospital twice a day, at noon and in the early evening. He did some brief interrogations of his own, visiting Frank Lombard's law partner, his mother, and a few of his political associates. For these interviews Delaney wore his uniform and badge, risking Broughton's wrath if he should somehow discover what Delaney was up to. But it was all a waste of time; he learned nothing of value.

One evening, despairing of his failure to make any meaningful progress, he took a long pad of legal notepaper, yellow and ruled, and headed it "The Suspect." He then drew a line down the center of the page. The lefthand column he headed "Physical," the righthand column "Psychological." He resolved to write down everything he knew or suspected about the killer.

Under "Physical" he listed:

"Probably male, white."

"Tall, probably over six feet."

"Strong and young. Under 35?"

"Of average or good appearance. Possibly well-dressed."

"Very quick with good muscular coordination. An athlete?"

Under "Psychological" he listed:

"Cool, determined."

"Driven by unknown motive."

"Psycopath? Unruh type?"

At the bottom of the page he made a general heading he called "Additional Notes." Under this he listed:

"Third person involved? Because of stolen license as 'proof of homicide'."

"Resident of 251st Precinct?"

Then he reread his list. It was, he admitted, distressingly skimpy. But just the act of writing down what he knew—or guessed, rather; he *knew* nothing—made him feel better. It was all smoke and shadows. But he began to feel someone was there. Someone dimly glimpsed . . .

He read the list again, and again, and again. He kept coming back to the notation "Driven by unknown motive."

In all his personal experiences with and research on psychopathic killers he had never come across or read of a killer totally without motive. Certainly the motive might be irrational, senseless, but in every case, particularly those involving multiple murders, the killer had a "motive." It might be as obvious as financial gain; it might be an incredible philosophical structure as creepy and cheap as an Eiffel Tower built of glued toothpicks.

But however mad the assassin, he had his reasons: the slights of society, the whispers of God, the evil of man, the demands of political faith, the fire of ego, the scorn of women, the terrors of loneliness . . . whatever. *But he had his reasons.* Nowhere, in Delaney's experience or in his readings, existed the truly motiveless killer, the quintessentially evil man who slew as naturally and casually as another man lighted a cigarette or picked his nose.

There was no completely good man alive upon this earth and, Delaney believed—hoped!—there was no completely evil man. It was not a moral problem; it was just that no man was complete, in any way. So the killer of Frank Lombard had crushed his skull for a reason, a reason beyond logic and sense, but for a purpose that had meaning to him, twisted and contorted though it might be.

Sitting there in the gloom of his study, reading and rereading his sad little "Portrait of a Killer," Edward Delaney thought of this man existing, quite possibly not too far from where he now sat. He wondered what this man might be thinking and dreaming, might be hoping and planning.

In the morning he made his own breakfast, since it had been arranged that their day-only maid, Mary, would go directly from her home to the hospital, bringing Barbara fresh nightgowns and an address book she had requested. Delaney drank a glass of tomato juice, doggedly ate his way through two slices of unbuttered whole wheat toast, and drank two cups of black coffee. He scanned the morning paper as he ate. The Lombard story had fallen back to page 14. It said, in essence, there was nothing to say.

Wearing his winter overcoat, for the November day was chill, and the air smelled of snow, Delaney left the house before ten a.m. and walked over to Second Avenue, to a phone booth in a candy store. He dialed Deputy Inspector Thorsen's answering service, left his phone booth number, hung up, waited patiently. Thorsen was back to him within five minutes.

"I have nothing to report," Delaney said flatly. "Nothing."

Thorsen must have caught something in his tone, for he attempted to soothe.

"Take it easy, Edward. Broughton doesn't have anything either."

"I know."

"But I have some good news for you."

"What's that?"

"We were able to get your Lieutenant Dorfman a temporary

191

appointment as Acting Commander of the Two-five-one Precinct."

"That's fine. Thank you."

"But it's only for six months. After that, either you'll be back on the job or we'll have to put in a captain or deputy inspector."

"I understand. Good enough. It'll help with the problem of Lombard's driver's license."

"What's the problem?"

"I'm on leave of absence, but I'm still on the Department list. I've got to report the license is missing."

"Edward, you worry too much."

"Yes. I do. But I've got to report it."

"That means Broughton will learn about it."

"Possibly. But if there is another killing, and I think there will be, and Chief Pauley's boys find the victim's license is missing—or anything like it—they'll check back with Lombard's widow down in Florida. She'll tell them I asked about the license and she couldn't find it. Then my ass will be in a sling. Broughton will have me up for withholding evidence."

"How do you want to handle it?"

"I've got to check the book, but as I recall, precinct reports of lost or stolen drivers' licenses are sent to Traffic Department personnel who then forward the report to the New York State Department of Motor Vehicles. I'll tell Dorfman about it and ask him to file the usual form. But Broughton might learn about it from Traffic. If they get a report that Frank Lombard's license is missing, someone will start screaming."

"Not to worry. We have a friend in Traffic."

"I thought you might have."

"Tell Dorfman to make out the usual form, but to call me before he sends it in. I'll tell him the man to send it to in Traffic. It will get to the State, but no one will tip Broughton. Does that satisfy you?"

"Yes."

"You're playing this very cautiously, Edward."

"Aren't you?"

"Yes, I guess we are. Edward, tell me . . ."

"What?"

"Are you making any progress at all? Even if it's something you don't want to talk about yet?"

"Yes," Delaney lied, "I'm making progress."

He walked back to his home, head bent, hands deep in overcoat pockets, trundling through the damp, gloomy day. His lie to Thorsen depressed him. It always depressed him when it was necessary to manipulate people. He would do it, but he would not enjoy it.

Why was it necessary to keep Thorsen's morale high? Because . . . because, Delaney decided, the Lombard homicide was more than just an intramural feud between the Broughton forces and the Thorsen-Johnson forces. In fact, he acknowledged, he had accepted their offer, not because he instinctively disliked Broughton and wanted him put down, or had any interest in Departmental politics, but because . . . because . . .

He groaned aloud, knowing he was once again at the bone, gnawing. Was it the intellectual challenge? The atavistic excitement of the chase? The belief he was God's surrogate on earth? Why did he do it! For that universe of harmony and rhythm he had described so glowingly to Thomas Handry? Oh shit! He only knew, mournfully, that the time, mental effort and creative energy spent exploring his own labyrinthine motives might better be spent finding the man who sent a spike smashing into the skull of Frank Lombard.

He came up to his own stoop, and there was Lieutenant Dorfman ringing his bell. The lieutenant turned as he approached, saw Delaney, grinned, came bouncing down the steps. He caught up Delaney's hand, shook it enthusiastically.

"I got it, Captain!" he cried. "Acting Commander for six months. I thank you!"

"Good, good," Delaney smiled, gripping Dorfman's shoulder. "Come in and have a coffee and tell me about it."

They sat in the kitchen, and Delaney was amused to note that Dorfman was already assuming the prerogatives of his new rank; he unbuttoned his uniform blouse and sat sprawled, his long, skinny legs thrust out. He would never have sat in such a position in the Captain's office, but Delaney could understand, and even approve.

He read the teletype Dorfman had brought over and smiled again.

"All I can tell you is what I said before: I'm here and I'll be happy to help you any way I can. Don't be shy of asking. There's a lot to learn."

"I know that, Captain, and I appreciate anything you can do. You've already done plenty recommending me."

Delaney looked at him closely. Here it was again: using people. He forced ahead.

"I was glad to do it," he said. "In return, there is something you can do for me."

"Anything, Captain."

"Right now, I am going to ask you for two favors. In the future, I will probably ask for more. I swear to you I will not ask you to do anything that will jeopardize your record or your career. If you decide my word is not sufficient—and believe me, I wouldn't blame you if you thought that—then I won't insist. All right?"

Dorfman straightened in his chair, his expression puzzled at first, then serious. He stared at Delaney a long moment, their eyes locked.

"Captain, we've worked together a long time."

"Yes. We have."

"I can't believe you'd ask me to do anything I shouldn't do."

"Thank you."

"What is it you want?"

"First, I want you to file a report with the Traffic Department of a missing driver's license. I want it clearly stated on the report that I was the one who brought this matter to your attention. Before the report is sent in, I ask you to call Deputy Inspector Thorsen. He will give you the name of the man in the Traffic Department to send the report to. Thorsen has assured me the report will be forwarded to the New York State Department of Motor Vehicles in the usual manner."

Dorfman was bewildered.

"That's not much of a favor, Captain. That's just routine. Is it your license?"

"No. It's Frank Lombard's."

Dorfman stared at him again, then slowly began to button up his uniform jacket.

"Lombard's?"

"Yes. Lieutenant, if you want to ask questions, I'll try to answer them. But please don't be insulted if I say that in this matter, the less you know, the better."

The tall, red-headed man stood, began to pace about the kitchen, hands thrust into his trouser pockets. He counted the walls, didn't look at Delaney.

"I've been hearing things," he said. "Rumors."

"I imagine you have," Delaney nodded, knowing there was scarcely a man in the Department, down to the lowliest probationary patrolman, who wasn't dimly aware of the feuds and schisms amongst high-level commanders. "You don't want to get involved in it, do you?"

Dorfman stopped and gripped the top rail of a kitchen

chair with reddish hands, knuckles bulging. Now he looked directly at Delaney.

"No, Captain, I don't want to get involved at all."

"What I've asked so far is pure routine, is it not? I'm asking you to report a missing driver's license. That's all."

"All right. I'll call Thorsen, get the name of the man at the Traffic Department, and file a report. Do you know the license number?"

"No."

"What is the second favor you want, Captain?"

There was something in his voice, something sad. The Captain knew Dorfman would do as he, Delaney, requested. But somehow, subtly, their relationship had changed. Dorfman would pay his debt as long as he was not compromised. But once he paid what he felt was enough, they would no longer be mentor and student, captain and lieutenant. They would no longer be friends. They would be professional associates, cautious, pleasant but reserved, watchful. They would be rivals.

Delaney had, he acknowledged, already destroyed a cordial relationship. In some small way he had corrupted faith and trust. Now, to Dorfman, he was just another guy who wanted a favor. But there was no help for it, no turning back.

"The second favor," Delaney said, accenting the word "favor" somewhat ironically, "is that I would appreciate it, lieutenant—" and again he deliberately accented the word "lieutenant"—"if you would keep me personally informed of any assaults or homicides in the Two-five-one Precinct in which the circumstances and particularly the wound are similar to the Lombard homicide."

"That's all?" Dorfman asked, and now the irony was his.

"Yes."

"All right, Captain," Dorfman nodded. He hooked his collar, tugged his jacket straight. The stains and crumbs were missing now. He was Acting Commander of the 251st Precinct.

He strode to the door without another word. Then, hand on the knob, he paused, turned to face Delaney, and seemed to soften.

"Captain," he said, "in case you're interested, I already have orders to report any assault or homicide like that to Chief Pauley."

"Of course," Delaney nodded. "He couldn't do anything else. Report to him first."

"Then to you?"

"Then to me. Please."

Dorfman nodded, and was gone.

Delaney sat without moving. Then he held out his right hand. It was trembling, a bit. It had not gone as well as he had hoped or as badly as he had feared. But, he assured himself again, it had to be done—and perhaps it would have happened in the ordinary course of events. Dorfman was a natural worshipper, almost a hanger-on, and if he was to make anything of himself, eventually he would have to be cast adrift, sink or swim. And Delaney laughed ruefully at his own rationalizing. There was, he admitted disgustedly, too goddamn much Hamlet in him.

It was almost time to leave for the hospital. He consulted his little pocket notebook and checked off the items Mary had taken care of. He had already donned his overcoat and hard Homburg, his hand reaching for the outside doorknob, when the phone rang. He picked up the extension in the hall and said; "Captain Edward X. Delaney here."

"Captain, this is Christopher Langley."

"Mr. Langley. Good to hear from you. How are you, sir?"

"Very well. And you?"

"Fine. I've been intending to call, but I didn't want you to feel I was pressuring you. So I thought it best to say *nothing*. You understand?"

There was silence for a moment, then Langley said, "I think I do understand. Gee, this is great! But it's been over a week since we met. Could we have lunch today, Captain? There's something I'd like your advice on."

"Oh?" Delaney said. "I'm afraid I can't make lunch. My wife is in the hospital, and I'm just leaving to visit her."

"I'm sorry to hear that, Captain. Nothing serious, I hope?"

"Well . . . we don't know. But it will take time. Listen, Mr. Langley, what you wanted to talk to me about—is it important?"

"It might be, Captain," the thin, flutey voice came back, excited now. "It's not anything final, but it's a beginning. That's why—"

"Yes, yes," Delaney interrupted. "Mr. Langley, would it be possible for you to meet me at the hospital? I do want to see you. Unfortunately, I can't have lunch with you, but we'll have a chance to talk and discuss your problem."

"Excellent!" Christopher Langley chortled, and Delaney knew he was enjoying this cloak-and-dagger conversation. "I'll be glad to meet you there. I hope you may be able to help me. At least it will give me an opportunity to meet your wife."

Delaney gave him the address and room number, and then rang off. The Captain stood a moment, his hand still on the dead phone, and hoped, not for the first time, that he had acted correctly in entrusting the important job of weapon identification to this elderly dandy. He started to analyze his motives for enlisting Langley's aid: the man's expertise; the need to recruit a staff, however amateur; Langley's plea for "important" work; Delaney's need—

He snorted with disgust at his own maunderings. He wanted to *move* on the Lombard homicide, and it seemed to him he had spent an unconscionable amount of time interrogating himself, probing his own motives, as if he might be guilty of— of what? Dereliction of duty? He resolved to be done, for this day at least, with such futile searchings. What was necessary was to *do*.

Barbara was seated in a wheelchair at the window, and she turned her head to give him a dazzling smile when he entered. But he had come to dread that appearance of roseate good health—the bright eyes and flushed cheeks—knowing what it masked. He crossed the room swiftly, smiling, kissed her cheek, and presented her with what might have been the biggest, reddest Delicious apple ever grown.

"An apple for the teacher," he said.

"What did I ever teach you?" she laughed, touching his lips.

"I'd tell you, but I don't want to get you unnecessarily excited."

She laughed again and turned the enormous apple in her slim fingers, stroking it. "It's beautiful."

"But probably mealy as hell. The big ones usually are."

"Maybe I won't eat it," she said faintly. "Maybe I'll just keep it next to my bed and look at it."

He was concerned. "Well . . . yes," he said finally. "Why not? Listen, how *are* you? I know you must be bored with me asking that, but you know I *must* ask it."

"Of course." She reached out to put a hand on his. "They started the new injections this morning. Two days before they know." *She* was comforting *him*.

He nodded miserably. "Is everything all right?" he asked anxiously. "I mean the food? The nurses?"

"Everything is fine."

"I asked for Temples at that stand on First Avenue. They expect them next week. I'll bring them over then."

"It's not important."

"It *is* important," he said fiercely. "You like Temples, you'll get Temples."

"All right, Edward," she smiled, patting his hand. "It's important, and I'll get Temples."

Then she was gone. It had happened several times recently, and it frightened him. Her body seemed to stiffen, her eyes took on an unfocused stare. She ceased speaking but her lips moved, pouting and drawing apart, kissing, over and over, like a babe suckling, and with the same soft, smacking sound.

"Listen," he said hurriedly, "when Eddie was here last week, I thought he looked thin. Didn't you think he looked thin?"

"Honey Bunch," she said

"What?" he asked, not understanding and wanting to weep.

"My Honey Bunch books," she repeated patiently, still looking somewhere. "What happened to them?"

"Oh," he said. "Your Honey Bunch books. Don't you remember? When Liza told us she was pregnant, we packed up all the children's books and sent them off to her."

"Maybe she'll send them back," she murmured, turning her head to look at him with blind eyes. "My Honey Bunch books."

"I'll get some for you."

"I don't want new ones. I want the old ones."

"I know, I know," he said desperately. "The old ones with the red covers and the drawings. I'll get them for you, Barbara. Barbara? Barbara?"

Slowly the focus of her eyes shortened. She came back. He saw it happen. Then she was looking at him.

"Edward?"

"Yes," he said, "I'm here."

She smiled, gripped his hand. "Edward," she repeated.

"Listen, Barbara, there is someone coming here to meet me. Christopher Langley. He's an ex-curator of the Metropolitan. I told you about him."

"Oh, yes," she nodded. "You told me. He's trying to identify the weapon in the Lombard case."

"Exactly!" he cried delightedly, and leaned forward to kiss her cheek.

"What was that for?" she laughed.

"For being you."

"Edward, when Eddie was here last week, didn't you think he looked a little thin?"

"Yes," he nodded. "I thought he looked a little thin."

He lurched his chair closer, clasping her hands, and they talked of little things: the drapes in the study, whether or not to draw out accumulated dividends on his insurance policy to help pay hospital costs, what he had for breakfast, a rude attendant in the X-ray lab, a nurse who had unaccountably broken into tears while taking Barbara's temperature. He told her about Dorfman's promotion. She told him about a pigeon that came to her windowsill every morning at the same time. They spoke in low, droning voices, not really hearing each other, but gripping hands and singing a lovely duet.

They came out of it, interrupted by a timid but persistent rapping on the hospital room door. Delaney turned from the waist. "Come in," he called.

And into the room came dashing the dapper Christopher Langley, beaming. And behind him, like a battle-ship plowing in the wake of a saucy corvette, came the massive Widow Zimmerman, also beaming. Both visitors carried parcels: brown paper bags of curious shape.

Delaney sprang to his feet. He shook Langley's little hand and bowed to the Widow. He introduced his wife to both. Barbara brightened immediately. She liked people, and she particularly liked people who knew what they were and could live with it.

There was talk, laughter, confusion. Barbara insisted on being moved back to the bed, knowing Edward would want to talk to Langley privately. The Widow Zimmerman planted her monumental butt in a chair alongside the bed and opened her brown paper bag. Gefilte fish! And homemade at that. The two men stood by, nodding and smiling, as the Widow expounded on the nutritive and therapeutic qualities of gefilte fish.

Within moments the good Widow had leaned forward over the bed, grasped one of Barbara's hands in her own meaty fists, and the two women were deep in a whispered discussion of such physical intimacy that the men hastily withdrew to a corner of the hospital room, pulled up chairs, leaned to each other.

"First of all, Captain," the little man said, "let me tell you immediately that I have not identified the weapon that killed Frank Lombard. I went through my books, I visited museums, and I saw several weapons—antique weapons—that could have made that skull puncture. But I agree with you: it was a modern weapon or tool. Gosh, I *thought* about it! Then, last week, I was walking down my street, and a Con Edison crew was tearing up the pavement. To lay a new cable, I suppose. They do it all the time. Anyway, they had a trench dug. There was a man in the trench, a huge black, and even in this weather he was stripped to the waist. A magnificent torso. Heroic. But what interested me was the tool he was using. It was a pick, Captain. An ordinary pick. A wooden handle as long as a woodsman's ax, and then a steel head with a pick on each side, tapering to a point. Much too large to be the Lombard weapon, of course. And I remembered you felt the killer carried it concealed. Extremely difficult to carry a concealed pick."

"Yes," Delaney nodded, "it would be. But the pick idea is interesting."

"The shape!" Langley said, hunching forward. "That's what caught my eye. A square spike tapering to a sharp point. More than that, each spike of the pick curved downward, just as your surgeon described the wound. So I began wondering if that pick, customarily used in excavation and construction work, might have a smaller counterpart—a one-handed pick with a handle no longer than that of a hatchet."

Delaney brooded a moment. "I can't recall ever seeing a tool like that."

"I don't think there is one," Langley agreed. "At least, I visited six hardware stores and none of them had anything like what I described. But at the seventh hardware store I found this. It was displayed in their window."

He opened his brown paper bag and withdrew a tool: magician and rabbit. He handed it to Delaney. The Captain took it in his blunt fingers, stared, turned it over and over, hefted it, gripped it, swung it by the handle, peered at the head. He sniffed at the wood handle.

"What the hell *is* it?" he asked finally.

"It's a bricklayer's hammer," Langley said rapidly. "Handle of seasoned hickory. Head of forged steel. Notice the squared hammer on one side of the head? That's for tapping bricks into place in the mortar. Now look at the spike. The top surface curves downward, but the bottom side is horizontal. The spike itself doesn't curve downward. In addition, the spike ends in a sharp chisel point, used to split bricks. I knew at once it wasn't the weapon we seek. But it's a start, don't you think?"

"Of course it is," Delaney said promptly. He swung the hammer in short, violent strokes. "My God, I never knew such a tool existed. You could easily split a man's skull with this."

"But it isn't what we want, is it?"

"No," Delaney acknowledged, "it isn't. The spike doesn't curve downward, and the end comes to a chisel edge about— oh, I'd guess an inch across. Mr. Langley, there's something else I should have mentioned to you. This has a wooden handle. I admit Lombard might well have been killed with a wood-handle weapon, but my experience has been that with wood-handled implements, particularly old ones, the handle breaks. Usually at the point where it's been compressed into the steel head. I'd feel a lot better if we could find a tool or weapon that was made totally of steel. This is just a feeling I have, and I don't want it to inhibit your investigation, sir."

"Oh, it won't, it won't!" the little man cried, bouncing up and down on his chair in his excitement. "I agree, I agree! Steel would be better. But I haven't told you everything that happened. In the store where I found this bricklayer's hammer, I asked the proprietor why he stocked them and how many he sold. After all, Captain, how many bricklayers are there in this world? And how many hammers would they need? Look at that tool. Wouldn't you judge that an apprentice brick-layer, buying a tool as sturdy as that, would use it for the rest of his professional career?"

Delaney hefted the hammer again, swinging it experimentally.

"Yes," he nodded, "I think you're right. The handle might possibly break, but this thing could last fifty, a hundred years."

"Exactly. Well, the hardware store owner said—and it's amazing how willing and eager men are to talk about their jobs and specialties—"

"I know," Delaney smiled.

"Well, he said he stocked those hammers because he sold twenty or thirty a year. And not only to bricklayers! He sold them, he said, to 'rock hounds'—a term, as he explained it, that applies to people who search for precious and semi-precious stones—gemmologists and others of their ilk. In addition, he sold a few hammers to amateur archeologists. I then asked if he knew of a similar hammer on which the spike, instead of ending in a wide chisel edge, came to a sharp, ta-pered point. He said he had heard of such a hammer but had never seen it—a hammer made especially for rock hounds, prospectors, and archeologists. And this hammer had a spike, a pick, that tapered to a sharp point. I asked him where it might be available, but he couldn't say, except that I might try hobby and outdoor stores. What do you think, Captain?"

Delaney looked at him. "First of all," he said, "I think you have done remarkably well. Much better than I could have done." He was rewarded by Langley's beam of pleasure. "And I hope you will be willing to track this thing down, to try to find the rock hound's hammer with a spike that curves downward and tapers to a point."

"Willing?" Christopher Langley shouted delightedly. "Willing?" And the two women at the bed, still speaking softly, broke off their conversation and looked over inquiringly.

"Willing?" Langley asked in a quieter voice. "Captain, I cannot stop now. I never knew detective work could be so fascinating."

"Oh yes," Delaney nodded solemnly, "fascinating."

"Well, I haven't had so much fun in my life. After we leave here, Myra and I—"

"Myra?" Delaney interrupted.

"The Widow Zimmerman," the old dandy said, casting his eyes downward and blushing. "She has several admirable qualities."

"I'm sure."

"Well, I made a list of hobby shops from the Yellow Pages. We're going to have lunch in the Times Square area, and then we're going around to all the addresses I have and try to locate a rock hound's hammer. Is that the right way, Captain?"

"Exactly the right way," Delaney assured him. "It's just what I'd do. Don't be discouraged if you don't find it in the first four or five or dozen or fifty places you visit. Stick to it."

"Oh, I intend to," Langley said stoutly, straightening up. "This is important, isn't it, Captain?"

Delaney looked at him strangely. "Yes," he nodded, "it *is* important. Mr. Langley, I have a feeling about you and what you're doing. I think it's *very* important."

"Well," Christopher Langley said, "then I better get to it."

"May I keep this hammer?"

"Of course, of course. I have no use for it. I'll keep you informed as to our progress."

"*Our?*"

"Well . . . you know. I must take the Widow Zimmerman to lunch. She has been very kind to me."

"Of course."

"But I've told her nothing, Captain. *Nothing*, I swear. She thinks I'm looking for a rock hammer for my nephew."

"Good. Keep it that way. And I must apologize for my phone conversation this morning. I'm probably being over-cautious. I doubt very much if my phone is being tapped, but there's no point in taking chances. When you want to reach me from now on, just dial my home phone and say something innocuous. I'll get back to you within ten or fifteen minutes from an outside phone. Will that be satisfactory?"

Then the ex-curator did something exceedingly curious. He made an antique gesture Delaney had read about in Dickens' novels but had never seen. Langley laid a forefinger alongside his nose and nodded wisely. Captain Delaney was delighted.

"Exactly," he nodded.

Then they were gone, waving goodby to Barbara and promising to visit her again. When the door closed behind them, Barbara and Edward looked at each other, then simultaneously broke into laughter.

"I like her," Barbara told him. "She asked very personal questions on short acquaintance, but I think it was from genuine interest, not just idle curiosity. A very warm, out-going, good-hearted woman."

"I think she's after Langley."

"So?" she challenged. "What's wrong with that? She told me she's been very lonely since her husband died, and he's all alone, too. It's not good to be alone when you get old."

"Look at this," he said, changing the subject hastily. "It's a bricklayer's hammer. This is what Langley's come up with so far."

"Is that what killed Lombard?"

"Oh no. But it's close. It's an ugly thing, isn't it?"

"Yes. Evil-looking. Put it away, please, dear."

He put it back in the brown paper sack and placed it atop his folded overcoat, so he wouldn't forget it when he left. Then he drew up a chair alongside her bed.

"What are you going to do with the gefilte fish?" he smiled.

"I may try a little. Unless you'd like it, Edward?"

"No, thank you!"

"Well, it was nice of her to bring it. She's one of those women who think food solves all problems and you can't be miserable on a full stomach. Sometimes they're right."

"Yes."

"You're discouraged, aren't you, Edward?"

He rose and began to stalk up and down at the foot of her bed, hands shoved into his hip pockets.

"Nothing is happening!" he said disgustedly. "I'm not *doing* anything."

"You're convinced the killer is crazy?"

"It's just an idea," he sighed, "but the only theory that makes any sense at all. But if I'm right, it means we have to wait for another killing before we learn anything more. That's what's so infuriating."

"Isn't that hammer Langley brought a lead?"

"Maybe. Maybe not. But even if Lombard had been murdered with a hammer exactly like that, I'd be no closer to finding the killer. There must be hundreds—thousands!—of hammers exactly like that in existence, and more sold every day. So where does that leave me?"

"Come over here and sit down." She motioned toward the chair at the bedside. He slumped into it, took her proffered hand. She lifted his knuckles to her face, rubbed them softly on her cheek, kissed them. "Edward," she said. "Poor Edward."

"I'm a lousy cop," he grumbled.

"No," she soothed. "You're a good cop. I can't think of anything you could have done that you haven't done."

"Operation Lombard did it all," he said dispiritedly.

"You discovered his driver's license was missing."

"Oh sure. Whatever the hell that means."

After 30 years of living with this man, she was almost as familiar with police procedure as he. "Did they check license numbers of parked cars?" she asked.

"Of course. Chief Pauley saw to that. The license number of every parked car in a five-block area was taken down on three successive nights. Then the owners were looked up and asked if they saw anything on the night of the murder. What a job that must have been! But Broughton has the manpower to do it, and it had to be done. They got nothing. Just like the questioning of residents in the neighborhood. Zero."

"Occam's Razor," she said, and he smiled, knowing what she meant.

Several years ago he had come across the unfamiliar phrase "Occam's Razor" in a criminologist's report dealing with percentages and probabilities in homicide cases in the Boston area. Delaney trusted the findings since the percentages quoted were very close to those then current in New York: the great majority of homicides were committed by relatives or "friends" of the victim—mothers, fathers, children, husbands, wives, uncles, aunts, neighbors . . . In other words, most killings involved people who knew each other.

In light of these findings, the Boston criminologist had stated, it was always wise for investigating officers to be guided by the principle of "Occam's Razor."

Intrigued by the phrase, Delaney had spent an afternoon in the reading room of the 42nd Street library, tracking down Occam and his "Razor." Later he told Barbara what he had discovered.

"Occam was a fourteenth century philosopher," he reported. "His philosophy was 'nominalism,' which I don't understand except that I think he meant there are no universal truths. Anyway, he was famous for his hard-headed approach to problem solving. He believed in shaving away all extraneous details. That's why they call his axiom 'Occam's Razor.' He said that when there are several possible solutions, the right one is probably the most obvious. In other words, you should eliminate all the unnecessary facts."

"But you've been doing that all your life, Edward."

"I guess so," he laughed, "but I call it 'Cut out the crap.' Anyway, it's nice to know a fourteenth century philosopher agrees with me. I wish I knew more about philosophy and could understand it."

"Does it really bother you that you can't?"

"Nooo . . . it doesn't bother me, but it makes me realize the limitations of my intelligence. I just can't think in abstractions. You know I tried to learn to play chess three times and finally gave up."

"Edward, you're more interested in people than things, or ideas. You have a very good intelligence for people."

Now, in the hospital room, when Barbara mentioned Occam's Razor, he knew what she meant and smiled ruefully.

"Well," he said, rubbing his forehead, "I wonder if old Occam ever tried solving an irrational problem by rational means. I wonder if he wouldn't begin to doubt the value of logic and deductive reasoning when you're dealing with—"

But then the door to the hospital room swung open, and Dr. Louis Bernardi glided in, olive skin gleaming, his little eyes glittering. A stethoscope was draped about his neck.

He offered Delaney a limp hand, and with the forefinger of his left hand lovingly caressed his ridiculous stripe of a mustache.

"Captain," he murmured. "And you, dear lady," he inquired in a louder voice, "how are we feeling today?"

Barbara began to explain that her feet continued to be swollen uncomfortably, how the rash had reappeared on the insides of her thighs, that the attacks of nausea had seemed to worsen with the first injection of the antibiotic.

To each complaint Bernardi smiled, said, "Yes, yes," or "That doesn't bother me."

Why should it bother you, Delaney thought angrily. It's not happening to you, you little prick.

Meanwhile the doctor was taking her pulse, listening to her heart, gently pushing up eyelids to peer into her staring eyes.

"You're making a fine recovery from surgery," he assured her. "And they tell me your appetite is improving. I am so very happy, dear lady."

"When do you think—" Delaney began, but the doctor held up a soft hand.

"Patience," he said. "You must have patience. And I must have patients. He!"

Delaney turned away in disgust, not understanding how Barbara could trust this simpering popinjay.

Bernardi murmured a few more words, patted Barbara's hand, smiling his oleaginous smile, then turned to go. He was almost at the door when Delaney saw he was leaving.

"Doctor," he called, "I want to talk to you a minute." He said to Barbara, "Be right back, dear."

In the hall, the door of the room closed, he faced Bernardi and looked at him stonily. "Well?" he demanded.

The doctor spread his hands in that familiar bland gesture that said nothing. "What can I tell you? You can see for yourself. The infection still persists. That damned Proteus. We are working our way through the full spectrum of antibiotics. It takes time."

"There's something else."

"Oh? What is that?"

"Recently my wife has been exhibiting signs of—well, signs of irrationality. She gets a curious stare, she seems suddenly withdrawn, and she says things that don't make too much sense."

"What kind of things?"

"Well, a little while ago she wanted some children's books. I mean books she owned and read when she was a child. She's not under sedation, is she?"

"Not now, no."

206

"Pain-killers? Sleeping pills?"

"No. We are trying to avoid any possibility of masking or affecting the strength of the antibiotics. Captain, this does not worry me. Your wife has undergone major surgery. She is under medication. The fever is, admittedly, weakening her. It is understandable that she might have brief periods of—oh, call it wool-gathering. He! I suggest you humor her insofar as that is possible. Her pulse is steady and her heart is strong."

"As strong as it was?"

Bernardi looked at him without expression. "Captain," he said softly—and Delaney knew exactly what was coming— "your wife is doing as well as can be expected."

He nodded, turned, glided away, graceful as a ballet dancer. Delaney was left standing alone, impotent fury hot in his throat, convinced the man knew something, or suspected something, and would not put it into words. He seemed blocked and thwarted on all sides: in his work, in his personal life. What was it he had said to Thomas Handry about a divine order in the universe? Now order seemed slipping away, slyly, and he was defeated by a maniacal killer and unseen beasts feeding on his wife's flesh.

From the man on the beat to the police commissioner—all cops knew what to expect when the moon was full: sleep-walkers, women who heard voices, men claiming they were being bombarded by electronic beams from a neighbor's apartment, end-of-the-world nuts, people stumbling naked down the midnight streets, urinating as they ran.

Now Delaney, brooding on war, crime, senseless violence, cruel sickness, brutality, terror, and the slick, honeyed words of a self-satisfied physician, wondered if this was not The Age of the Full Moon, with order gone from the world and irrationality triumphant.

He straightened, set his features into a smile, reentered his wife's hospital room.

"I suddenly realized why solving the Lombard killing is so important to me," he told her. "It happened in the Two-five-one Precinct. That's my world."

"Occam's Razor," she nodded.

Later, he returned home and Mary fixed him a baked ham sandwich and brought that and a bottle of cold beer into his study. He propped the telephone book open on his desk, and as he ate he called second-hand bookstores, asking for original editions of the Honey Bunch books, the illustrated ones.

Everyone he called seemed to know immediately what he

wanted: the Grosset & Dunlap editions published in the early 1920s. The author was Helen Louise Thorndyke. But no one had any copies. One bookseller took his name and address and promised to try to locate them. Another suggested he try the chic "antique boutiques" on upper Second and Third Avenues, shops that specialized in nostalgic Americana.

Curiously, this ridiculous task seemed to calm him, and by the time he had finished his calls and his lunch, he was determined to get back to work, to work steadily and unquestioningly, just doing.

He went to his book shelves and took down every volume he owned dealing, even in peripheral fashion, with the histories, analyses and detection of mass murderers. The stack he put on the table alongside his club chair was not high; literature on the subject was not extensive. He sat down heavily, put on his thick, horn-rimmed reading glasses, and began to plow through the books, skipping and skimming as much as he could of material that had no application to the Lombard case.

He read about Gille de Raix, Verdoux, Jack the Ripper and in more recent times, Whitman, Speck, Unruh, the Boston strangler, Panzram, Manson, the boy in Chicago who wrote with the victim's lipstick on her bathroom mirror, "Stop me before I kill more." It was a sad, sad chronicle of human aberration, and the saddest thing of all was the feeling he got of killer as victim, dupe of his own agonizing lust or chaotic dreams.

But there was no pattern—at least none he could discern. Each mass killer, of tens, hundreds, reputedly thousands, was an individual and had apparently acted from unique motives. If there was any pattern it existed solely in each man: the *modus operandi* remained identical, the weapon the same. And in almost every case, the period between killings became progressively shorter. The killer was caught up in a crescendo: more! more! faster! faster!

One other odd fact: the mass killer was invariably male. There were a few isolated cases of women who had killed several times; the Ohio Pig Woman was one, the Beck-Fernandez case involved another. But the few female mass murderers seemed motivated by desire for financial gain. The males were driven by wild longings, insane furies, mad passions.

The light faded; he switched on the reading lamp. Mary stopped by to say good-night, and he followed her into the hall to double-lock and chain the front door behind her. He returned to his reading, still trying to find a pattern, a repeated cause-effect, searching for the percentages.

It was almost five in the evening when the front doorbell chimed. He put aside the article he was reading—a fascinating analysis of Hitler as a criminal rather than a political leader— and went out into the hallway again. He switched on the stoop light, peered out the etched glass panel alongside the door. Christopher Langley was standing there, a neat white shopping bag in one hand. Delaney unlocked the door.

"Captain!" Langley cried anxiously. "I hope I'm not disturbing you? But I didn't want to call, and since it was on my way home, I thought I'd take the chance and—"

"You're not disturbing me. Come in, come in."

"Gee, what a marvelous house!"

"Old, but comfortable."

They went into the lighted study.

"Captain, I've got—"

"Wait, just a minute. Please, let me get you a drink. Anything?"

"Sherry?"

"At the moment, I'm sorry to say, no. But I have some dry vermouth. Will that do?"

"Oh, that's jim-dandy. No ice. Just a small glass, please."

Delaney went over to his modest liquor cabinet, poured Langley a glass of vermouth, took a rye for himself. He handed Langley his wine, got him settled in the leather club chair. He retreated a few steps out of the circle of light cast by the reading lamp and stood in the gloom.

"Your health, sir."

"And yours. And your wife's."

"Thank you."

They both sipped.

"Well," Delaney said, "how did you make out?"

"Oh, Captain, I was a fool, *such* a fool! I didn't do the obvious thing, the thing I should have done in the first place."

"I know," Delaney smiled, thinking of Occam's Razor again. "I've done that many times. What happened?"

"Well, as I told you at the hospital, I had gone through the Yellow Pages and made a list of hobby shops in the midtown area, places that might sell a rock hound's hammer with a tapered pick. The Widow Zimmerman and I had lunch—I had stuffed sole: marvelous—and then we started walking around. We covered six different stores, and none of them carried rock hammers. Some of them didn't even know what I was talking about. I could tell Myra was getting tired, so I put her in a cab and sent her home. She is preparing dinner for me tonight. By the by, she's an awful cook. I thought I'd try a few more stores before calling it a day. The next one on my list was Abercrombie & Fitch. And of course they carried a rock hound's hammer. It was so obvious! It's the largest store of its kind in the city, and I should have tried them first. That's why I say I was a fool. Anyway, here it is."

He leaned over, pulled the tool from his white shopping bag, handed it to Captain Delaney.

The hammer was still in its vacuum-packed plastic coating, and the cardboard backing stated it was a "prospector's ax recommended for rock collectors and archeologists." Like the bricklayers' hammer, it had a wood handle and steel head. One side of the head was a square hammer. The other side was a pick, about four inches long. It started out as a square, then tapered to a sharp point. The tool came complete with a leather holster, enabling it to be worn on a belt. The whole thing was about as long as a hatchet: a one-handed implement.

"Notice the taper of the pick," Langley pointed out. "It comes to a sharp point, but still the pick itself does not curve downward. The upper surface curves, but the lower surface is almost horizontal, at right angles to the handle. And, of course, it has a wooden handle. But still, it's closer to what we're looking for—don't you think?"

"No doubt about it," Delaney said definitely. "If that pick had a downward curve, I'd say this is it. May I take off the plastic covering?"

"Of course."

"You're spending a lot of money."

"Nonsense."

Delaney stripped off the clear plastic covering and hefted the ax in his hand.

"This is almost it," he nodded. "A tapered spike coming to a sharp point. About an inch across at the base of the pick. And with enough weight to crush a man's skull. Easily. Maybe this really is it. I'd like to show it to the police surgeon who did the Lombard autopsy."

"No, no," Christopher Langley protested. "I haven't told you the whole story. That's why I stopped by tonight. I bought this in the camping department, and I was on my way out to the elevators. I passed through a section where they sell skiing and mountain climbing gear. You know, rucksacks and crampons and pitons and things like that. And there, hanging on the wall, was something very interesting. It was an implement I've never seen before. It was about three feet long, a two-handed tool. I ruled it out immediately as our weapon: too cumbersome to conceal. And the handle was wood. At the butt end was a sharp steel spike, about three inches long, fitted into the handle. But it was the head that interested me. It was apparently chrome-plated steel. On one side was a kind of miniature mattock coming to a sharp cutting edge, a chisel edge. And the other side was exactly what we're looking for! It was a spike, a pick, about four or five inches long. It started out from the head as a square, about an inch on each side. Then it was formed into a triangle with a sharp edge on top and the base an inch across. Then the whole thing tapered, and as it thinned, it curved downward. Captain, *the whole pick curved downward,* top and bottom! It came to a sharp point, so sharp in fact that the tip was covered with a little rubber sleeve to prevent damage when the implement wasn't being used. I removed the rubber protector, and the underside of the tip had four little saw teeth. It's serrated, for cutting. I finally got a clerk and asked him what this amazing tool was called. He said it's an ice ax. I asked him what it was used for, and he—"

"What?" Delaney cried. "What did you say?"

"I asked the clerk what it was used—"

"No, no," the Captain said impatiently. "What did the clerk say it was called?"

"It's an ice ax."

"Jesus Christ," Delaney breathed. "Leon Trotsky. Mexico City. Nineteen-forty."

"What? Captain, I don't understand."

"Leon Trotsky. He was a refugee from Stalin's Russia—or perhaps he escaped or was deported; I don't remember exactly; I'll have to look it up. Trotsky and Lenin and Stalin were equals at one time. Then Lenin died. Then Stalin wanted to be Numero Uno. So Trotsky got out of Russia, somehow, and made his way to Mexico City. They caught up with him in nineteen-forty. At least it was said the assassin was an agent of the Russian Secret Police. I don't recall the details. But he killed Trotsky with an ice ax."

"Surely you don't think there's any connection between that and Frank Lombard's death?"

"Oh no. I doubt that very much. I'll look into it, of course, but I don't think there's anything there."

"But you think Lombard may have been killed with an ice ax?"

"Let me freshen your drink," Delaney said. He went over to the liquor cabinet, came back with new drinks for both of them. "Mr. Langley, I don't know whether being a detective is a job, a career, a profession, a talent or an art. There are some things I do know. One, you can't teach a man to be a *good* detective, anymore than you can teach him to be an Olympic miler or a great artist. And two, no matter how much talent and drive a man starts out with, he can never become a *good* detective without experience. The more years, the better. After you've been at it awhile, you begin to see the patterns. People repeat, in motives, weapons, methods of entrance and escape, alibis. You keep finding the same things happening over and over again; forced windows, kitchen knives, slashed screens, tire irons, jammed locks, rat poison—the lot. It all becomes familiar. Well, what bugged me about the Lombard killing, what really bugged me from the very start, was that there was nothing *familiar* in it. Nothing! The first reaction, of course, going by percentages, was that it had been committed by a relative or acquaintance, someone known to Lombard. Negative. The next possibility was that it was an attempted robbery, a felony-homicide. Negative. His money hadn't even been touched. And worst of all, we couldn't even identify the weapon. But now you walk in here and say, 'Ice ax.' Magic words! Click! Trotsky was killed with an ice ax. Suddenly I've got something *familiar*. A murder weapon that's been used before. It's hard to explain, I know, Mr. Langley, but I feel better about this than I've felt since it started. I think we're moving now. Thanks to you."

The man glowed.

"But I'm sorry," Delaney said. "I interrupted you. You were telling me what the clerk at Abercrombie & Fitch said when you asked him what the ice ax was used for. What did he say?"

"What?" Langley asked again, somewhat dazed. "Oh. Well, he said it was used in mountain climbing. You could use it like a cane, leaning on the head. The spike on the butt of the handle bites into crusty snow or ice, if you're hiking across a glacier, for instance. He said you could get this ice ax with different ends on the butt—a spike, the way I saw it, or with a little wheel, like a ski pole, for soft snow, and so forth. So then I asked him if there was a shorter ice ax available, a one-handed tool, but with the head shaped the same way. He was very vague; he wasn't sure. But he thought there was such an implement, and he thought the whole thing might be made of steel. Think of that, Captain! A one-handed tool, all steel, with a spike that curves downward and tapers to a sharp point as it curves. How does that strike you?"

"Excellent!" Captain Delaney crowed. "Just excellent! It's now a familiar weapon, used in a previous homicide, and I feel very good about it. Mr. Langley, you've done wonders."

"Oh," the old man smiled, "it was mostly luck. Really."

"You make your own luck," Delaney assured him. "And my luck. Our luck. You followed through. Did the clerk tell you where you can buy a one-handed ice ax?"

"Well . . . no. But he did say there were several stores in New York that specialized in camping and mountain climbing equipment—axes, hatchets, crampons, special rucksacks, nylon rope and things of that sort. The stores must be listed somewhere. Probably in the Yellow Pages. Captain, can I stick with this?"

Delaney took two quick steps forward, clapped the little man on both arms.

"*Can* you?" he declaimed. "*Can* you? I should think you can! You're doing just fine. You try to pin down that one-handed, all-steel ice ax, who sells them, who buys them. Meanwhile, I want to dig into the Trotsky murder, maybe get a photo of the weapon. And I want to get more information on mountain climbers. Mr. Langley, we're moving. We're really *doing* now! I'll call you or you call me. The hell with security. I just feel—I *know*—we're heading in the right direction. Instinct? Maybe. Logic has nothing to do with it. It just *feels* right."

He got Langley out of there, finally, bubbling with enthusiasm and plans of how he intended to trace the ice ax. Delaney nodded, smiled, agreeing to everything Langley said until he could, with decency, usher him out, lock the front door, and come back into the study. He realized it was time to eat, but he was too excited. He paced up and down in front of his desk, hands shoved into hip pockets, chin on chest.

Then he grabbed up the telephone directory, looked up the number, and dialed Thomas Handry's newspaper. The switchboard operator gave him the City Room where they told him Handry had left for the day. He asked for Handry's home phone number, but they wouldn't give it to him.

"Is it an unlisted number?" he asked.

"Yes, it is."

"This is Captain Edward X. Delaney, New York Police Department," the Captain said in his most pontifical tones. "I'm calling on official business. I can get Handry's phone number from the telephone company, if you insist. It would save time if you gave it to me. If you want to check on me, call your man at Centre Street. Who is he—Slawson?"

"Slawson died last year."

"I'm sorry to hear that. He was a good reporter."

"Yes. Just a minute, Captain."

The man came back and read off Handry's home phone number. Delaney thanked him, hung up, waited a few seconds, then lifted the receiver again and dialed. No answer. He waited ten minutes and called again. Still no answer.

There wasn't much in the refrigerator: half of that same baked ham he had had for lunch and some salad stuff. He sliced two thick slices of ham, then sliced a tomato and cucumber. He smeared mustard on the ham, and salad dressing on the rest. He ate it quickly, crunching on a hard roll. He glanced several times at his watch as he ate, anxious to get back to the hospital.

He slid plate and cutlery into the sink, rinsed his hands, and went back into his study to call Handry again. This time he got through.

"Hello?"

"Thomas Handry?"

"Yes."

"Captain Edward X. Delaney here."

"Oh. Hello, Captain. How are you?"

"Well, thank you. And you?"

"Fine. I heard you're on leave of absence."

"Yes, that's true."

"I understand your wife is ill. Sorry to hear that. I hope she's feeling better."

"Yes. Thank you. Handry, I want a favor from you."

"What is it, Captain?"

"First of all, I want some information on the murder of Leon Trotsky in Mexico City in nineteen-forty. I thought you might be able to get it from your morgue."

"Trotsky in Mexico City in nineteen-forty? Jesus, Captain, that was before I was born."

"I know."

"What do you want?"

"Nothing heavy. Just what the newspapers of the time reported. How he was killed, who killed him, the weapon used. If there was a photograph of the weapon published, and you could get a photostat, that would help."

"What's this all about?"

"The second thing," Delaney went on, ignoring the question, "is that I'd like the name and address of the best mountain climber in New York—the top man, or most experienced, or most skillful. I thought you might be able to get it from your Sports Desk."

"Probably. Will you please tell me what the hell this is all about?"

"Can you have a drink with me tomorrow? Say about five o'clock?"

"Well . . . sure. I guess so."

"Can you have the information by then?"

"I'll try."

"Fine. I'll tell you about it then." Delaney gave him the address of the chop house where he had lunched with Dr. Ferguson. "Is that all right, Handry?"

"Sure. I'll see what I can do. Trotsky and the mountain climber. Right?"

"Right. See you tomorrow."

Delaney hurried out and got a cab on Second Avenue. He was at the hospital within fifteen minutes. When he gently opened the door of his wife's room, he saw at once she was sleeping. He tiptoed over to the plastic armchair, switched off the floor lamp, then took off his overcoat. He sat down as quietly as he could.

He sat there for two hours, hardly moving. He may have dozed off a few minutes, but mostly he stared at his wife. She was sleeping calmly and deeply. No one came into the room. He heard the corridor sounds dimly. Still he sat, his mind not so much blank as whirring, leaping, jumping about without order or connection: their children, Handry, Langley, Broughton, the Widow Zimmerman, the ice ax, Thorsen and Johnson, a driver's license—a smear of thoughts, quick frames of a short movie, almost blending, looming, fading . . .

At the end of the two hours he scrawled a message in his notebook, tore the page out, propped it on her bedside table. "I was here. Where were you? Love and violets. Ted." He tiptoed from the room.

He walked back to their home, certain he would be mugged, but he wasn't. He went back into his study and resumed his readings of the histories, motives and methods of mass murderers. There was no one pattern.

He put the books aside, turned off the study lights shortly after midnight. He toured the basement and street floor, checking windows and door locks. Then he trudged upstairs to undress, take a warm shower, and shave. He pulled on fresh pajamas. The image of his naked body in the bathroom mirror was not encouraging. Everything—face, neck, breasts, abdomen, ass, thighs—seemed to be sinking.

He got into bed, switched off the bedside lamp, and lay awake for almost an hour, turning from side to side, his mind churning. Finally he turned on the lamp, shoved his feet into wool slippers, went padding down to the study again. He dug out his list, the one headed "The Suspect." Under the "Physical" column he had jotted "An athlete?" He crossed this out and inserted "A mountain climber?" At the bottom, under "Additional Notes," he wrote "Possesses an ice ax?"

It wasn't much, he admitted. In fact, it was ridiculous. But when he turned out the study lights, climbed once more to the empty bedroom, and slid into bed, he fell asleep almost instantly.

2

"You didn't give me much time," Thomas Handry said, unlocking his attache case. "I guessed you'd be more interested in the assassination itself rather than the political background, so most of the stuff I've got is on the killing."

"You guessed right," Captain Delaney nodded. "By the way, I read all your articles on the Department. Pretty good, for an outsider."

"Thanks a whole hell of a lot!"

"You want to write poetry, don't you?"

Handry was astonished, physically. He jerked back in the booth, jaw dropping, took off his Benjamin Franklin reading glasses.

"How did you know that?"

"Words and phrases you used. The rhythm. And you were trying to get inside cops. It was a good try."

"Well . . . you can't make a living writing poetry."

"Yes. That's true."

Handry was embarrassed. So he looked around at the paneled walls, leather-covered chairs, old etchings and playbills, yellowed and filmed with dust.

"I like this place," he said. "I've never been here before. I suppose it was created last year, and they sprayed dirt on everything. But they did a good job. It really does look old."

"It is," Delaney assured him. "Over a hundred years. It's not a hype. How's your ale?"

"Real good. All right, let's get started." He took handwritten notes from his attache case and began reading rapidly.

"Leon Trotsky. Da-dah da-dah da-dah. One of the leaders of the Russian Revolution, and after. A theorist. Stalin drives him out of Russia, but still doesn't trust him. Trotsky, even overseas, could be plotting. Trotsky gets to Mexico City. He's suspicious, naturally. Very wary..But he can't live in a closet. A guy named Jacson makes his acquaintance. It's spelled two ways in newspaper reports: J-a-c-s-o-n and J-a-c-k-s-o-n. A white male. He visits Trotsky for at least six months. Friends. But Trotsky never sees *anyone* unless his secretaries and body-guards are present. August twentieth, nineteen-forty, Jacson comes to visit Trotsky, bringing an article he's written that he wants Trotsky to read. I couldn't find what it was about. Probably political. Jacson is invited into the study. For the first time the secretaries aren't notified. Jacson said later that Trotsky started reading the article. He sat behind his desk. Jacson stood at his left. He had a raincoat, and in the pockets were an ice ax, a revolver, and a dagger. He said—"

"Wait a minute, wait a minute," Delaney protested. "Jacson had an ice ax in his raincoat pocket? Impossible. It would never fit."

"Well, one report said it was in the raincoat pocket. Another said it was concealed by Jacson's raincoat."

" 'Concealed.' That's better."

"All right, so Trotsky is reading Jacson's article. Jacson takes the ice ax from under his raincoat, or out of the pocket, and smashes it down on Trotsky's skull. Trotsky shrieks and throws himself on Jacson, biting his left hand. Beautiful. Then he staggers backward. The secretaries come running in and grab Jacson."

"Why the revolver and dagger?"

"Jacson said they were to be used to kill himself after he killed Trotsky."

"It smells. Did Trotsky die then, in his study?"

"No. He lived for about twenty-six hours. Then he died."

"Any mention of the direction of the blow?"

"On top of Trotsky's head, as far as I can gather. Trotsky was seated, Jacson was standing."

"What happened to him?"

"Jacson? Imprisoned. One escape try failed, apparently planned by the GPU. That's what the Russian Secret Police was called then. I don't know where Jacson is today, or even if he's alive. There was a book published on Trotsky last year. Want me to look into it?"

"No. It's not important. Another ale?"

"Please. I'm getting thirsty with all this talking."

They sat silently until another round of drinks was brought. Delaney was drinking rye and water.

"Let's get back to the weapon," he said, and Handry consulted his notes.

"I couldn't locate a photo, but the wonderful old lady who runs our morgue, and who remembers *everything*, told me that a magazine ran an article on the killing in the 1950s and published a photo of the ice ax used, so apparently a photo does exist, somewhere."

"Anything else?"

"It was the kind of ice ax used in mountain climbing. First, Jacson said he bought it in Switzerland. Now the testimony gets confused. Jacson's mistress said she had never seen it in Paris or New York, prior to their trip to Mexico. Then Jacson said he like mountaineering and had bought the ax in Mexico and used it when climbing—wait a minute; I've got it here somewhere—when climbing the Orizaba and Popo in Mexico. But then later it turned out that Jacson had lived in a camp in Mexico for awhile, and the owner's son was an enthusiastic mountaineer. He and Jacson talked about mountain climbing several times. This son owned an ice ax, purchased four years previously. The day following the attack on Trotsky, and Jacson's arrest, the camp owner went looking for his son's ice ax, but it had disappeared. Confusing, isn't it?"

"It always is," Delaney nodded. "But Jacson could have purchased the ax in Switzerland, Paris, New York, or stolen it in Mexico. Right?"

"Right."

"Great," Delaney sighed. "I didn't know you could buy the damned thing like a candy bar. Was Jacson really a GPU agent?"

"Apparently no one knows for sure. But the ex-chief of the Secret Service of Mexican Police says he was. Says it in a book he wrote about the case anyway."

"You're sure Jacson hit Trotsky only once with the ice ax?"

"That's one thing everyone seems to agree on. One blow. You need anything else on this?"

"Nooo. Not right now. Handry, you've done excellently in such a short time."

"Sure. I'm good. I admit it. Now let's get to New York's best mountain climber. Two years ago—about eighteen months, to be exact—that would have been an easy question to answer. Calvin Case, thirty-one, married, internationally recognized as one of the most expert, bravest, most daring mountaineers in the world. Then, early last year, he was the last man on the rope of a four-man team climbing the north wall of the Eiger. That's supposed to be the most difficult climb in the world. The guy I spoke to on our Sports Desk said Everest is pure technology, but the north wall of the Eiger is pure guts. It's in Switzerland, in case you're wondering, and apparently it's practically sheer. Anyway, this guy Calvin Case was tail-end Charlie on the rope. He either slipped or an outcrop crumbled or a piton pulled free; my informant didn't remember the details. But he did remember that Case dangled, and finally had to cut himself loose from the others, and fell."

"Jesus."

"Yes. Incredibly, he wasn't killed, but he crushed his spine. Now he's paralyzed from the waist down. Bed-ridden. Can't control his bladder or bowels. My man tells me he's on the sauce. Won't give any interviews. And he's had some good offers for books."

"How does he live?"

"His wife works. No children. I guess they get along. But anyway, I got another guy, active, who's now the number one New York climber. But right now he's in Nepal, preparing for some climb. Who do you want?"

"Do I have a choice? I'll take this Calvin Case. Do you have his address?"

"Sure. I figured you'd want him. I wrote it down. Here." He handed Delaney a small slip of paper. The Captain glanced at it briefly.

"Greenwich Village," he nodded. "I know that street well. A guy took a shot at me on a rooftop on that street, years ago. It was the first time I had ever been shot at."

"He didn't hit?" Handry asked.

"No," Delaney smiled. "He didn't hit."

"Did you?"

"Yes."

"Kill him?"

"Yes. Another ale?"

"Well . . . all right. One more. You having another drink?"

"Sure."

"But I've got to go to the john first. My back teeth are floating."

"That door over there, in the corner."

When Handry came back, he slid into the booth and asked, "How did you know I want to write poetry?"

Delaney shrugged. "I told you. Just a guess. Don't be so goddamned embarrassed about it. It's not shameful."

"I know," Handry said, looking down at the table, moving his glass around. "But still . . . All right, Captain, now you talk. What the hell is this all about?"

"What do you think it's about?"

"You ask me for a run-down on Trotsky, killed with an ice ax. A mountaineer's tool. Then you ask me for the name of the top mountain climber in New York. It's something to do with mountain climbing, obviously. The ice ax is the main thing. What's it all about?"

Delaney, knowing he would be asked, had carefully considered his answers. He had prepared three possible replies, of increasing frankness, still not certain how far he could trust the reporter. But now that Handry had made the Trotsky-ice ax-mountain climbing connection, he went directly to his second reply.

"I am not on active duty," he acknowledged. "But Frank Lombard was killed in my precinct. You may think it's silly, but I consider that my responsibility. The Two-five-one Precinct is my home. So I'm conducting what you might call an unofficial investigation. Operation Lombard is handling the official investigation. I'm sure you know that. Whatever I do, whatever I ask you to do, is outside the Department. As of the date of my leave of absence, I have no official standing. Whatever you do for me is a personal favor—you to me."

Thomas Handry stared at him a long moment. Then he poured himself a full glass of ale and drained off half of it. He set the glass down, a white foam mustache on his upper lip.

"You're full of shit," he informed Captain Edward X. Delaney.

"Yes," Delaney nodded miserably. "That's true. I think Lombard was killed with an ice ax. That's why I asked you for background on Trotsky and mountain climbers. That's all I've got. I asked you to look into it because I trust you. All I can promise you is first whack at the story—if there is a story."

"Do you have a staff?"

"A staff? No, I don't have a staff. I have some people helping me, but they're not in the Department. They're civilians."

"I'll get the story? Exclusively?"

"You'll get it. If there is a story."

"I could get a story published right now. Leave-of-absence police captain personally investigating a murder in his old precinct. Harmonicas and violins. 'I want revenge,' states Captain Edward X. Delaney. Is that what you want?"

"No. What do you want?"

"To be in on it. Okay, Captain? Just to know what's going on. You can use me as much as you want. I'm willing. But I want to know what you're up to."

"It may be nothing."

"Okay, it's nothing. I'll take the gamble. A deal?"

"You won't publish anything without my go-ahead?"

"I won't."

"I trust you, Handry."

"The hell you do. But you've got no choice."

3

It was a faint dream. He followed a man down a misted street. Not a man, really, but something there, a bulk, in the gilded gloom. Like the night when Frank Lombard was killed: orange light and soft rain.

The figure stayed ahead of him, indecipherable, no matter how fast he moved to see what it was he chased. He never closed. He felt no fear nor panic; just a need, a want for the shadow moving through shadows.

Then there was a ringing; not the siren of a squad car or the buffalo whistle of a fire engine, but the ringing of an ambulance, coming closer, louder; he drifted up from sleep and fumbled for the telephone.

Before he could identify himself he recognized Dorfman's voice.

"Captain?"

"Yes."

"Dorfman. There's been an assault on East Eighty-fourth. About halfway between First and Second. Sounds like the Lombard thing. A man tentatively identified as Bernard Gilbert. He's not dead. They're waiting for the ambulance now. I'm on my way."

"Did you call Chief Pauley?"

"Yes."

"Good."

"You want to meet me there?"

"No. You can handle it. Go by the book. Where they taking him?"

"Mother of Mercy."

"Thank you for calling, lieutenant."

"You're welcome."

Then he switched on the light, stepped into slippers, pulled on a robe. He went down to the study, flipping wall switches as he went, and finally lighted the lamp on his desk. The house was cold and damp; he pulled his overcoat on over his bathrobe. Then he consulted his desk calendar: 22 days since the Frank Lombard homicide. He made careful note of this on a fresh sheet of paper, then called Deputy Inspector Thorsen's answering service. He left his name and number.

Thorsen called him in minutes, sounding sleepy but not angry.

"What is it, Edward?"

"I'm calling from my home, but it's important. There's been a Lombard-type assault in the Two-five-one. Eighty-fourth Street. A man tentatively identified as Bernard Gilbert. He's still alive. They're taking him to Mother of Mercy. That's all I've got."

"Jesus," Thorsen breathed. "Sounds like you were right."

"No comfort in that. I can't go over there."

"No. That wouldn't be wise. Is it certain it's a Lombard-type thing?"

"I told you all I know."

"All right, assuming it is, what will Broughton do now?"

"If the wound is similar to the one that killed Lombard, Chief Pauley will try to establish a link between Lombard and this Bernard Gilbert. If he can't, and I don't believe he will, unless it's pure coincidence, he'll realize they were both chance victims, and he's faced with a crazy. Then he'll check every mental institution in a five-state area. He'll have men checking private doctors and psychiatrists and recently released inmates. He'll pull in every known nut in the city for questioning. He'll do what he has to do."

"Do you think it'll work?"

"No. Broughton has had about five hundred dicks working for him. Figure each detective has a minimum of three or four snitches on his wire. That means about two thousand informers, all over the city, and they've come up with zilch. If there was a crazy running wild—a crazy with a record—*someone* would know about it, or notice something weird, or hear some talk. Our man is new. Probably no record. Probably normal-appearing. I've already got him on my list as of good appearance, possibly well-dressed."

"What list?"

Delaney was silent a moment, cursing his lapse. That list was *his*.

"A stupid list I made out of things I suspect about the guy. It's all smoke. I don't *know* anything."

Now Thorsen was silent a moment. Then . . .

"I think maybe you and Johnson and I better have a meeting."

"All right," Delaney said glumly.

"And bring your list."

"Can it wait until I see the reports on this Bernard Gilbert assault?"

"Sure. Anything I can do?"

"Will you have a man at the scene—or involved in the investigation?"

"Well . . ." Thorsen said cautiously, "maybe."

"If you do, a couple of things . . . Is anything missing from the victim's wallet? Particularly identification of any kind? And second, does he—or did he—use hair oil of any kind?"

"Hair oil? What the hell is that all about?"

Delaney frowned at the telephone. "I don't know. I honestly don't know. Probably not important. But can you check?"

"I'll try. Anything else?"

"One more thing. If this Bernard Gilbert dies, and it's proved similar to the Lombard snuff, the papers are going to get hold of it, so you better be prepared for 'Maniacal Killer on Loose' type of thing. It's going to get hairy."

"Oh God. I suppose so."

"Most of the pressure will be on Broughton."

"And the Commish."

"Him, too, of course. But it will affect Chief Pauley most. He's sure to get hundreds of phony leads and false confessions. They'll all have to be checked out, of course. And there's a good possibility there may be imitative assaults and homicides in other parts of the city. It usually happens. But don't be spooked by them. Eventually they'll be weeded out . . ."

He had more conversation with Deputy Inspector Thorsen. They agreed that since Dorfman was recently appointed Acting Commander of the 251st Precinct, and since Thorsen was head of personnel of the patrol division, it would be entirely logical and understandable if Thorsen went to the scene of the Gilbert assault, ostensibly to check up on how Dorfman was handling things. Thorsen promised to call Delaney back as soon as possible, and he would, personally, try to check out the question of missing identification from Bernard Gilbert's wallet and whether or not the victim used hair oil.

The moment he hung up, Delaney dialed the home number of Dr. Sanford Ferguson. It was getting on to 2:00 a.m., but the doctor was awake and cheerful.

"Edward!" he said. "How's by you? I just came in from an on-the-spot inspection of a luscious young piece. Couldn't have been over twenty-six or seven. Oh so lovely."

"Dead?"

"Oh so dead. Apparently cardiac arrest. But doesn't that strike you as odd, Edward? A luscious young piece with a shattered heart?"

"Married?"

"Not legally."

"Is the boy friend a doctor or medical student?"

There was silence a moment.

"You bastard," Ferguson said finally, "you scare me, you know that? In case you're interested, the boy friend is a pharmacist."

"Beautiful," Delaney said. "Well, he probably found a younger, more luscious piece. But doctor, why I called . . . There's been an assault in the Two-five-one Precinct. Tonight. Preliminary reports are that the wound and weapon used are similar to the Lombard homicide. The victim in this case, still alive, a man named Bernard Gilbert, will be taken or has been taken to Mother of Mercy."

"Dear old Mother."

"I wondered if you've been assigned to this?"

"No, I have not."

"I wondered if you could call the attending doctors and surgeons at Mother of Mercy and find out if it really is a Lombard-type penetration, and whether he'll live or not, and —you know—whatever they'll tell you."

Again there was silence. Then . . .

"You know, Edward, you want a lot for one lousy lunch."

"I'll buy you another lousy lunch."

Ferguson laughed. "You treat everyone differently, don't you?"

"Don't we all?"

"I guess so. And you want me to call you back with whatever I can get?"

"If you would. Please. Also, doctor, if this man should die, will there be an autopsy?"

"Of course. On every homicide victim. Or suspected victim."

"With or without next-of-kin's consent?"

"That's correct."

"If this man dies—this Bernard Gilbert—could you do the autopsy?"

"I'm not the Chief Medical Examiner, Edward. I'm just one of the slaves."

"But could you wangle it?"

"I might be able to wangle it."

"I wish you would. If he dies."

"All right, Edward. I'll try."

"One more thing . . ."

Ferguson's laughter almost broke his eardrum; Delaney held the phone up in the air until the doctor stopped spluttering.

"Edward," Ferguson said, "I love you. I really do. With you it's always 'I want two things' or 'I'd like three favors.' But then you always say, 'Oh, just one more thing.' You're great. Okay, what's your 'one more thing'?"

"If you should happen to talk to a doctor or surgeon up at Mother of Mercy, or if you should happen to do the post-mortem, find out if the victim used hair oil, will you?"

"Hair oil?" Ferguson asked. "Hair oil," Ferguson said. "Hair oil!" Ferguson cried. "Jesus Christ, Edward, you never forget a thing, do you?"

"Sometimes," Captain Delaney acknowledged.

"Nothing important, I'll bet. All right, I'll keep the hair oil in mind if I do the cut-'em-up. I'm certainly not going to bother the men in emergency at Mother of Mercy with a thing like that right now."

"Good enough. You'll get back to me?"

"If I learn anything. If you don't hear from me, it means I've drawn a blank."

Delaney rejected the idea of sleep, and went into the kitchen to put water on for instant coffee. While it was heating, he returned to the study and from a corner closet he dragged out a three-by-four ft. bulletin board to which he had pinned a black-and-white street map of the 251st Precinct. The map was covered with a clear plastic flap that could be wiped clean. In the past, while on active duty, Delaney had used the map to chart location and incidence of street crimes, breaking-and-entering, felonious assaults, etc. The map was a miniature of the big one on the wall of the commander's office in the precinct house.

Now he wiped the plastic overlay clean with a paper tissue, returned to the kitchen to mix his cup of black coffee, brought it back with him and sat at the desk, the map before him. He sharpened a red grease pencil and carefully marked two fat dots: on East 73rd Street where Lombard had been killed and on East 84th Street where Gilbert had been assaulted. Alongside each dot he wrote the last name of the victim and the date of the attack.

Two red dots, he acknowledged, hardly constituted a pattern, or even a crime wave. But from his experience and reading of the histories of mass murders, he was convinced additional assaults would be confined to a limited area, probably the 251st Precinct, and the assailant was probably a resident of the area. (Probably! Probably! Everything was probably.) The assassin's success in the Lombard killing would certainly make him feel safe in his home territory.

Delaney sat back and stared at the red dots. He gave Chief Pauley about three days to acknowledge there was no connection between the victims. Then Pauley would opt for a psychopathic killer and would do all those things Delaney had mentioned to Deputy Inspector Thorsen.

In addition, Delaney guessed, Chief Pauley, with no announcement and no publicity, would put out 10 or 20 decoys on the streets of the 251st Precinct, from about ten p.m. till dawn. In civilian clothes, newspapers clutched under one arm, the detectives would scurry up one street and down the next, apparently residents hurrying home in the darkness, but actually inviting attack. That's what Delaney would do. He was certain, knowing Pauley's thoroughness, that the Chief would do it, too. It might work. And it might only serve to drive the killer farther afield if he recognized the decoys for what they were. But you took your chances and hoped. You had to do *something*.

He was still staring at the red dots on the map overlay, sipping cooled black coffee and trying to compute percentages and probabilities, when the desk phone rang. He snatched it up after one ring.

"Captain Edward X. Delaney here."

"Thorsen. I'm calling from a tavern on Second Avenue. They had taken Gilbert to the hospital by the time I arrived. Broughton and Pauley are with him, hoping he'll regain consciousness and say something."

"Sure."

"Gilbert's wallet was on the sidewalk next to him, just like in the Lombard case. Someone's at his home now, trying to find out what, if anything, is missing."

"Was there money in it?"

"Dorfman tells me yes. He thinks it was about fifty dollars."

"Untouched?"

"Apparently."

"How is Dorfman managing?"

"Very well."

"Good."

"He's a little nervous."

"Naturally. Any prediction on whether Gilbert will live?"

"Nothing on that. He is a short man, about five-six or five-seven. He was hit from the front. The penetration went in high up on the skull, about an inch or so above where the hair line would have been."

" 'Would have been'?"

"Gilbert is almost completely bald. Dorfman says just a fringe of thin, grey hair around the scalp, above the ears. But not in front. He was wearing a hat, so I assume some of the hat material was driven into the wound. Jesus, Edward, I don't like this kind of work. I saw the blood and stuff where he lay. I want to get back to my personnel records."

"I know. So you have nothing on whether or not he used hair oil?"

"No, nothing. I'm a lousy detective, I admit."

"You did all you could. Why don't you go home and try to get some sleep?"

"Yes. I'll try. Anything else you need?"

"Copies of the Operation Lombard reports as soon as you can."

"I'll put the pressure on. Edward . . ."

"Yes?"

"When I saw the pool of blood there, on the sidewalk, I got the feeling . . ."

"What?"

"That this business with Broughton is pretty small potatoes. You understand?"

"Yes," Delaney said gently. "I know what you mean."

"You've got to get this guy, Edward."

"I'll get him."

"You sure?"

"I'm sure."

"Good. I think I'll go home now and try to get some sleep."

"Yes, you do that."

After he hung up, Delaney drew his list, "The Suspect," from his top drawer and went through it, item by item. None of his notations had been negated by what Thorsen had told him. If anything, his supposition had been strengthened. Certainly a swinging blow high on the skull of a short man would indicate a tall assailant. But why the attack from the front when the rear attack on Lombard had been so successful? And couldn't Gilbert see the blow coming and dodge or throw up an arm to ward it off? A puzzle.

He was almost ready to give it up for the night, to try to grab a few hours of sleep before dawn, when the phone rang. He reached for it, wondering again how much of his life was spent with that damned black thing pressing his ear flat and sticky.

"Captain Edward X. Delaney here."

"Ferguson. I'm tired, I'm sleepy, I'm irritable. So I'll go through this fast. And don't interrupt."

"I won't."

"You just did. Bernard Gilbert. White male. About forty years old. Five feet six or seven. About one-fifty. Around there. I'll skip the medical lingo. Definitely a Lombard-type wound. Struck from the front. The penetration went in about two inches above the normal hair line. But the man is almost totally bald. That answers your hair oil question."

"The hell it does. Just makes the cheese more binding."

"I'll ignore that. Foreign matter in the wound from the felt hat he was wearing. Penetration to a depth of four or five inches. Curving downward. He's in a deep coma. Paralyzed. Prognosis: negative. Any questions?"

"How long do they figure?"

"From this instant to a week or so. His heart isn't all that strong."

"Will he recover consciousness?"

"Doubtful."

Delaney could tell Ferguson's patience was wearing thin.

"Thank you, doctor. You've been a great help."

"Any time," Ferguson assured him. "Any two o'clock in the morning you want to call."

"Oh, wait a minute," Delaney said.

"I know," Ferguson sighed. " 'One more thing'."

"You won't forget about the autopsy."

Ferguson began to swear—ripe, sweaty curses—and Delaney

hung up softly, smiling. Then he went to bed, but didn't sleep.

It was something he hated and loved: hated because it kept his mind in a flux and robbed him of sleep; loved because it was a challenge: how many oranges could he juggle in the air at one time?

All difficult cases came eventually to this point of complexity: weapon, method, motives, suspects, alibis, timing. And he had to juggle them all, catching, tossing, watching them all every second, relaxed and laughing.

It had been his experience that when this point came in a difficult, involved investigation, when the time arrived when he wondered if he could hold onto all the threads, keep the writhings in his mind, at that point, at that time of almost total confusion, if he could just endure, and absorb more and more, then somehow the log jam loosened, he could see things beginning to run free.

Right now it was a jam, everything caught up and canted. But he began to see key logs, things to be loosened. Then it would all run out. Now the complexity didn't worry him. He could accept it, and more. Pile it on! There wasn't anything one man could do that a better man couldn't undo. That was a stupid, arrogant belief, he admitted. But if he didn't hold it, he really should be in another line of business.

4

Four days later Bernard Gilbert died without regaining consciousness. By that time Chief Pauley had established, to his satisfaction, that there was no link between Lombard and Gilbert, except the nature of the attack, and he had set in motion all those things Captain Delaney had predicted: the check-up of recent escapes from mental institutions, investigation of recently released inmates, questioning of known criminals with a record of mental instability, the posting of decoys in the 251st Precinct.

Delaney learned all this from copies of Operation Lombard reports supplied by Deputy Inspector Thorsen. Once again there were many of them, and they were long. He studied them all carefully, reading them several times. He learned details of Bernard Gilbert's life. He learned that the victim's wife, Monica Gilbert, had stated she believed the only thing missing from her husband's wallet was an identification card.

The accountants for whom Bernard Gilbert worked audited the books of a Long Island manufacturer doing secret work for the U. S. government. To gain access to the premises of the manufacturer, it was necessary for Bernard Gilbert to show a special identification card with his photo attached. It was this card that was missing. The FBI had been alerted by Chief Pauley but, as far as Delaney could determine, the federal agency was not taking an active role in the investigation at this time.

There was a long memo from Chief Pauley to Deputy Commissioner Broughton speculating on the type of weapon used in the Lombard and Gilbert assaults. The phrase "a kind of ax or pick" was used, and Delaney knew Pauley was not far behind him.

At this point the news media had not yet made the Lombard-Gilbert connection. In fact, Gilbert's attack earned only a few short paragraphs on inside pages. Just another street crime. Delaney considered a few moments whether to tip off Thomas Handry, then thought better of it. He'd learn soon enough, and meanwhile Chief Pauley would be free of the pressures of screaming headlines, crank calls, false confessions, and imitative crimes.

It was the timing of his own activities that concerned Captain Delaney most. He wanted to keep up with the flood of Operation Lombard reports. He wanted desperately to interrogate Monica Gilbert himself. He needed to visit Calvin Case, the crippled mountain climber, and learn what he could about ice axes. He wanted to check the progress of Christopher Langley without giving the sweet old man the feeling that he, Delaney, was leaning on him. And, of course, the two visits a day to Barbara in the hospital—that came first.

Two days after the Gilbert attack, while the victim floated off somewhere, living and not living, but still breathing, Delaney thought long and hard on how to approach Monica Gilbert. She was sure to be spending many hours at her husband's bedside. And it was certain she would be guarded by Operation Lombard detectives, probably a two-man team outside her house, although there might be an interior man, too.

The Captain considered and rejected several involved plans for a clandestine meeting with her, unobserved by Operation Lombard. They all seemed too devious. He decided the best solution would be the obvious: he would call for an appointment, give his name, and then walk right up to her door. If he was braced or recognized by Broughton's dicks he would use the same cover story he had prepared when he had gone to question the widow of Frank Lombard: as ex-commander of the 251st Precinct he had come to express his sympathy.

It worked—up to a point. He phoned, identified himself, made an appointment to see her at her home at 4:00 p.m., when she returned from Mother of Mercy. He thought it likely she would repeat the conversation to her guard, as she had been instructed. Or perhaps her phone was tapped. Anything was possible. So, when he walked over a few minutes before four, and one of the dicks in the unmarked police car parked outside her brownstone cranked down his window, waved, and called, "Hi, Captain," he wasn't surprised. He waved back, although he didn't recognize the man.

Monica Gilbert was a strong, handsome woman, hairy, wearing a shapeless black dress that didn't quite conceal heavy breasts, wide hips, pillar thighs. She had been brewing a pot of tea, and he accepted a cup gratefully. There were two little girls in the room, peeking out from behind their mother's skirts. They were introduced to him as Mary and Sylvia, and he rose to bow gravely. They ran giggling from the room. He saw no sign of an interior guard.

"Milk?" she asked. "Sugar?"

"Thank you, no. I take it straight. How is your husband?"

"No change. Still in a coma. They don't hold out much hope."

She said all that in a flat monotone, not blinking, looking at him directly. He admired her control, knowing what it cost.

Her thick black hair, somewhat oily, was combed back from a wide, smooth brow and fell almost to her shoulders. Her large eyes appeared blue-grey, and were her best feature. The nose was long but proportionate. All of her was big. Not so much big as assertive. She wore no makeup, had made no effort to pluck heavy eyebrows. She was, he decided, a complete woman, but he knew instinctively she would respond to soft speech and a gentle manner.

"Mrs. Gilbert," he said in a low voice, leaning forward to her, "I know you must have spent many hours with the police since the attack on your husband. This is an unofficial visit. I am not on active duty; I'm on leave of absence. But I was commander of this precinct for many years, and I wanted to express my regrets and sympathy personally."

"Thank you," she said. "That's very kind of you. I'm sure everything is being done . . ."

"I assure you it is," he said earnestly. "A great number of men are working on this case."

"Will they get the man who did it?"

"Yes," he nodded. "They will. I promise you that."

She looked at him strangely a moment.

"You're not involved in the investigation?"

"Not directly, no. But it did happen in my precinct. What was my precinct."

"Why are you on leave of absence?"

"My wife is ill."

"I'm sorry to hear that. You live in the neighborhood?"

"Yes. Right next door to the precinct house."

"Well, then you know what it's like around here—robberies and muggings, and you can't go out at night."

"I know," he nodded sympathetically. "Believe me, I know, and hate it more than you do."

"He never hurt anyone," she burst out, and he was afraid she might weep, but she did not.

"Mrs. Gilbert, will it upset you to talk about your husband?"

"Of course not. What do you want to know?"

"What kind of a man is he? Not his job, or his background —I've got all that. Just the man himself."

"Bernie? The dearest, sweetest man who ever lived. He wouldn't hurt a fly. He worked so hard, for me and the girls. I know that's all he thinks about."

"Yes, yes."

"Look around. Does it look like we're rich?"

Obediently he looked around. In truth it was a modest apartment: linoleum on the floor, inexpensive furniture, paper drapes. But it was clean, and there were some touches: a good hi-fi set, on one wall an original abstraction that had color and flash, a small wooden piece of primitive sculpture that had meaning.

"Comfortable," he murmured.

"Paradise," she said definitely. "Compared to what Bernie had and what I had. It's not right, Captain. It's just not right."

He nodded miserably, wondering what he could say to comfort her. There was nothing. So he got on with it, still speaking in a quiet, gentle voice, hoping to soothe her.

"Mrs. Gilbert," he asked, remembering Ferguson's comment about the victim's heart, "was your husband an active man?" Realizing he had used the past tense, he switched immediately to the present, hoping she hadn't caught it. But the focus of her eyes changed; he realized she had, and he cursed himself.

"I mean, is he active physically? Does he exercise? Play games?"

She stared at him without answering. Then she leaned forward to pour him another cup of tea. The black dress left her arms bare; he admired the play of muscle, the texture of her skin.

"Captain," she said finally, "for a man not involved in the investigation, you're asking a lot of unusual questions."

He realized then how shrewd she was. He could try lying to her, but was convinced she'd know.

"Mrs. Gilbert," he said, "do you really care how many men are working on this, or who they are, or what their motives are? The main thing is to catch the man who did it. Isn't that true? Well, I swear to you, I want to find the man who struck down your husband more than you do."

"No!" she cried. "Not more that I do." Her eyes were glittering now, her whole body taut. "I want the one who did it caught and punished."

He was astonished by her fury. He had thought her controlled, perhaps even phlegmatic. But now she was twanging, alive and fiery.

"What do you want?" he asked her. "Vengeance?"

Her eyes burned into his.

"Yes. That's exactly what I want. Vengeance. If I answer your questions, will it help me get it?"

"I think so."

"Not good enough, Captain."

"Yes, if you answer my questions it will help find the man who did this thing to your husband."

"Your husband" were the key words, as he had hoped they would be. She started talking.

Her husband was physically weak. He had a heart murmur, arthritis of the left wrist, intermittent kidney pains, although examinations and X-rays showed nothing. His eyes were weak, he suffered from periodic conjunctivitis. He did no exercise, he played no games. He was a sedentary man.

But he worked hard, she added in fierce tones; he worked so hard.

Delaney nodded. Now he had some kind of answer to what had been bothering him: why hadn't Bernard Gilbert made a response to a frontal attack, dodged or warded off the blow? It seemed obvious now: poor musculature, slow physical reactions, the bone-deep weariness of a man working up to and beyond his body's capacity. What chance did he have against a "strong, young, cool, determined psychopath with good muscular coordination?"

"Thank you, Mrs. Gilbert," Captain Delaney said softly. He finished his tea, rose to his feet. "I appreciate your giving me this time, and I hope your husband makes a quick recovery."

"Do you know anything about his condition?"

This time he did lie. "I'm sure you know more than I do. All I know is that he's seriously injured."

She nodded, not looking at him, and he realized she already knew.

She walked him to the door. The two delightful little girls came scampering out, stared at him, giggled, and pulled at their mother's skirt. Delaney smiled at them, remembering Liza at that age. The darlings!

"I want to do something," she said.

"What?" he asked, distracted. "I don't understand."

"I want to *do* something. To help."

"You have helped."

"Isn't there anything else I can do? You're doing something. I don't know what you're up to, but I trust you. I really feel you're trying to find who did it."

"Thank you," he said, so moved. "Yes, I'm trying to find who did it."

"Then let me help. Anything! I can type, take shorthand. I'm very good with figures. I'll do anything. Make coffee. Run errands. Anything!"

He couldn't trust himself to speak. He tried to nod brightly and smile. He left, closing the door firmly behind him.

Out on the street the unmarked police car was still parked in the same position. He expected a stare or a wave. But one of the detectives was sleeping, his head thrown back, his mouth open. The other was marking a racing sheet. They didn't even notice him. If they had been under his command he'd have reamed their ass out.

5

The next day started well, with a call from a book dealer informing Captain Delaney that he had located two volumes of the original Honey Bunch series. The Captain was delighted, and it was arranged that the books would be mailed to him, along with the invoice.

He took this unexpected find as a good omen, for like most policemen he was superstitious. He would tell others, "You make your own luck," knowing this wasn't exactly true; there was a good fortune that came unexpectedly, sometimes unasked, and the important thing was to recognize it when it came, for luck wore a thousand disguises, including calamity.

He sat at his study desk and reviewed a list of "Things to Do" he had prepared. It read:

"Interrogate Monica Gilbert.

"Calvin Case re ice ax.

"Ferguson re autopsy.

"Call Langley.

"Honey Bunch."

He drew a line through the final item. He was about to draw a line through the first and then, for a reason he could not understand, left it open. He searched, and finally found the slip of paper Thomas Handry had given him, bearing the name, address and telephone number of Calvin Case. He realized more and more people were being drawn into his investigation, and he resolved to set up some kind of a card file or simple directory that would list names, addresses, and phone numbers of all the people involved.

He considered what might be the best way to handle the Calvin Case interview. He decided against phoning; an unexpected personal visit would be better. Sometimes it was useful to surprise people, catch them off guard with no opportunity to plan their reaction.

He walked over to Lexington Avenue, shoulders hunched against the raw cold, and took the IRT downtown. It seemed to him each time he rode the subway—and his trips were rare —the graffiti covered more and more of interior and exterior surfaces of cars and platforms. Sexual and racist inscriptions were, thankfully, relatively rare, but spray cans and felt-tipped markers had been used by the hundreds for such records as: "Tony 168. Vic 134. Angie 127. Bella 78. Iron Wolves 127." He knew these to be the first names of individuals and the titles of street gangs, followed by their street number—evidence: "I was here."

He got off at 14th Street and walked west and south, looking about him constantly, noting how this section had changed and was changing since he had been a dick two in this precinct and thought he might leave the world a better place than he found it. Now if he left it no worse, he'd be satisfied.

The address was on West 11th Street, just off Fifth Avenue.

The rents here, Delaney knew, were enormous, unless Case was fortunate enough to have a rent-controlled apartment. The house itself was a handsome old structure in the Federal style. All the front windows had white-painted boxes of geraniums or ivy on the sills. The outside knob and number plate were polished brass. The garbage cans had their lids on; the entryway had been swept. There was a little sign that read "Please curb your dog." Under it someone had written, "No shit?"

Calvin Case lived in apartment 3-B. Delaney pushed the bell and leaned down to the intercom. He waited, but there was no answer. He pushed the bell again, three long rings. This time a harsh masculine voice said, "What the hell. Yes?"

"Mr. Calvin Case?"

"Yes. What do you want?"

"My name is Captain Edward X. Delaney. Of the New York Police Department. I'd like to talk to you for a few minutes."

"What about?" The voice was loud, slurred, and the mechanics of the intercom made it raucous.

"It's about an investigation I'm conducting."

There was silence. It lasted so long that Delaney was about to ring again when the door lock buzzed, and he grabbed the knob hastily, opened the door, and climbed carpeted steps to 3-B. There was another bell. He rang, and again he waited for what he thought was an unusually long time. Then another buzzer sounded. He was startled and did nothing. When you rang the bell of an apartment door, you expected someone to inquire from within or open the door. But now a buzzer sounded.

Then, remembering the man was an invalid, and cursing his own stupidity, Delaney rang again. The answering buzz seemed long and angry. He pushed the door open, stepped into the dark hallway of a small, cluttered apartment. Delaney shut the door firmly behind him, heard the electric lock click.

"Mr. Case?" he called.

"In here." The voice was harsh, almost cracked.

The captain walked through a littered living room. Someone slept in here, on a sofa bed that was still unmade. There were signs of a woman's presence: a tossed nightgown, a powder box and makeup kit on an end table, lipsticked cigarette butts, tossed copies of "Vogue" and "Bride." But there were a few plants at the windows, a tall tin vase of fresh rhododendron leaves. Someone was making an effort.

Delaney stepped through the disorder to an open door leading to the rear of the apartment. Curiously, the door frame between the cluttered living room and the bedroom beyond had been fitted with a window shade with a cord pull. The shade, Delaney guessed, could be pulled down almost to the floor, shutting off light, affording some kind of privacy, but not as sound-proof as a door. And, of course, it couldn't be locked.

He ducked under the hanging shade and looked about the bedroom. Dusty windows, frayed curtains, plaster curls from the ceiling, a stained rag rug, two good oak dressers with drawers partly open, newspapers and magazines scattered on the floor. And then the bed, and on the opposite wall a shocking big stain as if someone had thrown a full bottle, watched it splinter and the contents drip down.

The smell was . . . something. Stale whiskey, stale bedclothes, stale flesh. Urine and excrement. There was a tiny log of incense smoking in a cast iron pot; it made things worse. The room was rotting. Delaney had smelled odors more ferocious than this—was there a cop who had not?—but it never got easier. He breathed through his mouth and turned to the man in the bed.

It was a big bed, occupied at some time in the past, Delaney imagined, by Calvin Case and his wife. Now she slept on the convertible in the living room. The bed was surrounded, by tables, chairs, magazine racks, a telephone stand, a wheeled cart with bottles and an ice bucket, on the floor an open bedpan and plastic "duck." Tissues, a half-eaten sandwich, a sodden towel, cigarette and cigar butts, a paperback book with pages torn out in a frenzy, and even a hard-cover bent and partly ripped, a broken glass, and . . . and everything.

"What the fuck do you want?"

Then he looked directly at the man in the bed.

The soiled sheet, a surprising blue, was drawn up to the chin. All Delaney saw was a square face, a square head. Uncombed hair was spread almost to the man's shoulders. The reddish mustache and beard were squarish. And untrimmed. Dark eyes burned. The full lips were stained and crusted.

"Calvin Case?"

"Yeah."

"Captain Edward X. Delaney, New York Police Department. I'm investigating the death—the murder—of a man we believe—"

"Let's see your badge."

Delaney stepped closer to the bed. The stench was sickening. He held his identification in front of Case's face. The man hardly glanced at it. Delaney stepped back.

"We believe the man was murdered with an ice ax. A mountain climber's ax. So I came—"

"You think I did it?" The cracked lips opened to reveal yellowed teeth: a death's head grin.

Delaney was shocked. "Of course not. But I need more information on ice axes. And as the best mountain climber—you've been recommended to me—I thought you might be—"

"Fuck off," Calvin Case said wearily, moving his heavy head to one side.

"You mean you won't cooperate in finding a man who—"

"Be gone," Case whispered. "Just be gone."

Delaney turned, moved away two steps, stopped. There was Barbara, and Christopher Langley, and Monica Gilbert, and all the peripheral people: Handry and Thorsen and Ferguson and Dorfman, and here was this . . . He took a deep breath, hating himself because even his furies were calculated. He turned back to the cripple on the soiled bed. He had nothing to lose.

"You goddamned cock-sucking mother-fucking son-of-a-bitch," he said steadily and tonelessly. "You shit-gutted ass-licking bastard. I'm a detective, and I detect *you*, you punky no-ball frigger. Go ahead, lie in your bed of crap. Who buys the food? Your wife—right? Who tries to keep a home for you? Your wife—right? Who empties your shit and pours your piss in the toilet? Your wife—right? And you lie there and soak up whiskey. I could smell you the minute I walked in, you piece of rot. It's great to lie in bed and feel sorry for yourself, isn't it? You corn-holing filth. Go piss and shit in your bed and drink your whiskey and work your wife to death and scream at her, you crud. A man? Oh! You're some man, you lousy ass-kissing turd. I spit on you, and I forget the day I heard your name, you dirt-eating nobody. You don't exist. You understand? You're no one."

He turned away, almost out of control, and a woman was standing in the bedroom doorway, a slight, frail blonde, her hair brushing the window shade. Her face was blanched; she was biting on a knuckle.

He took a deep breath, tried to square his shoulders, to feel bigger. He felt very small.

"Mrs. Case?"

She nodded.

"My name is Edward X. Delaney, Captain, New York Police Department. I came to ask your husband's help on an investigation. If you heard what I said, I apologize for my language. I'm very sorry. Please forgive me. I didn't know you were there."

She nodded dumbly again, still gnawing her knuckle and staring at him with wide blue eyes.

"Good-day," he said and moved to pass her in the doorway.

"Captain," the man in the bed croaked.

Delaney turned back. "Yes?"

"You're some bastard, aren't you?"

"When I have to be," Delaney nodded.

"You'll use anyone, won't you? Cripples, drunks, the helpless and the hopeless. You'll use them all."

"That's right. I'm looking for a killer. I'll use anyone who can help."

Calvin Case used the edge of his soiled blue sheet to wipe his clotted eyes clear.

"And you got a big mouth," he added. "A *biiig* mouth." He reached to the wheeled cart for a half-full bottle of whiskey and a stained glass. "Honey," he called to his wife, "we got a clean glass for Mister Captain Edward X. Delaney, New York Police Department?"

She nodded, still silent. She ran out, then came back with two glasses. Calvin Case poured a round, then set the bottle back on the cart. The three raised glasses in a silent toast, although what they were drinking to they could not have said.

"Cal, are you hungry?" his wife asked anxiously. "I've got to get back to work soon."

"No, not me. Captain, you want a sandwich?"

"Thank you, no."

"Just leave us alone, hon."

"Maybe I should just clean up a—"

"Just leave us alone. Okay, hon?"

She turned to go.

"Mrs. Case," Delaney said.

She turned back.

"Please stay. Whatever your husband and I have to discuss, there is no reason why you can't hear it."

She was startled. She looked back and forth, man to man, not knowing.

Calvin Case sighed. "You're something," he said to Captain Delaney. "You're really something."

"That's right," Delaney nodded. "I'm something."

"You barge in here and you take over."

"You want to talk now?" Delaney asked impatiently. "Do you want to answer my questions?"

"First tell me what it's all about."

"A man was killed with a strange weapon. We think it was an ice ax and—"

"Who's 'we'?"

"*I* think it was an ice ax. I want to know more about it, and your name was given to me as the most experienced mountaineer in New York."

"Was," Case said softly. "*Was.*"

They sipped their drinks, looked at each other stonily. For once, there were no sirens, no buffalo whistles, no trembles of blasting or street sounds, no city noises. It was on this very block, Delaney recalled, that a fine old town house was accidentally demolished by a group of bumbling revolutionaries, proving their love of the human race by preparing bombs in the basement. Now, in the Case apartment, they existed in a bubble of silence, and unconsciously they lowered their voices.

"A captain comes to investigate a crime?" Case asked quietly. "Even a murder? No, no. A uniformed cop or a detective, yes. A captain, no. What's it all about, Delaney?"

The Captain took a deep breath. "I'm on leave of absence. I'm not on active duty. You're under no obligation to answer my questions. I was commander of the Two-five-one Precinct. Uptown. A man was killed there about a month ago. On the street. Maybe you read about it. Frank Lombard, a city councilman. A lot of men are working on the case, but they're getting nowhere. They haven't even identified the weapon used. I started looking into it on my own time. It's not official; as I told you, I'm on leave of absence. Then, three days ago, another man was attacked not too far from where Lombard was killed. This man is still alive but will probably die. His wound is like Lombard's: a skull puncture. I think it was done with an ice ax."

"What makes you think so?"

"The nature of the wound, the size and shape. And an ice ax has been used as a murder weapon before. It was used to assassinate Leon Trotsky in Mexico City in nineteen-forty."

"What do you want from me?"

"Whatever you can tell me about ice axes, who makes them, where you buy them, what they're used for."

Calvin Case looked at his wife. "Will you get my axes, hon? They're in the hall closet."

While she was gone the men didn't speak. Case motioned toward a chair, but Delaney shook his head. Finally Mrs. Case came back, awkwardly clutching five axes. Two were under an arm; she held the handles of the other three in a clump.

"Dump 'em on the bed," Case ordered, and she obediently let them slide onto the soiled sheet.

Delaney stood over them, inspected them swiftly, then grabbed. It was an all-steel implement, hatchet-length, the handle bound in leather. From the butt of the handle hung a thong loop. The head had a hammer on one side, a pick on the other. The pick was exactly like that described by Christopher Langley; about five inches long, it was square-shaped at the shaft, then tapered to a thinning triangle. As it tapered, the spike curved downward and ended in a sharp point. On the underside were four little saw teeth. The entire head was a bright red, the leather-covered handle a bright blue. Between was a naked shaft of polished steel. There was a stamping on the side of the head: a small inscription. Delaney put on his glasses to read it: "Made in West Germany."

"This—" he began.

"That's not an ice ax," Calvin Case interrupted. "Technically, it's an ice hammer. But most people call it an ice ax. They lump all these things together."

"You bought it in West Germany?"

"No. Right here in New York. The best mountain gear is made in West Germany, Austria and Switzerland. But they export all over the world."

"Where in New York did you buy it?"

"A place I used to work. I got an employees' discount on it. It's down on Spring Street, a place called 'Outside Life.' They sell gear for hunting, fishing, camping, safaris, mountaineering, back-packing—stuff like that."

"May I use your phone?"

"Help yourself."

He was so encouraged, so excited, that he couldn't remember Christopher Langley's phone number and had to look it up in his pocket notebook. But he would not put the short ice ax down; he held it along with the phone in one hand while he dialed. He finally got through.

"Mr. Langley? Delaney here."

"Oh, Captain! I should have called, but I really have nothing to report. I've made a list of possible sources, and I've been visiting six or seven shops a day. But so far I—"

"Mr. Langley, do you have your list handy?"

"Why yes, Captain. Right here. I was just about to start out when you called."

"Do you have a store named Outside Life on your list?"

"Outside Life? Just a minute . . . Yes, here it is. It's on Spring Street."

"That's the one."

"Yes, I have it. I've divided my list into neighborhoods, and I have that in the downtown section. I haven't been there yet."

"Mr. Langley. I have a lead they may have what we want. Could you get there today?"

"Of course. I'll go directly."

"Thank you. Please call me at once, whether you find it or not. I'll either be home or at the hospital."

He hung up, turned back to Calvin Case, still holding the ice ax. He didn't want to let it go. He swung the tool in a chopping stroke. Then he raised it high and slashed down.

"Nice balance," he nodded.

"Sure," Case agreed. "And plenty of weight. You could kill a man easily."

"Tell me about ice axes."

Calvin Case told him what he could. It wasn't much. He thought the modern ice ax had evolved from the ancient Alpinestock, a staff as long as a shepherd's crook. In fact, Case had seen several still in use in Switzerland. They were tipped with hand-hammered iron spikes, and used to probe the depth of snow, try the consistency of ice, test stone ledges and overhangs, probe crevasses.

"Then," Case said, "the two-handed ice ax was developed." He leaned forward from the waist to pick up samples from the foot of his bed. Apparently he was naked under the sheet. His upper torso had once been thick and muscular. Now it had gone to flab: pale flesh matted with reddish hair, smelling rankly.

He showed the long ice axes to Delaney, explaining how the implement could be used as a cane, driven into ice as a rope support, the mattock side of the head used to chop foot and hand holds in ice as capable of load-bearing as granite. The butt end of the handle varied. It could be a plain spike for hiking on glaciers, or fitted with a small thonged wheel for walking on crusted snow, or simply supplied with a small knurled cap.

"Where did you get all these?" Delaney asked.

"These two in Austria. This one in West Germany. This one in Geneva."

"You can buy them anywhere?"

"Anywhere in Europe, sure. Climbing is very big over there."

"And here?"

"There must be a dozen stores in New York. Maybe more. And other places too, of course. The West Coast, for instance."

"And this one?" Delaney had slipped the thong loop of the short ice ax over his wrist. "What's this used for?"

"Like I told you, technically it's an ice hammer. If you're on stone, you can start a hole with the pick end. Then you try to hammer in a piton with the other side of the head. A piton is a steel peg. It has a loop on top, and you can attach a line to it or thread it through."

Delaney drew two fingers across the head of the ax he held. Then he rubbed the tips of the two fingers with his thumb and grinned.

"You look happy," Case said, pouring himself another whiskey.

"I am. Oiled."

"What?"

"The ax head is oiled."

"Oh . . . sure. Evelyn keeps all my stuff cleaned and oiled. She thinks I'm going to climb again some day. Don't you, hon?"

Delaney turned to look at her. She nodded mutely, tried to smile. He smiled in return.

"What kind of oil do you use, Mrs. Case?"

"Oh . . . I don't know. It's regular oil. I buy it in a hardware store on Sixth Avenue."

"A thin oil," Calvin Case said. "Like sewing machine oil. Nothing special about it."

"Do all climbers keep their tools cleaned and oiled?"

"The good ones do. And sharp."

Delaney nodded. Regretfully he relinquished the short-handled ice ax, putting it back with the others on the foot of Case's bed.

"You said you worked for Outside Life, where you bought this?"

"That's right. For almost ten years. I was in charge of the mountaineering department. They gave me all the time off I wanted for climbs. It was good publicity for them."

"Suppose I wanted to buy an ice ax like that. I just walk in and put down my money. Right?"

"Sure. That one cost about fifteen dollars. But that was five years ago."

"Do I just get a cash register receipt, or do they write out an itemized sales check?"

Case looked at him narrowly. Then his bearded face opened into a smile; he showed his stained teeth again.

"Mr. Detective," he grinned. "Thinking every minute, aren't you? Well, as far as Outside Life goes, you're in luck. A sales slip is written out—or was, when I worked there. You got the customer's name and address. This was because Sol Appel, who owns the place, does a big mail order business. He gets out a Summer and Winter catalogue, and he's always anxious to add to his list. Then, on the slip, you wrote out the items purchased."

"After the customer's name and address were added to the mailing list, how long were the sales slips kept? Do you know?"

"Oh Jesus, years and years. The basement was full of them. But don't get your balls in an uproar, Captain. Outside Life isn't the only place in New York where you can buy an ice ax. And most of the other places just ring up the total purchase. There's no record of the customer's name, address, or what was bought. And, like I told you, most of these things are imported. You can buy an ice ax in London, Paris, Berlin, Vienna, Rome, Geneva, and points in between. And in Los Angeles, San Francisco, Boston, Portland, Seattle, Montreal, and a hundred other places. So where does that leave you?"

"Thank you very much," Captain Delaney said, without irony. "You have really been a big help, and I appreciate your cooperation. I apologize for the way I spoke."

Calvin Case made a gesture, a wave Delaney couldn't interpret.

"What are you going to do now, Captain?"

"Do now? Oh, you mean my next step. Well, you heard my telephone call. A man who is helping me is on his way to Outside Life. If he is able to purchase an ice ax like yours, then I'll go down there, ask if they'll let me go through their sales slips and make a list of people who have bought ice axes."

"But I just told you, there'll be thousands of sales checks. *Thousands!*"

"I know."

"And there are other stores in New York that sell ice axes with no record of the buyer. And stores all over the world that sell them."

244

"I know."

"You're a fool," Calvin Case said dully, turning his face away. "I thought for awhile you weren't, but now I think you are."

"Cal," his wife said softly, but he didn't look at her.

"I don't know what you think detective work is like," Delaney said, staring at the man in the bed. "Most people have been conditioned by novels, the movies and TV. They think it's either exotic clues and devilishly clever deductive reasoning, or else they figure it's all rooftop chases, breaking down doors, and shoot-outs on the subway tracks. All that is maybe five percent of what a detective does. Now I'll tell you how he mostly spends his time. About fifteen years ago a little girl was snatched on a street out on Long Island. She was walking home from school. A car pulled up alongside her and the driver said something. She came over to the car. A little girl. The driver opened the door, grabbed her, pulled her inside, and took off. There was an eyewitness to this, an old woman who 'thought' it was a dark car, black or dark blue or dark green or maroon. And she 'thought' it had a New York license plate. She wasn't sure of anything. Anyway, the parents got a ransom note. They followed instructions exactly: they didn't call the cops and they paid off. The little girl was found dead three days later. *Then* the FBI was called in. They had two things to work on: it *might* have been a New York license plate on the car, and the ransom note was hand-written. So the FBI called in about sixty agents from all over, and they were given a crash course in handwriting identification. Big blow-ups of parts of the ransom note were pasted on the walls. Three shifts of twenty men each started going through every application for an automobile license that originated on Long Island. They worked around the clock. How many signatures? Thousands? Millions, more likely. The agents set aside the possibles, and then handwriting experts took over to narrow it down."

"Did they get the man?" Evelyn Case burst out.

"Oh, sure," Delaney nodded. "They got him. Eventually. And if they hadn't found it in the Long Island applications, they'd have inspected every license in New York State. Millions and millions and millions. I'm telling you all this so you'll know what detective work usually is: common sense; a realization that you've got to start somewhere; hard, grinding, routine labor; and percentages. That's about it. Again, I thank you for your help."

He was almost at the shaded doorway to the living room when Calvin Case spoke in a faint, almost wispy voice.

"Captain."

Delaney turned. "Yes?"

"If you do find the ax at Outside Life, who'll go through the sales slips?"

Delaney shrugged. "I will. Someone will. They'll be checked."

"Sometimes the items listed on the sales slips are just by stock number. You won't know what they are."

"I'll get identification from the owner. I'll learn what the stock numbers mean."

"Captain, I've got all the time in the world. I'm not going any place. I could go through those sales checks. I know what to look for. I could pull out every slip that shows an ice ax purchase faster than you could."

Delaney looked at him a long moment, expressionless. "I'll let you know," he nodded.

Evelyn Case saw him to the outside door.

"Thank you," she said softly.

When he left the Case home he walked directly over to Sixth Avenue and turned south, looking for a hardware store. Nothing. He returned to 11th Street and walked north. Still nothing. Then, across Sixth Avenue, on the west side, he saw one.

"A little can of oil," he told the clerk. "Like sewing machine oil."

He was offered a small, square can with a long neck sealed with a little red cap.

"Can I oil tools with this?" he asked.

"Of course," the clerk assured him. "Tools, sewing machines, electric fans, locks . . . anything. It's the biggest selling all-purpose oil in the country."

Thanks a lot, Delaney thought ruefully. He bought the can of oil.

He shouldn't have taken a cab. They still had sizable balances in their savings and checking accounts, they owned securities (mostly tax-exempt municipal bonds) and, of course, they owned their brownstone. But Delaney was no longer on salary, and Barbara's medical and hospital bills were frightening, So he really should have taken the subway and changed at 59th Street for a bus. But he felt so encouraged, so optimistic, that he decided to buy a cab to the hospital. On the way uptown he took the little red cap off the oil can and squeezed a few drops of oil onto his fingertips. He rubbed it against his thumb. Thin oil. It felt good, and he smiled.

But Barbara wasn't in her room. The floor nurse explained she had been taken down to the lab for more X-rays and tests. Delaney left a short note on her bedside table: "Hello. I was here. See you this evening. I love you. Edward."

He hurried home, stripped off overcoat and jacket, loosened his tie, rolled up his cuffs, put on his carpet slippers. Mary was there and had a beef stew cooking in a Dutch oven. But he asked her to let it cool after it was done; he had too much to do to think about eating.

He had cleaned out the two upper drawers of a metal business file cabinet in the study. In the top drawer he had filed the copies of the Operation Lombard reports. Methodically, he had divided this file in two: Frank Lombard and Bernard Gilbert. Under each heading he had broken the reports down into categories: Weapon, Motive, Wound, Personal History, etc.

In the second drawer he had started his own file, a thin folder that consisted mostly, at this time, of jotted notes.

Now he began to expand these notes into reports, to whom or for what purpose he could not say. But he had worked this way on all his investigations for many years, and frequently found it valuable to put his own instinctive reactions and questions into words. In happier times Barbara had typed out his notes on her electric portable, and that was a big help. But he had never solved the mysteries of the electric, and now would have to be content with handwritten reports.

He started with the long-delayed directory of all the people involved, their addresses and telephone numbers, if he had them or could find them in the book. Then he wrote out reports of his meeting with Thorsen and Johnson, of his interviews with Lombard's widow, mother, and associates, his talks with Dorfman, with Ferguson. He wrote as rapidly as he could, transcribing scribbles he had made in his pocket notebook, on envelopes of letters, on scraps of paper torn from magazines and newspaper margins.

He wrote of his meetings with Thomas Handry, with Christopher Langley, with Calvin Case. He described the bricklayers' hammer, the rock hounds' hammer, and Case's ice ax—where they had been purchased, when, what they cost, and what they were used for. He wrote a report of his interrogation of Monica Gilbert, his purchase of the can of light machine oil, his filing of a missing driver's license report.

He should have done all this weeks ago, and he was anxious to catch up and then to keep his file current with daily additions. It might mean nothing, it probably meant nothing, but it seemed important to him to have a written record of what he had done, and the growing mass of paper was, somehow, reassuring. At the rear of the second file drawer he placed the bricklayers' hammer, the rock hounds' hammer, and the can of oil: physical evidence.

He worked steadily, stopping twice just long enough to get bottles of cold beer from the kitchen. Mary was upstairs, cleaning, but she had turned the light out under the stew. He lifted the lid and sniffed experimentally. The steam smelled great.

He wrote as clearly and as swiftly as he could, but he admitted his handwriting was miserable. Barbara could read it, but who else could? Still, his neat manila file folders grew: "The Suspect," Weapon, Motive, Interrogations, Timing, Autopsies, etc. It all looked very official and impressive.

Late in the afternoon, still writing as fast as he could, Mary departed, with a firm command to eat the stew befo e he collapsed from malnutrition. He locked the door behind her, went back to his reports and then, a few minutes later, the front door bell chimed. He threw his pen down in anger, thought, then said aloud, "Please, God, let it be Langley. With the ax."

He peered through the narrow glass side panels, and it was Langley. Bearing a paper-wrapped parcel. And beaming. Delaney threw open the door.

"Got it!" Langley cried.

The Captain could not tell him he had held the same thing in his hands a few hours previously; he would not rob this wonderful little man of his moment of triumph.

In the study they inspected the ice ax together. It was a duplicate of the one Calvin Case owned. They went over it, pointing out to each other the required features: the tapering pick, the downward curve, the sharp point, the all-steel construction.

"Oh yes," Delaney nodded. "Mr. Langley, I think this is it. Congratulations."

"Oh . . ." Langley said, waving in the air. "You gave me the lead. Who told you about Outside Life?"

"A man I happened to meet," Delaney said vaguely. "He was interested in mountain climbing and happened to mention that store. Pure luck. But you'd have gotten there eventually."

"Excellent balance," Langley said, hefting the tool. "Very well made indeed. Well . . ."

"Yes?" Delaney said.

"Well, I suppose my job is finished," the old man said. "I mean, we've found the weapon, haven't we?"

"What we think is the weapon."

"Yes. Of course. But here it is, isn't it? I mean, I don't suppose you have anything more for me to do. So I'll . . ."

His voice died away, and he turned the ice ax over and over in his hands, staring at it.

"Nothing more for you to do?" Delaney said incredulously. "Mr. Langley, I have a great deal more I'd like you to do. But you've done so much already, I hesitate to ask."

"What?" Langley interrupted eagerly. "What? Tell me what. I don't want to stop now. Really I don't. What's to be done? Please tell me."

"Well . . ." Delaney said, "we don't know that Outside Life is the only store in New York that sells this type of ice ax. You have other stores on your list you haven't visited yet, don't you?"

"Oh my yes."

"Well, we must investigate and make a hard list of every place in New York that sells this ice ax. This one or one like it. That involves finding out how many American companies manufacture this type of ax and who they wholesale to and who the wholesalers retail to in the New York area. Then— you see here? On the side of the head? It says 'Made in West Germany.' Imported. And maybe from Austria and Switzerland as well. So we must find out who the exporters are and who, over here, they sell to. Mr. Langley, that's a hell of a lot of work, and I hesitate to ask—"

"I'll do it!" Christopher Langley cried. "My goodness, I had no idea detective work was so—so involved. But I can understand why it's necessary. You want the source of every ice ax like this sold in the New York area. Am I correct?"

"Exactly," Delaney nodded. "We'll start with the New York area, and then we'll branch out. But it's so much work. I can't—"

Christopher Langley held up a little hand.

"Please," he said. "Captain, I *want* to do it. I've never felt so *alive* in my life. Now what I'll do is this: first I'll check out all the other stores on my list to see if they carry ice axes. I'll keep a record of the ones that do. Then I'll go to the library and consult a directory of domestic tool manufacturers. I'll query every one of them, or write for their catalogues to determine if they manufacture a tool like this. At the same time I'll check with European embassies, consulates and trade commissions and find out who's importing these implements to the U.S. How does that sound?"

Delaney looked at him admiringly. "Mr. Langley, I wish I had had you working with me on some of my cases in the past. You're a wonder, you are."

"Oh . . ." Langley said, blushing with pleasure, "you know . . ."

"I think your plan is excellent, and if you're willing to work at it—and it's going to be a lot of hard, grinding work—all I can say is 'Thank you' because what you'll be doing is important."

Key word.

"Important," Langley repeated. "Yes. Thank you."

They agreed Delaney could retain possession of the Outside Life ice ax. He placed it carefully in the rear of the second file cabinet drawer. His "exhibits" were growing. Then he walked Langley to the door.

"And how is the Widow Zimmerman?" he asked.

"What? Oh. Very well, thank you. She's been very kind to me. You know . . ."

"Of course. My wife thought very well of her."

"Did she!"

"Oh yes. Liked her very much. Thought she was a very warm hearted, sincere, out-going woman."

"Oh yes. Oh yes. She is all that. Did you eat any of the gefilte fish, Captain?"

"No, I didn't."

"It grows on you. An acquired taste, I suspect. Well . . ."

The little man started out. But the Captain called, "Oh, Mr. Langley, just one more thing," and he turned back.

"Did you get a sales check when you bought the ice ax at Outside Life?"

"A sales check? Oh, yes. Here it is."

He pulled it from his overcoat pocket and handed it to Delaney. The Captain inspected it eagerly. It bore Langley's name and address, the time ("Mountain ax—4B54C") and the price, $18.95, with the city sales tax added, and the total.

"The clerk asked for my name and address because they send out free catalogues twice a year and want to add to their mailing list. I gave my right name. That was all right, wasn't it, Captain?"

"Of course."

"And I thought their catalogue might be interesting. They do carry some fascinating items."

"May I keep this sales check?"

"Naturally."

"You're spending a lot of money on this case, Mr. Langley."

He smiled, tossed a hand in the air, and strutted out, the debonair boulevardier.

After the door was locked behind him, the Captain returned to his study, determined to take up his task of writing out the complete reports of his investigation. But he faltered. Finally he gave it up; something was bothering him. He went into the kitchen. The pot of stew was on the cold range. Using a long-handled fork, he stood there and ate three pieces of luke-warm beef, a potato, a small onion, and two slices of carrot. It all tasted like sawdust but, knowing Mary's cooking, he supposed it was good and the fault was his.

Later, at the hospital, he told Barbara what the problem was. She was quiet, almost apathetic, lying in her bed, and he wasn't certain she was listening or, if she was, if she understood. She stared at him with what he thought were fevered eyes, wide and brilliant.

He told her everything that had happened during the day, omitting only the call from the bookseller about the Honey Bunch books. He wanted to surprise her with that. But he told her of Langley buying the ice ax and how he, Delaney, was convinced that a similar tool had been used in the Lombard and Gilbert attacks.

"I know what should be done now," he said. "I already have Langley working on other places where an ice ax can be bought. He'll be checking retailers, wholesalers, manufacturers and importers. It's a big job for one man. Then I must try to get a copy of Outside Life's mailing list. I don't know how big it is, but it's bound to be extensive. Someone's got to go through it and pull the names and addresses of every resident of the Two-five-one Precinct. I'm almost certain the killer lives in the neighborhood. Then I want to get all the sales slips of Outside Life, for as many years as they've kept them, again to look for buyers of ice axes who live in the Precinct. And that checking and cross-checking will have to be done at every store where Langley discovers ice axes are sold. And I'm sure some of them won't have mailing lists or itemized sales checks, so the whole thing may be a monumental waste of time. But I think it has to be done, don't you?"

"Yes," she said firmly. "No doubt of it. Besides, it's your only lead, isn't it?"

"The only one," he nodded grimly. "But it's going to take a lot of time."

She looked at him a few moments, then smiled softly.

"I know what's bothering you, Edward. You think that even with Mr. Langley and Calvin Case helping you, checking all the lists and sales slips will take too much time. You're afraid someone else may be wounded or killed while you're messing around with mailing lists. You're wondering if perhaps you shouldn't turn over what you have right now to Operation Lombard, and let Broughton and his five hundred detectives get on it. They could do it so much faster."

"Yes," he said, grateful that she was thinking clearly now, her mind attuned to his. "That's exactly what's worrying me. How do you feel about it?"

"Would Broughton follow up on what you gave him?"

"Chief Pauley sure as hell would. I'd go to him. He's getting desperate now. And for good reason. He's got *nothing*. He'd grab at this and really do a job."

They were silent then. He came over to sit by her bedside and hold her hand. Neither spoke for several minutes.

"It's really a moral problem, isn't it?" she said finally.

He nodded miserably. "It's my own pride and ambition and ego . . . And my commitment to Thorsen and Johnson, of course. But if I don't do it, and someone else gets killed, I'll have a lot to answer for."

She didn't ask to whom.

"I could help you with the lists," she said faintly. "Most of the time I just lie here and read or sleep. But I have my good days, and I could help."

He squeezed her hand, smiled sadly. "You can help most by telling me what to do."

"When did you ever do what I told you to do?" she scoffed. "You go your own way, and you know it."

He grinned. "But you help," he assured her. "You sort things out for me."

"Edward, I don't think you should do anything immediately. Ivar Thorsen is deeply involved in this, and so is Inspector Johnson. If you go to Broughton, or even Chief Pauley, and tell them what you've discovered and what you suspect, they're sure to ask who authorized you to investigate."

"I could keep Thorsen and Johnson out of it. Don't forget, I have that letter from the Commissioner."

"But it would still be a mess, wouldn't it? And Broughton would probably know Thorsen is involved; the two of you have been so close for so long. Edward, why don't you have a talk with Ivar and Inspector Johnson? Tell them what you want to do. Discuss it. They're reasonable men; maybe they can suggest something. I know how much this case means to you."

"Yes," he said, looking down, "it does. More every day. And when Thorsen went to the scene of the Gilbert attack, he was really spooked. He as much as said that this business of cutting Broughton down was small stuff compared to finding the killer. Yes, that's the best thing to do. I'll talk to Thorsen and Johnson, and tell them I want to go to Broughton with what I've got. I hate the thought of it—that shit! But maybe it has to be done. Well, I'll think about it some more. I'll try to see them tomorrow, so I may not be over at noon. But I'll come in the evening and tell you how it all came out."

"Remember, don't lose your temper, Edward."

"When did I ever lose my temper?" he demanded. "I'm always in complete control."

They both laughed.

6

He shaved with an old-fashioned straight razor, one of a matched pair his father had used. They were handsome implements of Swedish steel with bone handles. Each morning, alternating, he took a razor from the worn, velvet-lined case and honed it lightly on a leather strop that hung from the inside knob of the bathroom door.

Barbara could never conceal her dislike of the naked steel. She had bought him an electric shaver one Christmas and, to please her, he had used it a few times at home. Then he had taken it to his office in the precinct house where, he assured her, he frequently used it for a "touch-up" when he had a meeting late in the afternoon or evening. She nodded, accepting his lie. Perhaps she sensed that the reason he used the straight razors was because they had belonged to his father, a man he worshipped.

Now, this morning, drawing the fine steel slowly and carefully down his lathered jaw, he listened to a news broadcast from the little transistor radio in the bedroom and learned, from a brief announcement, that Bernard Gilbert, victim of a midnight street attack, had died without regaining consciousness. Delaney's hand did not falter, and he finished his shave steadily, wiped off excess lather, splashed lotion, powdered lightly, dressed in his usual dark suit, white shirt, striped tie, and went down to the kitchen for breakfast, bolstered and carried along by habit. He stopped in the study just long enough to jot a little note to himself to write a letter of condolence to Monica Gilbert.

He greeted Mary, accepted orange juice, one poached egg on unbuttered toast, and black coffee. They chatted about the weather, about Mrs. Delaney's condition, and he approved of Mary's plan to strip the furniture in Barbara's sewing room of chintz slipcovers and send them all to the dry cleaner.

Later, in the study, he wrote out a pencilled rough of his letter of condolence to Mrs. Gilbert. When he had it the way he wanted—admitting it was stilted, but there was no way of getting around *that*—he copied it in ink, addressed and stamped the envelope and put it aside, intending to mail it when he left the house.

It was then almost 9:30, and he called the Medical Examiner's office. Ferguson wasn't in yet but was expected momentarily. Delaney waited patiently for fifteen minutes, making circular doodles on a scratch pad, a thin line that went around and around in a narrowing spiral. Then he called again and was put through to Ferguson.

"I know," the doctor said, "he's dead. I heard when I got in."

"Did you get it?"

"Yes. The lump is on the way down now. The big problem in my life, Edward, is whether to do a cut-'em-up before lunch or after. I finally decided before is better. So I'll probably get to him about eleven or eleven-thirty."

"I'd like to see you before you start."

"I can't get out, Edward. No way. I'm tied up here with other things."

"I'll come down. Could you give me about fifteen minutes at eleven o'clock?"

"Important?"

"I think so."

"You can't tell me on the phone?"

"No. It's something I've got to show you, to give you."

"All right, Edward. Fifteen minutes at eleven."

"Thank you, doctor."

First he went into the kitchen. He tore a square of paper towel off the roller, then a square of wax paper from the package, then a square of aluminum foil. Back in the study he took from the file drawer the can of light machine oil and the ice ax Christopher Langley had purchased at Outside Life.

He removed the cap from the oil can and impregnated the paper towel with oil. He folded it carefully into wax paper, then wrapped the whole thing in aluminum foil, pressing down hard on the folds so the oil wouldn't seep out. He put the package in a heavy manila envelope.

Then he sharpened a pencil, using his penknife to scrape the graphite to a long point. He placed the ice ax head on a sheet of good rag stationery and carefully traced a profile with his sharpened pencil, going very slowly, taking particular care to include the four little saw teeth on the underside of the point.

Then he took out his desk ruler and measured the size of the spike where it left the head, as a square. Each of the four sides, as closely as he could determine, was 15/16th of an inch. He then drew a square to those dimensions on the same sheet of paper with the silhouette of the pick. He folded the sheet, tucked it into his breast pocket. He took the envelope with the oil impregnated paper towel and started out. He pulled on his overcoat and hat, shouted upstairs to Mary to tell her he was leaving, and heard her answering shout. At the last minute, halfway out the door, he remembered his letter of condolence to Monica Gilbert and went back into the study to pick it up. He dropped it in the first mailbox he passed.

"Better make this quick, Edward," Dr. Ferguson said. "Broughton is sending one of his boys down to witness the autopsy. He wants a preliminary verbal report before he gets the official form."

"I'll make it fast. Did the doctors at Mother of Mercy tell you anything?"

"Not much. As I told you, Gilbert was struck from the front, the wound about two inches above the normal hair line. The blow apparently knocked him backward, and the weapon was pulled free before he fell. As a result, the penetration is reasonably clean and neat, so I should be able to get a better profile of the wound than on the Lombard snuff."

"Good." Delaney unfolded his paper. "Doctor, this is what I think the penetration profile will look like. It's hard to tell from this, but the spike starts out as a square. Here, in this little drawing, are the dimensions, about an inch on each side. If I'm right, that should be the size of the outside wound, at scalp and skull. Then the square changes to a triangular pick, and tapers, and curves downward, coming to a sharp point."

"Is this your imagination, or was it traced from an actual weapon?"

"It was traced."

"All right. I don't want to know anything more. What are these?"

"Four little saw teeth on the underside of the point. You may find some rough abrasions on the lower surface of the wound."

"I may, eh? The brain isn't hard cheddar, you know. You want me to work with this paper open on the table alongside the corpse?"

"Not if Broughton's man is there."

"I didn't think so."

"Couldn't you just take a look at it, doctor? Just in case?"

"Sure," Ferguson said, folding up the paper and sliding it into his hip pocket. "What else have you got?"

"In this envelope is a folded packet of aluminum foil, and inside that is an envelope of wax paper, and inside that is a paper towel soaked in oil. Light machine oil."

"So?"

"You mentioned there were traces of oil in the Lombard wound. You thought it was probably Lombard's hair oil, but it was too slight for analysis."

"But Gilbert was bald—at least where he was hit he was bald."

"That's the point. It couldn't be hair oil. But I'm hoping there will be oil in the Gilbert wound. Light machine oil."

Ferguson pushed back in his swivel chair and stared at him. Then the doctor pulled his wool tie open, unbuttoned the neck of his flannel shirt.

"You're a lovely man, Edward," he said, "and the best detective in town, but Gilbert's wound was X-rayed, probed and flushed at Mother of Mercy."

"If there was any oil in it, there couldn't be any now?"

"I didn't say that. But it sure as hell cuts down on your chances."

"What about the Olfactory Analysis Indicator?"

"The OAI? What about it?"

"How much do you know about it, doctor?"

"About as much as you do. You read the last bulletin, didn't you?"

"Yes. Sort of inconclusive, wasn't it?"

"It surely was. The idea is to develop a sniffer not much larger than a vacuum cleaner. Portable. It could be taken to the scene of a crime, inhale an air sample, and either identify the odors immediately or store the air sample so it could be taken back to the lab and analyzed by a master machine. Well, they're a long way from that right now. It's a monstrous big thing at this point, very crude, but I saw an impressive demonstration the other day. It correctly identified nine smokes from fifteen different brands of cigarettes. That's not bad."

"In other words, it's got to have a comparison to go by? Like the memory bank in a computer?"

"That's right. Oh-ho. I see what you're getting at. All right, Edward. Leave me your machine oil sample. I'll try to get a reading on tissue from Gilbert's wound. But don't count on it. The OAI is years away. It's just an experiment now."

"I realize that. But I don't want to neglect any possibility."

"You never did," Dr. Ferguson said.

"Should I wait around?"

"No point in it. The OAI analysis will take three days at least. Probably a week. As far as your drawing goes, I'll call you this afternoon or this evening. Will you be home?"

"Probably. But I may be at the hospital. You could reach me there."

"How's Barbara?"

"Getting along."

Ferguson nodded, stood, took off his tweed jacket, hung it on a coat tree, began to shrug into a stained white coat.

"Getting anywhere, Edward?" he asked.

"Who the hell knows?" Captain Delaney grumbled. "I just keep going."

"Don't we all?" the big man smiled.

Delaney called Ivar Thorsen from a lobby phone. The answering service got back to him a few minutes later and said Mr. Thorsen was not available and would he please call again at three in the afternoon.

It was the first time Thorsen had not returned his call, and it bothered Delaney. It might be, of course, that the deputy inspector was in a meeting or on his way to a precinct house, but the Captain couldn't shake a vague feeling of unease.

He consulted his pocket notebook in which he had copied the address of Outside Life. He took a taxi to Spring Street, and when he got out of the cab, he spent a few minutes walking up and down the block, looking around. It was a section of grimy loft buildings, apparently mostly occupied by small manufacturers, printers, and wholesalers of leather findings. It seemed a strange neighborhood for Outside Life.

That occupied the second and third floors of a ten-story building. Delaney walked up the stairs to the second floor, but the sign on the solid door said "Offices and Mailing. Store on third floor." So he climbed another flight, wanting to look about before he talked to—to— He consulted his notebook again: Sol Appel, the owner.

The "store" was actually one enormous, high-ceilinged loft with pipe racks, a few glass showcases, and with no attempts made at fashionable merchandizing. Most of the stock was piled on the floor, on unpainted wooden shelves, or hung from hooks driven into the whitewashed walls.

As Langley had said, it was a fascinating conglomeration: rucksacks, rubber dinghies, hiking boots, crampons, dehydrated food, kerosene lanterns, battery-heated socks, machetes, net hammocks, sleeping bags, outdoor cookware, hunting knives, fishing rods, reels, creels, pitons, nylon rope, boating gear—an endless profusion of items ranging from five-cent fishhooks to a magnificent red, three-room tent with a mosquito-netted picture window, at $1,495.00.

Outside Life seemed to have its devotees, despite its out-of-the-way location; Delaney counted at least 40 customers wandering about, and the clerks were busy writing up purchases. The Captain found his way to the mountaineering department and inspected pitons, crampons, web belts and harnesses, nylon line, aluminum-framed backpacks, and a wide variety of ice axes. There were two styles of short-handled axes: the one purchased by Langley and another, somewhat similar, but with a wooden handle and no saw-tooth serrations under the spike. Delaney inspected it, and finally found "Made in U.S.A." stamped on the handle butt.

He halted a scurrying clerk just long enough to ask for the whereabouts of Mr. Appel. "Sol's in the office," the departing clerk called over his shoulder. "Downstairs."

Delaney pushed open the heavy door on the second floor and found himself in a tiny reception room, walled with unfinished plywood panels. There was a door of clear glass leading to the open space beyond, apparently a combination warehouse and mailing room. In one corner of the reception room was a telephone operator wearing a wired headset and sitting before a push-pull switchboard that Delaney knew had been phased out of production years and years ago. Outside Life seemed to be a busy, thriving enterprise, but it was also obvious the profits weren't going into fancy offices and smart decoration.

He waited patiently until the operator had plugged and unplugged half-a-dozen calls. Finally, desperately, he said, "Mr. Appel, please. My name is—"

She stuck her head through the opening into the big room beyond and screamed, "Soll Guy to see you!"

Delaney sat on the single couch, a rickety thing covered with slashed plastic. He was amused to note an overflowing ashtray on the floor. The single decoration in the room was a plaque on the plywood wall attesting to Mr. Solomon Appel's efforts on behalf of the United Jewish Appeal.

The glass door crashed back, and a heavy, sweating man rushed in. Delaney caught a confused impression of a round, plump face (the man in the moon), a well-chewed, unlit cigar, a raveled, sleeveless sweater of hellish hue, unexpectedly "mod" jeans of dark blue with white stitching and a darker stain down one leg, and Indian moccasins decorated with beads.

"You from Benson & Hurst?" the man demanded, talking rapidly around his cigar. "I'm Sol Appel. Where the hell are those tents? You promised—"

"Wait, wait," Delaney said hastily. "I'm not from Benson & Hurst. I'm—"

"Gatters," the man said positively. "The fiberglass rods. You guys are sure giving me the rod—you know where. You said—"

"Will you wait a minute," Delaney said again, sighing. "I'm not from Gatters either. My name is Captain Edward X. Delaney. New York Police Department. Here's my identification."

Sol Appel didn't even glance at it. He raised his hands above his head, palms outward, in mock surrender.

"I give up," he said. "Whatever it was, I did it. Take me away. Now. Please get me out of this nuthouse. Do me a favor. Jail will be a pleasure."

"No, no," Delaney laughed. "Nothing like that. Mr. Appel, I wanted—"

"You're putting on a dance? A dinner? You want a few bucks? Of course. Why not? Always. Any time. So tell me—how much?"

He was already reaching for his wallet when Delaney held out a restraining hand and sighed again.

"Please, Mr. Appel, it's nothing like that. I'm not collecting for anything. All I want is a few minutes of your time."

"A few minutes? Now you're really asking for something valuable. A few minutes!" He turned back to the opened glass door. "Sam!" he screamed. "You, Sam! Get the cash. No check. The cash! You understand?"

"Is there any place we can talk?" the Captain asked.

"We're talking, aren't we?"

"All right," Delaney said doubtfully, glancing at the switchboard operator. But she was busy with her cords and plugs. "Mr. Appel, your name was given to me by Calvin Case, and I—"

"Cal!" Appel cried. He stepped close and grabbed Delaney's overcoat by the lapels. "That dear, sweet boy. How is he? Will you tell me?"

"Well . . . he's—"

"Don't tell me. He's on the booze. I know. I heard. I wanted him back. 'So you can't walk,' I told him. 'Big deal. You can think. No? You can work. No?' That's the big thing—right, Captain—uh, Captain—"

"Delaney."

"Captain Delaney. That's Irish, no?"

"Yes."

"Sure. I knew. The important thing is to work. Am I right?"

"You're right."

"Of course I'm right," Sol Appel said angrily. "So any time he wants a job, he's got it. Right here. We can use him. Tell him that. Will you tell him that?" Suddenly Appel struck his forehead with the heel of his hand. "I should have been to see him," he groaned. "What kind of a *schmuck* am I? I'm really ashamed. I'll go see him. Tell him that, Chief Delaney."

"Captain."

"Captain. Will you tell him that?"

"Yes, certainly, if I speak to him again. But that isn't the—"

"You're taking up a collection for him? You're making a benefit, Captain? It will be my pleasure to take a table for eight, and I'll—"

Delaney finally got him calmed down, a little, and seated on the plastic couch. He explained he was involved in an investigation, and the cigar-chomping Sol Appel asked no questions. Within five minutes Delaney had discovered that Outside Life had a mailing list of approximately 30,000 customers who were sent Summer and Winter catalogues. The mailings were done with metal address plates and printed labels. There was also a typed master list, and Sol Appel would be happy to provide a copy for Captain Delaney whenever he asked.

"I assure you, it'll be held in complete confidence," the Captain said earnestly.

"Who cares?" Appel shouted. "My competitors can meet my prices? Hah!"

Delaney also learned that Outside Life kept sales checks for seven years. They were stored in cardboard cartons in the basement of the loft building, filed by month and year.

"Why seven years?" he asked.

"Who the hell knows?" Appel shrugged. "My father—God rest his soul—he only died last year—I should live so long— Mike Appel—a *mensch*. You know what a *mensch* is, Captain?"

"Yes. I know. My father was an Irish *mensch*."

"Good. So he told me, 'Sol,' he said a hundred times, 'always keep the copies of the sales checks for seven years.' Who the hell knows why? That's the way he did it, that's the way I do it. Taxes or something; I don't know. Anyway, I keep them seven years. I add this year's, I throw the oldest year's away."

"Would you let me go through them?"

"Go through them? Captain, there's got to be like a hundred thousand checks there."

"If I have to, can I go through them?"

"Be my guest. Sarah! Sol Appel suddenly screamed. "You, Sarah!"

An elderly Jewish lady thrust her head through the switchboard operator's window,

"You called, Sol?" she asked.

"Tell him 'No'!" Appel screamed, and the lady nodded and withdrew.

Now that Delaney wanted to leave, Appel wouldn't let him depart. He shook his hand endlessly and talked a blue streak . . .

"Go up to the store. Pick out anything you like. Have them call me before you pay. You'll get a nice discount, believe me. You know, you Irish and us Jews are much alike. We're both poets—am I right? And who can talk these days? The Irish and the Jews only. You need a cop, you find an Irishman. You need a lawyer, you find a Jew. This stuff I sell, you think I understand it? Hah! For me, I go camping on Miami Beach or Nassau. You float on the pool there in this plastic couch with a nice, tall drink and all around these girlies in their little bitty bikinis. That, to me, is outside life. Captain, I like you. Delaney—right? You in the book? Sure, you're in the book. Next month, a Bar-Mitzvah for my nephew. I'll call you. Bring nothing, you understand? Nothing! I'll go see Calvin Case. I swear I'll go. You've got to work. Sarah! Sarah!"

Delaney finally got out of there, laughing aloud and shaking his head, so that people he passed on the stairway looked at him strangely. He didn't think Appel would remember to invite him to the Bar-Mitzvah. But if he did, Delaney decided he would go. How often do you meet a *live* man?

Well, he had found out what he wanted to know—and, as usual, it wasn't as bad as he had feared or as good as he had hoped. He walked west on Spring Street and, suddenly, pierced by the odor of frying sausage and peppers, he joined a throng of Puerto Ricans and blacks at an open luncheonette counter and had a slice of sausage pizza and a glass of sweet cola, resolutely forgetting about his diet. Sometimes . . .

He took two subways and a bus back to his home. Mary was having coffee in the kitchen, and he joined her for a cup, telling her he had already eaten lunch, but not saying what it was.

"Whatever it was, it had garlic in it," she sniffed, and he laughed.

He worked in his study until 3:00 p.m., bringing his reports up to date. The file of his own investigation was becoming pleasingly plump. It was nowhere near as extensive as the Operation Lombard reports, of course, but still, it had width to it now, it had width.

At 3:00 p.m., he called Deputy Inspector Thorsen. This time the answering service operator asked him to hold while she checked. She was back on again in a few minutes and told him Thorsen asked him to call again at seven in the evening. Delaney hung up, now convinced that something was happening, something was awry.

He put the worry away from him and went back to his notes and reports. If "The Suspect" was indeed a mountain climber —and Delaney believed he was—weren't there other possible leads to his identity other than the mailing list of Outside Life? For instance, was there a local or national club or association of mountain climbers whose membership list could be culled for residents of the 251st Precinct? Was there a newsletter or magazine devoted to mountaineering with a subscription list that could be used for the same purpose? What about books on mountain climbing? Should Delaney inquire at the library that served the 251st Precinct and try to determine who had withdrawn books on the subject?

He jotted down notes on these questions as fast as they occurred to him. Mountain climbing was, after all, a minor sport. But could you call it a *sport?* It really didn't seem to be a pastime or diversion. It seemed more of a—of a—well, the only word that came to his mind was "challenge." He also thought, for some reason, of "crusade," but that didn't make too much sense, and he resolved to talk to Calvin Case about it, and carefully made a note to himself to that effect.

Finally, almost as a casual afterthought, he came back to the problem that had been nagging him for the past few days, and he resolved to turn over everything he had to Broughton and Chief Pauley. They could follow through much faster than he could, and their investigation might, just might, prevent another death. He would have liked to stick to it on his own, but that was egotism, just egotism.

He was writing out a detailed report of his meeting with Sol Appel when the desk phone rang. He lifted the receiver and said absently, "Hello."

" 'Hello'?" Dr. Sanford Ferguson laughed. "What the hell kind of a greeting is that—'Hello?' Whatever happened to 'Captain Edward X. Delaney here'?"

"All right. Captain Edward X. Delaney here. Are you bombed?"

"On my way, m'lad. Congratulations."

"You mean the drawing was accurate?"

"Right on. The outside wound—I'm talking about the skull now—was a rough square, about an inch on each side. For the probe I used glass fiber. You know what that is?"

"A slender bundle of glass threads, flexible and transmitting light from a battery-powered source."

"You know everything, don't you, Edward? Yes, that's what I used. Tapering, curving downward to a sharp point, and I even found some evidence of heavier abrasions on the lower surface, a tearing. That could be accounted for by those little saw teeth. Not definite enough to put in my official report, but a possible, Captain, a possible."

"Thank you, doctor. And the oil?"

"No obvious sign of it. But I sent your rag and a specimen of tissue to the lab. I told you, it'll take time."

"They won't talk?"

"The lab boys? Only to me. It's just a job. They know from nothing. Happy, Edward?"

"Yes. Very. Why are you getting drunk?"

"He was so small. So small, so frail, so wasted and his heart wasn't worth a damn and he had a prick about the size of a thimble. So I'm getting drunk. Any objections?"

"No. None."

"Get the bastard, Edward."

"I will."

"Promise?"

"I promise," Captain Edward X. Delaney said.

He got to the hospital shortly after 5:30, but the visit was a disaster. Barbara immediately started talking of a cousin of hers who had died twenty years ago, and then began speaking of "this terrible war." He thought she was talking about Vietnam, but then she spoke of Tom Hendricks, a lieutenant of Marines, and he realized she was talking about the Korean War, in which Tom Hendricks had been killed. Then she sang a verse of "Black is the color of my true love's hair," and he didn't know what to do.

He sat beside her, tried to soothe her. But she would not be still. She gabbled of Mary, of the drapes in the third-floor bedrooms, Thorsen, violets, a dead dog—and who had taken her children away? He was frightened and close to weeping. He pushed the bell for the nurse, but when no one came, he rushed into the corridor and almost dragged in the first nurse he saw.

Barbara was still babbling, eyes closed, an almost-smile on her lips, and he waited anxiously, alone, while the nurse left for a moment to consult her medication chart. He listened to a never-ending stream of meaningless chatter: Lombard and Honey Bunch and suddenly, "I need a hundred dollars," and Eddie and Liza, and then she was at the carrousel in the park, describing it and laughing, and the painted horses went round and round, and then the nurse came back with a covered tray, removed a hypodermic, gave Barbara a shot in the arm, near the wrist. In a few moments she was calm, then sleeping.

"Jesus Christ," Delaney breathed, "what happened to her? What was that?"

"Just upset," the nurse smiled mechanically. "She's all right now. She's sleeping peaceably."

"Peacefully," the Captain said.

"Peacefully," the nurse repeated obediently. "If you have any questions, please contact your doctor in the morning."

She marched out. Delaney stared after her, wondering if there was any end to the madness in the world. He turned back to the bed. Barbara was, apparently, sleeping peacefully. He felt so goddamned frightened, helpless, furious.

It wasn't 7:00 p.m., so he couldn't call Thorsen. He walked home, hoping, just hoping, he might be attacked. He was not armed, but he didn't care. He would kick them in the balls, bite their throats—he was in that mood. He looked around at the shadowed streets. "Try me," he wanted to shout. "Come on! I'm here."

He got inside, took off his hat and coat, treated himself to two straight whiskies. He calmed down, gradually. What a thing that had been. He was home now, unhurt, thinking clearly. But Barbara . . .

He sat stolidly sipping his whiskey until 7:00 p.m. Then he called Thorsen's number, not really caring. Thorsen called him back almost immediately.

"Edward?"

"Yes."

"Something important?"

"I think so. Can you get Johnson?"

"He's here now."

Then Delaney became aware of the tone of the man's voice, the tightness, urgency.

"I've got to see you," the Captain said. "The sooner the better."

"Yes," Thorsen agreed. "Can you come over now?"

"Your office or home?"

"Home."

"I'll take a cab," Captain Delaney told him. "About twenty minutes, at the most."

He hung up, then said, "Fuck 'em all," in a loud voice. But he went into the kitchen, found a paper shopping bag in the cabinet under the sink, brought it back to the study. In it he placed the three hammers and the can of machine oil—all his "physical evidence." Then he set out.

Mrs. Thorsen met him at the door, took his coat and hat and hung them away. She was a tall silver-blonde, almost gaunt, but with good bones and the most beautiful violet eyes Delaney had ever seen. They chatted a few moments, and she asked about Barbara. He mumbled something.

"Have you eaten tonight, Edward?" she asked suddenly.

He tried to think, not remembering, then shook his head.

"I'm making some sandwiches. Ham-and-cheese all right? Or roast beef?"

"Either or both will be fine, Karen."

"And I have some salad things. In about an hour or so. The others are in the living room—you know where."

There were three men in the room, all seated. Thorsen and Inspector Johnson rose and came forward to shake his hand. The third man remained seated; no one offered to introduce him.

This man was short, chunky, swarthy, with a tremendous mustache. His hands lay flat on his knees, and his composure was monumental. Only his dark eyes moved, darting, filled with curiosity and a lively intelligence.

It was only after he was seated that Delaney made him: Deputy Mayor Herman Alinski. He was a secretive, publicity-shy politico, reputed to be the mayor's trouble-shooter and one of his closest confidants. In a short biographical sketch in the *Times*, the writer, speculating on Alinski's duties, had come to the conclusion that, "Apparently, what he does most frequently is listen, and everyone who knows him agrees that he does that very well indeed."

"Drink, Edward?" Thorsen asked. "Rye highball?"

Delaney looked around. Thorsen and Johnson had glasses. Alinski did not.

"Not right now, thank you. Maybe later."

"All right. Karen is making up some sandwiches for us. Edward, you said you had something important for us. You can talk freely."

Again Delaney became conscious of the tension in Thorsen's voice, and when he looked at Inspector Johnson, the big black seemed stiff and grim.

"All right," Delaney said. "I'll take it from the top."

He started speaking, still seated, and then, in a few moments, rose to pace around the room, or pause with his elbow on the mantel. He thought and spoke better, he knew, on his feet, and could gesture freely. None of the three men interrupted, but their heads or eyes followed him wherever he strode.

He began with Lombard's death. The position of the body. His reasons for thinking the killer had approached from the front, then whirled to strike Lombard down from behind. The shape and nature of the wound. Oil in the wound. The missing driver's license. His belief that it was taken as evidence of the kill. Then Langley, his expertise, and the discovery of the bricklayers' hammer which led to the rock hounds' hammer which led to the ice ax.

At this point he unpacked his shopping bag and handed

around the tools. The three men examined them closely, their faces expressionless as they tested sharp edges with thumbs, hefted the weight and balance of the tools.

Delaney went on: the Bernard Gilbert attack. The missing ID card. His belief that the assailant was psychopathic. A resident of the 251st Precinct. And would kill again. The information supplied by Handry: the Trotsky assassination and the name of Calvin Case. Then the interview with Case. The oil on the ice ax heads. He handed around the can of oil.

He had them now, and the three were leaning forward intently, Thorsen and Johnson neglecting their drinks, the Deputy Mayor's sharp eyes darting and glittering. There wasn't a sound from them.

Delaney told them about the interview with Sol Appel at Outside Life. The mailing list and itemized sales checks. Then he related how he had traced a profile of the ice ax head. How he had given that and a sample of machine oil to the surgeon who did the autopsy on Gilbert. How the profile of the wound checked out. How the oil would be analyzed on the OAI.

"Who did the post?" Inspector Johnson asked.

Alinski's head swivelled sharply, and he spoke for the first time. "Post?" he asked. "What's post?"

"Post-mortem," Delaney explained. "I promised to keep the surgeon's name out of it."

"We could find out," Alinksi said mildly.

"Of course," the Captain said, just as mildly. "But not from me."

That seemed to satisfy Alinski. Thorsen asked how much Delaney had told the surgeon, had told Langley, Handry, Case, Mrs. Gilbert, Sol Appel.

Only as much as they needed to know, Delaney assured him. They knew only that he was engaged in a private investigation of the deaths of Lombard and Gilbert, and they were willing to help.

"Why?" Alinski asked.

Delaney shrugged. "For reasons of their own."

There was silence for a few minutes, then Alinski spoke softly:

"You have no proof, do you, Captain?"

Delaney looked at him in astonishment.

"Of course not. It's all smoke, all theory. I haven't told you or shown you a single thing that could be taken into court at this time."

"But you believe in it?"

"I believe in it. For one reason only—there's nothing else to believe in. Does Operation Lombard have anything better?"

The three men turned heads to stare wordlessly at each other. Delaney could tell nothing from their expressions.

"That's really why I'm here," he said, addressing Thorsen. "I want to turn—"

But at that moment there was a kicking at the door; not a knocking, but three sharp kicks. Thorsen sprang up, stalked over, opened the door and relieved his wife of a big tray of food.

"Thank you, dear," he smiled.

"There's plenty more of everything," she called to the other men. "So don't be polite if you're hungry; just ask."

Thorsen put the loaded tray on a low cocktail table, and they clustered around. There were ham-and-cheese sandwiches, roast beef sandwiches, chunks of tomato, radishes, dill pickles, slices of Spanish onions, a jar of hot mustard, olives, potato chips, scallions.

They helped themselves, all standing, and Thorsen mixed fresh drinks. This time Delaney had a rye and water, and Deputy Mayor Alinski took a double Scotch.

Unwilling to sacrifice the momentum of what he had been saying, and the impression he had obviously made on them, Delaney began talking again, speaking between bites of his sandwich and pieces of scallion. This time he looked at Alinski as he spoke.

"I want to turn over everything I've got to Chief Pauley. I admit it's smoke, but it's a lead. I've got three or four inexperienced people who can check sources of the ax and the Outside Life mailing list and sales checks. But Pauley's got five hundred dicks and God knows how many deskmen if he needs them. It's a question of time. I think Pauley should take this over; he can do it a lot faster than I can. It might prevent another kill, and I'm convinced there will be another, and another, and another, until we catch up with this nut."

The other three continued eating steadily, sipping their drinks and looking at him. Once Thorsen started to speak, but Alinski held up a hand, silencing him. Finally the Deputy Mayor finished his sandwich, wiped his fingers on a paper napkin, took his drink back to his chair. He sat down, sighed, stared at Delaney.

"A moral problem for you, isn't it, Captain?" he asked softly.

"Call it what you like," Delaney shrugged. "I just feel what I

268

have is strong enough to follow up on, and Chief Pauley is—"

"Impossible," Thorsen said.

"Why impossible?" Delaney cried angrily. "If you—"

"Calm down, Edward," Inspector Johnson said quietly. He was on his third sandwich. "That's why we wanted to talk to you tonight. You obviously haven't been listening to radio or TV in the last few hours. You can't turn over what you have to Chief Pauley. Broughton canned him a few hours ago."

"Canned him?"

"Whatever you want to call it. Relieved him of command. Kicked him off Operation Lombard."

"Jesus Christ!" Delaney said furiously. "He can't do that."

"He did it," Thorsen nodded. "And in a particularly—in a particularly brutal way. Didn't even tell the Chief. Just called a press conference and announced he was relieving Pauley of all command responsibilities relating to Operation Lombard. He said Pauley was inefficient and getting nowhere."

"But who the hell is—"

"And Broughton is going to take over personal supervision of all the detectives assigned to Operation Lombard."

"Oh God," Delaney groaned. "That tears it."

"You haven't heard the worst," Thorsen went on, staring at him without expression. "About an hour ago, Pauley filed for retirement. After what Broughton said, Pauley knows his career is finished, and he wants out."

Delaney sat down heavily in an armchair, looked down at his drink, swirling the ice cubes.

"Son of a bitch," he said bitterly. "Pauley was a good man. You have no idea how good. He was right behind me. Only because I had the breaks, and he didn't. But he would have been on to this ice ax thing in another week or so. I know he would; I could tell it by the reports. God damn it! The Department can't afford to lose men like Pauley. Jesus! A good brain and thirty years' experience down the drain. It just makes me sick!"

None of them said anything, giving him time to calm down. Alinski rose from his chair to go over to the food tray again, take a few radishes and olives. Then he came over to stand before Delaney's chair, popping food.

"You know, Captain," he said gently, "this development really doesn't affect your moral problem, does it? I mean, you can still take what you have to Broughton."

"I suppose so," Delaney said morosely. "Canning Pauley, for

God's sake. Broughton's out of his mind. He just wanted a goat to protect his own reputation."

"That's what we think," Inspector Johnson said.

Delaney looked up at Deputy Mayor Alinski, still standing over him.

"What's it all about?" he demanded. "Will you please tell me what the hell this is all about?"

"Do you really want to know, Captain?"

"Yeah, I want to know," Delaney grunted. "But I don't want you to tell me. I'll find out for myself."

"I think you will," Alinski nodded. "I think you are a very smart man."

"Smart? Shit! I can't even find one kill-crazy psycopath in my own precinct."

"It's important to you, isn't it, Captain, to find the killer? It's the most important thing."

"Of course it's the most important thing. This nut is going to keep killing, over and over and over. There will be shorter intervals between murders. Maybe he'll hit in the daytime. Who the hell knows? But I can guarantee one thing: he won't stop now. It's a fever in his blood. He can't stop. Wait'll the newspapers get hold of this. And they will. Then the shit will hit the fan."

"Going to take what you have to Broughton?" Thorsen asked, almost idly.

"I don't know. I don't know what I'll do. I have to think about it."

"That's wise," Alinski said unexpectedly. "Think about it. There's nothing like thought—long, deep thought."

"I just want all of you to know one thing," Delaney said angrily, not understanding why he was angry. "The decision is mine. Only mine. What I decide to do, I'll do."

They would have offered him something, but they knew better.

Johnson came over to put a heavy hand on Delaney's shoulder. The big black was grinning. "We know that, Edward. We knew you were a hard-nose from the start. We're not going to lean on you."

Delaney drained his drink, rose, put the empty glass on the cocktail table. He repacked his paper shopping bag with hammers and the can of oil.

"Thank you," he said to Thorsen. "Thank Karen for me for the food. I can find my own way out."

"Will you call and tell me what you've decided, Edward?"

"Sure. If I decide to go to Broughton, I'll call you first."

"Thank you."

"Gentlemen," Delaney nodded around, and marched out. They watched him go, all of them standing.

He had to walk five blocks and lost two dimes before he found a public phone that worked. He finally got through to Thomas Handry.

"Yes?"

"Captain Edward X. Delaney here. Am I interrupting you?"

"Yes."

"Working?"

"Trying to."

"How's it coming?"

"It's never as good as you want it to be."

"That's true," Delaney said, without irony and without malice. "True for poets and true for cops. I was hoping you could give me some help."

"That photo of the ice ax that killed Trotsky? I haven't been able to find it."

"No, this is something else."

"You're something else too, Captain—you know that? All for you and none for me. When are you going to open up?"

"In a day or so."

"Promise?"

"I promise."

"All right. What do you want?"

"What do you know about Broughton?"

"Who?"

"Broughton, Timothy A. Deputy Commissioner."

"That prick? Did you see him on TV tonight?"

"No, I didn't."

"He fired Chief Pauley. For inefficiency and, he hinted, dereliction of duty. A sweet man."

"What does he want?"

"Broughton? He wants to be commissioner, then mayor, then governor, then President of these here You-nited States. He's got ambition and drive you wouldn't believe."

"I gather you don't approve of him."

"You gather right. I've had one personal interview with him. You know how most men carry pictures of their wives and children in their wallets? Broughton carries pictures of himself."

"Nice. Does he have any clout? Political clout?"

"Very heavy indeed. Queens and Staten Island for starters.

The talk is that he's aiming for the primary next year. On a 'law and order' platform. You know, 'We must clamp down on crime in the streets, no matter what it costs'."

"You think he'll make it?"

"He might. If he can bring off this Operation Lombard thing, it's bound to help. And if Lombard's killer turns out to be a black heroin addict on welfare who's living with a white fifteen-year-old hippie with long blonde hair, there'll be no stopping Broughton."

"You think the mayor's worried?"

"Wouldn't you be?"

"I guess. Thank you, Handry. You've made a lot of things a lot clearer."

"Not for me. What the hell is going on?"

"Will you give me a day—or two?"

"No more. Gilbert died, didn't he?"

"Yes. He did."

"There's a connection, isn't there?"

"Yes."

"Two days," Handry said. "No more. If I don't hear from you by then, I'll have to start guessing. In print."

"Good enough."

He walked home, the shopping bag bumping against his knee. Now he could understand something of what was going on—the tension of Thorsen, Johnson's grimness, Alinski's presence. He really didn't want to get involved in all that political shit. He was a cop, a professional. Right now, all he wanted to do was catch a killer, but he seemed bound and strangled by this maze of other men's ambitions, feuds, obligations.

What had happened, he realized, was that his search for the killer of Lombard and Gilbert had become a very personal thing to him, a private thing, and he resented the intrusion of other men, other circumstances, other motives. He needed help, of course—he couldn't do everything himself—but essentially it was a duel, a two-man combat, and outside advice, pressures, influence were to be shunned. You knew what you could do, and you respected your opponent's ability and didn't take him lightly. Whether it was a fencing exhibition or a duel to the death, you put your cock on the line.

But all that was egotism he admitted, groaning aloud. Stupid male *machismo*, believing that nothing mattered unless you risked your balls. It should not, it *could* not affect his decision which, as Barbara and Deputy Mayor Alinski had recognized, was essentially a moral choice.

Thinking this way, brooding, his brain in a whirl, he turned into his own block, head down, *schlepping* along with his heavy shopping bag, when a harsh voice called, "Delaney!"

He stopped slowly. Like most detectives in New York—in the world!—he had helped send men up. To execution, or to long or short prison terms, or to mental institutions. Most of them vowed revenge—in the courtroom, in threats phoned by their friends, in letters. Very few of them, thankfully, ever carried out their threats. But there were a few . . .

Now, hearing his name called from a dark sedan parked on a poorly lighted street, realizing he was unarmed, he turned slowly toward the car. He let the shopping bag drop to the sidewalk. He raised his arms slightly, palms turned forward.

But then he saw the uniformed driver in the front seat. And in the back, leaning toward the cranked-down window, the bulk and angry face of Deputy Commissioner Broughton. The cigar, clenched in his teeth, was burning furiously.

"Delaney!" Broughton said again, more of a command than a greeting. The Captain stepped closer to the car. Broughton made no effort to open the door, so Delaney was forced to bow forward from the waist to speak to him. He was certain this was deliberate on Broughton's part, to keep him in a supplicant's position.

"Sir?" he asked.

"Just what the fuck do you think you're doing?"

"I don't understand, sir."

"We sent a man to Florida. It turns out that Lombard's driver's license is missing. The widow says you spoke to her about it. You were seen entering her house. You knew the license was missing. I could rack you up for withholding evidence."

"But I reported it, sir."

"You reported it? To Pauley?"

"No, I didn't think it was that important. I reported it to Dorfman, Acting Commander of the Two-five-one Precinct. I'm sure he sent a report to the Traffic Department. Check the New York State Department of Motor Vehicles, sir. I'm certain you'll find a missing license report was filed with them."

There was silence for a moment. A cloud of rank cigar smoke came billowing out the window, into Delaney's face. Still he stooped.

"Why did you go see Gilbert's wife?" Broughton demanded.

"For the same reason I went to see Mrs. Lombard," Delaney said promptly. "To present my condolences. As commander

273

and ex-commander of the precinct in which the crimes occurred. Good public relations for the Department."

Again there was a moment's silence.

"You got an answer for everything, you wise bastard," Broughton said angrily. He was in semi-darkness. Delaney, bending down, could barely make out his features. "You been seeing Thorsen? And Inspector Johnson?"

"Of course I've been seeing Deputy Inspector Thorsen, sir. He's been a friend of mine for many years."

"He's your 'rabbi'—right?"

"Yes. And he introduced me to Johnson. Just because I'm on leave of absence doesn't mean I have to stop seeing old friends in the Department."

"Delaney, I don't trust you. I got a nose for snots like you, and I got a feeling you're up to something. Just listen to this: you're still on the list, and I can stomp on you any time I want to. You know that?"

"Yes, sir."

"Don't fuck me, Delaney. I can do more to you than you can do to me. You *coppish*?"

"Yes. I understand."

So far he had held his temper under control and now, in a split-second, he made his decision. His anger wasn't important, and neither was Broughton's obnoxious personality. He brought the shopping bag closer to the car window.

"Sir," he said, "I have something here I'd like to show you. I think it may possibly help—"

"Go fuck yourself," Broughton interrupted roughly, and Delaney heard the belch. "I don't need your help. I don't want your help. The only way you can help me is to crawl in a hole and pull it in over your head. Is that clear?"

"Sir, I've been—"

"Jesus Christ, how can I get through to you? Fuck off, Delaney. That's all I want from you. Just fuck off, you shithead."

"Yes, sir," Captain Edward X. Delaney said, almost delirious with pleasure. "I heard. I understand."

He stood and watched the black sedan pull away. See? You worry, brood, wrestle with "moral problems" and such crap, and then suddenly a foul-mouthed moron solves the whole thing for you. He went into his own home happily, called Deputy Inspector Thorsen and, after reporting his meeting with Broughton, told Thorsen he wanted to continue the investigation on his own.

"Hang on a minute, Edward," Thorsen said. Delaney

274

guessed Inspector Johnson and Deputy Mayor Alinski were still there, and Ivar was repeating the conversation to them. Thorsen was back again in about two minutes.

"Fine," he said. "Go ahead. Good luck."

7

He seemed to be spending a lot of time doodling, staring off into space, jotting down almost incomprehensible notes, outlining programs he tore up and discarded as soon as they were completed. But he was, he knew, gradually evolving a sensible campaign in the two weeks following the meeting in Thorsen's home.

He sat down with Christopher Langley in the Widow Zimmerman's apartment and, while she fussed about, urging them to more tea and crumbcake, they went over Langley's firm schedule for his investigation. The little man had already discovered two more stores in Manhattan that sold ice axes, neither of which had mailing lists or kept a record of customers' purchases.

"That's all right," Delaney said grimly. "We can't be lucky all the time. We'll do what we can with what we have."

Langley would continue to look for stores in Manhattan where the ice ax was sold, then broadening his search to the other boroughs. Then he would check tool and outdoor equipment jobbers and wholesalers. Then he would try to assemble a list of American manufacturers of ice axes. Then he would assemble a list of names and addresses of foreign manufacturers of mountaineering gear who exported their products to the U.S., starting with West Germany, then Austria, then Switzerland.

"It's a tremendous job," Delaney told him.

Langley smiled, seemingly not at all daunted by the dimensions of his task.

"More crumbcake?" the Widow Zimmerman asked brightly. "It's homemade."

Langley had told the truth; she was a lousy cook.

Delaney had another meeting with Calvin Case, who announced proudly that he was now refraining from taking his first drink of the day until his bedside radio began the noon news broadcast.

"I have it prepared," Case said, "but I don't touch it until I hear that chime. Then . . ."

275

Delaney congratulated him, and when Case repeated his offer of help, they began to figure out how to handle the Outside Life sales checks.

"We got a problem," Case told him. "It'll be easy enough to pull every sales slip that shows a purchase of an ice ax during the past seven years. But what if your man bought it ten years ago?"

"Then his name should show up on the mailing list. I'll have someone working on that."

"Okay, but what if he bought the ice ax some place else but maybe bought some other mountain gear at Outside Life?"

"Well, couldn't you pull every slip that shows a purchase of mountain climbing gear of any type?"

"That's the problem," Case said. "A lot of stuff used in mountaineering is used by campers, back-packers, and a lot of people who never go near a mountain. I mean stuff like rucksacks, lanterns, freeze-dried foods, gloves, web belts and harnesses. Hell, ice fishermen buy crampons, and yachtsmen buy the same kind of line mountaineers use. So where does that leave us?"

Delaney thought a few minutes. Case took another drink.

"Look," Delaney said, "I'm not going to ask you to go through a hundred thousand sales checks more than once. Why don't you do this: why don't you pull every check that has anything at all to do with mountain climbing? I mean *anything*. Rope, rucksacks, food—whatever. That will be a big stack of sales checks—right? And it will include a lot of non-mountain climbers. That's okay. At the same time you make a separate file of every sales check that definitely lists the purchase of an ice ax. After you've finished with all the checks, we'll go through your ice ax file first and pull every one purchased by a resident of the Two-five-one Precinct, and look 'em up. If that doesn't work, we'll pull every resident of the Precinct from your general file of mountaineering equipment purchases. And if that doesn't work, we'll branch out and take in everyone in that file."

"Jesus Christ. And if that doesn't work, I suppose you'll investigate every one of those hundred thousand customers in the big file?"

"There won't be that many. There have got to be people who bought things at Outside Life several times over the past seven years. Notice that Sol Appel estimates a hundred thousand sales checks in storage, but only thirty thousand on his mailing list. I'll check with him, or you can, but I'd guess he's got someone winnowing out repeat buyers, and only *new* customers are added to the mailing list."

"That makes sense. All right, suppose there are thirty thousand individual customers. If you don't get anywhere with the sales checks I pull, you'll investigate all thirty thousand?"

"If I have to," Delaney nodded. "But I'll cross that bridge when I come to it. Meanwhile, how does the plan sound to you—I mean your making two files: one of ice ax purchases, one of general mountaineering equipment purchases?"

"It sounds okay."

"Then can I make arrangements with Sol Appel to have the sales checks sent up here?"

"Sure. You're a nut—you know that, Captain?"

"I know."

The meeting with Monica Gilbert called for more caution and deliberation. He walked past her house twice, on the other side of the street, and could see no signs of surveillance, no uniformed patrolmen, no unmarked police cars. But even if the guards had been called off, it was probable that her phone was still tapped. Remembering Broughton's threat to "stomp" him, he had no desire to risk a contact that the Deputy Commissioner would learn about.

Then he remembered her two little girls. One of them, the older, was surely of school age—perhaps both of them. Monica Gilbert, if she was sending her children to a public school, and from what Delaney had learned of her circumstances she probably was, would surely walk the children to the nearest elementary school, three blocks away, and call for them in the afternoon.

So, the next morning, he stationed himself down the block, across the street, and waited, stamping his feet against the cold and wishing he had worn his earmuffs. But, within half an hour, he was rewarded by the sight of Mrs. Gilbert and her two little girls, bundled up in snowsuits, exiting from the brownstone. He followed them, across the street and at a distance, until she left her daughters at the door of the school. She started back, apparently heading home, and he crossed the street, approached her, raised his hat.

"Mrs. Gilbert."

"Why, it's Captain . . . Delaney?"

"Yes. How are you?"

"Well, thank you. And thank you for your letter of condolence. It was very kind of you."

"Yes, well . . . Mrs. Gilbert, I was wondering if I could talk to you for a few minutes. Would you like a cup of coffee? We could go to a luncheonette."

She looked at him a moment, debating. "Well . . . I'm on my way home. Why don't you come back with me? I always have my second cup after the girls are in school."

"Thank you. I'd like that."

He had carefully brought along the Xerox copy of the Outside Life mailing list, three packs of 3X5 filing cards, and a small, hand-drawn map of the 251st Precinct, showing only its boundaries.

"Good coffee," he said.

"Thank you."

"Mrs. Gilbert, you told me you wanted to help. Do you still feel that way?"

"Yes. More than ever. Now . . ."

"It's just routine work. Boring."

"I don't care."

"All right."

He told her what he wanted. She was to go through the 30,000 names and addresses on the mailing list, and when she found one within the 251st Precinct, she was to make out a typed file card for each person. When she had finished the list, she was then to type out her own list, with two carbons, of her cards of the Precinct residents.

"Do you have any questions?" he asked her.

"Do they have to live strictly within the boundaries of this Precinct?"

"Well . . . use your own judgment on that. If it's only a few blocks outside, include them."

"Will this help find my husband's killer?"

"I think it will, Mrs. Gilbert."

She nodded. "All right. I'll get started on it right away. Besides, I think it's best if I have something to keep me busy right now."

He looked at her admiringly.

Later, he wondered why he felt so pleased with himself after his meetings with Calvin Case and Mrs. Gilbert. He realized it was because he had been discussing names and addresses. Names! Up to now it had all been steel tools and cans of oil. But now he had names—a reservoir, a Niagara of names! And addresses! Perhaps nothing would come of it. He was prepared for that. But meanwhile he was investigating *people*, not things, and so he was pleased.

The interview with Thomas Handry was ticklish. Delaney

told him only as much as he felt Handry should know, believing the reporter was intelligent enough to fill in the gaps. For instance, he told Handry that both Lombard and Gilbert had been killed with the same weapon—had *apparently* been killed with the same weapon. He didn't specify an ice ax, and Handry, writing notes furiously, nodded without asking more questions on the type of weapon used. As a newspaperman he knew the value of such qualifiers as "apparently," "allegedly," and "reportedly."

Delaney took complete responsibility for his own investigation, made no mention of Thorsen, Johnson, Alinski or Broughton. He said he was concerned because the crimes had occurred in his precinct, and he felt a personal responsibility. Handry looked up from his notebook to stare at Delaney a long time, but made no comment. Delaney told him he was convinced the killer was a psychopath, that Lombard and Gilbert were chance victims, and that the murderer would slay again. Handry wrote it all down and, thankfully, didn't inquire why Delaney didn't take what he had to Operation Lombard.

Their big argument involved when Handry could publish. The reporter wanted to go at once with what he had been told; the Captain wanted him to hold off until he got the go-ahead from him, Delaney. It developed into a shouting match, louder and louder, about who had done more for whom, and who owed whom what. Finally, realizing simultaneously how ridiculous they sounded, they dissolved into laughter, and the Captain mixed fresh drinks. They came to a compromise: Handry would hold off for two weeks. If he hadn't received the Captain's go-ahead by then, he could publish anything he liked, guess at anything he liked, but with no direct attribution to Delaney.

His biggest disappointment during this period came when he happily, proudly brought Barbara the two Honey Bunch books he had received in the mail. She was completely rational, apparently in flaming good health. She inspected the books, and gave a mirthful shout, looking at him and shaking her head.

"Edward," she said, "what on *earth?*"

He was about to remind her she had requested them, then suddenly realized she obviously didn't remember. He hid his chagrin.

"I thought you'd like them," he smiled. "Just like the ones you sent to Liza."

"Oh, you're such an old dear," she said, holding up her face to be kissed.

He leaned over the hospital bed eagerly, hoping her cheerfulness was a presage of recovery. When he left, the two books were alongside her bed, on the floor. When he returned the next day, one was opened, spread, pages down, on her bedside table. He knew she had been reading it, but he didn't know if this was a good sign or a bad sign. She made no reference to the book, and he didn't either.

So his days were spent mostly on plans, programs, meetings, interviews, and there was absolutely no progress to report when he called Thorsen twice a week. Having assigned his amateur "staff" their tasks, he called each of them every other day or so, not to lean on them, but to talk, assure them of the importance of what they were doing, answer their questions, and just let them know that he was there, he knew it would take time, and not to become discouraged. He was very good at this, because he liked these people, and he knew or sensed their motives for helping him.

But when all his plans and programs were in progress, when all his amateurs were busy at their tasks, he found himself with nothing to do. He went back through his own notes and reports, and found the suggestions about a mountain climbers' magazine, an association or club of mountain climbers, a mention to check the local library on withdrawals of books on mountaineering.

Then he came across his list, "The Suspect." He had not made an addition to it in almost six weeks. He looked at his watch. He had returned from his evening visit to the hospital; it was almost 8:00 p.m. Had he eaten? Yes, he had. Mary had left a casserole of shrimp, chicken, rice, and little pieces of ham. And walnuts. He didn't like the walnuts, but he picked them out, and the rest was good.

He called Calvin Case.

"Captain Edward X. Delaney here. How are you?"

"Okay."

"And your wife?"

"Fine. What's on your mind?"

"I'd like to talk to you. Now. It's not about the sales checks. I know you're working away at them. It's something else. If I can find a cab, I could be at your place in half an hour."

"Sure. Come ahead. I've got something great to show you."

"Oh? I'll be right down."

Evelyn Case met him at the door. She was flushed, happy,

and looked about 15 years old, in faded jeans, torn sneakers, one of her husband's shirts tied about her waist. Unexpectedly, she went up on her toes to kiss his cheek.

"Well!" he said. "I thank you."

"We're working on the sales checks, Captain," she said breathlessly. "Both of us. Every night. And Cal taught me what the stock numbers mean. And sometimes I come home during my lunch hour and help him."

"Good," he smiled, patting her shoulder. "That's fine. And you look just great."

"Wait till you see Cal!"

The apartment was brighter now, and smelled reasonably clean. The windows of Case's bedroom were washed, there were fresh paper drapes, a pot of ivy on his cart, a new rag rug on the floor.

But the cartons of Outside Life sales checks were everywhere, stacked high against walls in the hallway, living room, bedroom. Delaney had to thread his way through, walking sideways in a few places, sidling through the open bedroom doorway from which, he noted, the window shade had been removed.

"Hi," Calvin Case called, gesturing around. "How do you like this?"

He was waving at an incredible contraption, a framework of two-inch iron pipe that surrounded his bed and hung over it, like the bare bones of a canopy. And there were steel cables, weights, handles, pulleys, gadgets.

Delaney stared in astonishment. "What the hell *is* it?" he asked.

Case laughed pleased at his wonderment.

"Sol Appel gave it to me. He came up to see me. The next day a guy showed up to take measurements. A few days later three guys showed up with the whole thing and just bolted it together. It's a gym. So I can exercise from the waist up. Look at this . . ."

He reached up with both hands, grabbed a trapeze that hung from wire cables. He pulled his body off the bed. The clean sheet dropped away to his waist. His naked torso was still flaccid, soft muscles trembling with his effort. He let go, let himself fall back onto the bed.

"That's all," he gasped. "So far. But strength is coming back. Muscle tone. I can feel it. Now look at this . . ."

Two handles hung above his head. They were attached to steel cables that ran over pulleys on the crossbar above him.

The cables ran down over the length of the bed, across pulleys on the lower crossbar, and then down. They were attached to stainless steel weights.

"See?" Case said, and demonstrated by pulling the handles down to his chest alternately: right, left, right, left. "I'm only raising the one-pound weights now," he admitted. "But you can add up to five pounds on each cable."

"And when he started he couldn't even raise the one-pound weights," Evelyn Case said eagerly to Captain Delaney. "Next week we're going to two-pound weights."

"And look at this," Case said, showing what appeared to be a giant steel hairpin hanging from his pipe cage. "It's for your grip. For biceps and pectorals."

He grasped the hairpin in both hands and tried to squeeze the two arms together, his face reddening. He barely moved them.

"That's fine," Delaney said. "Just fine."

"The best thing is this," Case said, and showed how a steel arm was hinged to swing out sideways from the gym. "I talked to the guys who put this thing together. They're from some physical therapy outfit that specializes in stuff like this. Well, they sell a wheelchair with a commode built into it. I mean, you sit on a kind of a potty seat. You wheel yourself around, and when you've got to shit, you shit. But Jesus Christ, you're mobile. I'm too heavy for Ev to lift me into a chair like that, but when I get my strength back, I'll be able to move this bar out and swing onto that potty chair by myself, and swing back into bed whenever I want to. I know I'll be able to do it. My arms and shoulders were always good. I've hung from my hands lots of times, and then pulled myself up."

"That sounds great," Delaney said admiringly. "But don't overdo it. I mean, take it easy at first. Build your strength up gradually."

"Oh sure. I know how to do it. We ordered one of those chairs, but it won't be delivered for a couple of weeks. By that time I hope I'll be able to flip myself in and out of bed with no sweat. The chair's got a brake you can set so it won't roll away from you while you're getting into it. You realize what that means, Delaney? I'll be able to sit up at that desk while I'm going through the sales checks. That'll help."

"It surely will," the Captain smiled. "How you doing with the booze?"

"Okay. I haven't stopped, but I've cut down—haven't I, hon?"

"Oh yes," his wife nodded happily. "I know because I'm only buying about half the bottles I did before."

The two men laughed, and then she laughed.

"Incidentally," Case said, "the sales checks are going a lot faster than I expected."

"Oh? Why is that?"

"I hadn't realized how much of Outdoor Life's business was in fishing and hunting gear, tennis, golf, even croquet and badminton and stuff like that. About seventy-five percent, I'd guess. So I can just take a quick glance at the sales slip and toss it aside if it has nothing to do with mountaineering."

"Good. I'm glad to hear that. Can I talk to you a few minutes? Not about the sales checks. Something else. Do you feel up to it?"

"Oh sure. I feel great. Hon, pull up a chair for the Captain."

"I'll get it," Delaney told her, and brought the straight-backed desk chair over to the bedside and sat where he could watch Case's face.

"A drink, Captain?"

"All right. Thank you. With water."

"Hon?"

She went out into the kitchen. The two men sat in silence a few moments.

"What's it all about?" Case asked finally.

"Mountain climbers."

Later, in his own study, Captain Delaney took out his list, "The Suspect," and began to add what Calvin Case had told him about mountain climbers while it was still fresh in his mind. He extrapolated on what Case had said, based on his own instinct, experience, and knowledge of why men acted the way they did.

Under "Physical" he added items about ranginess, reach, strength of arms and shoulders, size of chest, resistance to panic. It was true Case had said mountain climbers come "in all shapes and sizes," but he had qualified that later, and Delaney was willing to go with the percentages.

Under "Psychological" he had a lot to write: love of the outdoors, risk as an addiction, a disciplined mind, no obvious suicide compulsion, total egotism, pushing to—what was it Case had said?—the 'edge of life," with nothing between you and death but your own strength and wit. Then, finally, a deeply religious feeling, becoming one with the universe—"one with everything." And compared to that, everything else was "just mush."

Under "Additional Notes" he listed "Probably moderate drinker" and "No drugs" and "Sex relations probable after murder but not before."

He read and reread the list, looking for something he might have forgotten. He couldn't find anything. "The Suspect" was coming out of the gloom, looming. Delaney was beginning to get a handle on the man, grabbing what he was, what he wanted, why he had to do what he did. He was still a shadow, smoke, but there was an outline to him now. He began to exist, on paper and in Delaney's mind. The Captain had a rough mental image of the man's physical appearance, and he was just beginning to guess what was going on in the fool's mind. "The poor, sad shit," Delaney said aloud, then shook his head angrily, wondering why he should feel any sympathy at all for this villain.

He was still at it, close to 1:00 a.m., when the desk phone rang. He let it ring three times, knowing—*knowing*—what the call was, and dreading it. Finally he picked up the receiver.

"Yes?" he asked cautiously.

"Captain Delaney?"

"Yes."

"Dorfman. Another one."

Delaney took a deep breath, then opened his mouth wide, tilted his head back, stared at the ceiling, took another deep breath.

"Captain? Are you there?"

"Yes. Where was it?"

"On Seventy-fifth Street. Between Second and Third."

"Dead?"

"Yes."

"Identified?"

"Yes. His shield was missing but he still had his service revolver."

"What?"

"He was one of Broughton's decoys."

PART VI

1

"I didn't want him to suffer," he said earnestly, showing her Bernard Gilbert's ID card. "Really I didn't."

"He didn't suffer, dear," she murmured, stroking his cheek. "He was unconscious, in a coma."

"But I wanted him to be happy!" Daniel Blank cried.

"Of course," she soothed. "I understand."

He had waited for Gilbert's death before he had run to Celia, just as he had run to her after Lombard's death. But this time was different. He felt a sense of estrangement, withdrawal. It seemed to him that he no longer needed her, her advice, her lectures. He wanted to savor in solitude what he had done. She said she understood, but of course she didn't. How could she?

They were naked in the dreadful room, dust everywhere, the silent house hovering about them. He thought he might be potent with her, wasn't sure, didn't care. It was of no importance.

"The mistake was in coming from in front," he said thoughtfully. "Perhaps the skull is stronger there, or the brain not as frail, but he fell back, and he lived for four days. I won't do that again. I don't want anyone to suffer."

"But you saw his eyes?" she asked softly.

"Oh yes."

"What did you see?"

"Surprise. Shock. Recognition. Realization. And then, at the final moment, something else . . ."

"What?"

"I don't know. I'm not sure. Acceptance, I think. And a kind of knowing calm. It's hard to explain."

"Oh!" she said. "Oh yes! Finitude. That's what we're all looking for, isn't it? The last word. Completion. Catholicism or Zen or Communism or Meaninglessness. Whatever. But Dan, isn't it true we need it? We all need it, and will abase ourselves or enslave others to find it. But is it one for all of us, or one for each of us? Isn't that the question? I think it's one absolute for all, but I think the paths differ, and each must find his own way. Did I ever tell you what a beautiful body you have, darling?"

As she spoke she had been touching him softly, arousing him slowly.

"Have you shaved a little here? And here?"

"What?" he asked vaguely, drugged by her caresses. "I don't remember. I may have."

"Here you're silk, oiled silk. I love the way your ribs and hip bones press through your skin, the deep curve from chest to waist, and then the flare of your hips. You're so strong and hard, so soft and yielding. Look how long your arms are, and how wide your shoulders. And still, nipples like buds and your sweet, smooth ass. How dear your flesh is to me. Oh!"

She murmured, still touching him, and almost against his will he responded and moved against her. Then he lay on his back, pulled her over atop him, spread his legs, raised his knees.

"How lovely if you could come into me," he whispered and, knowing, she made the movements he desired. "If you had a penis, too . . . Or better yet, if we both had both penis and vagina. What an improvement on God's design! So that we both might be inside each other, simultaneously, penetrating. Wouldn't that be wonderful?"

"Oh yes," she breathed. "Wonderful."

He held her weight down onto him, calling her "Darling" and "Honey" and saying, "Oh love, you feel so good," and it seemed to him the fabric of his life, like a linen handkerchief laundered too often, was simply shredding apart. Not rotting, but pulling into individual threads; light was coming through.

In her exertions, sweat dripped from her unshaven armpits onto his shoulders; he turned his head to lick it up, tasting salty life.

"Will you kill someone for me?" she gasped.

He pulled her down tighter, elevating his hips, linking his ankles around her slender back.

"Of course not," he told her. "That would spoil everything."

2

He grew up in that silent, loveless, white-tiled house and, an only child, had no sun to turn to and so turned inward, becoming contemplative, secretive even. Almost all he thought and all he felt concerned himself, his wants, fears, hates, hopes, despairs. Strangely, for a young boy, he was aware of this intense egoism and wondered if everyone else was as self-centered. It didn't seem possible; there were boys his age who were jolly and out-going, who made friends quickly and easily, who could tease girls and laugh. But still . . .

"Sometimes it seemed I might be two persons: the one I presented to my parents and the world, and the one I *was*, whirling in my own orbit. The outward me was the orderly, organized boy who was a good student, who collected rocks and stowed them away in compartmented trays, each specimen neatly labeled: 'Blank, Daniel: Good boy.'

"But from my earliest boyhood—from my infancy, even—I have dreamed in my sleep, almost every night: wild, disjointed dreams of no particular meaning: silly things, happenings, people all mixed up, costumes, crazy faces, my parents and kids in school and historical and literary characters—all in a churn.

"Then—oh, perhaps at the age of eight, but it may have been later—I began to lose myself in daytime fantasies, as turbulent and incredible as my nighttime dreams. This daydreaming had no effect on my outward life, on the image I presented to the world. I could do homework efficiently, answer up in class, label the stones I collected, kiss my parents' cold cheeks dutifully . . . and be a million miles away. No, not away, but down inside myself, dreaming.

"Gradually, almost without my being aware of it, daytime fantasies merged with nighttime dreams. How this developed, or exactly when, I cannot say. But daytime fantasies became extensions of nighttime dreams, and it happened that I would imagine a 'plot' that continued, day and night, for perhaps a week. And then, having been rejected in favor of a new 'plot,' I might come back to the old one for a day or two, simply recalling it or perhaps embellishing it with fanciful details.

"For instance, I might imagine that I was actually not the child of my mother and father, but was a foster child placed with them for romantic reasons. My true father was, perhaps, a well-known statesman, my mother a great beauty who had sinned for love. For various reasons, whatever, they were unable to acknowledge me, and had placed me with this dull, putty-faced, childless Indiana couple. But the day would come . . .

"There was something else I became aware of during my early boyhood, and this may serve to illustrate my awareness of myself. Like most young boys of the same age—I was about twelve at the time—I was capable of certain acts of nastiness, even of minor crimes: wanton vandalism, meaningless violence, 'youthful high spirits,' etc. Where I differed from other boys of that age, I believe, was that even when caught and punished, I felt no guilt. No one could make me feel guilty. My only regret was in being caught.

"Is it so strange that someone can live two lives? No, I honestly believe most people do. Most, of course, play the public role expected of them: they marry, work, have children, establish a home, vote, try to keep clean and reasonably law-abiding. But each—man, woman, and child—has a secret life of which they rarely speak and hardly ever display. And this secret life, for each of us, is filled with ferocious fantasies and incredible wants and suffocating lusts. Not shameful in themselves, except as we have been taught so.

"I remember reading something a man wrote—he was a famous author—and he said if it was definitely announced that the world would end in one hour, there would be long lines before each phone booth, with people waiting to call other people to tell them how much they loved them. I do not believe that, I believe most of us would spend the last hour mourning, 'Why didn't I do what I *wanted* to do?'

"Because I believe each of us is a secret island ('No man is an island'? What shit!) and even the deepest, most intense love cannot bridge the gap between individuals. Much of what we feel and dream, that we cannot speak of to others, is shameful, judged by what society says we are allowed to feel and dream. But if humans are capable of it, how can it be shameful? Rather do as our natures dictate. It may lead to heaven or it may lead to hell—what does 'heaven' mean or 'hell'?—but the most terrible sin is to deny. *That* is inhuman.

"When I fucked that girl in college, and later with my wife, and all those in between, I found it exciting and pleasurable, naturally. Satisfying enough to ignore the grunts, coughs, farts, belches, bad breath, blood and . . . and other things. But a moment later my mind would be on my collection of semiprecious stones or the programming of AMROK II. I had enjoyed masturbation as much, and began to wonder how much so-called 'normal sex' is really masturbation à deux. All the groans and protestations of love and ecstasy are the public face;' the secret reactions are hidden from the partner. I once fucked a woman, and all the time I was thinking of—well,

288

someone I had seen at a health club I belonged to. God knows what *she* was thinking of. Island lives.

"Celia Montfort was the most intelligent woman I had ever met. Much more intelligent than I was, as a matter of fact, although I think she lacked my sensitivity and understanding. But she was complex, and I had never met a complex woman before. Or perhaps I had, but could not endure the complexity. But in Celia's case, it attracted me, fascinated me, puzzled me—for a time.

"I wasn't certain what she wanted from me, if she wanted anything at all. I enjoyed her lectures, the play of her mind, but I could never quite pin down who she was. Once, when I called for a dinner date, she said, 'There is something I want to ask you.'

" 'Yes?' I said.

"There was a pause.

" 'I'll ask you tonight,' she said finally. 'At dinner.'

"So, at dinner, I said, 'What did you want to ask me?'

"She looked at me and said, 'I think I better put it in a letter. I'll write you a letter, asking it.'

" 'All right,' I nodded, not wanting to push.

"But, of course, she never wrote me a letter asking anything. She was like that. It was maddening, in a way, until I began to understand . . .

"Understand that she was as deep and moiling as I, and subject, as I was, to sudden whims, crazy passions, incoherent longings, foolish dreams . . . the whole bit. Irrational, I suppose you might say. If I didn't lie to myself—and it's extremely difficult not to lie to yourself—I had to recognize that some of my hostility toward her—and I recognized I was beginning to feel a certain hostility, because she *knew*—well, some of this was because I was a man and she was a woman. I am not a great admirer of the women's liberation movement, but I agree men are victims of a conditioning difficult to recognize and analyze.

"But once I stopped lying to myself, I could acknowledge that she upset me because she had a secret life of her own, an intelligence greater than mine and, when it pleased her, a sexuality more intense than mine.

"I could realize that and admit it to myself: she was the first woman I had been intimate with who existed as an individual, not just as a body. The Jewish girl from Boston had been a body. My wife had been a body. Now I knew a person— call it a 'soul' if it amuses you—as unfathomable as myself.

289

And it was no more logical for me to expect to understand her than to expect her to understand me.

"Item: We have come from a sweated bed where we have been as intimate as man and woman can be physically intimate. I have tasted her. Then, dressed, composed, on our way to dinner, I grab her arm to pull her out of the way of a careening cab. She looks at me with loathing. 'You touched me!' she gasps.

"Item: She has been tender, sympathetic, but somewhat withdrawn all evening. We returned to her home and, only because I need to use the john, does she allow me inside the door. I know there will be no sex that night. That's all right with me. It is her prerogative; I am not a mad rapist. But, from the bathroom, I return to the study. She is seated in the leather armchair and, standing behind her, Valenter is softly massaging her neck and bare shoulders with loving movements. Curled in a corner, Tony is watching them curiously. What am I to make of all that?

"Item: She disappears, frequently and without notice, for hours, days, a week at a time. She returns without explanation or excuse, usually weary and bruised, sometimes wounded and bandaged. I ask no questions; she volunteers no information. We have an unspoken pact: I will not pry; she will not ask. Except about the killing. She can't get enough of *that!*

"Item: She buys an imported English riding crop, but I refuse. Either way.

"In fact, there is no end to her.

"Item: She treats a cab driver shamefully for taking us a block out of our way, and tells me loudly not to tip him. Three hours later she insists I give money to a filthy, drunken panhandler who smells of urine. Well . . .

"I think what was happening was this: we had started on one level, trying to find a satisfactory relationship. Then, sated or bored, the wild sex had calmed and we began to explore the psychic part of sex in which she, and I, believed so strongly. After that—it proving not completely satisfactory—we went on digging deeper, inserting ourselves into each other, yet remaining essentially strangers. I tried to tell her: to achieve the final relationship, you must penetrate. Is that not so?

"I must not see her again. I would resolve that, unable to cope with her *humanity*, and, at the last moment, when I was certain our affair was over, she would call and say things to me on the phone. Oh! So we would once again have lunch or dinner, and under the table cloth, beneath our joined napkins, she would touch me, looking into my eyes. And it would start again.

"I do owe her one thing: the killings. You see, I can acknowledge them openly. The murders. Daniel, I love you! I know what I have done, and will do, and I feel no guilt. It is not someone else doing them. It is I, Daniel Blank, and I do not deny them, apologize or regret. Any more than when I stand naked before a dim mirror and once again touch myself. To deny your secret, island life and die unfulfilled—that is the worst.

"I need, most of all, to go deeper and deeper into myself, peeling layers away—the human onion. I am in full possession of my faculties. I know most people would think me vicious or deranged. But is that of any importance? I don't think so. I think the important thing is to fulfill yourself. If you can do that, you come to some kind of completion where both of you, the two you's, become one, and that one merges and becomes part of and adds to the Cosmic One. What *that* might be, I do not know—yet. But I am beginning to glimpse its outlines, the glory it is, and I think, if I continue on my course, I will know it finally.

"With all this introspection, all this intent searching for the eternal verity, which may make you laugh—do *you* have the courage to try it?—the incredible thing, the amazing thing is that I have been able to keep intact the image I present to the world. That is, I function: I awake each morning, bathe and dress in a fashion of careless elegance, take a cab to my place of work, and there, I believe, I do my job in an efficient and useful manner. It is a charade, of course, but I perform well. In all honesty, perhaps not as I did before . . . Am I going through the movements, marching out the drill? It's probably my imagination but, a few times, I thought members of my X-1 computer team looked at me a bit queerly.

"And one day my secretary, Mrs. Cleek, was wearing a pants suit—it's allowed at Javis-Bircham—and I complimented her on how well it looked. Actually, it was much too snug for her. But later in the day, while she was standing by me, waiting while I signed some letters, I suddenly reached to stroke her pudendum, obvious beneath the crotch of her pants. I didn't grab or squeeze; I just stroked. She drew away, making a small cry. I went back to signing letters; neither of us spoke of what had happened.

"There was one other thing, but since nothing came of it, it hardly seems worth mentioning. I had a dream, a nighttime dream that merged into a daytime fantasy, of doing something to the computer, AMROK II. That is, I wanted to—well, I suppose in some way I wanted to destroy it. How, I didn't know. It was just a vagrant thought. I didn't even consider it. But the thought did come to me. I think I was searching for more humanity, not less. For more *human*-ness, with all its terrible mystery.

"Now we must consider why I killed those men and why (Sigh! Sob! Groan!) I suppose I will kill again. Well . . . again, it's *human*-ness, isn't it? To come close, as close as you can possibly come. Because love—I mean physical love (sex) or romantic love—isn't the answer, is it? It's a poor, cheap substitute, and never quite satisfactory. Because, no matter how good physical love or romantic love may seem, the partners still have, each, their secret, island life.

"But when you kill, the gap disappears, the division is gone, you are one with the victim. I don't suppose you will believe me, but it is so. I assure you it is. The act of killing is an act of love, ultimate love, and though there is no orgasm, no sexual feeling at all—at least in my case—you do, you really do, enter into another human being, and through that violent conjunction—painful perhaps, but just for a split-second—you enter into all humans, all animals, all vegetables, all minerals. In fact, you become one with everything: stars, planets, galaxies, the great darkness beyond, and . . .

"Oh. Well. What this is, the final mystery, is what I'm searching for, isn't it? I'm convinced it is not in books or beds or conversation or churches or sudden flashes of inspiration or revelation. It must be worked for, and it will be, in me.

"What I'm saying is that I want to go into myself, penetrate myself, as deeply as I possibly can. I know it will be a long and painful process. It may prove, eventually, to be impossible —but I don't believe that. I think that I can go deep within myself—I mean *deep!*—and there I'll find it.

"Sometimes I wonder if it's a kind of masturbation, as when I stand naked before my full-length mirror, golden chains about wrist and waist, and look at my own body and touch myself. The wonder! But then I come back, always come back, to what I seek. And it has nothing to do with Celia or Tony or the Mortons or my job or anything else but me. Me! That's where the answer lies. And who can uncover it but me? So I keep trying, and it is not too difficult, too painful or exhausting. Except, in all truth, I must tell you this: If I had my life to live over again, I would want to lie naked in the sun and watch women oil their bodies. That's all I've ever wanted."

He should have stopped there; it was a logical end to his musings. But he would not, could not. He thought of Tony Montfort, what they had done, what they might do. But the dream was fleeting, flicking away a mosquito or something else that might bite. He thought of Valenter, and of a professor in his college who had smelled of earth, and of going into a women's lingerie shop to buy white bikini panties for himself. Because they fit better? Once a man on a Fifth Avenue bus had smiled at him.

He still had the nighttime dreams, the daytime fantasies, but he was aware that the images were becoming shorter. That is, they no longer overlapped from night to day, the "plots" were abbreviated, visions flickered by sharply. His mind was so charged, so jumping, that he became vaguely alarmed, went to a doctor, received a prescription for a mild tranquilizer. They worked on him as a weak sleeping pill. But his mind still jumped.

He could not penetrate deeply enough into himself. He lied to himself; he admitted it; he caught himself at it. It was difficult not to lie to himself. He had to be on guard, not every day or every hour but every minute. He had to question every action, every motive. Probing. Penetrating. If he wanted to discover . . . what?

He soothed an engorged penis in a Vaselined hand, probed his own rectum with a stiff forefinger pointing toward Heaven, opened his empty mouth to a white ceiling and waited for bliss. Throbbing warmth engulfed him, eventually, but not what he sought.

There was more. He knew there was more. He had experienced it, and he set out to find it again, bathing, dusting, perfuming, dressing, preparing for an assignation. We all—all of us—must fulfill our island life. Oh yes, he thought, we must. Taking up the ice ax . . .

"Blood is thicker than water," he said aloud, "and semen is thicker than blood."

He laughed, having no idea what that meant, or if, indeed, it meant anything at all.

3

A week or so after the death of Bernard Gilbert, Daniel Blank went on the stalk. It was not too unlike learning to

293

climb. You had to master the techniques, you had to test your strength and, of course, you had to try your nerve, pushing it to its limit, but not beyond. You did not learn how to murder by reading a book, anymore than you could learn how to swim or ride a bicycle by looking at diagrams.

He had already acquired several valuable techniques. The business of concealing the ice ax under his top coat, holding it through the pocket slit by his left hand, then transferring it swiftly to his right hand shoved through the opened fly of his coat—that worked perfectly, with no fumbling. The death of Lombard had been, he thought, instantaneous, while Gilbert lingered four days. He deduced from this that a blow from the back apparently penetrated a more sensitive area of the skull, and he resolved to make no more frontal attacks.

He was convinced his basic method of approach was sound: the quick, brisk step; the eye-to-eye smile; the whole appearance of ease and neighborliness. Then the fast turn, the blow.

He had, of course, made several errors. For instance, during the attack on Frank Lombard, he had worn his usual black calfskin shoes with leather soles. At the moment of assault his right foot had slipped on the pavement, leather sliding on cement. It was not, fortunately, a serious error, but he had been off-balance, and when Lombard fell backward the ice ax was pulled from Blank's grasp.

So, before the murder of Bernard Gilbert, Blank had purchased a pair of light-weight crepe-soled shoes. It was getting on to December, with cold rain, sleet, snow flurries, and the rubber-soled shoes gave much better traction and stability.

Similarly, in the attack on Lombard, the leather handle of the ice ax had twisted in his sweated hand. Reflecting on this, he had, before the Gilbert assault, roughed the leather handle by rubbing it gently with fine sandpaper. This worked well enough, but he still was not satisfied. He purchased a pair of black suede gloves, certainly a common enough article of apparel in early winter weather. The grip between suede glove and the roughened leather of the ice ax handle was all that could be desired.

These were details, of course, and those who had never climbed mountains would shrug them off as of no consequence. But a good climb depended on just such details. You could have all the balls in the world, but if your equipment was faulty, or your technique wasn't right, you were dead.

There were other things to consider; you just didn't go out

and murder the first man you met. He cancelled out rainy and sleety nights; he needed a reasonably dry pavement for that quick whirl after he had passed his victim. A cloudy or moonless night was best, with no strong wind to tug at his unbuttoned coat. And he carried as few objects and as little identification as possible; less to drop accidentally at the scene.

He went to his health club twice a week and worked out, and he did his stretch exercises at home every night, so strength was no problem. He was, he knew, in excellent physical condition. He could lift, turn, bend, probably better than most boys half his age. He watched his diet; his reactions were still fast. He meant to keep them that way, and looked forward to climbing Devil's Needle again in the Spring, or perhaps taking a trip to the Bavarian Alps for more technical climbs. That would be a joy.

So there was the passion—just as in mountain climbing—and there was also the careful planning, the mundane details—weapon, shoes, gloves, smile—just as any great art is really, essentially, a lot of little jobs. Picasso mixed paints, did he not?

He took the same careful and thoughtful preparation in his stalk after Gilbert's death. A stupid assassin might come home from his job and eat, or dine out and then come home, and start out again each evening at the same time, reconnoiter, and return to his apartment house at the same time. Sooner or later, the apartment house doorman on duty would become aware of this routine.

So Daniel Blank varied his arrivals and departures, carefully avoiding a regular schedule, knowing one doorman went off duty at 8:00 p.m., when his relief arrived. Blank came and he went, casually, and usually these departures and arrivals went unobserved by a doorman busy with cabs or packages or other tasks. He didn't prowl every night. Two nights in a row. One night in. Three out. No pattern. No formal program. Whatever occurred to him; irregularity was best. He thought of everything.

There was, he admitted, something strange that to this enterprise that meant so much to him emotionally, privately, he should bring all his talents for finicky analysis, careful classifying, all the cold, bloodless skills of his public life. It proved, he supposed, he was still two, but in this case it served him well; he never made a move without thinking out its consequences.

For instance, he debated a long time whether or not, during an actual murder, he should wear a hat. At this time of year, in this weather, most men wore hats.

But it might be lost by his exertions. And, supposing he made a murder attempt and was not successful—the possibility had to be faced—and the intended victim lived to testify. Surely he would remember the presence of a hat more strongly than he would recall the absence of a hat.

"Sir, did he wear a hat?"

"Yes, he wore a black hat. A soft hat. The brim was turned down in front."

That would be more likely than if Blank wore no hat at all.

"Sir, did he wear a hat?"

"What? Well . . . I don't remember. A hat? I don't know. Maybe. I really didn't notice."

So Daniel Blank wore no hat on his forays. He was that careful.

But his cool caution almost crumbled when he began his nighttime reconnaissance following the death of Bernard Gilbert. It was on the third night of his aimless meanderings that he became aware of what seemed to be an unusual number of single men, most of them tall and well proportioned, strolling through the shadowed streets of his neighborhood. The pavements were alive with potential victims!

He might have been mistaken, of course; Christmas wasn't so far away, and people were out shopping. Still . . . So he followed a few of these single males, far back and across the street. They turned a corner. He turned a corner. They turned another corner. He turned another corner. But none of them, none of the three he followed cautiously from a distance, ever entered a house. They kept walking steadily, not fast and not slow, up one street and down another.

He stopped suddenly, half-laughing but sick with fear. Decoys! Policemen. Who else could they be? He went home immediately, to think.

He analyzed the problem accurately: (1) He could cease his activities at once. (2) He could continue his activities in another neighborhood, even another borough. (3) He could continue his activities in his own neighborhood, welcoming the challenge.

Possibility (1) he rejected immediately. Could he stop now, having already come so far, with the final prize within recognizable reach? Possibility (2) required a more reasoned dissection. Could he carry a concealed weapon—the ice ax--by taxi, bus, subway, his own car, for any distance without eventual detection? Or (3), might he risk it?

He thought of his options for two whole days, and the solution, when it came, made him smack his thigh, smile, shake his head at his own stupidity. Because, he realized, he had been analyzing, thinking along in a vertical, in-line, masculine fashion —as if such a problem could be solved so!

He had come so far from this, so far from AMROK II, that he was ashamed he had fallen into the same trap once again. The important thing here was to trust his instincts, follow his passions, do as he was compelled, divorced from cold logic and bloodless reason. If he was finally to know truth, it would come from heart and gut.

And besides, there was risk—the sweet attraction of risk.

There was a dichotomy here that puzzled him. In the planning of the crime he was willing to use cool and formal reason: the shoes, the gloves, the weapon, the technique—all designed with logic and precision. And yet when it came to the *reason* for the act, he deliberately shunned the same method of thought and sought the answer in "heart and gut."

He finally came to the realization that logic might do for method but not for motive. Again, to use the analogy of creative art, the artist thought out the techniques of his art, or learned them from others and, with patience, became a skilled craftsman. But where craft ended and art began was at the point where the artist had to draw on his own emotions, dreams, fervors and fears, penetrating deep into himself to uncover what he needed to express by his skill.

The same could be said of mountain climbing. A man might be an enormously talented and knowledgeable mountaineer. But it was just a specialized skill if, within him, there was no drive to push himself to the edge of life and know worlds that the people of the valley could not imagine.

He spent several evenings attempting to observe the operations of the decoys. So far as he could determine, the detectives were not being followed by "back-up men" or trailed by unmarked police cars. It appeared that each decoy was assigned a four-block area, to walk up one street and down the next, going east to west, then west to east, then circling to cover the north-south streets. And unexpectedly, hurrying past a decoy who had stepped into a shadowed store doorway, he saw they were equipped with small walkie-talkies and were apparently in communication with some central command post.

It was, he decided, of little significance.

Sixteen days after the attack on Bernard Gilbert, Daniel Blank returned home directly from work. It was a cold, dry evening with a quarter moon rarely visible through a clouded sky. There was some wind, a hint of rain or snow in a day or so. But generally it was a still night, cold enough to tingle nose, ears, ungloved hands. There was one other factor: the neighborhood theatre was showing a movie Daniel Blank had seen a month ago when it opened on Times Square.

He mixed himself a single drink, watched the evening news on TV. Americans were killing Vietnamese. Vietnamese were killing Americans. Jews were killing Arabs. Arabs were killing Jews. Catholics were killing Protestants. Protestants were killing Catholics. Pakistani were killing Indians. Indians were killing Pakistani. There was nothing new. He fixed a small dinner of broiled calves' liver and an endive salad. He brought his coffee into the living room and had that and a cognac while he listened to a tape of the Brandenburg Concerto No. 3. Then he undressed, got into bed, took a nap.

It was a little after nine when he awoke. He splashed cold water on his face, dressed in a black suit, white shirt, modestly patterned tie. He put on his crepe-soled shoes. He donned his topcoat, pulled on the black suede gloves, held the ice ax under the coat by his left hand, through the pocket slit. The leather thong attached to the handle butt of the ax went around his left wrist.

In the lobby, doorman Charles Lipsky was at the desk, but he rose to unlock and hold the outer door open for Blank. The door was kept locked from 8:00 p.m., when the shift of doormen changed, to 8:00 a.m. the following morning.

"Charles," Blank asked casually, "do you happen to know what movie's playing at the Filmways over on Second Avenue?"

"Afraid I don't, Mr. Blank."

"Well, maybe I'll take a walk over. Nothing much on TV tonight."

He strolled out. It was that natural and easy.

He actually did walk over to the theatre, to take a look at the movie schedule taped to the ticket seller's window. The feature film would begin again in 30 minutes. He had the money ready in his righthand trouser pocket. He bought a ticket with the exact sum, receiving no change. He went into the half-empty theatre, sat in the back row without removing his coat or gloves. When the movie ended and at least fifty people left, he left with them. No one glanced at him, certainly not the usher, ticket taker, or ticket seller. They would never remember his arrival or departure. But, of course, he had the ticket stub in his pocket and had already seen the film.

He walked eastward, toward the river, both hands now

thrust through the coat's pocket slits. On a deserted stretch of street he carefully slipped the leather loop off his left wrist. He held the ax by the handle with his left hand. He unbuttoned his coat, but he didn't allow the flaps to swing wide, holding them close to his body with hands in his pockets.

Now began the time he liked best. Easy walk, a good posture, head held high. Not a scurrying walk, but not dawdling either. When he saw someone approaching, someone who might or might not have been a police decoy, he crossed casually to the other side of the street, walked to the corner and turned, never looking back. It was too early; he wanted this feeling to last.

He *knew* it was going to be this night, just as you know almost from the start of a climb that it will be successful, you will not turn back. He was confident, alert, anxious to feel once again that moment of exalted happiness when the eternal was in him and he was one with the universe.

He was experienced now, and knew what he would feel before that final moment. First, the power: should it be you or shall it be you? The strength and glory of the godhead fizzing through his veins. And second, the pleasure that came from the intimacy and the love, soon to be consummated. Not a physical love, but something much finer, so fine indeed that he could not put it into words but only felt it, knew it, floated with the exaltation.

And now, for the first time, there was something else. He had been frightened and wary before, but this night, with the police decoys on the streets, held a sense of peril that was almost tangible. It was all around him, in the air, in the light, on the mild wind. He could almost *smell* the risk; it excited him as much as the odor of new-fallen snow or his own scented body.

He let these things—power, pleasure, peril—grow in him as he walked. He opened himself to them, cast off all restraint, let them flood and engulf him. Once he had "shot the rapids" in a rubber dinghy, on a western river, and then and now he had the not unpleasant sensation of helplessness, surrender, in the hands of luck or an unknown god, swept along, this way, that, the world whirling, and, having started, no way to stop, no way, until passion ran its course, the river finally flowed placid between broad banks, and risk was a happy memory.

He turned west on 76th Street. Halfway down the block a man was also walking west, at about the same speed, not hurrying but not dallying either. Daniel Blank immediately

299

stopped, turned around, and retraced his steps to Second Avenue. The man he had seen ahead of him had the physical appearance, the *feel*, of a police decoy. If Blank's investigations and guesses were accurate, the man would circle the block to head eastward on 75th Street. So Blank walked south on Second Avenue and paused on the corner, looking westward toward Third Avenue. Sure enough, his quarry turned the corner a block away and headed toward him.

"I love you," Daniel Blank said softly.

He looked about. No one else on the block. No other pedestrians. All parked cars dark. Weak moon behind clouds. Pavement dry. Oh yes. Walk toward the approaching man. Pacing himself so they might meet about halfway between Second and Third Avenues.

Ice ax gripped lightly in fingertips of left hand, beneath his unbuttoned coat. Right arm and gloved hand swinging free. Then the hearty tramp down the street. The neighborly smile. That smile! And the friendly nod.

"Good evening!"

He was of medium height, broad through the chest and shoulders. Not handsome, but a kind of battered good looks. Surprisingly young. A physical awareness, a tension, in the way he walked. Arms out a little from his sides, fingers bent. He stared at Blank. Saw the smile. His whole body seemed to relax. He nodded, not smiling.

They came abreast. Right hand darting into the open coat. The smooth, practised transfer of the ax to the free right hand. Weight on left foot. Whirl as smooth as a ballet step. An original art form. Murder as a fine art: all sensual kinetics. Weight onto the right foot now. Right arm rising. Lover sensing, hearing, pausing, beginning his own turn in this dear *pas de deux*.

And then. Oh. Up onto his toes. His body arching into the blow. Everything: flesh, bone, sinew, muscle, blood, penis, kneecaps, elbows and biceps, whatever he was . . . giving freely, completely, all of him. The crunch and sweet thud that quivered his hand, wrist, arm, torso, down into his bowels and nuts. The penetration! And the ecstasy! Into the grey wonder and mystery of the man. Oh!

Plucking the ax free even as the body fell, the soul soaring up to the cloudy sky. Oh no. The soul entering into Daniel Blank, becoming one with his soul, the two coupling even as he had imagined lost astronauts embracing and drifting through all immeasurable time.

He stooped swiftly, not looking at the crushed skull. He was not morbid. He found the shield and ID card in a leather folder. He no longer had to prove his deeds to Celia, but this was for him. It was not a trophy, it was a gift from the victim. I love you, too.

So simple! It was incredible, his luck. No witnesses. No shouts, cries, alarms. The moon peeped from behind clouds and withdrew again. The mild wind was there. The night. Somewhere, unseen, stars whirled their keening courses. And tomorrow the sun might shine. Nothing could stop the tides.

"Good movie, Mr. Blank?" Charles Lipsky asked.

"I liked it," Daniel Blank nodded brightly. "Very enjoyable. You really should see it."

He went through the now familiar drill: washing and sterilizing the ice ax, then oiling the exposed steel. He put it away with his other climbing gear in the front hall closet. The policeman's badge represented a problem. He had tucked Lombard's driver's license and Gilbert's ID card under a stack of handkerchiefs in his top dresser drawer. It was extremely unlikely the cleaning woman, or anyone else, would uncover them. But still . . .

He wandered through the apartment, looking for a better hiding place. His first idea was to tape the identification to the backs of three of the larger mirrors on the living room wall. But the tape might dry, the gifts fall free, and then . . .

He finally came back to his bedroom dresser. He pulled the top drawer out and placed it on his bed. There was a shallow recess under the drawer, between the bottom and the runners. All the identification fitted easily into a large white envelope, and this he taped to the bottom of the drawer. If the tape dried, and the envelope dropped, it could only drop into the second drawer. And, while taped, it was in a position where he could easily check its security every day, if he wanted to. Or open the envelope flap and look at his gifts.

Then he was home free—weapon cleansed, evidence hidden, all done that reason told him should be done. He even saved the ticket stub for the neighborhood movie. Now was the time for reflection and dreaming, for pondering significance and meaning.

He bathed slowly, scrubbing, then rubbing scented oil onto his wet skin. He stood on the bathroom mat, staring at himself in the full-length mirror. Unaccountably, he began to make the gyrations of a strip-tease dancer: hands clasped behind his head, knees slightly bent, pelvis pumping in and out, hips grinding. He became excited by his own mirror image. He became erect, not fully but sufficiently to add to his pleasure. So there he stood, pumping his turgid shaft at the mirror.

Was he mad? he wondered. And, laughing, thought he might very well be.

4

The following morning he was having breakfast—a small glass of apple juice, a bowl of organic cereal with skim milk, a cup of black coffee—when the nine o'clock news came on the kitchen radio and a toneless voice announced the murder of Detective third grade Roger Kope on East 75th Street the previous midnight. Kope had been promoted from uniformed patrolman only two weeks previously. He left a widow and three small children. Deputy Commissioner Broughton, in charge of the investigation, stated several important leads were being followed up, and he hoped to make an important statement on the case shortly.

Daniel Blank put his emptied dishes into the sink, ran hot water into them, went off to work.

When he left his office in the evening, he purchased the afternoon *Post*, but hardly glanced at the headline: "Killer Loose on East Side." He carried the paper home with him and collected his mail at the lobby desk. He opened envelopes in the elevator: two bills, a magazine subscription offer, and the winter catalogue from Outside Life.

He fixed himself a vodka on the rocks with a squeeze of lime, turned on the television set and sat in the living room, sipping his drink, leafing through the catalogue, waiting for the evening news.

The coverage of Kope's murder was disappointingly brief. There was a shot of the scene of the crime, a shot of the ambulance moving away, and then the TV reporter said the details of the death of Detective Kope were very similar to those in the murders of Frank Lombard and Bernard Gilbert, and police believed all three killings were the work of one man. "The investigation is continuing."

Later that evening Blank walked over to Second Avenue to buy the early morning editions of the *News* and the *Times*. "Mad Killer Strikes Again," the *News'* headline screamed. The *Times* had a one-column story low on the front page: "Detective Slain on East Side." He brought the papers home, added them to the afternoon *Post* and settled down with a kind of bored dread to read everything that had been printed on Kope's death.

The most detailed, the most accurate report, Blank acknowledged, appeared under the byline "Thomas Handry." Handry, quoting "a high police official who asked that his name not be used," stated unequivocally that the three murders were committed by the same man, and that the weapon used was "an ax-like tool with an elongated spike." The other papers identified the weapon as "a small pick or something similar."

Handry also quoted his anonymous informant in explaining how a police decoy, an experienced officer, could be struck down from behind without apparently being aware of the approach of his attacker or making any effort to defend himself. "It is suggested," Handry wrote, "the assailant approached from the front, presenting an innocent, smiling appearance to his victim, then, at the moment of passing, turned and struck him down. It is believed by the usually reliable source that the killer carried his weapon concealed under a folded newspaper or under his coat. Although Gilbert died from a frontal attack, the method used in Kope's murder closely parallels that in the Lombard killing."

Handry's report ended by stating that his informant feared there would be additional attacks unless the killer was caught. Another paper spoke of an unprecedented assignment of detectives to the case, and the third paper stated that a curfew in the 251st Precinct was under consideration.

Blank tossed the papers aside. It was disquieting, he admitted, that the term "ax-like tool" had been used in Handry's report. He had to assume the police knew exactly what the weapon was, but were not releasing the information. He did not believe they could trace the purchase of an ice ax to him; his ax was five years old, and hundreds were sold annually all over the world. But it did indicate he would be wise not to underestimate the challenge he faced, and he wondered what kind of a man this Deputy Commissioner Broughton was who was trying so hard to take him by the neck. Or, if not Broughton, who Handry's anonymous "high police official" was. That business of approaching from the front, then whirling to strike —who had guessed *that?* There were probably other things known or guessed, and not released to the newspapers—but *what?*

Blank went over his procedures carefully and could find only two obvious weak links. One was his continued possession of the victims' identification. But, after pondering, he realized that if it ever came to a police search of his apartment, they would already have sufficient evidence to tie him to the murders, and the identification would merely be the final confirmation.

The other problem was more serious: Celia Montfort's knowledge of what he had done.

5

Erotica, the sex boutique owned by Florence and Samuel Morton was located on upper Madison Avenue, between a gourmet food shop and a 100-year-old store that sold saddles and polo mallets. Erotica's storefront had been designed by a pop-art enthusiast and consisted of hundreds of polished automobile hubcaps which served as distorting mirrors of the street scene and passing pedestrians.

"It boggles the mind," Flo nodded.

"It blows the brain," Sam nodded.

Between them, they had come up with this absolutely marvy idea for decorating their one window for the Christmas shopping season. They had, at great expense, commissioned a display house to create a naked Santa Claus. He had the requisite tasseled red cap and white beard, but otherwise his plump and roseate body was nude except for a small, black patent leather bikini equipped with a plastic codpiece, an item of masculine attire Erotica was attempting to revive in New York, with limited success.

The naked Santa was displayed in the Madison Avenue window for one day. Then Lieutenant Marty Dorfman, Acting Commander of the 251st Precinct, paid a personal visit to Erotica and politely asked the owners to remove the display, citing a number of complaints he had received from local churches, merchants, and outraged citizens. So the bikini-clad Saint Nicholas was moved to the back of the store, the window filled with miscellaneous erotic Christmas gifts, and Flo and Sam decided to inaugurate the extended-hours shopping season with an open house; free Swedish glug for old and new customers and a dazzling buffet that included such exotic items as fried grasshoppers and chocolate-covered ants.

Daniel Blank and Celia Montfort were specifically invited to this feast and asked to return to the Mortons' apartment later for food and drink of a more substantial nature. They accepted.

The air was overheated—and scented. Two antique Byzantine censers hung suspended in corners; from their pierced shells drifted fumes of a musky incense called "Orgasm," one of Erotica's best sellers. Customers checked their coats and hats with a dark, exquisite, sullen Japanese girl clad in diaphanous Arabian Nights pajamas beneath which she wore no brassiere —only sheer panties imprinted with small reproductions of Mickey Mouse. Incredibly, her pubic hair was blond.

Celia and Daniel stood to one side, observing the hectic scene, sipping small cups of the spiced, steaming glug. The store was crowded with loud-voiced, flush-faced customers, most of them young, all wearing the kinky, trendy fashions of the day. They weren't clothed; they were costumed. Their laughter was shrill, their movements jerky as they pushed through the store, examining phallic candles, volumes of Aubrey Beardsley prints, leather brassieres, jockstraps fashioned in the shape of a clutching hand.

"They're so excited," Daniel Blank said. "The whole world's excited."

Celia looked up at him and smiled faintly. Her long black hair, parted in the middle, framed her witch's face. As usual, she was wearing no makeup, though her eyes seemed shadowed with a bone-deep weariness.

"What are you thinking?" she asked him, and he realized once again how ideas, abstract ideas, aroused her.

"About the world," he said, looking around the frantic room. "The ruttish world. About people today. How stimulated they all are."

"Sexually stimulated?"

"That, of course. But in other ways. Politically. Spiritually, I guess. Violence. The new. The terrible hunger for the new, the different, the 'in thing.' And what's in is out in weeks, days. In sex, art, politics, everything. It all seems to be going faster and faster. It wasn't always like this, was it?"

"No," she said, "it wasn't."

"The in thing," he repeated. "Why do they call it 'in?' Penetration?"

Now she looked at him curiously. "Are you drunk?" she asked.

He was surprised. "On two paper cups of Swedish glug? No," he laughed, "I am not drunk."

He touched her cheek with warm fingers. She grabbed his

hand, turned her head to kiss his fingertips, then slid his thumb into her wet mouth, tongued it, drew it softly out. He looked swiftly about the room; no one was staring.

"I wish you were my sister," he said in a low voice.

She was silent a moment, then asked, "Why did you say that?"

"I don't know. I didn't think about it. I just said it."

"Are you tired of sex?" she asked shrewdly.

"What? Oh no. No. Not exactly. It's just . . ." He waved at the crowded room. "It's just that they're not going to find it this way."

"Find what?"

"Oh . . . you know. The answer."

The evening had that chopped, chaotic tempo that now infected all his hours: life speeding in disconnected scenes, a sharply cut film, images and distortions in an accelerating frenzy: faces, places, bodies, speech and ideas swimming up to the lens, enlarging, then dwindling away, fading. It was difficult to concentrate on any one experience; it was best simply to open himself to sensation, to let it all engulf him.

"Something's happening to me," he told her. "I see these people here, and on the street, and at work, and I can't believe I belong with them. The same race, I mean. They seem to me dogs, or animals in a zoo. Or perhaps I am. But I can't relate. But if they are human, I am not. And if I am, they are not. I just don't recognize them. I'm apart from them."

"You *are* apart from them," she said softly. "You've done something so meaningful that it sets you apart."

"Oh yes," he said, laughing happily. "I have, haven't I? If they only knew . . ."

"How does it feel?" she asked him. "I mean . . . knowing? Satisfaction? Pleasure?"

"That, of course," he nodded, feeling an itch of joy at talking of these things in a crowded, noisy room (he was naked but no one could see). "But mostly a feeling of—of gratification that I've been able to accomplish so much."

"Oh yes, Dan," she breathed, putting a hand on his arm.

"Am I mad?" he asked. "I've been wondering."

"Is it important?"

"No. Not really."

"Look at these people," she gestured. "Are they sane?"

"No," he said. "Well . . . maybe. But whether they're sane or mad, I'm different from them."

"Of course you are."

"And different from you," he added, smiling.

She shivered, a bit, and moved closer to him.

"Do we have to go to the Mortons?" she murmured.

"We don't have to. I think we should."

"We could go to your place. Or my place. Our place."

"Let's go to the Mortons," he said, smiling again and feeling it on his face.

They waited until Flo and Sam were ready to leave. Then they all shared a big cab back to the Mortons' apartment. Flo and Sam gabbled away in loud voices. Daniel Blank sat on the monkey seat, smiled and smiled.

Blanche had prepared a roast duckling garnished with peach halves. And there were small roasted potatoes and a tossed salad of romaine and Italian water cress. She brought the duckling in on a carving board to show it around for their approval before returning it to the kitchen to quarter it.

It looked delicious, they agreed, with its black, crusty skin and gleaming peach juice. And yet, when Daniel Blank's full plate was put before him, he sat a moment and stared; the food offended him.

He could not say why, but it happened frequently of late. He would go into a familiar restaurant, alone or with Celia, order a dish that he had had before, that he knew he liked, and then, when the food was put before him, he had no appetite and could scarcely toy with it.

It was just so—so *physical*. That steaming mixture to be cut into manageable forkfuls and shoved through the small hole that was his mouth, to emerge, changed and compounded, a day later via another small hole. Perhaps it was the vulgarity of the process that offended him. Or its animality. Whatever, the sight of food, however well prepared, now made him queasy. It was all he could do, for politeness' sake, to eat a bit of his duckling quarter, two small potatoes, dabble in the salad. He wasn't comfortable until, finally, they were seated on sofas and in soft chairs, having black coffee and vodka stingers.

"Hey, Dan," Samuel Morton said abruptly, "you got any money to invest?"

"Sure," Blank said amiably. "Not a lot, but some. In what?"

"First of all, this health club you belong to—what does it cost you?"

"Five hundred a year. That doesn't include massage or food, if you want it. They have sandwiches and salads. Nothing fancy."

"Liquor?"

"You can keep a bottle in your locker if you like. They sell set-ups."

"A swimming pool?"

"A small one. And a small sundeck. Gymnasium, of course. A sauna. What's this all about?"

"Can you swim naked in the pool?"

"Naked? I don't know. I suppose you could if you wanted to. It's for men only. I've never seen anyone do it. Why do you ask?"

"Sam and I had this marvy idea," Florence Morton said.

"A natural," Sam said. "Can't miss."

"There's this health club on East Fifty-seventh Street," Flo said. "It started as a reducing salon, but it's not making it. It's up for grabs now."

"Good asking price." Sam nodded. "And they'll shave."

"It's got a big pool," Flo nodded. "A gym with all the machines, two saunas, locker room, showers. The works."

"And a completely equipped kitchen," Sam added. "A nice indoor-outdoor lounge with tables and chairs."

"The decor is hideous," Flo added. "Hideous. But all the basic stuff is there."

"You're thinking of opening a health club?" Celia Montfort asked.

"But different," Flo laughed.

"Totally different," Sam laughed.

"For men *and* women," Flo grinned.

"Using the same locker room and showers," Sam grinned.

"With nude sunbathing on the roof," Sam noted.

Blank looked from one to the other. "You're kidding?"

They shook their heads.

"You'd take only married couples and families for members?"

"Oh no," Flo said. "Swinging singles only."

"That's just the point," Sam said. "That's where the money comes from. Lonely singles. And it won't be cheap. We figure five hundred members at a thousand a year each. We'll try to keep the membership about sixty-forty."

"Sixty percent men and forty percent women," Flo explained.

Blank stared at them, shook his head. "You'll go to jail," he told them. "And so will your members."

"Not necessarily," Flo said. "We've had our lawyers looking into it."

"There are some encouraging precedents," Sam said. "There

308

are beaches out in California set aside for swimming in the nude. All four sexes. The courts have upheld the legality. The law is very hazy in New York. No one's ever challenged the right to have mixed nude bathing in a private club. We think we can get away with it."

"It all hinges on whether or not you're 'maintaining a public nuisance'," Flo explained.

"If it's private and well-run and no nudity in public, we think we can do it," Sam explained.

"No nudity in public?" Daniel Blank asked. "You mean fornication in the sauna or in a mop closet or underwater groping is okay?"

"It's all private," Flo shrugged.

"Who's hurting whom?" Sam shrugged. "Consenting adults."

Daniel looked at Celia Montfort. She sat still, her face expressionless. She seemed waiting for his reaction.

"We're forming a corporation," Flo said.

"We figure we'll need a hundred thousand tops," Sam said, "for lease, mortgage, conversion, insurance, etcetera."

"We're selling shares," Flo said.

"Interested?" Sam asked.

Daniel Blank patted his Via Veneto wig gently.

"Oh," he said. "No," he said. "I don't think so. Not my cup of tea. But I think, if you can get around the legal angle, it's a good idea."

"You think it'll catch on?" Sam asked.

"Profitable?" Flo asked.

"No doubt about it," Blank assured them. "If the law doesn't close you down, you'll make a mint. Just walk down Eighth Avenue, which I do almost every day. Places where you can get a woman to give you a rub-down, or you can paint her body, or watch films, or get tickled with feathers. And ordinary prostitution too, of course. Mixed nude bathing in a private pool? Why not? Yes, I think it's a profitable idea."

"Then why don't you want to invest?" Celia asked him.

"What? Oh . . . I don't know. I told you—not my style. I'm tired of it all. Maybe just bored. Anyway, it puts me off. I don't like it."

They stared at him, the three of them, and waited. But when he said nothing more, Celia spurred him on.

"What don't you like?" she asked quietly. "The idea of men and women swimming naked together? You think it's immoral?"

309

"Oh God no!" he laughed loudly. "I'm no deacon. It's just that . . ."

"It's just what?"

"Well," he said, showing his teeth, "sex is so—so inconsequential, isn't it? I mean, compared to death and—well, virginity. I mean, they're so absolute, aren't they? And sex never is. Always something more. But with death and virginity you're dealing with absolutes. Celia, that word you used? Finitudes. Was that it? Or finalities. Something like that. It's so nice to—it's so warm to—I know life is trouble, but still . . . What you're planning is wrong. Not in the moral sense. Oh no. But you're skirting the issue. You know? You're wandering around and around, and you don't see the goal, don't even glimpse it. Oh yes. Profitable? It will surely be profitable. For a year or two. Different. New. The in-thing. But then it will fall away. Just die. Because you're not giving them the answer, don't you see? Fucking underwater or in a sauna. And then. No, no! It's all so—so superficial. I told you. Those people tonight. Well, there you are. What have they learned or won? Maybe masturbation is the answer. Have you ever considered that? I know it's ridiculous. I apologize for mentioning it. But still . . . Because, you see, in your permissive world they say porn, perv and S-M. That's how much it means, that you can abbreviate it. So there you are. And it offends me. The vulgarity. Because it might have been a way, a path, but is no longer. Sex? Oh no. Shall we have another martini or shall we fuck? That important. I knew a girl once . . . Well. So you've got to go beyond. I tell you, it's just not enough. So, putting aside sex, you decide what comes next. What number bus to the absolute. And so you—"

Celia Montfort interrupted swiftly.

"What Daniel is trying to say," she told the astounded Mortons, "is that in a totally permissive society, virginity becomes the ultimate perversion. Isn't that what you wanted to say, dear?"

He nodded dumbly. Finally, they got out of there. She was trembling but he was not.

6

He propped himself on his left elbow, let his right palm slide lightly down that silky back.

"Are you awake?"

"Yes."

"Tell me about this woman, Celia Montfort."

Soft laughter.

"What do you want to know about 'this woman, Celia Montfort'?"

"Who is she? What is she?"

"I thought you knew all about her."

"I know she is beautiful and passionate. But so mysterious and withdrawn. She's so locked up within herself."

"Yes, she is, luv. Very deep, is our Celia."

"When she goes away, unexpectedly, where does she go?"

"Oh . . . places."

"To other men?"

"Sometimes. Sometimes to other women."

"Oh."

"Are you shocked, darling?"

"Not really. I guess I suspected it. But she comes back so weary. Sometimes she's been hurt. Does she want to be? I mean, does she deliberately seek it?"

"I thought you knew. You saw those bandages on her wrists. I saw you staring at them. She tried to slash her veins."

"My God."

"She tried it before and will probably try it again. Pills or driving too fast or a razor."

"Oh sweetheart, why does she do it?"

"Why? She really doesn't know. Except life has no value for her. No real value. She said that once."

He kissed those soft lips and with his fingertips touched the closed eyes gently. The limpid body moved to him, pressed sweetly; he smelled again that precious flesh, skin as thin, as smooth as watered silk.

"I thought I made her happy."

"Oh you did, Dan. As much as any man can. But it's not enough for her. She's seen everything, done everything, and still nothing has meaning for her. She's run through a dozen religions and faiths, tried alcohol and all kinds of drugs, done things with men and women and children you wouldn't believe. She's burned out now. Isn't it obvious? Celia Montfort. Poor twit."

"I love her."

"Do you? I think it's too late for her, Dan. She's—she's beyond love. All she wants now is release."

"Release from what?"

"From living, I suppose. Since she's trying so hard to kill herself. Perhaps her problem is that she's too intelligent. She's painted and written poetry. She was very good but couldn't endure the thought of being just 'very good.' If she didn't have the talent of a genius, she couldn't settle for second-best. Always, she wants the best, the most, the final. I think her problem is that she wants to be *sure*. Of something, anything. She wants final answers. I think that's why she was attracted to you, darling. She felt you were searching for the same thing."

"You're so old for your age."

"Am I? I'm ancient. I was born ancient."

They laughed gently, together, and moved together, holding each other. Then kissing, kissing, with love but without passion, wet lips clinging. Blank stroked webbed hair and with a fingertip traced convolution of delicate ear, slender throat, thrust of rib beneath satin skin.

Finally they drew apart, lay on their backs, side by side, inside hands clasped loosely.

"What about Valenter?"

"What about him?"

"What is his role in your house?"

"His *role*? He's a servant, a houseman."

"He seems so—so sinister."

Mocking: "Do you think he's sleeping with brother or sister? Or both?"

"I don't know. It's a strange house."

"It may be a strange house, but I assure you Valenter is only a servant. It's your imagination, Dan."

"I suppose so. That room upstairs. Are there peepholes where other people can watch? Or is the place wired to pick up conversation?"

"Now you're being ridiculous."

"I suppose so. Perhaps I was believing what I wanted to believe. But why that room?"

"Why did I take you there? Because it's at the top of the house. No one ever goes there. It's private, and I knew we wouldn't be interrupted. It's shabby, I know, but it was fun, wasn't it? Didn't you think it was fun? Why are you laughing?"

"I don't know. Because I read so much into it that doesn't exist. Perhaps."

"Like what?"

"Well, this woman—"

"I know, 'this Celia Montfort'."

312

"Yes. Well, I thought this Celia Montfort might be manipulating me, using me."

"For what?"

"I don't know. But I feel she wants something from me. She's waiting for something. From me. Is she?"

"I don't know, Dan. I just don't know. She is a very complex woman. I don't know too much about women; most of my experience has been with men, as you very well know. But I don't think Celia Montfort knows exactly what she wants. I think she senses it and is fumbling toward it, making all kinds of false starts and wrong turnings. She's always having accidents. Slipping, upsetting things, knocking things over, falling and breaking this or that. But she's moving toward something. Do you have that feeling?"

"Yes. Oh yes. Are you rested now?"

"Yes, darling, I'm rested."

"Can we make love again?"

"Please. Slowly."

"Tony, Tony, I love you."

"Oh pooh," Tony Montfort said.

7

The strange thing, the strange thing, Daniel Blank decided, was that the world, his world, was expanding at the same time he, himself, was contracting. That is, Tony and Mrs. Cleek and Valenter and the Mortons—everyone he knew and everyone he saw on the streets—well, he loved them all. So sad. They were all so sad. But then, just as he had told Celia that night at the Erotica, he felt apart from them. But still he could love them. That was curious and insolvable.

At the same time his love and understanding were going out to encompass all living things—people, animals, rocks, the whirling skies—he pulled in within himself, chuckling, to nibble on his own heart and hug his secret life. He was condensing, coiling in upon himself, penetrating deeper and deeper. It was a closed life of shadow, scent, and gasps. And yet, and yet there were stars keening their courses, a music in the treacherous world.

Well, it came to this: should he or should he not be a hermit? He could twirl naked before a mirrored wall and embrace himself in golden chains. That was one answer. Or he could go out into the clotted life of the streets, and mingle. Join. Penetrate, and know them all. Loving.

He opted for the streets, the evil streets, and openness. The answer, he decided, was there. It was not in AMROK II; it was in Charles Lipsky, and all the other striving, defeated clods. He hated them for their weaknesses and vices, and loved them for their weaknesses and vices. Was he a Christ? It was a vagrant thought. Still, he acknowledged, he could be. He had Christ's love. But, of course, he was not a religious man.

So. Daniel Blank on the prowl. Grinning at the dull winter sky, determined to solve the mystery of life.

This night he had bathed, oiled and scented his slender body, dressed slowly and carefully in black suit, black turtle-neck sweater, crepe-soled shoes, the slit-pocket topcoat with the ice ax looped over his left wrist within. He sauntered out to search for his demon lover, a Mongol of a man, so happy, so happy. It was eleven days after the murder of Detective third grade Roger Kope.

It had become increasingly difficult, he acknowledged. Since the death of the detective, the neighborhood streets at night were not only patrolled by plain-clothes decoys, but two-man teams of uniformed officers appeared on almost every block and corner, wary and not at all relaxed after what happened to Kope. In addition, the assignment of more squad cars to the area was evident, and Daniel Blank supposed that unmarked police cars were also being used.

Under the circumstances he would have been justified in seeking another hunting ground, perhaps another borough. But he considered it more challenge than risk. Did you reject a difficult climb because of the danger? If you did, why climb at all? The point, the whole point, was to stretch yourself, probe new limits of your talent and courage. Resolution was like a muscle: exercised it grew larger and firmer; unused it became pale and flabby.

The key, he reasoned, might be the time factor. His three killings had all taken place between 11:30 p.m. and 12:30 a.m. The police would be aware of this, of course, and all officers warned to be especially alert during that midnight hour. They might be less vigilant before and after. He needed every advantage he could find.

He decided on an earlier time. It was the Christmas shopping season. It was dark by seven p.m., but the stores were open until nine, and even at ten o'clock people were scurrying home, laden with parcels and bundles. After 12:30 the streets were almost deserted except for the decoys and uniformed patrols. Neighborhood residents had read the newspaper reports following Kope's death; few ventured out after midnight. Yes, earlier would be best: any time from nine to ten-thirty. Mountain climbers judged carefully the odds and percentages; they were not deliberate suicides.

He needed camouflage, he decided, and after long consideration determined what he must do. The previous evening, on his way home from work, he stopped in a store on 42nd Street that sold Christmas cards, artificial trees, ornaments, wrapping paper, and decorations. The store had opened six weeks before Christmas and would go out of business on Christmas Eve. He had seen it happen frequently, all over the city.

He purchased two boxes, one about the size of a shoe box, the other flat and long, designed for a man's necktie or a pair of gloves. He bought a roll of Christmas wrapping paper, the most conventional he could find: red background with reindeer pulling Santa's sled imprinted on it. The roll itself was wrapped in cellophane. He bought a small package of stickers and a ball of cord that was actually a length of knitting yarn wound about a cardboard square.

He wore his thin, black suede gloves while making the purchase. The store was mobbed; the clerk hardly glanced at him. At home, still wearing the gloves, he prepared the two empty boxes as Christmas packages, wrapping them neatly in the reindeer paper, sticking down the end flaps with the gummed Santa Claus heads, then tying them up with the red yarn, making very attractive bows on top. Finished, he had what were apparently two Christmas gifts, handsomely wrapped. He intended to leave them at the scene; the chances of their being traced to him, he believed, were absolutely minimal. He then shoved excess wrapping, stickers, cord and paper bag into his garbage can, took it to the incinerator room down the hall, and dumped it all down. Then he came back to his apartment and took off his gloves.

As he had expected, the doorman on duty when he left the following evening—it was not Charles Lipsky—hardly looked up when Daniel Blank passed, carrying his two empty Christmas boxes; he was too busy signing for packages and helping tenants out of cabs with shopping bags stuffed with bundles. And if he had noted him, what of that? Daniel Blank on his way to an evening with friends, bringing them two gaily wrapped presents. Beautiful.

He was so elated with his own cleverness, so surprised by the number of shoppers still on the streets, that he decided to walk over to The Parrot on Third Avenue, have a leisurely drink, kill a little time. "Kill time." He giggled, the ax clasped beneath his coat, the Christmas packages in his right arm.

The Parrot was almost empty. There was one customer at the bar, a middle-aged man talking to himself, making wide gestures. The lone waiter sat at a back table, reading a religious tract. The bartender was marking a racing form. They were the two who had been on duty when he had had the fight with the homosexual the previous year. They both looked up when he came in, but he saw no recognition in their faces.

He ordered a brandy, and when it was brought he asked the bartender if he'd have something, too.

"Thanks," the man said with a cold smile. "Not while I'm working."

"Quiet tonight. Everyone Christmas shopping, I suppose."

"It ain't that," the man said, leaning toward him. "Other Christmases we used to get a crowd when the stores closed. This year, no one. Know why?"

"Why?"

"This nutty killer on the loose," the man said angrily, his reddish wattles wagging. "Who the hell wants to be out on the streets after dark? I hope they catch him soon and cut his balls off. The son-of-a-bitch, he's ruining our business."

Blank nodded sympathetically and paid for his drink. The ax was still under his coat. He sat at the bar, coated, gloved, although the room was warm, and sipped his brandy with pleasure. The Christmas boxes were placed on the bar next to him. It was quiet and restful. And amusing, in a way, to learn that what he was doing had affected so many people. A stone dropped in a pool, the ripples going out, spreading . . .

He had the one drink, left a modest tip, walked out with his packages. He turned at the door to see if he should make a half-wave to the bartender or waiter, but no one was looking at him. He laughed inwardly; it was all so easy. No one cared.

The shoppers were thinning out; those still on the streets were hurrying homeward, packages under their arms or shopping bags swinging. Blank imitated their appearance: his two Christmas presents under one arm, his head and shoulders slightly bent against the cruel wind. But his eyes flicked everywhere. If he couldn't finish his business before 11:00, he would give it up for another night; he was determined on that.

He lost one good prospect when the man suddenly darted up the stairway of a brownstone and was gone while Daniel

Blank was still practicing his smile. He lost another who stopped to talk to the doorman of an apartment house. A third looked promising, but too much like a detective decoy; a civilian wouldn't be walking *that* slowly. Another was lost because a uniformed patrol turned the corner after him unexpectedly and came sauntering toward Blank.

He would not be frustrated and tried to keep his rage under control. But still . . . what were they doing to him? He pulled his left wrist far enough from his coat pocket to read the time under a street lamp. It was almost 10:30. Not much left. Then he'd have to let it go for another night. But he couldn't. *Couldn't.* The fever was in his blood, blazing. The hell with . . . Damn the . . . Fix bayonets, lads, and over . . . Now or . . . It had to be. His luck was so good. A winning streak. Always ride a winning streak.

And so it was. For there—incredibly, delightfully, free of prowling cars and uniformed patrols—the block was empty and dim, and toward him came striding a single man, walking swiftly, under one arm a package in Christmas wrapping. And in the buttonhole of his tweed overcoat, a small, sweetheart rose. Would a police decoy carry a Christmas package? Wear a rose? Not likely, Daniel Blank decided. He began his smile.

The lover passed under a street lamp. Blank saw he was young, slender, mustached, erect, confident and, really, rather beautiful. Another Daniel Blank.

"Good evening!" Daniel called out, a pace away, smiling.

"Good evening!" the man said in return, smiling.

At the moment of passing, Blank transferred the ax and started his turn. And even as he did he was aware that the victim had suddenly stopped and started *his* turn. He had a dim feeling of admiration for a man whose instincts, whose physical reactions were so right and so swift, but after that it was all uncertain.

The ax was raised. The Christmas packages dropped to the sidewalk. Then there were two hands clamped on his lifted wrist. The man's package fell also. But his grip didn't loosen. Blank was pulled tight. Three arms were high in the air. They stood a second, carved in sweet embrace, breathing wintry steam into each other's open lips, close. The physical contact was so delicious that Daniel was fuddled, and pressed closer. Warmth. Lovely warmth and strength.

Sense came flooding back. He hooked a heel behind the man's left knee, pulled back and pushed. It wasn't enough. The man staggered but would not go down. But his grip on

Blank's wrist loosened. He hooked again and shoved again, his entire body against the other body. Oh. He thought he heard a distant whistle but wasn't sure. They fell then, and Daniel Blank, rolling, heard and felt his bent left elbow crack against the pavement and wondered, idly, if it was broken, and thought perhaps it was.

Then they were flat, Blank lying on top of the man whose eyes were dull with a kind of weariness. His hands fell free from Blank's wrist. So he brought the ice ax up and down, up and down, up and down, hacking furiously, in an ecstasy, pressing close, for this was the best yet, and hardly aware of weak fingers and nails clawing at his face. Something warm there.

Until the young man was still, black eyes glaring now. Blank laid the ax aside a moment to snatch at the lapel rose, picked up the ax again, staggered to a snarling crouch, looked about wildly. There were whistles now, definitely. A uniformed cop came pounding down from the far corner, hand fumbling at his hip, and his partner across the avenue, blowing and blowing at that silly whistle. Blank watched a few seconds, looping the ax about his dead left wrist under his coat.

He was suddenly conscious of the pain, in his left elbow, in his bleeding face. Then he was running, holding his injured left elbow close to his body, calculating possibilities and probabilities, but never once considered casting aside the sweetheart rose.

The body on the sidewalk should stop them for a moment, one of them at least, and as he turned onto First Avenue he stopped running, shoved the rose into his righthand coat pocket, fished out a handkerchief from the breast pocket of his jacket and held it across his bleeding face, coughing and coughing. He went into a luncheonette, two doors down from the corner. Still coughing, his bleeding face concealed by his handkerchief, he walked steadily to the phone booth in the rear. He actually clamped the handkerchief with his shoulder and took a coin from his righthand pocket to put in and dial the weather service. He was listening to a disembodied voice say, "Small craft warnings are in effect from Charleston to Block Island," when, watching, he saw a uniformed cop run by the luncheonette with drawn gun. Blank left the phone booth immediately, still coughing, handkerchief to face. There was an empty cab stopped for a light at 81st Street. Luck. Wasn't it all luck?

He asked the driver, politely, to take him to the west side

bus terminal. His voice—to his own ears, at least—was steady. When the light changed and the cab started off, he pushed to the far left corner where the driver couldn't see him in his rear view mirror without obviously craning. Then Blank held out his right hand, fingers spread. They didn't seem to be trembling. ·

It was almost a twenty-minute trip to the bus terminal and he used every one of them, looking up frequently to make certain the driver wasn't watching. First he swung open his top-coat, unbuttoned his jacket, unhooked his belt. Then he gently slid the loop of the ice ax off his nerveless left wrist, put his belt through the loop, and buckled it again. Now the ax would bump against his thigh as he walked, but it was safe. He buttoned his jacket.

Then he spit onto his handkerchief and softly rubbed his face. There was blood, but much less than he had feared. He put the handkerchief beside him on the seat and, gripping his left hand in his right, slowly bent his left arm. It hurt, it ached, but the pain was endurable, the elbow seemed to be functioning, and he hoped it was a bad bruise, not a break or a chip. He bent his left elbow and put the forearm inside his jacket, resting on the buttons, like a sling. It felt better that way.

He spit more into his handkerchief, wiped his face again, and there was hardly any fresh blood. The shallow wounds were already clotting. Blank pushed his reddened handkerchief into his breast pocket. He dragged out his wallet with one hand, glanced at the taxi meter, then extracted three one-dollar bills, replaced his wallet, sat back in the seat, drew a deep breath and smiled.

The bus station was mobbed. No one stared at him, and he didn't even bother covering his face with his handkerchief. He went directly to the men's room. It, too, was crowded, but he was able to get a look at himself in the mirror. His wig was awry, his left cheek scratched deeply—they'd surely scab—his right cheek roughened but not cut. Only one scratch on his left cheek was still welling blood, but slowly.

There was a man washing his hands in the basin alongside. He caught Blank's eye in the mirror.

"Hope the other guy looks as bad," he said.

"Never laid a hand on him," Blank said ruefully, and the man laughed.

Daniel moistened two paper towels under the tap and went into one of the pay toilets. When he had locked the door, he used one wet towel to wipe his face again, then plastered toilet paper onto his scratched, wet cheek. He used the other dampened towel to sponge his coat and suit. He discovered an abrasion on the left knee of his trousers; the cloth had been scraped through and skin showed. He would have to throw away the entire suit, wrap it in brown paper and dump it in a trash basket on his way to work. Chances were a derelict would fish it out before the sanitation men got to the basket. In any event, Blank could tear out the labels and burn them. It wasn't important.

He tried his left arm again. The elbow joint worked, but painfully—no doubt about that. He took off his jacket and rolled up his sleeve. A lovely swelling there, already discolored. But the elbow worked. He adjusted all his clothes and managed his topcoat so that it hung from his shoulders, continental style, both his arms inside, the ax swinging from his belt. He peeled the toilet paper carefully from his face and looked at it. Faintly pinkish. He had a sudden, uncontrollable need to defecate, and did. He flushed paper and towels down the drain, tugged his clothing smooth, and opened the toilet door, smiling faintly.

In the mirror over the basin he adjusted his wig and combed it slowly with his right hand.

Another man, a hatless, bald-headed man, was drying his hands nearby. He stared at Blank. Daniel turned to stare back.

"Looking at something?" he asked.

The man gestured apologetically. "Your hair," he said, "it's a rug. Right?"

"Oh yes."

"I've been thinking," the man said. "You recommend?"

"Absolutely. No doubt about it. But get the best you can afford. I mean, don't skimp."

"It don't blow off?"

"Not a chance. I never wear a hat. You can swim in it. Even shower in it if you like."

"You really think so?"

"Definitely," Blank nodded. "Change your whole life."

"No kidding?" the man breathed, enthused.

He took a cab back to his apartment house, his coat hanging loosely from his shoulders.

"Hey, Mr. Blank," the doorman said. "Another guy got killed tonight. Not two blocks from here."

"Is that right?" Daniel said, and shook his head despairingly. "From now on I'm taking cabs *everywhere.*"

"That's the best way, Mr. Blank."

He drew a hot tub, poured in enough scented bath oil to froth the water and spice the bathroom. He undressed and slid in carefully, leaving the cleaning of the ice ax until later. But, atop the sudsy water, he floated the sweetheart rose. He watched it, immersed to his chin in the steaming tub, soaking his sore elbow. After awhile his erection came up until the flushed head of his penis was above the surface, and the small rose bobbed about it. He had never been so happy in his life. He dreamed.

PART VII

1

"They had stopped at a wharf painted white, and now Honey Bunch followed her daddy and her mother up this and found herself at the steps of the cunningest bungalow she had ever seen. It was painted white and it had green window boxes and green shutters with little white acorns painted on them. Honey Bunch had never seen a white acorn, but she thought they looked very pretty on the shutters. There was a little sign over the porch of this bungalow and on it were the words 'Acorn House'."

Captain Edward X. Delaney stopped. At his wife's request he had been reading aloud from "Honey Bunch: Her First Days in Camp," but when he glanced up at the hospital bed Barbara seemed asleep, breathing heavily, thin arms and white hands lying limply atop the single blanket. She never got out of bed any more, not even to sit in a wheelchair.

He had arrived in time to help her with the evening meal. She nibbled a muffin, ate a little mashed potatoes, a few string beans, but wouldn't taste the small steak.

"You've got to eat, dear," he said, as firmly as he could, and she smiled wanly as he took the spoon and held some custard to her lips. She ate almost all the custard, then pushed his hand away, averted her face; he didn't have the heart to insist.

"What have you been doing, Edward?" she asked weakly.

"Oh . . . you know; trying to keep myself busy."

"Is there anything new on the case?"

"What case?" he asked, and then was ashamed and dropped his eyes. He did not want to dissemble but it seemed cruel, in her condition, to speak of violent death.

"What is it, Edward?" she asked, guessing.

"There's been another one," he said in a low voice. "A detective. One of Broughton's decoys."

"Married?"

"Yes. Three small children."

Her eyes closed slowly, her face took on a waxen hue. It was then she asked him to read aloud to her from one of the "Honey Bunch" books he had brought her. He took it up gladly, eager to change the subject, opened the book at random and began reading aloud in a resolute, expressive voice.

But now, after only two pages, she seemed to be sleeping. He put the book aside, pulled on his overcoat, took his hat, started to step quietly from the room. But she called, "Edward," and when he turned, her eyes were open, she was holding a hand out to him. He returned immediately to her bedside, pulled up a chair, sat holding her hot, dry fingers.

"That makes three," she said.

"Yes," he nodded miserably. "Three."

"All men," she said vaguely. "Why all men? It would be so much easier to kill women. Or children. Wouldn't it, Edward? Not as dangerous for the killer."

He stared at her, the import of what she was saying growing in his mind. It could be nothing, of course. But it could be something. He leaned forward to kiss her cheek softly.

"You're a wonder, you are," he whispered. "What would I ever do without you?"

Back in his study, a rye highball in his big fist, he forgot about the chicken pie Mary had left on the kitchen table, and thought only of the significance of what his wife had suggested.

It certainly wasn't unusual for a psychopathic killer to be uninterested in or fearful of sex before killing (or even impotent) and then, during or after the murder, to become an uncontrollable satyr. There had been many such cases, but all, to his knowledge, involved women or children as victims.

But now the three victims were men, and Lombard and Kope had been big, muscular men, well able to defend themselves, given half a chance. Still, so far the killer had selected only men, slaying with an ice ax. As Barbara had said, it was a dangerous way to kill—dangerous for the assassin. How much easier to strike down a woman or use a gun against a man. But he had not. Only men. With an ax. Did that mean anything?

It might, Delaney nodded, it just might. Of course, if the next victim was a woman, the theory would be shot to hell, but just consider it a moment. The killer, a male, had killed three other men, risking. Playing amateur psychologist, Delaney considered the sexual symbolism of the weapon used: a pointed ice ax, an ax with a rigid spike. Was that so farfetched? An ice ax with a drooping spike! Even more farfetched?

He took his "Expert File" from the bottom drawer of his desk and found the card he wanted: "PSYCHIATRIST-CRIMINOLOGIST. Dr. Otto Morgenthau." There were short additional notes in Delaney's handwriting on the card, recalling the two cases in which Dr. Morgenthau had assisted the Department. One involved a rapist, the other a bomber. Delaney called the number listed: the doctor's office on Fifth Avenue in the 60s, not in the 251st Precinct.

A feminine voice: "Dr. Morgenthau's office."

"Could I speak to Dr. Morgenthau, please? This is Captain Edward X. Delaney, New York Police Department."

"I'm sorry, Captain, the doctor is unavailable at the moment."

That meant Morgenthau had a patient.

"Could he call me back?" Delaney asked.

"I'll try, sir. May I have your number?"

He gave it to her, hung up, then went into the kitchen. He tried some of the chicken pie; it was good but he really wasn't hungry. He covered the remainder carefully with plastic wrap and put it into the refrigerator. He mixed another rye highball and sat hunched in the swivel chair behind his study desk, sipping his drink, staring blankly at the telephone. When it rang, half an hour later, he let it ring three times before he picked it up.

"Captain Edward X. Delaney here."

"And here is Dr. Otto Morgenthau. How are you, Captain?"

"Well, thank you, doctor. And you?"

"Weary. What is it, Captain?"

"I'd like to see you, sir."

"*You*, Captain? Personally? Or Department business?"

"Department."

"Well, what is it?"

"It's difficult to explain over the phone, doctor. I was wondering—"

"Impossible," Morgenthau interrupted sharply. "I have patients until ten o'clock tonight. And then I must—"

"The three men who were axed to death on the east side," Delaney interrupted in his turn. "You must have read about it."

There was a moment of silence.

"Yes," Dr. Morgenthau said slowly, "I have read about it. Interesting. The work of one man?"

"Yes, sir. Everything points to it."

"What do you have?"

"Bits and pieces. I hoped you could fill in some of the gaps."

Dr. Morgenthau sighed. "I suppose it must be immediately?"

"If possible, sir."

"Be here promptly at ten o'clock. Then I will give you fifteen minutes. No more."

"Yes, sir. I'll be there. Thank you, doctor."

Delaney arrived five minutes early. The morose, matronly nurse was pulling on an ugly cloth coat, fastened in front with wooden toggles.

"Captain Delaney?"

"Yes."

"Please to doublelock the door after I leave," she said. "Doctor will call you when he is ready."

Delaney nodded, and after she marched out, he obediently turned the latch, then sat down in a straight chair, his hat hooked over one knee, and waited patiently, staring at nothing.

When the doctor finally appeared from his consulting room, Delaney rose to his feet, shocked at the man's appearance. The last time the Captain had seen him, Morgenthau was somewhat corpulent but robust, alert, with erect posture, healthy skin tone, clear and active eyes. But now Delaney was confronted by a wheyfaced man shrunken within clothing that seemed three sizes too large in all dimensions. The eyes were dull and hooded, the hair thinning and uncombed. There was a tremor to the hands and, Delaney noted, fingernails were dirty and untrimmed.

They sat in the consulting room, Morgenthau slumped behind his desk, Delaney in an armchair at one side.

"I'll be as brief as possible, doctor," he began. "I know how busy—"

"Just a moment," Morgenthau muttered, gripping the edge of the desk to pull himself upright. "Sorry to interrupt you, Captain, but I have just remembered a phone call I must make at once. A disturbed patient. I shall only be a few minutes. You wait here."

He hurried out, not to the reception room but to an inner office. Delaney caught a quick glimpse of white medical cabinets, a stainless steel sink. Morgenthau was gone almost ten minutes. When he returned, his walk was swift and steady, his eyes wide and shiny. He was rubbing his palms together, smiling.

"Well now," he said genially, "what have we got, Captain?"

Not pills, Delaney thought; the reaction was too swift for pills. Probably an amphetamine injection. Whatever it was, it had worked wonders for Dr. Otto Morgenthau; he was relaxed, assured, listened closely, and when he lighted a cigar his hands were unhurried and steady.

Delaney went through it all: the deaths of the three victims, the ice ax, what he had learned about mountaineers, the way he believed the crimes were committed, the missing identification—everything he felt Morgenthau needed to know, omitting the fact, naturally, that he, Delaney, was not on active duty and was not in charge of the official investigation.

"And that's about all we've got, doctor."

"No possible link between the three men?"

"No, sir. Nothing we've been able to discover."

"And what do you want from me?"

"What you were able to provide us before—a psychiatric profile of the criminal. They were of great help, doctor."

"Oh yes," Morgenthau nodded. "Rape and bombing. But they are sufficiently popular pastimes so that there is a large history available, many similar cases. So it is possible to analyze and detect a pattern. You understand? Make a fairly reasonable guess as to motivation, *modus operandi*, perhaps even physical appearance and habits. But in this case—impossible. Now we are dealing with multiple murder. It is, fortunately for all of us, a relatively rare activity. I am now eliminating political assassination which, I would guess, does not apply here."

"No, sir. I don't believe it does."

"So . . . the literature on the subject is not extensive. I tried my hand at a short monograph but I do not believe you read it."

"No, doctor, I didn't."

"No wonder," Morgenthau giggled. "It was published in an obscure German psychiatric journal. So then, I cannot, regretfully, provide you with a psychiatric profile of the mass murderer."

"Well, listen," Delaney said desperately, "can you give me *anything?* About motivation, I mean. Even general stuff might help. For instance, do you think this killer is insane?"

Dr. Morgenthau shook his head angrily. "Sane. Insane. Those are legal terms. They have absolutely no meaning in the world of mental health. Well, I will try . . . My limited research leads me to believe mass murderers are generally of one of three very broad, indefinite types. But I warn you, motivations frequently overlap. With multiple killers, we are dealing with individuals; as I told you, there are no definitive patterns I can discern. Well, then . . . the three main types . . . One:

biological. Those cases in which mass murder is triggered by a physical defect, although the killer may have been psychologically predisposed. As an example, that rifleman up in the Texas tower who killed—how many people? I understand he had a brain tumor and had been trained as a skilled marksman and killer in the military service. Two: psychological. Here the environment in general is not at fault, but the specific pressures—usually familial or sexual—on the individual are of such an extreme nature that killing, over and over again, is the only release. Bluebeard might be such a case, or Jack the Ripper, or that young man in New Jersey—what was his name?"

"Unruh."

"Yes, Unruh. And then the third cause: sociological. This might be when the killer, in a different environment, might live out his days without violence. But his surroundings are so oppressive that his only recourse is fighting back, by killing, against a world he never made, a world that grinds him down to something less than human. This sociological motivation involves not only the residents of ghettoes, the brutalized minorities. There was a case a few years ago—again in New Jersey, I believe—where a 'solid citizen,' a middle-aged, middle-class gentleman who worked for a bank or insurance company—something like that—and passed the collection—"

The fifteen minutes Dr. Morgenthau had allotted Delaney had long since passed. But the doctor kept talking, as Delaney knew he would. It was hard to stop a man riding his hobby.

"—and passed the collection plate at his church every Sunday," Morgenthau was saying. "And then one day this fine, mild, upstanding citizen kills his wife, children, and his mother. Mark that—his mother! And then he takes off."

"I remember that case," Delaney nodded.

"Have they caught him yet?"

"No, I don't think so."

"Well, anyway, Captain, in the investigation, according to newspaper reports, it was discovered this pillar of the community was living in a much larger house than he could afford; it was heavily mortgaged and he was deeply in debt: insurance, cars, clothes, furniture, his children's education—all the social pressures to consider. A sociological motivation here, obviously, but as I told you, mass killers do not fit into neat classifications. What of the man's personality, background, childhood, his crimes considered as a part of the nation's or the world's social history? Charles Manson, for instance. What I am trying to prove to you is that despite these three quite loose classifications, each case of mass murder is specific and different from the others. Men who kill children and the man who killed all those nurses in Chicago and Panzram all seem to have had a similar childhood: physical abuse and body contact at an early age. Sexual pleasure at an infantile level. And yet, of the three I just mentioned, one kills children, one kills young women, and one kills young boys—or buggers them. So where is the pattern? Well, there is a superficial one perhaps. Most mass murderers tend to be quiet, conservative, neat. They attract no attention until their rampage. Often they wear the same suit or the same cut and color suit for days on end."

Delaney had been taking notes furiously in his pocket notebook. Now he looked up, eyes gleaming.

"That's interesting, doctor. But Manson wasn't like that."

"Exactly!" Morgenthau cried triumphantly. "That's just what I've been telling you: in this field it is dangerous to generalize. Here is something else interesting . . . Wertham says mass murderers are not passionless; they only appear to be so. But—and this is what is significant—he says that when their orgy of killing is finished, they once again become apparently passionless and are able to describe their most blood-curdling acts in chilling detail, without regret and without remorse. You know, Captain, my field has its own jargon, just as yours does. And the—the—what do you call it?—the lingo changes frequently, just like slang. Five or ten years ago we spoke of 'CPI's.' These were 'Constitutional Psychopathic Inferiors.' Apparently normal, functioning effectively in society, the CPI's feel no guilt, apparently are born without conscience, have no remorse, and cannot understand what the fuss is all about when the law objects to them holding a child's hand over a gas flame, throwing a puppy out of a ten-story window, or giving apples studded with razor blades and broken glass to a Halloween trick-or-treat visitor. Most mass murderers are CPI's, I would guess. Was that lecture of any help to you, Captain?"

"A very great help," Delaney said gravely. "You've made a number of things clear. But doctor . . . well, the fault is mine, I suppose, in asking you about 'motives.' You spoke mostly about causes. But what about *motives?* I mean, how does the killer justify to himself what he has done or is doing?"

Dr. Morgenthau stared at him a moment, then laughed shortly. His exhilaration was wearing off, his body seemed to be shrinking as he slumped down into his swivel chair. "Now I know why they call you 'Iron Balls,'" he said. "Oh yes, I know your nickname. During our first—ah—cooperation—I believe it was that Chelsea rapist—I made certain inquiries about you. You interested me."

"Did I?"

"You still do. The nickname is a good one for you, Captain."

"Is it?"

"Oh yes. You are surprisingly intelligent and perceptive for a man in your position. You are remarkably well-read, and you ask the right questions. But do you know what you are, Captain Edward X. Delaney? I mean beneath the intelligence, perception, patience, understanding. Do you know what you are, really?"

"What am I?"

"You are a cop."

"Yes," Delaney agreed readily. "That's what I am all right: a cop." The doctor was drifting away from him; he better finish it up fast.

"Iron balls," Dr. Morgenthau muttered. "Iron soul."

"Yes," Delaney nodded. "Let's get back to this problem of motives. How does the killer justify to himself what he is doing?"

"Highly irrational," Morgenthau said in a slurred voice. "Highly. Most fascinating. They all have elaborate rationalizations. It allows them to do what they do. It absolves them. It makes no sense to so-called 'normal' men, but it relieves the killer of guilt. What they are doing is *necessary*."

"Such as?"

"What? Well, now we are getting into metaphysics, are we not? Have some ideas. Do a monograph some day. Captain, will you excuse . . ."

He started to lift himself from his chair, but Delaney held out an arm, the palm of his hand turned downward.

"Just a few more minutes," he said firmly, "and then I'll be out of your hair."

Morgenthau fell back into his chair, looked at the Captain with dull, weary eyes.

" 'Iron Balls'," he said. "The mass killer seeks to impose order on chaos. Not the kind of order you and I want and welcome, but *his* kind of order. World in a ferment. He organizes it. He can't cope. He wants the security of prison. That dear, familiar prison. 'Catch me before I kill again.' You understand? He wants the institution. And if not that, order in the universe. Humanity is disorderly. Unpredictable. So he must work for order. Even if he must kill to attain it. Then he will find peace, because in an ordered world there will be no responsibility."

Delaney wasn't making notes now, but leaning forward listening intently. Dr. Morgenthau looked at him and suddenly yawned, a wide, jaw-cracking yawn. Delaney, unable to help himself, yawned in return.

"Or," Dr. Morgenthau went on, and yawned again (and Delaney yawned in reply), "we have the graffiti artist. Pico 137. Marv 145. Slinky 179. Goddamn it, world, I exist. I am Pico, Marv, Slinky. I have made my mark. You are required to acknowledge my existence. You mother-fuckers, *I am!* So he kills fifteen people or assassinates a President so the world says, 'Yes, Pico, Marv, Slinky, you do exist!' "

Delaney wondered if the man would last. Puffed lids were coming down over dulled eyes, the flesh was slack, swollen fingers plucked at folds of loose skin under the chin. Even the voice had lost its timbre and resolve.

"Or," Morgenthau droned, "or . . ."

Eyes rolled up into his skull until all Delaney could see were clotted whites. But suddenly, pulling himself partly upright, the doctor shook his head wildly, side to side, tiny drops of spittle splattering the glass top of his desk.

"Or alienation," he said thickly. "You cannot relate. Worse. You cannot feel. You want to come close. You want to understand. Truly you do. Come close. To another human being and through him to all humanity and the secret of existence. Captain? Iron Balls? You want to enter into life. Because emotion, feeling, love, ecstasy—all that has been denied you. I said metaphysical. But. That's what you seek. And you cannot find, except by killing. To find your way. And now, Captain Iron Balls, I must . . ."

"I'm going," Delaney said hastily, rising to his feet. "Thank you very much, doctor. You've been a big help."

"Have I?" Morgenthau said vaguely. He staggered upward, made it on the second try, headed toward his inner office.

Delaney paused with his hand on the knob of the reception room door. Then he turned.

"Doctor," he said sharply.

Morgenthau turned slowly, staggered, looked at him through unseeing eyes.

"Who?" he asked.

"Captain Delaney. One more thing . . . This killer we've been discussing has snuffed three men. No women or children.

330

He kills with an ice ax, with a pointed pick. A phallus. I know I'm talking like an amateur now. But could he be a homosexual? Latent maybe? Fighting it. Is it possible?"

Morgenthau stared at him, and before Delaney's eyes he melted farther into his oversize clothes, his face decayed and fell, the light vanished from his eyes.

"Possible?" he whispered. "Anything is possible."

2

Delaney watched, with anger and dismay, as Operation Lombard fell apart. It had been a viable concept—a temporary horizontal organization cutting across precinct lines and the chain of command—and under Chief Pauley, with his talent for organization and administrative genius, it had had a good chance of succeeding. But Pauley had been fired, and under the direction of Deputy Commissioner Broughton, Operation Lombard was foundering.

It was not for lack of energy; Broughton had plenty of that —too much. But he simply didn't have the experience to oversee a manhunt of this size and complexity. And he didn't know the men working for him. He sent weapons specialists halfway across the country to interrogate a recaptured escapee from a mental institution, and he used interrogation experts to check birth and marriage records in musty libraries. He dispatched four men in a car with screaming siren to question a suspect, where one man on foot would have obtained better results. And his paper work was atrocious; from reading the operation Lombard reports, Delaney could tell it was getting out of hand; Broughton was detailing men to tasks that had been checked out weeks ago by Chief Pauley; reports were in the file, if Broughton knew where to look.

It was Thomas Handry, now calling Delaney at least twice a week, who described another of Broughton's failures: his ineptitude at handling the news media. Broughton made the fatal error of continually promising more than he could deliver, and newsmen became disillusioned with his "An arrest is expected momentarily" or "I'll have a *very* important announcement tomorrow" or "We have a suspect in custody who looks very hot." According to Handry, few reporters now bothered to attend Broughton's daily news briefings; he had earned the sobriquet of "Deputy Commissioner Bullshit."

Medical Examiner Sanford Ferguson also called. He wanted to tell Delaney that the Olfactory Analysis Indicator report on tissue taken from Bernard Gilbert's wound had been inconclusive. There could have been trace elements of a light machine oil; it could also have been half a dozen similar substances. Ferguson was trying again with scrapings from the fatal wound of Detective Roger Kope.

"Did you tell Broughton anything about this?"

"That son of a bitch? Don't be silly. He's caused us more trouble—I can't begin to tell you. It's not the work we mind, it's the bastard's *manner*."

Then Ferguson detailed some Departmental gossip:

Broughton was in real trouble. Demands from wealthy east side residents of the 251st Precinct for a quick solution to the three street murders were growing. A citizens' group had been formed. The Mayor was leaning on the Commissioner, and there were even rumors of the Governor appointing a board of inquiry. The murder of Frank Lombard was bad enough—he had wielded a lot of political clout—but the killing of a police officer had intensified editorial demands for a more productive investigation. Broughton, said Ferguson, had a lighted dynamite stick up his ass.

"It couldn't happen to a nicer guy," he added cheerfully.

Delaney wasted no time savoring the comeuppance of Deputy Commissioner Broughton. Nor did he dwell too long on his own personal guilt in the death of Detective third grade Roger Kope. He had done all he could to alert Broughton to the weapon used and the method of attack. And besides, if the truth be known, he blamed Kope; no officer on decoy should have allowed himself to be taken that way. Kope knew what he was up against and what the stakes were. You could feel horror and sympathy for a man shot down from ambush. But Kope had failed—and paid for it.

Delaney had enough on his plate without guilt feelings about Detective Kope. His amateurs needed constant mothering: telephone calls, personal visits and steady, low-key assurance that what they were doing was of value. So when Christopher Langley called to invite him to dinner with the Widow Zimmerman, and to discuss Langley's progress and future activities later, Delaney accepted promptly. He knew Langley's business could be decided in that phone conversation, but he also knew his physical presence was important to Langley, and he gave up the time gladly.

The dinner, thankfully, was prepared by the dapper little

gourmet and served in his apartment, although the Widow Zimmerman had provided an incredibly renitent cheese cake. Delaney brought two bottles of wine, white and red, and they drank them both with Langley's *poulet en cocotte du midi,* since he assured them the business of red for meat and white for fish was pure poppycock.

After the meal, the Widow Zimmerman cleaned up, moving about Christopher Langley's apartment as if she was already mistress—as indeed she probably was, Delaney decided, having intercepted their affectionate glances, sly touchings, and sudden giggles at comments the humor of which he could not detect.

Langley and Delaney sat at the cleared table, sipped brandy, and the ex-curator brought out his lists, records, and notes, all beautifully neat, written out in a scholar's fine hand.

"Now then," he said, handing a paper over to Delaney, "here is a list of all stores and shops in the New York area selling the ice ax. Some call it 'ice ax' and some call it 'ice hammer.' I don't think that's important, do you?"

"No. Not at all."

"Of the five, the three I have checked in red itemize their sales checks, so that the purchase of an ice ax would be on record. Of these three, one does no mail order business and hence has no mailing list. The other two do have mailing lists and send out catalogues."

"Good," Delaney nodded. "I'll try to get copies of the mailing lists and their sales checks."

"I should warn you," Langley said, "not all these stores carry the same ax I found at Outside Life. The axes are similar in design, but they are not identical. I found one from Austria, one from Switzerland, and one made in America. The other two were identical to the Outside Life ax made in West Germany. I've marked all this on the list."

"Fine. Thank you. Well . . . where do we go from here?"

"I think," Christopher Langley said thoughtfully, "I should first concentrate on the West German ax, the one Outside Life sells. They're by far the largest outlet for mountaineering equipment in this area—and the least expensive, incidentally. I'll try to identify the manufacturer, the importer, and all retail outlets in this country that handle that particular ax. How does that sound?"

"Excellent. Just right. You're doing a marvelous job on this, Mr. Langley."

"Oh well, you know . . ."

When he left them, the Widow Zimmerman was washing dishes, and Christopher Langley was drying.

Delaney spent the next two days checking out Langley's list of stores in the New York area that sold ice axes and kept itemized sales checks. The one that did no mail order business and had no mailing list was willing to cooperate and lend Delaney the sales slips. He made arrangements to have them delivered to Calvin Case. The Captain wasn't optimistic about results; this particular store kept the checks for only six months.

Of the other two stores, Delaney was able to obtain checks and mailing lists from only one. The owner of the other simply refused to cooperate, claiming his mailing list was a carefully guarded business secret, of value to competitors, and Delaney couldn't have it without a court order. The Captain didn't push it; he could always come back to it later.

So he now had two more shipments of itemized sales checks for Calvin Case and another mailing list for Monica Gilbert. He decided to tackle Case first. He called, then subwayed down about noon.

The change in Calvin Case was a delight. He was clean, his hair cut and combed, his beard trimmed. He sat in pajamas in his aluminum and plastic wheelchair at his desk, flipping through Outside Life sales checks. Delaney had brought him a bottle, the same brand of whiskey Case had been drinking when Delaney first met him. The crippled mountaineer looked at the bottle and laughed.

"Thanks a lot," he said, "but I never touch the stuff now until the sun goes down. You?"

"No. Thanks. It's a bribe. I've got bad news for you."

"Oh?"

"We've found two more stores that sell ice axes. Ice hammers, I guess you'd say. Anyway, these stores have itemized sales checks."

Unexpectedly, Calvin Case smiled. "So?" he asked.

"Will you be willing to go through them?"

"Is it going to help?"

"Damned right," Delaney said fervently.

"Pile it on," Case grinned. "I ain't going no place. The more the merrier."

"Very few receipts," Delaney assured him. "I mean," he added hastily, "compared to Outside Life. One store keeps them for six months, and the other store for a year. How you coming?"

"Okay. Another three days, I figure. Then what happens?"

"Then you'll have a file of all ice ax purchases made at Outside Life in the past seven years. Right? Then I'll give you a map of the Two-five-one Precinct, and you'll go through your file and pull every sales check for an ice ax in the precinct."

Case stared at him a long moment, then shook his head.

"Delaney," he said, "you're not a detective; you're a fucking bookkeeper. You know that?"

"That's right," the Captain agreed readily. "No doubt about it."

He was going down the stairs when he met Evelyn Case coming up. He took off his hat, nodded, and smiled. She put down her shopping bag to grab him in her arms, hug him, kiss his cheek.

"He's wonderful," she said breathlessly. "Just the way he used to be. And it's all your doing."

"Is it?" Delaney asked wonderingly.

His next meet had to be with Monica Gilbert, for he now had another mailing list for her to check. But she called him first and told him she had completed the Outside Life mailing list, had made out a file card for every resident of the 251st Precinct on the list, and had a typed record of those residents, a master and two carbon copies, just as he had instructed.

He was amazed and delighted she had completed her job so quickly . . . and a little worried that she had not been as meticulous as he wanted her to be. But he had to work with what he had, and he arranged to meet her at her home the following evening. She asked him if he would care to come for dinner but he declined, with thanks; he would dine early (he lied) before he visited his wife at the hospital, and then be over later. Though why he had accepted Christopher Langley's dinner invitation and not Monica Gilbert's, he could not have said.

He bought two stuffed toys for the young daughters: a black and a white poodle. When you pressed their stomachs, they made a funny barking, squeaking sound. When he arrived, Mary and Sylvia were already in their little nightgowns, but Mrs. Gilbert allowed them out of their bedroom to say hello to the visitor. They were delighted with their presents and finally retired (pushed) to their bedroom, arguing about which poodle had the more ferocious expression. For a half-hour afterwards the adults heard the squeal of pressed toys. But the sounds gradually grew more infrequent, then ceased, and then Monica Gilbert and Edward Delaney were alone, in silence.

Finally: "Thank you for thinking of the girls," she said warmly.

"My pleasure. They're lovely kids."

"It was very kind of you. You like children?"

"Oh yes. Very much. I have a son and a daughter."

"Married?"

"My daughter is. She's expecting. Any day now."

"Her first?"

"Yes."

"How wonderful. You'll be a grandfather."

"Yes," he laughed with delight. "So I will."

She served coffee and almond-flavored cookies, so buttery he knew immediately they were homemade. His mother had made cookies like that. He put on his heavy glasses to inspect what she had done, while he sipped black coffee and nibbled cookies.

He saw immediately he needn't have doubted her swift efficiency. There had been 116 residents of the 251st Precinct on the Outside Life mailing list. She had made out a file card for each one: last name first in capital letters, followed by the given name and middle initial. Beneath the name was typed the address, in two lines. Then she had made a master list and two carbons from the cards, now neatly filed alphabetically in a wooden box.

"Very good," he nodded approvingly. "Excellent. Now I have some bad news for you; I have another mailing list from another store." He smiled at her. "Willing?"

She smiled in return. "Yes. How many names?"

"I estimate about a third of the number on the Outside Life list; maybe less. And you'll probably find duplications. If you do, don't make out a separate card, just note on the Outside Life card that the individual is also on this list. Okay?"

"Yes. What happens now?"

"To your typed list, you mean? You keep one carbon. Just stick it away somewhere as insurance. I'll keep the other carbon. The original will go to friends in the Department. They'll check the names with city, state, and federal files to see if anyone listed has a criminal record."

"A record?"

"Sure. Been charged, been convicted of any crime. Been sentenced. Fined, on probation, or time in jail."

She was disturbed; he could see it.

"Will this help find the man who killed my husband?"

"Yes," he said decisively, paused a moment, staring at her, then asked, "What's bothering you?"

"It seems so—so unfair," she said faintly.

He became suddenly aware of her as a woman: the solid, warm body beneath the black dress, the strong arms and legs, the steady look of purpose. She was not a beautiful woman, not as delicate as Barbara nor as fine. But there was a peasant sensuality to her; her smell was deep and disturbing.

"What's unfair?" he asked quietly.

"Hounding men who have made one mistake. You do it all the time I suppose."

"Yes," he nodded, "we do it all the time. You know what the recidivist rate is, Mrs. Gilbert? Of all the men presently in prison, about eighty percent have been behind bars at least once before."

"It still seems—"

"Percentages, Mrs. Gilbert. We've got to use them. We know that if a man rapes, robs, or kills once, the chances are he'll rape, rob, or kill again. We can't deny that. We didn't create that situation, but we'd be fools to overlook it."

"But doesn't police surveillance, the constant hounding of men with records, contribute to—"

"No," he shook his great head angrily. "If an ex-con wants to go straight, really wants to, he will. I'm not going to tell you there have never been frames of ex-cons. Of course there have. But generally, when a man repeats, he wants to go back behind bars. Did you know that? There's never been a study of it, to my knowledge, but my guess is that most two-and three-time losers are asking for it. They need the bars. They can't cope on the outside. I'm hoping a check on your list will turn up a man or men like that. If not, it may turn up *something*. A similar case, a pattern of violence, *something* that may give me a lead."

"Does that mean if you get a report that some poor man on this list forged a check or deserted his wife, you'll swoop down on him and demand to know where he was on the night my husband and those other men were killed?"

"Of course not. Nothing like that. First of all, criminals can be classified. They have their specialties, and rarely vary. Some deal strictly in white-collar crime: embezzlement, bribery, patent infringement—things like that. Crimes against property, mostly. Then there's a grey area: forgery, swindling, fraud, and so forth. Still crimes against property, but now the victim tends to be an individual rather than the government or the public. And then there's the big area of conventional crime: homicide, kidnapping, robbery, and so forth. These are usually crimes of violence during which the criminal actually sees and has physical contact with his victim; and infliction of injury or death usually results. Or, at least, the potential is there. I'm looking for a man with a record in this last classification, a man with a record of violence, physical violence."

"But—but how will you *know?* What if one of the men on that list was arrested for beating his wife? That's certainly violent, isn't it? Does that make him the killer?"

"Not necessarily, though I'd certainly check him out. But I'm looking for a man who fits a profile."

She stared at him, not understanding. "A profile?"

He debated if he should tell her, but felt a need to impress her, couldn't resist it, and wondered why that was.

"Mrs. Gilbert, I have a pretty good idea—a pretty good *visualization* of the man who's doing these killings. He's young—between thirty-five and forty—tall and slender. He's in good health and strong. His physical reactions are very fast. He's probably a bachelor. He may be a latent homosexual. He dresses very well, but conservatively. Dark suits. If you passed him on the street at night, you'd feel perfectly safe. He probably has a good job and handles it well. There's nothing about him that would make people suspect him. But he's addicted to danger, to taking risks. He's a mountain climber. He's cool, determined, and I'm positive he's a resident of this neighborhood. Certainly of this precinct. And tall. Did I say he was tall? Yes, I did. Well, he's probably six feet or over."

Her astonishment was all he could have asked, and he cursed his own ego for showing off in this fashion.

"But how do you know all this?" she said finally.

He rose to his feet and began to gather his papers together. He was so disgusted with himself.

"Sherlock Holmes," he said sourly. "It's all guesswork, Mrs. Gilbert. Forget it. I was just shooting off my mouth."

She followed him to the door.

"I'm sorry about what I said," she told him, putting a strong hand on his arm. "I mean about how cruel it is to check men with records. I know you've got to do it."

"Yes," he nodded, "I've got to do it. Percentages."

"Captain, please do everything you think should be done. I don't know anything about it. This is all new to me."

He smiled at her without speaking.

"I'll get going on the new list tonight. And thank you, Captain."

"For what?"

"For doing what you're doing."

"I haven't done anything yet except give you work to do."

"You're going to get him, aren't you?"

"Listen," Delaney said, "could we—"

He stopped suddenly and was silent. She was puzzled. "Could we what?" she asked finally.

"Nothing," he said. "Good-night, Mrs. Gilbert. Thank you for the coffee and cookies."

He walked home, resolutely turning his mind from the thought of what a fool he had made of himself—in his own eyes if not in hers. He stopped at a phone booth to call Deputy Inspector Thorsen, and waited five minutes until Thorsen called him back.

"Edward?"

"Yes."

"Anything new?"

"I have a list of a hundred and sixteen names and addresses. I need them checked out against city, state, and federal records."

"My God."

"It's important."

"I know, Edward. Well . . . at least we've got some names. That's more than Broughton has."

"I hear he's in trouble."

"You hear right."

"Heavy?"

"Not yet. But it's growing. Everyone's leaning on him."

"About this list of mine—I'll get it to your office tomorrow by messenger. All right?"

"Better send it to my home."

"All right, and listen, please include the State Department of Motor Vehicles and the NYPD's Special Services Branch. Can you do that?"

"We'll have to do it."

"Yes."

"Getting close, Edward?"

"Well . . . closer."

"You think he's on the list?"

"He better be," Delaney said. Everyone was leaning on him, too.

He was weary now, wanting nothing but a hot shower, a rye highball, perhaps a sleeping pill, and bed. But he had his paper work to do, and drove himself to it. What was it Case called him—a fucking bookkeeper?

He finished his writing, his brain frazzled, and filed his neat folders away. He drained his highball, watery now, and considered the best way to handle results from the search of records of those 116 individuals, when they began to come in on printouts from city, state, and federal computers.

What he would do, he decided, was this: he would ask Monica Gilbert to make notations of any criminal history on the individual cards. He would buy five or six packages of little colored plastic tabs, the kind that could be clipped on the upper edge of file cards. He would devise a color code: a red tab attached to a card would indicate a motor vehicle violation, a blue tab would indicate a New York City criminal record . . . and so forth. When reports were in from all computers, he could then look at Monica Gilbert's file box and, without wasting time flipping through 116 cards, see at a glance which had one, two, three or more plastic tabs attached to their upper edges. He thought it over, and it seemed an efficient plan.

His mind was working so sluggishly that it was some time before he wondered why he hadn't brought Monica Gilbert's card file home with him, to keep in his own study. The computer printouts Thorsen would obtain would be delivered to him, Delaney. He could make handwritten notations on individual cards himself and attach the color-coded plastic tabs. It wasn't necessary for him to run over to Mrs. Gilbert's apartment to consult the file every time he needed to. So why . . . Still . . . She *was* efficient and he couldn't do everything . . . Still . . . Had he angered her? If she . . . Barbara . . .

He dragged himself up to bed, took no shower and no sleeping pill, but lay awake for at least an hour, trying to understand himself. Not succeeding, he finally slid into a thin sleep.

3

It began to come together. Slowly. What he had set in motion. The first report on the 116 names came from the New York State Department of Motor Vehicles: a neatly folded computer printout, an original and six copies. Delaney took a quick look, noted there were 11 individuals listed, tore off a carbon for his own file, and took the report over to Monica Gilbert. He explained what he wanted:

"It's easy to read once you get the hang of it. It's computer printing—all capitals and no punctuation—but don't let that throw you. Now the first one listed is AVERY JOHN H on East Seventy-ninth Street. You have Avery's card?"

Obediently she flipped through her file and handed him the card.

"Good. Now Avery was charged with going through an unattended toll booth without tossing fifty cents in the hopper. Pleaded guilty, paid a fine. It's printed here in a kind of official lingo, but I'm sure you can make it out. Now I'd like you to make a very brief notation on his card. If you write, 'Toll booth—guilty—fine,' it will be sufficient. I'd also like you to note his license number and make of car, in this case a blue Mercury. All clear?"

"I think so," she nodded. "Let me try the next one myself. 'BLANK DANIEL G on East Eighty-third Street; two arrests for speeding, guilty, fined. Black Corvette and then his license number.' Is that what you want on his card?"

"Right. In case you're wondering, I'm not going to lean on these particular people. This report is just possible background stuff. The important returns will come from city and federal files. One more thing . . ."

He showed her the multicolored plastic tabs he had purchased in a stationery store, and explained the color code he had written out for her. She consulted it and clipped red tabs onto the top edges of the AVERY and BLANK cards. It looked very efficient, and he was satisfied.

Calvin Case called to report he had finished going through the Outside Life sales checks and had a file of 234 purchases of ice axes made in the past seven years. Delaney brought him a hand-drawn map of the 251st Precinct, and by the next day Case had separated those purchases made by residents of the Precinct. There were six of them. Delaney took the six sales checks, went home, and made two lists. One was for his file, one he delivered to Monica Gilbert so she could make notations on the appropriate cards and attach green plastic tabs. He had hardly returned home when she called. She was troubled because one of the six ice ax purchasers was not included in her master file of Outside Life customers. She gave him the name and address.

Delaney laughed. "Look," he said, "don't let it worry you. We can't expect perfection. It was probably human error; it usually is. For some reason this particular customer wasn't included on the mailing list. Who knows—maybe he said he didn't want their catalogue; he doesn't like junk mail. Just make out a card for him."

"Yes, Edward."

He was silent. It was the first time she had used his given name. She must have realized what she had done for suddenly she said, in a rush, "Yes, Captain."

"Edward is better," he told her, and they said goodby.

Now he could call her Monica.

Back to his records, remembering to start a new list for Thorsen headed by the single ice ax purchaser not included on the original list. Two days later Monica Gilbert had finished going through the new mailing list he had given her, and 34 more names were added to her master file and to the new list for Thorsen. And two days after that, Calvin Case had finished flipping through sales checks of the two additional New York stores that sold ice axes, and the names of three more purchasers in the 251st Precinct were added to Monica's file, green plastic tabs attached, and the names also added to the new Thorsen list. Delaney had it delivered to the Deputy Inspector.

Meanwhile computer printouts were coming in on the original 116, and Monica Gilbert was making notations on her cards, and attaching colored tabs to indicate the source of the information. Meanwhile Calvin Case was breaking down his big file of Outside Life receipts of sales of any type of mountaineering equipment, to extract those of residents of the 251st Precinct. Meanwhile Christopher Langley was visiting official German agencies in New York to determine the manufacturer, importer, jobbers and retail outlets that handled the ice ax in the U.S. Meanwhile, Captain Edward X. Delaney was personally checking out the six people who had purchased ice axes at Outside Life, and then three additional purchasers from the other two stores. And reading "Honey Bunch" to his wife.

Ever since he had been promoted from uniformed patrolman to detective third grade, Delaney, following the advice of his first partner—an old, experienced, and alcoholic detective who called him "Buddy Boy"—had collected business cards. If he was given a card by a banker, shoe salesman, mortician, insurance agent, private investigator—whatever—he hung onto it, and it went into a little rubber-banded pack. Just as his mentor had promised, the business cards proved valuable. They provided temporary "cover." People were impressed by them; often they were all the identification he needed to be banker, shoe salesman, mortician, insurance agent, private investigator—whatever. That little bit of pasteboard was a passport; few people investigated his identity further. When he passed printing shops advertising "100 Business Cards for $5.00" he could understand how easily conmen and swindlers operated.

Now he made a selection of his collected cards and set out to investigate personally the nine residents of the 251st Precinct who had purchased ice axes in the past seven years. He had arranged the nine names and addresses according to location, so he wouldn't have to retrace his steps or end the day at the other end of the Precinct. This was strictly a walking job, and he dug out an old pair of shoes he had worn on similar jobs in the past. They were soft, comfortable kangaroo leather with high laced cuffs that came up over his ankles.

He waited until 9:00 a.m., then began his rounds, speaking only to doormen, supers, landlords, neighbors . . .

"Good morning. My name's Barrett, of Acme Insurance. Here's my card. But I don't want to sell you anything. I'm looking for a man named David Sharpe. He was listed as beneficiary on one of our policies and has some money coming to him. He live here?"

"Who?"

"David Sharpe."

"I don' know him."

"This is the address we have for him."

"Nah, I never—wait . . . What's his name?"

"David Sharpe."

"Oh yeah. Chris', he move away almost two years ago."

"Oh. I don't suppose you have any forwarding address?"

"Nah. Try the post office."

"That's a good idea. I'll try them."

And plucking his business card back, Delaney trudged on.

"Good morning. My name's Barrett, of Acme Insurance. Here's my card. But I don't want to sell you anything. I'm looking for a man named Arnold K. Abel. He was listed as beneficiary on one of our policies and has some money coming to him. He—"

"Tough shit. He's dead."

"Dead?"

"Yeah. Remember that plane crash last year? It landed short and went into Jamaica Bay."

"Yes, I remember that."

"Well, Abel was on it."

"I'm sorry to hear that."

"Yeah, he was a nice guy. A lush but a nice guy. He always give me a tenner at Christmas."

And then something happened he should have expected.

"Good morning," he started his spiel, "I'm—"

"Hell, I know you, Captain Delaney. I was on that owners' protective committee you started. Don't you remember me? The name's Goldenberg."

"Of course, Mr. Goldenberg. How are you?"

"Healthy, thank God. And you, Captain?"

"Can't complain."

"I was sorry to hear you retired."

"Well . . . not retired exactly. Just temporary leave of absence. But things piled up and I'm spending a few hours a day helping out the new commander. You know?"

"Oh sure. Breaking him in—right?"

"Right. Now we're looking for a man named Simmons. Walter J. Simmons. He's not wanted or anything like that, but he was a witness to a robbery about a year ago, and now we got the guy we think pulled the job, and we hoped this Simmons could identify him."

"Roosevelt Hospital, Captain. He's been in there almost six months now. He's one of these mountain climbers, and he fell and got all cracked up. From what I hear, he'll never be the same again."

"I'm sorry to hear that. But he still may be able to testify. I better get over there. Thank you for your trouble."

"My pleasure, Captain. Tell me the truth, what do you think about this new man, this Dorfman?"

"Good man," Delaney said promptly.

"With these three murders we've had in the last few months and the dingaling still running around free? What's this Dorfman doing about that?"

"Well, it's out of his hands, Mr. Goldenberg. The investigation is being handled personally by Deputy Commissioner Broughton."

"I read, I read. But it's Dorfman's precinct—right?"

"Right," Delaney said sadly.

So the day went. It was a disaster. Of the nine ice ax purchasers, three had moved out of the precinct, one had died, one was hositalized, and one had been on a climbing tour in Europe for the past six months.

That left three possibles. Delaney made a hurried visit to Barbara, then spent the evening checking out the three, this time questioning them personally, giving his name and showing his shield and identification. He didn't tell them the reasons for his questions, and they didn't ask. The efforts of Delaney, New York Police Department, were no more productive than those of Barrett, Acme Insurance.

One purchaser was an octogenarian who had bought the ax as a birthday present for a 12-year-old great-grandson.

One was a sprightly, almost maniacal young man who assured Delaney he had given up mountain climbing for skydiving. "Much more *machismo,* man!" At Delaney's urging, he dug his ax out of a back closet. It was dusty, stained, pitted with rust, and the Captain wondered if it had ever been used, for anything.

The third was a young man who, when he answered Delaney's ring, seemed at first sight to fit the profile: tall, slender, quick, strong. But behind him, eyeing the unexpected visitor nervously and curiously, was his obviously pregnant wife. Their apartment was a shambles of barrels and cartons; Delaney had interrupted their packing; they were moving in two days since, with the expected new arrival, they would need more room. When the Captain brought up the subject of the ice ax, they both laughed. Apparently, one of the conditions she had insisted on, before marrying him, was that he give up mountain climbing. So he had, and quite voluntarily he showed Delaney his ice ax. They had been using it as a general purpose hammer; the head was scarred and nicked. Also, they had tried to use the spike to pry open a painted-shut window and suddenly, without warning, the pick of the ice ax had just snapped off. And it was supposed to be steel. Wasn't that the damndest thing? they asked. Delaney agreed despondently it was the damndest thing he ever heard.

He walked home slowly, thinking he had been a fool to believe it would be easy. Still, it was the obvious thing to trace weapon to source to buyer. It had to be done, and he had done it. Nothing. He knew how many other paths he could now take, but it was a disappointment; he admitted it. He had hoped—just hoped—that one of those cards with the green plastic tab would be the one.

His big worry was time. All this checking of sales receipts and list making and setting up of card files and questioning innocents—time! It all took days and weeks, and meanwhile this nut was wandering the streets and, as past histories of similar crimes indicated, the intervals between murders became shorter and shorter.

When he got home he found a package Mary had signed for. He recognized it as coming from Thorsen by commercial messenger. He tore it open and when he saw what it was, he didn't look any further. It was a report from the Records Division, New York Police Department, including the Special Services Branch. That completed the check on criminal records of the original 116 names.

He had been doing a curious thing. As reports came in from federal, state, and local authorities, he had been tearing off a carbon for his files, then delivering the other copies to Monica Gilbert for notation and tabbing in her master file. He didn't read the reports himself; he didn't even glance at them. He told himself the reason for this was that he couldn't move on individuals with criminal records until *all* the reports were in and recorded on Monica's file cards. Then he'd be able to see at a glance how many men had committed how many offenses. That's what he told himself.

He also told himself he was lying—to himself.

The real reason he was following this procedure was very involved, and he wasn't quite sure he understood it. First of all, being a superstitious cop, he had the feeling that Monica Gilbert had brought him and would bring him luck. Somehow, through her efforts, solely or in part, he'd find the lead he needed. The second thing was that he hoped these computer printouts of criminal records would lead to the killer and thus prove to Monica he had merely been logical and professional when he had requested them. He had seen it in her eyes when he told her what he was about to do; she had thought him a brutal, callous—well, a *cop*, who had no feeling or sympathy for human frailty. That was, he assured himself, simply not true.

Unlacing his high shoes, peeling off his sweated socks, he paused a moment, sock in hand, and wondered why her good opinion of him was so important to him. He thought of her, of her heavy muscular haunches moving slowly under the thin black dress, and he realized to his shame that he was beginning to get an erection. He had had no sex since Barbara became ill, and his "sacrifice" seemed so much less than her pain that he couldn't believe what he was dreaming: the recent widow of a murder victim . . . while Barbara . . . and he . . . He

346

snorted with disgust at himself, took a tepid shower, donned fresh pajamas, and got out of bed an hour later, wide-eyed and frantic, to gulp two sleeping pills.

He delivered the new report to her the next morning and refused her offer to stay for coffee and Danish. Did she seem hurt? He thought so. Then, sighing, he spent a whole day—time! time!—doing what he had to do and what he knew would be of no value whatsoever: he checked those purchasers of ice axes who had moved, died, were abroad, or hospitalized. The results, as he knew they would, added up to zero. They really had moved, died, were abroad, or hospitalized.

Mary had left a note that Mrs. Gilbert had called, and would the Captain please call her back. So he did, immediately, and there was no coolness in her voice he could detect. She told him she had completed noting all the reported criminal records in her master file, and had attached appropriately colored plastic tabs. He asked her if she'd care to have lunch with him at 1:00 p.m. the following day, and she accepted promptly.

They ate at a local seafood restaurant and had identical luncheons: crabmeat salads with a glass of white wine. They spent a pleasant hour and half together, talking of the pains and pleasures of life in the city. She told him of her frustrated efforts to grow geraniums in window boxes; he told her of how, for years, Barbara and he had tried to grow flowers and flowering shrubs in their shaded backyard, had finally surrendered to the soot and sour soil, and let the ivy take over. Now it was a jungle of ivy and, surprisingly, rather pretty.

He told her about Barbara while they sipped coffee. She listened intently and finally asked:

"Do you think you should change doctors?"

"I don't know what to do," he confessed. "He's always been her physician, and she has great faith in him. I couldn't bring someone else in without her permission. He's trying everything he can, I'm sure. And there are consultants in on this. But she shows no improvement. In fact, it seems to me she's just wasting away, just fading. My son was up to visit a few weeks ago and was shocked at how she looked. So thin and flushed and drawn. And occasionally now she's irrational. Just for short periods of time."

"That could be the fever, or even the antibiotics she's getting."

"I suppose so," he nodded miserably. "But it frightens me. She was always so—so sharp and perceptive. Still is, when she isn't floating off in never-never land. Well . . . I didn't invite you to lunch to cry on your shoulder. Tell me about your girls. How are they getting along in school?"

She brightened, and told him about their goodness and deviltry, things they had said and how different their personalities were, one from the other. He listened with interest, smiling, remembering the days when Eddie and Liza were growing up, and wondering if he was now paying for that happiness.

"Well," he said, after she finished her coffee, "can we go back to your place? I'd like to take a look at that card file. All the reports finished?"

"Yes," she nodded, "everything's entered. I'm afraid you're going to be disappointed."

"I usually am," he said wryly.

"Oh well," she smiled, "these are only the unsuccessful criminals."

"Pardon?" he asked, not realizing at first that she was teasing him.

"Well, when a man has a record, it proves he was an inefficient criminal, doesn't it? He got caught. If he was good at his job, he wouldn't have a record."

"Yes," he laughed. "You're right."

They stood and moved to the cashier's desk, Delaney had his wallet out, but the manager, who had apparently been waiting for this moment, moved in close, smiling, and said to the cashier, "No check for Captain Delaney."

He looked up in surprise. "Oh . . . hello, Mr. Varro. How are you?"

"Bless God, okay, Captain. And you?"

"Fine. Thanks for the offer, but I'm afraid I can't accept it. I'm not on active duty, you know. Leave of absence. And besides—" He gestured toward Monica Gilbert who was watching this scene closely. "—this young lady is a witness, and I wouldn't want her to think I was accepting a bribe."

They all laughed—an easy laugh.

"Tell you what," Delaney said, paying his bill, "next time I'll come in alone, order the biggest lobster in the house, and let you pick up the tab. Okay?"

"Sure, okay," Varro smiled. "You know me. Anytime, Captain."

They walked toward Monica's apartment, and she looked up at him curiously. "Will you?" she asked. "Stop in for a free meal, I mean?"

"Sure," he said cheerfully. "He'd be hurt if I didn't. Varro is all right. The beat men stop in for coffee almost every day. The squad car men do, too. Not all of them take, but I'd guess most of them do. It doesn't mean a thing. Happens in a hundred restaurants and bars and hotdog stands and pizza parlors in the Precinct. Are you going to say, 'Petty graft'? You're right, but most cops are struggling to get their kids to college on a cop's pay, and a free lunch now and then is more important than you think. When I said it doesn't mean a thing, I meant that if any of these generous owners and managers get out of line, they'll be leaned on like anyone else. A free cup of coffee doesn't entitle them to anything but a friendly hello. Besides, Varro owes me a favor. About two years ago he discovered he was losing stuff from his storeroom. It wasn't the usual pilferage—a can or package now and then. This stuff was disappearing in *cases*. So he came to me, and I called in Jeri Fernandez who was lieutenant of our precinct detective squad at that time. Jeri put a two-man stakeout watching the back alley. The first night they were there—the *first* night!—this guy pulls up to the back door in a station wagon, unlocks the door cool as you please, and starts bringing up cases and cartons and bags from the basement and loading his wagon. They waited until he had the wagon full and was locking the back door. Then they moved in."

"What did they do?" she asked breathlessly.

Delaney laughed. "They made him unload his station wagon and carry all that stuff back down to the basement again and store it neatly away. They said he was puffing like a whale by the time he got through. He was one of the assistant chefs there and had keys to the back door and storeroom. It really wasn't important enough to bring charges. It would have meant impounding evidence, a lot of paperwork for everyone, time lost in court, and the guy probably would have been fined and put on probation if it was his first offense. So after he finished putting everything back the way it was, Jeri's boys worked him over. Nothing serious. I mean he didn't have to go to the hospital or anything like that, but I suppose they marked him up some—a few aches and pains. And of course he was fired. The word got around, and Varro hasn't lost a can of salad oil since. That's why he wanted to buy our lunch."

He looked at her, smiling, and saw her shiver suddenly.

"It's a whole different world," she said in a low voice.

"What is?"

But she didn't answer.

She was right; the criminal records were a disappointment.

What he had been hoping was that when the computer print-outs were collated and entered on the file cards, there would be a few or several cards with a perfect forest of multicolored plastic tabs clipped to their upper edges, indicating significant criminal records that might show a pattern of psychopathic and uncontrollable violence.

Instead, the card file was distressingly bare. There was one card with three tabs, two with two tabs, and 43 with one tab. None of the nine purchasers of ice axes, who Delaney had already checked out, had a criminal record.

While he went through the tabbed cards, slowly, working at Monica's kitchen table, she had brought in mending, donned a pair of rimless spectacles, and began making a hem on one of the girl's dresses, working swiftly, making small stitches, a thimble and scissors handy. When he had finished the cards, he pushed the file box away from him, and the sound made her look up. He gave her a bleak smile.

"You're right," he said. "A disappointment. One rape, one robbery, one assault with a deadly weapon. And my God, have you ever seen so many income tax frauds in your life!"

She smiled slightly and went back to her sewing. He sat brooding, tapping his pencil eraser lightly on the table top.

"Of course, this is a good precinct," he said, thinking aloud as much as he was talking to her. "I mean 'good' in the sense of better than East Harlem and Bedford-Stuyvesant. The per capita income is second highest of all the precincts in the city, and the rates of crimes of violence are in the lower third. I'm speaking of Manhattan, Bronx, and Brooklyn now. Not Queens and Staten Island. So I should have expected a high preponderance of white-collar crime. Did you notice the tax evasions, unscrupulous repair estimates, stock swindles—things like that? But still . . . What I didn't really consider is that all these cards, all these individuals—by the way, did you see that there are only four women in the whole file?—these individuals are all presumably mountain climbers or have bought gifts for mountain climbers or are outdoorsmen of one type or another: hunters, fishermen, boat owners, hikers, campers, and so forth. That means people with enough money for a leisure hobby. And lack of money is usually the cause of violent crime. So what we've got is a well-to-do precinct and a file of people who can afford to spend money, heavy money, on their leisure-time activities. I guess I was foolish to expect mountain climbers and deep-sea fishermen to have the same percentage of records as people in the ghettoes. Still . . . it is a disappointment."

"Discouraged?" she asked quietly, not looking up.

"Monica," he said, and at his tone of voice she did look up to find him smiling at her. "I'm never discouraged," he said. "Well . . . hardly ever. I'll check out the rape, the robbery, and the assault. If nothing comes of that, there's a lot more I can do. I'm just getting started."

She nodded, and went back to her mending. He took notes on the three records of violent crimes included on the file cards. For good measure, although he thought the chances were nil, he added the names and addresses of men convicted of vandalism, extortion, and safe-breaking. He glanced at his watch, a thick hunter his grandfather had owned, and saw he had time to check out three or four of the men with records.

He rose, she put aside her sewing and stood up, and they took off their glasses simultaneously, and laughed together, it seemed like such an odd thing.

"I hope your wife is feeling better soon," she said, walking him to the door.

"Thank you."

"I'd—I'd like to meet her," she said faintly. "That is, if you think it's all right. I mean, I have time on my hands now that the file is finished, and I could go over and sit with—"

He turned to her eagerly. "Would you? My God, that would be wonderful! I know you two will get along. She'll like you, and you'll like her. I try to get there twice a day, but sometimes I don't. We have friends who come to see her. At least at first they did. But—you know—they don't come too often anymore. I'll go over with you and introduce you, and then if you could just stop by occasionally . . ."

"Of course. I'll be happy to."

"Thank you. You're very kind. And thank you for having lunch with me. I really enjoyed it."

She held out her hand. He was surprised, a second, then grasped it, and they shook. Her grip was dry, her flesh firm, the hand unexpectedly strong.

He went out into the dull winter afternoon, the sky tarnished pewter, and glanced at his list to see who he should hit first. But curiously he was not thinking of the list, nor of Monica Gilbert, nor of Barbara. Something was nibbling at the edge of his mind, something that had to do with the murders. It was something he had heard recently; someone had said something. But what it was he could not identify. It hovered there, tantalizing, teasing, until finally he shook his head, put it away from him, and started tramping the streets.

He got home a little after ten that evening, his feet aching (he had not worn his "cop shoes"), and so soured with frustration that he whistled and thought of daffodils—anything to keep from brooding on false leads and time wasted. He soaked under a hot shower and washed his hair. That made him feel a little better. He pulled on pajamas, robe, slippers, and went down to the study.

During the afternoon and evening he had checked out five of the six on his list. The rapist and the robber were still in prison. The man convicted of assault with a deadly weapon had been released a year ago, but was not living at the address given. It would have to be checked with his parole officer in the morning. Of the other three, the safe-breaker was still in prison, the vandal had moved to Florida two months ago and considerately left a forwarding address, and Delaney was just too damned tired to look for the extortionist, but would the next day.

He stolidly wrote out reports on all his activities and added them to his files. Then he made his nightly tour of inspection, trying locks on all windows and outside doors. Lights out and up to bed. It wasn't midnight, but he was weary. He was really getting too old for this kind of nonsense. No pill tonight. Blessed sleep would come easily.

While he waited for it, he wondered if it was wise to introduce Monica Gilbert to his wife. He had said they would hit it off, and they probably would. Barbara would certainly feel sympathy for a murder victim's widow. But would she think . . . would she imagine . . . But she had asked him to . . . Oh, he didn't know, couldn't judge. He'd bring them together, once at least, and see what happened.

Then he turned his thoughts to what had been nagging his brain since he left Monica's apartment that afternoon. He was a firm believer in the theory that if you fell asleep with a problem on your mind—a word you were trying to remember, an address, a name, a professional or personal dilemma—you would awake refreshed and the magic solution would be there, the problem solved in your subconscious while you slept.

He awoke the next morning, and the problem still existed, gnawing at his memory. But now it was closer; it was something Monica had said at their luncheon. He tried to remember their conversation in every detail: she had talked about her geraniums, he had talked about his ivy; she had talked about her children, he had talked about Barbara. Then Varro tried to pick up the check, and he, Delaney, told her about the break-in at the restaurant. But what the hell did all that have to do with the price of eggs in China? He shook his head disgustedly and went in to shave.

He spent the morning tracking down the extortionist, the last man of the six in Monica Gilbert's file with a record of even mildly violent crime. Delaney finally found him pressing pants in a little tailor shop on Second Avenue. The extortionist was barely five feet tall, at least 55 and 175 lbs., pasty-faced, with trembling hands and watery eyes. What in God's name did he ever extort? Delaney muttered something about "mistaken identity" and departed as fast as he could, leaving the fat little man in a paroxysm of trembling and watering.

He went directly to the hospital, helped feed Barbara her noon meal, and then read to her for almost an hour from "Honey Bunch: Her First Little Garden." Strangely, the reading soothed him as much as it did her, and when he returned home he was in a somber but not depressed mood—a mood to work steadily without questioning the why's or wherefore's.

He spent an hour on his personal affairs: checks, investments, bank balances, tax estimates, charitable contributions. He cleaned up the month's accumulated shit, paid what he had to pay, wrote a letter to his accountant, made out a deposit for his savings account and a withdrawal against his checking account for current expenses.

Envelopes were sealed, stamped, and put on the hall table where he'd be sure to see them and pick them up for mailing the next time he went out. Then he returned to the study, drew the long legal pad toward him, and began listing his options.

1. He could begin personally investigating *every* name in Monica's card file. He estimated there were now about 155.

2. He could wait for Christopher Langley's report, and then contact, by mail or phone, every retail outlet for the West German ice ax in the U.S.

3. He could wait for Calvin Case's file of everyone in the 251st Precinct who had bought any kind of mountaineering equipment whatsoever from Outside Life and that other store that had supplied a mailing list, and then he could ask Monica to double-check her file to make certain she had a card for every customer.

4. He could go back to the store that refused to volunteer sales checks and mailing list, and he could lean on them. If that

didn't work, he could ask Thorsen what the chances were for a search warrant.

5. He could recheck his own investigations of the nine ice ax purchasers and the six men in the file with a record of violent crime.

6. He could finally get to his early idea of determining if there was a magazine for mountain climbers and he could borrow their subscription list; if there was a club or society of mountain climbers and he could borrow their membership list; and if it was possible to check the local library on residents of the 251st Precinct who had withdrawn books on mountaineering.

7. If it came to it, he would personally check out every goddamn name of every goddamn New Yorker on the goddamn Outside Life mailing list. There were probably about 10,000 goddamn New Yorkers included, and he'd hunt down every goddamn one of them.

But he was just blathering, and he knew it. If he was commanding the 500 detectives in Operation Lombard he could do it, but not by himself in much less than five years. How many murder victims would there be by then? Oh? . . . probably not more than a thousand or so.

But all this was cheesy thinking. One thing was bothering him, and he knew what it was. When Monica called him to report that one of the ice ax purchasers in Calvin Case's file hadn't been included on her Outside Life mailing list, he had laughed it off as "human error." No one is perfect. People do make mistakes, errors of commission or omission. Quite innocently, of course.

What if Calvin Case, late at night and weary, flipped by the sales check of an ice ax purchaser?

What if Christopher Langley had missed a store in the New York area that sold ice axes?

What if Monica Gilbert had somehow skipped a record of violent crime on one of the computer reports she noted on her file cards?

And what if he, Captain Edward X. Delaney, had the solution to the whole fucking mess right under his big, beaky nose and couldn't see it because he was stupid, stupid, stupid?

Human errors. And professionals were just as prone to them as Delaney's amateurs. That was why Chief Pauley sent different men back to check the same facts, why he repeated interrogations twice, sometimes three times. My God, even com-

354

puters weren't perfect. But was there anything he could do about it? No.

So the Captain read over his list of options again and tossed it aside. A lot of shit. He called Monica Gilbert.

"Monica? Edward. Am I disturbing you?"

"Oh no."

"Do you have a few minutes?"

"Do you want to come over?"

"Oh no. I just want to talk to you. About our lunch yesterday. You said something, and I can't remember what it was. I have a feeling it's important, and it's been nagging at me, and I can't for the life of me remember it."

"What was it?"

He broke up: a great blast of raucous laughter. Finally he spluttered, "If I knew, I wouldn't be calling, would I? What did we talk about?"

She wasn't offended by his laughter. "Talk about?" she said. "Let's see . . . I told you about my window boxes, and you told me about your backyard. And then you spoke about your wife's illness, and then we talked about my girls. Going out, the manager tried to pick up the check, and you wouldn't let him. On the way home you told me about the assistant chef who was robbing him."

"No, no," he said impatiently. "It must have been something to do with the case. Did we discuss the case while we were eating?"

"Nooo . . ." she said doubtfully. "After we finished coffee you said we'd come back to my place and you'd go over the cards. Oh yes. You asked if I had finished entering all the reports on the cards, and I said I had."

"And that's all?"

"Yes. Edward, what is this— No, wait a minute. I was teasing you. I said something about the records from the computers just showing unsuccessful criminals, because if they were good at their jobs, they wouldn't have any record, and you laughed and said that was so."

He was silent a moment.

"Monica," he said finally.

"Yes, Edward?"

"I love you," he said, laughing and keeping it light.

"You mean *that's* what you wanted?"

"That's *exactly* what I wanted."

His erratic memory flashed back now, and he recalled talking to Detective Lieutenant Jeri Fernandez on the steps leading up to the second floor of the precinct house. That was when they were breaking up the precinct detective squads.

"What did you get?" Delaney had asked.

"I drew a Safe, Loft and Truck Division in midtown," Fernandez had said disgustedly.

Now Delaney called Police Information, identified himself, told the operator what he wanted: the telephone number of the new Safe, Loft and Truck Division in midtown Manhattan. He was shunted twice more—it took almost five minutes—but eventually he got the number and, carefully crossing his fingers, dialed and asked for Lieutenant Fernandez. His luck was in; the detective picked up the phone after eight rings.

"Lieutenant Fernandez."

"Captain Edward X. Delaney here."

There was a second of silence, then a jubilant, "Captain! Jesus Christ! This is great! How the hell are you, Captain?"

"Just fine, lieutenant. And you?"

"Up to my ears in shit. Captain, this new system just ain't working. I can tell you. It's a lot of crap. You think I know what's going on? I don' know what's going on. No one knows what's going on. We got guys in here from every precinct in town. They set us all down here, and we're supposed to know all about the garment business. Pilferage, hijacking, fraud, arson, safecracking, the mob—the whole bit. Captain, it's wicked. I tell you, it's *wicked!*"

"Take it easy," Delaney soothed. "Give it a little time. Maybe it'll work out."

"Work out my ass," Fernandez shouted. "Yesterday two of my boys caught a spade taking packages out of the back of a U.S. Mail parcel post truck. Can you imagine that? In broad daylight. It's parked at Thirty-fourth and Madison, and this nut is calmly dragging out two heavy packages and strolling off with them. The U.S. Mail!"

"Lieutenant," Delaney said patiently, "the reason I called, I need some help from you."

"Help?" Fernandez cried. "Jesus Christ, Captain, you name it you got it. You know that. What is it?"

"I remember your telling me, just before the precinct squad was broken up, that you had been working on your open files and sending them to the new detective districts, depending on the nature of the crime."

"That's right, Captain. Took us weeks to get cleaned out."

"Well, what about the garbage? You know—the beef sheets, reports on squeals, tips, diaries, and so forth?"

"All the shit? Most of it was thrung out. What could we do with it? We was sent all over the city, and maybe only one or too guys would be working in the Two-five-one. It was all past history anyway—right? So I told the boys to trash the whole lot and—"

"Well, thanks very much," Delaney said heavily. "I guess that—"

"—except for the last year," Fernandez kept talking, ignoring the Captain's interruption. "I figured the new stuff might mean something to somebody, so we kept the paper that came in the last year, but everything else was thrung out."

"Oh?" Delaney said, still alive. "What did you do with it?"

"It's down in the basement of the precinct house. You know when you go down the stairs and the locker room is off to your right and the detention cells on your left? Well, you go past the cells and past the drunk tank, then turn right. There's this hallway that leads to a flight of stairs and the back door."

"Yes, I remember that. We always closed off that hallway during inspections."

"Right. Well, along that hallway is this broom closet where they keep mops and pails and all that shit, and then farther on toward the back door there's this little storage room with a lot of crap in it. I think it used to be a torture chamber in the old days."

"Yes," Delaney laughed. "Probably was."

"Sure, Captain. The walls are thick and that room's got no windows, so who could hear the screams? Who knows how many crimes got solved in there—right? Anyways, that's where we dumped all the garbage files. But just for the last year. That any help?"

"A lot of help. Thank you very much, lieutenant."

"My pleasure, Captain. Listen, can I ask you a favor now?"

"Of course."

"It's a one-word favor: HELP! Captain, you got influence and a good rep. Get me out of here, will you? I'm dying here. I don' like the spot and I don' like the guys I'm with. I shuffle papers around all day like some kind of Manchurian idiot, and you think I know what I'm doing? I don' know my ass from my elbow. I want to get out on the street again. The street I know. Can you work it, Captain?"

"What do you want?"

"Assault-Homicide or Burglary," Fernandez said promptly. "I'll even take Narcotics. I know I can't hope for Vice; I ain't pretty enough."

"Well . . ." Delaney said slowly, "I can't promise you anything, but let me see what I can do. Maybe I can work something."

'That's good enough for me," Fernandez said cheerfully. "Many thanks, Captain."

"Thank *you*, lieutenant."

He hung up and stared at the telephone, thinking of what Fernandez had told him. It was a long shot, of course, but it shouldn't take more than a day, and it was better than resigning himself to one of those seven options on his list, most of which offered nothing but hard, grinding labor with no guarantee of success.

When Monica Gilbert had repeated her teasing remark about successful criminals having no record, he had to recognize its truth. But Monica wasn't aware that between a criminal's complete freedom and formal charges against him existed a half-world of documentation: of charges dismissed, of arrests never made because of lack of adequate evidence, of suits settled out of court, of complaints dropped because of dollar bribery or physical threats, of trials delayed or rejected simply because of the horrific backlog of court cases and the shortage of personnel.

But most of these judicial abortions had a history, a written record that existed *somewhere*. And part of it was in detectives' paperwork: the squeals and beef sheets and diaries and records of "Charge dropped," "Refused to press charges," "Agreed to make restitution," "Let off with warning,"—all the circumlocutions to indicate that the over-worked detective, using patient persuasion in most cases, with or without the approval of his superior officer, had kept a case off the court calendar.

Most judicial adjustments were of a minor nature, and a product of the investigating officer's experience and common sense. Two men in a bar, both liquored up, begin beating on each others' faces with their fists. The police are called. Each antagonist wants the other arrested on charges of assault. What is the cop to do? If he's smart, he gives both a tongue-lashing, threatens to arrest both for disturbing the peace, and sends them off in opposite directions. No pain, no strain, no paperwork with formal charges, warrants, time lost in court—an ache in the ass to everyone. And the judge would probably listen incredulously for all of five minutes and then throw both plaintiff and defendant out of his court.

But if the matter is a little more serious than a barroom

squabble, if damage has been done to property or someone has suffered obvious injury, then the investigating officer might move more circumspectly. It can still be settled out of court, with the cop acting as judge and jury. It can be settled by voluntary withdrawal of charges, by immediate payment of money to the aggrieved party by the man who has wronged him, by mutual consent of both parties when threatened with more substantial charges by the investigating officer, or by a bribe to the cop.

This is "street justice," and for every case that comes to trial in a walnut-paneled courtroom, a hundred street trials are held every hour of every day in every city in the country, and the presiding magistrate is a cop—plainclothes detective or uniformed patrolman. And honest or venal, he is the kingpin of the whole ramshackle, tottering, ridiculous, working system of "street justice," and without him the already overclogged formal courts of the nation would be inundated, drowned in a sea of pettifoggery, and unable to function.

The conscientious investigating officer will or will not make a written report of the case, depending on his judgment of its importance. But if the investigating officer is a plainclothes detective, and if the case involves people of an obviously higher social status than sidewalk brawlers, and if formal charges have been made by *anyone*, and one or more visits to the precinct house have been made, then the detective will almost certainly make a written report of what happened, who did what, who said what, how much injury or damage resulted. Even if the confrontation simply dissolves—charges withdrawn, no warrants issued, no trial—the detective, sighing, fills out the forms, writes his report, and stuffs all the paper in the slush heap, to be thrown out when the file is overflowing.

Knowing all this, knowing how slim his chances were of finding anything meaningful in the detritus left behind by the Precinct's detective squad when it was disbanded, Delaney followed his cop's instinct and phoned Lt. Marty Dorfman at the 251st Precinct, next door.

Their preliminary conversation was friendly but cool. Delaney asked after the well-being of Dorfman's family, and the lieutenant inquired as to Mrs. Delaney's health. It was only when the Captain inquired about conditions in the Precinct that Dorfman's voice took on a tone of anguish and anger.

It developed that Operation Lombard was using the 251st Precinct house as command headquarters. Deputy Commissioner Broughton had taken over Lt. Dorfman's office, and his men were filling the second floor offices and bull pen formerly occupied by the Precinct detective squad. Dorfman himself was stuck at a desk in a corner of the sergeants' room.

He could have endured this ignominy, he suggested to Delaney, and even endured Broughton's slights that included ignoring him completely when they met in the hallway and commandeering the Precinct's vehicles without prior consultation with Dorfman. But what really rankled was that apparently residents of the Precinct were blaming him, Dorfman, personally for not finding the killer. In spite of what they read in the papers and saw on television about Operation Lombard, headed by Deputy Commissioner Broughton, they knew Dorfman was commander of their precinct, and they blamed him for failing to make their streets safe.

"I know," Delaney said sympathetically. "They feel it's your neighborhood and your responsibility."

"Oh yes," Dorfman sighed. "Well, I'm learning. Learning what you had to put up with. I guess it's good experience."

"It is," Delaney said definitely. "The best experience of all —being on the firing line. Are you going to take the exam for captain?"

"I don't know what to do. My wife says no. She wants me to get out, get into something else."

"Don't do that," Delaney said quickly. "Hang in there. A little while longer anyway. Things might change before you know it."

"Oh?" Dorfman asked, interested now, curious, but not wanting to pin Delaney down. "You think there may be changes?"

"Yes. Maybe sooner than you think. Don't make any decisions now. Wait. Just wait."

"All right, Captain. If you say so."

"Lieutenant, the reason I called—I want to come into the Precinct house around eight or nine tomorrow morning. I want to go down to that storage room in the basement. It's off the hallway to the back door. You know, when you pass the pens and drunk tank and turn right. I want to go through some old files stored in there. It's slush left by the detective squad. It'll probably take me all day, and I may remove some of the files. I want your permission."

There was silence, and Delaney thought the connection might have been cut.

"Hello? Hello?" he said.

"I'm still here," Dorfman said finally in a soft voice. "Yes, you have my permission. Thank you for calling first, Captain. You didn't have to do that."

"It's your precinct."

"So I've been learning. Captain . . ."

"What?"

"I think I know what you've been doing. Are you getting anywhere?"

"Nothing definite. Yet. Coming along."

"Will the files help?"

"Maybe."

"Take whatever you need."

"Thank you. If I meet you, just nod and pass by. Don't stop to talk. Broughton's men don't have to—"

"I understand."

"Dorfman . . ."

"Yes, Captain?"

"Don't stop studying for the captain's exam."

"All right. I won't."

"I know you'll do fine on the written, but on the oral they ask some tricky questions. One they ask every year, but it takes different forms. It goes something like this: You're a captain with a lieutenant three sergeants, and maybe twenty or thirty men. There's this riot. Hippies or drunks off a Hudson River cruise or some kind of a nutty mob. Maybe a hundred people hollering and breaking windows and raising hell. How do you handle it?"

There was silence. Then Dorfman said, not sure of himself, "I'd have the men form a wedge. Then, if I had a bullhorn, I'd tell the mob to disperse. If that didn't work, I'd tell the men to—"

"No," Delaney said. "That isn't the answer they want. The right answer is this: you turn to your lieutenant and say, 'Break 'em up.' Then you turn your back on the mob and walk away. It might not be the *right* way. You understand? But it's the right answer to the question. They want to make sure you know how to use command. Watch out for a question like that."

"Thank you, Captain," Dorfman said, and Delaney hoped they might be easing back into their earlier, closer relationship.

He thought it out carefully in his methodical way. He would wear his oldest suit, since that basement storeroom was sure to be dusty. It was probably adequately lighted with an overhead bulb, but just in case he would take along his flashlight.

Now, the room itself might be locked, and then he'd be forced to make a fuss until he found someone with the proper key. But he had never turned in his ring of master keys which, his predecessor had assured him, opened every door, cell and locker in the Precinct house. So he'd take his ring of keys along.

He didn't know how long it would take to go through the detectives' old files, but he judged it might be all day. He wouldn't want to go out to eat; the less chance of being seen by Broughton's men, or by Broughton himself, moving around the stairs and corridors, the better for everyone. So he would need sandwiches, two sandwiches, that he would ask Mary to make up for him in the morning, plus a thermos of black coffee. He would carry all this, plus the flashlight and keys, in his briefcase, which would also hold the typed lists of the cards included in Monica Gilbert's file.

Anything else? Well, he should have some kind of cover story just in case, by bad luck, Broughton saw him, braced him, and wanted to know what the fuck he was up to. He would say, he decided, that he had just stopped by to reclaim some personal files from the basement storeroom. He would keep it as vague as possible; it might be enough to get by.

He awoke the next morning, resolutely trying not to hope, but attempting to treat this search as just another logical step that had to be taken, whether it yielded results or not. He ate an unusually large breakfast for him: tomato juice, two poached eggs on whole wheat toast, a side order of pork sausages, and two cups of black coffee.

While Mary was preparing his luncheon sandwiches and his thermos, he went into the study to call Barbara, to explain why he would be unable to see her that day. Thankfully, she was in an alert, cheery mood, and when he told her exactly what he planned to do, she approved immediately and made him promise to call her as soon as his search was completed, to report results.

His entry into the 251st Precinct house went easily, without incident. That intimidating woman, the blonde sergeant, was on the blotter when he walked in. She was leaning across the desk, talking to a black woman who was weeping. The sergeant looked up, recognized the Captain, and flapped him a half-salute. He waved in return and marched steadily ahead, carrying his briefcase like a salesman. He went down the worn wooden staircase and turned into the detention area.

The officer on duty—on limited duty since his right arm had

been knifed open by an eleven-year-old on the shit—was tilted back against the wall in an ancient armchair. He was reading a late edition of the *Daily News*; Delaney could see the headline: MANIAC KILLER STILL ON LOOSE. The officer glanced up, recognized the Captain, and started to scramble to his feet. Delaney waved him down, ashamed at himself for not remembering the man's name.

"How you coming along?" he asked.

"Fine, Captain. It's healing real good. The doc said I should be mustering in a week or so."

"Glad to hear it. But don't hurry it; take all the time you need. I'm going to that storeroom in the back hallway. I've got some personal files there I want to get."

The officer nodded. He couldn't care less.

"I don't know how long it'll take, so if I'm not out by the time you leave, please tell your relief I'm back there."

"Okay, Captain."

He walked past the detention cells: six cells, four occupied. He didn't look to the right or to the left. Someone whispered to him; someone screamed. There were three men in the drunk tank lying in each others' filth and moaning. It wasn't the noise that bothered him, it was the smell; he had almost forgotten how bad it was: old urine, old shit, old blood, old vomit, old puss—90 years of human pain soaked into floors and walls. And coming through the miasma, like a knife thrust, the sharp, piercing carbolic odor that stung his nostrils and brought tears to his eyes.

The storeroom was locked, and it took him almost five minutes to find the right key on the big ring. And when the latch snapped open, he paused a few seconds and wondered why he hadn't turned that ring of keys over to Dorfman. Officially, they should be in the lieutenant's possession; it was his precinct.

He shoved the door open, found the wall switch, flipped on the overhead light, closed the door behind him and looked around. It was as bad as he had expected.

The precinct house had opened for business in 1882 and, inspecting the storeroom, Delaney guessed that every desk blotter for every one of those 90 years was carefully retained and never looked at again. They were stacked to the ceiling. An historian might do wonders with them. The Captain was amused by the thought: "A Criminal History of Our Times"—reconstructing the way our great-grandparents, grandparents, and parents lived by analyzing the evidence in those yellowing police blotters. It could be done, he thought, and it might prove revealing. Not the usual history, not the theories of philosophers, discoveries of scientists, programs of statesmen; not wars, explorations, revolutions, and new religions.

Just the petty crimes, misdemeanors, and felonies of a weak and sinning humanity. It was all there: the mayhem, frauds, child-beating, theft, drug abuse, alcoholism, kidnapping, rape, murder. It would make a fascinating record, and he wished an historian would attempt it. Something might be learned from it.

He took off his coat, hat and jacket and laid them on the least dusty crate he could find. The windowless room had a single radiator that clanked and hissed constantly, spitting out steam and water. Delaney opened the door a few inches. The air that came in was carbolic-laden, but a little cooler.

He put on his glasses and looked at what else the room held.

Mostly cardboard cartons, overflowing with files and papers.

The cartons bore on their sides the names of whiskies, rums, gins, etc., and he knew most of them came from the liquor store on First Avenue, around the corner. There were also rough wooden cases filled with what appeared to be physical evidence of long forgotten crimes: a knitted woolen glove, moth-eaten; a rusted cleaver with a broken handle; a stained upper denture; a child's Raggedy-Ann doll; a woman's patent leather purse, yawning empty; a broken crutch; a window-weight with black stains; a man's fedora with one bullet hole through the crown; sealed and bulging envelopes with information jotted on their sides; a bloodied wig; a corset ripped down with a knife thrust.

Delaney turned away and found himself facing a carton of theatrical costumes. He fumbled through them and thought they might have been left from some remote Christmas pageant performed in the Precinct house by neighborhood children, the costumes provided by the cops. But beneath the cheap cotton—sleazy to begin with and now rotting away—he found an ancient Colt revolver, at least 12 inches long, rusted past all usefulness, and to the trigger guard was attached a wrinkled tag with the faded inscription: "Malone's gun. July 16, 1902." Malone. Who had he been—cop or killer? It made no difference now.

He finally found what he was looking for: two stacks of relatively fresh cardboard cartons containing the last year's garbage from the detective squad's files. Each carton held folders in alphabetical order, but the cartons themselves were stacked helter-skelter, and Delaney spent almost an hour organizing them. It was then past noon, and he sat down on a nailed wooden crate (painted on the top: "Hold for Capt. Kelly") and ate one of his sandwiches, spiced salami and thickly sliced Spanish onion on rye bread thinly spread with mayonnaise—which he dearly loved—and drank half his thermos of coffee.

Then he got out his list of names from Monica's cards and went to work. He had to compare list to files, and had to work standing up or kneeling or crouching. Occasionally he would spread his arms wide and bend back his spine. Twice he stepped out into the hallway and walked up and down a few minutes, trying to shake the kinks out of his legs.

He felt no elation whatsoever when he found the first file labeled with a name on his list. The address checked out. He merely put the file aside and went on with the job. It was lumbering work, like a stake-out or a 24-hour shadow. You didn't stop to question what you were doing; it was just something that had to be done, usually to prove the "no" rather than discover the "yes."

When he finished the last file in the last cardboard carton, it was nearly 7:00 p.m. He had long ago finished his second sandwich and the remainder of his coffee. But he wasn't hungry; just thirsty. His nostrils and throat seemed caked with dust, but the radiator had never stopped clanking, hissing steam and water, and his shirt was plastered to armpits, chest, and back; he could smell his own sweat.

He packed carefully. Three files. Three of the people on Monica's cards had been involved in cases of "street justice." He tucked the files carefully in his brief case, added the empty thermos and wax paper wrappings from the sandwiches. He pulled on jacket and overcoat, put on his hat, took a final look around. If he ever came back to the Two-five-one, the first thing he'd do was have this room cleaned up. He turned off the light, stepped out into the hallway, made certain the spring lock clicked.

He walked past the drunk tank and detention cells. Two of the drunks were gone, and only one cell was occupied. There was no uniformed officer about, but he might have gone upstairs for coffee. Delaney walked up the rickety staircase and was surprised to feel his knees tremble from tiredness. Lt. Dorfman was standing near the outside door, talking to a civilian Delaney didn't recognize. When he passed, the Captain nodded, smiling slightly, and Dorfman nodded in return, not interrupting his conversation.

In his bedroom, Delaney stripped down to his skin as quickly as he could, leaving all his soiled clothing in a damp heap on the floor. He soaked in a hot shower and soaped his hands three times but was unable to get the grime out of the pores or from under his nails. Then he found a can of kitchen cleanser in the cabinet under the sink; that did the trick. After he dried, he used cologne and powder, but he still smelled the carbolic.

He dressed in pajamas, robe, slippers, then glanced at the bedside clock. Getting on . . . He decided to call Barbara, rather than wait until he went through the retrieved files. But when she answered the phone, he realized that she had drifted away. Perhaps it was sleep or the medication, perhaps the illness; he just didn't know. She kept repeating his name. Laughing: "Edward!" Questioning: "Edward?" Demanding: "Edward!" Loving: "Ed-d-w-ward . . ."

Finally he said, "Good-night, dear," hung up, took a deep breath, tried not to weep. In his study, moving mechanically, he mixed a heavy rye highball, then unpacked his briefcase. Flashlight back to the drawer in the kitchen cabinet. Crumpled wax paper into the garbage can. Thermos rinsed out, then filled with hot water and left to soak on the sink sideboard. Ring of keys into his top desk drawer, to be handed over to Lt. Dorfman. Delaney knew now, in somber realization, he would never again command the Two-five-one.

And the three files stacked neatly in the center of his desk blotter. He got a square of paper towel, wiped off their surface dust, stacked them neatly again. He washed his hands, sat down behind his desk, put on his glasses. Then he just sat there and slowly, slowly sipped away half his strong highball, staring at the files. Then he leaned forward, began to read.

The first case was amusing, and the officer who had handled the beef, Detective second grade Samuel Berkowitz, had recognized it from the start; his tart, ironic reports understated and heightened the humor. A man named Timothy J. Lester had been apprehended shortly after throwing an empty garbage can through the plate glass window of a Madison Avenue shop that specialized in maternity clothes. The shop was coyly called "Expectin'." Berkowitz reported the suspect was "apparently intoxicated on Jamesons"—a reasonable deduction since next door to "Expectin'" was a tavern called "Ye Olde Emerald Isle." Detective Berkowitz had also determined that Mr. Lester, although only 34, was the father of seven children and had, that very night, been informed by his wife that it would soon be eight. Timothy had immediately departed for "Ye Olde Emerald Isle" to celebrate, had celebrated, and on his way home had paused to toss the garbage can through the window of "Expectin'." Since Lester was, in Berkowitz's words, "apparently an exemplary family man," since he had a good job as a typesetter, since he offered to make complete restitution for the shattered window, Detective Berkowitz felt the cause of justice would best be served if Mr. Lester was allowed to pay for his mischievous damage and all charges dropped.

Captain Edward X. Delaney, reading this file and smiling, concurred with the judgment of Detective Berkowitz.

The second file was short and sad. It concerned one of the few women included on Monica Gilbert's list. She was 38 years old and lived in a smart apartment on Second Avenue near 85th Street. She had taken in a roommate, a young woman of 22. All apparently went well for almost a year. Then the younger woman met a man, they became engaged, and she announced the news to her roommate and was congratulated. She returned home the following evening to discover the older woman had slashed all her clothes to thin ribbons with a razor blade and had trashed all her personal belongings. She called the police. But after consultation with her fiancé, she refused to press charges, moved out of the apartment, and the case was dropped.

The third file, thicker, dealt with Daniel G. Blank, divorced, living alone on East 83rd Street. He had been involved in two separate incidents about six months apart. In the first he had originally been charged with simple assault in an altercation involving a fellow tenant of his apartment house who apparently had been beating his own dog. Blank had intervened, and the dog owner had suffered a broken arm. There had been a witness, Charles Lipsky, a doorman, who signed a statement that Blank had merely pushed the other man after being struck with a folded newspaper. The man had stumbled off the curb and fell, breaking his arm. Charges were eventually dropped.

The second incident was more serious. Blank had been in a bar, The Parrot on Third Avenue, and was allegedly solicited by a middle-aged homosexual. Blank, according to testimony of witnesses, thereupon hit the man twice, breaking his jaw with the second blow. While the man was helpless on the floor, Blank had kicked him repeatedly in the groin until he was dragged away and the police were called. The homosexual refused to sign a complaint, Blank's lawyer appeared, and apparently the injured man signed a release.

The same officer, Detective first grade Ronald A. Blankenship, had handled both beefs. His language, in his reports, was official, clear, concise, colorless, and implied no judgments.

Delaney read through the file slowly, then read it through again. He got up to mix another rye highball and then, standing at his desk, read it through a third time. He took off his glasses, began to pace about his chilly study, carrying his drink, sipping occasionally. Once or twice he came back behind his desk to stare at the Daniel Blank manila folder, but he didn't open the file again.

Several years previously, when he had been a Detective lieutenant, he had contributed two articles to the Department's monthly magazine. The first monograph was entitled "Common Sense and the New Detective." It was a very basic, down-to-earth analysis of how the great majority of crimes are solved: good judgment based on physical evidence and experience—the ability to put two and two together and come up with four, not three or five. It was hardly a revolutionary argument.

The second article, entitled "Hunch, Instinct, and the New Detective," occasioned a little more comment. Delaney argued that in spite of the great advances in laboratory analysis, the forensic sciences, computerized records and probability percentages, the new detective disregarded his hunches and instinct at his peril, for frequently they were not a sudden brainstorm, but were the result of observation of physical evidence and experience of which the detective might not even be consciously aware. But stewing in his subconscious, a rational and reasonable conclusion was reached, thrust into his conscious thought, and should never be allowed to wither unexplored, since it was, in many cases, as logical and empirical as common sense.

(Delaney had prepared a third article for the series. This dealt with his theory of an "adversary concept" in which he explored the Dostoevskian relationship between detective and criminal. It was an abstruse examination of the "sensual" (Delaney's word) affinity between hunter and hunted, of how, in certain cases, it was necessary for the detective to penetrate and assume the physical body, spirit, and soul of the criminal in order to bring him to justice. This treatise, at Barbara's gentle persuasion, Delaney did not submit for publication.)

Now, thinking over the facts included in the Daniel Blank file, Captain Delaney acknowledged he was halfway between common sense and instinct. Intelligence and experience convinced him that the man involved in the two incidents described was worth investigating further.

The salient point in the second incident was the raw savagery Blank had displayed. A normal man—well, an average man—might have handled the homosexual's first advance by merely smiling and shaking his head, or moving down the bar, or even leaving The Parrot. The violence displayed by Blank was excessive. Protesting too much?

The first incident—the case of the injured dog-owner—might not be as innocent as it appeared in Detective Blankenship's report. It was true that the witness, the doorman—what was his name? Delaney looked it up. Charles Lipsky—it was true that Lipsky stated that Blank had been struck with a folded newspaper before pushing his assailant. But witnesses can be bribed; it was hardly an uncommon occurrence. Even if Lipsky had told the truth, Delaney was amazed at how this incident fit into a pattern he had learned from experience: men prone to violence, men too ready to use their fists, their feet, even their teeth, somehow became involved in situations that were obviously not their fault, and yet resulted in injury or death to their antagonist.

Delaney called Monica Gilbert.

"Monica? Edward. I'm sorry to disturb you at this hour. I hope I didn't wake the children."

"Oh no. That takes more than a phone ring. What is it?"

"Would you mind looking at your card file and see if you have anything on a man named Blank. Daniel G. He lives on East Eighty-third Street."

"Just a minute."

He waited patiently. He heard her moving about. Then she was back on the phone.

"Blank, Daniel G.," she read. "Arrested twice for speeding. Guilty and fined. Do you want the make of car and license number?"

"Please."

He took quick notes as she gave him the information.

"Thank you," he said.

"Edward, is it—anything?"

"I don't know. I really don't. It's interesting. That's about all I can say right now. I'll know more tomorrow."

"Will you call?"

"Yes, if you want me to."

"Please do."

"All right. Sleep well."

"Thank you. You, too."

Two arrests for speeding. Not in itself significant, but within the pattern. The choice of car was similarly meaningful. Delaney was glad Daniel Blank didn't drive a Volkswagen.

He called Thomas Handry at the newspaper office. He had left for home. He called him at home. No answer. He called Detective Lieutenant Jeri Fernandez at his office. Fernandez had gone home. Delaney felt a sudden surge of anger at these people who couldn't be reached when he needed them. Then he realized how childish that was, and calmed down.

He found Fernandez' home phone number in the back of his pocket notebook where he had carefully listed home phone numbers of all sergeants and higher ranks in the 251st Precinct. Fernandez lived in Brooklyn. A child answered the phone.

"Hello?"

"Is Detective Fernandez there, please?"

"Just a minute. Daddy, it's for you!" the child screamed.

In the background Delaney could hear music, shouts, loud laughter, the thump of heavy dancing. Finally Fernandez came to the phone.

"Hello?"

"Captain Edward X. Delaney here."

"Oh. Howrya, Captain?"

"Lieutenant, I'm sorry to disturb you at this hour. Sounds like you're having a party."

"Yeah, it's the wife's birthday, and we have some people in."

"I won't keep you long. Lieutenant, when you were at the Two-five-one, you had a dick one named Blankenship. Right?"

"Sure. Ronnie. Good man."

"What did he look like? I can't seem to remember him."

"Sure you do, Captain. A real tall guy. About six-three or four. Skinny as a rail. We called him 'Scarecrow.' Remember now?"

"Oh yes. A big Adam's apple?"

"That's the guy."

"What happened to him?"

"He drew an Assault-Homicide Squad over on the West Side. I think it's up in the Sixties-Seventies-Eighties—around there. I know it takes in the Twentieth Precinct. Listen, I got his home phone number somewhere. Would that help?"

"It certainly would."

"Hang on a minute."

It was almost five minutes, but eventually Fernandez was back with Blankenship's phone number. Delaney thanked him. Fernandez seemed to want to talk more, but the Captain cut him short.

He dialed Blankenship's home phone. A woman answered. In the background Delaney could hear an infant wailing loudly.

"Hello?"

"Mrs. Blankenship?"

"Yes. Who is this?"

"My name is Delaney, Captain Edward X. Delaney, New York Police Depart—"

"What's happened? What's happened to Ronnie? Is he all right? Is he hurt? What—"

"No, no, Mrs. Blankenship," he said hurriedly, soothing her fears. "As far as I know, your husband is perfectly all right."

He could sympathize with her fright. Every cop's wife lived with that dread. But she should have known that if anything had happened to her husband, she wouldn't learn of it from a phone call. Two men from the Department would ring her bell. She would open the door and they would be standing there, faces twisted and guilty, and she would know.

"I'm trying to contact your husband to get some information, Mrs. Blankenship," he went on, speaking slowly and distinctly. This was obviously not an alert woman. "I gather he's not at home. Is he working?"

"Yes. He's on nights for the next two weeks."

"Could you give me his office phone number, please?"

"All right. Just a minute."

He could also have told her not to give out any information about her husband to a stranger who calls in the middle of the night and claims he's a captain in the NYPD. But what would be the use? Her husband had probably told her that a dozen times. A dull woman.

He got the number and thanked her. It was now getting on toward eleven o'clock; he wondered if he should try or let it go till morning. He dialed the number. Blankenship had checked in all right, but he wasn't on the premises. Delaney left his number, without identifying himself, and asked if the operator would have him call back.

"Please tell him it's important," he said.

" 'Important'?" the male operator said. "How do you spell that, Mr. Important?"

Delaney hung up. A wise-ass. The Captain would remember. The Department moved in involved and sometimes mysterious ways. One day that phone operator in that detective division might be under Delaney's command. He'd remember the high, lilting, laughing voice. It was stupid to act like that.

He started a new file, headed BLANK, Daniel G., and in it he stowed the Blankenship reports, his notes on Blank's record of arrests for speeding, the make of car he drove and his license number. Then he went to the Manhattan telephone directory and looked up Blank, Daniel G. There was only one listing of that name, on East 83rd Street. He made a note of the phone number and added that to his file.

He was mixing a fresh rye highball—was it his second or third?—when the phone rang. He put down the glass and bottle carefully, then ran for the phone, catching it midway through the third ring.

"Hello?"

"This is Blankenship. Who's this?"

"Captain Edward X. Delaney here. I was—"

"Captain! Good to hear from you. How are you, sir?"

"Fine, Ronnie. And you?" Delaney had never before called the man by his first name, hadn't even known what it was before his call to Fernandez. In fact, he couldn't remember ever speaking to Blankenship personally, but he wanted to set a tone.

"Okay, Captain. Getting along."

"How do you like the new assignment? Tell me, do you think this reorganization is going to work?"

"Captain, it's great!" Blankenship said enthusiastically. "They should have done it years ago. Now I can spend some time on important stuff and forget the little squeals. Our arrest rate is up, and morale is real good. The case load is way down, and we've got time to think."

The man sounded intelligent. His voice was pleasingly deep, vibrant, resonant. Delaney remembered that big, jutting Adam's apple.

"Glad to hear it," he said. "Listen, I'm on leave of absence, but something came up and I agreed to help out on it."

He let it go at that, keeping it vague, waiting to see if Blankenship would pick up on it and ask questions. But the detective hesitated a moment, then said, "Sure, Captain."

"It concerns a man named Daniel Blank, in the Two-five-one. He was involved in two beefs last year. You handled both of them. I have your reports. Good reports. Very complete."

"What was that name again?"

"Blank, B-l-a-n-k, Daniel G. He lives on East Eighty-third Street. The first thing was a pushing match with a guy who was allegedly beating his dog. The second—"

"Oh sure," Blankenship interrupted. "I remember. Probably because his name is Blank and mine is Blankenship. At the time I thought it was funny I should be handling him. Two beefs in six months. In the second, he kicked the shit out of a faggot. Right?"

"Right."

"But the victim wouldn't sign a complaint. What do you want to know, Captain?"

"About Blank. You saw him?"

"Sure. Twice."

"What do you remember about him?"

Blankenship recited: "Blank, Daniel G. White, male, approximately six feet or slightly taller, about—"

"Wait, wait a minute," Delaney said hastily. "I'm taking notes. Go a little slower."

"Okay, Captain. You got the height?"

"Six feet or a little over."

"Right. Weight about one seventy-five. Slim build but good shoulders. Good physical condition from what I could see. No obvious physical scars or infirmities. Dark complexion. Sunburned, I'd say. Long face. Sort of Chinese-looking. Let's see—anything else?"

"How was he dressed?" Delaney asked, admiring the man's observation and memory.

"Dark suits," Blankenship said promptly. "Nothing flashy, but well-cut and expensive. Some funny things I remember. Gold link chain on his wrist watch. Like a bracelet. The first time I saw him I think it was his own hair. The second time I swear it was a rug. The second time he was wearing a real crazy shirt open to his *pipik*, with some kind of necklace. You know—hippie stuff."

"Accent?" Delaney asked.

"Accent?" Blankenship repeated, thought a moment, then said, "Not a native New Yorker. Mid-western, I'd guess. Sorry I can't be more specific."

"You're doing great," Delaney assured him, elated. "You think he's strong?"

"Strong? I'd guess so. Any guy who can break another man's jaw with a punch has got to be strong. Right?"

"Right. What was your personal reaction to him? Flitty?"

"Could be, Captain. When they punish an obvious faggot like that, it's got to mean something. Right?"

"Right."

"I wanted to charge him, but the victim refused to sign anything. So what could I do?"

"I understand," Delaney said. "Believe me, this has nothing to do with that beef."

"I believe you, Captain."

"Do you know where he works, what he does for a living?"

"It's not in my reports?"

"No, it isn't."

"Sorry about that. But you've got his lawyer's name and address, haven't you?"

"Oh yes, I have that. I'll get it from him," Delaney lied. It was Blankenship's first mistake, and a small one. No use going to the lawyer; he'd simply refuse to divulge the information, then surely mention to Blank that the police had been around asking questions.

"That just about covers it," Delaney said. "Thanks very much for your help. What are you working on now?"

"It's a beaut, Captain," Blankenship said in his enthusiastic way. "This old dame got knocked off in her apartment. Strangled. No signs of forcible entry. And as far as we can tell, nothing stolen. A neighbor smelled it; that's how we got on to it. A poor little apartment, but it turns out the old dame was loaded."

"Who inherits?"

"A nephew. But we checked him out six ways from the middle. He's got an alibi that holds up. He was down in Florida for two weeks. We checked. He really was there. Every minute."

"Check his bank account, back for about six months or a year. See if there was a heavy withdrawal—maybe five or ten big ones."

"You mean he hired—? Son of a bitch!" Blankenship said bitterly. "Why didn't I think of that?"

"Stick around for twenty-five years," Delaney laughed. "You'll learn. Thanks again. If there's ever anything I can do for you, just let me know."

"I'll hold you to that, Captain," Blankenship said in his deep, throaty voice.

"You do that," Delaney said seriously.

After he hung up, he finished mixing his highball. He took a deep swallow, then grinned, grinned, grinned. He looked around at walls, ceiling, floor, furniture, and grinned at everything. It felt good. It had gone beyond his first article on common sense: the value of personally observed evidence and experience. It had even gone beyond the second article that extolled the value of hunch and instinct. Now he was in the realm of the third, unpublished article which Barbara had convinced him should never be printed. Quite rightly, too. Because in that monograph, exploring the nature of the detective-criminal relationship—his theory of the adversary concept—he had rashly dwelt on the "joy" of the successful detective.

That was what he felt now—*joy!* He worked at his new file —BLANK, Daniel G.—adding to it everything Detective Blankenship had reported, and not a thing, not one single thing, varied in any significant aspect from his original "The Suspect" outline. He gained surety as he amplified his notes. It was beautiful, beautiful, all so beautiful. And, just as he had written in his unpublished article, there was sensuous pleasure —was it sexual?—in the chase. So intent was he on his rapid writing, his reports, his new, beautiful file, that the phone rang five times before he picked it up. As a matter of fact, he kept writing as he answered it.

"Captain Edward X. Delaney here."

"Dorfman. There's been another one."

"Captain—*what?*"

"Lieutenant Dorfman, Captain. Sorry to wake you up. There's been another killing. Same type, with extras."

"Where?"

"Eighty-fifth. Between First and York."

"A man?"

"Yes."

"Tall?"

"Tall? I'd guess five-ten or eleven."

"Weight?"

There was silence, then Dorfman's dull voice: "I don't know what he weighed, Captain. Is it important?"

"Extras? You said 'Extras.' What extras?"

"He was struck at least three times. Maybe more. There are signs of a struggle. Christmas packages, three of them, thrown

375

around. Scuff marks on the sidewalk. His coat was torn. Looks like he put up a fight."

"Identified?"

"A man named Feinberg. Albert Feinberg."

"Anything missing? Identification of any kind?"

"We don't know," Dorfman said wearily. "They're checking with his wife now. His wallet wasn't out like in the Lombard kill. We just don't know."

"All right," Delaney said softly. "Thank you for calling. Sounds like you could use some sleep, lieutenant."

"Yes, I could. If I could sleep."

"Where was it again?"

"Eighty-fifth, between First and York."

"Thank you. Good-night."

He looked at his desk calendar and counted carefully. It had been eleven days since the murder of Detective Kope. His research was proving out; the intervals between killings were becoming shorter and shorter.

He got out his Precinct map with the plastic overlay and, with a red grease pencil, carefully marked in the murder of Albert Feinberg, noting victim's name, date of killing, and place. The locations of the four murders formed a rough square on the map. On impulse, he used his grease pencil and a ruler to connect opposite corners of the square, making an X. It intersected at 84th Street and Second Avenue, right in the middle of the crossing of the two streets. He checked Daniel Blank's address. It was on 83rd Street, about a block and a half away. The map didn't say yes and it didn't say no.

He was staring at the map, nodding, and awoke fifteen minutes later, startled, shocked that he had been sleeping. He pulled himself to his feet, drained the watery remains of his final highball, and made his rounds, checking window locks and outside doors.

Then to bed, groaning with weariness. What he really wanted to do . . . what he wanted to do . . . so foolish . . . was to go to Daniel Blank . . . go to him right now . . . introduce himself and say, "Tell me all about it."

Yes, that was foolish . . . idiotic . . . but he was sure . . . well, maybe not sure, but it was a chance, and the best . . . and just before he fell asleep he acknowledged, with a sad smile, that all this shitty thinking about patterns and percentages and psychological profile was just that—a lot of shit. He was following up on Daniel Blank because he had no other lead. It was as simple and obvious as that. Occam's Razor. So he fell asleep.

4

His bedside alarm went off at 8:00 a.m. He slapped it silent, swung his legs out from under the blankets, donned his glasses, consulted a slip of paper he had left under the phone. He called Thomas Handry at home. The phone rang eight times. He was about to give up when Handry answered.

"Hello?" he asked sleepily.

"Captain Edward X. Delaney here. Did I wake you up?"

"Why no," Handry yawned. "I've been up for hours. Jogged around the reservoir, wrote two deathless sonnets, and seduced my landlady. All right, what do you want, Captain?"

"Got a pencil handy?"

"A minute . . . okay, what is it?"

"I want you to check a man in your morgue file."

"Who is he?"

"Blank, Daniel G. That last name is Blank, B-l-a-n-k."

"Why should he be in our morgue?"

"I don't know why. It's just a chance."

"Well, what has he done? I mean, has he been in the news for any reason?"

"Not to my knowledge."

"Then why the hell should we have him in the morgue?"

"I told you," Delaney said patiently, "it's just a chance. But I've got to cover every possibility."

"Oh Jesus. All right. I'll try. I'll call you around ten, either way."

"No, don't do that," the Captain said quickly. "I may be out. I'll call you at the paper around ten."

Handry grunted and hung up.

After breakfast he went into the study. He wanted to check the dates of the four murders and the intervals between them. Lombard to Gilbert: 22 days. Gilbert to Kope: 17 days. Kope to Feinberg: 11 days. By projection, the next murder should occur during the week between Christmas and New Year's Day, and probably a few days after Christmas. He sat suddenly upright. Christmas! Oh God.

He called Barbara immediately. She reported she was feeling

377

well, had had a good night's sleep, and ate all her breakfast. She always said that.

"Listen," he said breathlessly, "it's about Christmas . . . I'm sorry, dear. I forgot all about gifts and cards. What are we to do?"

She laughed. "I knew you were too busy. I've mailed things to the children. I saw ads in the newspapers and ordered by phone. Liza and John are getting a nice crystal ice bucket from Tiffany's, and I sent Eddie a terribly expensive sweater from Saks. How does that sound?"

"You're a wonder," he told her.

"So you keep saying," she teased, "but do you *really* mean it? Give Mary some money, as usual, and maybe you can get her something personal, just some little thing, like a scarf or handkerchief or something like that. And put the check in the package."

"All right. What about the cards?"

"Well, we have some left over from last year—about twenty, I think—and they're in the bottom drawer of the secretary in the living room. Now if you buy another three boxes, I'm sure it'll be enough. Are you coming over today?"

"Yes. Definitely. At noon."

"Well, bring the cards and the list. You know where the list is, don't you?"

"Bottom drawer of the secretary in the living room."

"Detective!" she giggled. "Yes, that's where it is. Bring the list and cards over at noon. I feel very good today. I'll start writing them. I won't try to do them all today, but I should have them finished up in two or three days, and they'll get there in time."

"Stamps?"

"Yes, I'll need stamps. Get a roll of a hundred. A roll is easier to handle. I make such a mess of a sheet. Oh Edward, I'm sorry . . . I forgot to ask. Did you find anything in the old files?"

"I'll tell you all about it when I see you at noon."

"Does it look good?"

"Well . . . maybe."

She was silent, then sighed. "I hope so," she said. "Oh, how I hope so."

"I do, too. Listen, dear . . . what would you like for Christmas?"

"Do I have a choice?" she laughed. "I know what I'm going

378

to get—perfume from any drugstore you find that's open on Christmas Eve."

He laughed too. She was right.

He hung up and glanced at his watch. It was a little past 9:00 a.m., later than he wanted it to be. He dug hurriedly through his pack of business cards and found the one he was looking for: Arthur K. Ames. Automobile Insurance.

Blank's apartment house occupied an entire block on East 83rd Street. Delaney was familiar with the building and, standing across the street, looking up, thought again of how institutional it looked. All steel and glass. A hospital or a research center, not a place to live in. But people did, and he could imagine what the rents must be.

As he had hoped, men and women were still leaving for work. Two doormen were constantly running down the driveway to flag cabs and, even as he watched, a garage attendant brought a Lincoln Continental to the entrance, hopped out and ran back to the underground garage to drive up another tenant's car.

Delaney walked resolutely up the driveway, turned right and walked down a short flight of steps to the underground garage. A light blue Jaguar came roaring by him, the garage man at the wheel. Delaney waited patiently at the entrance until the black attendant came trotting back.

"Good morning," he said proffering his business card. "My name is Ames, of Cross-Country Insurance."

The attendant glanced at the card. "You picked a bad time to sell insurance, man."

"No, no," Delaney said quickly, smiling. "I'm not selling anything. One of the cars we cover was involved in an accident with a nineteen-seventy-one Chevy Corvette. The Corvette took off. The car we cover was trashed. The driver's in the hospital. Happened over on Third Avenue. We think the Corvette might be from the neighborhood, so I'm checking all the garages around here. Just routine."

"A nineteen-seventy-one Corvette?"

"Yes."

"What color?"

"Probably dark blue or black."

"When did this happen?"

"Couple of days ago."

"We got one Corvette. Mr. Blank. But it couldn't be him. He hasn't had his car out in weeks."

"The police found glass at the scene and pieces of fiberglass from the left front fender."

"I'm telling you it couldn't be Mr. Blank's Corvette. There's not a scratch on it."

"Mind if I take a look?"

"Help yourself," the man shrugged. "It's back there in the far corner, behind the white Caddy."

"Thank you."

The man took a phone call, hopped into a Ford station wagon, began to back out into the center of the garage so he could turn around. He was busy, which was why Delaney had picked this time. He walked slowly over to the black Corvette. The license number was Blank's.

The door was unlocked. He opened it and looked in, sniffing. A musty, closed-window smell. There was an ice-scraper for the windshield, a can of defogger, a dusty rag, a pair of worn driving gloves. Between the two seats was tucked a gasoline station map that had been handled, unfolded and refolded several times. Delaney opened it far enough to look. New York State. With a route marked on it in heavy black pencil: from East 83rd Street, across town, up the West Side Highway to the George Washington Bridge, across to New Jersey, up through Mahwah into New York again, then north to the Catskill Mountains, ending at a town named Chilton. He reshuffled the map, put it back where he found it.

He closed the car door gently and started out. He met the attendant coming back.

"It sure wasn't that car," he smiled.

"I told you that, man."

Delaney wondered if the attendant would mention the incident to Blank. He thought it likely, and he tried to guess what Blank's reaction would be. It wouldn't spook him but, if he was guilty, it might start him thinking. There was an idea there, Delaney acknowledged, but it wasn't time for it . . . yet.

Back in his study, he looked up Chilton in his world atlas. All it said was, "Chilton, N.Y. Pop.: 3,146." He made a note about Chilton and added it to the Daniel Blank file. He looked at his watch. It wasn't quite ten, but close enough. He called Handry at his office.

"Captain? Sorry. No soap."

"Well . . . it was a long shot. Thank you very much for—"

"Hey, wait a minute. You give up too easily. We got other files of people. For instance, the sports desk keeps a file of living personalities and so does the theatre and arts section. Could your boy be in either?"

"Maybe in the sports file, but I doubt it."

"Well, can you tell me *anything* about him?"

"Not much. He lives in an expensive apartment house and drives an expensive car, so he must be loaded."

"Thanks a lot," Handry sighed. "Okay, I'll see what I can do. If I have something, I'll call you. If you don't hear from me, you'll know I didn't turn up a thing. Okay?"

"Yes. Sure. Fine," Delaney said heavily, feeling this was just a polite kiss-off.

He got over to the hospital as Barbara's noon meal was being served and he watched, beaming, as she ate almost all of it, feeding herself. She really was getting better, he told himself happily. Then he showed her the Christmas cards he had purchased, in three different price ranges; the most expensive for their "important" friends and acquaintances, the least expensive for—well, for people. And the twenty cards left over from last year, the list, the stamps.

Then he told her about Daniel Blank, stalking about the room, making wide gestures. He told her the man's history, what he had been able to dig up, what he suspected.

"What do you think?" he asked finally, eager for her opinion.

"Yes," she said thoughtfully. "Maybe. But you've really got nothing, Edward. You know that."

"Of course."

"Nothing definite. But certainly worth following up. I'd feel a lot better if you could tie him up with an ice ax purchase."

"I would too. But right now he's all I've got."

"Where do you go from here?"

"Where? Checking out everything. Charles Lipsky. The Parrot, where he had that fight. Trying to find out who he is and what he is. Listen, dear, I won't be over this evening. Too much to do. All right?"

"Of course," she said. "Are you sticking to your diet?"

"Sure," he said, patting his stomach. "I'm up only three pounds this week."

They laughed, and he kissed her on the lips before he left. Then they kissed again. Soft, clinging, wanting kisses.

He clumped down to the lobby, dug out his pocket notebook, looked up the number. Then he called Calvin Case from the lobby booth.

"How you coming?"

"All right," Case said. "I'm still working on the general mountaineering equipment sales checks, pulling those in the Two-five-one Precinct."

Delaney was amused at Case's "Two-five-one Precinct." His amateur was talking officialese.

"Am I doing any good?" Case wanted to know.

"You are," Delaney assured him. "I've got a lead. Name is Daniel Blank. Know him?"

"What's it?"

"Blank. B-l-a-n-k. Daniel G. Ever hear of him?"

"Is he a climber?"

"I don't know. Could be."

"Hey, Captain, there're two hundred thousand climbers in the country and more every year. No, I don't know any Daniel G. Blank. What does the G. stand for?"

"Gideon. All right, let me try this one on you: Ever hear of Chilton? It's a town in New York."

"I know. Up in the Catskills. Sleepy little place."

"Would a mountain climber go there?"

"Sure. Not Chilton itself, but about two miles out of town is a state park. A small one, but nice. Benches, tables, barbecues —crap like that."

"What about climbing?"

"Mostly for hiking. There are some nice outcrops. There's one good climb, a monolith. Devil's Needle. It's a chimney climb. As a matter of fact, I left two pitons up there to help whoever came after me to crawl out onto the top. I used to go up there to work out."

"Is it an easy climb?"

"Easy? Well . . . it's not for beginners. I'd say an intermediate climb. If you know what you're doing, it's easy. Does that help?"

"At this point everything helps."

Back home, he added the information Calvin Case had given him about Chilton and the Devil's Needle to the Daniel Blank file. Then he checked the address of The Parrot in Blankenship's report. He went through his pack of business cards, found one that read: "Ward M. Miller. Private Investigations. Discreet—Reliable—Satisfaction Guaranteed." He began to plan his cover story.

He was still thinking it out an hour later, so deeply engrossed with the deception he was plotting that the phone must have rung several times without his being aware of it.

Then Mary, who had picked up the hall extension, came in to tell him Mr. Handry was on the phone.

"Got him," Handry said.

"What?"

"I found him. Your Daniel G. Blank."

"Jesus Christ!" Delaney said excitedly. "Where?"

Handry laughed. "Our business-finance desk keeps a personality file, mostly on executives. They get tons of press releases and public relations reports every year. You know, Joe Blow has been promoted from vice president to executive vice president, or Harry Hardass has been hired as sales manager at Wee Tots Bootery, or some such shit. Usually it's a one-page release with a small photo, a head-and-shoulders shot. You know what the business desk calls that stuff?"

"What?"

"The 'Fink File.' And if you got a look at those photos, you'd understand why. You wouldn't believe! They print about one out of every ten releases they get, depending on the importance of the company. Anyway, that's where I found your pigeon. He got a promotion a couple of years ago, and there's a photo of him and a few paragraphs of slush."

"Where does he work?"

"Ohhh no," Handry said. "You haven't a bloody chance. I'll have a Xerox made of the release and a copy of the photo. I'll bring them up to your place tonight if you'll tell me why you're so interested in Mr. Blank. It's the Lombard thing, isn't it?"

Delaney hesitated. "Yes," he said finally.

"Blank a suspect?"

"Maybe."

"If I bring the release and photo tonight, will you tell me about it?"

"There isn't much to tell."

"Let me be the judge of that. Is it a deal?"

"All right. About eight or nine."

"I'll be there."

Delaney hung up, exultant. Information *and* a photo! He knew from experience the usual sequence of a difficult case. The beginning was long, slow, muddled. The middle began to pick up momentum, pieces coming together, fragments fitting. The end was usually short, fast, frequently violent. He judged he was in the middle of the middle now, the pace quickening, parts clicking into place. It was all luck. It was all fucking luck.

The Parrot was no worse and no better than any other ancient Third Avenue bar that served food (steak sandwich, veal
cutlet, beef stew; spaghetti, home fries, peas-and-carrots; apple
pie, tapioca pudding, chocolate cake). With the growth of
high-rise apartment houses, there were fewer such places every
year. As he had hoped, the tavern was almost empty. There
were two men wearing yellow hardhats drinking beer at the
bar and matching coins. There was a young couple at a back
table, holding hands, dawdling over a bottle of cheap wine.
One waiter at this hour. One bartender.

Delaney sat at the bar, near the door, his back to the plate
glass window. He ordered a rye and water. When the bartender poured it, the Captain put a ten-dollar bill on the
counter.

"Got a minute?" he asked.

The man looked at him. "For what?"

"I need some information."

"Who are you?"

Delaney slid the "Ward M. Miller—Private Investigations"
business card across the bar. The man picked it up and read
it, his lips moving. He returned the card.

"I don't know nothing," he said.

"Sure you do," the Captain smiled genially. He placed the
card atop the ten-dollar bill. "It's a matter of public record.
Last year there was a fight in here. A guy kicked the shit out of
a faggot. Were you on duty that night?"

"I'm on duty every night. I own the joint. Part of it
anyways."

"Remember the fight?"

"I remember. How come you know about it?"

"I got a friend in the Department. He told me about it."

"What's it got to do with me?"

"Nothing. I don't even know your name, and I don't want
to know it. I'm interested in the guy who broke the other guy's
jaw."

"That sonofabitch!" the bartender burst out. "That guy
should have been put away and throw away the key. A
maniac!"

"He kicked the faggot when he was down?"

"That's right. In the balls. He was a wild man. It took three
of us to pull him away. He would have killed him. I came
close to sapping him. I keep a sawed-off pool cue behind the
bar. He was a raving nut. How come you're interested in
him?"

"Just checking up. His name is Daniel Blank. He's about thirty-six, thirty-seven—around there. He's divorced. Now he's got the hots for this young chick. She's nineteen, in college. This Blank wants to marry her, and she's all for it. Her old man is loaded. He thinks this Blank smells. The old man wants me to check him out, see what I can dig up."

"The old man better kick his kid's tail or get her out of the country before he lets her marry Blank. That guy's bad news."

"I'm beginning to think so," Delaney agreed.

"Bet your sweet ass," the bartender nodded. He was interested now, leaned across the bar, his arms folded. "He's a wrongo. Listen, I got a young daughter myself. If this Blank ever came near her, I'd break his arms and legs. He was in trouble with the cops before, you know."

Delaney took back his business card, moved the ten-dollar bill closer to the man's elbow.

"What happened?" he asked.

"He got in trouble with some guy who lives in his apartment house. Something about the guy's dog. Anyway, this guy got a busted arm, and this Blank was hauled in on an assault rap. But they fixed it up somehow and settled out of court."

"No kidding?" the Captain said. "First I heard about it. When did this happen?"

"About six months before he had the fight in here. The guy's a trouble-maker."

"Sure sounds like it. How did you find out about it—the assault charge I mean?"

"My brother-in-law told me. His name's Lipsky. He's a doorman in the apartment house where this Blank lives."

"That's interesting. You think your brother-in-law would talk to me?"

The bartender looked down at the ten-dollar bill, slid it under his elbow. The two construction workers down at the other end of the bar called for more beer; he went down there to serve them. Then he came back.

"Sure," he said. "Why not? He thinks this Blank stinks on ice."

"How can I get in touch with him?"

"You can call him on the lobby phone. You know where this Blank lives?"

"Oh sure. That's a good idea. I'll call Lipsky there. Maybe this Blank is shacking up or something and is playing my client's daughter along for kicks or maybe he smells money."

"Could be. Another drink?"

"Not right now. Listen, have you seen Blank since he got in that fight in here?"

"Sure. The bastard was in a few nights ago. He thought I didn't recognize him, the shit, but I never forget a face."

"Did he behave himself?"

"Oh sure. He was quiet. I didn't say word one to him. Just served him his drink and left him alone. He had some Christmas packages with him so I guess he had been out shopping."

Christmas packages. It could be the night Albert Feinberg was killed. But Delaney didn't dare press it.

"Thanks very much," he said, sliding off the stool. He started toward the door, then stopped and came back. The ten-dollar bill had disappeared.

"Oh," he said, snapping his fingers, "two more things . . . Could you call your brother-in-law and tell him I'm going to call him? I mean, it would help if I didn't just call him cold. You can tell him what it's all about, and there'll be a couple of bucks in it for him."

"Sure," the bartender nodded, "I can do that. I talk to him almost every day anyway. When he's on days, he usually stops by for a brew when he gets off. But he's on nights this week. You won't get him before eight tonight. But I'll call him at home."

"Many thanks. I appreciate that. The other thing is this: if Blank should stop in for a drink, tell him I was around asking questions about him. You don't have to give him my name; just tell him a private investigator was in asking questions. You can describe me." He grinned at the bartender. "Might put the fear of God in him. Know what I mean?"

"Yeah," the man grinned back, "I know what you mean."

He returned home to find a packet of Operation Lombard reports Mary had signed for. He left them on the hallway table, went directly to the kitchen, still wearing his stiff Homburg and heavy, shapeless overcoat. He was so hungry he was almost sick, and realized he had eaten nothing since breakfast. Mary had left a pot of lamb stew on the range. It was still vaguely warm, not hot, but he didn't care. He stood there in Homburg and overcoat, and forked out pieces of lamb, a potato, onions, carrots. He got a can of beer from the refrigerator and drank deeply from that, not bothering with a glass. He gulped everything, belching once or twice. After awhile he began to feel a little better; his knees stopped trembling.

He took off hat and coat, opened another can of beer, brought that and the Operation Lombard reports into the study. He donned his glasses, sat at his desk. He began writing an account of his interview with the bartender at The Parrot.

He filed away his account, then opened the package of Operation Lombard reports dealing with the murder of the fourth victim, Albert Feinberg. There were sketchy preliminary statements from the first uniformed patrolmen on the scene, lengthier reports from detectives, temporary opinion of the Medical Examiner (Dr. Sanford Ferguson again), an inventory of the victim's effects, the first interview with the victim's widow, photos of the corpse and murder scene, etc., etc.

As Lt. Dorfman had said, there were "extras" that were not present in the three previous homicides. Captain Delaney made a careful list of them:

1. Signs of a struggle. Victim's jacket lapel torn, necktie awry, shirt pulled from belt. Scuff marks of heels (rubber) and soles (leather) on the sidewalk.

2. Three Christmas packages nearby. One, which contained a black lace negligee, bore the victim's fingerprints. The other two were empty—dummy packages—and bore no prints at all, neither on the outside wrapping paper nor the inside boxes.

3. Drops of blood on the sidewalk a few feet from where the victim's battered skull rested. Careful scrapings and analysis proved these several drops were not of the victim's blood type and were presumed to be the killer's. (Delaney made a note to call Ferguson and find out exactly what blood types were involved.)

4. The victim's wallet and credit card case appeared to be intact in his pockets. His wife stated that, to her knowledge, no identification was missing. However, pinned behind the left lapel of the victim's overcoat and poking through the buttonhole, examiners had found a short green stem. The forensic men had identified it as genus *Rosa*, family *Rosaceae*, order *Rosales*. Investigation was continuing to determine, if possible, exactly what type of rose the victim had been sporting on his overcoat lapel.

He was going over the reports once again when the outside door bell rang. Before he answered it, he slid the Operation Lombard material and his own notes into his top desk drawer and closed it tightly. Then he went out to the door, brought Thomas Handry back into the study, took his coat and hat. He poured a Scotch on the rocks for Handry, drained the warm dregs of his own beer, then mixed himself a rye and water, sat down heavily behind the desk. Handry slumped in the leather club chair, crossed his knees.

"Well . . ." Delaney said briskly. "What have you got?"

"What have *you* got, Captain? Remember our deal?"

Delaney stared at the neatly dressed young man a moment. Handry seemed tired; his forehead was seamed, diagonal lines that hadn't been there before now ran from the corners of his nose down to the sides of his mouth. He bit continually at the hard skin around his thumbnails.

"Been working hard?" Delaney asked quietly.

Handry shrugged. "The usual. I'm thinking of quitting."

"Oh?"

"I'm not getting any younger, and I'm not doing what I want to do."

"How's the writing coming?"

"It's not. I get home at night and all I want to do is take off my shoes, mix a drink, and watch the boob tube."

Delaney nodded. "You're not married, are you?"

"No."

"Got a woman?"

"Yes."

"What does she think about your quitting?"

"She's all for it. She's got a good job. Makes more than I do. She says she'll support us until I can get published or get a job I can live with."

"You don't like newspaper work?"

"Not anymore."

"Why not?"

"I didn't know there was so much shit in the world. I can't take much more of it. But I didn't come here to talk about my problems."

"Problems?" the Captain said, surprised. "That's what it's all about. Some you have to handle. Some there's nothing you can do about. Some go away by themselves if you wait long enough. What were you worrying about five years ago?"

"Who the hell knows."

"Well . . . there you are. All right, here's what I've got . . ."

Handry knew about the Captain's amateurs, of the checkings of mailing lists and sales slips, of the setting up of Monica Gilbert's master file of names, the investigation of their criminal records.

Now the Captain brought him up-to-date on Daniel Blank,

how he, Delaney, had found the year-old beef sheets in the Precinct house basement, the search of Blank's car, the interview with the bartender at The Parrot.

". . . and that's all I've got," he concluded. "So far."

Handry shook his head. "Pretty thin."

"I know."

"You're not even sure if this guy is a mountain climber."

"That's true. But he was on the Outside Life mailing list, and that map in his car could be marked to a place where he climbs in this area."

"Want to go to the D.A. with that?"

"Don't be silly."

"You don't even know if he owns an ice ax."

"That's true; I don't."

"Well, what I've got isn't going to help you much more."

He drew an envelope from his breast pocket, leaned forward, scaled it onto Delaney's desk. The envelope was unsealed. The Captain drew out a 4X5 glossy photo and a single Xerox sheet that he unfolded and smoothed out on his desk blotter. He tilted his desk lamp to cast a stronger beam, took up the photo. He stared at it a long time. There. You. Are.

It was a close-up. Daniel Blank was staring directly at the lens. His shoulders were straight and wide. There was a faint smile on his lips, but not in his eyes.

He seemed remarkably youthful. His face was smooth, unlined. Small ears set close to the skull. A strong jaw. Prominent cheek bones. Large eyes, widely spaced, with an expression at once impassive and brooding. Straight hair, parted on the left, but combed flatly back. Heavy brows. Sculpted and unexpectedly tender lips, softly curved.

"Looks a little like an Indian," Delaney said.

"No," Handry said. "More Slavic. Almost Mongol. Look like a killer to you?"

"Everyone looks like a killer to me," Delaney said, not smiling. He turned his attention to the copy of the press release.

It was dated almost two years previously. It was brief, only two paragraphs, and said merely that Daniel G. Blank had been appointed Circulation Director of all Javis-Bircham Publications and would assume his new duties immediately. He was planning to computerize the Circulation Department of Javis-Bircham and would be in charge of the installation of AMROK II, a new computer that had been leased and would occupy almost an entire floor of the Javis-Bircham Building on West 46th Street.

Delaney read through the release again, then pushed it away from him. He took off his heavy glasses, placed them on top of the release. Then he leaned back in his swivel chair, clasped his hands behind his head, stared at the ceiling.

"I told you it wouldn't be much help," Handry said.

"Oh . . . I don't know," Delaney murmured dreamily. "There are some things . . . Fix yourself a fresh drink."

"Thanks. You want some more rye?"

"All right. A little."

He waited until Handry was settled back in the club chair again. Then the Captain sat up straight, put on his glasses, read the release again. He moved his glasses down on his nose, stared at Handry over the rims.

"How much do you think the Circulation Director of Javis-Bircham earns?"

"Oh, I'd guess a minimum of thirty thousand. And if it ran to fifty, I would be a bit surprised."

"That much?"

"Javis-Bircham is a big outfit. I looked it up. It's in the top five hundred of all the corporations in the country."

"Fifty thousand? Pretty good for a young man."

"How old is he?" Handry asked.

"I don't know exactly. Around thirty-five I'd guess."

"Jesus. What does he do with his money?"

"Pays a heavy rent. Keeps an expensive car. Pays alimony. Travels, I suppose. Invests. Maybe he owns a summer home; I don't know. There's a lot I don't know about him."

He got up to add more ice to his drink. Then he began to wander about the room, carrying the highball.

"The computer," he said. "What was it—AMROK II?"

Handry, puzzled, said nothing.

"Want to hear something funny?" Delaney asked.

"Sure. I could use a good laugh."

"This isn't funny-haha; this is funny strange. I was a detective for almost twenty years before I transferred to the Patrol Division. In those twenty years I had my share of cases involving sexual aberrations, either as a primary or secondary motive. And you know, a lot of those cases—many more than could be accounted for by statistical averages—involved electronic experts, electricians, mechanics, computer programmers, bookkeepers and accountants. Men who worked with things, with machinery, with numbers. These men were rapists or Peeping Toms or flashers or child molesters or sadists or exhibitionists. This is my own experience, you understand. I have never seen any study that breaks down sex offenders according to occupation. I think I'll suggest an analysis like that to Inspector Johnson. It might prove valuable."

"How do you figure it?"

"I can't. It might just be my own experience with sex offenders, too limited to be significant. But it does seem to me that men whose jobs are—are mechanized or automated, whose daily relations with people are limited, are more prone to sex aberrations than men who have frequent and varied human contacts during their working hours. Whether the sex offense is due to the nature of the man's work, or whether the man unconsciously sought that type of work because he was already a potential sex offender and feared human contact, I can't say. How would you like to go talk to Daniel Blank in his office?"

Handry was startled. His drink slopped over the rim of the glass.

"What?" he asked incredulously. "What did you say?"

Delaney started to repeat his question, but the phone on his desk shrilled loudly.

"Delaney here."

"Edward? Thorsen. Can you talk?"

"Not very well."

"Can you listen a moment?"

"Yes."

"Good news. We think Broughton's on the way out. This fourth killing did it. The Mayor and Commissioner and their top aides are meeting tonight on it."

"I see."

"If I hear anything more tonight, I'll let you know."

"Thank you."

"How are you coming?"

"So-so."

"Got a name?"

"Yes."

"Good. Hang in there. Things are beginning to break."

"All right. Thank you for calling."

He hung up, turned back to Handry. "I asked how you'd like to go talk to Daniel Blank in his office."

"Oh sure," Handry nodded. "Just waltz in and say, 'Mr. Blank, Captain Edward X. Delaney of the New York Police Department thinks you axed four men to death on the east side. Would you care to make a statement'?"

"No, not like that," Delaney said seriously. "Javis-Bircham will have a publicity or public relations department, won't they?"

"Bound to."

"I'd do this myself, but you have a press card and identifications man. Identify yourself. Make an appointment. The *top* man. When you go see him, flash your buzzer. Say that your paper is planning a series of personality profiles on young, up-and-coming executives, the—"

"Hey, wait a minute!"

"The new breed of young executives who are familiar with computers, market sampling, demographic percentages and all that shit. Ask the public relations man to suggest four or five young, progressive Javis-Bircham executives who might fit the type your paper is looking for."

"Now see here—"

"Don't—repeat, *do not*—ask for Blank by name. Just come down hard on the fact that you're looking for a young executive familiar with the current use and future value of computers in business operations. Blank is certain to be one of the four or five men he suggests to you. Ask a few questions about each man he suggests. Then you pick Blank. See how easy it is?"

"Easy?" Handry shook his head. "Madness! And what if the Javis-Bircham PR man checks back with the finance editor of my paper and finds out no such series of articles is planned?"

"Chances are he won't. He'll be happy to get the publicity for Javis-Bircham, won't he?"

"But what if he does check? Then I'll be out on my ass."

"So what? You're thinking of quitting anyway, aren't you? So one of your problems is solved right there."

Handry stared at him, shaking his head. "You really are a special kind of bastard," he said in wonderment.

"Or," Delaney went on imperturbably, "if you like, you can give the finance editor on your paper a cover story. Tell him it's a police case—which it is—and if he asks questions, tell him it involves a big embezzlement or fraud or something like that. Don't mention the Lombard case. He'd probably cover for you if the Javis-Bircham PR man called and say, yes, the paper was planning a series of articles on young, progressive executives. He'd do that for you, wouldn't he?"

"Maybe."

"So you'll do it?"

"Just one question: why the fuck should I?"

"Two answers to that. One, if Blank turns out to be the killer, you'll be the only reporter in the world who had a personal interview with him. That's worth something, isn't it? Two, you want to be a poet, don't you? Or some kind of writer other than a reporter or rewrite man. How can you expect to be a good writer if you don't understand people, if you don't know what makes them tick? You've got to learn to get inside people, to penetrate their minds, their hearts, their souls. What an opportunity this is—to meet and talk to a man who might have slaughtered four human beings!"

Handry drained his drink in a gulp. He rose, poured himself another, stood with his back to Delaney.

"You really know how to go for the jugular, don't you?"

"Yes."

"Aren't you ever ashamed of the way you manipulate people?"

"I don't manipulate people. Sometimes I give them the chance to do what they want to do and never had the opportunity. Will you do it, Handry?"

There was silence. The reporter took a deep breath, then blew it out. He turned to face Delaney.

"All right," he said.

"Good," the Captain nodded. "Set up the appointment with Blank the way I've outlined it. Use your brains. I know you've got a good brain. The day before your interview is scheduled, give me a call. We'll have a meet and I'll tell you what questions to ask him. Then we'll have a rehearsal."

"A rehearsal?"

"That's right. I'll play Blank, to give you an idea of how he might react to your questions and how you can follow up on things he might or might not say."

"I've interviewed before," Handry protested. "Hundreds of times."

"None as important as this. Handry, you're an amateur liar. I'm going to make you a professional."

The reporter nodded grimly. "If anyone can, you can. You don't miss a trick, do you?"

"I try not to."

"I hope to Christ if I ever commit a crime you don't come after me, Iron Balls."

He sounded bitter.

After Handry left, Delaney sat at his study desk, staring again at the photo of Daniel Blank. The man was handsome, no doubt about it: dark and lean. His face seemed honed; beneath the thin flesh cover the bones of brow, cheeks and jaw were undeniably there. But the Captain could read nothing from that face: neither greed, passion, evil nor weakness. It was a closed-off mask, hiding its secrets.

On impulse, not bothering to analyze his own motive, he took out the Daniel G. Blank file, flipped throught it until he found Blank's phone number and dialed it. It rang four times, then:

"Hello?"

"Lou?" Delaney asked. "Lou Jackson?"

"No, I'm afraid you've got the wrong number," the voice said pleasantly.

"Oh. Sorry."

Delaney hung up. It was an agreeable voice, somewhat musical, words clearly enunciated, tone deep, a good resonance. He stared at the photo again, matching what his eyes saw to what his ears had heard. He was beginning, just beginning, to penetrate Daniel Blank.

He worked on his records and files till almost 11:00 p.m., then judged the time was right to call Charles Lipsky. He looked up the apartment house number and called from his study phone.

"Lobby," a whiny voice answered.

"Charles Lipsky, please."

"Yeah. Talking. Who's this?" Delany caught the caution, the suspicion in that thin, nasal voice. He wondered what doom the doorman expected from a phone call at this hour.

"Mr. Lipsky, my name is Miller, Ward M. Miller. Did your brother-in-law speak to you about me?"

"Oh. Yeah. He called." Now Delaney caught a note of relief, of catastrophe averted or at least postponed.

"I was hoping we might get together, Mr. Lipsky. Just for a short talk."

"Yeah. Well, listen . . ." Now the voice became low, conspiratorial. "You know I ain't supposed to talk to anyone about the tenants. We got a very strict rule against that."

Delaney recognized this virtuous reminder for what it was: a ploy to drive the price up.

"I realize that, Mr. Lipsky, and believe me, you don't have to tell me a thing you feel you shouldn't. But a short talk would be to our mutual advantage. You understand?"

"Well . . . yeah."

"I have an expense account."

"Oh, well, okay then."

394

"And your name will be kept out of it."

"You're sure?"

"Absolutely. When and where?"

"Well, how soon do you want to make it?"

"As soon as possible. Wherever you say."

"Well, I get off tomorrow morning at four. I usually stop by this luncheonette on Second and Eighty-fifth for coffee before I go home. It's open twenty-four hours a day, but it's usually empty at that hour except for some hackies and hookers."

Delaney knew the place Lipsky referred to, but didn't mention he knew it.

"Second Avenue and Eighty-fifth," he repeated. "About four-fifteen, four-thirty tomorrow morning?"

"Yeah. Around there."

"Fine. I'll be wearing a black Homburg and a double-breasted black overcoat."

"Yeah. All right."

"See you then."

Delaney hung up, satisfied. Lipsky sounded like a grifter, and penny ante at that. He jotted a note to have Thorsen check Department records to see if there was a sheet on Charles Lipsky. Delaney would almost bet there was.

He went immediately to bed, setting his alarm for 3:30 a.m. Thankfully, he fell asleep within half an hour, even as he was rehearsing in his mind how to handle Lipsky and what questions to ask.

The luncheonette had all the charm and ambience of a subway station. The walls and counter were white linoleum tiles, dulled with grease. Counter and table tops were plastic, scarred with cigarette burns. Chairs and counter stools were molded plastic, unpadded to reduce the possibility of vandalism. Rancid grease hung in the air like a wet sheet, and signs taped to the walls would have delighted a linguist: "Turky and all the tremens: $2.25." "Fryed Shrims—$1.85 with French pots and cold slaw." "Our eggs are strickly fresh."

Down at the end of the counter, two hookers, one white, one black, both in orange wigs, were working on plates of steak and eggs, conversing in low voices as fast as they were eating. Closer to the door, three cabbies were drinking coffee, trading wisecracks with the counterman and the black short order cook who was scraping thick rolls of grease off the wide griddle.

Delaney was early, a few minutes after four. When he entered, talk ceased, heads swivelled to inspect him. Apparently he didn't look like a holdup man; when he orderd black coffee

395

and two sugared doughnuts, the other customers went back to their food and talk.

The Captain carried his coffee and doughnuts to a rear table for two. He sat where he could watch the door and the plate glass window. He didn't remove his hat but he unbuttoned his overcoat. He sat patiently, sipping the bitter coffee that had a film of oil glinting on the surface. He ate half a doughnut, then gave up.

His man came in about ten minutes later. Short, almost stunted, but heavy through the waist and hips, like an old jockey gone to seed. His eyes drifted, seemed to float around the room. The other customers glanced at him, but didn't stop eating or talking. The newcomer ordered a cup of light coffee, a piece of apple pie, and brought them over to Delaney's table.

"Miller?"

Delaney nodded. "Mr. Lipsky?"

"Yeah."

The doorman sat down opposite the Captain. He was still wearing his doorman's overcoat and uniform but, incongruously, he was wearing a beaked cap, a horseman's cap, in an horrendous plaid. He looked at Delaney briefly, but then his yellowish eyes floated off, to his food, the floor, the walls, the ceiling.

A grifter. Delaney was sure of it now. And seedy. Always with the shorts. On the take. A sheet that might include gambling arrests, maybe soome boosting, receiving stolen property, bad debts, perhaps even an attempted shakedown. Cheap, dirty stuff.

"I ain't got much time," Lipsky said in his low, whiny voice. "I start on days again at noon." He shoveled pie into his surprisingly prim little mouth. "So I got to get home and catch a few hours of shuteye. Then back on the door again at twelve."

"Rough," Delaney said sympathetically. "Did your brother-in-law tell you what this is all about?"

"Yeah," Lipsky nodded, gulping his hot coffee. "This Blank is after some young cunt and her father wants to break it up. Right?"

"That's about it. What can you tell me about Blank?"

Lipsky scraped pie crust crumbs together on his plate with his fingers, picked them up, tossed them down his throat like a man downing a shot of liquor neat.

"Thought you was on an expense account."

Delaney glanced at the other customers. No one was observing them. He took his wallet from his hip pocket, held it on the far side of the table where only Lipsky could see it. He opened it wide, watched Lipsky's hungry eyes slide over and estimate the total. The Captain took out a ten, proffered it under the table edge. It was gone.

"Can't you do better than that?" Lipsky whined. "I'm taking an awful chance."

"Depends," Delaney said. "How long has Blank been living there?"

"I don't know exactly. I been working there four years, and he was living there when I started."

"He was married then?"

"Yeah. A big *zoftig* blonde. A real piece of push. Then he got divorced."

"Know where his ex-wife is living?"

"No."

"Does he have any woman now? Anyone regular who visits him?"

"Yeah. What does this young cunt look like? The one her father doesn't want her to see Blank?"

"About eighteen," Delaney said smoothly. "Long blonde hair. About five-four or five. Maybe one-twenty. Blue eyes. Peaches-and-cream complexion. Big jugs."

"Yum-yum," the doorman said, licking his lips. "I ain't seen anyone like that around."

"Anyone else? Any woman?"

"Yeah. A rich bitch. Mink coat down to her feet. About thirty, thirty-five. No tits. Black hair. White face. No makeup. A weirdo."

"Know her name?"

"No. She comes and she goes by cab."

"Sleep over?"

"Sure. Sometimes. What do you think?"

"That's interesting."

"Yeah? How interesting?"

"You're getting there," Delaney said coldly. "Don't get greedy. Anyone else?"

"No women. A boy."

"A boy?"

"Yeah. About eleven, twelve. Around there. Pretty enough to be a girl. I heard Blank call him Tony."

"What's going on there?"

"What the hell do you think?"

"This Tony ever sleep over?"

"I never seen it. One of the other doors tells me yes. Once or twict."

"This Blank got any close friends? In the building, I mean?"

"The Mortons."

"A family?"

"Married couple. No children. You want a lot for your sawbuck, don't you?"

Sighing, Delaney reached for his wallet again. But he looked up, saw a squad car roll to a stop just outside the luncheonette, and he paused. A uniformed cop got out of the car and came inside. The cabbies had gone, but the two hookers were picking their teeth, finishing their coffee. The cop glanced at them, then his eyes slid over to Delaney's table.

He recognized the Captain, and Delaney recognized him. Handrette. A good man. Maybe a little too fast with his stick, but a good, brave cop. And smart enough not to greet a plainclothesman or superior officer out of uniform in public unless spoken to first. His eyes moved away from Delaney. He ordered two hamburgers with everything, two coffees, and two Danish to go. Delaney gave Charles Lipsky another ten.

"Who are the Mortons?" he asked. "Blank's friends."

"Loaded. Top floor penthouse. They own a store on Madison Avenue that sells sex stuff."

"Sex stuff?"

"Yeah," Lipsky said with his wet leer. "You know, candles shaped like pricks. Stuff like that."

Delaney nodded. Probably the Erotica. When he had commanded the 251st, he had made inquiries about the possibility of closing the place down and making it stick. The legal department told him to forget it; it would never hold up in court.

"Blank got any hobbies?" he asked Lipsky casually. "Is he a baseball or football nut? Anything like that?"

"Mountain climbing," Lipsky said. "He likes to climb mountains."

"Climb mountains?" Delaney said, with no change of expression. "He must be crazy."

"Yeah. He's always going away on weekends in the Spring and Fall. He takes all this crap with him in his car."

"Crap? What kind of crap?"

"You know—a knapsack, a sleeping bag, a rope, things you tie on your shoes so you don't slip."

"Oh yes," Delaney said. "Now I know what you mean.

And an ax for chipping away ice and rocks. Does he take an ax with him on these trips?"

"Never seen it. What's this got to do with cutting him loose from the young cunt?"

"Nothing," Delaney shrugged. "Just trying to get a line on him. Listen, to get back to this woman of his. The skinny one with black hair. You know her name?"

"No."

"She come around very often?"

"She'll be there like three nights in a row. Then I won't see her for a week or so. No regular schedule, if that's what you're hoping." He grinned shrewdly at Delany. Two of his front teeth were missing, two were chipped; the Captain wondered what kind of bet he had welshed on.

"Comes and goes by cab?"

"That's right. Or they walk out together."

"The next time you're on duty, if she comes or goes by cab, get the license number of the hack, the date, and the time. That's all I need—the date, the time, the license number of the cab. There's another tenner in it for you."

"And then all you got to do is check the trip sheets. Right?"

"Right," Delaney said, smiling bleakly. "You're way ahead of me."

"I could have been a private eye," Lipsky bragged. "I'd make a hell of a dick. Listen, I got to go now."

"Wait. Wait just a minute," Delaney said, making up his mind that moment. He watched the cop pay for the hamburgers, coffee, Danish and carry the bag out to his partner in the parked squad. He wondered idly if the cop insisted on paying because he, the Captain, was there.

"In your apartment house," Delaney said slowly, "you keep master keys? Or dupes to all the door locks on tenants' doors, locks they put on themselves?"

"Sure we got dupes," Lipsky frowned. "What do you think? I mean, in case of fire or an emergency, we got to get in—right?"

"And where are all these keys kept?"

"Right outside the assistant manager's office we got—" Lipsky stopped suddenly. His lips drew back from his chipped teeth. "If you're thinking what I think you're thinking," he said, "forget it. Not a chance. No way."

"Look, Mr. Lipsky," Delaney said earnestly, sincerely, hunching forward on the table. "It's not like I want to loot the place. I wouldn't take a cigarette butt out of there. All I want to do is look around."

"Yeah? For what?"

"This woman he's been sleeping with. Maybe a photo of them together. Maybe a letter from her to him. Maybe she's keeping some clothes up there in his closet. Anything that'll help my client convince his daughter that Blank has been cheating on her all along."

"But if you don't take anything, how . . ."

"You tell me," Delaney said. "You claim you could have been a private eye. How would you handle it?"

Lipsky stared at him, puzzled. Then his eyes widened. "Camera!" he gasped. "A miniature camera. You take pictures!"

Delaney slapped the table top with his palm. "Mr. Lipsky, you're all right," he chuckled. "You'd make a hell of a detective. I take a miniature camera. I shoot letters, photos, clothes, any evidence at all that Blank has been shacking up with this black-haired twist or even this kid Tony. I put everything back exactly where it was. Believe me, I know how to do it. He'll never know anyone's been in there. He leaves for work around nine and comes back around six. Something like that—correct?"

"Yeah."

"So the apartment's empty all day?"

"Yeah."

"Cleaning woman?"

"Two days a week. But she comes early and she's out by noon."

"So . . . what's the problem? It'll take me an hour. No more, I swear. Would anyone miss the keys?"

"Nah. That board's got a zillion keys."

"So there you are. I come into the lobby. You've already got the keys off the board. You slip them to me. I'm up and down in an hour. Probably less. I pass the keys back to you. You replace them. You're going on duty days starting today—right? So we make it about two or three in the afternoon. Right?"

"How much?" Lipsky said hoarsely.

Got him, Delaney thought.

"Twenty bucks," the Captain said.

"Twenty?" Lipsky cried, horrified. "I wouldn't do it for less than a C. If I'm caught, it's my ass."

Five minutes later they had agreed on fifty dollars, twenty immediately, thirty when Delaney returned the keys, and an extra twenty if Lipsky could get the license number of the cab used by Blank's skinny girl friend.

"If I get it," Lipsky said, "should I call your office?"

"I'm not in very much," Delaney said casually. "In this business you've got to keep moving around. I'll call you every day on the lobby phone. If you go back on nights, leave a message with your brother-in-law. I'll find out from him when to call. Okay?"

"I guess," Lipsky said doubtfully. "Jesus, if I didn't need the dough so bad, I'll tell you to go suck."

"Sharks?" the Captain asked.

"Yeah," Lipsky said wonderingly. "How did you know?"

"A guess," Delaney shrugged. He passed twenty under the table to the doorman. "I'll see you at two-thirty this afternoon. What's the apartment number?"

"Twenty-one H. It's on a tag attached to the keys."

"Good. Don't worry. It'll go like silk."

"Jesus, I hope so."

The Captain looked at him narrowly. "You don't like this guy much, do you?"

Lipsky began to curse, ripe obscenities spluttering from his lips. Delaney listened awhile, serious and unsmiling, then held up a hand to cut off the flow of invective.

"One more thing," he said to Lipsky. "In a few days, or a week from now, you might mention casually to Blank that I was around asking questions about him. You can describe me, but don't tell him my name. You forgot it. Just say I was asking personal questions, but you wouldn't tell me a goddamned thing. Got that?"

"Well . . . sure," Lipsky said, puzzled. "But what for?"

"I don't know," Captain Delaney said. "I'm not sure. Just to give him something to think about, I guess. Will you do it?"

"Yeah. Sure. Why not?"

They left the luncheonette together. There were early workers on the streets now. The air was cold, sharp. The sky was lightening in the east; it promised to be a clear day. Captain Delaney walked home slowly, leaning against the December wind. By the time he unlocked his door he could hardly smell the rancid grease.

The projected break-in had been a spur-of-the-moment thing. He hadn't planned that, hadn't even considered it. But Lipsky had tied Daniel Blank to mountain climbing: the first time that was definitely established. And that led to the ice ax. That damned ax! Nothing so far had tied Blank to the purchase or possession of an ice ax. Delaney wanted things tidy. Possession would be tidy enough; purchase could be traced later.

He wasn't lying when he told Lipsky he'd be in and out of Blank's apartment in an hour. My God, he could find an ice ax in Grand Central Station in that time. And why should Blank hide it? As far as he knew, he wasn't suspected. He owned rucksack, pitons, crampons, ice ax. What could be more natural? He was a mountaineer. All Delaney wanted from that break-in was the ice ax. Anything else would be gravy on the roast.

He wrote up his reports and noted, gratified, how fat the Daniel G. Blank file was growing. More important, how he was beginning to penetrate his man. Tony, a twelve-year-old boy pretty enough to be a girl. A thin, black-haired woman with no tits. Friends who owned a sex boutique. Much, much there. But if the ice ax didn't exist in Blank's apartment, it was all smoke. What would he do then? Start in again—someone else, another angle, a different approach. He was prepared for it.

He worked on his reports until Mary arrived. She fixed him coffee, dry toast, a soft-boiled egg. No grease. After breakfast, he went into the living room, pulled the shades, took off his shoes and jacket, unbuttoned his vest. He lay down on the couch, intending to nap for only an hour. But when he awoke, it was almost 11:30, and he was angry at himself for time wasted.

He went into the downstairs lavatory to rub his face with cold water and comb his hair. In the mirror he saw how he looked, but he had already felt it: blueish bags swelling down beneath his eyes, the greyish, unhealthy complexion, lines deeper, wrinkled forehead, bloodless lips pressed tighter, everything old and troubled. When all this was over, and Barbara was well again, they'd go somewhere, groan in the sun, stuff until their skins were tight, eyes clear, memories washed, blood pure and pumping. And they'd make love. That's what he told himself.

He called Monica Gilbert.

"Monica, I'm going over to visit my wife. I was wondering if —if you're not busy—if you'd like to meet her."

"Oh yes. I would. When?"

"Fifteen minutes or so. Too soon? Would you like lunch first?"

"Thank you, but I've had a salad. That's all I'm eating these days."

"A diet?" he laughed. "You don't need that."

"I do. I've been eating so much since—since Bernie died. Just nerves, I guess. Edward . . ."

"What?"

"You said you'd call me about Daniel Blank, but you didn't. Was it anything?"

"I think so. But I'd like my wife to hear it, too. I trust her judgment. She's very good on people. I'll tell you both at the same time. All right?"

"Of course."

"Be over in fifteen minutes."

Then he called Barbara and told her he was bringing Monica Gilbert to meet her, the widow of the second victim. Barbara said of course. She was happy to talk to him and told him to hurry.

He had thought about it a long time—whether or not to bring the two women together. He recognized the dangers and the advantages. He didn't want Barbara to think, even to suspect, that he was having a relationship—even an innocent relationship—with another women while she, Barbara, was ill, confined to a hospital room, despite what she had said about his marrying again if anything happened to her. That was just talk, he decided firmly: an emotional outburst from a woman disturbed by her own pain and fears of the future. But Barbara would enjoy company—that he knew. She really did like people, much more than he did. He could tell her of a man arrested for molesting women—there was one crazy case: this nut would sneak into bedrooms out in Queens, always coming through unlocked windows, and he would kiss sleeping women and then run away. He never put his hands on them or injured them physically. He just kissed them. When he told Barbara about it, she gave a troubled sigh and said, "Poor fellow. How lonely he must have been."—and her sympathies were frequently with the suspect, unless violence was involved.

Monica Gilbert needed a confidante as well. Her job was finished, her file complete. He wanted to continue giving her a feeling of involvement. So, finally, he had decided to bring them together.

It wasn't a disaster, as he had feared, but it didn't go marvelously well, as he had hoped. Both women were cordial, but nervous, guarded, reserved. Monica had brought Barbara a little African violet, not from a florist's shop but one she had nurtured herself. That helped. Barbara expressed her condolences in low tones on the death of Monica's husband. Delaney stayed out of it, standing away from Barbara's bed, listening and watching anxiously.

Then they began speaking about their children, exchanging photographs and smiling. Their talk became louder than sickroom tones; they laughed more frequently; Barbara touched Monica's arm. Then he knew it was going to be all right. He relaxed, sat in a chair away from them, listening to their chatter, comparing them: Barbara so thin and fine, wasted and elegant, a silver sword of a woman. And Monica with her heavy peasant's body, sturdy and hard, bursting with juice. At that moment he loved them both.

For awhile they leaned close, conversing in whispers. He wondered if they might be talking about women's ailments, women's plumbing—a complete mystery to him—or perhaps, from occasional glances they threw in his direction, he wondered if they might be discussing him, although what there was about him to talk about he couldn't imagine.

It was almost an hour before Barbara held out a hand to him. He came over to her bedside, smiling at both of them.

"Daniel Blank?" Barbara asked.

He told them about the interviews with the bartender, with Handry, with Lipsky. He told them everything except his plan to be inside Blank's apartment within two hours.

"Edward, it's beginning to take form," Barbara nodded approvingly. As usual, she went to the nub. "At least now you know he's a mountain climber. I suppose the next step is to find out if he owns an ice ax?"

Delaney nodded. She would never even consider asking him how he might do this.

"Can't you arrest him now?" Monica Gilbert demanded. "On suspicion or something?"

The Captain shook his head. "Not a chance," he said patiently. "No evidence at all. Not a shred. He'd be out before the cell door was slammed behind him, and the city would be liable for false arrest. That would be the end of that."

"Well, what can you do then? Wait until he kills someone else?"

"Oh . . ." he said vaguely, "there are things. Establish his guilt without a doubt. He's just a suspect now, you know. The only one I've got. But still just a suspect. Then, when I'm sure of him, I'll—well. at this moment I'm not sure what I'll do. Something."

"I'm sure you will," Barbara smiled, taking Monica's hand. "My husband is a very stubborn man. And he's neat. He doesn't like loose ends."

They all laughed. Delaney glanced at his watch, saw he had to leave. He offered to take Monica Gilbert home, but she wanted to stay awhile and said she'd leave when it was time to pick up her girls at school. Delaney glanced at Barbara, realized she wanted Monica's company a while longer. He kissed Barbara's cheek, nodded brightly at both, lumbered from the room. Outside in the hall, adjusting his Homburg squarely atop his head, he heard a sudden burst of laughter from inside the room, quickly suppressed. He wondered if they could be laughing at him, something he had done or said. But he was used to people finding him amusing; it didn't bother him.

He had never, of course, had any intention of taking a camera to Blank's apartment. What would a photograph of an ice ax prove? But he did take a set of locksmith's picks, of fine Swedish steel, fitted into individual pockets in a thin chamois case. Included in the set were long, slender tweezers. The case went into his inside jacket pocket. In the lefthand pocket he clipped a two-battery penlite. Into his overcoat pocket he folded a pair of thin black silk gloves. Barbara called them his "undertaker's gloves."

At 2:30, Captain Delaney walked steadily up the driveway, pushed through the lobby door. Lipsky saw him almost at once. His face was pale, sheeny with sweat. His hand dipped into his lefthand jacket pocket. Brainless idiot, Delaney thought mournfully. The whole idea had been to transfer the keys during a normal handshake. Well, it couldn't be helped now . . .

He advanced, smiling, holding out his right hand. Lipsky grabbed it with a damp palm and only then realized the keys were gripped in his left fist. He dropped Delaney's hand, transferred the keys, almost losing them in the process. Delaney plucked them lightly from Lipsky's nerveless fingers. The Captain slid them into his overcoat pocket, still smiling slightly, and said, "Any trouble, give me three fast rings on the intercom."

Lipsky turned even paler. It was a warning Delaney had deliberately avoided giving the doorman at the luncheonette; it might have queered the whole thing right then.

He sauntered slowly toward the elevator banks, turning left to face the cars marked 15-34. Two other people were waiting: a man flipping through a magazine, a woman with an overflowing Bloomingdale's shopping bag. A door slid open on a self-service elevator; a young couple with a small child came out. Delaney hung back a moment, then followed the other two into the elevator. The man punched 16, the woman pushed 21 —Blank's floor. Delaney pressed 24.

Both men removed their hats. They rode up in silence. The magazine reader got off at 16. The woman with the shopping bag got off at 21. Delaney rode up to ·24 and stepped out. He killed a few minutes pinpointing the direction of apartment H, assuming it was in the same location on every floor.

He came back to the elevators to push the Down button. Thankfully, the elevator that stopped for him a moment later was empty. He pushed 21, suddenly became aware of the soft music. He didn't recognize the tune. The door opened at 21. He pushed the Lobby button, then stepped out quickly before the doors closed.

The 21st Floor corridor was empty. He took off his fleece-lined leather gloves, stuffed them in an overcoat pocket, pulled on his "undertaker's gloves." As he walked the carpeted corridor, he scraped soles and heels heavily, hoping to remove whatever mud or dog shit or dust or dirt that had accumulated, possibly to show up in Blank's apartment. And he noted the peephole in every door.

He rang the bell of apartment 21-H twice, heard it peal quietly inside. He waited a few moments. No answer. He went to work.

He had no trouble with two of the keys, but the third lock, the police bar, took more time. His hands were so large that he could not slip his fingers inside the partly opened door to disengage the diagonal rod. He finally took the tweezers from his pick case and, working slowly and without panic, moved the bar up out of its slot. The door swung open.

He stepped inside, closed the door gently behind him but did not lock it. He moved through the apartment swiftly, opening closet doors, glancing inside, closing them. He peeked behind the shower curtain in the bathroom, went down on his knees to peer under the bed. When he was satisfied the apartment was unoccupied, he returned to the front door, locked it, set the police bar in place.

The next step was silly, but basic. But perhaps not so silly. He remembered the case of a dick two who had spent four hours tossing the wrong apartment. Delaney went looking for subscription magazines, letters . . . anything. He found a shelf of books on computer technology. Each one, on the front end paper, bore an engraved bookplate neatly pasted in place. A nude youth with bow and arrow leaping through a forest glade. "Ex Libris. Daniel G. Blank." Good enough.

He returned to the front door again, put his back against it, then began to stroll, to wander through the apartment. Just to absorb it, to try to understand what kind of a man lived here.

But did anyone live here? Actually breathe, sleep, eat, fart, belch, defecate in these sterile operating rooms? No cigarette butts, no tossed newspapers, no smells, no photos, personal mementoes, vulgar little geegaws, souvenirs, no unwashed glass or chipped paint or old burns or a cracked ceiling. It was all so antiseptic he could hardly believe it; the cold order and cleanliness were overwhelming. Furniture in black leather and chrome. Crystal ashtrays precisely arranged. An iron candelabra with each taper carefully burned down to a different length.

He thought of his own home: his, Barbara's, their family's.

Their home sang their history, who they were, their taste and lack of taste, worn things, used things, roots, smells of living, memories everywhere. You could write a biography of Edward X. Delaney from his home. But who was Daniel G. Blank? This decorator's showroom, this model apartment said nothing. Unless . . .

That heavy beveled mirror in the foyer, handsomely framed. That long wall in the living room bearing at least 50 small mirrors of various shapes, individually framed. A full-length mirror on the bedroom door. Another on the inside of the bathroom door. A double medicine cabinet, both sliding doors mirrored. Did that plethora of mirrors say anything about the man who lived there?

There was another sure tip-off, to anyone's life style: the contents of the refrigerator, kitchen cabinets, the bathroom cabinet. In the refrigerator, a bottle of vodka, three bottles of juice—orange, grapefruit, tomato. Salad fixings. Apples, tangerines, plums, peaches, dried apricots and dried prunes. In the cabinets, coffee, herbal tea, spices, health foods, organic cereals. No meats anywhere. No cheese. No coldcuts. No bread. No potatoes. But sliced celery and carrots.

In the bathroom, behind the sliding cabinet doors, he found the scented soaps, oils, perfumes, colognes, lotions, unguents, powders, deodorants, sprays. One bottle of aspirin. One bottle of pills, almost full, he recognized as Librium. One envelope of pills he could not identify. One bottle of vitamin B-12 pills. Shaving gear. He closed the doors with the tips of his gloved fingers. Was the toilet paper scented? It was. He glanced at his watch. About ten minutes so far.

Once again he returned to the entrance, trying to walk softly in case the tenant in the apartment below might hear footsteps and wonder who was in Mr. Blank's apartment at this hour.

He switched on the overhead light, opened the door of the foyer closet.

On the top shelf: six closed hatboxes and a trooper's winter hat of black fur.

On the rod: two overcoats, three topcoats, two raincoats, a thigh-length coat of military canvas, olive-drab, fleece-lined, with an attached hood, a waist-length jacket, fur-lined, two light-weight nylon jackets.

On the floor: a sleeping bag rolled up and strapped, heavy climbing boots with ridged soles, a set of steel crampons, a rucksack, a webbed belt, a coil of nylon line, and . . .

One ice ax.

There it was. It was that easy. An ice ax. Delaney stared at it, feeling no elation. Perhaps satisfaction. No more than that.

He stared at it for almost a minute, not doubting his eyes but memorizing its exact position. Balanced on the handle butt. The head leaning against two walls in the corner. The leather thong loop from the end of the handle curved to the right, then doubled back upon itself.

The Captain reached in, picked it up in his gloved hand. He examined it closely. "Made in West Germany." Similar to those sold by Outside Life. He sniffed at the head. Oiled steel. The handle darkened with sweat stains. Using one of his lock picks, he gently prized the leather covering away from the steel shaft, just slightly. No stains beneath the leather. But then, he hadn't expected to find any.

He stood gripping the ax, loath to put it down. But it could tell him nothing more; he doubted very much if it could tell the forensic men anything either. He replaced it as carefully as he could, leaning it into the corner at the original angle, arranging the leather thong in its double-backed loop. He closed the closet door, looked at his watch. Fifteen minutes.

The living room floor was a checkerboard pattern, alternating black and white tiles, 18 inches square. Scattered about were six small rugs in bright colors and modern design. Scandinavian, he guessed. He lifted each rug, looked underneath. He didn't expect to find anything; he didn't.

He wasted a few minutes staring at that long mirrored wall,

watching his image jerk along as he moved. He would have liked to search behind each mirror but knew it would take forever, and he'd never get them back in their precise pattern. He turned instead to a desk near the window. It was a slim, elegant spider of chrome and glass. One center drawer, one deep file drawer on the left side.

The top drawer was marvelously organized with a white plastic divider: paper clips (two sizes), sharpened pencils, stamps, built-in Scotch tape dispenser, scissors, ruler, letter opener, magnifying glass—all matching. Delaney was impressed. Not envious, but impressed.

There were three documents. One was a winter catalogue from Outside Life; the Captain smiled, without mirth. One, in a back corner, was obviously half a salary check, the half that listed taxes, pension payment, hospitalization, and similar deductions. Delaney put on his glasses to read it. According to his calculations, Blank was earning about $55,000 a year. That was nice.

The third document was an opened manila envelope addressed to Mr. Daniel G. Blank from something called Medical Examiners Institute. Delaney drew out the stapled report, scanned it quickly. Apparently, six months ago, Blank had undergone a complete physical checkup. He had had the usual minor childhood illnesses, but the only operation noted was a tonsillectomy at the age of nine. His blood pressure was just slightly below normal, and he had a 20 percent impairment of hearing in his left ear. But other than that, he seemed to be in perfect physical condition for a man his age.

Delaney replaced this document and then, recalling something, drew it out again. In his pocket notebook he made a notation of Blank's blood type.

The deep file drawer contained one object: a metal document box. Delaney lifted it out, placed it atop the desk, examined it. Grey steel. Locked, with the lock on top. White plastic handle in front. About 12 inches long, eight inches wide, four inches deep. He could never understand why people bought such boxes for their valuables. It was true the box might be fire-resistant, but no professional thief would waste time forcing or picking the lock; he'd just carry the entire box away by its neat plastic handle, or slip it into a pillowcase with his other loot.

Delaney took a closer look at the lock. Five minutes at the most, but was it worth it? Probably checkbooks, bank books, maybe some cash, his lease, passport, a few documents not valuable enough to put in his safe deposit box. Blank, he was certain, would have a safe deposit box. He was that kind of a man. He replaced the document box in the desk, closed the drawer firmly. If he had time, he'd come back to it. He glanced at his watch; almost 25 minutes.

He moved toward the bedroom. But he paused before an ebony and aluminum liquor cabinet. He could not resist it, and opened the two doors. Matching glassware on one side: Baccarat crystal, and beautiful. What was it Handry had asked? What does Blank do with his money? He could tell Handry now: he buys Baccarat crystal.

The liquor supply was curious: one gin, one Scotch, one rye, one bourbon, one rum, and at least a dozen bottles of brandies and cordials. Curiouser and curiouser. What did a grown man want with an ink-colored liqueur called "Fleur d'Amour"?

There was a technique to a good search; some dicks were better at it than others. It was a special skill. Delaney knew he was good at it, but he knew others who were better. There was an old detective—the Captain thought he was probably retired by now—who could go through a six-room house in an hour and find the cancelled stamp he was looking for, or a single earring, or a glassine envelope of shit. You simply could not hide anything with absolute certainty that it could never be found. Given enough time, enough men, anything could be found, anywhere. Swallow a metal capsule? Stick a microfilm up your ass? Put a microdot in a ground-out tooth and have it capped? Tattoo your skull and let the hair grow over? Forget it. Anything could be found.

But those methods were rare and exotic. Most people with something to hide—documents, money, evidence, drugs—hid it in their own home or apartment. Easy to check its safety. Easy to destroy fast in an emergency. Easy to get to when needed.

But within their homes—as the cops good at tossing well knew—most people had two tendencies: one rational, one emotional. The rational was that, if you lived a reasonably normal life, you had visitors: friends and neighbors dropping in, sometimes unexpectedly. So you did not hide your secret in the foyer, living room, or dining room: areas that were occupied by others at various times, where the hidden object might, by accident, be uncovered or be discovered by a drunken and/or inquisitive guest. So you selected bathroom or bedroom, the two rooms in your home indisputably *yours*.

The emotional reason for choosing bathroom or bedroom was this: they were intimate rooms. You were naked there.

You slept there, bathed, performed your bodily functions. They were your "secret places." Where else would you conceal something secret, of great value to you alone, something you could not share?

Delaney went directly to the bathroom, removed the top of the toilet tank. An old trick but still used occasionally. Nothing in there except, he was amused to note, a plastic daisy and a bar of solid deodorant that kept Daniel Blank's toilet bowl sweet-smelling and clean. Beautiful.

He tapped the wall tiles rapidly, lifted the tufted bathmat from the floor and looked underneath, made a closer inspection of the medicine cabinets, used his penlite to tap the length of the shower curtain rod. All hollow. What was he looking for? He knew but would not admit it to himself. Not at this moment. He was just looking.

Into the bedroom. Under the rug again. A long wiggle under the bed to inspect the spring. A careful hand thrust between spring and mattress. Under the pillows. Then the bed restored to its taut neatness. Nothing in the Venetian blinds. Base of the lamp? Nothing. Two framed French posters on the walls. Nothing on their backs. The paper appeared intact. That left the wall-length closet and the two dressers in pale Danish wood. He looked at his watch. Coming up to forty minutes. He was sweating now; he had not removed hat or overcoat or taken anything from his pockets that he did not immediately replace.

He tried the closet first. Two wide, hinged, louvered doors that could be folded back completely. So he did, and gazed in astonishment. He himself was a tidy man, but compared to Daniel Blank he was a lubber. Delaney liked his personal linen folded softly, neatly stacked with fold forward, newly laundered to the bottom. But this display in Blank's closet, this was—was mechanized!

The top shelf, running the length of both closets, held linen: sheets, pillowcases, beach towels, bath towels, bathmats, hand towels, dish towels, washcloths, napkins, tablecloths, mattress covers, mattress pads, and a stack of heavy things whose function Delaney could only guess at, although they might have been dustcloths for covering furniture during an extended absence.

But what was so amazing was the precision with which these stacks had been arranged. Was it a militaristic cleaning woman or Blank himself who had adjusted these individual stacks, and then aligned all stacks as if with a stretched string? And the colors! No white sheets and pillowcases here, no dull towels and washcloths, but bright, jumping colors, floral designs, abstract patterns: an eye-jarring display. How reconcile this extravagance with the white-and-black sterility of the living room, the architectural furniture?

On the floors of both closets were racks of shoes. In the left-hand closet, summer shoes—whites, sneakers, multi-colors—each pair fitted with trees, encased in clear plastic bags. In the other closet, winter shoes, also with trees but not bagged. Practically all blacks these, mostly slip-ons, moccasin styles, two pair of buckled Guccis, three pairs of boots, one knee-high.

Similarly, hanging from the rod, summer clothing on the left, winter on the right. The summer suits were bagged in clear plastic, jackets on wooden hangers, trousers suspended from their cuffs on clamps. The uncovered winter suits were almost all black or midnight blue. There was a suede sports jacket, a tartan, a modest hound's tooth. Four pairs of slacks: two grey flannel, one tartan, one a bottle-green suede. Two silk dressing gowns, one in a bird print, one with purple orchids.

Delaney did the best he could in a short time, feeling between and under the stacks of linen, shaking the shoes heels downward, pressing between his palms the bottoms of the plastic bags that protected the summer suits. He went into the living room, removed a small metal mirror from its hook on the wall, and by stretching, using the mirror and his penlite, he was able to see behind the stacks of linen on the top shelf. It was, he admitted, a cursory search, but better than nothing. That's what he found—nothing. He returned the mirror to its hook, adjusted it carefully.

That left the two dressers. They were matching pieces, each with three full drawers below and two half-drawers on top. He looked at his watch. About 46 minutes gone now. He had promised Lipsky an hour, no more.

He started on the dresser closest to the bedroom window. The first half-drawer he opened was all jewelry, loose or in small leather cases: tie pins, cufflinks, studs, tie tacks, a few things he couldn't immediately understand—a belt of gold links, for instance, and a gold link wristwatch band, three obviously expensive identification bracelets, two heavy masculine necklaces, seven rings, a hand-hammered golden heart strung on a fine chain. He cautiously pried under everything.

The other half-drawer contained handkerchiefs, and how long had it been since he had seen Irish linen laundered to a silken feel? Nothing underneath.

Top full drawer: hosiery, at least fifty pair, from black silk formal to knee-length Argyle-patterned knits. Nothing there.

Second and third full drawers: shirts. Obviously business shirts in the second: white and light blue in a conservative cut. In the third drawer, sports shirts, wilder hues, patterns, knits, polyesters. Again he thrust his hand carefully between and beneath the neat piles. His silk-covered fingers slid on something smooth. He drew it out.

It was, or had been originally, an 8X10 glossy photo of Daniel Blank taken in the nude. Not recently. He looked younger. His hair was thicker. He was standing with his hands on his hips, laughing at the camera. He had, Delaney realized, a beautiful body. Not handsome, not rugged, not especially muscular. But beautiful: wide shoulders, slender waist, good arms. It was impossible to judge his legs since the photograph had been cut across just above the pubic hair, by scissors, razor, or knife. Blank stood smiling at Delaney, hands on hips, prick and balls excised and missing. The Captain carefully slid the mutilated photo back beneath the knitted sports shirts.

He went to the second dresser now, feeling certain he would find little of significance, but wanting to learn this man. He had already observed enough to keep him pondering for weeks, but there might be more.

One half-drawer of the second dresser contained scarves: mostly foulard ascots, squares, a formal white silk scarf, a few patterned handkerchiefs. The second half-drawer contained a miscellany: two crushable linen beach hats, two pairs of sunglasses, a bottle of suntan lotion in a plastic bag, a tube of "Cover-All" sunscreen cream, and timetables of airline flights to Florida, the West Indies, Britain, Brazil, Switzerland, France, Italy, Sweden—all bound together with a rubber band.

The top full drawer was underwear. Delaney looked at the assortment, oddly moved. It was a feeling he had had before when searching the apartment of a stranger: secret intimacy. He remembered once sitting around in a squad room, just relaxing with two other detectives, gossiping, telling stories about their cases and experiences. One of the dicks was telling about a recent toss he had made of the premises of a hooker who had been beaten to death by one of her customers.

"My God," the cop said, "I handled all her underwear and that frilly stuff, her garter belt and that thing they pin their napkins on and blue baby-doll pajamas she had, and the smell of it all, and I damned near came in my pants."

The others laughed, but they knew what he meant. It wasn't

only that she had been a whore with lacy things that smelled sexy. It was the secret sharing, entering into another's life as a god might enter—unseen, unsuspected, but penetrating into a human being and knowing.

That was something of what Captain Edward X. Delaney felt, staring at Blank's precise stacks of briefs, bikinis, shorts, stretch panties, trimmed garments in colors he could not believe were sold anywhere but in women's lingerie shops. But stolidly he felt beneath each stack after flipping them through, replaced everything meticulously, and went on.

The second full drawer was pajamas: jackets and pants in nylon, cotton, flannel. Sleep coats. Even a bright red nightshirt.

The bottom drawer was bathing suits—more than one man could use in a lifetime: everything from the tiniest of bikinis to long-legged surfing trunks. Three jockstraps, one no larger than an eyepatch. And in with it all, unexpectedly, six pairs of winter gloves: thin, black leather; rough cowhide, fleece-lined; bright yellow suede; grey formal with black stitching along the knuckles; etc. Nothing. Between items or underneath.

Delaney closed the final drawer, drew a deep breath. He looked at his watch again. Five minutes to go. He might stretch it a minute or two, but no more. Then, he was certain, he'd hear three frantic intercom rings from a spooked Charles Lipsky.

He could open that document case in the living room desk. He could take a look at the bottom kitchen cabinets. He could try several things. On impulse, nothing more, he got down on his hands and knees, felt beneath the bottom drawer of one of the dressers. Nothing. He crawled on hands and knees, felt beneath the other. Nothing. But as he felt about, the wood panel pressed slightly upward.

Now that was surprising. In chests of drawers as expensive and elegant as these appeared to be, he would have guessed a solid piece of wood beneath the bottom drawer, and between each pair of drawers another flat layer of wood. They were called "dust covers," he remembered. Good furniture had them. Cheaply made chests had no horizontal partitions between the bottom of one drawer and the open top of the one beneath.

He climbed to his feet, brushed his overcoat, knees, and trouser cuffs free of carpet lint. There was lint; he picked it off carefully, put it into a vest pocket. Then he opened a few dresser drawers at random. It was true; there were no wooden

414

partitions between drawers; they were simply stacked. Well, it would only take a minute . . .

He pulled out the first full drawer of one dresser, reached in and felt the bottom surfaces of the two half-drawers above it. Nothing. He closed the first full drawer, opened the second and ran his fingers over the bottom surface of the first full drawer. Nothing. He continued in this fashion. It only took seconds. Seconds of nothing.

He started on the second dresser. Closed the drawer containing Blank's incredible underwear, opened the drawer containing pajamas, thrust his hand in to feel the undersurface of the drawer above. And stopped. He withdrew his hand a moment, wiped his silk-clad fingertips on his overcoat, reached in again, felt cautiously. Something there.

"Please, God," he said aloud.

Slowly, with infinite caution, he closed the pajama drawer and then drew out the one above it, the underwear drawer. He drew it halfway out of the dresser. Then, fearful there might be wood splinters on the runners, sawdust, stains, anything, he took off his overcoat and laid it out on Daniel Blank's bed, lining side up. Then he carefully removed the underwear drawer completely from the chest, placed it softly on his overcoat. He didn't look at his watch now. Fuck Charles Lipsky.

He removed the stacks of underwear, placing them on the other side of the bed in the exact order in which he removed them. Four stacks across, two stacks back to front. They'd be returned to the drawer in the same order. When the drawer was empty, he slowly turned it upside down and placed it on his opened overcoat. He stared at the taped envelope. He could appreciate Blank's reasoning: if the tape dried out and the envelope dropped, it could only drop into the next drawer down.

He pressed the envelope gently with his fingertips. Things stiffer than paper, and something hard. Leather maybe, wood or metal. The envelope was taped to the wooden bottom of the drawer on all its four sides. He put on his glasses again, bent over it. He used one of his lock picks, probed gently at the corners of the envelope where the strips of tape didn't quite meet.

He wanted to avoid, if possible, removing the four strips of tape completely. He finally determined, to his satisfaction, the top of the envelope. Using a pick, he lifted a tiny corner of the top tape. Then he switched to tweezers. Slowly, slowly, with infinite caution, he peeled the tape away from the wood,

415

making certain he did not pull the tape away from the paper envelope. Tape peeled off the rough wood stickily; he tried to curl it back without tearing it or folding it. He heard, dimly, three sharp rings on the intercom, but he didn't pause. Screw Lipsky. Let him sweat for his fifty bucks.

When the top tape was free of the wood, he switched back to a locksmith's pick, slender as a surgeon's scalpel. He knew the envelope flap would be unsealed, he *knew* it! Well, it wasn't just luck or instinct. Why should Blank want to seal the envelope? He'd want to gloat over his goodies, and add more to them later.

Gently Delaney prized out the envelope flap, lifted it. He leaned forward to smell at the open envelope. A scent of roses. Back to the tweezers again, and he carefully withdrew the contents, laying them out on his overcoat lining in the order in which they had been inserted in the envelope: Frank Lomband's driver's license. Bernard Gilbert's ID card. Detective Kope's shield and identification. And four withered rose petals. From Albert Feinberg's boutonniere. Delaney turned them over and over with his tweezers. Then he left them alone, lying there, walked to the window, put his hands in his pockets, stared out.

It really was a beautiful day. Crisp, clear. Everyone had been predicting a mild winter. He hoped so. He'd had his fill of snow, slush, blizzards, garbage-decked drifts—all the crap. He and Barbara would retire to some warm place, some place quiet. Not Florida. He didn't enjoy the heat that much. But maybe to the Carolinas. Some place like that. He'd go fishing. He had never fished in his life, but he could learn. Barbara would have a decent garden. She'd love that.

God damn it, it wasn't the murders! He had seen the results of murder without end. Murders by gun, by knife, by strangling, by bludgeoning, by drowning, by stomping, by—by anything. You name it; he had seen it. And he had handled homicides where the corpse was robbed: money taken, fingers cut off to get the rings, necklaces wrenched from a dead neck, even shoes taken and, in one case, gold teeth pulled out with pliers.

He turned back to that display on his overcoat. This was the worst. He could not say exactly why, but this was an obscenity so awful he wasn't certain he wanted to live, to be a member of the human race. This was despoiling the dead, not for vengeance, want, or greed, but for— For what? A souvenir? A trophy? A scalp? There was something godless about it, something he could not endure. He didn't know. He just didn't know. Not right now. But he'd think about it.

He cleaned up fast. Everything back into the envelope with tweezers, in the exact order in which they had originally been packed. The envelope flap tucked under with no bend or crease. The top tape pressed down again upon the wood. It held. The drawer turned rightside up. Underwear back in neat stacks in the original order. Drawer slid into the dresser. He inspected the lining of his overcoat. Some wood dust there, from the drawer runners. He went into the bathroom, moistened two sheets of toilet paper at the sink, came back into the bedroom, sponged his overcoat lining clean. Back into the bathroom, used tissues into the toilet. But before he flushed, he used two more squares to wipe the sink dry. Then those went into the toilet also; he flushed all away. He would, he thought sardonically—and not for the first time—have made a hell of a murderer.

He made a quick trip of inspection through the apartment. All clean. He was at the front door, his hand on the knob, when he thought of something else. He went back into the kitchen, opened the lower cabinets. A plastic pail, detergents, roach spray, floor wax, furniture polish. And, what he had hoped to find, a small can of light machine oil.

He tore a square of paper towel from the roll hanging from the kitchen wall. Could this man keep track of pieces of toilet paper or sections of paper towel? Delaney wouldn't be a bit surprised. But he soaked the paper towel in the machine oil, folded it up, put it inside one of his fleece-lined gloves in his overcoat pocket. Machine oil can returned to its original position.

Then back to the outside door, unlocking, a quick peer outside at an empty corridor. He stepped out, locked up, tried the knob three times. Solid. He walked toward the elevators, stripping off his black silk gloves stuffing them away into an inside pocket. He rang the Down button and while he waited, he took three ten-dollar bills from his wallet, folded them tightly about the keys, held them in his right hand.

There were six other people on the elevator. They stood back politely to let him get on. He edged slowly toward the back. Music was playing softly. In the lobby, he let everyone else off first, then walked out, looked about for Lipsky. He finally saw him, outside, helping an old woman into a cab. He waited patiently until Lipsky came back inside. Lipsky saw him, and the Captain thought he might faint. Delaney moved forward smiling, holding out his right hand. He felt Lipsky's wet palm as keys and money were passed.

Delaney nodded, still smiling, and walked outside. He walked down the driveway. He walked home. He was thinking a curious thought: that his transfer to the Patrol Division had been a mistake. He didn't want administrative experience. He didn't want to be Police Commissioner. This was what he did best. And what he liked best.

He called Thorsen from his home. It was no time to be worrying about tapped phones, if that ever had any validity to begin with. But Thorsen did not return his call, not for 15 minutes. Delaney then called his office. The Deputy Inspector was "in conference" and could not be disturbed.

"Disturb him," Delaney said sharply. "This is Captain Edward X. Delaney. It's an emergency."

He waited a few moments, then:

"Jesus Christ, Edward, what's so—"

"I've got to see you. At once."

"Impossible. You don't know what's going on down here. All hell is breaking loose. It's the showdown."

Delaney didn't ask what "showdown." He wasn't interested. "I've got to see you," he repeated.

Thorsen was silent a minute. Then: "Will it wait till six o'clock? There's another meeting with the Commissioner at seven, but I'll be able to see you at six. Can it hold till then?"

Delaney thought. "All right. Six o'clock. Where?"

"Uptown. The seven o'clock meeting's at the Mansion. Better make it my house at six."

"I'll be there."

He pressed the phone prongs just long enough to break the connection, then dialed Dr. Sanford Ferguson.

"Captain Edward X. Delaney here."

"Neglect, neglect, neglect," Ferguson said sorrowfully. "You haven't called me for 'two more things' in weeks. Not sore at me, are you, Edward?"

"No," Delaney laughed, "I'm not sore at you."

"How you coming along?"

"All right. I read your preliminary report on the Feinberg kill, but I didn't see the final PM."

"Completed it today. The usual. Nothing new."

"The preliminary report said that blood found on the sidewalk was not the victim's type."

"That's correct."

"What type was it?"

418

"You're *asking* me? Edward, you're losing your grip. I thought you'd be telling me."

"Just a minute." Delaney took his notebook from his inside coat pocket. "All right, I'll tell you. AB-Rh negative."

There was a swift intake of breath. "Edward, you *are* getting somewhere, aren't you? You're right. AB-Rh negative. A rare type. Who has it?"

"A friend of mine," Delaney said tonelessly. "A close friend."

"Well, when you take him, make it clean, will you?" the Medical Examiner said. "I'm getting bored with crushed skulls. A single pop through the heart would be nice."

"Too good for him," Delaney said savagely.

Silence then. Finally: "Edward, you're not losing your cool, are you?" Ferguson asked, concern in his voice.

"I've never been colder in my life."

"Good."

"One more thing . . ."

"Now I know you're normal."

"I'm mailing you a sample of a light machine oil. It's a different brand from the one I gave you before. Will you try to get a match with oil in the tissue from Feinberg's wounds?"

"I'll try. Sounds like you're close, Edward."

"Yes. Thank you, doctor."

He looked at his watch. Almost two hours to kill before his meeting with Thorsen. He sat down at his study desk, put on his glasses, picked up a pencil, drew a pad toward him. He began to head the page "Report on—" then stopped, thinking carefully. Was it wise to have an account of that illegal break-in, in his handwriting? He pushed pad and pencil away, rose, began to pace around the room, hands jammed in his hip pockets.

If, for some reason he could not yet foresee, it came to a court trial or the taking of sworn depositions, it was Lipsky's word against his. All Lipsky could swear to was that he had passed the keys. He had not seen Delaney in Blank's apartment. He could not honestly swear to that, only that he had given Delaney the keys and *presumed* he was going to search the apartment. But presumptions had no value. Still, the Captain decided, he would not make a written report of the search. Not at this moment, at any rate. He continued his pacing.

The problem, he decided—the *essential problem*—was not how to take Blank. That had to wait for his meeting with

Thorsen at six o'clock. The essential problem was Blank, the man himself, who he was, what he was, what he might do.

That apartment was a puzzle. It displayed a dichotomy (the Captain was familiar with the word) of personality difficult to decipher. There was the incredible orderliness, almost a fanatical tidiness. And the ultramodern furnishings, black and white, steel and leather, no warmth, no softness, no personal "give" to the surroundings.

Then there were the multi-hued linens, luxurious personal belongings, the excess of silk and soft fabrics, feminine underwear, the perfumes, oils, scented creams, the jewelry. That mutilated nude photograph. And, above all, the mirrors. Mirrors everywhere.

He went over to the cabinet, flipped through the Daniel G. Blank file, pulled out the thick report he had written after his interview with Dr. Otto Morgenthau. Delaney stood at his desk, turning pages until he found the section he wanted, where Morgenthau, having discussed causes, spoke about motives, how the mass murderer justified his actions to himself. The Captain had jotted short, elliptic notes:

"Elaborate rationalizations. No guilt. Killings necessary . . .

"1. Impose order on chaos. Cannot stand disorder or the unpredictable. Needs rules of institution: prison, army, etc. Finds peace, because no responsibility in completely ordered world.

"2. Graffiti artist. Make his mark by murder. I exist! Statement to world.

"3. Alienation. Cannot relate to anyone. Cannot feel. Wants to come close to another human being. To love? Through love to all humanity and secret of existence. God? Because (in youth?) emotion, feeling, love have been denied to him. Cannot find (feel) except by killing. Ecstasy."

Delaney reread these notes again, and recalled Dr. Morgenthau's warning that in dealing with multiple killers, there were no precise classifications. Causes overlapped, and so did motives. These were not simple men who killed from greed, lust or vengeance. They were a tangled complex, could not recognize themselves where truth ended and fantasy began. But perhaps in their mad, whirling minds there were no endings and no beginnings. Just a hot swirl, with no more outline than a flame and as fluid as blood.

He put the notes away, no closer to Dan's heart. The thing about Dan was— He stopped suddenly. Dan? He was thinking of him as "Dan" now? Not Blank, or Daniel G. Blank, but Dan. Very well, he would think of him as Dan. "A friend," he had told Dr. Ferguson. "A close friend." He had smelled his soap, handled his underwear, felt his silken robes, heard his voice, seen a photo of him naked. Discovered his secrets.

The trouble with Dan, the trouble with understanding Dan, was the question he had posed to Barbara: Was it possible to solve an irrational problem by rational means? He hadn't the answer to that. Yet. He glanced at his watch, hurriedly emptied his pockets of penlite, black silk gloves, case of lock picks. He wrapped the oil-soaked wad of paper towel in a square of aluminum foil, put it into an envelope addressed to Dr. Sanford Ferguson, and mailed it on his way to the home of Deputy Inspector Thorsen.

It was strange; he could smell cigar smoke on the sidewalk outside Thorsen's brownstone. He walked up the stoop; the smell was stronger. He hoped to hell Karen was visiting or up in her bedroom; she hated cigars.

He rang. And rang. Rang. Finally Thorsen pulled open the door.

"Sorry, Edward. Lots of noise."

Thorsen, he noted, was under pressure. The "Admiral" was hanging on tight, but the fine silver hair was unbrushed, blue eyes dimmed, the whites bloodshot, lines in his face Delaney had never seen before. And a jerkiness to his movements.

The door of the living room was closed. But the Captain heard a loud, angry babble. He saw a pile of overcoats, at least a dozen, thrown over hallway chairs. Civilian and uniform coats, civilian hats and cop caps. One cane. One umbrella. The air was hot and swirling—cigar smoke, and harsh. Thorsen didn't ask for his hat and coat.

"Come in here," he commanded.

He led Delaney down a short hall to a dining room, flicked on a wall switch. There was a Tiffany lampshade over the heavy oak dining table. Thorsen closed the door, but the Captain could still hear the voices, still smell the coarse cigars.

"What is it?" Thorsen demanded.

Delaney looked at him. He could forgive that tone; the man was obviously exhausted. Something was happening, something big.

"Ivar," he said gently—perhaps the second or third time in his life he had used the Deputy Inspector's given name—"I've found him."

Thorsen looked at him, not comprehending.

"Found him?"

Delaney didn't answer. Thorsen, staring at him, suddenly knew.

"Oh Jesus," he groaned. "Now of all times. Right now. Oh God. No doubt at all?"

"No. No doubt. It's absolute."

Thorsen took a deep breath.

"Don't—" he started to say, then stopped, smiled wanly at the Captain. "Congratulations, Edward."

Delaney didn't say anything.

"Don't move from here. Please. I want Johnson and Alinski in on this. I'll be right back."

The Captain waited patiently. Still standing, he ran his fingers over the waxed surface of the dining table. Old, scarred oak. There was something about wood, something you couldn't find in steel, chrome, aluminum, plastic. The wood had lived, he decided; that was the answer. The wood had been seedling, twig, trunk, all pulsing with sap, responding to the seasons, growing. The tree cut down eventually, and sliced, planed, worked, sanded, polished. But the sense of life was still there You could feel it.

Inspector Johnson seemed as distraught as Thorsen; his black face was sweated, and Delaney noted the hands thrust into trouser pockets. You did that to conceal trembling. But Deputy Mayor Herman Alinski was still expressionless, the short, heavy body composed, dark, intelligent eyes moving from man to man.

The four men stood around the dining room table. No one suggested they sit. From outside, Delaney could still hear the loud talk going on, still smell the crude cigar smoke.

"Edward?" Thorsen said in a low voice.

Delaney looked at the other two men. Then he addressed himself directly to Alinski.

"I have found the killer of Frank Lombard, Bernard Gilbert, Detective Kope, and Albert Feinberg," he said, speaking slowly and distinctly. "There is no possibility of error. I know the man who committed the four homicides."

There was silence. Delaney looked from Alinski to Johnson to Thorsen.

"Oh Jesus," Johnson said. "That tears it."

"No possibility of error?" Alinski repeated softly.

"No, sir. None."

"Can we make a collar, Edward?" Thorsen asked. "Now?"

"No use. He'd be out in an hour."

"Run him around the horn?" Johnson said in a cracked voice.

Delaney: "What for? A waste of time. He'd float free eventually."

Thorsen: "Search warrant?"

Delaney: "Not even from a pet judge."

Johnson: "Anything for the DA?"

Delaney: "Not a thing."

Thorsen: "Will he sweat in the slammer?"

Delaney : "No."

Johnson: "Break-in?"

Delaney: "What do you think?"

Thorsen: "You left it?"

Delaney: "What else could I do?"

Thorsen: "But it was there?"

Delaney: "Three hours ago. It may be gone by now."

Johnson: "Witnesses to the break-in?"

Delaney: "Presumption only."

Thorsen: "Then we've got nothing?"

Delaney: "Not right now."

Johnson: "But you can nail him?"

Delaney (astonished): "Of course. Eventually."

Deputy Mayor Herman Alinski had followed this fast exchange without interrupting. Now he held up a hand. They fell silent. He carefully relighted a cold cigar he had brought into the room with him.

"Gentlemen," he said quietly, "I realize I am just a poor pol, one generation removed from the Warsaw ghetto, but I did think I had mastered the English language and the American idiom. But I would be much obliged, gentlemen, if you could inform me just what the fuck you are talking about."

They laughed then. The ice was broken—which was, Delaney realized, exactly what Alinski had intended. The Captain turned to Thorsen.

"Let me tell it my way?"

Thorsen nodded.

"Sir," the Captain said, addressing the Deputy Mayor directly, "I will tell you what I can. Some things I will not tell you. Not to protect myself. I don't give a damn. But I don't think it wise that you and these other men should have guilty knowledge. You understand?"

Alinski, smoking his cigar, nodded. His dark eyes deepened even more; he stared at Delaney with curious interest.

"I know the man who committed these homicides," the Captain continued. "I have seen the evidence. Conclusive, incontrovertible evidence. You'll have to take my word for that. The evidence exists, or did exist three hours ago, in this man's apartment. But the evidence is of such a nature that it doesn't justify a collar—an arrest. Why not? Because it exists in his apartment, his home. How could I swear to what I have seen? Legally, I have seen nothing. And if, by any chance, a sympathetic judge issued a search warrant, what then? Served on the man while he was home, he could stall long enough to destroy the evidence. Somehow. Then what? Arrest him on a charge—any charge? And run the risk of a false arrest suit? What for? Run him around the horn? That's probably some of our cop talk you didn't understand. It means collaring a suspect, keeping him in a precinct house detention cell, trying to sweat him —getting him to talk. He calls his lawyer. We're required to let him do that. His lawyer gets a release. By the time the lawyer shows up with the paper, we've moved him to another precinct house tank. No one knows where. By the time the lawyer finds out, we've moved him again. We waltz him 'around the horn.' It's an old routine, not used much these days, originally used when cops needed to keep an important witness in the slammer, or needed another day or two days or three days to nail the guy good. It wouldn't work here. Sweating him wouldn't work either. Don't ask me how I know—I just know. He won't talk. Why should he? He makes fifty-five thousand a year. He's an important business executive with a big corporation in the city. He's no street ponce with a snoot full of shit. We can't lean on him. He's got no record. He's got a good lawyer. He's got friends. He carries weight. Got it now?"

"Yes . . ." Alinski said slowly, "I've got it now. Thank you, Captain."

"Fifty-five thousand a year?" Inspector Johnson said incredulously. "Jesus H. Christ!"

"One thing," the Deputy Mayor said. "Inspector Johnson asked if you could nail him, and you said yes. How do you propose to do that?"

"I don't know," Delaney admitted. "I haven't thought it through yet. That's not why I came here tonight."

"Why did you come?"

"This crazy's coming up to another kill. I figure it should be in the week between Christmas and New Year's. But it may be sooner. I can't take the chance."

Strangely, no one asked him how he had estimated the killer's schedule. They simply believed him.

"So," Delaney went on, "I came here tonight for three men, plainclothes, on foot, and one unmarked car, with two men, to cover this guy tonight. I either get this cover or I'll have to dump what I have in Broughton's lap, let him own it, and take my lumps. Before, I just had a lead to offer him. Now I've got the guy he's bleeding for."

His demand came so suddenly, so abruptly, that the other three were startled. They looked at each other; the noise and smells from outside, men talking, arguing, smoking in the living room, seemed to invade this quiet place and envelope them all.

"Now," Thorsen said bitterly. "It would have to be tonight."

"You can do it," Delaney said stonily, staring at the Deputy Inspector. "I don't give a fuck where you get them. Bring them in from Staten Island. This guy has got to be covered. Tonight and every night until I can figure our how to take him."

Silence then, in the dining room, the four men standing. Only Delaney looked at Thorsen; the other men's eyes were turned downward, unseeing.

Was it a minute, or five, or ten? The Captain never knew. Finally Deputy Mayor Alinski sighed deeply, raised his head to look at Thorsen and Johnson.

"Would you excuse us?" he asked gently. "I would like to speak to Captain Delaney privately. For just a few moments. Would you wait outside, please?"

Wordlessly, they filed out, Johnson closing the door behind them.

Alinski looked at Delaney and smiled. "Could we sit down?" he asked. "It seems to me we have been standing much too long."

Delaney nodded. They took padded armchairs on opposite sides of the oak table.

"You don't smoke cigars?" Alinski asked.

"No more. Oh, occasionally. But not very often."

"Filthy habit," Alinski nodded. "But all enjoyable habits are filthy. I looked up your record. 'Iron Balls.' Am I right?"

"Yes."

"In my younger days I was called 'Bubble Head'."

Delaney smiled.

"Good record," Alinski said. "How many commendations?"

"I don't know."

"You've lost count. Many. You were in the Army in World War Two. Military Police."

"That's correct."

"Yes. Tell me something, Captain: Do you feel that the military—the Army, Navy, Air Force—should be, at the top, under control of civilian authority—President, Secretary of Defense, and so forth?"

"Of course."

"And do you also believe that the Police Department of the City of New York should also, essentially, be under civilian control? That is, that the Commissioner, the highest ranking police officer, should be appointed by the Mayor, a civilian politician?"

"Yes . . . I guess I believe that," Delaney said slowly. "I don't like civilian interference in Department affairs anymore than any other cop. But I agree the Department should be subject to some civilian control authority, not be a totally autonomous body. Some form of civilian control is the lesser of two evils."

Alinski smiled wryly. "So many decisions in this world come down to that," he nodded. "The lesser of two evils. Thorsen and Johnson tell me you are an apolitical man. That is, you have very little interest in Department politics, in feuds, cliques, personality conflicts. Is that correct?"

"Yes."

"You just want to be left alone to do your job?"

"That's right."

The Deputy Mayor nodded again. "We owe you an explanation," he said. "It won't be a complete explanation because there are some things you have no need to know. Also, time is growing short. We must all be at the Mansion by seven. Well then . . .

"About three years ago it became apparent that there was a serious breach of security in the Mayor's 'Inner Circle.' This is an informal group, about a dozen men—the Mayor's closest personal friends, advisors, various media experts, campaign contributors, labor leaders, and so forth—on whom he depends for advice and ideas. Meetings are held once a month, or more often when needed. Well, someone in that group was leaking. Newspapers were getting rumors they shouldn't get, and some individuals were profiting from plans still in the discussion stage, before the public announcement was made. The problem was dumped in my lap; one of my responsibilities is internal security. It wasn't hard to discover who was leaking—his name's of no importance to you."

"How did you do it?" Delaney asked. "I'm just interested in the technique you used."

"The most obvious," Alinski shrugged. "Various fictitious documents planted with every man in the Inner Circle. Only one was leaked. It was that easy. But before we kicked this bastard downstairs to a job inspecting monuments or potholes— you don't fire a man like that; the public scandal helps no one —I put him under twenty-four hour surveillance and discovered something interesting. Once a week he was having dinner with five men, always the same five men. They were meeting at one of their homes or in a hotel room or renting a private dining room in a restaurant. It was a curious group. Chairman of the Board of a downtown bank, real estate speculator, editor of a news magazine, a corporation VP, our squealer, and Deputy Commissioner Broughton. I didn't like the smell of it. What did those men have in common? They didn't even all belong to the same political party. So I kept an eye on them. A few months later, the six had grown to twelve, then to twenty. And they were entertaining occasional guests from Albany, and once a man from the Attorney-General's office in Washington. By this time there were almost thirty members, dining together every week."

"Including the man you infiltrated," Delaney said.

Alinski smiled distantly but didn't answer. "It took me a while to catch on," he continued. "As far as I could determine, they had no name, no address, no letterhead, no formal organization, no officers. Just an informal group who met for dinner. That's what I called them in my verbal reports to the Mayor—the 'Group.' I kept watching. It was fascinating to see how they grew. They split into three divisions; three separate dinners every week: one of the money men; one of editors, writers, publishers, TV producers; one of cops—local, state, a few federal. Then they began recruiting. Nothing obvious, but a solid cadre. Still no name, no address, no program —nothing. But odd things began happening: certain editorials, hefty campaign contributions to minor league pols, pressure for or against certain bills, some obviously planned and extremely well organized demonstrations, heavy clout that got a certain man off on probation on a tax evasion rap that should have netted him five years. The Group was growing, fast. And the members were Democrats, Republicans, Liberals, Conservatives—you name it, they had them. Still no public an-

nouncements, no formal program, no statement of principles—
nothing like that. But it came increasingly clear what they
were after: an authoritarian city government, 'law and order,'
let the cops use their sticks, guns for everyone. Except the
blacks. More muscle in government. Tell people, don't ask
them. Because people really want to be told, don't they? All
they need or want is a cold six-pack and a fourth rerun of 'I
Love Lucy'."

Alinski glanced at his watch. "I've got to cut this short," he
said. "Time's running out. But I get carried away. Half my
family got made into soap at Treblinka. Anyway, Deputy
Commissioner Broughton began to throw his weight around.
The man is good; I don't deny it. Shrewd, strong, active. And
loud. Above all, loud. So when Frank Lombard was killed, the
Group's agit-prop division went to work. It was a natural.
After all, Frank Lombard was a member of the Group."

Delaney looked at him, astounded. "You mean these four
victims had something in common after all—a political angle?
Were the other three members of the Group, too?"

"No, no," Alinski shook his head. "Don't get me wrong. Detective Kope couldn't have been a member because the Group
doesn't recruit cops under the rank of lieutenant. And Bernard Gilbert and Albert Feinberg couldn't have been members
because there are no Jews in the Group. No, Lombard's death
was just a coincidence, a chance killing, and I'd guess the man
you've found has never even heard of the Group. Not many
people have. But Lombard's murder was a marvelous opportunity for the Group. First of all, he was a very vocal advocate of
'law and order.' 'Let us crush completely crime on our city
streets.' Broughton saw his opportunity. He got command of
Operation Lombard. With the political pressures the Group organized, he got everything he wanted—men, equipment, unlimited funds. You've met Broughton?"

"Yes."

"Don't underestimate him. He has the confidence of the
devil. He thought he'd wrap up the Lombard murder in record time. Score one for his side, and an important step toward
becoming the next Commissioner. But in case he didn't find
Lombard's killer, the Group would be left with their thumbs
up their assholes. So I asked Thorsen and Johnson who were
the best detectives in New York. They named you and Chief
Pauley. Broughton took Pauley. Thorsen and Johnson asked
for you, and we went along with them."

"Who is 'we'?"

"Our Group," Alinski smiled. "Or call it our 'Anti-Group.' Anyway, here is the situation of this moment. At the meeting tonight, we think we can get Broughton dumped from Operation Lombard. No guarantee, but we think we can do it. But not if you go to him now and give him the killer."

"Fuck Broughton," Delaney said roughly. "I couldn't care less about his ambitions, political or otherwise. I won't go to him if you'll just give me my three plainclothesmen on foot and two in an unmarked car."

"But you see," Alinski explained patiently, "we cannot possibly do that. How could we? From where? You don't realize how big the Group has grown, how powerful. They are everywhere, in every precinct, in every special unit in the Department. Not the men; the officers. How can we risk alerting Broughton that we have the killer and want to put a watch on him? You know exactly what would happen. He would come galloping with sirens screaming, flashing lights, a hundred men and, when all the TV cameras were in place, he'd pull your man out of his apartment in chains."

"And lose him in the courts," Delaney said bitterly. "I'm telling you, at this moment you couldn't even indict this man, let alone convict him."

The Deputy Mayor looked at his watch again and grimaced. "We're going to be late," he said. He strode to the door, yanked it open. Thorsen and Johnson were waiting outside, in hats and overcoats. Alinski waved them into the dining room, then closed the door behind them. He turned to Delaney. "Captain," he said. "Twenty-four hours. Will you give us that? Just twenty-four hours. After that, if Broughton still heads Operation Lombard, you better go to him and tell him what you have. He'll crucify you, but he'll have the killer—and the headlines—whether or not the man is ever convicted."

"You won't give the guards?" Delaney asked.

"No. I can't stop you from going to Broughton right now, if that's what you want to do. But I will not cooperate in his triumph by furnishing the men you want."

"All right," the Captain said mildly. He pushed by Alinski, Thorsen, Johnson, and pulled open the door. "You can have your twenty-four hours."

He made his way through the hallway, crowded now with men pulling on hats and coats. He looked at no one, spoke to no one, although one man called his name.

Back in the dining room, Alinski looked at the two officers in astonishment. "He agreed so easily," he said, puzzled. "Maybe he was exaggerating. Perhaps there is no danger tonight. He certainly didn't fight very hard for the guards he wanted."

Thorsen looked at him, then looked out into the hallway where the others were waiting.

"You don't know Edward," he said, almost sadly.

"That's right," Inspector Johnson agreed softly. "He's going to freeze his ass off tonight."

He wasn't furious, wasn't even angry. They had their priorities, and he had his. They had the "Group" and "Anti-Group." He had Daniel G. Blank. It was interesting, listening to the Deputy Mayor, and he supposed their concern was important. But he had been in the Department a long time, had witnessed many similar battles between the "Ins" and the "Outs," and it was difficult for him to become personally involved in this political clash. Somehow the Department always survived. At the moment, his only interest was Dan, his close friend Dan.

He walked home rapidly, called Barbara immediately. But it was Dr. Louis Bernardi who answered the phone.

"What's wrong?" Delaney demanded. "Is Barbara all right?"

"Fine, fine, Captain," the doctor soothed. "We're just conducting a little examination."

"So you think the new drug is helping?"

"Coming along," Bernardi said blithely. "A little fretful, perhaps, but that's understandable. It doesn't worry me."

Oh you bastard, Delaney thought again. Nothing worries *you*. Why the hell should it?

"I think we'll give her a little something to help her sleep tonight," Bernardi went on in his greasy voice. "Just a little something. I think perhaps you might skip your visit tonight, Captain. A nice, long sleep will do our Barbara more good."

"Our Barbara." Delaney could have throttled him, and cheerfully.

"All right," he said shortly. "I'll see her tomorrow."

He looked at his watch: almost seven-thirty. He didn't have much time; it was dark outside; the street lights were on, had been since six. He went up to the bedroom, stripped down to his skin. He knew, from painful experience, what to wear on an all-night vigil in the winter.

Thermal underwear, a two-piece set. A pair of light cotton socks with heavy wool socks over them. An old winter uniform, pants shiny, jacket frayed at the cuffs and along the seams. But there was still no civilian suit as warm as that good, heavy blanket wool. And the choker collar would protect his chest and throat. Then his comfortable "cop shoes" with a pair of rubbers over them, even though the streets were dry and no rain or snow predicted.

He unlocked his equipment drawer in the bedroom taboret. He owned three guns: his .38 service revolver, a .32 "belly gun" with a two-inch barrel, and a .45 automatic pistol which he had stolen from the U.S. Army in 1946. He selected the small .32, slid it from its flannel bag and, flicking the cylinder to the side, loaded it slowly and carefully from a box of ammunition. He didn't bother with an extra gun belt. The gun was carried on his pants belt in a black leather holster. He adjusted it under his uniform jacket so the gun hung down over his right groin, aimed toward his testicles: a happy thought. He checked the safety again.

His identification into his inside breast pocket. A leather-covered sap slid into a special narrow pocket alongside his right leg. Handcuffs into his righthand pants pocket and, at the last minute, he added a steel-linked "come-along"—a short length of chain, just long enough to encircle a wrist, with heavy grips at both ends.

Downstairs, he prepared a thick sandwich of bologna and sliced onion, wrapped it in waxed paper, put it into his civilian overcoat pocket. He filled a pint flask with brandy; that went into the inside overcoat breast pocket. He found his fleece-lined earmuffs and fur-lined leather gloves; they went into outside overcoat pockets.

Just before he left the house, he dialed Daniel Blank. He knew the number by heart now. The phone rang three times, then that familiar voice said, "Hello?" Delancy hung up softly. At least his friend was home, the Captain wouldn't be watching an empty hole.

He put on his stiff Homburg, left the hall light burning, double-locked the front door, went out into the night. He moved stiffly, hot and sweating under his layers of clothing. But he knew that wouldn't last long.

He walked over to Daniel Blank's apartment house, pausing once to transfer the come-along to his lefthand pants pocket so it wouldn't clink against the handcuffs. The weighted blackjack knocked against his leg as he walked, but he was familiar with that feeling; there was nothing to be done about it.

It was an overcast night, not so much cold as damp and raw. He pulled on his gloves and knew it wouldn't be long before he clamped on the earmuffs. It was going to be a long night.

Plenty of people still on the streets; laden Christmas shoppers hurrying home. The lobby lights of Dan's apartment house were blazing. Two doormen on duty now, one of them Lipsky. They were hustling tips. Why not—it was Christmas, wasn't it? Cabs were arriving and departing, private cars were heading into the underground garage, tenants on foot were staggering up with shopping bags and huge parcels.

Delaney took up his station across the street, strolling up and down the length of the block. The lobby was easily observable during most of his to-and-from pacing, or could be glimpsed over his shoulder. When it was behind him, he turned his head frequently enough to keep track of arrivals and departures. After every five trips, up and down, he crossed the street and walked along the other side once, directly in front of the apartment house, then crossed back again and continued his back-and-forth vigil. He walked at a steady pace, not fast, not slow, stamping each foot slightly with every step, swinging his arms more than he would ordinarily.

He could perform this job automatically, and he welcomed the chance it gave him to consider once again his conversation with Thorsen, Johnson, Deputy Mayor Alinski.

What disturbed him was that he was not positive he had been entirely accurate in his comments regarding the admissibility of evidence and the possibility of obtaining a search warrant. Ten years ago he would have been absolutely certain. But recent court decisions, particularly those of the Supreme Court, had so confused him—and all cops—that he no longer comprehended the laws of evidence and the rights of suspects.

Even such a Philadelphia lawyer as Lt. Marty Dorfman had admitted his confusion. "Captain," he had said, "they've demolished the old guidelines without substituting a new, definite code. Even the DA's men are walking on eggs. As I see it, until all this gets straightened out and enough precedents established, each case will be judged on its own merits, and we'll have to take our chances. It's the old story: 'The cop proposes, the judge disposes.' Only now even the judges aren't sure. That's why the percentage of appeals is way, way up."

Well, start from the beginning . . . His search of Dan's apartment had been illegal. Nothing he saw or learned from that search could be used in court. No doubt about that. If he had taken away Dan's "trophies," it would have served no purpose other than to alert Blank that his apartment had been tossed, that he was under suspicion.

Now what about a search warrant? On what grounds? That Dan owned an ice ax of a type possibly used to kill four men?

And, of course, of a type owned by hundreds of people all over the world. That blood of Dan's type had been found at the scene of the most recent homicide? How many people had that blood type? That he possessed a can of light machine oil that a thousand other New Yorkers owned? And all of these facts established only by an illegal break-in. Or tell the judge that Daniel G. Blank was a known mountaineer and was suspected of carrying two dummy Christmas packages the night Albert Feinberg was slain? Delaney could imagine the judge's reaction to a request for a search warrant on those grounds.

No, he *had* been correct. As of this moment, Dan was untouchable. Then why hadn't he taken the whole mess to Broughton and dumped it on him? Because Alinski had been exactly right, knowing his man. Broughton would have said, "Fuck the law," would have come on like Gang Busters, would have collared Blank, got the headlines and TV exposure he wanted.

Later, when Blank was set free, as he was certain to be, Broughton would denounce "permissive justice," "slack criminal laws," "handcuffing the cops, not the crooks." The fact that Blank walked away a free man would have little importance to Broughton compared to the publicity of the suspect's release, the public outcry, the furtherance of exactly what the Group wanted.

But if Dan couldn't legally—

Delaney ceased pondering, his head crooked over his shoulder. There was a man standing in the lighted lobby, talking to one of the doormen. The man was tall, slender, wearing a black topcoat, no hat. Delaney stopped midstride, took a sham look at a nonexistent wristwatch, made a gesture of impatience, turned in his tracks, walked toward the lobby. He should apply for an Actors Equity card, he thought; he really should.

He came abreast of the lobby, across the street, just as Daniel Blank exited from the glass doors and stood a moment. It was undeniably him: wide shoulders, slim hips, handsome with vaguely Oriental features. His left hand was thrust into his topcoat pocket. Delaney glanced long enough to watch him sniff the night air, button up his coat with his right hand, turn up the collar. Then Blank walked down the driveway, turned west in the direction Delaney was moving across the street.

Ah there, the Captain thought. Out for a stroll, Danny boy?

"Danny Boy." The phrase amused him; he began to hum the tune. He matched Blank's speed, and when Dan crossed Second Avenue, Delaney crossed on his side, keeping just a little behind his target. He was good at tailing, but not nearly as good as, say, Lt. Jeri Fernandez, known to his squad as the "Invisible Man."

The problem was mainly one of physical appearance. Delaney was obvious. He was tall, big, stooped, lumbering, with a shapeless black overcoat, a stiff Homburg set squarely atop his heavy head. He could change his costume but not the man he was.

Fernandez was average and middle. Average height, middle weight, no distinguishing features. On a tail, he wore clothes a zillion other men wore. More than that, he had mastered the rhythm of the streets, a trick Delaney could never catch. Even within a single city, New York, people moved differently on different streets. In the Garment District they trotted and shoved. On Fifth Avenue they walked at a slower tempo, pausing to look in shop windows. On Park Avenue and upper eastside cross streets they sauntered. Wherever he tailed, Fernandez picked up the rhythm of the street, unconsciously, and moved like a wraith. Set him down in Brussels, Cairo, or Tokyo, the Captain was convinced, and Lt. Jeri Fernandez would take one quick look around and become a resident. Delaney wished he could do it.

But he did what he could, performed what tricks he knew. When Blank turned the corner onto Third Avenue, Delaney crossed the street to move up behind him. He increased his speed to tail from in front. The Captain stopped to look in a store window, watched the reflection in the glass as Blank passed him. Delaney took up a following tail again, dropping behind a couple, dogging their heels closely. If Blank looked back, he'd see a group of three.

Dan was walking slowly. Delaney's covering couple turned away. He continued his steady pace, passing his quarry again. He was conscious that Blank was now close behind him, but he felt no particular fear. The avenue was well-lighted; there were people about. Danny Boy might be crazy, but he wasn't stupid. Besides, Delaney was certain, he always approached his victims from the front.

Delaney walked another half-block and stopped. He had lost him. He knew it, without turning to look. Instinct? Something atavistic? Fuck it. He just knew it. He turned back, searched, cursed his own stupidity. He should have known, or at least wondered.

Halfway down the block was a pet shop, still open, front

window brilliantly lighted. Behind the glass were pups—fox terriers, poodles, spaniels—all frolicking on torn newspaper, and gumming each other, pissing, shitting up a storm, pressing noses and paws against the window where at least half a dozen people stood laughing, tapping the glass, saying things like "Kitchy-koo." Daniel Blank was one of them.

He should have guessed, he repeated to himself. Even the dullest dick three learned that a high percentage of killers were animal lovers. They kept dogs, cats, parakeets, pigeons, even goldfish. They treated their pets with tender, loving care, feeding them at great expense, hustling them to the vet at the first sign of illness, talking to them, caressing them. Then they killed a human being, cutting off the victim's nipples or slicing open the abdomen or shoving a beer bottle up the ass. Captain Edward X. Delaney really didn't want to know the explanation of this predilection of animal lovers for homicide. It was difficult enough, after years of experience, to assimilate the facts of these things happening. The facts themselves were hard enough to accept; who had the time or stomach for explanations?

Then Blank moved off, crossed the street, dodging oncoming traffic. Delaney tailed him on his side of the avenue, but when Dan went into a large, two-window liquor store, the Captain crossed and stood staring at the shop's window display. He was not alone; there were two couples inspecting Christmas gift packages, wicker baskets of liqueurs, cases of imported wine. Delaney inspected them, too, or appeared to. His head was tilted downward just enough so that he could observe Daniel Blank inside the store.

Dan's actions were not puzzling. He took a paper from his righthand pocket, unfolded it, handed it to the clerk. The clerk glanced at it and nodded. The clerk took a bottle of Scotch from a shelf, showed it to Blank. The bottle was in a box, gift-wrapped, a red plastic bow on top. Blank inspected it and approved. The clerk replaced the bottle on the shelf. Blank took several sealed cards from his pocket. They looked to Delaney, standing outside, like Christmas cards. The clerk ran off a tape on an electric adding machine, showed it to Blank. Dan took a wallet from his pocket, extracted some bills, paid in cash. The clerk gave him change. The clerk kept the sheet of paper and the envelopes. They smiled at each other. Blank left the store. It wasn't difficult to understand; Dan was sending several bottles of holiday-wrapped Scotch to several people, several addresses. He left his list and identical cards to

435

be enclosed with each gift. He paid for the liquor and the delivery fee. So?

Delaney tailed him away from the store, south three blocks, east two blocks, north four blocks. Dan walked steadily, alertly; the Captain admired the way he moved: balls of feet touching before the heels came down. But he didn't dawdle, apparently wasn't inspecting, searching. Just getting a breath of air. Delaney was back and forth, across, behind, in front, quartering like a good pointer. Nothing.

In less than a half-hour, Dan was back in his apartment house, headed for the bank of elevators, and eventually disappeared. Delaney, across the street, took a swallow of brandy, ate half his bologna and onion sandwich as he paced, watching. He belched suddenly. Understandable. Brandy and bologna and onion?

Was Dan in for the night? Maybe, maybe not. In any event, Delaney would be there until dawn. Blank's stroll had been—well, inconclusive. It made sense, but the Captain had a nagging feeling of having missed something. What? The man had been under his direct observation for—oh, well, say 75 percent of the time he had been out on the street. He had acted like any other completely innocent evening stroller, out to buy some Christmas booze for friends, doormen, acquaintances. So?

It did nag. Something. Delaney re-wrapped his half-sandwich, continued his routine pacing. Now the thing to do was to take it from the start, the beginning, and remember everything his friend had done, every action, every movement.

He had first glimpsed him inside the lobby, talking to a doorman. Blank came outside, looked up at the sky, buttoned his coat, turned up the collar, started walking west. Nothing in all that.

He recalled it all again. The slow walk along Third Avenue, Blank's stop outside the pet shop, the way—

Suddenly there was a car pulling up alongside Delaney at the curb. A dusty, four-door, dark blue Plymouth. Two men in the front seat in civilian clothes. But the near man, not the driver, turned a powerful flashlight on Delaney.

"Police," he said. "Stop where you are, please."

Delaney stopped. He turned slowly to face the car. He raised his arms slightly from his body, turned his palms outward. The man with the flashlight got out of the car, his right hand near his hip. His partner, the driver, dimly seen, was cuddling something in his lap. Delaney admired their competence. They were professionals. But he wondered, not for the first

436

time, why the Department invariably selected three-year-old, dusty, four-door, dark blue Plymouths for their unmarked cars. Every villain on the streets could spot one a block away.

The detective with the flashlight advanced two steps, but still kept a long stride away from Delaney. The light was directly in the Captain's eyes.

"Live in the neighborhood?" the man asked. His voice was dry gin, on the rocks.

"Yes," the Captain nodded.

"Do you have identification?"

"Yes," Delaney said. "I am going to reach up slowly with my left hand, open my overcoat, then my jacket. I am going to withdraw my identification from the inside right breast pocket of my jacket with my left hand and hand it to you. Okay?"

The detective nodded.

Delaney, moving slowly, meticulously, handed over his buzzer and ID card in the leather folder. It was a long reach to the detective. The flashlight turned down to the badge and photo, then up again to Delaney's face. Then it was snapped off.

"Sorry, Captain," the man said, no apology in his voice. He handed the leather back.

"You did just right," Delaney said. "Operation Lombard?"

"Yeah," the detective said, and asked no unnecessary questions. "You'll be around awhile?"

"Until dawn."

"We won't roust you again."

"That's all right," Delaney assured him. "What's your name?"

"You're not going to believe it, Captain, but it's William Shakespeare."

"I believe it," Delaney laughed. "There was a football player named William Shakespeare."

"You remember him?" the dick said with wonder and delight. "He probably had the same trouble I have. You should see the looks I get when I register at a motel with my wife."

"Who's your partner?"

The dick turned his flashlight on the driver. He was black, grinning. "A spook," the man on the sidewalk said. "Loves fried chicken and watermelon. Sam Lauder."

The black driver nodded solemnly. "Don't forget the pork chops and collard greens," he said in a marvelously rich bass voice.

"How long you two been partners?" Delaney asked.

"About a thousand years," the driver called.

"Naw," the sidewalk man said. "A year or two. It just *seems* like a thousand."

They all laughed.

"Shakespeare and Lauder," Delaney repeated. "I'll remember. I owe you one."

"Thanks, Captain," Shakespeare said. He got back in the car; they drove away. Delaney was pleased. Good men.

But to get back to Dan . . . He resumed his pacing, the lobby never out of his glance for more than 30 seconds. It was quiet in there now. One doorman.

After the stop at the pet shop, Dan had crossed to the liquor store, presented his Christmas list, paid for his purchases, then sauntered home. So what was bugging Delaney? He reached into his inner overcoat pocket for a swig of brandy from the flask. Reached into his outer pocket for a bit of sandwich. Reached—

Ah. Ah. Now he had it.

Blank had been talking to a doorman inside the lobby when Delaney first spotted him. Unbuttoned black topcoat, left hand thrust into topcoat pocket. Then Dan had come out under the portico, buttoning up his topcoat, turning up the collar with his right hand. No action from left hand so far—correct?

Then the stroll. Both hands jammed into topcoat pockets. The walk, the tail, the stop at the pet shop—all that was nothing. But now Delaney, from under the brim of his wooden Homburg, is observing Blank inside the liquor store. The right hand dips into the righthand topcoat pocket and comes out with a folded list. The right hand unfolds it on the counter. The right hand holds it out to the clerk. The clerk offers a Christmas-wrapped bottle of Scotch to Blank. Dan takes it in his right hand, inspects it, approves, hands it back to the clerk. Still no action from that left hand. It's dead. Right hand goes back into the topcoat pocket. Out come a half-dozen Christmas cards to be taped to the gifts of liquor. The right hand comes out again with a wallet. The tape is run off. Money paid. The change goes back into the righthand pocket of the topcoat. Left hand, where are you?

Captain Delaney stopped, stood, remembering and suddenly laughing. It was so beautiful. The details always were. What man would carry his Christmas list, Christmas cards and wallet in the outer pocket of his topcoat? Answer: no man. Because Delaney owned a handsome, custom-made, uniform overcoat that had flapped slits just inside the pocket openings so that he

438

could reach inside to equipment on his gun belt without unbuttoning the overcoat. During World War II he had a lined trench coat with the same convenience, and for his birthday in 1953, Barbara had given him an English raincoat with the identical feature; it could be raining cats and dogs, but you didn't have to unbutton your coat, you just reached through those flapped slits for wallet, tickets, identification—whatever.

Sure. That's how Dan had paid for his liquor purchase. He had reached *through* his topcoat pocket for the list in his jacket pocket. *Through* his topcoat pocket to take the wallet off his hip. *Through* his topcoat pocket to find, somewhere, in some jacket or trouser pocket, the addressed and sealed Christmas cards to be taped to the bottles he was sending. Beautiful.

Beautiful not because this was how Daniel G. Blank was sending Christmas gifts, but because this was how Danny Boy was killing men. Slit pockets. Left hand in pocket, through the slit, holding the ice ax handle. Coat unbuttoned. Right hand swinging free. Then, at the moment of meeting, the quick transfer of the ax to the right hand—that innocent, open, swinging right hand—and then the assault. It was slick. Oh God, was it slick.

Delaney continued his patrol. He knew, he *knew*, Blank would not come out again this night. But that was of no consequence. Delaney would parade until dawn. It gave him time to think things out.

Time to consider The Case of the Invisible Left Hand. What was the solution to that? Two possibilities, Delaney thought. One: The left hand was through the slit of the topcoat pocket and was actually holding the ax under the coat by its handle or leather loop. But the Captain didn't think it likely. Dan's coat had been open when Delaney first saw him in the brightly lighted lobby. Would he risk the doorman or another tenant glimpsing the ax beneath his open coat? From then on, the topcoat was buttoned. Why would Dan carry an ice ax beneath a buttoned coat? He obviously wasn't on the prowl for a victim.

Possibility Two: The left hand was injured or incapacitated in some way. Or the wrist, arm, elbow, or shoulder. Danny Boy couldn't use it normally and tucked it away into the topcoat pocket as a kind of sling. Yes, that listened, and it would be easy to check. Thomas Handry could do it in his interview or, better yet, when Delaney called Charles Lipsky tomorrow, he'd ask about any sign of injury to Blank's left arm. The Captain planned to call Lipsky every day to ask if the doorman had been able to get the taxi license number of Dan's dark, skinny girl friend.

All Delaney's interest in a possible injury to Dan's left arm was due, of course, to the evidence of a scuffle, a fight, at the scene of the most recent homicide. Albert Feinberg had made his killer bleed a few drops on the sidewalk. He might have done more.

What time was it? Getting on toward midnight, Delaney guessed. On a long stake-out like this he very deliberately avoided looking at his watch. Start watching the clock, and you were dead; time seemed to go backwards. When the sky lightened, when it was dawn, then he could go home and sleep. Not before.

He varied his patrol, just to keep himself alert. Three up-and-downs across the street, then two up-and-downs on the apartment side. Crossing at different corners. Stopping in the middle of the block to retrace his steps. Anything to keep from walking in a dream. But always watching that lobby entrance. If his friend came out again, he'd come through there.

He finished his sandwich but saved the remainder of the brandy for later. It must be in the low 40's or high 30's by now; he put on his earmuffs. They were cops' style, connected with a strip of elastic that went entirely around his head, and they fitted snugly. No metal band clamping them to his ears. That clamp could get so cold you thought your skull was coming off.

So what was all this business about right hand, left hand, and slit pockets? He knew—no doubt at all—that Daniel Blank was guilty of four homicides. But what he needed was hard evidence, good enough to take to the DA and hope for an indictment. That was the reason for the Handry interview, and the follow-ups he'd have to make on Blank's girl friend, the boy Tony, the Mortons. They were leads that any detective would investigate. They might peter out—probably would—but one of them might, just might, pay off. Then he could nail Danny Boy and bring him to trial. And then?

Then Delaney knew exactly what would happen. Blank's smart, expensive lawyer would cop an insanity plea—"This sick man killed four complete strangers for no reason whatsoever. I ask you, Your Honor, were those the acts of a sane man?"—and Dan would be hidden away in an acorn academy for a period of years.

It would happen, and Delaney couldn't object too strongly; Blank *was* sick, no doubt of that. Hospitalization, in his case, was preferable to imprisonment. But still . . . Well, what was it he, Delaney, wanted? Just to get this nut out of circulation? Oh no. No. More than that.

It wasn't only Dan's motives he couldn't understand; it was his own as well. His thoughts about it were nebulous; he would have to do a lot more pondering. But he knew that never in his life had he felt such an affinity for a criminal. He had a sense that if he could understand Dan, he might better understand himself.

Later in the morning, the sky lightening now, Delaney continued his patrol, swinging his arms, stamping his feet because the brandy had worn off; it was goddamned cold. He got back to the problem of Daniel G. Blank, and to his own problems.

The truth came to him slowly, without shock. Well, it was *his* "truth." It was that he wanted this man dead.

What was in Daniel Blank, what was in him, what he hoped to demolish by putting Dan to death was evil, all evil. Wasn't that it? The idea was so irrational that he could not face, could not consider it.

He looked up to the sky again; it was once again black. It had been a false dawn. He resumed his patrol, flinging his arms sideways to smack his own shoulders, slapping his feet on the pavement, shivering in the darkness.

The phone awoke him. When he looked at the bedside clock it was almost 11:00 a.m. He wondered why Mary hadn't picked it up downstairs, then remembered it was her day off. And he had left a note for her on the kitchen table. He really hadn't been functioning too well when he came off that patrol, but he felt okay now. He must have slept "fast"—as they said in the Army; those four hours had been as good as eight.

"Captain Edward X. Delaney here."

"This is Handry. I got that interview set up with Blank."

"Good. When's it for?"

"The day after Christmas."

"Any trouble?"

"Noo . . . not exactly."

"What happened?"

"I did just what you said, contacted the Javis-Bircham PR man. He was all for it. So I went to see him. You know the type: a big laugh and lots of teeth. I showed him my press pass but he didn't even look at it. He'll never check with the paper. He can't believe anyone could con him. He's too bright —he thinks."

"So what went wrong?"

"Nothing went wrong . . . exactly. He suggested the names of four young, up-and-coming J-B executives—that's the way he kept referring to the corporation, J-B, like IBM, GE and GM—but none of the four names was Blank's."

"Did you tell him you wanted to interview a guy familiar with the uses and future of the computer in business?"

"Of course. But he didn't mention Blank. That's odd—don't you think?"

"Mmm. Maybe. So how did you handle it?"

"Told him I was particularly interested in AMROK II. That's the computer mentioned in that release about Blank I dredged out of the Fink File. Remember?"

"I remember. What did he say to that?"

"Well, then, he mentioned Blank, and agreed when I said I wanted to interview him. But he wasn't happy about it, I could tell."

"It might be personal animosity. You know—office politics. Maybe he hates Blank's guts and doesn't want him to get any personal publicity."

"Maybe," Handry said doubtedly, "but that's not the impression I got."

"What impression did you get?"

"Just a crazy idea."

"Let's have it," Delaney said patiently.

"That maybe Blank's stock is falling. That maybe he hasn't been doing a good job. That maybe the rumor is around that they're going to get rid of him. So naturally the PR man wouldn't want an article in the paper that says what a great genius Blank is, and a week later J-B ties a can to him. Sound crazy?"

Delaney was silent, thinking it over. "No," he said finally, "not so crazy. In fact, it may make a lot of sense. Can you have lunch today?"

"You paying?"

"Sure."

"Then I can have lunch today. Where and when?"

"How about that chophouse where we ate before?"

"Sure. Fine. Great ale."

"About twelve-thirty? In the bar?"

"I'll be there."

The Captain went in to shave. As he scraped his jaw, he thought that Handry's impression might possibly be correct. Blank's little hobby could be affecting his efficiency during office hours; that wasn't hard to understand He had been the corporation's fairhaired boy when that Fink File release was sent out. But now they weren't happy about his being interviewed by the press. Interesting.

Wiping away excess lather and splashing after-shave lotion on his face, Delaney decided he better brief Handry on the upcoming interview during lunch. The interview was scheduled for the day after Christmas. By that time Handry might be reporting the results to Broughton, if he wanted to. But Delaney was determined to do everything he possibly could right up to that 24-hour deadline Alinski had promised which, when the Captain left the house, was now only six hours away.

Handry ordered a broiled veal chop and draft ale. Delaney had a rye highball and steak-and-kidney pie.

"Listen," the Captain said to the reporter "we've got a lot to get through, so let's get started on it right away."

Handry stared at him. "What's up?" he asked.

"What's up?" Delaney repeated, puzzled. "What do you mean, 'What's up'?"

"We've been sitting here five minutes at the most. You've already looked at your watch twice, and you keep fiddling with the silverware. You never did that before."

"You should be a detective," Delaney growled, "and go looking for clues."

"No, thanks. Detectives lie too much, and they always answer a question with a question. Right?"

"When did I ever answer a question with a question?"

Handry shook with laughter, spluttering. Finally, when he calmed down, he said: "On the way over, just before I left the office, I met a guy at the water cooler. He's on the political side. City. He says there was a big meeting at the Mansion last night. Heavy brass. He says the rumor is that Deputy Commissioner Broughton is on the skids. Because of his flop with Operation Lombard. You know anything about that?"

"No."

"Doesn't affect you one way or another?"

"No."

"All right," Handry sighed. "Have it your own way. So, like you said, let's get started."

"Look," Delaney said earnestly, leaning forward across the table on his elbows, "I'm not conning you. Sure, there are some things I'm not telling you, but they're not mine to tell. You've been a great help to me. This interview with Blank is

443

important. I don't want you to think I'm deliberately lying to you."

"All right, all right," Handry said, holding up a hand. "I believe you. Now, what I'd guess you'd like to know most from this Blank interview is whether or not he's a mountain climber, and if he owns an ice ax. Right?"

"Right," the Captain said promptly, not bothering to mention that he had already established these facts. It was necessary that Handry continue to believe his interview was important. "Sure, I want to know what he does at Javis-Bircham, what his job is, how many people work for him, and so on. That has to be the bulk of the interview or he'll get suspicious. But what I *really* want is his personal record, his history, his background, the man himself. Can you get that?"

"Sure."

"You can? All right, let's suppose I'm Blank. You're interviewing me. How do you go about it?"

Handry thought a moment, then: "Could you tell me something about your personal life, Mr. Blank? Where you were born, schools you attended—things like that."

"What for? I thought this interview was about the installation of AMROK II and the possibilities for the computer in business?"

"Oh, it is, it is. But in these executive interviews, Mr. Blank, we always try to include a few personal items. It adds to the readability of the article and to make the man interviewed a real person."

"Good, good," Delaney nodded. "You've got the right idea. Play up to his ego. There are millions of readers out there who want to know about *him*, not just the job he does."

Their food and drinks arrived, and they dug in, but Delaney wouldn't pause.

"Here's what I need about him," he said, and took a deep swallow from his glass. "Where and when he was born, schools, military service, previous jobs, marital status. All right—let's take marital status. I'm Blank again. You ask questions."

"Are you married, Mr. Blank?" Handry asked.

"Is that important to the article?"

"Well, if you'd rather not . . ."

"I'm divorced. I guess it's no secret."

"I see. Any children?"

"No."

"Any plans for marriage in the near future?"

444

"I really don't think that has any place in your article, Mr. Handry."

"No. You're right. I guess not. But we have a lot of women readers, Mr. Blank—more than you'd guess—and things like that interest them."

"You're doing great," Delaney said approvingly. "Actually, he's got a girl friend, but I doubt if he'll mention her. Now let's rehearse the mountain climbing thing. How will you go about that?"

"Do you have any hobbies, Mr. Blank? Stamp collecting, skiing, boating, bird watching—anything like that?"

"Well . . . as a matter of fact, I'm a mountain climber. An amateur one, I assure you."

"Mountain climbing? That *is* interesting. Where do you do that?"

"Oh . . . here, in the States. And in Europe."

"Where in Europe?"

"France, Switzerland, Italy, Austria. I don't travel as much as I'd like to, but I try to include some climbing wherever I go."

"Fascinating sport—but expensive, isn't it, Mr. Blank? I mean, outside the travel. I'm just asking out of personal curiosity, but don't you need a lot of equipment?"

"Oh . . . not so much. Outdoor winter wear, of course. A rucksack. Crampons. Nylon rope."

"And an ice ax?"

"No," Delaney said definitely. "Don't say that. If Blank doesn't mention it, don't you suggest it. If he's guilty, I don't want to alert him. Handry, this stuff could be important, very important, but don't say anything or suggest anything that might make him think your conversation is anything but what it's supposed to be—an interview with a young executive who works with a computer."

"You mean if he suspects it's not what it seems, I may be in danger."

"Oh yes," the Captain nodded, digging into his meat pie. "You may be."

"Thanks a whole hell of a lot," Handry said, trying to keep his voice light. "You're making me feel much better about the whole thing."

"You'll do all right," Delaney assured him. "You take shorthand on these interviews?"

"My own kind. Very short notes. Single words. No one else can read it. I transcribe as soon as I get home or back to the office."

"Good. Just take it easy. From what you've said, I don't think you'll have any trouble with the personal history, the background. Or with the hobby of mountain climbing. But on the ice ax and his romantic affairs, don't push. If he wants to tell you, fine. If not, drop it. I'll get it some other way."

They each had another drink, finished their food. Neither wanted dessert, but Captain Delaney insisted they have espresso and brandy.

"That's a great flavor," Handry said, having taken a sip of his cognac. "You're spoiling me. I'm used to a tuna fish sandwich for lunch."

"Yes," Delaney smiled. "Me, too. Oh, by the way, a couple of other little things."

Handry put down his brandy snifter, looked at him with wonderment, shaking his head. "You're incredible," he said. "Now I understand why you insisted on the cognac. 'A couple of little things?' Like asking Blank if he's the killer, or putting my head in the lion's mouth at the zoo?"

"No, no," Delaney protested. "Really little things. First of all, see if you can spot any injury to his left hand. Or wrist, arm or elbow. It might be bandaged or in a sling."

"I don't get it."

"Just take a look, that's all. See if he uses his left arm normally. Can he grip anything in his left hand? Does he hide it beneath his desk? Just observe—that's all."

"All right," Handry sighed, "I'll observe. What's the other 'little thing'?"

"Try to get a sample of his handwriting."

Handry looked at him in astonishment. "You *are* incredible," he said. "How in Christ's name am I supposed to do that?"

"I have no idea," Delaney confessed. "Maybe you can swipe something he signed. No, that's no good. I don't know. You think about it. You've got a good imagination. Just some words he's written and his signature. That's all I need. If you can manage it."

Handry didn't answer. They finished their brandy and coffee. The Captain paid the check, and they left. Outside on the sidewalk, they turned coat collars up against the winter wind. Delaney put his hand on Handry's arm.

"I want the stuff we talked about," he said in a low voice. "I really do. But what I want most of all are your *impressions* of the man. You're sensitive to people; I know you are. How could you want to be a poet and not be sensitive to

446

people, what they are, what they think, what they feel, who they hate, who they love? That's what I want you to do. Talk to this man. Observe him. Notice all the little things he does—bites his fingernails, picks his nose, strokes his hair, fidgets, crosses his legs back and forth—anything and everything. Watch him. And absorb him. Let him seep into you. Who is he and what is he? Would you like to know him better? Does he frighten you, disgust you, amuse you? That's really what I want —your *feeling* about him. All right?"

"All right," Thomas Handry said.

As soon as he got home, Delaney called Barbara at the hospital. She said she had had a very good night's sleep and was feeling much better. Monica Gilbert was there, they were having a nice visit, she liked Monica very much. The Captain said he was glad, and would come over to see her in the evening, no matter what.

"I send you a kiss," Barbara said, and made a kissing sound on the phone.

"And I send you one," Captain Edward X. Delaney said, and repeated the sound. What he had always considered silly sentimentality now didn't seem silly to him at all, but meaningful and so touching he could hardly endure it.

He called Charles Lipsky. The doorman was low-voiced and cautious.

"Find anything?" he whispered.

For a moment, Delaney didn't know what he was talking about, then realized Lipsky was referring to the previous afternoon's search.

"No," the Captain said. "Nothing. The girl friend been around?"

"Haven't seen her."

"Remember what I said; you get the license number and—"

"I remember," Lipsky said hurriedly. "Twenty. Right?"

"Yes," Delaney said. "One other thing, is anything wrong with Blank's left arm? Is it hurt?"

"He was carrying it in a sling for a couple of days."

"Was he?"

"Yeah. I asked him. He said he slipped on a little rug in his living room. His floors was just waxed. He landed on his elbow. And he hit his face on the edge of a glass table, so it was scratched up."

"Well," the Captain said, "they say most accidents happen in the home."

"Yeah. But the scratches are gone and he ain't wearing the sling no more. That worth anything?"

"Don't get greedy," Delaney said coldly.

"Greedy?" Lipsky said indignantly. "Who's greedy? But one hand washes the other—right?"

"I'll call you tomorrow," the Captain said. "You still on days?"

"Yeah. Until Christmas. Jesus, you know, when you was up there over an hour, and I buzzed you, and you—"

The Captain hung up. A little of Charles Lipsky went a long, long way.

He wrote up reports of his meeting with Thomas Handry and his conversation with the doorman. The only thing he deliberately omitted was his final talk with Handry on the sidewalk outside the restaurant. That exchange would mean nothing to Broughton.

It was past 4:00 p.m. when he finished putting it all down on paper. The reports were added to the Daniel G. Blank file. He wondered if he'd ever see that plump folder again. Alinski and the Anti-Group had about two more hours. Delaney didn't want to think of what would happen if he didn't hear from them. He'd have to deliver Blank's file to Broughton, of course, but *how* he'd deliver it was something he wouldn't consider until the crunch.

He went into the living room, slipped off his shoes, lay down on the couch, intending only to relax, rest his eyes, think of happier times. But the weariness he hadn't yet slept off, the two drinks and brandy at lunch—all caught up with him; he slept lightly and dreamed of the wife of a homicide victim he had interrogated years and years ago. "He was asking for it," she said, and no matter what questions he put to her, that's all she'd say: "He was asking for it, he was asking for it."

When he awoke, the room was dark. He laced on his shoes, walked through to the kitchen before he put on a light. The wall clock showed almost 7:00 p.m. Well, it was time . . . Delaney opened the refrigerator door, looked for a cold can of beer to cleanse his palate and his dreams. He found it, was just peeling back the tab when the phone rang.

He walked back into the study, let the phone ring while he finished opening the beer and taking a deep swallow. Then:

"Captain Edward X. Delaney here."

There was no answer. He could hear the loud conversation of several men, laughter, an occasional shout, the clink of bottles and glasses. It sounded like a drunken party.

"Delaney here," he repeated.

"Edward?" It was Thorsen's voice, slurred with drink, weariness, happiness.

"Yes. I'm here."

"Edward, we did it. Broughton is out. We pooped him."

"Congratulations," Delaney said tonelessly.

"Edward, you've got to return to active duty. Take over Operation Lombard. Whatever you want—men, equipment, money. You name it, you've got it. Right?" Thorsen shouted; Delaney grimaced, held the phone away from his ear. He heard two or three voices shout, "Right!" in reply to Thorsen's question.

"Edward? You still there?"

"I'm still here."

"You understand? You back on active duty. Head of Operation Lombard. Whatever you need. What do you say?"

"Yes," Captain Edward X. Delaney said promptly.

"Yes? You said yes?"

"That's what I said."

"He said yes!" Thorsen screamed. Again Delaney held the phone away, hearing the loud gabble of many voices. This was fraternity house stuff, and it displeased him.

"My God, that's great," the Deputy Inspector said in what Delaney was sure Thorsen thought was a sober and solemn voice.

"But I want complete control," the Captain said stonily. "Over the whole operation. No written reports. Verbal reports to you only. And—"

"Whatever you want, Edward."

"And no press conferences, no press releases, no publicity from anyone but me."

"Anything, Edward, anything. Just wrap it up fast. You understand? Show Broughton up for the stupid *schmuck* he is. He gets canned and three days later you've solved it. Right? Shows up the bastard."

"Canned?" the Captain asked. "Broughton?"

" 'mounts to the same thing," Thorsen giggled. "Filed for retirement. Stupid sonofabitch. Says he's going to run for mayor next year."

"Is he?" Delaney said, still speaking in a dull, toneless voice. "Ivar, are you certain you've got this straight? I'll take it on, but only on the conditions that I have complete control, verbal reports only to you, pick my own men, handle all the publicity personally. Is that understood?"

"Captain Delaney," a quiet voice said, "this is Deputy Mayor Herman Alinski. I apologize, but I have been listening in on an extension. There is a certain celebration going on here."

"I can hear it."

"But I assure you, your conditions will be met. You will have complete control. Whatever you need. And nothing in the press or TV on Operation Lombard will come from anyone but you. Satisfactory?"

"Yes."

"Great!" Deputy Inspector Thorsen burbled. "The Telex will go out immediately. We'll get out a press release right away—just so we can make the late editions—that Broughton has put in for retirement and you're taking over Operation Lombard. Is that all right, Edward? Just a short, one-paragraph release. Okay?"

"Yes. All right."

"Your personal orders have already been cut. The Commissioner will sign them tonight."

"You must have been very sure of me," Delaney said.

"I wasn't," Thorsen laughed, "and Johnson wasn't. But Alinski was."

"Oh?" Delaney said coldly. "Are you there, Alinski?"

"I am here, Captain," the soft voice came back.

"You were sure of me? That I'd take this on?"

"Yes," Alinski said, "I was sure."

"Why?"

"You don't have any choice, do you, Captain?" the Deputy Mayor asked gently.

Delaney hung up, just as gently.

The first thing the Captain did was finish his beer. It helped. Not only the tang of it, the shock of coldness in his throat, but it stimulated the sudden realization of the magnitude of the job he had agreed to, the priorities, big responsibilities and small details, and the fact that "first things first" would be the only guide that might see him through. Right now, the first thing was finishing a cold beer.

"You don't have any choice, do you, Captain?" the Deputy Mayor had asked gently.

What had he meant by that?

He switched on the desk lamp, sat down, put on his glasses, pulled the yellow, legal-lined pad toward him, began to doodle —squares, circles, lines. Rough diagrams, very rough, and random ideas expressed in arrowheads, lightning bolts, spirals.

First things first. First of the first was around-the-clock surveillance of Daniel G. Blank. Three plainclothesmen on foot and two unmarked cars of two men each should do it. Seven men. Working eight-hour shifts. That was 21 men. But a police commander with any experience at all didn't multiply his personnel requirements by three: he multiplied by four, at least. Because men are entitled to days off, vacations, sick leave, family emergencies, etc. So the basic force watching Danny Boy was 28, and Delaney wondered if he had been too optimistic in thinking he could reduce the 500 detectives assigned to Operation Lombard by two-thirds.

That was one division: the outside force shadowing Blank. A second division would be inside, keeping records, monitoring walkie-talkie reports from the Blank guards. That meant a communications set-up. Receivers and transmitters. Somewhere. Not in the 251st Precinct house. Delaney owed Lt. Dorfman that one. He'd get Operation Lombard out of there, establish his command post somewhere else, anywhere. Isolate his men. That would help cut down leaks to the press.

A third division would be research: the suspect's history, background, credit rating, bank accounts, tax returns, military record—anything and everything that had ever been recorded about the man. Plus interviews with friends, relatives, acquaintances, business associates. Cover stories could be concocted so Blank wasn't alerted.

(But what if he was? That blurry idea in the back of Delaney's mind began to take on a definite outline.)

A possible fourth division might investigate the dark, skinny girl friend, the boy Tony, the friends—what was their name? Morton. That was it. They owned the Erotica. All that might take another squad.

It was all very crude, very tentative. Just a sketching-in. But it was a beginning. He doodled on for almost an hour, starting to firm it up, thinking of what men he wanted where, who he owed favors to. Favors. "I owe you one." "That's one you owe me." The lifeblood of the Department. Of politics. Of business. Of the thrusting, scheming, rude world. Wasn't that the rough cement that kept the whole rickety machine from falling apart? You be nice to me and I'll be nice to you. Charles Lipsky: "One hand washes the other—right?"

It was an hour—more than that—since his conversation with Thorsen. The Telex would now be clicked out in every precinct house, detective division, and special unit in the city. Captain Delaney went up to his bedroom, stripped down to

451

his underwear and took a "whore's bath," soaping hands, face and armpits with a washcloth, then drying, powdering, combing his hair carefully.

He put on his Number Ones, his newest uniform, used, so far, only for ceremonies and funerals. He squared his shoulders, pulled the blouse down tautly, made certain his decorations were aligned. He took a new cap from a plastic bag on the closet shelf, wiped the shield bright on his sleeve, set the cap squarely atop his head, the short beak pulled down almost over his eyes. The uniform was a brutal one: choker collar, shielded eyes, wide shoulders, tapered waist. Menace there.

He inspected himself in the downstairs hallway mirror. It was not egotism. If you had never belonged to church, synagogue or mosque, you might think so. But the costume was continuing tradition, symbol, myth—whatever you like. The clothing, decorations, insignia went beyond clothing, decorations, insignia. They were, to those of the faith, belief.

He decided against an overcoat; he wouldn't be going far. He went into the study just long enough to take the photo of Daniel G. Blank from the file and scrawl the man's address, but not his name, on the back. He slipped the photo into his hip pocket. He left his glasses on the desk. If possible, you did not wear eyeglasses when you exercised command, or exhibit any other signs of physical infirmity. It was ridiculous, but it was so.

He locked up, marched next door to the 251st Precinct house. The Telex had obviously come through; Dorfman was standing near the sergeant's desk, his arms folded, waiting. When he saw Delaney, he came forward at once, his long, ugly face relaxing into a grin. He held out a hand eagerly.

"Congratulations, Captain."

"Thank you," Delaney said, shaking his hand. "Lieutenant, I'll have this gang out of your hair as soon as possible. A day or two at the most. Then you'll have your house back."

"Thank you, Captain," Dorfman said gratefully.

"Where are they?" Delaney asked.

"Detectives' squad room."

"How many?"

"Thirty, forty—around there. They got the word, but they don't know what to do."

Delaney nodded. He walked up the old creaking stairway, past the commander's office. The frosted glass door of the detectives' squad room was closed. There was noise from inside,

452

a lot of men talking at once, a buzz of confused sound, angry turbulence. The Captain opened the door, and stood there.

The majority were in plainclothes, a few in uniform. Heads turned to look at him, then more. More. All. The talk died down. He just stood there, looking coldly out from under the beak of his cap. They all stared at him. A few men rose grudgingly to their feet. Then a few more. Then more. He waited unmoving, watching them. He recognized a few, but his aloof expression didn't change. He waited until they were all standing, and silent.

"I am Captain Edward X. Delaney," he said crisply. "I am now in command. Are there any lieutenants here?"

Some of the men looked around uneasily. Finally, from the back, a voice called, "No, Captain, no lieutenants."

"Any detective sergeants?"

A hand went up, a black hand. Delaney walked toward the raised hand, men stepping aside to let him through. He walked to the back of the room until he was facing the black sergeant, a short, heavyset man with sculpted features and what appeared to be a closely-fitted knitted cap of white wool. He was, Delaney knew, called "Pops," and he looked like a professor of Middle English literature. Strangely enough, he had professorial talents.

"Detective sergeant Thomas MacDonald," Captain Delaney said loudly, so everyone could hear him.

"That's right, Captain."

"I remember. We worked together. A warehouse job over on the west side. About ten years ago."

"More like fifteen, Captain."

"Was it? You took one in the hip."

"In the ass, Captain."

There were a few snickers. Delaney knew what MacDonald was trying to do, and fed him his lines.

"In the ass?" he said. "I trust it healed, sergeant?"

The black professor shrugged. "Just one more crease, Captain," he said. The listening men broke up, laughing and relaxing.

Delaney motioned to MacDonald. "Come with me." The sergeant followed him out into the hallway. The Captain closed the door, shutting off most of the laughter and noise. He looked at MacDonald. MacDonald looked at him.

"It really was the hip," Delaney said softly.

"Sure, Captain," the sergeant agreed. "But I figured—"

"I know what you figured," the Captain said, "and you figured right. Can you work till eight tomorrow morning?"

"If I have to."

"You have to," Delaney said. He drew Blank's photo from his pocket, handed it to MacDonald. "This is the man," he said tonelessly. "His address is on the back. You don't have to know his name—now. It's a block-size apartment building. Entrance and exit through a lobby on East Eighty-third. One doorman this time of night. I want three men, plain, covering the lobby. If this man comes out, I want them close to him."

"How close?"

"Close enough."

"So if he farts, they can smell it?"

"Not that close. But don't let this guy out of their sight. Not for a second. If he spots them, all right. But I wouldn't like it."

"I understand, Captain. A crazy?"

"Something like that. Just don't play him for laughs. He's not a nice boy."

The sergeant nodded.

"And two cars. Two men each, in plain. At both ends of the block. In case he takes off. He's got a black Chevy Stingray in the underground garage, or he might take a cab. Got all that?"

"Sure, Captain."

"You know Shakespeare and Lauder?"

"The 'Gold Dust Twins?' I know Lauder."

"I'd like them in one of the cars. If they're not on duty, any good men will do. That makes seven men. You pick six more, three in plain and three in uniform, and have them stand by here until eight tomorrow morning. Everyone else can go home. But everyone back by eight tomorrow, and anyone else you can reach by phone or who calls in. Got it?"

"Where do you want me, Captain?"

"Right here. I've got to go out for an hour or so, but I'll be back. We'll have some coffee together and talk about that extra crease in your ass."

"Sounds like a jolly night."

Delaney looked at him a long time. They had started in the Department the same year, had been in the same Academy class. Now Delaney was a captain, and MacDonald was a sergeant. It wasn't a question of ability. Delaney wouldn't mention what it was, and MacDonald never would either.

"What's Broughton had you on?" he asked the sergeant finally.

"Rousting street freaks," MacDonald said.

"Shit," Delaney said disgustedly.

"My sentiments exactly, Captain," the sergeant said.

"Well, lay it all on," the Captain said. "I'll be back in an hour or so. Your men should be in position by then. The sooner, the better. Show them that photo, but you hang onto it. It's the only one I've got. I'll have copies run off tomorrow."

"Is he it, Captain?" Detective sergeant MacDonald asked. Delaney shrugged. "Who knows?" he said.

He turned, walked away. He was at the staircase when the sergeant called softly: "Captain." He turned around.

"Good to be working with you again, sir," MacDonald said.

Delaney smiled faintly but didn't answer. He walked down the stairway thinking of Broughton's stupidity in using Mac-Donald to pull in street freaks. MacDonald! One of the best professors in the Department. No wonder those forty men had been sour and grumbling. It wasn't that Broughton hadn't kept them busy, but he had misused their individual abilities and talents. No one could take that for long without losing drive, ambition, even interest in what he was doing. And what was he, Delaney? What were his abilities and talents? He waved a hand in answer to the desk sergeant's salute as he walked out. He knew what he was. He was a cop.

He would have commandeered a squad car, but there was none around. So he walked over to Second Avenue, got a cab heading downtown. He walked into the hospital and, for once, the white tiled walls and the smell couldn't depress him. Wait until Barbara heard!

Then he pushed open the door of her room. There was a nurses' aide sitting alongside the bed. Barbara appeared to be sleeping. The aide motioned to him, beckoning him outside into the corridor.

"She's had a bad evening," she whispered. "Earlier it took two of us to hold her down, and we had to give her something. Doctor said it would be all right."

"Why?" the Captain demanded. "What is it? Is it the new drug?"

"You'll have to ask doctor," the aide said primly. Delaney wondered again, in despair, why they always just said "doctor." Never "the doctor." "You have to consult engineer." "You'll have to talk to architect." "You'll have to discuss that with lawyer." It made the same sense, and it all made no sense whatever.

"I'll sit with her awhile," Delaney told the aide. She was so young; he couldn't blame her. Who could he blame?

She nodded brightly. "Tell me when you leave. Unless she's asleep by then."

"She's not asleep now?"

"No. Her eyes are closed, but she's awake. If you need any help, ring the bell or call."

She walked away quickly, leaving him wondering what help he might need. He went softly back into the hospital room, still wearing his uniform cap. He pulled a chair over to Barbara's bedside, sat looking at her. She did seem to be sleeping; her eyes were shut tight, she was breathing deeply and regularly. But, while he watched, her eyelids flicked open, she stared at the ceiling.

"Barbara?" he called gently. "Darling?"

Her eyes moved, but her head didn't turn. Her eyes moved to look at him, into him, through him, not seeing him.

"Barbara, it's Edward. I'm here. I have so much to tell you, dear. So much has happened."

"Honey Bunch?" she said.

"It's Edward, dear. I have a lot to tell you. A lot has happened."

"Honey Bunch?" she said.

He found the books in the metal taboret alongside her bed. He took the top one, not even glancing at the title, and opened it at random. Not having his glasses, he had to hold the book almost at arm's length. But the type was large, there was good white space between the lines.

Sitting upright in his Number One uniform, gleaming cap squarely atop his head, the commander of Operation Lombard began reading:

"Honey Bunch picked her nasturtiums that morning and she gave away her first bouquet. That is always a lovely garden experience—to give away your first bouquet. Of course Honey Bunch gave hers to Mrs. Lancaster and the little old lady said that she would take the flowers home and put them in water and make them last as long as possible.

" 'Haven't you any garden at all?' asked Honey Bunch. 'Just a little one?'

" 'No garden at all,' replied the old lady sadly. 'This is the first year I can remember that I haven't had a piece of ground to do with as . . .' "

He slept when he could, but it wasn't much: perhaps four or five hours a night. But, to his surprise and pleasure, it didn't slow him down. Within three days he had it all organized. It was functioning.

He took Lt. Jeri Fernandez out of the Garment Center division he hated, put him in command of the squad shadowing Daniel Blank. Delaney let him select his own spooks; the "Invisible Man" almost wept with gratitude. It was exactly the kind of job he loved, that he did best. It was his idea to borrow a Consolidated Edison van and tear up a section of East 83rd Street near the driveway leading to Blank's apartment house. Fernandez' men wore Con Ed uniforms and hard hats, and worked slowly on the hole they dug in the pavement. It played hell with traffic, but the van was filled with communication gear and weapons, and served as Fernandez' command post. Delaney was delighted. Fuck the traffic jams.

For "Mr. Inside," the Captain requisitioned Detective first grade Ronald Blankenship, the man who had handled the two original beefs on Daniel Blank. Working together closely, Delaney and Blankenship transferred the command post of Operation Lombard from the 251st Precinct house to the living room of Delaney's home, next door. It wasn't as spacious as they would have liked, but it had its advantages; the communications men could run wires out the window, up to Delaney's roof, then across to tie in with the antennae on the precinct house roof.

Detective sergeant Thomas MacDonald, "Pops," was Delaney's choice to head up the research squad, and MacDonald was happy. He got as much pleasure from an afternoon of sifting through dusty documents as another man might get in an Eighth Avenue massage parlor. Within 24 hours his men had compiled a growing dossier on Daniel G. Blank, taking him apart, piece by piece.

Captain Delaney appreciated the unpaid labors of his amateurs, but he couldn't deny the advantages and privileges of being on active duty, in official command, with all the resources of the Department behind him, and a promise of unlimited men, equipment, funds.

Item: A tap was put on the home telephone of Daniel Blank. It was installed in the central telephone office servicing his number.

Item: The next day's call to Charles Lipsky had resulted in the time of departure and license number of a cab picking up Blank's dark-haired girl friend at his apartment house. Delaney told Blankenship what he wanted. Within three hours the license number had been traced, the fleet identified, and a dick was waiting in the garage for the driver to return. His trip sheet was checked, and the Captain had the address where the cab had dropped her off. One of Fernandez' boys went over to check it; it turned out to be a townhouse on East End Avenue. After consultation with the lieutenant, Delaney decided to establish surveillance: one plainclothesman around-the-clock. Fernandez suggested detailing a two-man team to comb the neighborhood, to learn what they could about that house.

"It's an expensive section," Delaney said thoughtfully. "Lots of VIP's around there. Tell them to walk softly."

"Sure, Captain."

"And lots of servants. You got a good-looking black who could cuddle up to some of the maids and cooks on the street?"

"Just the man!" Fernandez said triumphantly. "A big, handsome stud. He don' walk, he glides. And smart as a whip. We call him 'Mr. Clean'."

"Sounds good," the Captain nodded. "Turn him loose and see what he can come up with."

He then put on his civilian clothes, went over to Blank's apartment house to slip Lipsky his twenty dollars. The doorman thanked him gratefully.

Item: An hour later, Blankenship handed him the trace on Charles Lipsky. As Delaney had suspected, the man had a sheet. As a matter of fact, he was on probation, having been found guilty of committing a public nuisance, in that he did "with deliberate and malicious intent," urinate on the hood of a parked Bentley on East 59th Street.

Item: Christopher Langley called to report he had completed a list of all retail outlets of the West German ice ax in the U.S. With his new authority, Delaney was able to dispatch a squad car to go up to Langley's, pick up the list, bring it back to the command post. The list was assigned to one of Detective sergeant MacDonald's research men and, on the phone, he struck gold with his first call. Daniel G. Blank had purchased such an ax five years ago from Alpine Haven, a mail order house in Stamford, Conn., that specialized in mountaineering gear. A man was immediately sent to Stamford to bring back a photostatic copy of the sales check made out to Daniel G. Blank.

Item: Fernandez' men, particularly "Mr. Clean," made progress on that East End Avenue townhouse. At least, they now had the names of the residents: Celia Montfort, Blank's dark, thin girl friend; her young brother Anthony; a houseman named Valenter; and a middle-aged housekeeper. The names were turned over to MacDonald; the professor set up a separate staff to check them out.

During these days and nights of frantic activity, in the week before Christmas, Captain Delaney took time out to perform several personal chores. He gave Mary her Christmas gift early and, in addition, two weeks' vacation. Then he brought in an old uniformed patrolman, on limited duty, waiting for retirement, and told him to buy a 20-cup coffee urn and keep it going 24 hours a day in the kitchen; to keep the refrigerator filled with beer, cold cuts, cheese; and have enough bread and rolls on hand so anyone in Operation Lombard coming off a cold night's watch, or just stopping by during the day to report, would be assured of a sandwich and a drink.

He ordered folding cots, pillows and blankets brought in, and they were set up in the living room, hallway, kitchen, dining room—any place except in his study. They were in use almost constantly. Men who lived out on Long Island or up in Westchester sometimes preferred to sleep in, rather than make the long trip home, eat, sleep a few hours, turn around and come right back again.

He also found time to call his amateurs, wish them a Merry Christmas, thank them for their help and support and tell them, as gently as he could, that their efforts were no longer needed. He assured them their aid had been of invaluable assistance in developing a "very promising lead."

He did this on the phone to Christopher Langley and Calvin Case. He took Monica Gilbert to lunch and told her as much as he felt she should know: that partly through her efforts, he had a good chance to nail the killer but, because of the press of work, he wouldn't be able to call her or see her as often as he'd like. She was understanding and sympathetic.

"But take care of yourself," she entreated. "You look so tired."

"I feel great," he protested. "Sleep like a baby."

"How many hours?"

"Well . . . as much as I can."

"And you have regular, nourishing meals, I'm sure," she said sardonically.

He laughed. "I'm not starving," he assured her. "With luck, this may be over soon. One way or another. Are you still visiting Barbara?"

"Almost every day. You know, we're so dissimilar, but we have so much in common."

"Do you? That's good. I feel so guilty about Barbara. I dash in and dash out. Just stay long enough to say hello. But she's been through this before. She's a cop's wife."

"Yes. She told me."

Her sad voice gave him a sudden, vague ache, of something he should have done but did not do. But he couldn't think about it now.

"Thank you for visiting Barbara and for liking her," he said. "Did I tell you we're now grandparents?"

"Barbara did. *Mazeltov.*"

"Thank you. An ugly little boy."

"Barbara told me," she repeated. "But don't worry; within six months he'll be a beautiful little boy."

"Sure."

"Did you send a gift?"

"Well . . . I really didn't have time. But I did talk to Liza and her husband on the phone."

"It's all right. Barbara sent things. I picked them out for her and had them sent."

"That was very kind of you." He rubbed his chin, felt the bristle, realized he had neglected to shave that morning. That was no good. He had to present the image of a well-groomed, crisply uniformed, confident commander to his men. It was important.

"Edward," she said, in a low voice, with real concern, "are you all right?"

"Of course I'm all right," he said stonily. "I've been through things like this before."

"Please don't be angry with me."

"I'm not angry, Monica. I'm all right. I swear it. I could be sleeping more and eating better, but it's not going to kill me."

"You seem so—so wound up. This is important to you, isn't it?"

"Important? That I nail this guy? Of course it's important to me. Isn't it to you? He killed your husband."

460

She flinched at his brutality. "Yes," she said faintly, "it's important to me. But I don't like what it's doing to you."

He wouldn't think of what she had said, or what she had meant. First things first.

"I've got to get back," he said, and signaled for a check.

During that wild week he found time for two more personal jobs. Still not certain in his mind why he was doing it, he selected the business card of a certain J. David McCann, representative of something called the Universal Credit Union. Wearing his stiff Homburg and floppy civilian overcoat, he walked into the effete, scented showroom of the Erotica on Madison Avenue and asked to speak to Mr. or Mrs. Morton, hoping neither would recognize him as the former commander of the precinct in which they lived and worked.

He spoke to both in their backroom office. Neither glommed him; he realized that except for members of business associations, VIP's, community groups and social activists, the average New Yorker hadn't the slightest idea of the name or appearance of the man who commanded the forces of law and order in his precinct. An ego-deflating thought.

Delaney took off his hat, bowed, presented his phony business card, did everything but tug his forelock.

"I'm not selling anything," he said ingratiatingly. "Just a routine credit investigation. Mr. Daniel G. Blank has applied for a loan and given us your names as references. We just want to make sure you actually do know him."

Flo looked at Sam. Sam looked at Flo.

"Of course we know him," Sam said, almost angrily. "A very good friend."

"Known him for years," Flo affirmed. "Lives in the same apartment house we do."

"Mm-hmm," Delaney nodded. "A man of good character, you'd say? Dependable? Honest? Trustworthy?"

"A Boy Scout," Sam assured him. "What the hell's this all about?"

"You mentioned a loan," Flo said. "What kind of a loan? How big?"

"Well . . . I really shouldn't reveal these details," Delaney said in soft confidential tones, "but Mr. Blank has applied for a rather large mortgage covering the purchase of a townhouse on East End Avenue."

The Mortons looked at each other in astonishment. Then to Delaney's interest, they broke into pleased smiles.

"Celia's house!" Sam shouted, smacking his thighs. "He's buying her place!"

"It's on!" Flo screamed, hugging her arms. "They're really getting together!"

Captain Delaney nodded at both, snatched his business card back from Sam's fingers, replaced his Homburg, started from the office.

"Wait, wait, wait," Sam called. "You don't mind if we tell him you were here?"

"That you were checking up?" Flo asked. "You don't mind if we kid him about it?"

"Of course not," Captain Delaney smiled. "Please do."

On the second call he wore the same clothes, used the same business card. But this time he had to sit on his butt in an overheated outer office for almost a half-hour before he was allowed to see Mr. René Horvath, Personnel Director of the Javis-Bircham Corp. Eventually he was ushered into the inner sanctum where Mr. Horvath inspected the Captain's clothing with some distaste. As well he might; he himself was wearing a black raw silk suit, a red gingham plaid shirt with stiff white collar and cuffs, a black knitted tie. What Delaney liked most, he decided, were the black crinkle-patent leather moccasins with bright copper pennies inserted into openings on the top flaps. Exquisite.

Delaney went through the same routine he used with the Mortons, varying it to leave out any mention of a mortgage on a townhouse, saying only that Mr. Daniel G. Blank had applied for a loan, and that he, Mr. J. David McCann—"My card, sir" —and the Universal Credit Union were simply interested in verifying that Mr. Blank was indeed, as he claimed to be, employed by Javis-Bircham Corp.

"He is," the elegant Mr. Horvath said, handing back the soiled business card with a look that suggested it might be a carrier of VD. "Mr. Daniel Blank is presently employed by this company."

"In a responsible capacity?"

"Very responsible."

"I suppose you'd object to giving me a rough idea of Mr. Blank's annual income?"

"You suppose correctly."

"Mr. Horvath, I assure you that anything you tell me will be held in strictest confidence. Would you say that Mr. Blank is honest, dependable, and trustworthy?"

462

Horvath's pinched face closed up even more. "Mr. Mc-Closky—"

"McCann."

"Mr. McCann, *all* J-B executives are honest, dependable and trustworthy."

Delaney nodded, replaced the Homburg on his big head.

"Thank you for your time, sir. I certainly do appreciate it. Just doing my job—I hope you realize that."

"Naturally."

Delaney turned away, but suddenly a squid hand was on his arm, gripping limply.

"Mr. McCann . . ."

"Yes?"

"You said Mr. Blank has applied for a loan?"

"Yes, sir."

"How large a loan?"

"That I am not allowed to say sir. But you've been so cooperative that I can tell you it's a very large loan."

"Oh?" said Mr. Horvath. "Hmm," said Mr. Horvath, staring at the bright pennies inserted into his moccasin tongues. "That's very odd. Javis-Bircham, Mr. McCann, has its own loan program for all employees, from cafeteria busboy to Chairman of the Board. They can draw up to five thousand dollars, interest-free, and pay it back by salary deductions over a period of several years. Why didn't Mr. Blank apply for a company loan?"

"Oh well," Delaney laughed merrily, "you know how it is; everyone gets caught by the shorts sooner or later—right? And I guess he wanted to keep it private."

He left a very perturbed Mr. René Horvath behind him, and he thought, if Handry's impression was right and Blank's position with the company was shaky, it was shakier now.

In that week before Christmas, while the Delaney's living room furniture was being pushed back to the walls, deal tables and folding chairs brought in, cots set up, and communications men were still fiddling with their equipment, including three extra telephone lines, a "council of war" was scheduled every afternoon at 3:00 p.m. It was held in the Captain's study where the doors could be closed and locked. Attending were Captain Delaney, Lt. Jeri Fernandez, Detective first grade Ronald Blankenship, and Detective sergeant Thomas Mac-Donald. Delaney's liquor cabinet was open or, if they preferred, there was cold beer or hot coffee from the kitchen.

The first few meetings were concerned mostly with planning, organization, division of responsibility, choice of personnel, chain of command. Then, as information began to come in, they spent part of their time discussing the "Time-Habit Charts" compiled by Blankenship's squad. They were extremely detailed tabulations of Daniel Blank's daily routine: the time he left for work, his route, time of arrival at the Javis-Bircham Building, when he left for lunch, where he usually went, time of arrival back at the office, departure time, arrival at home, when he departed in the evening, where he went, how long he stayed. By the end of the fourth day, his patterns were pretty well established. Daniel Blank appeared to be a disciplined and orderly man.

Problems came up, were hashed out. Delaney listened to everyone's opinion. Then, after the discussion, he made the final decision.

Question: Should an undercover cop, with the cooperation of the management, be placed in Daniel Blank's apartment house as a porter, doorman, or whatever? Delaney's decision: No.

Question: Should an undercover cop be placed in Javis-Bircham, as close to Blank's department as he could get? Delaney's decision: Yes. It was assigned to Fernandez to work out as best he could a cover story that might seem plausible to the J-B executives he'd be dealing with.

Question: Should a Time-Habit Chart be set up for the residents of that townhouse on East End Avenue? Delaney's decision: No, with the concurring opinions of all three assistants.

"It's a screwy household," MacDonald admitted. "We can't get a line on them. This Valenter, the butler—or whatever you want to call him—has a sheet on molesting juvenile males. But no convictions. But that's all I've got so far."

"I don't have much more," Fernandez confessed. "The dame —this Celia Montfort—was admitted twice to Mother of Mercy Hospital for suicide attempts. Slashed wrists, and once her stomach had to be pumped out. We're checking other hospitals, but nothing definite yet."

"The kid seems to be a young fag," Blankenship said, "but no one's given me anything yet that makes a pattern. Like Pops said, it's a weird set-up. I don't think anyone knows what's going on over there. Nothing we can chart, anyway. She's in, she's out, at all hours of the day and night. She was gone for two days. Where was she? We don't know and won't until we put a special tail on her. Captain?"

"No," Delaney said. "Not yet. Keep at it."

Keep at it. Keep at it. That's all they heard from him, and they did because he seemed to know what he was doing, radiated an aura of confidence, never appeared to doubt that if they all kept at it, they'd nail this psycho and the killings would stop.

Daniel G. Blank. Captain Delaney knew his name, and now the others did, too. Had to. The men on the street, in the Con Ed van, in the unmarked cars adopted, by common consent, the code name "Danny Boy" for the man they watched. They had his photo now, reprinted in the hundreds, they knew his home address and shadowed his comings and goings. But they were told only that he was a "suspect."

Sometime during that week, Captain Delaney could never recall later exactly when, he scheduled his first press conference. It was held in the now empty detectives' squad room of the 251st Precinct house. There were reporters from newspapers, magazines, local TV news programs. The cameras were there, too, and the lights were hot. Captain Delaney wore his Number Ones and delivered, from memory, a brief statement he had labored over a long time the previous evening.

"My name is Captain Edward X. Delaney," he started, standing erect, staring into the TV cameras, hoping the sweat on his face didn't show. "I have been assigned command of Operation Lombard. This case, as you all know, involves the apparently unconnected homicides of four men: Frank Lombard, Bernard Gilbert, Detective Roger Kope, and Albert Feinberg. I have spent several days going through the records of Operation Lombard during the time it was commanded by former Deputy Commissioner Broughton. There is nothing in that record that might possibly lead to the indictment, conviction, or even identification of a suspect. It is a record of complete and utter failure."

There was a gasp from the assembled reporters; they scribbled furiously. Delaney didn't change expression, but he was grinning inwardly. Did Broughton really think he could talk to Delaney the way he had and not pay for it, eventually? The Department functioned on favors. It also functioned on vengeance. Run for mayor, would he? Lots of luck, Broughton!

"So," Captain Delaney continued, "because there is such a complete lack of evidence in the files of Operation Lombard while it was under the command of former Deputy Commissioner Broughton, I am starting from the beginning, with the death of Frank Lombard, and intend to conduct a totally new investigation into the homicides of all four men. I promise you nothing. I prefer to be judged by my acts rather than by my words. This is the first and last press conference I intend to hold until I either have the killer or am relieved of command. I will not answer any questions."

An hour after this brief interview, shown in its entirety, appeared on local TV news programs, Captain Delaney received a package at his home. It was brought into his study by one of the uniformed patrolmen on guard duty at the outside door—a 24-hour watch. No one went in or out without showing a special pass Delaney had had printed up, issued only to bona fide members of *his* Operation Lombard. The patrolman placed the package on Delaney's desk.

"Couldn't be a bomb, could it, Captain?" he asked anxiously. "You was on TV tonight, you know."

"I know," the Captain nodded. He inspected the package, then picked it up gingerly. He tilted it gently, back and forth. Something sloshed.

"No," he said to the nervous officer, "I don't think it's a bomb. But you did well to suggest it. You can return to your post."

"Yes, sir," the young patrolman said, saluted and left.

Handsome, Delaney thought, but those sideburns were too goddamned long.

He opened the package. It was a bottle of 25-year-old brandy with a little envelope taped to the side. Delaney opened the bottle and sniffed; first things first. He wanted to taste it immediately. Then he opened the sealed envelope. A stiff card. Two words: "Beautiful" and "Alinski."

The mood of the "war councils" changed imperceptibly in the three days before Christmas. It was obvious they now had a working, efficient organization. Danny Boy was blanketed by spooks every time he stepped outside home or office. Blankenship's bookkeeping and communications were beyond reproach. Detective sergeant MacDonald's snoops had built up a file on Blank that took up three drawers of a locked cabinet in Delaney's study. It included the story of his refusal to attend his parents' funeral and a revealing interview with a married woman in Boston who agreed to give her impressions of Daniel Blank while he was in college, under the cover story that Blank was being considered for a high-level security government job. Her comments were damning, but nothing that could be presented to a grand jury. Blank's ex-wife had remarried and was presently on an around-the-world honeymoon cruise.

During those last three days before Christmas, the impression was growing amongst Delaney's assistants—he could *feel* the mood—that they were amassing a great deal of information about Daniel G. Blank—a lot of it fascinating and libidinous reading—but it amounted to a very small hill of beans. The man had a girl friend. So? Maybe he was or was not sleeping with her brother Tony. So? He came out occasionally at odd hours, wandered about the streets, looked in shop windows, stopped in at The Parrot for a drink. So?

"Maybe he's on to us," Blankenship. "Maybe he knows the decoys are out every night, and he's being tailed."

"Can't be," Fernandez growled angrily. "No way. He don' even *see* my boys. As far as he's concerned, we don' exist."

"I don't know what else we can do," MacDonald confessed. "We've got him sliced up so thin I can see right through him. Birth certificate, diplomas, passport, bank statements—everything. You've seen the file. The man's laid out there, bareassed naked. Read the file and you've got him. Sure, maybe he's a psychopath, capable of killing I guess. He's a cold, smart, slick sonofabitch. But take him into court on what we've got? Uh-uh. Never. That's my guess."

"Keep at it," Captain Edward X. Delaney said.

Things slowed down on Christmas Eve. That was natural; men wanted to be home with their families. Squads were cut to a minimum (mostly bachelors or volunteers), and men sent home early. Delaney spent that quiet afternoon in his study, reading once again through his original Daniel G. Blank file and the great mass of material assembled by Pops and his squad who seemed to get their kicks sifting through dusty documents, military records, tax returns.

He read it all once more, sipping slowly from a balloon glass of that marvelous brandy Alinski had sent. He would have to call the Deputy Mayor to thank him, or perhaps mail a thank-you note, but meanwhile Alinski's envelope was added to the stack of unopened Christmas cards and presents that had accumulated in a corner of the study. He'd get to them, eventually, or take them over to Barbara when she was well enough to open them and enjoy them.

So he sipped brandy through a long Christmas Eve afternoon (the usual conference had been cancelled). As he read, the belief grew in him that the chilling of Danny Boy would come about through the man's personality, not by any clever police work, the discovery of a "clue," or by a sudden revelation of friend or lover.

Who was Daniel G. Blank? Who *was* he? MacDonald had said he was sliced thin, that he was laid out in that file bare-assed naked. No, Delaney thought, just the facts of the man's life were there. But no one is a simple compilation of official documents, of interviews with friends and acquaintances, of Time-Habit schedules. The essential question remained: Who *was* Daniel G. Blank?

Delaney was fascinated by him because he seemed to be two men. He had been a cold, lonely boy who grew up in what apparently had been a loveless home. No record of juvenile delinquency. He was quiet, collected rocks and, until college, didn't show any particular interest in girls. Then he refused to attend his parents' funeral. That seemed significant to Delaney. How could anyone, no matter how young, do a thing like that? There was a callous brutality about it that was frightening.

Then there was his marriage—what was it Lipsky had called her? A big *zoftig* blonde—the divorce, the girl friend with a boy's body, then possibly the boy himself, Tony. And meanwhile the sterile apartment with mirrors, the antiseptic apartment with silk bikini underwear and scented toilet paper. And according to one of MacDonald's beautifully composed and sardonic reports, a fast climb up the corporate ladder.

Delaney went back to an interview one of MacDonald's snoops had with a man named Robert White who had been Blank's immediate superior at Javis-Bircham. He had, from all the evidence and statements available, been knifed and ousted by Daniel Blank. The interview with White had been made under the cover story that Blank was being considered for a high executive position with a corporation competing with J-B.

"He's a nice lad," Bob White had stated ("Possibly under the influence of alcohol," the interrogating detective had noted carefully in his report). "He's talented. Lots of imagination. Too much maybe. But he gets the job done: I'll say that for him. But no blood. You understand? No fucking blood."

Captain Delaney stared up at the ceiling. "No fucking blood." What did that mean? Who *was* Daniel G. Blank? Of such complexity . . . Disgusting and fascinating. Courage—no doubt about that; he climbed mountains and he killed. Kind? Of course. He objected when he saw a man hit a dog, and he kept sentimental souvenirs of the men he murdered. Talented and imaginative? Well, his previous boss had said so. Talented and imaginative enough to fuck a 30-year-old woman and her 12-year-old brother, but Delaney didn't suppose Bob White knew anything about *that!*

Who *was* Dan?

Captain Delaney rose to his feet, brandy glass in hand, about to propose a toast: "Here's to you, Danny Boy," when there was a knock on his study door. He sat down sedately behind his desk.

"Come in," he called.

Lt. Jeri Fernandez stuck his head through the opened door. "Busy, Captain?" he asked. "Got a few minutes?"

"Of course, of course," Delaney gestured. "Come on in. Got some fine brandy here. How about it?"

"Ever know me to refuse?" Fernandez asked in mock seriousness, and they both laughed.

Then Delaney was in his swivel chair, swinging back and forth gently, holding his glass, and Fernandez was in the leather club chair. The lieutenant sipped the brandy, said nothing, but his eyes rolled to Heaven in appreciation.

"Thought you'd be home by now," the Captain said.

"On my way. Just making sure everything's copasetic."

"I know I've told you this before, lieutenant, but I'll say it again: tell your boys not to relax, not for a second. This monkey is fast."

Fernandez hunched over in the club chair, leaning forward, head lowered, moving the brandy snifter between his palms.

"Faster than a thirty-eight, Captain?" he asked in a voice so low that Delaney wasn't sure he heard him.

"What?" he demanded.

"Is this freak faster than a thirty-eight?" Fernandez repeated. This time he raised his head, looked directly into Delaney's eyes.

The Captain rose immediately, went to the study doors, closed them and locked them, then came back to sit behind his desk again.

"What's on your mind?" he asked quietly, looking directly at Fernandez.

"Captain, we been at this for—how long? Over a week now. Almost ten days. We got this Danny Boy covered six ways from Sunday. You keep calling him a 'suspect.' But I notice we're not out looking for other suspects, digging into anyone else. Everything we do is about this guy Blank."

"So?" Delaney said coldly.

"So," Fernandez sighed, looking down at his glass, "I figure maybe you know something we don' know, something you're not telling us." He held up a hand hastily, palm out. "This isn't a beef, Captain. If there's something we don' have to know, that's your right and privilege. Just thought—maybe—you might be sure of this guy but can't collar him. For some reason. No witnesses. No evidence that'll hold up. Whatever. But I figure you know it's him. *Know* it!"

The Captain resumed his slow swinging back and forth in his swivel chair. "Supposing," he said, "just *supposing*, mind you, that you're right, that I know as sure as God made little green apples that Blank is our pigeon, but we can't touch him. What do you suggest then?"

Fernandez shrugged. "Supposing," he said, "just *supposing* that's the situation, then I can't see us collaring Danny Boy unless we grab him in the act. And if he's as fast as you say he is, we'll have another stiff before we can do that. Right?"

Delaney nodded. "Yes," he said, "I've thought of that. So what's your answer?"

Fernandez took a sip of brandy, then looked up.

"Let me take him, Captain," he said softly.

Delaney set his brandy glass on the desk blotter, poured himself another small portion of that ambrosia, then carried the bottle over to Fernandez and added to his snifter. He returned to his swivel chair, set the bottle down, began to drum gently on his desk top with one hand, watching the moving fingers.

"You?" he asked Fernandez. "You alone?"

"No. I got a friend. The two—"

"A friend?" Delaney said sharply, looking up. "In the Department?"

The lieutenant was astonished. "Of course in the Department. Who's got any friends outside the Department?"

"All right," Delaney nodded. "How would you handle it?"

"The usual," Fernandez shrugged. "We go up to his apartment and roust him. He resists arrest and tries to escape, so we ice him. Clean and simple and neat."

The Captain sighed, shook his head. "It doesn't listen," he said.

"Captain, it's been done before."

"Goddamn it, don't try to tell me my business," Delaney shouted furiously. "I know it's been done before. But we do it your way, and we all get pooped."

He jerked to his feet, unbuttoned his uniform jacket, jammed his hands in his hip pockets. He began to pace about the study, not glancing at Fernandez as he talked.

"Look, lieutenant," he said patiently, "this guy is no alley cat with a snoot full of shit, that no one cares if he lives or dies. Burn a guy like that, and he's just a number in potter's field. But Danny Boy is *somebody*. He's rich, he lives in a luxury apartment house, drives an expensive car, works for a big corporation. He's got friends, influential friends. Chill him, and people are going to ask questions. And we better have the answers. If it's done at all, it's got to be done *right*."

Fernandez opened his mouth to speak, but Delaney held up a hand. "Wait a minute. Let me finish. Now let's take your plan. You and your friend go up to brace him. How you going to get inside his apartment? I happen to know that guy's got more locks on his door than you'll find in a Tombs' cellblock. You think you'll knock, say, 'Police officers,' and he'll open up and let you in? The hell he will; he's too smart for that. He'll look at you through the peephole and talk to you through the locked door."

"Search warrant?" Fernandez suggested.

"Not a chance," Delaney shook his head. "Forget it."

"Then how about this: One of us goes up and waits outside his door, before he gets home from work. The other guy waits in the lobby until he comes in and rides up in the elevator with him. Then we got him in his hallway between us."

"And then what?" the Captain demanded. "You weight him right there in the corridor, while he's between you, and then claim he was trying to escape or resisting arrest? Who'd buy that?"

"Well . . ." Fernandez said doubtfully, "I guess you're right. But there's got to—"

"Shut up a minute and let me think," Delaney said. "Maybe we can work this out."

The lieutenant was silent then, sipping a little brandy, his bright eyes following the Captain as he lumbered about the room.

"Look," Delaney said, "there's a doorman over there. Guy named Charles Lipsky. He's got access to duplicate keys to every apartment in the building. They hang on a board outside the assistant manager's office. This Lipsky's got a sheet. As a matter of fact, he's on probation, so you can lean on him. Now . . . you hear on the radio that Danny Boy has left work and is heading home. You and your friend get the keys from Lipsky, go upstairs and get inside Blank's apartment. Then you relock the door from the inside. So when he comes home, unlocks his door and marches in, you're already in there."

"I like it," Fernandez grinned.

"When the time comes I'll draw you a floor plan so you'll know where to be when he comes in. Then you—"

"A floor plan?" the lieutenant interrupted. "But how—"

"Just don't worry about it. Don't even think about it. When the time comes, you'll have a floor plan. But you give him time to get inside before you show yourselves. Maybe even give him time to relock his door so he can't make a fast run for it. He's sure to relock once he's inside his apartment; that's the kind of a guy he is. *Then* you show yourselves. Now here's where it begins to get cute. Can you get hold of a piece that can't be traced?"

"Oh sure. No trouble."

"What is it?"

"A Saturday-night special."

The Captain took a deep breath, blew it out in an audible sigh.

"Lieutenant," he said gently, "Danny Boy makes fifty-five big ones a year, drives a Stingray, and wears silk underwear. Do you really think he's the kind of guy who'd own a piece of crap like that? What else can you get?"

The "Invisible Man" thought a moment, his teeth clenched.

"A nine-millimeter Luger," he said finally. "Brand-new. Right off the docks. Never been used. Still in the oiled envelope."

"What kind of grips."

"Wood."

"Yesss . . ." Delaney said thoughtfully. "He might own a gun like that. But the brand-new part is no good. It'll have to have at least three magazines fired through with a complete breakdown and cleaning between firings. Can you manage that?"

"No sweat, Captain."

"And it's got to be banged up a little. Not a lot. A few nicks on the grips. A little scratch here and there. You understand?"

"Like he's owned it for a long time?"

"Right. And took it on those mountain climbing trips of his to plink at tin cans or some such shit. Now here's something else: keep the box or envelope it came in, get the right cleaning tools and some oil-soaked rags. You know, the usual crap. This stuff you turn over to me."

"To *you*, Captain?"

"Yes, to me. All right, now you and your buddy are inside the apartment, and the door is locked. You've both got your

472

service revolvers, and one of you has also got the used Luger. It's loaded. Full magazine. As soon as Danny Boy is inside his apartment, and has locked the door, you show. And for God's sake, have your sticks out. Don't relax for a second. Keep this guy covered."

"Don' worry, he'll be covered."

"Don't say a word to him, not a word. Just back him toward the bedroom door. You'll see where it is on that floor plan I'll draw for you. Now this is where you've got to work fast. As soon as he's in the bedroom doorway, or near it, facing you, weight him. Make it fast and—this is important—make certain you both ice him. I don't know how good a friend this pal of yours is, but you've *both* got to do it. You understand?"

Fernandez smiled slyly. "You're a smart man, Captain."

"Yes. Now you're working fast. He's down, and for Christ's sake make certain he's gone."

"He'll have enough weight in him to sink him," the lieutenant assured him. "He'll be a clunk before he hits the floor."

"I'll take your word for it," Delaney grunted. "Now, the moment he's down, one of you—I don't care who it is—straddles his body, facing in the direction he was facing just before he bought it. And then—"

"And then we fire two or three shots from the Luger into the opposite wall," Fernandez said rapidly. "Where the two of us was just standing."

"Now you're catching it," the Captain said approvingly. "But it's got to be done fast—so that if anyone hears the shots, it's just a lot of shots, no pauses. No witness is going to remember how many shots were fired, when, or in what order. But just to play safe, the Luger should be fired into the opposite wall as soon as possible after you've iced him."

"I've got it," Fernandez smiled. "Two or three shots into the wall. Not too high. Like he really was firing at us."

"Right. Splinter a couple of mirrors if you can. That opposite wall is full of mirrors. Then what do you do?"

"Easy," Fernandez said. "Wipe the Luger clean. Put it in his hand and—"

"His *right* hand," Delaney cautioned. "He's right-handed. Don't forget it."

"I won't forget it. The Luger gets wiped clean and put in his right hand."

"Try it," Delaney said, "but don't get spooked if it doesn't work. It's tougher than you think to get a clunk's hand to grip a gun—even a fresh clunk. Just make sure you get a couple of good prints on it. They probably won't show on the wood grips, especially if they're checkered, but put them on the metal. Anywhere. The gun can even be on the floor, near his right hand. But a couple of good prints are what we need. What do you do next?"

"Let's see . . ." Fernandez thought deeply. He took a sip of his brandy. "Well, we've still got the keys to the guy's apartment."

"Right," Delaney said promptly. "So your friend has got to go down to the lobby and slip the keys back to Lipsky. Tell him to leave Danny Boy's apartment door open on the way out. Not open, but unlocked. And while he's doing that, what are you doing?"

"Me? Well, I guess I could start tossing—"

"Forget it," the Captain said. "Don't touch a goddamn thing. The first thing you do is call me on Blank's phone. I'll be waiting for your call. I'll collect a squad and be right over. But don't do a thing until I get there. Don't even sit down in a chair. Just stand there. If you get any flak from neighbors, just identify yourself, tell them more cops are on the way, and keep them out in the corridor. All right, I come in with a squad. You tell us what happened, and keep it as short as possible. I make the calls I have to make—the ME, lab, and so forth. Then we start a search, and then I'll plant the oily rag, the cleaning tools, the extra Luger magazines, and so forth. I don't know how I'll carry them up there, but I'll—"

"But why should you do it, Captain?" Fernandez protested. "We could take that stuff up there with us."

Delaney grinned cynically. "In cases like this, it's best that everyone be involved, as equally as possible. It's insurance. That's why I want you to make certain that both you and your friend feed Danny Boy the pills."

The lieutenant puzzled over this. Then his face cleared.

"Smart," he nodded. "So no one talks, ever, and knows none of the others is going to spill."

"Something like that," Delaney agreed, not smiling. "Mutual trust. Now here's the cover story: Operation Lombard determined that the weapon used in the four homicides was an ice ax. That's a tool used by mountain climbers. Danny Boy is a mountain climber. There's hard evidence for all this. We checked into purchasers of ice axes in the Two-five-one Precinct, where all the killings occurred, and you and your friend were given a list of ice ax owners to question. Just to put the icing on the cake, I'll give you two or three names and addresses to check out before you get to Danny Boy. Then you say you identified yourselves as police officers, he let you in, and you asked to examine his ice ax. He said it was in his bedroom and went in there to get it. It's really in the outside hall closet, but he went into the bedroom and came out with the Luger, blasting. But he missed. The two of you went for your sticks and iced him. How does it sound?"

The lieutenant shook his head admiringly. "You're a wonder, Captain," he said. "It sounds great, just great."

"And, with any luck, while I'm planting the Luger equipment, I'll turn up the evidence that will put the finger on Danny Boy but good. It was there a few weeks ago. If it's still there, believe me, no one will ask any questions. But even if he's destroyed it by now, it won't make any difference. He'll be wasted, and it'll all be over."

"Sounds perfect, Captain."

"No," Delaney said, "it's not perfect. There are some loose ends we'll have to take care of. For instance, this friend of yours—I'll have to meet him."

"You already know him."

"He's in Operation Lombard?"

"Yes."

"Good. That makes it easier. This was just a quick outline, lieutenant. The three of us will have to go over it again and again and again until we've got it just right and our timing set. Maybe we could even have a dry-run to work out any bugs, but essentially I think it's a logical and workable plan."

"I think it's a winner, Captain. Can't miss."

"It can miss," Delaney said grimly, "Anything can miss. But I think it's worth a chance."

"Then it's on, Captain? Definitely?"

Delaney took a deep breath, came back to sit behind his desk again. He sat erect in his swivel chair, put his big hands flat on the desk top.

"Well . . . maybe not definitely," he said finally. "I like it because it gives me another option, and I'm practically running out of those. I've got just one other idea that's been percolating in my brain. I tell you what: Go ahead and get the Luger. Fire it, clean it, and bang it up a little. But don't mention a word to your friend. If I decide to go ahead, I'll let you know. Got it?"

"Sure," Fernandez nodded. "I do what you said about the Luger but hold up on anything else until I get the word from you."

"Exactly."

They both rose to their feet. The lieutenant put out his hand; Delaney grasped it.

"Captain," Lt. Fernandez said seriously, "I want to wish a Merry Christmas and a very happy New Year to you and yours. I hope Mrs. Delaney is feeling much better real soon."

"Thank you, lieutenant," Delaney said. "The very merriest of Christmases to you and your family, and I hope the New Year brings you everything you want. It's a real pleasure working with you."

"Thank you, Captain," Fernandez said. "Likewise."

Delaney closed the door, came back into the study.

He sat down at his desk, wished he had a fresh Cuban cigar, and considered the plan he had discussed with Lt. Fernandez. It wasn't foolproof; such plans never were. There was always the possibility of the unexpected, the unimagined: a scream from somewhere, a sudden visitor, a phone call. Danny Boy might even charge the two police officers, going right into their naked guns. He was capable of such insanity.

But essentially, Delaney decided, it was a logical and workable program. It was a solution. There were a lot of loose ends: how would he carry the Luger tools and cleaning equipment up to the apartment when he answered Fernandez' call, where would he plant them (in the bedroom, obviously), what if the souvenirs were no longer taped to the bottom of the dresser drawer? A hundred questions would be asked, by newsmen and by his superiors. How had Operation Lombard determined that an ice ax was the weapon used in the four homicides? How had they latched onto Daniel Blank? There would be many, many such questions; he would have to anticipate them all and have his answers ready.

He looked at his watch. Almost 4:15; it was a long afternoon. He sighed, pulled himself to his feet, unlocked the study door to the living room, wandered in.

The two big transceivers were on plain pine planks, placed across sawhorses. A uniformed officer was seated in front of each instrument, hunched over a table microphone. A separate table, not as large, held the three new telephones. There was a uniformed officer on duty there, reading a paperback novel. Two men, stripped to their scivvies, were sleeping on cots alongside the wall. One was snoring audibly. Detective second grade Samuel Wilding—he was one of Blankenship's assistants —was seated at a card table, making notes on a chart. Delaney raised a hand to him.

He stood a moment near the radios, hands clasped behind his back. He was probably, he thought regretfully, making the operators nervous. But there was no answer for that.

The room was quiet. No, not quiet; except for the low snoring, it was absolutely silent. Late afternoon darkness crept through open drapes, and with it came a—what? A sweetness, Captain Delaney admitted, laughing at himself, but it was a kind of sweetness.

The uniformed men had taken off their blouses. They were working at their desks in sweaters or T-shirts, but still wearing gun belts. Only Detective Wilding wore a jacket, and his was summer-weight, with lapels. So what was it? Delaney wondered. Why the sweetness? It came, he decided, from men on duty, doing their incredibly boring jobs, enduring. The fraternity. Of what? (Delaney: "A friend? In the Department?" Fernandez ((astonished)): "Of course in the Department. Who's got any friends outside the Department?") A kind of brotherhood.

A phone rang on the deal desk. The officer on duty put aside his paperback, picked up the ringing phone. "Barbara," he said.

They had devised a radio and telephone code as simple and brief as they could make it. Not because Danny Boy might be listening in, but to keep away the short-wave nuts who tuned to police frequencies.

"Danny Boy"—Daniel G. Blank.

"Barbara"—the command post in Delaney's home.

"White House"—Blank's apartment house.

"Factory"—the Javis-Bircham Building.

"Castle"—the East End Avenue townhouse.

"Bulldog One"—the phony Con Ed van on the street outside the White House. It was Lt. Fernandez' command post.

"Bulldog Two, Three, Four, etc."—code names for Fernandez' unmarked cars and spooks on foot.

"Tiger One"—the man watching the Montfort townhouse. "Tiger Two" and "Tiger Three" were the street men sweeping the neighborhood.

Other than that, the Operation Lombard investigators used their actual names in transmissions, keeping their calls, in compliance with frequently repeated orders, informal and laconic.

When the phone rang, the officer who answered it said "Barbara." Then he listened awhile, turned to look at Detective Wilding. "Stryker at the Factory," he reported. "Danny

Boy has his coat and hat on, looks like he's ready to leave." Stryker was the undercover man planted at Javis-Bircham. He was a tabulating clerk—and a good one—in Blank's department.

Detective Wilding nodded. He turned to a man at the radio. "Alert Bulldog Three." He looked at Delaney. "Okay for Stryker to cut out?"

The Captain nodded. The detective called to the man on the phone, "Tell Stryker he can take off. Report back the day after Christmas."

The officer spoke into the phone, then grinned. "That Stryker," he said to everyone listening. "He doesn't want to take off. He says they've got an office party going, and he ain't going to miss it."

"The greatest cocksman in the Department," someone said.

The listening men broke up. Captain Delaney smiled thinly. He leaned forward to hear one of the radio operators say, "Bulldog Three from Barbara. Got me?"

"Yes. Very nice." It was a bored voice.

"Danny Boy on his way down."

"Okay."

There was a quiet wait of about five minutes. Then: "Barbara from Bulldog Three. We've got him. Heading east on Forty-sixth Street. A yellow cab. License XB sixty-one—dash—forty-nine—dash—three—dash—one. Got it?"

"XB sixty-one—dash—forty-nine—dash—three—dash—one."

"Right on."

It was all low key; it was routine. The logs were kept carefully, and the 24-hour Time-Habit Charts were marked in. But nothing was happening.

Delaney stalked back into his study, put on his glasses, drew his yellow pad toward him. He jotted two lists. The first consisted of five numbered items:

1. Garage attendant.
2. Bartender at Parrot.
3. Lipsky.
4. Mortons.
5. Horvath at J-B.

The second list came slower, over a period of almost an hour. It finally consisted of four numbered items.

Delaney put it aside, rose, lumbered back into the living room. He went directly to Detective Samuel Wilding.

"When's Blankenship coming back on?" he demanded.

478

"Tomorrow at noon, Captain. We're splitting up because of Christmas."

Delaney nodded. "Tell him, or leave a note for him, that I want to be informed immediately of any change in Danny Boy's Time-Habit pattern. Got that?"

"Yes, sir."

"Informed immediately," the Captain repeated.

He marched through to his dining room and up to the lone man of Detective sergeant MacDonald's squad on duty. The man looked up, startled.

"When's MacDonald due back?" Delaney asked.

"Tomorrow at four in the afternoon, Captain. We're splitting—"

"I know, I know," Delaney said testily. "Christmas. I want to leave a message for him." The duty officer took up a pad and waited, pencil in hand. "Tell him I want a photograph of Detective Kope."

The officer's pencil hesitated.

"Kope? The guy who got chilled?"

"Detective third grade Roger Kope, homicide victim," Delaney said grimly. "I need a photograph of him. Preferably with his family. A photograph of the entire Kope family. Got that?"

He looked down at the officer's pad. It was covered with squiggles.

"You know shorthand?" he asked.

"Yes, sir. I took a course."

"Very good. It's valuable. I wish I knew it. But I guess I'm too old to learn now."

He started to explain to the officer that MacDonald would do best to send a man for the photo who had known Kope, who had been a friend of the family. But he stopped. The sergeant was an old cop; he'd know how to handle it.

He tramped back into his study, closed the doors. He looked at his watch. Almost 7:00 p.m. It was time. He looked at the list on his desk, then dialed the number of Daniel G. Blank. The phone rang and rang. No one answered. He walked back into the living room, over to the radio operator keeping the log.

"Danny Boy in the White House?" he asked.

"Yes, sir. No departure. About half an hour ago Tiger One called in. Princess left the Castle in a cab." ("Princess" was the code name for Celia Montfort.) "About ten minutes later

Bulldog One reported her arrival at the White House. They're both still in there, as far as we know."

Delaney nodded, went back into his study, closing the door. He called Blank's number again. No answer. Maybe Danny Boy and the Princess were having a sex scene and weren't answering the phone. Maybe. And maybe they were at a Christmas Eve party. At the Mortons, possibly? Possibly. He went to the file cabinet, took out the thin folder on the Mortons that MacDonald's snoops had assembled. Their home phone number was there.

Delaney came back to his desk, dialed the number.

"Mortons' residence," a female voice answered, after the seventh ring.

In the background Delaney could hear the loud voices of several people, shouts, laughter. A party. He didn't grin.

"I'm trying to reach Mr. Daniel Blank," he said slowly, distinctly, "and I was given this number to call. Is he there?"

"Yes, he is. Just a minute, please."

He heard her call, "Mr. Blank! Phone!" Then that familiar voice was there, curious and cautious. Delaney knew what Danny Boy was wondering: how had anyone traced him to the Mortons' Christmas Eve party?

"Hello?"

"Mr. Daniel G. Blank?"

"Yes. Who is this?"

"Frank Lombard."

There was a sound at the other end of the phone: part moan, part groan, part gasp—something sick and unbelieving.

"Who?"

"Frank Lombard," Delaney said in a low, soft voice. "You know me. We've met before. I just wanted to wish you—"

But the connection went dead. Delaney hung up gently, smiling now. Then he put on overcoat and cap and went out into the dark night to find a drugstore that was still open so he could buy a bottle of perfume and take it to the hospital, a Christmas gift for his wife.

PART VIII

1

Something was happening. What was happening? Something . . .

Daniel Blank thought it had started two weeks ago. Or perhaps it was three; it was difficult to remember. But the garage attendant in his apartment house casually mentioned that an insurance examiner had been around, asking about Blank's car.

"He thought you had been in some kind of accident," the man said. "But he took one look at your car and knew you wasn't. I told him so. I told him you ain't had that car out in months."

Blank nodded and asked the man to wash the Stingray, check the battery, oil, gas. He thought no more about the insurance examiner. It had nothing to do with him.

But then, one night, he stopped in at The Parrot. The bartender served him his brandy, then asked if his name was Blank. When Daniel acknowledged it—a tickle of agitation there—the bartender told him a private detective had been in, asking questions about him. He couldn't recall the man's name, but he described him. Troubled now, Blank went back to the garage attendant; his description of the "insurance examiner" tallied with that of the bartender's "private detective."

Not two days later, doorman Charles Lipsky reported that a man had been around asking "very personal questions" about Daniel Blank. The man, Lipsky said, had not stated his name or occupation, but Lipsky could describe him, and did.

From these three descriptions Blank began to form a picture of the man dogging him. Not so much a picture as a silhouette. A dark, hulking figure, rough as a woodcut. Big, with stooped shoulders. Massive. Wearing a stiff Homburg set squarely atop his head, an old-fashioned, double-breasted, shapeless overcoat.

Then, with great glee, Flo and Sam Morton told him of the visit of the credit investigator, and Dan—you devil!—why hadn't you told your best friends about your plans to marry

Celia Montfort and purchase her townhouse? He grinned bleakly.

Then that numbing, mumbling meeting with René Horvath, Javis-Bircham's Director of Personnel. Blank finally got it straight that a credit investigator had been making inquiries; apparently Blank had applied for a "very large loan" —much larger than that offered by the J-B employees' loan program. Horvath had felt it his duty to report the investigator's visit to his superiors, and he had been assigned to ask Daniel Blank the purpose of the loan.

Blank finally got rid of the disgusting little creep, but not before eliciting a physical description of the "credit investigator." Same man.

He knew now his days at Javis-Bircham were numbered, but it wasn't important. The phony credit investigation would just be the last straw. But it wasn't important. He'd be fired, or allowed to resign, and given a generous severance payment. It wasn't important. He knew that during the last few months he simply hadn't been doing his job. He wasn't interested. It wasn't important.

What was important, right now, was the insurance examiner-private detective-credit investigator—a composite man who had become more than a silhouette, a vague image, but was now assuming a rotundity, a solidity, with heavy features and gross gestures, a shambling walk and eyes that never stopped looking. Who was he? God in a stiff Homburg and floppy overcoat?

Blank looked for him wherever he went, on the street, in bars and restaurants, at night, alone in his apartment. On the streets he would search the faces of approaching strangers, then whirl suddenly to see if that big, huddled man was lumbering along behind him. In restaurants, he strolled to the men's room, looking casually at patrons, walking into the kitchen "by accident," glancing into occupied phone booths, inspecting toilet cubicles. Where was he? At home, at night, the door locked, bolted, jammed tight, he would lie awake in the darkness and suddenly hear night noises: thumpings, creakings, a short snap. Then he would rise, put on all the lights, stalk through the apartment, wanting to meet him face to face. But he was not there.

Then, finally, it was Christmas Eve. Javis-Bircham would not fire him until after the holidays; he knew that. So he could accept happily an invitation to the Mortons' Christmas Eve party and ask Celia to join him. He would drink a little, laugh,

482

put his arm around Celia's slender, hard waist, and surely the dark, thrusting shadow could not be there.

The call shattered him. For how could anyone know he was at the Mortons'? He approached the phone cautiously, picked it up as if expecting it to explode in his hand. Then that soft, insinuating voice said: "Frank Lombard. You know me. We've met before. I just wanted—"

Then he was out of there, leaving Celia behind him, saying goodnight to no one. The elevator took a decade; it was a generation before he got his door unlocked and locked again; it was a century before he had the drawer out, turned upside down on his bed. He inspected the taped envelope carefully but, as far as he could see, it had not been touched. He opened it; everything was there. He sat on his bed, fingering his mementoes, and became aware that he had wet his pants. Not a lot. But a few drops. It was degrading.

He stuffed the black velvet suit, white cashmere turtleneck sweater, and flowered bikini panties into the bathroom laundry hamper. He peeled off the Via Veneto wig before getting under a shower as hot as he could stand it. When he soaped his bare skull, he felt the light fuzz and knew he'd soon need another shave.

He dried, smoothed on cologne, powdered, stuck the wig firmly back into place. Then he put on one of his silk robes, the crane design, and padded barefoot into the living room to pour himself a warm vodka and light one of his dried lettuce cigarettes.

Then he realized the apartment doorbell was chiming, had been for several rings. He stubbed his cigarette out carefully and drained his vodka before going into the hallway to peer at Celia Montfort through the peephole. He unlocked the door to let her in, bolted it again behind her.

"You're not ill, are you, Dan?"

"You don't talk in your sleep, do you?" he asked. Even in his own ears his laugh sounded wild and forced.

She stared at him, expressionless.

She sat on the living room couch, waited patiently while he opened a bottle of bordeaux, poured her a stemmed glass and for himself the glass still wet from the vodka he had finished. She sipped the wine cautiously.

"Good," she nodded. "Dry as dust."

"What? Oh yes. I should have bought more. The price has almost doubled. Did you tell anyone about me?"

"What are you talking about, Dan?"

"What I've done. Did you tell anyone?"

Her answer was prompt, but it was no answer at all: "Why should I do a thing like that?"

She was wearing a tube of black jersey, high at the neck, long-sleeved, hanging to her dull black satin evening pumps. About her neck was what appeared to be a six-foot rope of cultured pearls, wound tightly, around and around, so it formed a gleaming collar that kept her head erect, chin raised.

He had the sense—as he had at their first meeting—of never being able to recognize her, of forgetting what she looked like when she was out of his sight. The long, black, almost purple hair; drawn, witch-like face; slender, tapering hands; but the eyes—were they grey or blue? Were the lips full or flat? Was the nose Egyptian—or merely pinched? And the pallid complexion, bruised weariness, aura of corruption, of white flesh punished to a puddle—where did those fantasies come from? She was as much a mystery to him now as at their first meeting. Was it a thousand years ago?

She sat on the couch, composed, withdrawn, sipping her wine as he passed back and forth. He never took his eyes from her as he told her about the man who had been dogging him—the insurance examiner-private detective-credit investigator man—and the people this man had seen, the questions he had asked, what he had said.

As he talked, words spilling out so fast that he spluttered a few times and white spittle gathered in the corners of his mouth—well, as he chattered, he saw her cross her legs slowly, high up, at her thighs, hidden by her long dress. But from the bent knee, one ankle showed, a satin evening pump hung down. As he told her what had happened, that loose foot, that black shoe, began to bob up and down, lower leg swinging from the hidden knee, slow at first, nodding in a graceful rhythm, then moving faster in stronger jerks. Her face was still expressionless.

Watching Celia's bobbing foot, the leg from the knee down swinging faster under her long dress, he thought she must be masturbating, sitting there on his couch, naked thighs pressed tightly together beneath her gown. The rhythm of that jerking foot became faster and faster until when he told her about the telephone call he had just received at the Mortons, she began to pant, her eyes glazed, pearls of sweat to match her necklace formed on brow and upper lip. Then, eyes closed now, her entire body stiffened for a moment. He stopped talking to watch her. When she finally relaxed, shuddering, looked about with vacant eyes, uncrossed her legs, he thought she must have been sexually excited by his danger, but for what reason he did not know, could not guess.

"Could the man be Valenter?" he asked her.

"Valenter?" She took a deep sip of wine. "How could he know? Besides, Valenter is skinny, a scarecrow. You said this man following you about is heavy, lumbering. It couldn't be Valenter."

"No. I suppose not."

"How could this man—the one on the phone—know about Frank Lombard?"

"I don't know. Perhaps there was an eyewitness—to Lombard or one of the others—and he followed me home and got my address and then my name."

"For what reasons?"

"It's obvious, isn't it? He didn't go to the police, so it must be blackmail."

"Mmm, possibly. Are you frightened?"

"Well . . . disturbed." Then he told her about what he had been doing since he left the Mortons' apartment so abruptly: trying to make his mind into a blank blackboard, erasing thoughts as quickly as they appeared in chalk script.

"Oh no," she shook her head, and in her voice was an imploring tone he had never heard her use before, "you shouldn't do that. Open your mind wide. Let it expand. Let it shatter into a million thoughts, sensations, memories, fears. That's how you'll find perception. Don't erase your consciousness. Let it flower as it will. Anything is possible. Remember that: anything is possible. Something will come to you, something that will explain the man following you and the phone call. Open your mind; don't close it down. Logic won't help. You must become increasingly aware, increasingly sensitive. I have a drug at home. Do you want to use it?"

"No."

"All right. But don't shut yourself in, inside yourself. Be open to everything."

She stood, picked up the remainder of the wine.

"Let's go to your bedroom," she said. "I'll stay the night."

"I won't be any good."

Her free hand slid inside the opening of his robe. He felt her slim, cool fingers drift across his nakedness to find him, to hold him.

"We'll play with each other," she murmured.

And so they did.

2

On the day following Christmas, Captain Delaney worked all morning in his study, in his shirtsleeves—it was unseasonably warm, the house overheated—trying to prepare estimates of his manpower and vehicle requirements for the coming week. The holiday season complicated things; men wanted to spend time at home with their families. That was understandable, but it meant schedules had to be reshuffled, and it was impossible to satisfy everyone.

Delaney's three commanders—Fernandez, MacDonald, and Blankenship—had prepared tentative schedules for their squads, but had appended suggestions, questions, requests. From this tangled mess of men available for duty, men on vacation or about to go, sick leave, hardship cases, special pleadings (one of Fernandez' spooks had an appointment with a podiatrist to have his bunions trimmed), Delaney tried to construct a master schedule for Operation Lombard that would, at least, have every important post covered 24 hours a day but still leave enough "wiggle room" so last-minute substitutions could be made, and there would always be a few men playing poker for matchsticks in the radio room, available for emergency duty if needed.

By noon he had a rough timetable worked out; he was shocked at the number of men it required. The City of New York was spending a great deal of money to monitor the activities of Daniel G. Blank. That didn't bother Delaney; the City spent more money for more frivolous projects. But the Captain was concerned about how long Thorsen, Johnson, et al., would give him a free hand and a limitless budget before screaming for results. Not too long, he thought grimly; perhaps another week.

He pulled on jacket, civilian overcoat and hat, and checked out with the uniformed patrolman keeping an entrance-exit log at a card table set up just inside the outer door. Delaney gave him destination and phone number where he could be reached. Then he had one of the unmarked cars parked outside drive him over to the hospital. Another breach of regulations, but at least it gave the two dicks in the car a few minutes' relief from the boredom of their job: sitting and waiting.

Barbara seemed in a subdued mood, and answered his conversational offerings with a few words, a wan smile. He helped her with her noon meal and, that finished, just sat with her for another hour. He asked if she'd like him to read to her, but when she shook her head, he just sat stolidly, in silence, hoping his presence might be of some comfort, not daring to think of how long her illness would endure, or how it might end.

He returned home by cab, dutifully showed his Operation Lombard pass for entrance, even though the uniformed outside guard recognized him immediately and saluted. He was hungry for a sandwich and a cold beer, but the kitchen was crowded with at least a dozen noisy men taking a lunch-hour break for coffee, beer, or some of the cheese and cold cuts for which they all contributed, a dollar a day per man.

The old uniformed patrolman on kitchen duty saw the Captain walk through to his study. A few minutes later he knocked on the door to bring Delaney a beer and ham-and-Swiss on rye. The Captain smiled his thanks; it was just what he wanted.

About an hour later a patrolman knocked and came in to relay a request from Detective first grade Blankenship: could the Captain come into the living room for a minute? Delaney hauled himself to his feet, followed the officer out. Blankenship was standing behind the radio operators, bending over the day's Time-Habit log of Daniel Blank's activities. He swung around when Delaney came up.

"Captain, you asked to be informed of any erratic change in Danny Boy's Time-Habit Pattern. Take a look at this." Delaney leaned forward to follow Blankenship's finger pointing out entries in the log. "This morning Danny Boy comes outside the White House at ten minutes after nine. Spotted by Bulldog One. Nine-ten is normal; he's been leaving for work every day around nine-fifteen, give or take a few minutes. But this morning he doesn't leave. According to Bulldog One, he turns around and goes right back into the White House. He comes out again almost an hour later. That means he just didn't forget something—right? Okay . . . he gets a cab. Here it is: at almost ten a.m. Bulldog Two tails him. But he doesn't go right to the Factory. His cab goes around and around Central Park for almost forty-five minutes. What a meter tab he must have had! Then, finally, he gets to his office. It's close to eleven o'clock when Stryker calls to clock him in, almost two hours late. Captain, I realize this all might be a lot of crap.

487

After all, it's the day after Christmas, and Danny Boy might just be unwinding. But I thought you better know."

"Glad you did," Delaney nodded thoughtfully. "Glad you did. It's interesting."

"All right, now come over here and listen to this. It's a tape from Stryker, recorded about a half-hour ago. I wasn't here then so I couldn't talk to him. He asked the operator to put it on tape for me. Spin it, will you, Al?"

One of the operators at the telephone table started his deck recorder. The other men in the room quieted to listen to the tape.

"Ronnie, this is Stryker, at the Factory. How you doing? Ronnie, I just came back from lunch with the cunt I been pushing down here. A little bony, but a wild piece. At lunch I got the talk around to Danny Boy. He was almost two hours late getting to work. This cunt of mine—she's the outside receptionist in Danny Boy's department—she told me that just before I met her for lunch, she was in the ladies' john talking to Mrs. Cleek. That's C-l-e-e-k. She's Danny Boy's personal secretary. A widow. First name Martha or Margaret. White, female, middle thirties, five-three, one-ten or thereabouts, dark brown hair, fair complexion, no visible scars, wears glasses all the time. Well, anyway, in the can, this Mrs. Cleek tells my cunt that Danny Boy was acting real queer this morning. Wouldn't dictate or sign any letters. Wouldn't read anything. Wouldn't even answer any important phone calls. Probably a sack of shit, Ronnie—but I figured I better report it. If you think it's important, I can cozy up to this Cleek dame and see what else I can find out. No problem; she's hungry I can tell. Nice ass. Let me know if you want me to follow up on this. Stryker at the Factory, off."

There was silence in the radio room after the tape was stopped. Then someone laughed. "That Stryker," someone said softly, "all he thinks about is pussy."

"Maybe," Captain Delaney said coldly, speaking to no one man, speaking to them all, "but he's doing a good job." He turned to Blankenship. "Call Stryker. Tell him to cozy up to the Cleek woman and keep us informed—of anything."

"Will do, Captain."

Delaney walked slowly back into his study, heavy head bowed, hands shoved into his hip pockets. The altered Time-Habit Pattern and Danny Boy's strange behavior in his office: the best news he'd had all day. It might be working. It just might be working.

488

He searched for the sheet of yellow paper on which he had jotted his nine-point plan. It wasn't in his locked top desk drawer. It wasn't in the file. Where was it? His memory was really getting bad. He finally found the plan under his desk blotter, alongside the plus-minus list he used to evaluate the performance of men under his command. Before looking at the plan, he added the name of Stryker to the plus column of the performance list.

Peering at the plan closely through his reading glasses, he checked off the first six items: Garage attendant, Parrot bartender, Lipsky, the Mortons at Erotica, Visit to Factory, Lombard Christmas Eve call to Blank. The seventh item was: "Monica's call to Blank." He sat back in his swivel chair, stared at the ceiling, tried to think out the best way to handle *that*.

He was still pondering his options—what *he* would say and what *she* would say—when the outside guard knocked on his study door and didn't enter until he heard Delaney's shouted, "Come in!" The officer said a reporter named Thomas Handry was on the sidewalk and claimed he had an appointment with the Captain.

"Sure," Delaney nodded. "Let him in. Tell the man at the desk to make certain he's logged in and out."

He went into the kitchen for some ice cubes. When he came back Handry was standing in front of the desk.

"Thanks for coming," Delaney smiled genially. "I had it marked down: 'Day after Christmas; Handry interviews Blank.' "

Handry sat in the leather club chair, then rose immediately, took two folded sheets from his inside breast pocket, tossed them onto Delaney's desk.

"Background stuff on this guy," he said, slumping back into his soft chair. "His job, views on the importance of the computer in industry, biography, personal life. But I imagine you've got all this by now."

The Captain took a quick look at the two typed pages. "Got most of it," he acknowledged. "But you've got a few things here we'll follow up on—a few leads."

"So my interview was just wasted time?"

"Oh Handry," Delaney sighed. "At the time I asked you to do this, I was on my own. I had no idea I'd be back on active duty with enough dicks to run all this down. Besides, all this background shit isn't so important. I told you that at the restaurant. I wanted your personal impressions of the man. You're sensitive, intelligent. Since I couldn't interview him myself, I wanted you to meet him and tell me what your reactions were. That *is* important. Now give me the whole thing, how it went, what you said and what he said."

Thomas Handry took a deep breath, blew it out. Then he began talking. Delaney never interrupted once, but leaned forward, cupping one ear, the better to hear Handry's low-voiced recital.

The newspaperman's report was fluid and concise. He had arrived precisely at 1:30 p.m., the time previously arranged for the interview by Javis-Bircham's Director of Public Relations. But Blank had kept him waiting almost a half-hour. It was only after two requests to Blank's secretary that Handry had been allowed into the inner office.

Daniel G. Blank had been polite, but cold and withdrawn. Also, somewhat suspicious. He had asked to inspect Handry's press card—an odd act for a business executive giving an interview arranged by his own PR man. But Blank had spoken lucidly and at length about the role played by AMROK II in the activities of Javis-Bircham. About his personal background, he had been cautious, uncommunicative, and frequently asked Handry what his questions had to do with the interview in progress. As far as the reporter could determine, Blank was divorced, had no children, had no plans to marry again. He lived a bachelor's life, found it enjoyable, had no ambitions other than to serve J-B as best he might.

"Very pretty," Delaney nodded. "You said he was 'withdrawn.' Your word. What did you mean by that?"

"Were you in the military, Captain?"

"Yes. Five years U.S. Army."

"I did four with the Marines. You know the expression 'a thousand-yard stare'?"

"Oh yes. On the range. For an unfocussed vision."

"Right. That's what Blank has. Or had a few hours ago during the interview. He was looking at me, in me, through me, and somewhere beyond. I don't know what the hell he was focussing on. Most of these high-pressure business executives are all teeth, hearty handshake, sincere smile, focussing between your eyes, over the bridge of your nose, so it looks like they're returning your stare frankly, without blinking. But this guy was gone somewhere, off somewhere. I don't know where the hell he was."

490

"Good, good," Delaney muttered, taking quick notes. "Anything else? Physical peculiarities? Habits? Bite his nails?"

"No . . . But he wears a wig. Did you know that?"

"No," the Captain said in apparent astonishment. "A wig? He's only in his middle-thirties. Are you sure?"

"Positive," Handry said, enjoying the surprise. "It wasn't even on straight. And he didn't give a goddamn if I knew. He kept poking a finger up under the edge of the rug and scratching his scalp. Anything?"

"Mmm. Maybe. How was he dressed?"

" 'Conservative elegance' is the phrase. Black suit well-cut. White shirt, starched collar. Striped tie. Black shoes with a dull gloss, not shiny."

"You'd make a hell of a detective."

"You told me that before."

"Smell any booze on his breath?"

"No. But a high-powered cologne or after-shave lotion."

"That figures. Scratch his balls?"

"*What?*"

"Did he play with himself?"

"Jesus, no! Captain, you're wild."

"Yes. Did he look drawn, thin, emaciated? Like he hasn't been eating well lately?"

"Not that I could see. Well . . ."

"What?" Delaney demanded quickly.

"Shadows under his eyes. Puffy bags. Like he hasn't been sleeping so well lately. But all the rest of his face was tight. He's really a good-looking guy. And his handshake was firm and dry. He looked to be in good physical shape. Just before I left, when we were both standing, he handed me a promotion booklet Javis-Bircham got out on AMROK II. It slipped out of my hand. It was my fault; I dropped it. But Blank stooped and caught it before it hit the floor. The guy's quick."

"Oh yes," Delaney nodded grimly, "he's quick. All right, this is all interesting and valuable. Now tell me what you think about him, what you *feel* about him."

"A drink?"

"Of course. Help yourself."

"Well . . ." Thomas Handry said, pouring Scotch over ice cubes, "he's a puzzle. He's not one thing and he's not another. He's a between-man, going from A to B. Or maybe from A to Z. I guess that doesn't make much sense."

"Go on."

"He's just not *with* it. He's not *there*. The impression I got was of a guy floating. He's out there somewhere. Who the hell knows where? That thousand-yard stare. And it was obvious he couldn't care less about Javis-Bircham and AMROK II. He was just going through the motions; a published interview couldn't interest him less. I don't know what's on his mind. He's lost and floating, like I said. Captain, the guy's a balloon! He's got no anchor. He puzzles me and he interests me. I can't solve him." A long pause. "Can you?"

"Getting there," Captain Delaney said slowly. "Just beginning to get there."

There was a lengthy silence, while Handry sipped his drink and Delaney stared at a damp spot on the opposing wall.

"It's him, isn't it?" Handry said finally. "No doubt about it."

Delaney sighed. "That's right. It's him. No doubt about it."

"Okay," the reporter said, surprisingly chipper. He drained his glass, rose, walked toward the hallway door. Then, knob in hand, he turned to stare at the Captain. "I want to be in on the kill," he stated flatly.

"All right."

Handry nodded, turned away, then turned back again. "Oh," he said nonchalantly, "one more thing . . . I got a sample of his handwriting."

He marched back to Delaney's desk, tossed a photo onto the blotter. Delaney picked it up slowly, stared. Daniel G. Blank: a copy of the photo taken from the "Fink File," the same photo that was now copied in the hundreds and in the hands of every man assigned to Operation Lombard. Delaney turned it over. On the back, written with a felt-tipped pen, was: "With all best wishes. Daniel G. Blank."

"How did you get this?"

"The ego-trip. I told him I kept a scrapbook of photos and autographs of famous people I interviewed. He went for it."

"Beautiful. Thank you for your help."

After Handry left, Delaney kept staring at that inscription: "With all best wishes. Daniel G. Blank." He rubbed his fingers lightly over the signature. It seemed to bring him closer to the man.

He was still staring at the handwriting, trying to see beyond it, when Detective sergeant Thomas MacDonald came in sideways, slipping his bulk neatly through the hallway door, left partly open by Handry.

The black moved a step into the study, then stopped.

"Interrupting you, Captain?"

"No, no. Come on in. What's up?"

The short, squat detective came over to Delaney's desk.

"You wanted a photo of Roger Kope, the cop who got wasted. Will this do?"

He handed Delaney a crisp white cardboard folder, opening sideways. On the front it said, in gold script, "Holiday Greetings." Inside, on the left, in the same gold script, it read: "From the Kope Family." On the right side was pasted a color photo of Roger Kope, his wife, three little children. They were posed, grinning self-consciously, before a decorated Christmas tree. The dead detective had his arm about his wife's shoulders. It wasn't a good photo: obviously an amateur job taken a year ago and poorly copied. The colors were washed out, the face of one of the children was blurred. But they were all there.

"It was all we could get," MacDonald said tonelessly. "They had about a hundred made up a month ago, but I guess Mrs. Kope won't send them this year. Will it do?"

"Yes," Delaney nodded. "Just fine." Then, as MacDonald turned to go, he said, "Sergeant, a couple of other things . . . Who's the best handwriting man in the Department?"

MacDonald thought a moment, his sculpted features calm, carved: a Congo mask or a Picasso sketch. "Handwriting," he repeated. "That would be Willow, William T., Detective lieutenant. He works out of a broom-closet office downtown."

"Ever have any dealings with him?"

"About two years ago. It was a forged lottery ticket ring. He's a nice guy. Prickly, but okay. He sure knows his stuff."

"Could you get him up here? No rush. Whenever he can make it."

"I'll give him a call."

"Good. The next day or so will be fine."

"All right, Captain. What's the other thing?"

"What?"

"You said you had a couple of things."

"Oh. Yes. Who's controlling the men on the tap on Danny Boy's home phone?"

"I am, Captain. Fernandez set it up; technically they're his boys. But he asked me to take over. He's got enough on his plate. Besides, these guys are just sitting on their ass. They've come up with zilch. Danny Boy makes one or two calls a week, usually to the Princess in the Castle. Maybe to the Mortons. And he gets fewer calls. So far it's nothing."

"Uh-huh," Delaney nodded. "Listen, sergeant, would it be

possible to make some clicks or buzzes the next time Danny Boy makes or gets a call?"

MacDonald picked up on it instantly. "So he thinks or knows his phone is tapped?"

"Right."

"Sure. No sweat; we could do that. Clicks, buzzes, hisses, an echo—something. He'll get the idea."

"Fine."

MacDonald stared at him a long time, putting things together. Finally: "Spooking him, Captain?" he asked softly.

Captain Delaney put his hands, palms down on his desk blotter, lowered his massive head to stare at them.

"Not spooking," he said in a gentle voice. "I mean to split him. To crack him open. Wide. Until he's in pieces and bleeding. And it's working. I know it is. Sergeant, how do *you* know when you're close?"

"My mouth goes dry."

Delaney nodded. "My armpits begin to sweat something awful. Right now they're dripping like old faucets. I'm going to push this guy right over the edge, right off, and watch him fall."

MacDonald's smooth expression didn't change. "You figure he'll suicide, Captain?"

"Will he suicide . . ." Delaney said thoughtfully. Suddenly, that moment, something began that he had been hoping for. *He* was Daniel G. Blank, penetrating deep into the man, smoothing his body with perfumed oils, dribbling on scented powders, wearing silk bikini underwear and a fashionable wig, living in sterile loneliness, fucking a boy-shaped woman, buggering a real boy, and venturing out at night to find loves who would help him to break out, to feel, to discover what he was, and meaning.

"Suicide?" Delaney repeated, so quietly that MacDonald could hardly hear him. "No. Not by gunshot, pills, or defenestration." He smiled slightly when he pronounced the last word, knowing the sergeant would pick up the mild humor. Defenestration: throwing yourself out a window to smash to jelly on the concrete below. "No, he won't suicide, no matter how hard the pressure. Not his style. He likes risk. He climbs mountains. He's at his best when he's in danger. It's like champagne."

"Then what will he do, Captain?"

"I'm going to run," Delaney said in a strange, pleading voice. "I've *got* to run."

3

The second day after Christmas, Daniel Blank decided the worst thing—the *worst* thing—was committing these irrational acts, and *knowing* they were irrational, and not being able to stop.

For instance, this morning, completely unable to get to work at his usual hour, he sat stiffly in his living room, dressed for a normal day at Javis-Bircham. And between 9:00 and 11:00 a.m., he rose from his chair at least three times to check the locks and bolts on the front door. They were fastened—he *knew* they were fastened—but he had to check. Three times.

Then suddenly he darted through the apartment, flinging open closet doors, thrusting an arm between hanging clothes. No one there. He knew it was wrong to be acting the way he was.

He mixed a drink, a morning drink, thinking it might help. He picked up a knife to slice a wedge of lime, looked at the blade, let it clatter into the sink. No temptation there, none, but he didn't want the thing in his hand. He might reach up to wipe his eyes and . . .

What about the sandals? That was odd. He owned a pair of leather strap-sandals, custom-made. He still remembered the shop in Greenwich Village, the cool hands of the young Chinese girl tracing his bare feet on a sheet of white paper. He frequently wore the sandals at night, when he was home alone. The straps were loose enough so that he could slip the sandals onto his feet without unbuckling and buckling. He had been doing it for years. But this morning the straps had been unbuckled, the sandals there beside his bed with straps flapping wide. Who had done that?

And time—what was happening to his sense of time? He thought ten minutes had elapsed, but it turned out to be an hour. He guessed an hour, and it was 20 minutes. What was happening?

And what was happening to his penis? It was his imagination, of course, but it seemed to be shrinking, withdrawing into his scrotum. Ridiculous. And he no longer had his regular bowel movement a half-hour after he awoke. He felt stuffed and blocked.

Other things . . . Little things . . .

Going from one room to another and, when he got there, forgetting why he had made the trip.

Hearing a phone ring on a television program and leaping up to answer his own phone.

Finally, when he got to the office, things didn't go well at all. Not that he couldn't have handled it; he was thinking logically, he was lucid. But what was the point?

Near noon, Mrs. Cleek came in and found him weeping at his desk, head bent forward, palms gripping his temples. Her eyes blurred immediately with sympathy.

"Mr. Blank," she said, "what *is* it?"

"I'm sorry," he gasped, and then, saying the first thing that came into his mind: "A death in the family."

What caused his tears was this: do mad people know they are mad? That is, do they know they are acting abnormally but cannot help it? That was why he wept.

"Oh," Mrs. Cleek mourned, "I'm so sorry."

He got home, finally. He was as proud as a drunk who walks out of a bar without upsetting anything, steadfast, steps slowly through the doorway without brushing the frame, follows a sidewalk seam slowly and carefully homeward, never wavering.

It was early in the evening. Was it 6:00 p.m.? It might be eight. He didn't want to look at his watch bracelet. He wasn't sure he could trust it. Perhaps it might not be his own faulty time sense; it might be his wristwatch running wild. Or time itself running wild.

He picked up his phone. There was a curious, empty echo before he got a dial tone. He heard it ring. Someone picked up the phone. Then Blank heard two sharp clicks.

"Mith Montforth rethidenth," he heard Valenter say.

"This is Daniel Blank. Is Miss Montfort in?"

"Yeth, thir. I'll call—"

But then Daniel Blank heard a few more soft clicks, a strange hissing on the line. He hung up abruptly. Jesus! He should have known. He left the apartment immediately. What time *was* it? It didn't matter.

"He's tapping my phone," he said to Celia indignantly. "I definitely heard it. Definitely."

They were in that tainted room at the top of the house; city sounds came faintly. He told her he had followed her advice, had opened his mind to instinct, to all the primitive fears and passions that had come flooding in. He told her how he had been acting, the irrational fits and starts of his daily activities, and he told about the clicks, hisses, and echo on the phone when he had called her.

"Do you think I'm going mad?" he demanded.

"No," she said slowly, almost judiciously, "I don't think so. I think that in the time I have known you, you have been moving from the man you were to the man you are to be. What that is, I don't believe either of us know for sure. But it's understandable that this growth should be painful, perhaps even frightening. You're leaving everything familiar behind you and setting out on a journey, a search, a climb, that's leading . . . somewhere. Forget for a moment the man who has been following you and the phone call you received. These pains and dislocations have nothing to do with that. Dan, you're being born again, and you're feeling all the anguish of birth, being yanked from the safety of a warm womb into a foreign world. The wonder is that you've endured it as well as you have."

As usual, her flood of murmured words soothed and assured him; he felt as relaxed as if she was stroking his brow. She *did* make sense; it *was* true that he had changed since he met her, and was changing. The murders were part of it, of course—she was wrong to deny that—but they were not the cause but just one effect of the monumental upheaval inside him, something hot and bubbling there thrusting to the surface.

They made love slowly then, with more tenderness than passion, more sweetness than joy. In the eerie light of that single orange bulb he leaned close to see her for the first time, microscopically.

Her nipples, under his tongue's urging, engorged and, peering close, he saw the flattened tops with ravines and gorges, tiny, tiny, a topographic map. And threaded through the small breasts a network of bluish veins, tangled as a silken skein.

Along the line of curved hip sprouted a Lilliputian wheatfield of surprisingly golden hairs, and more at the dimpled small of her back. These tender sprouts tickled dry and dusty on his tongue. The convoluted navel returned his stare in a lascivious wink. Inside, prying, he found a sharp bitterness that tingled.

Far up beneath her long hair, at nape of neck, was swamp dampness and scent of pond lilies. He stared at flesh of leg and groin, so close his eyelashes brushed and she made a small sound. There was hard, shiny skin on her soles, a crumbling softness between her toes. It all became clear to him, and dear, and sad.

They fenced with tongues—thrust, parry, cut—and then he was tasting creamy wax from her ear and in her armpits a sweet liquor that bit and melted on his lips like snow. Behind her knees more blue veins meandered, close to a skin that felt like suede and twitched faintly when he touched.

He spread her buttocks; the rosebud glared at him, withdrawing and expanding—a time-motion film of a flower reacting to light and darkness. He put his erect penis in her soft palm, slowly guided her fingers to stroke, circle, gently probe the opening, their hands clasped so they might share. He touched his lips to her closed eyes, thought he might suck them out and gulp them down like oysters, seasoned with her tears.

"I want you inside me," she said suddenly, lay on her back, spread her knees wide, guided his cock up into her. She wrapped arms and legs about him and moaned softly, as if they were making love for the first time.

But there was no love. Only a sweetness so sad it was almost unendurable. Even as they fucked he knew it was the sadness of departure; they would never fuck again; both knew it.

She was quickly slick, inside and out; they grappled to hold tight. He spurted with a series of great, painful lunges and, stunned, he continued to make the motions long after he was drained and surfeited. He could not stop his spasm, had no desire to, and felt her come again.

She looked at him through half-opened eyes, glazed; he thought she felt what he did: the defeat of departure. In that moment he knew she had told. She had betrayed him.

But he smiled, smiled, smiled, kissed her closed mouth, went home early. He took a cab because the darkness frightened him.

If it was a day of departure and defeat for Daniel Blank, it was a day of arrival and triumph for Captain Edward X. Delaney. He dared not feel confident, lest he put the whammy on it, but it did seem to be coming together.

Paper work in the morning: requisitions, reports, vouchers— the whole schmear. Then over to the hospital to sit awhile with Barbara, reading to her from "Honey Bunch: Her First Little Garden." Then he treated himself to a decent meal in one of those west side French restaurants: *coq au vin* with a half-bottle of a heavy burgundy to help it along. He paid his bill and then, on the way out, stopped at the bar for a Kirsch. He felt good.

It was good; everything was good. He had no sooner returned

to his home when Blankenship came in to display Danny Boy's Time-Habit Pattern. It was very erratic indeed: Arrived at the Factory at 11:30 a.m. Skipped lunch completely. Took a long zigzag walk along the docks. Sat on a wharf for almost an hour —"Just watching the turds float by" according to the man tailing him. Report from Stryker: He had taken Mrs. Cleek to lunch, and she told him she had found Danny Boy weeping in his office, and he had told her there had been a death in the family. Danny Boy returned to the White House at 2:03 p.m.

"Fine," the Captain nodded, handing the log back to Blankenship. "Keep at it. Is Fernandez on?"

"Comes on at four, Captain."

"Ask him to stop by to see me, will you?"

After Blankenship left, Delaney closed all the doors to his study, paced slowly around the room, head bowed. "A death in the family." That was nice. He paused to call Monica Gilbert and ask if he could come over to see her that evening. She invited him for dinner but he begged off; they arranged that he would come over at 7:00 p.m. He told her it would only be for a few minutes; she didn't ask the reason. Her girls were home from school during the holiday week so, she explained, she hadn't been able to visit Barbara as much as she wanted to, but would try to get there the following afternoon. He thanked her.

More pacing, figuring out options and possibilities. He walked into the radio room to tell Blankenship to requisition four more cars, two squads and two unmarked, and keep them parked on the street outside, two men in each. He didn't want to think of the increase in manpower that entailed, and went back into his study to resume his pacing. Was there anything he should have done that he had not? He couldn't think of anything, but he was certain there would be problems he hadn't considered. No help for that.

He took out his plan and, alongside the final three items, worked out a rough time schedule. He was still fiddling with it when Lt. Jeri Fernandez knocked and looked in.

"Want me, Captain?"

"Just for a minute, lieutenant. Won't take long. How's it going?"

"Okay. I got a feeling things are beginning to move. Don' ask me how I know. Just a feeling."

"I hope you're right. I've got another job for you. You'll have to draw more men. Get them from wherever you can. If you have any shit with their commanders, tell them to call me.

It's a woman—Monica Gilbert. Here's her address and telephone number. She's the widow of Bernard Gilbert, the second victim. There was a guard on her right after he was iced, so there may be a photo of her in the files and some Time-Habit reports. I want a twenty-four tap on her phone, two men in an unmarked car outside her house, and two uniformed men outside her apartment door. She's got two little girls. If she goes out with the girls, both the buttons stick with them, and I mean close. If she goes out alone, one man on her and one on the kids. Got all that?"

"Sure, Captain. A tight tail?"

"But I mean *tight*. Close enough to touch."

"You think Danny Boy'll try something?"

"No, I don't. But I want her and her children covered, around the clock. Can you set it up?"

"No sweat, Captain. I'll get on it right away."

"Good. Put your first men on at eight tonight. Not before."

Fernandez nodded. "Captain . . ."

"Yes?"

"The Luger's almost ready."

"Fine. Any problems?"

"Nope, not a one."

"You spending any money on this?"

"Money?" Fernandez looked at him incredulously. "What money? Some guys owed me some favors."

Delaney nodded. Fernandez opened the hallway door to depart, and there was a man standing there, his arm bent, knuckles raised, about to knock on the Captain's door.

"Captain Delaney?" the man asked Fernandez.

The lieutenant shook his head, jerked a thumb over his shoulder at the Captain, stepped around the newcomer and disappeared.

"I'm Captain Edward X. Delaney."

"My name is William T. Willow, Detective lieutenant. I believe you wanted to consult me."

"Oh yes," Delaney said, rising from his chair. "Please come in, lieutenant, and close the door behind you. Thank you for coming up. Please sit down over there. Sergeant MacDonald tells me you're the best man in your field."

"I agree," Willow said, with a sweet smile.

Delaney laughed. "How about a drink?" he asked. "Anything?"

"You don't happen to have a glass of sherry, do you, Captain?"

"Yes, I do. Medium dry. Will that be all right?"

"Excellent, thank you."

The Captain walked over to his liquor cabinet, and while he poured the drink, he inspected the handwriting expert. A queer bird. The skin and frame of a plucked chicken, and clad in a hairy tweed suit so heavy Delaney wondered how the man's frail shoulders could support it. On his lap was a plaid cap, and his shoes were over-the-ankle boots in a dark brown suede. Argyle socks, wool Tattersall shirt, woven linen tie secured with a horse's head clasp. Quite a sight.

But Willow's eyes were washed blue, lively and alert, and his movements, when he took the glass of sherry from Delaney, were crisp and steady.

"Your health, sir," the lieutenant said, raising his glass. He sipped. "Harvey's," he said.

"Yes."

"And very good, too. I would have been up sooner, Captain, but I've been in court."

"That's all right. No rush about this."

"What is it?"

Delaney searched in his top desk drawer, then handed Willow the photo Thomas Handry had delivered, with the inscription on the back: "With all best wishes. Daniel G. Blank."

"What can you tell me about the man who wrote this?"

Detective lieutenant William T. Willow didn't even glance at it. Instead, he looked at the Captain with astonishment.

"Oh dear," he said, "I'm afraid there's been a frightful misunderstanding. Captain, I'm a QD man, not a graphologist."

Pause.

"What's a QD man?" Delaney asked.

"Questioned Documents. All my work is with forgeries or suspected forgeries, comparing one specimen with another."

"I see. And what is a graphologist?"

"A man who allegedly is able to determine character, personality, and even physical and mental illness from a man's handwriting."

" 'Allegedly'," Delaney repeated. "I gather you don't agree with graphologists?"

"Let's just say I'm an agnostic on the matter," Willow smiled his sweet smile. "I don't agree and I don't disagree."

The Captain saw the sherry glass was empty. He rose to refill it, and left the bottle on the little table alongside Willow's elbow. Then the Captain sat down behind his desk again, regarded the other man gravely.

"But you're familiar with the theories and practice of graphology?"

"Oh my yes, Captain. I read everything on the subject of handwriting analysis, from whatever source, good and bad."

Delaney nodded, laced his fingers across his stomach, leaned back in his swivel chair.

"Lieutenant Willow," he said dreamily, "I am going to ask a very special favor of you. I am going to ask you to pretend you are a graphologist and not a QD man. I am going to ask you to inspect this specimen of handwriting and analyze it as a graphologist would. What I want is your opinion. I do not want a signed statement from you. You will not be called upon to testify. This is completely unofficial. I just want to know what you think—putting yourself in the place of a graphologist, of course. It will go no further than this room."

"Of course," Willow said promptly. "Delighted."

From an inner pocket he whipped out an unusual pair of glasses: prescription spectacles with an additional pair of magnifying glasses hinged to the top edge. The lieutenant shoved on the glasses, flipped down the extra lenses. He held the Daniel Blank inscription so close it was almost touching his nose.

"Felt-tipped pen," he said immediately. "Too bad. You lose the nuances. Mmm. Uh-huh. Mmm. Interesting, very interesting. Captain, does this man suffer from constipation?"

"I have no idea," Delaney said.

"Oh, my, look at this," Willow said, still peering closely at Blank's handwriting. "Would you believe . . . Sick, sick, sick. And this . . . Beautiful capitals, just beautiful." He looked up at the Captain. "He grew up in a small town in middle America —Ohio, Indiana, Iowa—around there?"

"Yes."

"He's about forty, or older?"

"Middle-thirties."

"Well . . . yes, that could be. Palmer Method. They still teach it in some schools. Goodness, look at that. This *is* interesting."

Suddenly he jerked off his glasses, tucked them away, half-rose to his feet to flip the photo of Blank onto Delaney's desk, then settled back to pour himself another glass of sherry.

"Schizoid," he said, beginning to speak rapidly. "On one side, artistic, sensitive, imaginative, gentle, perceptive, outgoing, striving, sympathetic, generous. The capitals are works of art. Flowing. Just blooming. On the other side, lower case now, tight, very cold, perfectly aligned: the mechanical mind, ordered, disciplined, ruthless, without emotion, inhuman, dead. It's very difficult to reconcile."

"Yes," Delaney said. "Is the man insane?"

"No. But he's breaking up."

"Why do you say that?"

"His handwriting is breaking up. Even with the felt-tipped pen you can see it. The connections between letters are faint. Between some there are no connections at all. And in his signature, that should be the most fluid and assured of anyone's handwriting, he's beginning to waver. He doesn't know who he is."

"Thank you very much, Lieutenant Willow," Captain Delaney said genially. "Please stay and finish your drink. Tell me more about handwriting analysis—from a graphologist's point of view, of course. It sounds fascinating."

"Oh yes," the bird-man said, "it is."

Later that evening Delaney went into the living room to inspect the log. Danny Boy had returned to the White House at 2:03 p.m. At 5:28 p.m., he had called the Princess in the Castle, hung up abruptly after speaking only a few minutes and then, at 5:47 p.m., had taken a cab to the Castle. He was still inside as of that moment, reported by Bulldog Three.

Delaney went over to the telephone desk.

"Did you get a tape of Danny Boy's call to the Castle at five twenty-eight?"

"Yes, sir. The man on the tap gave it to us over the phone. Spin it?"

"Please."

He listened to Daniel Blank talking to the lisping Valenter. He heard the clicks, hisses, and echo they were feeding onto the tapped line. He smiled when Blank slammed down his phone in the middle of the conversation.

"Perfect," Delaney said to no one in particular.

He had planned his meeting with Monica Gilbert with his usual meticulous attention to detail, even to the extent of deciding to keep on his overcoat. It would make her think he could only stay a moment, he was rushed, working hard to convict her husband's killer.

But when he arrived at 7:00 p.m., the children were still awake, but in their nightgowns, and he had to play with them, inspect their Christmas gifts, accept a cup of coffee. The atmosphere was relaxed, warm, pleasant, domestic—all wrong for his

503

purpose. He was glad when Monica packed the girls off to bed.

Delaney went back to the living room, sat down on the couch, took out the single sheet of paper he had prepared, with the speech he wanted her to deliver.

She came in, looking at him anxiously.

"What is it, Edward? You seem—well, tense."

"The killer is Daniel Blank. There's no doubt about it. He killed your husband, and Lombard, Kope, and Feinberg. He's a psycho, a crazy."

"When are you going to arrest him?"

"I'm not going to arrest him. There's no evidence I can take into court. He'd walk away a free man an hour after I collared him."

"I can't believe it."

"It's true. We're watching him, every minute, and maybe we can prevent another killing or catch him in the act. But I can't take the chance."

Then he told her of what he had been doing to smash Daniel Blank. When he described the Christmas Eve call as Frank Lombard, her face went white.

"Edward, you didn't." she gasped.

"Oh yes. I did. And it worked. The man is breaking apart. I know he is. A couple of more days, if I keep the pressure on, he's going to crack wide open. Now here's what I want you to do."

He handed her the sheet of dialogue he had written out. "I want you to call him, now, at his home, identify yourself and ask him why he killed your husband."

She looked at him with shock and horror. "Edward," she choked, "I can't do that."

"Sure you can," he urged softly. "It's just a few words. I've got them all written down for you. All you've got to do is read them. I'll be right here when you call. I'll even hold your hand, if you want me to. It'll just take a minute or so. Then it'll all be over. You can do it."

"I can't, I *can't!*" She turned her head away, put her hands to her face. "Please don't ask me to," she said, her voice muffled. "Please don't. Please."

"He murdered your husband," he said stonily.

"But even if—"

"And three other innocent strangers. Cracked their skulls with his trusty little ice ax and left them on the sidewalk with their brains spilling out."

"Edward, please . . ."

504

"You're the woman who wanted revenge, aren't you? 'Vengeance,' you said. 'I'll do anything to help,' you said. 'Type, run errands, make coffee.' That's what you told me. A few words is all I want, spoken on the phone to the man who slaughtered your husband."

"He'll come after me. He'll hurt the children."

"No. He doesn't hurt women and children. Besides, you'll be tightly guarded. He couldn't get close even if he tried. But he won't. Monica? Will you do it?"

"Why me? Why must I do it? Can't you get a policewoman—"

"To call him and say it's you? That wouldn't lessen any possible danger to you and the girls. And I don't want any more people in the Department to know about this."

She shook her head, knuckles clenched to her mouth. Her eyes were wet.

"Anything but this," she said faintly. "I just can't do it. I *can't*."

He stood, looked down at her, his face pulled into an ugly smile.

"Leave it to the cops, eh?" he said in a voice he scarcely recognized as his own. "Leave it to the cops to clean up the world's shit, and vomit, and blood. Keep your own hands clean. Leave it all to the cops. Just so long as you don't know what they're doing."

"Edward, it's so cruel. Can't you see that? What you're doing is worse than what he did. He killed because he's sick and can't help himself. But you're killing him slowly and deliberately, knowing exactly what you're doing, everything planned and—"

Suddenly he was sitting close beside her, an arm about her shoulders, his lips at her ear.

"Listen," he whispered, "your husband was Jewish and you're Jewish—right? And Feinberg, the last guy he chilled, was a Jew. Four victims; two Jews. Fifty percent. You want this guy running loose, killing more of your people? You want—"

She jerked away from under his arm, swung from the waist, and slapped his face, an open-handed smack that knocked his head aside and made him blink.

"Despicable!" she spat at him. "The most despicable man I've ever met!"

He stood suddenly, looming over her.

"Oh yes," he said, tasting the bile bubbling up. "Despicable.

Oh yes. But Blank, he's a poor, sick lad—right? Right? Smashed your husband's skull in, but it's Be Nice to Blank Week. Right? Let me tell you—let me tell you—" He was stuttering now in his passion to get it out. "He's dead. You understand that? Daniel G. Blank is a dead man. Right now. You think—you think I'm going to let him walk away from this just because the law . . . You think I'm going to shrug, turn away, and give up? I tell you, he's *dead!* There's no way, *no* way, he can get away from me. If I have to blow his brains out with my service revolver at high noon on Fifth Avenue, I'll do it. Do it! And wait right there for them to come and take me away. I don't care. The man is *dead!* Can't you get that through your skull? If you won't help me, I'll do it another way. No matter what you do, it doesn't matter, doesn't matter. He's gone. He's just gone."

He stood there quivering with his anger, trying to draw deep breaths through his open mouth.

She looked up at him timidly. "What do you want me to say?" she asked in a small voice.

He sat beside her on the couch, holding her free hand, his ear pressed close to the phone she held so he could overhear the conversation. The script he had composed lay on her lap.

Blank's phone rang seven times before he picked it up.

"Hello?" he said cautiously.

"Daniel Blank?" Monica asked, reading her lines. There was a slight quaver in her voice.

"Yes. Who is this?"

"My name is Monica Gilbert. I'm the widow of Bernard Gilbert. Mr. Blank, why did you kill Bernie? My children and I want—"

But she was interrupted by a wild scream, a cry of panic and despair that frightened both of them. It came wailing over the wire, loud enough to be painful in their ears, shrill enough to pierce into their hearts and souls and set them quivering. Then there was the heavy bumping of a dropped phone, a thick clatter.

Delaney took the phone from Monica's trembling hand, hung it up gently. He stood, buttoned his overcoat, reached for his hat.

"Fine," he said softly. "You did just fine."

She looked at him.

"You're a dreadful man," she whispered. "The most dreadful man I've ever met."

"Am I?" he asked. "Dreadful and despicable, all in one evening. Well . . . I'm a cop."

"I never want to see you again, ever."

"All right," he said, saddened. "Good-night, and thank you."

There were two uniformed men outside her apartment door. He showed them his identification, made certain they had their orders straight. Both had been given copies of Daniel Blank's photo. Outside the house, two plainclothesmen sat in an unmarked car. One of them recognized Delaney, raised a hand in greeting. Fernandez had done an efficient job; he was good on this kind of thing.

The Captain shoved his hands into his overcoat pockets and, trying not to think of what he had done to Monica Gilbert, walked resolutely over to Blank's apartment house and into the lobby. Thank God Lipsky wasn't on duty.

"I have a letter for Daniel Blank," he told the doorman. "Could you put it in his box? No rush. If he gets it tomorrow, it'll be okay."

Delaney gave him two quarters and handed over the Holiday Greetings from Roger Kope and Family, sealed in a white envelope addressed to Mr. Daniel G. Blank.

4

After that call from Monica Gilbert, Daniel Blank had dropped the phone and gone trotting through the rooms of his apartment, mouth open, scream caught in his throat; he could not end it. Finally, it dribbled away to moans, heaves, gulps, coughs, tears. Then he was in the bedroom, forehead against the full-length mirror, staring at his strange, contorted face, torn apart.

When he quieted, fearful that his shriek had been heard by neighbors, he went directly to the bedroom phone extension, intending to call Celia Montfort and ask one question: "Why did you betray me?" But there was an odd-sounding dial tone, and he remembered he had dropped the living room handset. He hung up, went back into the living room, hung up that phone, too. He decided not to call Celia. What could she possibly say?

He had never felt such a sense of dissolution and, in self-preservation, undressed, checked window and door locks, turned out the lights and slid into bed naked. He rolled back and forth until silk sheet and wool blanket were wrapped about him tightly, mummifying him, holding him together.

He thought, his mind churning, that he might be awake forever, staring at the darkness and wondering. But curiously, he fell asleep almost instantly: a deep, dreamless slumber, more coma than sleep, heavy and depressing. He awoke at 7:18 a.m. the next morning, sodden with weariness. His eyelids were stuck shut; he realized he had wept during the night.

But the panic of the previous day had been replaced by a lethargy, a non-thinking state. Even after going through the motions of bathing, shaving, dressing, breakfasting, he found himself in a thoughtless world, as if his overworked brain had said, "All right! Enough already!" and doughtily rejected all fears, hopes, passions, visions, ardors. Even his body was subdued; his pulse seemed to beat patiently at a reduced rate, his limbs were slack. Dressed for work, like an actor waiting for his cue, he sat quietly in his living room, staring at the mirrored wall, content merely to exist, breathing.

His phone rang twice, at an hour's interval, but he did not answer. It could be his office calling. Or Celia Montfort. Or . . . or anyone. But he did not answer, but sat rigidly in a kind of catalepsy, only his eyes wandering across his mirrored wall. He needed this time of peace, quiet, non-thinking. He might even have dozed off, there in his Eames chair, but it wasn't important.

He roused early in the afternoon, looked at his watch; it seemed to be 2:18 p.m. That was possible; he was willing to accept it. He thought vaguely that he should get out, take a walk, get some fresh air.

But he only got as far as the lobby. He walked past the locked mail boxes. The mail had been delivered, but he just didn't care. Late Christmas cards, probably. And bills. And . . . well, it wasn't worth thinking about. Had Gilda sent him a Christmas card this year? He couldn't remember. He hadn't sent her one; of that he was certain.

Charles Lipsky stopped him.

"Message for you, Mr. Blank," he said brightly. "In your box." And he stepped behind the counter.

Blank suddenly realized he hadn't given the doormen anything for Christmas, nor the garage attendant, nor his cleaning woman. Or had he? Had he bought a Christmas gift for Celia? He couldn't remember. Why did she betray him?

He looked at the plain white envelope Lipsky thrust into his hand. "Mr. Daniel G. Blank." That was his name. He knew

508

that. He suddenly realized he better not take that short walk—not right now. He'd never make it. He knew he'd never make it.

"Thank you," he said to Lipsky. That was a funny name—Lipsky. Then he turned around, took the elevator back up to his apartment, still moving in that slow, lethargic dream, his knees water, his body ready to melt into a dark, scummed puddle on the lobby carpet if an elevator didn't come soon. He took a deep breath. He'd make it.

When the door was bolted, he leaned back against it and slowly opened the white envelope. Holiday Greetings from the Kope Family. Ah well. Why had she betrayed him? What possible reason could she have, since everything he had done had been at her gentle urging and wise tutelage?

He went directly to the bedroom, took out the drawer, turned it upside down on the bed, scattering the contents. He ripped the sealed envelope free. The souvenirs had been a foolish mistake, he thought lazily, but no harm had been done. There they were. No one had taken them. No one had seen them.

He brought in a pair of heavy shears from the kitchen and chopped Lombard's license, Gilbert's ID card, Kope's identification and leatherette holder, and Feinberg's rose petals into small bits, cutting, cutting, cutting. Then he flushed the whole mess down the toilet, watching to make sure it disappeared, then flushing twice more.

That left only Detective third grade Roger Kope's shield. Blank sat on the edge of the bed, bouncing the metal on his palm, wondering dreamily how to get rid of it. He could drop it down the incinerator, but it might endure, charred but legible enough to start someone thinking. Throw it out the window? Ridiculous. Into the river would be best—but could he walk that far and risk someone seeing? The most obvious was best. He would put the shield in a small brown paper bag, walk no more than two blocks or so, and push it down into a corner litter basket. Picked up by the Sanitation Department, dumped into the back of one of those monster trucks, squashed in with coffee grounds and grape fruit rinds, and eventually disgorged onto a dump or landfill in Brooklyn. Perfect. He giggled softly.

He pulled on gloves, wiped the shield with an oily rag, then dropped it into a small brown paper bag. He put on his topcoat; the bag went into the righthand pocket. Through the lefthand pocket he carried his ice ax, beneath the coat, though for what reason he could not say.

He walked over to Third Avenue, turned south. He paused halfway down the block, spotting a litter basket on the next corner. He paused to look in a shop window, inspecting an horrendous display of canes, walkers, wheelchairs, prosthetic devices, trusses, pads and bandages, emergency oxygen bottles, do-it-yourself urinalysis kits. He turned casually away from the window and inspected the block. No uniformed cops. No squad cars or anything that looked like an unmarked police car. No one who could be a plainclothes detective. Just the usual detritus of a Manhattan street—housewives and executives, hippies and hookers, pushers and priests: the swarm of the city, swimming in the street current.

He walked quickly to the litter basket at the corner, took out the small brown paper bag with the shield of Detective Kope inside, thrust it down into the accumulated trash: brown paper bags just like his, discarded newspapers, a dead rat, all the raw garbage of a living city. He looked about quickly. No one was watching him; everyone was busy with his own agonies.

He turned and walked home quickly, smiling. The simplest and most obvious was best.

The phone was ringing when he entered his apartment. He let it ring, not answering. He hung away his topcoat, put the ice ax in its place. Then he mixed a lovely vodka martini, stirring endlessly to get it as chilled as possible and, humming, took it into the living room where he lay full-length upon the couch, balanced his drink on his chest, and wondered why she had betrayed him.

After awhile, after he had taken a few sips of his drink, still coming out of his trance, rising to the surface like something long drowned and hidden, rising on a tide or cannon shot or storm to show itself, the phone rang again. He got up immediately, set his drink carefully and steadily on the glass cocktail table, went into the kitchen and selected a knife, a razor-sharp seven-inch blade with a comfortable handle.

Strange, but knives didn't bother him anymore; they felt good. He walked back into the living room, almost prancing, stooped, and with his sharp, comfortable knife, sawed through the coiled cord holding the handset to the telephone body. He put the severed part gently aside, intestine dangling.

With that severance, he cut himself loose. He felt it. Free from events, the world, all reality.

Captain Delaney awoke with a feeling of nagging unease.

He fretted that he had neglected something, overlooked some obvious detail that would enable Danny Boy to escape the vigil, fly off to Europe, slide into anonymity in the city streets, or even murder once again. The Captain brooded over the organization of the guard, but could not see how the net could be drawn tighter.

But he was in a grumpy mood when he went down for breakfast. He drew a cup of coffee in the kitchen, wandered back through the radio room, dining room, hallways, and he did become aware of something. There were no night men sleeping on the cots in their underwear. Everyone was awake and dressed; even as he looked about, he saw three men strapping on their guns.

Most of the cops in Operation Lombard were detectives and carried the standard .38 Police Special. A few lucky ones had .357 Magnums or .45 automatics. Some men had two weapons. Some holstered on the hip; some in front, at the waist. One man carried an extra holster and a small .32 at his back. One man carried an even smaller .22 strapped to his calf, under his trouser leg.

Delaney had no objection to this display of unofficial hardware. A dick carried what gave him most comfort on a job in which the next opened door might mean death. The Captain knew some carried saps, brass knuckles, switch-blade knives. That was all right. They were entitled to anything that might give them that extra edge of confidence and see them through.

But what was unusual was to see them make these preparations now, as if they sensed their long watch was drawing to a close. Delaney could guess what they were thinking, what they were discussing in low voices, looking up at him nervously as he stalked by.

First of all, they were not unintelligent men; you were not promoted from patrolman to detective by passing a "stupid test." When Captain Delaney took over command of Operation Lombard, all their efforts were concentrated on Daniel G. Blank, with investigations of other suspects halted. The dicks realized the Captain knew something they didn't know: Danny Boy was their pigeon. Delaney was too old and experienced a cop to put his cock on the line if he wasn't sure, of that they were certain.

Then the word got around that he had requested the Kope photo. Then the telephone men heard the taped replay, from the man tapping Danny Boy's phone, of the phone call from Monica Gilbert. Then the special guard was placed on the Gilbert widow and her children. All that was chewed over in radio room and squad car, on lonely night watches and long hours of patrol. They knew now, or guessed, what he was up to. It was a wonder, Delaney realized, he had been able to keep it private as long as he had. Well, at least it was his responsibility. His alone. If it failed, no one else would suffer from it. If it failed . . .

There was no report of any activity by Danny Boy at 9:00 a.m., 9:15, 9:30, 9:45, 10:00. Early on, when the vigil was first established, they had discovered a back entrance to Blank's apartment house, a seldom-used service door that opened onto a walk leading to 82nd Street. An unmarked car, with one man, was positioned there, in full view of this back exit, with orders to report in every fifteen minutes. This unit was coded Bulldog 10, but was familiarly known as Ten-O. Now, as Delaney passed back and forth through the radio room, he heard the reports from Ten-O and from Bulldog One, the Con Ed van parked on the street in front of the White House.

10:15, nothing, 10:30, nothing. No report of Danny Boy at 10:45, 11:00, 11:15, 11:30. Shortly before 12:00, Delaney went into his study and called Blank's apartment. The phone rang and rang, but there was no answer. He hung up; he was worried.

He took a cab over to the hospital. Barbara seemed in a semi-comatose state and refused to eat her meal. So he sat helplessly alongside her bed, holding her limp hand, pondering his options if Blank didn't appear for the rest of the day.

It might be that he was up there, just not answering his phone. It might be that he had slipped through their net, was long gone. And it might be that he had slit his throat after receiving the Kope photo, and was up there all right, leaking blood all over his polished floor. Delaney had told Sergeant MacDonald that Danny Boy wouldn't suicide, but he was going by patterns, by percentages. No one knew better than he that percentages weren't certainties.

He got back to his brownstone a little after 1:00 p.m. Ten-O and Bulldog One had just reported in. No sign of Danny Boy. Delaney had Stryker called at the Factory. Blank hadn't arrived at the office. The Captain went back into his study and called Blank's apartment again. Again the phone rang and rang. No answer.

By this time, without intending to, he had communicated his mood to his men; now he wasn't the only one pacing through the rooms, hands in pockets, head lowered. The men, he noticed, were keeping their faces deliberately expressionless, but he knew they feared what he feared: the pigeon had flown.

By two o'clock he had worked out a contingency plan. If Danny Boy didn't show within another hour, at 3:00 p.m., he'd send a uniformed officer over to the White House with a trumped-up story that the Department had received an anonymous threat against Daniel Blank. The patrolman would go up to Blank's apartment with the doorman, and listen. If they heard Blank moving about, or if he answered his bell, they would say it was a mistake and come away. If they heard nothing, and if Blank didn't answer his bell, then the officer would request the doorman or manager to open Blank's apartment with the pass-keys "just to make certain everthing is all right."

It was a sleazy plan, the Captain acknowledged. There were a hundred holes in it; it might endanger the whole operation. But it was the best he could come up with; it had to be done. If Danny Boy was long gone, or dead, they couldn't sit around watching an empty hole. He'd order it at exactly 3:00 p.m.

He was in the radio room, and at 2:48 p.m. there was a burst of static from one of the radio speakers, then it cleared.

"Barbara from Bulldog One."

"Got you, Bulldog One."

"Fernandez," the voice said triumphantly. "Danny Boy just came out."

There was a sigh in the radio room; Captain Delaney realized part of it was his.

"What's he wearing?" he asked the radioman.

The operator started to repeat the question into his mike, but Fernandez had heard the Captain's loud voice.

"Black topcoat," he reported. "No hat. Hands in pockets. He's not waiting for a cab. Walking west. Looks like he's out for a stroll. I'll put Bulldog Three on him, far back, and two sneaks on foot. Officer LeMolle, designated Bulldog Twenty. Officer Sanchez, designated Bulldog Forty. Got that?"

"LeMolle is Bulldog Twenty, Sanchez is Forty."

"Right. You'll get radio checks from them as soon as possible. Danny Boy is nearing Second Avenue now, still heading west. I'm out."

Delaney stood next to the radio table. The other men in the room closed in, heads turned, ears to the loudspeaker.

Silence for almost five minutes. One man coughed, looked apologetically at the others.

Then, almost a whisper: "Barbara from Bulldog Twenty. Read me?"

"Soft but good, Twenty."

"Danny Boy between Second and Third on Eighty-third, heading west. Out." It was a woman's voice.

"Who's Lemolle?" Delaney asked Blankenship.

"Policewoman Martha LeMolle. Her cover is a housewife—shopping bag, the whole bit."

Delaney opened his mouth to speak, but the radio crackled again.

"Barbara from Bulldog Forty. Make me?"

"Yes, Forty. Good. Where is he?"

"Turning south on Third. Out."

Blankenship turned to Delaney without waiting for his question. "Forty is Detective second grade Ramon Sanchez. Dressed like an orthodox Jewish rabbi."

So when Daniel G. Blank deposited the brown paper bag in the litter basket, the housewife was less than twenty feet behind him and saw him do it, and the rabbi was across the avenue and saw him do it. They both shadowed Danny Boy back to his apartment house, but by the time he arrived they had both reported he had discarded something in a litter basket, they had given the exact location (northeast corner, Third and 82nd; and, at Delaney's command, Blankenship had an unmarked car on the way with orders to pick up the entire basket and bring it back to the brownstone. Delaney thought it might be the ice ax.

At least twenty men crowded into the kitchen when the two plainclothesmen carried in the garbage basket and set it on the linoleum.

"I always knew you'd end up in Sanitation, Tommy," someone called. There were a few nervous laughs.

"Empty it," Delaney ordered. "Slowly. Put the crap on the floor. Shake out every newspaper. Look into every bag."

The two detectives pulled on their gloves. They began to snake out the sodden packages, the neatly wrapped bags, the dead rat (handled by the tip of its tail), loose garbage, a blood-soaked towel. The stench filled the room, but no one left; they had all smelled worse odors than that.

It went slowly, for almost ten minutes, as bags were pulled out, emptied onto the floor, and tied packages were cut open and unrolled. Then one of the dicks reached in, came out with a small brown paper bag, opened it, looked inside.

"Jesus Christ!"

The waiting men said nothing, but there was a tightening of the circle; Captain Delaney felt himself pressed closer until his

514

thighs were tight against the kitchen table. Holding the bag by the bottom, the detective slowly slid the contents out onto the tabletop. Cop's shield.

There was something: a collective moan, a gasp, something of anguish and fear. The men peered closer.

"That's Kope's tin," someone cried, voice crackling with fury. "I worked with him. That's Kope's number. I know it."

Someone said: "Oh, that dirty cocksucker."

Someone said, over and over: "Motherfucker, motherfucker, motherfucker . . ."

Someone said: "Let's get him right now. Let's waste him."

Delaney had been bending over, staring at the buzzer. It wasn't hard to imagine what had happened: Daniel G. Blank had destroyed the evidence, the ID cards and rose petals flushed down the toilet or thrown into the incinerator. But this was good metal, so he figured he better ditch it. Not smart, Danny Boy.

"Let's waste him," someone repeated, in a louder voice.

And here was another problem, one he had hoped to avoid by keeping his knowledge of Daniel Blank's definite guilt to himself. He knew that when a cop was killed, all cops became Sicilians. He had seen it happen: a patrolman shot down, and immediately his precinct house was flooded with cops from all over the city, wearing plaid windbreakers and business suits, shields pinned to lapels, offering to work on their own time. Was there anything they could do? Anything?

It was a mixture of fear, fury, anguish, sorrow. You couldn't possibly understand it unless you belonged. Because it was a brotherhood, and corrupt cops, stupid cops, cowardly cops had nothing to do with it. If you were a cop, then *any* cop's murder diminished you. You could not endure that.

The trouble was, Captain Edward X. Delaney acknowledged to himself, the trouble was that he could understand all this on an intellectual level without feeling the emotional involvement these men were feeling now, staring at a murdered cop's tin. It wasn't so much a lack in him, he assured himself, as that he looked at things differently from these furious men. To him *all* murders, in sanity and without conscience, demanded judgment, whether assassinated President, child thrown from rooftop, drunk knifed to death in a tavern brawl, whatever, wherever, whomever. His brotherhood was wider, larger, broader, and encompassed all, all, all . . .

But meanwhile, he was surrounded by a ring of blood-charged men. He knew he had only to say, "All right,

515

let's take him," and they would be with him, surging, breaking down doors. Daniel G. Blank would dissolve in a million plucking bullets, torn and falling into darkness.

Captain Delaney raised his head slowly, looked around at those faces: stony, twisted, blazing.

"We'll do it my way," he said, keeping his voice as toneless as he could. "Blankenship, have the shield dusted. Get this mess cleaned up. Return the basket to the street corner. The rest of you men get back to your posts."

He strode into his study, closed all the doors. He sat stolidly at his desk and listened. He heard the mutterings, shufflings of feet. He figured he had another 24 hours, no more. Then some hothead would get to Blank and gun him down. Exactly what he told Monica Gilbert he would do. But for different reasons.

About 7:30 p.m., he dressed warmly and left the house, telling the log-man he was going to the hospital. But instead, he went on his daily unannounced inspection. He knew the men on duty were aware of these unscheduled tours; he wanted them to know. He decided to walk—he had been inside, sitting, for too many hours—and he marched vigorously over to East End Avenue. He made certain Tiger One—the man watching the Castle—was in position and not goofing off. It was a game with him to spot Tiger One without being spotted. This night he won, bowing his shoulders, staring at the sidewalk, limping by Tiger One with no sign of recognition. Well, at least the kid was on duty, walking a beat across from the Castle and, Delaney hoped, not spending too much time grabbing a hot coffee somewhere or a shot of something stronger.

He walked briskly back to the White House and stood across the street, staring up at Blank's apartment house. Hopefully, Danny Boy was tucked in for the night. Captain Delaney stared and stared. Once again he had the irrational urge to go up there and ring the bell.

"My name is Captain Edward X. Delaney, New York Police Department. I'd like to talk to you."

Crazy. Blank wouldn't let him in. But that's all Delaney really wanted—just to talk. He didn't want to collar Blank or injure him. Just talk, and maybe understand. But it was hopeless; he'd have to imagine.

He knocked on the door of the Con Ed van; it was unlocked and opened cautiously. The man at the door recognized him and swung the door wide, throwing a half-assed salute. Delaney stepped inside; the door was locked behind him. There was one man with binoculars at the concealed flap, another man at the radio desk. Three men, three shifts; counting the guy in the hole and extras, there were about 20 men assigned to Bulldog One.

"How's it going?" he asked.

They assured him it was going fine. He looked around at the hot plate they had rigged up, the coffee percolator, a miniature refrigerator they had scrounged from somewhere.

"All the comforts of home," he nodded.

They nodded in return, and he wished them a Happy New Year. Outside again, he paused at the hole they had dug through the pavement of East 83rd Street, exposing steam pipes, sewer lines, telephone conduits. There was one man down there, dressed like a Con Ed repairman, holding a transistor radio to his ear under his hardhat. He took it away when he recognized Delaney.

"Get to China yet?" the Captain asked, gesturing toward the shovel leaning against the side of the excavation.

The officer was black.

"Getting there, Captain," he said solemnly, "Getting there. Slowly."

"Many complaints from residents?"

"Oh, we got plenty of those, Captain. No shortage."

Delaney smiled. "Keep at it. Happy New Year."

"Same to you, sir. Many of them."

He walked away westward, disgusted with himself. He did this sort of thing badly, he knew: talking informally with men under his command. He tried to be easy, relaxed, jovial. It just didn't work.

One of his problems was his reputation. "Iron Balls." But it wasn't only his record; they sensed something in him. Every cop had to draw his own boundaries of heroism, reality, stupidity, cowardice. In a dicey situation, you could go strictly by the book and get an inspector's funeral. Captain Edward X. Delaney would be there, wearing his Number Ones and white gloves. But all situations didn't call for sacrifice. Some called for a reasoned response. Some called for surrender. Each man had his own limits, set his own boundaries.

But what the men sensed was that Delaney's boundaries were narrower, stricter than theirs. Too bad there wasn't a word for it: coppishness, copicity, copanity—something like that. "Soldiership" came close, but didn't tell the whole story. What was needed was a special word for the special quality of being a cop.

What his men sensed, why he could never communicate with

them on equal terms, was that he had this quality to a frightening degree. He was the quintessential cop, and they didn't
need any new words to know it. They understood that he
would throw them into the grinder as fast as he would throw
himself.

He got to the florist's shop just as it was closing. They didn't
want to let him in, but he assured them it was an order for the
following day. He described exactly what he wanted: a single
longstem rose to be placed, no greenery, in a long, white
florists' box and delivered at 9:00 a.m. the next morning.

"Deliver one rose?" the clerk asked in astonishment. "Oh sir,
we'll have to charge extra for that."

"Of course," Delaney nodded. "I understand. I'll pay whatever's necessary. Just make certain it gets there first thing tomorrow morning."

"Would you like to enclose a card, sir?"

"I would."

He wrote out the small white card: "Dear Dan, here's a
fresh rose for the one you destroyed." He signed the card "Albert Feinberg," then slid the card in the little envelope, sealed
the flap, addressed the envelope to Daniel G. Blank, including
his street address and apartment number.

"You're certain it will get there by nine tomorrow
morning?"

"Yes, sir. We'll take care of it. That's a lot of money to
spend on one flower, sir. A sentimental occasion?"

"Yes," Captain Edward X. Delaney smiled. "Something like
that."

5

The next morning Delaney awoke, lay staring somberly at
the ceiling. Then, for the first time in a long time, he got out
of bed, kneeled, and thought a prayer for Barbara, for his own
dead parents, for all the dead, the weak, the afflicted. He did
not ask that he be allowed to kill Daniel Blank. It was not the
sort of thing you asked of God.

Then he showered, shaved, donned an old uniform, so aged
it was shiny enough to reflect light. He also loaded his .38 revolver, strapped on his gun belt and holster. It was not with
the certainty that this would be the day he'd need it, but it was

another of his odd superstitions: if you prepared carefully for an event, it helped hasten it.

Then he went downstairs for coffee. The men on duty noted his uniform, the bulge of his gun. Of course, no one commented on it, but a few men did check their own weapons, and one pulled on an elaborate shoulder holster that buckled across his chest.

Fernandez was in the kitchen, having a coffee and Danish. Delaney drew him aside.

"Lieutenant, when you're finished here, I want you to go to Bulldog One and stay there until relieved. Got that?"

"Sure, Captain."

"Tell your lookout to watch for a delivery by a florist. Let me know the minute he arrives."

"Okay," Fernandez nodded cheerfully. "You'll know as soon as we spot him. Something cooking, Captain?"

Delaney didn't answer, but carried his coffee back into the radio room. He set it down on the long table, then went back into his study and wheeled in his swivel chair. He positioned it to the right of the radio table, facing the operators.

He sat there all morning, sipping three black coffees, munching on the dry, stale heel of a loaf of Italian bread. Calls came in at fifteen-minute intervals from Bulldog One and Ten-O. No sign of Danny Boy. At 9:20, Stryker called from the Factory to report that Blank hadn't shown up for work. A few minutes later, Bulldog One was back on the radio.

Fernandez: "Tell Captain Delaney a boy carrying a long, white florist's box just went into the White House lobby."

Delaney heard it. Leaving as little as possible to chance, he went into his study, looked up the florist's number called, and asked if his single red rose had been delivered. He was assured the messenger had been sent and was probably there right now. Satisfied, the Captain went back to his chair at the radio table. The waiting men had heard Fernandez' report but what it meant, they did not know.

Sergeant MacDonald leaned over Delaney's chair.

"He's freaking, Captain?" he whispered.

"We'll see. We'll see. Pull up a chair, sergeant. Stay close to me for a few hours."

"Sure, Captain."

The black sergeant pulled over a wooden, straight-backed chair, sat at Delaney's right, slightly behind him. He sat as solidly as the Captain, wearing steel-rimmed spectacles, carved face immobile.

So they sat and waited. So everyone sat and waited. Quiet enough to hear a Sanitation truck grinding by, an airliner overhead, a far-off siren, hoot of tugboat, the bored fifteen-minute calls from Ten-O and Bulldog One. Still no sign of Danny Boy. Delaney wondered if he could risk a quick trip to the hospital.

Then, shortly before noon, a click loud enough to galvanize them, and Bulldog One was on:

"He's coming out! He's carrying stuff. A doorman behind him carrving stuff. What? A jacket, knapsack. What? What else? A coil of rope. Boots. What?"

Delaney: "Jesus Christ. Get Fernandez on."

Fernandez: "Fernandez here. Wearing black topcoat, no hat, left hand in coat pocket, right hand free. No glove. Knapsack, coil of rope, some steel things with spikes, jacket, heavy boots, knitted cap."

Delaney: "Ice ax?"

Barbara: "Bulldog One, ice ax?"

Fernandez: "No sign. Car coming up from garage. Black Chevy Corvette. His car."

Captain Delaney turned slightly to look at Sergeant MacDonald. "Got him," he said.

"Yes," MacDonald nodded. "He's running."

Fernandez: "They're pushing his stuff into the car. Left hand still in coat pocket, right hand free."

Delaney (to MacDonald): Two unmarked cars, three men each. Start the engines and wait. You come back in here."

Fernandez: "He's loaded. Getting into the driver's seat. Orders?"

Delaney: "Fernandez to trail in Bulldog Two. Keep in touch."

Fernandez: "Got it. Out."

Captain Delaney looked around. Sergeant MacDonald was just coming back into the room.

MacDonald: "Cars are ready, Captain."

Delaney: "Designated Searcher One and Searcher Two. If we both go, I'll take One, you take Two. If I stay, you take both."

MacDonald nodded. He had taken off his glasses.

Fernandez: "Barbara from Bulldog Two. He's circling the block. I think he's heading for the Castle. Out."

Delaney: "Alert Tiger One. Send Bulldog Three to Castle."

Fernandez: "Bulldog Two. It's the Castle all right. He's pulling up in front. We're back at the corner, the south corner. Danny Boy's parked in front of the Castle. He's getting out. Left hand in pocket, right hand free. Luggage still in car."

Bulldog Three: "Barbara from Bulldog Three."

Barbara: "Got you."

Bulldog Three: "We're in position. He's walking up to the Castle door. He's knocking at the door."

Delaney: "Where's Tiger One?"

Fernandez: "He's here in Bulldog Two with me. Danny Boy is parked on the wrong side of the street. We can plaster him."

Delaney: "Negative."

Barbara: "Negative, Bulldog Two."

Fernandez (laughing): "Thought it would be. Shit. Look at that . . . Barbara from Bulldog Two."

Barbara: "You're still on, Bulldog Two."

Fernandez: "Something don' smell right. Danny Boy knocked at the door of the Castle. It was opened. He went inside. But the door is still open. We can see it from here. Maybe I should take a walk up there and look."

Delaney: "Tell him to hold it."

Barbara: "Hold it, Bulldog Two."

Delaney: "Ask Bulldog Three if they're receiving our transcriptions to Bulldog Two."

Barbara: "Bulldog Three from Barbara. Are you monitoring our conversation with Bulldog Two?"

Bulldog Three: "Affirmative."

Delaney: "To Bulldog Two. Affirmative for a walk past Castle but put Tiger One with walkie-talkie on the other side of the street. Radio can be showing."

Fernandez: "Bulldog Two here. Got it. We're starting."

Bulldog Three: "Bulldog Three here. Got it. Fernandez is getting out of Bulldog Two. Tiger One is getting out, crossing to the other side of the street."

Delaney: "Hold it. Check out Tiger One's radio."

Barbara: "Tiger One from Barbara. How do you read?"

Tiger One: "T-One here. Lots of interference but I can read."

Delaney: "Tell him to cover. Understood?"

Barbara: "Tiger One, cover Lieutenant Fernandez on the other side of the street. *Coppish?*"

Tiger One: "Right on."

Delaney: "Bring in Bulldog Three."

Bulldog Three: "They're both walking toward us, slowly. Fernandez is passing the Castle, turning his head, looking at it.

Tiger One is right across the street. No action. They're coming toward us. Walking slowly. No sweat. Fernandez is crossing the street toward us. He'll probably want to use our mike. Ladies and gentlemen, the next voice you hear will be that of Lieutenant Jeri Fernandez."

Delaney (stonily): "Get that man's name."

Fernandez: "Fernandez in Bulldog Three. Is the Captain there?"

Delaney bent over the desk mike.

Delaney: "Here What is it, lieutenant?"

Fernandez: "It smells, Captain. The door to the Castle is half-open. Something's propping it open. Looks like a man's leg to me."

Delaney: "A leg?"

Fernandez: "From the knee down. A leg and a foot propping the door open. How about I take a closer look?"

Delaney: "Where's Tiger One?"

Fernandez: "Right here with me."

Delaney: "Both of you go back to Bulldog Two. Tiger One across the street, covering again. You take a closer look. Tell Tiger One to give us a continuous. Got that?"

Fernandez: "Sure."

Delaney: "Lieutenant . . ."

Fernandez: "Yeah?"

Delaney: "He's fast."

Fernandez (chuckling): "Don' give it a second thought, Captain."

Tiger One: "We're walking south. Slowly. Fernandez is across the street."

Delaney: "Gun out?"

Barbara: "Is your gun out, Tiger One?"

Tiger One: "Oh Jesus, it's been out for the last fifteen minutes. He's coming up to the Castle. He's slowing, stopping. Now Fernandez is kneeling on one knee He's pretending to tie his shoelace. He's looking toward the Castle door. He's—Oh my God!"

Daniel Blank awoke in an antic mood, laughing at a joke he had dreamed but could not remember. He looked to the windows; it promised to be a glorious day He thought he might go over to Celia Montfort's house and kill her. He might kill Charles Lipsky, Valenter, the bartender at The Parrot. He might kill a lot of people, depending on how he felt. It was that kind of a day.

522

It took off like a rocket: hesitating, almost motionless, moving, then spurting into the sky. That's the way the morning went, until he'd be out of the earth's pull, and free. There was nothing he might not do. He remembered that mood, when he was atop Devil's Needle, weeks, months, years ago.

Well, he would go back to Devil's Needle and know that rapture again. The park was closed for the winter, but it was just a chain-link fence, the gate closed with a rusty padlock. He could smash it open easily with his ice ax. He could smash anything with his ice ax.

He bathed and dressed carefully, still in that euphoria he knew would last forever.

So the chime at his outside door didn't disturb him at all.

"Who is it?" he called.

"Package for you, Mr. Blank."

He heard retreating footsteps, waited a few moments, then unbolted his door. He brought the long, white florist's box inside, relocked the door. He took the box to the living room and stared at it, not understanding.

Nor did he comprehend the single red rose inside. Nor the card. Albert Feinberg? Feinberg? Who was Albert Feinberg? Then he remembered that last death with longing: the close embrace, warm breath in his face, their passionate grunts. He wished they could do it again. And Feinberg had sent him another rose! Wasn't that sweet. He sniffed the fragrance, stroked the velvety petals against his cheek, then suddenly crushed the whole flower in his fist. When he opened his hand, the petals slowly came back to shape, moving as he watched, forming again the whole exquisitely shaped blossom, as lovely as it had been before.

He drifted about the apartment, dreaming, nibbling at the rose. He ate the petals, one by one; they were soft, hard, moist, dry on his tongue, with a tang and flavor all their own. He ate the flower down to the stem, grinning and nodding, swallowing it all.

He took his gear from the hallway closet: ice ax, rucksack, nylon line, boots, crampons, jacket, knitted watch cap. He wondered about sandwiches and a thermos—but what did he need with food and drink? He was beyond all that, outside the world's pull and the hunger to exist.

It was remarkable, he thought happily, how efficiently he was operating: the call to the garage to bring his car around, the call to a doorman—who turned out to be Charles Lipsky—to help him down with his gear. He moved through it all smiling. The day was sharp, clear, brisk, open, and so was he. He was in the lemon sun, in the thin blue sac filled with amniotic fluid. He was one with it all. He hummed a merry tune.

When Valenter opened the door and said, "I'm thorry, thir, but Mith Montfort ith not—" he smashed his fist into Valenter's face, feeling the nose crunch under his blow, seeing the blood, feeling the blood slippery between his knuckles. Then, stepping farther inside, he hit the shocked Valenter again, his fist going into the man's throat, crushing that jutting Adam's apple. Valenter's eyes rolled up into his skull and he went down.

So Daniel Blank walked easily across the entrance hall, still humming his merry tune. What was it? Some early American folksong; he couldn't remember the title. He climbed the stairs steadily, the ice ax out now, transferred to his right hand. He remembered the first time he had followed her up these stairs to the room on the fifth floor. She had paused, turned, and he had kissed her, between navel and groin, somewhere on the yielding softness, somewhere . . . Why had she betrayed him?

But even before he came to that splintered door, a naked Anthony Montfort darted out, gave Daniel one mad, frantic glance over his shoulder, then dashed down the hall, arms flinging. Watching that young, bare, unformed body run, all Blank could think of was the naked Vietnamese girl, burned by napalm, running, running, caught in pain and terror.

Celia was standing. She, too, was bare.

"Well," she said, her face a curious mixture of fear and triumph. "Well . . ."

He struck her again and again. But after the first blow, the fear faded from her face; only the triumph was left. The certitude. Was this what she wanted? He wondered, hacking away. Was this her reason? Why she had manipulated him. Why she had betrayed him. He would have to think about it. He hit her long after she was dead, and the sound of the ice ax ceased to be crisp and became sodden.

Then, hearing screams from somewhere, he transferred the ice ax to his left hand, under the coat, hidden again, and rushed out. Down the stairs. Over the fallen Valenter. Out into the bright, sharp, clear day. The screams pursued him: screams, screams, screams.

They were all on their feet in the radio room, listening white-faced to Tiger One's furious shouts, a scream from somewhere, "Fernandez is—", shots, roar of a car engine, squeal of tires, metallic clatter. Tiger One's radio went dead.

Captain Delaney stood stock-still for almost 30 seconds, hands on hips, head lowered, blinking slowly, licking his lips. The men in the room looked to him, waiting.

He was not hesitating as much as deliberating. He had been through situations as fucked-up as this in the past. Instinct and experience might see him through, but he knew a few seconds of consideration would help establish the proper sequence of orders. First things first.

He raised his head, caught MacDonald's eye.

"Sergeant," he said tonelessly, raised a hand, jerked a thumb over his shoulder, "on your way. Take both cars. Sirens. I'll stay here. Report as soon as possible."

MacDonald started out. Delaney caught up with him before he reached the hallway door, took his arm.

"In the outside toilet," he whispered, "in the cabinet under the sink. A pile of clean white towels. Take a handful with you."

The sergeant nodded, and was gone.

The Captain came back into the middle of the room. He began to dictate orders to the two radiomen and the two telephone men.

"To Bulldog Two, remain on station and assist."

"To Bulldog Three, take Danny Boy. Extreme caution."

Both cars cut in to answer; the waiting men heard more shots, curses, shouts.

"To downtown Communications. Operation Lombard top priority. Four cars New York entrance to George Washington Bridge. Detain black Chevy Corvette. Give them license number, description of Danny Boy. Extreme caution. Armed and dangerous."

"You and you. Take a squad. Up to George Washington Bridge. Siren and flasher. Grab a handful of those photos of Danny Boy and distribute them."

"To Communications. Officer in need of assistance. Ambulance. Urgent. Give address of Castle."

"To Deputy Inspector Thornsen: 'He's running. Will keep you informed. Delaney'."

"To Assault-Homicide Division. Crime in progress at Castle. Give address. Urgent. Please assist Operation Lombard."

"To Bulldog Ten. Recall to Barbara with car."

"To Bulldog One. Seal Danny Boy's apartment in White House. Twenty-one H. No one in, no one out."

"To Stryker. Seal Danny Boy's office. No one in, no one out."

"You and you, down to the Factory to help Stryker. Take Ten-O's car when he arrives."

"To Special Operations. Urgently need three heavy cars. Six men with vests, shotguns, gas grenades, subs, the works. Three snipers, completely equipped, one in each car. Up here as soon as possible. Oh yes . . . cars equipped with light bars, if possible."

"You and you, pick up the Mortons, at the Erotica on Madison Avenue, for questioning."

"You, pick up Mrs. Cleek at the Factory. You, pick up the owner of The Parrot on Third Avenue. You, pick up Charles Lipsky, doorman at the White House. Hold all of them for questioning."

"To Communications. All-precinct alert. Give description of car and Danny Boy. Photos to come. Wanted for multiple homicide. Extreme caution. Dangerous and armed. Inform chief inspector."

Delaney paused, drew a deep breath, looked about dazedly. The room was emptying out now as he pointed at men, gave orders, and they hitched up their guns, donned coats and hats, started out.

The radio crackled.

"Barbara from Searcher One."

"Got you, Searcher One."

"MacDonald. Outside the Castle. Fernandez down and bleeding badly. Tiger One down. Unconscious. At least a broken leg. Bulldog Three gone after Danny Boy. Bulldog Two and Searcher Two blocking off the street. Send assistance. Am now entering Castle."

Delaney heard, began speaking again.

"To Communications. Repeat urgent ambulance. Two officers wounded."

"To Assault-Homicide Division. Repeat urgent assistance needed. Two officers wounded."

"Sir, Deputy Inspector Thorsen is on the line," one of the telephone operators interrupted.

"Tell him two officers wounded. I'll get back to him. Recall guard on Monica Gilbert and get men and car over here. Recall taps on Danny Boy's phone and Monica Gilbert's phone. Tell them to remove all equipment, clean up, no sign."

"Barbara from Searcher One."

"Come in, Searcher One."

"MacDonald here. We have one homicide: female, white, black hair, early thirties, five-four or five, a hundred and ten, slender, skull crushed, answering description of the Princess. White, male boy, about twelve, naked and hysterical, answering description of Anthony Montfort. One white male, six-three or four, about one-sixty or sixty-five, unconscious, answering description of houseman Valenter, broken nose, facial injuries, bad breathing. Need two ambulances and doctors. Fernandez is alive but still bleeding. We can't stop it. Ambulance? Soon, please. Tiger One had broken right leg, arm, bruises, scrapes. Ambulances and doctors, please."

Delaney took a deep breath, started again.

"To Communications. Second repeat urgent ambulance. One homicide victim, four serious injuries, one hysteria victim. Need two ambulances and doctors soonest."

"To Assault-Homicide. Second repeat urgent assistance. Anything on those cars Communications sent to block the George Washington Bridge?"

"Cars in position, sir. No sign of Danny Boy."

"Our men there with photos?"

"Not yet, sir."

"Anything from Bulldog Three?"

"Can't raise them, sir."

"Keep trying."

Blankenship came over to the Captain, looking down at a wooden board with a spring clamp at the top. He had been making notes. Delaney noted the man's hands were trembling slightly but his voice was steady.

"Want a recap, sir?" he asked softly.

"A tally?" Delaney said thankfully. "I could use that. What have we got left?"

"One car, unmarked, and four men. But the recalls should be here soon, and Lieutenant Dorfman next door sent over two men in uniform to stand by. He also says he's holding a squad car outside the precinct house in case we need it. The three cars from Special Operations are on the way."

"No sign of Danny Boy at the Bridge, sir. Traffic beginning to back up."

"What?" the other radio operator said sharply. "Louder. Louder! I'm not making you."

Then they heard the hoarse, agonized whisper:

"Barbara . . . Bulldog Three . . . cracked up . . . lost him . . ."

527

"Where?" Delaney roared into the mike. "God damn you, stay on your feet! Where are you? Where did you lose him?"

". . . north . . . Broadway . . . Broadway . . . Ninety-fifth . . . hurt . . ."

"You and you," Delaney said, pointing. "Take the car outside. Over to Broadway and Ninety-fifth. Report in as soon as possible. You, get on to Communications. Nearest cars and ambulance. Officers injured in accident. Son of a bitch!"

"Barbara from Searcher One."

"Got you, Searcher One."

"MacDonald. One ambulance here. Fernandez is all right. Lost a lot of blood but he's going to make it. The doc gave him a shot. Thanks for the towels. Another ambulance pulling up. Cars from Assault-Homicide. Mobile lab . . ."

"Hold it a minute, sergeant." Delaney turned to the other radio operator. "Did you check the cars on the Bridge?"

"Yes, sir. The photos got there, but no sign of Danny Boy."

Delaney turned back to the first radio. "Go on, sergeant."

"Things are getting sorted out. Fernandez and Tiger One (what the hell *is* his name?) on their way to the hospital. The way I make it, Danny Boy came running out of the Castle and caught Fernandez just as he was straightening up, beginning his draw. Swung his ax at the lieutenant's skull. Fernandez moved and turned to take it on his left shoulder, back, high up, curving in near the neck. Danny Boy pulled the ax free, jumped into his car. Tiger One rushed the car from across the street, firing as he ran. He got off there. Two hits on the car, he says, with one through the front left window. But Danny Boy apparently unhurt. He got started fast, pulled away, sideswiped Tiger One, knocked him down and out. The whole goddamned thing happened so *fast*. The men in Bulldog Two and Three were left with their mouths open."

"I know," Delaney sighed. "Remain on station. Assist Assault-Homicide. Guards on the kid and Valenter until we can get statements."

"Understood. Searcher One out."

"Any word from the Bridge?" Delaney asked the radio operator.

"No, sir. Traffic backing up."

"Captain Delaney, the three cars from Special Operations are outside."

"Good. Hold them. Blankenship, come into the study with me."

They went in; Delaney closed all the doors. He searched a

moment, pulled from the bookshelves a folded road map of New York City and one of New York State. He spread the city map out on his desk, snapped on the table lamp. The two men bent over the desk. Delaney jabbed his finger at East End Avenue.

"He started here," he said. "Went north and made a left onto Eighty-sixth Street. That's what I figure. Went right past Bulldog Three who still had their thumbs up their asses. Oh hell, maybe I'm being too hard on them."

"We heard a second series of shots and shouts when we alerted Bulldog Three," Blankenship reminded him.

"Yes. Maybe they got some off. Anyway, Danny Boy headed west."

"To the George Washington Bridge?"

"Yes," the Captain said, and paused. If Blankenship wanted to ask any questions about why Delaney had sent blocking cars to the Bridge, now would be the time to ask them. But the detective had too much sense for that, and was silent.

"So now he's at Central Park," Delaney went on, his blunt finger tracing the path on the map. "I figure he turned south for Traverse Three and crossed to the west side at Eighty-sixth, went over to Broadway, and turned north. Bulldog Three said he was heading north. He probably turned left onto Ninety-sixth to get on the West Side Drive."

"He could have continued north and got on the Drive farther up. Or taken Broadway or Riverside Drive all the way to the Bridge."

"Oh shit," Captain Delaney said disgustedly, "he could have done a million things."

Like all cops, he was dogged by the unpredictable. Chance hung like a black cloud that soured his waking hours and defiled his dreams. Every cop lived with it: the meek, humble prisoner who suddenly pulls a knife, a shotgun blast that answers a knock on a door during a routine search, a rifle shot from a rooftop. The unexpected. The only way to beat it was to live by percentages, trust in luck, and—if you needed it—pray.

"We have a basic choice," Delaney said dully, and Blankenship was intelligent enough to note the Captain had said, "We have . . ." not "I have . . ." He was getting sucked in. This man, the detective reflected, didn't miss a trick. "We can send out a five-state alarm, then sit here on our keisters and wait for someone else to take him, or we can go get him and clean up our own shit."

"Where do you think he's heading, Captain?"

"Chilton," Delaney said promptly. "It's a little town in Orange County. Not ten miles from the river. Let me show you."

He opened the map of New York State, spread it over the back of the club chair, tilted the lampshade to spread more light.

"There it is," he pointed out, "just south of Mountainville, west of the Military Academy. See that little patch of green? It's Chilton State Park. Blank goes up there to climb. He's a mountain climber." He closed his eyes a moment, trying to remember details of that marked map he had found in Danny Boy's car a million years ago. Once again Blankenship was silent and asked no questions. Delaney opened his eyes, stared at the detective. "Across the George Washington Bridge," he recited, delighted with his memory. "Into New Jersey. Onto Four. Then onto Seventeen. Over into New York near Mahwah and Suffern. Then onto the Thruway, and turn off on Thirty-two to Mountainville. Then south to Chilton. The Park's a few miles out of town."

"New Jersey?" Blankenship cried. "Jesus Christ, Captain, maybe we better alert them."

Delaney shook his head. "No use. The Bridge was blocked before he got there. He couldn't possibly have beat that block. No way, city traffic being what it is. No, he by-passed the Bridge. If he hadn't he'd have been spotted by now. But he's still heading for Chilton. I've got to believe that. How can he get across the river north of the George Washington Bridge?"

They bent over the state map again. Blankenship's unexpectedly elegant forefinger traced a course.

"He gets on the Henry Hudson Parkway, say at Ninety-sixth. Okay, Captain?"

"Sure."

"He gets up to the George Washington Bridge, but maybe he sees the block."

"Or the traffic backing up because of the search."

"Or the traffic. So he sticks on the Henry Hudson Parkway, going north. My God, he can't be far along right now. He may be across this bridge here and into Spuyten Duyvil. Or maybe he's in Yonkers, still heading north."

"What's the next crossing?"

"The Tappan Zee Bridge. Here. Tarrytown to South Nyack."

"What if we closed that off?"

"And he kept going north, trying to get across? Bear Mountain Bridge is next. He's still south of Chilton."

"And if we blocked the Bear Mountain Bridge?"

"Then he's got to go up to the Newburgh-Beacon Bridge. Now he's north of Chilton."

Delaney took a deep breath, put his hands on his waist. He began to pace about the study.

"We could block every goddamned bridge up to Albany," he said, speaking to himself as much as to Blankenship. "Keep him on the east side of the river. What the hell for? I want him to go to his hole. He's heading for Chilton. He feels safe there. He's alone there. If we block him, he'll just keep running, and God only knows what he'll do."

Blankenship said, almost timidly, "There's always the possibility he might have made it across the George Washington Bridge, sir. Shouldn't we alert Jersey? Just in case."

"The hell with them."

"And the FBI?"

"Fuck 'em."

"And the New York State cops?"

"Those shitheads? With their sombreros. You think I'm going to let those apple-knockers waltz in and grab the headlines? Fat chance! This boy is mine. You got your pad?"

"Yes, sir. Right here."

"Take some notes. No . . . wait a minute."

Captain Delaney strode to the door of the radio room, yanked it open. There were more men; the recalls were coming in. Delaney pointed at the first man he saw. "You. Come here."

"Me, sir?"

The Captain grabbed him by the arm, pulled him inside the study, slammed the door behind him.

"What's your name?"

"Javis, John J. Detective second grade."

"Detective Javis, I am about to give orders to Detective first grade Ronald Blankenship. I want you to do nothing but listen and, in case of a Departmental hearing, testify honestly as to what you heard."

Javis' face went white.

"It's not necessary, sir," Blankenship said.

Delaney gave him a particularly sweet smile. "I know it isn't," he said softly. "But I'm cutting corners. If it works, fine. If not, it's my ass. It's been in a sling before. All right, let's go. Take notes on this. You listen carefully, Javis.

"Do all this through Communications. To New Jersey State Police, to the FBI, to New York State Police, a fugitive alert on Danny Boy. Complete description of him and car. Photos to follow. Apprehend and hold for questioning. Exercise extreme caution. Wanted for multiple homicide. Armed and dangerous. Got that?"

"Yes, sir."

"A *general* alert. The fugitive can be anywhere. You understand?"

"Yes, sir. I understand."

"Phone calls from here to police in Tarrytown, Bear Mountain, Beacon. Same alert. But tell them, do not stop or interfere with suspect. Let him run. If he crosses their bridge, call us. Let him get across the river but inform us immediately. Tell them he's a cop-killer. Got that?"

"Yes, sir," Blankenship nodded, writing busily. "If he tries to cross at the Tappan Zee, Bear Mountain, or Newburgh-Beacon Bridges, they are to let him cross but observe and call us. Correct?"

"Correct," Delaney said definitely. He looked at Javis. "You heard all that?"

"Yes, sir," the man faltered.

"Good," Delaney nodded. "Outside and stand by."

When the door closed behind the detective, Blankenship repeated, "You didn't have to do that, Captain."

"Screw it."

"You're going after him?"

"Yes."

"Can I come?"

"No. I need you here. Get those alerts off. I'll take the three cars from Special Operations and more men. I don't know the range of the radios. If they fade, I'll check by phone. I'll call on my private line here." He put his hand on his desk phone. "Put a man in here. No out-going calls. Keep it clear. I'll keep calling. You keep checking with Tarrytown, Bear Mountain and Beacon, to see where he goes across. You got all this?"

"Yes," Blankenship said, still jotting notes. "I'm caught up."

"Bring MacDonald back to Barbara. The two of you start on the paperwork. You handle the relief end: schedules, manpower, cars, and so forth. MacDonald is to get the statements, the questioning of everyone we took in. Clean up all the crap. He'll know what to do."

"Yes, sir."

"If Deputy Inspector Thorsen calls, just tell him I'm following and will contact him as soon as possible."

Blankenship looked up. "Should I call the hospital, sir?" he asked. "About your wife?"

Delaney looked at him, shocked. How long had it been?

"Yes," he said softly. "Thank you. And about Fernandez, Tiger One, and Bulldog Three. I'd appreciate that. I'll check with you when I call in. Let's see . . . Is there anything else? Any questions?"

"Can I come with you, sir?"

"Next time," Captain Edward X. Delaney said. "Get on those alerts right now."

The moment the door closed behind Blankenship, Delaney was on the phone. He got information, asking for police headquarters in Chilton, N.Y. It took time for the call to go through, but he wasn't impatient. If he was right, time didn't matter. And if he was wrong, time didn't matter.

Finally, he heard the clicks, the pauses, the buzzing, then the final regular ring.

"Chilton Police Department. Help you?"

"Could I speak to the commanding officer, please."

A throaty chuckle. "Commanding Officer? Guess that's me. Chief Forrest. What can I do you for?"

"Chief, this is Captain Edward X. Delaney, New York Police Department. New York *City*. I've got—"

"Well!" the Chief said. "This *is* nice. How's the weather down there?"

"Fine," Delaney said. "No complaints. A little nippy, but the sun's out and the sky's blue."

"Same here," the voice rumbled, "and the radio feller says it's going to stay just like this for another week. Hope he's right."

"Chief," Delaney said, "I've got a favor I'd like to ask of you."

"Why, yes," Forrest said. "Thought you might."

Delaney was caught up short. This was no country bumpkin.

"Got a man on the run," he said rapidly. "Five homicides known, including a cop. Ice ax. In a Chevy Corvette. Heading—"

"Whoa, whoa," the Chief said. "You city fellers talk so fast I can't hardly make sense. Just slow down a mite and spell it out."

"I've got a fugitive on the run," Delaney said slowly, obediently. "He's killed five people, including a New York City detective. He crushed their skulls with an ice ax."

"Mountain climber?"

"Yes," the Captain said, beginning to appreciate Chief Forrest. "It's just a slim chance, but I think he may be heading for the Chilton State Park. That's near you, isn't it?"

"Was, the last time I looked. About two miles out of town. What makes you think he's heading there?"

"Well . . . it's a long story. But he's been up there to climb. There's some rock—I forget the name—but apparently he—"

"Devil's Needle," Forrest said.

"Yes, that's it. He's been up there before, and I figured—"

"Park closed for the winter."

"If he wanted to get in, how would he do it, Chief?"

"It's a small park. Not like the Adirondacks. Nothing like that. Chain-link fence all around. One gate with a padlock. I reckon he could smash the gate or climb the fence. No big problem. This fugitive of yours—he a crazy?"

"Yes."

"Probably smash the gate. Well, Captain, what can I do you for?"

"Chief, I was wondering if you could send one of your men out there. Just to watch. You understand? If this nut shows up, I just want him observed. What he does. Where he goes. I don't want anyone trying to take him. I'm on my way with ten men. All I want is him holed up."

"Uh-huh," Chief Forrest said. "I think I got the picture. You call the State boys?"

"Alert going out right now."

"Uh-huh. Kinda out of your territory, isn't it, Captain?"

Shrewd bastard, Delaney thought desperately.

"Yes, it is," he confessed.

"But you're bringing up ten men?"

"Well . . . yes. If we can be of any help . . ."

"Uh-huh. And you just want a watch on the Park gate. Out of sight naturally. Just to see where this crazy goes and what he does. Have I got it right?"

"Exactly right," Delaney said thankfully. "If you could just send one of your men out . . ."

There was a silence that extended so long that finally Captain Delaney said, "Hello? Hello? Are you there?"

"Oh, I'm here, I'm here. But when you talk about sending out one of my men, I got to tell you, Captain: there ain't no men. I'm it. Chief Forrest. The Chilton Police Department. I suppose you think that's funny, a one-man po-*leece* department calling hisself 'Chief.' I know what a big-city 'Chief' means."

"I don't think it's funny," Delaney said. "Different places have different titles and different customs. That doesn't mean one is any better or any worse than another."

"Sonny," Chief Forrest rumbled, "I'm looking forward to meeting you. You sound like a real bright boy. Now you get up here with your ten men. Meanwhile, I'll mosey out to the Park and see what I can see. It's been a slow day."

"Thank you, Chief," Delaney said gratefully. "But it may take some time."

"Time?" the deep voice laughed. "Captain, we got plenty of that around here."

Delaney made one more call, to Thomas Handry. But the reporter wasn't in, so he left a message: "Break it. Blank running. After him. Call Thorsen. Delaney." Having paid his debt, he hitched up his gun belt, hooked his choker collar. He went into the radio room, pointed at three men; they all headed out to the heavy, armed cars waiting at the curb.

Still high, the air in his lungs as sharp and dry as good gin, Daniel Blank came dashing down the inside staircase of Celia Montfort's home leaped over the fallen Valenter, went sailing out into the thin winter sunlight, those distant screams pursuing him.

There was a man kneeling on the sidewalk between Blank and his car. This man saw Blank coming; his face twisted into an expression of wicked menace. He began to rise from his knee, one hand snaked beneath his jacket; Blank understood this man hated him and meant to kill him.

He performed his ax-transferring act as he rushed. He struck the man who was very quick and jerked aside so that the ax point did not enter his skull but crunched in behind his shoulder. But he went down. Daniel wrenched the ice ax free, ran to his car, conscious of shouts from across the avenue. Another man came dodging through traffic, pointing his finger at Blank. Then there were light, sharp explosions—snaps, really —and something smacked into and through the car body. Then there was a hole in the left window, another in the windshield, and he felt a stroke of air across his cheek, light as an angel's kiss.

The man was front left and seemed determined to yank

535

open the door or point his finger again. Blank caught a confused impression of black features contorted in fear and fury. There was nothing to do but accelerate, knock the man aside. So he did that, heard the thud as the body went flying, but he didn't look back.

He turned west onto 86th Street, saw a double-parked car with three men scrambling to get out. More shouts, more explosions, but then he was moving fast down 86th Street, hearing the rising and dwindling blare of horns, the squeal of brakes as he breezed through red lights, cut to the wrong side of the street to avoid a pile-up, cut back in, increasing speed, hearing a far-off siren, enjoying all this, loving it, because he had cut that telephone line that held him to the world, and now he was alone, all alone, no one could touch him. Ever again.

He took Traverse No. 3 across Central Park, turned right on Broadway, went north to 96th Street, made a left to get onto the Henry Hudson Parkway, which everyone called the West Side Drive. He went humming north on the Drive, keeping up with the traffic, no faster, no slower, and laughed because it had all been such a piece of cake. No one could touch him; not even the two police squads screaming by him, sirens open, could bring him down or spoil the zest of this bright, lively, *new* day.

But there was some kind of hassle at the Bridge—maybe an accident—and traffic was backing up. So he just stayed on the Parkway, went winging north as traffic thinned out and he could sing a little song—what was it? That same folksong he had been crooning earlier—and tap his hands in time on the steering wheel.

North of Yonkers he pulled onto the verge, stopped, unfolded his map. He could take the Parkway to the Thruway, cross the Tappan Zee Bridge to South Nyack. Around Palisades Interstate Park to 32, take that to Mountainville. Then south to Chilton. Simple . . . and beautiful. Everything was like that today.

He was folding up his map when a police car pulled alongside on the Parkway. The officer in the passenger's seat jerked his thumb north. Blank nodded, pulled off the verge, fell in behind the squad car, but kept his speed down until the cops were far ahead, out of sight. They hadn't even noticed the holes in window, windshield, car body.

He had no trouble, no trouble at all. Not even any toll to pay going west on the Tappan Zee. If he returned eastward, of course, he'd have to pay a toll. But he didn't think he'd be returning. He drove steadily, a mile or two above the limit, and almost before he knew it, he was in and out of Chilton, heading for the Park. Now his was the only car on the gravel road. No one else anywhere. Wonderful.

He turned into the dirt road leading to the Chilton State Park, saw the locked gate ahead of him. It seemed silly to stop and hack off the padlock with his ice ax, so he simply accelerated, going at almost 50 miles an hour at the moment of impact. He threw his forearm across his eyes when he hit, but the car slammed through the fence easily, the two wings of the gate flinging back. Daniel Blank braked suddenly and stopped. He was inside. He got out of the car and stretched, looking about. Not a soul. Just a winter landscape: naked black trees against a light blue sky. Clean and austere. The breeze was wine, the sun a tarnished coin that glowed softly.

Taking his time, he changed to climbing boots and lined canvas jacket. He threw his black moccasins and topcoat inside the car; he wouldn't need those anymore. At the last minute he also peeled off his formal "Ivy League" wig and left that in the car, too. He pulled the knitted watch cap over his shaved scalp.

He carried his gear to Devil's Needle, a walking climb of less than ten minutes, over a forest trail and rock outcrops. It was good to feel stone beneath his feet again. It was different from city cement. The pavement was a layer, insulating from the real world. But here you were on bare rock, the spine of the earth; you could feel the planet turning beneath your feet. You were close.

At the entrance to the chimney, he put on his webbed belt, attached one end of the nylon line, shook out the coils of rope carefully, attached the other end to all his gear; rucksack, crampons, extra sweater, his ice ax. He put on his rough gloves.

He began to climb slowly, wondering if his muscles had gone slack. But the climb went smoothly; he gained confidence as he hunched and wiggled upward. Then he reached to grasp the embedded pitons, pulled himself onto the flat. He rested a moment, breathing deeply, then rose and hauled up his gear. He unbuckled his belt, dumped everything in a heap. He straightened, put hands on his waist, inhaled deeply, forcing his shoulders back. He looked around.

It was a different scene, a winter scene, one he had never witnessed before from this elevation. It was a steel etching

537

down there: black trees spidery, occasional patches of un-melted snow, shadows and glints, all blacks, greys, browns, the flash of white. He could see the roofs of Chilton and, beyond, the mirror river, seemingly a pond, but moving, he knew, slowly to the sea, to the wide world, to everywhere.

He lighted one of his lettuce cigarettes, watched the smoke swirl away, enter into, disappear. The river became one with the sea, the smoke one with the air. All things became one with another, entered into and merged, until water was land, land water, and smoke was air, air smoke. Why had she smiled in triumph? Now he could think about it.

He sat on the bare stone, bent his legs, rested one cheek on his knee. He unbuttoned canvas jacket, suit jacket, shirt, and slid an ungloved hand inside to feel his own breast, not much flatter than hers. He worked the nipple slowly and thought she had been happy when her eyes turned upward to focus on that shining point of steel rushing downward to mark a period in her brain. She had been happy. She wanted the certitude. Everything she had told him testified to her anguished search for an absolute. And then, wearied of the endless squigglings of her quick and sensitive intelligence—so naked and aware it must have been as painful as an open wound—she had involved him in her plan, urging him on, then betraying him. Knowing what the end would be, wanting it. Yes, he thought, that was what happened.

He sat there a long time—the sky dulling to late afternoon—dreaming over what had happened. Not sorry for what had happened, but feeling a kind of sad joy, because he knew she had found her ultimate truth, and he would find his. So they both—but then he heard the sound of car engines, slam of car doors, and crawled slowly to the edge of Devil's Needle to peer down.

They came down the gravel road from Chilton, saw the sign: "One mile to Chilton State Park," then made their turn onto the dirt road. They pulled up outside the fence. The wings of the gate were leaning crazily. Inside was Daniel Blank's car. A big man, clad in a brown canvas windbreaker with a dirty sheepskin collar, was leaning against the car and watched them as they stopped. There was a six-pack of beer on the hood of the car; the man was sipping slowly from an opened can.

Captain Delaney got out, adjusted his cap, tugged down his jacket. He walked through the ruined gate toward Blank's car, taking out his identification. He inspected the big man as he advanced. Six-four, at least; maybe five or six if he straightened up. At least 250, maybe more, mostly in the belly. Had to be pushing 65. Wearing the worn windbreaker, stained corduroy pants, yellow, rubber-soled work shoes laced up over his ankles, a trooper's cap of some kind of black fur. Around his neck the leather cord of what appeared to be Army surplus field glasses from World War I. About his waist, a leather belt blotched with the sweat of a lifetime, supporting one of the biggest dogleg holsters Delancy had ever seen, flap buttoned. On the man's chest, some kind of a shield, star or sunburst; it was difficult to make out.

"Chief Forrest?" Delaney asked, coming up.

"Yep."

"Captain Edward X. Delaney, New York Police Department." He flipped open his identification, held it out.

The Chief took it in a hand not quite the size and color of a picnic ham, and inspected it thoroughly. He passed it back, then held a hand out to Delaney.

"Chief Evelyn F. Forrest," he rumbled. "Pleased to make your acquaintance, Captain. I suppose you think 'Evelyn' is a funny name for a man."

"No, I don't think that. My father's name was Marion. Not so important, is it?"

"Nooo . . . unless you've got it."

"I see our boy got here," Delaney said, patting the fender of the parked car.

"Uh-huh," Forrest nodded. "He arrived. Captain, I've got a cold six-pack here. Would you like . . ."

"Sure. Thank you. Go good right now."

The Chief selected a can, pulled the tab, handed over the beer. They both raised their drinks to each other, then sipped. The Captain inspected the label.

"Never had this brand before," he confessed. "Good. Almost like ale."

"Uh-huh," Chief Forrest nodded. "Local brewery. They don't go into the New York City area, but they sell all they can make."

He had, Delaney decided, the face of an old bloodhound, the skin a dark purplish-brown, hanging in wrinkles and folds: bags, jowls, wattles. But the eyes were unexpectedly young, mild, open; the whites were clear. Must have been quite a boy about 40 years ago, the Captain thought, before the beer got to him, ballooned his gut, slowed him up.

"Look here, Captain," Forrest said. "One of your men got some into him."

The Chief pointed out a bullet hole in the body of the car and another through the left front window.

"Come out here," he continued, pointing to a star-cracked hole in the windshield.

Delaney stooped to sight through the entrance hole in the window and the exit hole in the windshield.

"My God," he said, "by rights it should have taken his brains right along with it, if he was in the driver's seat. The man's got the luck of the Devil."

"Uh-huh," Chief Forrest nodded. "Some of 'em do. Well, here's what happened . . . I get here about an hour before he does, pull off the gravel road into the trees, opposite to the turnoff to the Park. Not such good concealment, but I figure he'll be looking to his right for the Park entrance and won't spot me."

"That makes sense."

"Yep. Well, I'm out of my station wagon, enjoying a brew, when he comes barreling along, pretty as you please. Turns into this here dirt road, sees the locked gate, speeds up, and just cuts right through; hot knife through butter. Then he gets out of the car, stretches, and looks around. I got him in my glasses by now. Handsome lad."

"Yes, he is."

"He starts changing to his outdoor duds: a jacket, boots, and so forth. I got a turn when he ducks into the car with a full head of hair and comes out balder'n a peeled egg."

"He wears a wig."

"Uh-huh. I found it, back there in the car. Looks like a dead muskrat. Also his coat and city shoes. Then he pulls on a cap, packs up his gear, and starts for Devil's Needle. I come across the road then and into the Park."

"Did he spot you?"

"Spot me?" the Chief said in some amazement. "Why no. I still move pretty good, and I know the land around here like the palm of my hand. No, he didn't spot me. Anyways, he gets there, attaches a line to his belt and to his gear, and goes into the chimney. Makes the climb in pretty good time. After awhile I see his line going out, and he pulls up his gear. Then I see him standing on top of Devil's Needle. I see him for just a few seconds, but he's up there all right, Captain; no doubt about that."

"Did you see any food in his gear? Or a canteen? Anything like that?"

"Nope. Nothing like that. But he had a rucksack. Might have had some food and drink in that."

"Maybe."

"Captain . . ."

"Yes, Chief?"

"That alert you phoned to the State boys . . . You know, they pass it on to all us local chiefs and sheriffs by radio. I was on my way out here when I heard the call. Didn't mention nothing about Chilton."

"Uh . . . well, I didn't mention Chilton to them. It was just a hunch, and I didn't want them charging out here on what might have been a wild-goose chase."

The Chief looked at him steadily a long moment. "Sonny," he said softly, "I don't know what your beef is with the State boys, and I don't want to know. I admit they can be a stiff-necked lot. But Captain, when this here is cleaned up, you're going back home. This is my home, and I got to deal with the State boys every day in the week. Now if they find out I knew a homicidal maniac was holed up on State property and didn't let them know, they'll be a mite put out, Captain, just a mite put out."

Delaney scuffed at the dirt with the toe of his city shoe, looking down. "Guess you're right," he muttered finally. "It's just . . ." He looked up at the Chief; his voice trailed away.

"Sonny," Forrest said in a kindly voice, "I been in this business a lot longer'n you, and I know what it means to be after a man, to track him a long time, and to corner him. Then the idea of anyone but you takin' him is enough to drive you right up into the rafters."

"Yes," Delaney nodded miserably. "Something like that."

"But you see my side of it, don't you, Captain? I got to call them. I'll do it anyway, but I'd rather you say, 'All right'."

"All right. I can understand it. How do you get them?"

"Radio in my wagon. I can reach the troop. I'll be right back."

The Chief moved off, up the dirt road, with a remarkably light stride for a man his age and weight. Captain Delaney stood by Blank's car, looking through the window at the coat, the shoes, the wig. They already had the shapeless, dusty look of possessions of a man long dead.

He should be feeling an exultation, he knew, at having snubbed Daniel Blank. But instead he felt a sense of dread.

Reaction to the excitement of the morning, he supposed, but there seemed to be more to it than that. The dread was for the future, for what lay ahead. "Finish the job," he told himself, "Finish the job." He refused to imagine what the finish might be. He remembered what his Army colonel had told him: "The best soldiers have no imagination."

He turned as Chief Forrest came driving through the sprung gate in an old, dilapidated station wagon with "Chilton Police Department" painted on the side in flaking red letters. He pulled up alongside Blank's car. "On their way," he called to Delaney. "About twenty minutes or so, I reckon."

He got from behind the wheel with some difficulty, grunting and puffing, then reached back inside to haul out two more six-packs of beer. He held them out to Delaney.

"For your boys," he said. "While they're waiting."

"Why, thank you, Chief. That's kind of you. Hope it's not leaving you short."

Forrest's big belly shook with laughter. "That'll be the day," he rumbled.

The Captain smiled, took the six-packs over to his cars.

"Better get out and stretch your legs," he advised his men. "Looks like we'll be here awhile. The State boys are on their way. Here's some beer, compliments of Chief Forrest of the Chilton Police Department."

The men got out of the cars happily, headed for the beer. Delaney went back to the Chief.

"Could we take a close look at Devil's Needle?" he asked.

"Why sure."

"I've got three snipers with me, and I'd like to locate a spot where they could cover the entrance to the chimney and the top of the rock. Just in case."

"Uh-huh. This fugitive of yours armed, Captain?"

"Just the ice ax, as far as I know. As for a gun, I can't guarantee either way. Chief, you don't have to come with me. Just point out the way, and I'll get there."

"Shit," Chief Forrest said disgustedly, "that's the first dumb thing you've said, sonny."

He started off with his light, flat-footed stride; Captain Delaney stumbled after him. They made their way down a faint dirt path winding through the skeleton trees.

Then they came to the out-crops. Captain Delaney's soles slipped on the shiny rocks while Chief Forrest stepped confidently, never missing his footing, not looking down, but striding and moving like a gargantuan ballet dancer to the base of Devil's Needle. When Delaney came up, breathing heavily, the Chief had opened his holster flap and was bending it back, tucking it under that sweat-stained belt.

Delaney jerked his chin toward the dogleg holster. "What do you carry, Chief?" he asked, one professional to another.

"Colt forty-four. Nine-inch barrel. It belonged to my daddy. He was a lawman, too. Replaced the pin and one of the grips, but otherwise it's in prime condition. A nice piece."

The Captain nodded and turned his eyes, unwillingly, to Devil's Needle. He raised his head slowly. The granite shaft poked into the sky, tapering slightly as it rose. There were mica glints that caught the late afternoon sunlight, and patches of dampness. A blotter of moss here and there. The surface was generally smooth and wind-worn, but there was a network of small cracks: a veiny stone torso.

He squinted at the top. It was strange to think of Daniel G. Blank up there. Near and far. Far.

"About eighty feet?" he guessed aloud.

"Closer to sixty-five, seventy, I reckon," Chief Forrest rumbled.

Up and down. They were separated. Captain Delaney had never felt so keenly the madness of the world. For some reason, he thought of lovers separated by glass or a fence, or a man and woman, strangers, exchanging an eye-to-eye stare on the street, on a bus, in a restaurant, a wall of convention or fear between them, yet unbearably close in that look and never to be closer.

"Inside," he said in a clogged voice, and stepped carefully into the opening of the vertical cleft, the chimney. He smelled the rank dampness, felt the chill of stone shadow. He tilted his head back. Far above, in the gloom, was a wedge of pale blue sky.

"A one-man climb," Chief Forrest said, his voice unexpectedly loud in the cavern. "You wiggle your way up, using your back and feet, then your hands and knees as the rock squeezes in. He's up there with an ice ax, ain't no man getting up there now unless he says so. You've got to use both hands."

"You've made the climb, Chief?"

Forrest grunted shortly. "Uh-huh. Many, many times. But that was years ago, before my belly got in the way."

"What's it like up there?"

543

"Oh, about the size of a double bedsheet. Flat, but sloping some to the south. Pitted and shiny. Some shallow rock hollows. Right nice view."

They came outside, Delaney looked up again.

"You figure sixty-five, seventy feet?"

"About."

"We could get a cherry-picker from the Highway Department, or I could bring up a ladder truck from the New York Fire Department. They can go up to a hundred feet. But there's no way to get a truck close enough; not down that path and across the rocks. Unless we build a road. And that would take a month."

They were silent then.

"Helicopter?" Delaney said finally.

"Yes," Forrest acknowledged. "They could blast him from that. Tricky in these downdrafts and cross-currents, but I reckon it could be done."

"It could be done," Captain Delaney agreed tonelessly. "Or we could bring in a fighter plane to blow him away with rockets and machineguns."

Silence again.

"Don't set right with you, does it, sonny?" the Chief asked softly.

"No, it doesn't. To you?"

"No. I never did hanker to shoot fish in a barrel."

"Let's get back."

On the way, they selected a tentative site for the snipers. It was back in a clump of firs, offering some concealment but providing a clear field of fire covering the entrance to the chimney and the top of Devil's Needle.

The State police had not yet arrived. Delaney's men were lounging in and out of the cars, nursing their beers. The three pale snipers stood a little apart from the others, talking quietly, hugging their rifles in canvas cases.

"Chief, I've got to make some phone calls. Do I go into Chilton?"

"No need. Right there." Forrest waved his hand toward the gate-keeper's cottage. He pointed out the telephone wire that ran on wooden poles back to the gravel road. "They keep that line open all winter. Highway crews plowing snow use it, and Park people who come in for early spring planting."

They walked over to the weathered wooden shack, stepped up onto the porch. Delaney inspected the hasp closed with a heavy iron padlock.

"Got a key?" he asked.

"Sure," the Chief said, pulling the massive revolver out of his holster. "Step back a mite, sonny."

The Captain backed away hastily, and Chief Forrest negligently shot the lock away. Delaney noted he aimed at the shackle, not the body of the lock where a bullet might do nothing but jam the works. He was beginning to admire the old man. The explosion was unexpectedly loud; echoes banged back and forth; Delaney's men rose uneasily to their feet. Two brown birds took off from the dry underbrush alongside the dirt road, went whirring off with raucous cries.

The Chief pushed the door open. The cabin smelled dusty and stale. An old, wood-based "cookie-cutter" phone was attached to the wall, operated by a little hand crank.

"Haven't seen one of those in years," Delaney observed.

"We still got a few around. The operator's name is Muriel. You might tell her I'm out here, in case she's got any words for me." He left Delaney alone in the shack.

The Captain spun the crank; Muriel came on with pleasing promptness. Delaney identified himself, and gave her the Chief's message.

"Well, his wife wants to know if she should hold supper," she said. "You tell him that."

"I will."

"You got the killer out there?" she asked sternly.

"Something like that. Can I get through to New York City?"

"Of course. What do you think?"

He called Blankenship first and reported the situation as briefly as he could. He told the detective to call Deputy Inspector Thorsen and repeat Delaney's message.

Then he called Barbara at the hospital. It was a harrowing call; his wife was weeping, and he couldn't find out the cause. Finally a nurse came on the phone and told the Captain his wife was hysterical; she didn't think the call should be continued. He hung up, bewildered and frightened.

Then he called Dr. Sanford Ferguson, and got him in his office.

"Captain Edward X. Delaney here."

"Edward! Congratulations! I hear you got him."

"Not exactly. He's on top of a rock, and we can't get to him."

"On top of a rock?"

"High. Sixty-five, seventy feet. Doctor, how long can a man live without food and water?"

"Food *or* water? About ten days, I'd guess. Maybe less."

"Ten days? That's all?"

"Sure. The food isn't so important. The water is. Dehydration is the problem."

"How long does it take to get to him?"

"Oh . . . twenty-four hours."

"Then what?"

"What you might expect. Tissue shrinks, strength goes, the kidneys fail. Joints ache. But by that time, the victim doesn't care. One of the first psychological symptoms is loss of will, a lassitude. Something like freezing to death. He'll lose from one-fifth to one-quarter of his body weight in fluids. Dizziness. Loss of voluntary muscles. Weakness. Can't see. Blurry images. Probably begin to hallucinate after the third day. The bladder goes. Just before death, the belly swells up. Not a pleasant way to die—but what is? Edward, is that what's going to happen?"

"I don't know. Thank you for your help."

He broke the connection, put in a call to Monica Gilbert. But when she recognized his voice, she hung up; he didn't try to call her again.

He came out onto the cottage porch and said to Forrest: "Your wife wants to know if she should hold supper."

"Uh-huh," the Chief nodded. "I'll let her know when I know. Captain, why don't—" He stopped suddenly, tilted his head. "Sireens," he said. "Coming fast. That'll be the troopers."

It was five seconds before Captain Delaney heard them. Finally, two cars careened around the curve into the Park entrance, skidded to a stop outside the fence, their sirens sighing slowly down. Four men in each car and, bringing up the rear, a beat-up Ford sedan with "Orange County Clarion" lettered on the side. One man in that.

Delaney came down off the porch and watched as the eight troopers piled out of their cars, put their hands on their polished holsters.

"Beautiful," he said aloud.

Then one man, not too tall, wider in the hips than the shoulders, stalked through the gate toward them.

"Oh-oh," Chief Forrest murmured. "Here comes Smokey the Bear."

The Captain took out his identification, watching the approaching officer. He was wearing the grey woolen winter uniform of the New York State Police, leather belt and holster gleaming wickedly. Squarely atop his head was the broad-brimmed, straight-brimmed, stiff-brimmed Stetson. He carried his chin out in front of him, a bare elbow, with narrow shoulders back, pigeon breast thrust. He marched up to them, stood vacant-faced. He glanced at Chief Forrest and nodded slightly, then stared at Delaney.

"Who are you?" he demanded.

The Captain looked at him a moment, then proffered his identification. "Captain Edward X. Delaney, New York Police Department. Who are you?"

"Captain Bertram Sneed, New York State Police."

"How do I know that?"

"Jesus Christ. What do I look like?"

"Oh, you look like a cop. No doubt about it; you're wearing a cop's uniform. But four men in cops' uniforms pulled the St. Valentine's Day Massacre. You just can't be too sure. Here's my ID. Where's yours?"

Sneed opened his trap mouth, then shut it suddenly with a snap of teeth. He opened one button of his woolen jacket, tugged out his identification. They exchanged.

As they examined each other's credentials, Delaney was conscious of men moving in, his men and Sneed's men. They sensed a confrontation of the brass, and they wouldn't miss it for the world.

Sneed and Delaney took back their ID cards.

"Captain," Sneed said harshly, "we got a jurisdiction problem here."

"Oh?" Delaney said. "Is that our problem?"

"Yes. This here Park is State property, under the protection of the New York State Police Organization. You're out of your territory."

Captain Delaney put away his identification, tugged down his jacket, squared his cap away.

"You're right," he smiled genially. "I'll just take my men and get out. Nice to have met you, captain. Chief. Goodby."

He was turning away when Sneed said, "Hey, wait a minute."

Delaney paused. "Yes?"

"What's the problem here?"

"Why," Delaney said blandly, "it's a problem of jurisdiction. Just like you said."

"No, no. I mean what have we got? Where's this here fugitive?"

"Oh . . . *him*. Well, he's sitting on top of Devil's Needle."

Chief Forrest had fished a wooden match from his side pocket and inserted the bare end into the corner of his mouth.

He appeared to be sucking on it, watching the two captains with a benign smile on his droopy features.

"Sitting on top of the rock?" Sneed said. "Shit, is that all? We got some good climbers in our outfit. I'll send a couple of men up there and we'll take him."

Delaney had turned away again, taken a few steps. His back was to Sneed when he halted, put his hands on his waist, paused a long moment, lowered his head, drew a deep breath, then turned back again. He came close to Sneed.

"You shit-headed, wet-brained sonofabitch," he said pleasantly. "By all rights, I should take my men and go and leave you to stew in your own juice, you fucking idiot. But when you talk about sending a brave man to his death because of your stupidity, I got to speak my piece. You haven't even made a physical reconnaissance, for Christ's sake. That's a one-man climb, captain, and every man you send up there will get his skull crushed in. Is that what you want?"

Sneed's puppet face had gone white under the lash of Delaney's invective. Then red blotches appeared on his cheeks, discs of rouge, and his hands worked convulsively. Everyone stood in silence, frozen. But there was an interruption. A heavy white van turned into the entrance from the gravel road; heads turned to look at it. It was a mobile TV van from one of the national networks. They watched it park outside the gate. Men got out and began unloading equipment. Sneed turned back to Delaney.

"Well . . . hell," he said, smiling triumphantly, "so I won't send a man up. But the first thing tomorrow morning, I'll have a helicopter up there and we'll pick him off. Make a great TV picture."

"Oh yes," Delaney agreed. "A great TV picture. Of course, this man is just a suspect right now. He hasn't been convicted of *anything*. Hasn't even been tried. But you send your chopper up and grease him. I can see the headlines now: 'State Cops Machine-gun Suspect on Mountaintop.' Good publicity for your outfit. Good public relations. Especially after Attica."

The last word stiffened Captain Bertram Sneed. He didn't breathe, his arms hanging like fluked anchors at his side.

"Another thing," Delaney went on. "See that TV truck out there? By dawn, there'll be two more. And reporters and photographers from newspapers and magazines. It's already been on radio. If you don't get the roads around here closed off in a hell of a hurry, by morning you'll have a hundred thousand creeps and nuts with their wives and kiddies and picnic baskets of fried chicken, all hurrying to be in on the kill. Just like Floyd Collins in the cave."

"I got to make a phone call," Captain Sneed said hoarsely. He looked around frantically. Chief Forrest jerked a thumb toward the gate-keeper's cottage. Sneed hurried toward it. "You stay here a minute," he called back to Delaney. "Please," he added.

He got up on the porch, saw the smashed lock.

"Who blew open this door?" he cried.

"I did," Chief Forrest said equably.

"State property," Sneed said indignantly, and disappeared inside.

"O Lord, will my afflictions never cease?" the Chief asked.

"I shouldn't have talked to him like that," Delaney said in a low voice, his head bowed. "Especially in front of his men."

"Oh, I don't know, Captain," the Chief said, still sucking on his matchstick. "I've heard better cussing-outs than that. Besides, you didn't say nothing his men haven't been saying for years. Amongst theirselves, of course."

"Who do you think he's calling?"

"I know exactly who he's calling: Major Samuel Barnes. He's in command of Sneed's troop."

"What's he like?"

"Sam? Cut from a different piece of cloth. A hard little man, smart as a whip. Knows his business. Sam comes from up near Woodstock. I knew his daddy. Hy Barnes made the best applejack in these parts, but Sam don't like to be reminded of that. Smokey the Bear will explain the situation, and Major Sam will listen carefully. Sneed will complain about you being here, and he'll tell Sam what you said about machinegunning that man from a chopper, and what you said about a mob of nuts descending on us tomorrow. Sneed will tell the Major *you* said those things, because he's too damned dumb to take credit for them hisself. Sam Barnes will think a few seconds, then he'll say, 'Sneed, you turd-kicking nincompoop, you get your fat ass out there and ask that New York City cop, just as polite as you can, if he'll stick around and tell you what to do until I can get on the scene. And if you haven't fucked things up too bad by the time I get there, you might—you just might—live to collect your pension, you asshole.' Now you stick around a few minutes, sonny, and see if I ain't exactly right."

A few moments later Captain Sneed came out of the cottage, pulling on his gloves. His face was still white, and he moved like a man who has just been kneed in the groin. He came over to them with a ghastly smile.

"Captain," he said, "I don't see why we can't cooperate on this."

"Cooperation!" the Chilton Chief cried unexpectedly. "That's what makes the world go 'round!"

They went to work, and by midnight they had it pretty well squared away, although many of the men and much of the equipment they had requisitioned had not yet arrived. But at least they had a tentative plan, filled it in and revised it as they went along.

The first thing they did was to establish a four-man walking patrol around the base of Devil's Needle, the sentries carrying shotguns and sidearms. The walkers did four hours on, and eight off.

Delaney's snipers established their blind in the fir copse, sitting crossed-legged atop folded blankets. They had mounted their scopes, donned black sweaters and pants, socks and shoes, jackets and tight black gloves. Each wore a flak vest on watch.

Squad cars were driven in as close as possible; their headlights and searchlights were used to illuminate the scene. Portable battery lanterns were set out to open up the shadows. Captain Delaney had called Special Operations and requisitioned a generator truck and a flatbed of heavy searchlights with cables long enough so the lights could be set up completely around Devil's Needle.

Captain Bertram Sneed was bringing in a field radio receiver-transmitter; the local power company was running in a temporary line. The local telephone company was bringing in extra lines and setting up pay phones for the press.

Major Samuel Barnes had not yet put in an appearance, but Delaney spoke to him on the phone. Barnes was snappish and all business. He promised to reshuffle his patrol schedules and send another twenty troopers over by bus as soon as possible. He was also working on the road blocks, and expected to have the Chilton area sealed off by dawn.

He and Delaney agreed on some ground rules. Delaney would be the on-the-spot commander with Sneed acting as his deputy. But Major Barnes would be nominal commander when the first report to the press was made, calling the siege of Devil's Needle a "joint operation" of New York State and New York City police. All press releases were to be okayed by both sides; no press conferences were to be held or interviews granted without representatives of both sides present.

Before agreeing, Captain Delaney called Deputy Inspector Thorsen to explain the situation and outline the terms of the oral agreement with the State. Thorsen said he'd call back; Delaney suspected he was checking with Deputy Mayor Alinski. In any event, Thorsen called back shortly and gave him the okay.

Little of what they accomplished would have been possible without the aid of Chief Evelyn Forrest. Laconic, unflappable, never rushing, the man was a miracle of efficiency, joshing the executives of the local power and telephone companies to get their men cracking.

It was Forrest who brought out a highway crew to open up the shut-off water fountains in the Park and set up two portable chemical toilets. The Chief also got the Chilton High School, closed for the Christmas holiday, to open up the gymnasium, to be used as a dormitory for the officers assigned to Devil's Needle. Cots, mattresses, pillows and blankets were brought in from the county National Guard armory. Forrest even remembered to alert the Chilton disaster unit; they provided a van with sides that folded down to form counters. They served hot coffee and doughnuts in the Park around the clock, the van staffed by lady volunteers.

Chief Forrest had offered Captain Delaney the hospitality of his home, but the Captain opted for a National Guard cot set up in the gate-keeper's cottage. But, the night being unexpectedly chill, he did accept the Chief's loan of a coat. What a garment it was! Made of grey herringbone tweed, it was lined with raccoon fur with a wide collar of beaver. It came to Delaney's ankles, the cuffs to his knuckles. The weight of it bowed his shoulders, but it was undeniably warm.

"My daddy's coat," Chief Forrest said proudly. "Made in Philadelphia in Nineteen-and-one. Can't buy a coat like that these days."

So they all worked hard, and Delaney had one moment of laughing fear when he thought of what fools they'd all look if it turned out that somehow Daniel G. Blank had already climbed down off his perch and escaped into the night. But he put that thought away from him.

Shortly after dark they started bullhorn appeals to the fugitive, to be repeated every hour on the hour:

"Daniel Blank, this is the police. You are surrounded and have no chance of escape. Come down and you will not be hurt. You will be given a fair trial, represented by legal counsel. Come down now and save yourself a lot of trouble. Daniel

Blank, you will not be injured in any way if you come down now. You have no chance of escape."

"Do any good, you think?" Forrest asked Delaney.

"No."

"Well," the Chief sighed, "at least it'll make it harder for him to get some sleep."

By 11:30 p.m., Delaney felt bone-weary and cruddy, wanted nothing more than a hot bath and eight hours of sleep. Yet when he lay down on his cold cot without undressing, just to rest for a few moments, he could not close his eyes, but lay stiffly awake, brain churning, nerves jangling. He rose, pulled on that marvelous coat, walked out onto the porch.

There were a lot of men still about—detectives and troopers, power and telephone repairmen, highway crews, reporters, television technicians. Delaney leaned against the railing, observed that all of them, sooner or later, went wandering off, affecting nonchalance, but looking back in guilt, anxious to see if anyone had noted their departure, half-ashamed of what they were doing. He knew what they were doing; they were going to Devil's Needle to stand, stare up and wonder.

He did the same thing himself, drawn against his will. He went as far as the rock outcrops, then stepped back into the shadow of a huge, leafless sugar maple. From there he could see the slowly circling sentries, the sniper sitting patiently on his blanket, rifle cradled on one arm. And there were all the men who had come to watch, standing with heads thrown back, mouths open, eyes turned upward.

Then there was the palely illumined bulk of Devil's Needle itself, looming like a veined apparition in the night. Captain Delaney, too, lifted his head, opened his mouth, turned his eyes upward. Above the stone, dimly, he could see stars whirling their courses in a black vault that went on forever.

He felt a vertigo, not so much of the body as of the spirit. He had never been so unsure of himself. His life seemed giddy and without purpose. Everything was toppling. His wife was dying and Devil's Needle was falling. Monica Gilbert hated him and that man up there, that man . . . he knew it all. Yes, Captain Edward X. Delaney decided, that man now knew it all, or was moving toward it with purpose and delight.

He became conscious of someone standing near him. Then he heard the words.

". . . soon as I could," Thomas Handry was saying. "Thanks for the tip. I filed a background story and then drove up. I'm staying at a motel just north of Chilton."

Delaney nodded.

"You all right, Captain?"

"Yes. I'm all right."

Handry turned to look at Devil's Needle. Like the others, his head went back, mouth opened, eyes rolled up.

Suddenly they heard the bullhorn boom. It was midnight.

The bullhorn clicked off. The watching men strained their eyes upward. There was no movement atop Devil's Needle.

"He's not coming down, is he, Captain?" Handry asked softly.

"No," Captain Delaney said wonderingly. "He's not coming down."

6

He awoke the first morning on Devil's Needle, and it seemed to him he had been dreaming. He remembered a voice calling, "Daniel Blank . . . Daniel Blank . . ." That could have been his mother because she always used his full name: "Daniel Blank, have you done your homework? Daniel Blank, I want you to go to the store for me. Daniel Blank, did you wash your hands?" That was strange, he realized for the first time—she never called him Daniel or Dan or son.

He looked at his watch; it showed 11:43. But that was absurd, he knew; the sun was just rising. He peered closer and saw the sweep second hand had stopped; he had forgotten to wind it. Well, he could wind it now, set it approximately, but time really didn't matter. He slipped the gold expansion band off his wrist, tossed the watch over the side.

He rummaged through his rucksack. When he found he had neglected to pack sandwiches and a thermos, he was not perturbed. It was not important.

He had slept fully clothed, crampons wedged under his ribs, spikes up, so he wouldn't roll off Devil's Needle in his sleep. Now he climbed shakily to his feet, feeling stiffness in shoulders and hips, and stood in the center of the little rock plateau where he could not be seen from the ground. He did stretching exercises, bending sideways at the waist, hands on hips; then bending down, knees locked, to place his palms flat on the chill stone; then jogging in place while he counted off five minutes.

He was gasping for breath when he finished, and his knees were trembling; he really wasn't in very good condition, he acknowledged, and resolved to spend at least an hour a day in stretching and deep-breathing exercises. But then he heard his name being called again. Lying on his stomach, he inched cautiously to the edge of Devil's Needle.

Yes, they were calling his name, asking him to come down, promising he wouldn't be hurt. He wasn't interested in that, but he was surprised by the number of men and vehicles down there. The packed dirt compound around the gate-keeper's cottage was crowded; everyone seemed very busy with some job they were all doing. When he looked directly downward, he could see armed men circling the base of Devil's Needle, but whether they were protecting the others from him or him from the others, he could not say and didn't care.

He felt a need to urinate, and did so, lying on his side, peeing so the stream went over the edge of the rock. There wasn't very much, and it seemed to him of a milky whiteness, not golden at all. There was a clogged heaviness in his bowels, but the difficulties of defecating up there, what he would do with the excrement, how he would wipe himself clean, were such that he resisted the urge, rolled back to the center of the stone, lay on his back, stared at the new sun.

At no time had he debated with himself and come to a conscious decision to stay up there, to die up there. It was just something his mind grasped instinctively and accepted. He was not driven to it; even now he could descend if he wanted to. But he didn't. He was content where he was, in a condition of almost drowsy ease. And he was safe; that was important. He had his ice ax and could easily smash the skull of any climber who came after him. But what if one should come in the dark, wiggling his way silently upward to kill Daniel G. Blank as he slept?

He didn't think it likely that anyone would attempt a night climb, but just to make it more difficult, he took his ice ax and using it as a hammer, knocked loose the two pitons that aided the final crawl from the chimney to the top of Devil's Needle. The task took a long time; he had to rest awhile after the pitons were free. Then he slid them skittering across the stone, watched them disappear over the side.

Then they were calling his name again, a great mechanical booming: "Daniel Blank . . . Daniel Blank . . ." He wished they wouldn't do that. For a moment he thought of shouting down and telling them to stop. But they probably wouldn't. The thing was, it was disturbing his reverie, intruding on his

554

isolation. He was enjoying his solitude, but it should have been a silent separateness.

He rolled over on his face, warming now as the watery sun rose higher. Beneath his eyes, close, close, he saw the rock itself, its texture. In all his years of mountain climbing and rock collecting, he had never looked at stone in that manner, seeing beneath the worn surface gloss, penetrating to the deep heart. He saw then what the stone was, and his own body, and the winter trees and glazed sun: infinite millions of bits, multicolored, in chance motion, a wild dance that went on and on to some silent tune.

He thought, for awhile, that these bits might be similar to the "bits" stored by a computer, recalled when needed to form a pattern, solve a problem, produce a meaningful answer. But this seemed to him too easy a solution, for if a cosmic computer did exist, who had programmed it, who would pose the questions and demand the answers? What answers? What questions?

He dozed off for awhile, awoke with that steel voice echoing, "Daniel Blank . . . Daniel Blank . . . ," and was forced to remember who he was.

Celia had found her certitude—whatever it was—and he supposed everyone in the world was searching for his own, and perhaps finding it, or settling, disappointed, for something less. But what was important, what was important was . . . What was important? It had been right there, he had been thinking of it, and then it went away.

There was a sudden griping in his bowels, a sharp pain that brought him sitting upright, gasping and frightened. He massaged his abdomen gently. Eventually the pain went away, leaving a leaden stuffiness. There was something in there, something in him . . . He fell asleep finally, dimly hearing the ghost voice calling, "Daniel Blank . . . Daniel Blank . . ." It might be his imagination, he admitted, but it seemed to him the voice was higher in pitch now, almost feminine in timbre, dawdling lovingly over the syllables of his name. Someone who loved him was calling.

Was it the second day or the third? Well . . . no matter. Anyway, a helicopter came over, dipped, circled his castle, tilted. He had been sitting with his knees drawn up, head down on folded arms, and he raised his head to stare at it. He thought they might shoot him or drop a bomb on him. He waited patiently, dreaming. But they just circled him, low, three or four times; he could see pale faces at the windows, peering down at him. He lowered his head again.

They came back, every day, and he tried to pay no attention to them, but the heavy throbbing of the rotor was annoying. It was slow enough to have a discernible rhythm, a heartbeat in the sky. Once they came so low over him that the downdraft blew his knitted watch cap off the stone. It went sailing out into space, then fell into the reaching spines of winter trees. He watched it go.

One morning—when was it?—he knew he was going to defecate and could not control himself. He fumbled at his belt with weak fingers, got it unbuckled and his pants down, but was too late to pull down his flowered bikini panties, and had to void. It was painful. Later he got his pants off his feet—he had to take his boots off first—then pulled down the panties and shook them out.

He looked at his feces curiously. They were small black balls, hard and round as marbles. He flicked them, one by one, with his forefinger; they rolled across the stone, over the edge. He knew he no longer had the strength to dress, but he could tug off socks, jacket, and shirt. Then he was naked, baring his shrunken body to pale sun.

He was no longer thirsty, no longer hungry. Most amazing, he was not cold, but suffused with a sleepy warmth that tingled his limbs. He was, he knew, sleeping more and more until on the fourth day—or perhaps it was the fifth—he was not conscious of sleep as a separate state. Sleep and wakefulness became so thin that they were no longer oil and water, but one fluid, grey and without flavor, that ebbed and flowed.

The days passed, he supposed, and so did the nights. But where one ended and the other began, he did not know. Days and darkness, all boundaries lost, became part of that grey, flavorless tide, warm, milky at times, without odor now. It was a great placid sea, endless; he wished he had the strength to stand and see just once more that silver river that flowed to everywhere.

But he could not stand, could not even make the effort to wipe away a thin, viscous liquid leaking from eyes, nose, mouth. When he moved his hand upon himself, he felt pulped nipples, knobbed joints, wrinkles, folds of scratchy skin. Pain had gone; will was going. But he held it tight, to think awhile longer with a slow, numbed brain.

"Daniel Blank . . . Daniel Blank . . . ," the voice called seductively. He knew who it was who called.

On the second day, an enterprising New York City newspaper hired a commercial helicopter; they flew over Devil's Needle and took a series of photos of Daniel Blank sitting on the rock, knees drawn up. The photograph featured on the newspaper's front page showed him with head raised, pale face turned to the circling 'copter.

Delaney was chagrined that he hadn't thought of aerial reconnaissance first and, after consultation with Major Samuel Barnes, all commercial flights over Devil's Needle were banned. The reason given to the press was that a light plane or helicopter approach might drive Blank to a suicide plunge, or the chopper's downdraft might blow him off the edge.

Actually, Captain Delaney was relieved by the publication of that famous photo; Danny Boy was up there, no doubt about it. At the same time, with the cooperation of Barnes, he initiated thrice-daily flights of a New York State Police helicopter over the scene. Aerial photographs were taken, portions greatly enlarged and analyzed by Air Force technicians. No signs of food or drink were found. As the days wore away and Blank spent more and more time on his back, staring at the sky, his physical deterioration became obvious.

Delaney went along on the first flight, taking a car north with Chief Forrest and Captain Sneed to meet Barnes at an Air Force field near Newburgh. It was his first face-to-face meeting with Sam Barnes. The Major was like his voice: hard, tight, peppery. His manner was cold, withdrawn, his gestures quick and short. He wasted little time on formalities, but hustled them aboard the waiting helicopter.

On the short flight south, he spoke only to Delaney. The Captain learned the State officer had consulted his departmental surgeon and was aware of what Delaney already knew: without food or liquid, Blank had about ten days to live, give or take a day or two. It depended on his physical condition prior to his climb, and to the nature and extent of his exposure to the elements. The Major, like Delaney, was monitoring the long-range weather forecasts daily. Generally, fair weather was expected to continue with gradually lowering temperatures. But there was a low-pressure system building up in northwest Canada that would bear watching.

They were all discussing their options when the 'copter came in view of Devil's Needle, then tilted to circle lower. Their talk died away; they stared out their windows at the rock. The cabin was suddenly cold as a crewman slid open the wide cargo door, and a police photographer positioned his long-lensed camera.

Captain Delaney's first reaction was one of shock at the small size of Daniel Blank's aerie. Chief Forrest had said it was "double bedsheet size," but from the air it was difficult to understand how Blank could exist up there for an hour without rolling or stumbling off the edge.

As the 'copter circled lower, the photographer snapping busily, Delaney felt a sense of awe and, looking at the other officers, suspected they were experiencing the same emotion. From this elevation, seeing Blank on his stone perch and the white, upturned faces of the men surrounding Devil's Needle on the ground, the Captain knew a dreadful wonder at the man's austere isolation and could not understand how he endured it.

It was not only the dangerous height at which he had sought refuge, lying atop a rock pillar that thrust into the sky, it was the absolute solitude of the man, deliberately cutting himself off from life and the living. Blank seemed, not on stone, but somehow floating in the air, not anchored, but adrift.

Only a few times before in his life had Delaney felt what he felt now. Once was when he forced his way into that concentration camp and saw the stick-men. Once was when he had taken a kitchen knife gently from the nerveless fingers of a man, soaked in blood, who had just murdered his mother, his wife, his three children, and then called the cops. The final time Delaney had helped subdue a mad woman attempting to crunch her skull against a wall. And now Blank . . .

It was the madness that was frightening, the loss of anchor, the float. It was a primitive terror that struck deep, plunged to something papered over by civilization and culture. It stripped away millions of years and said, "Look." It was the darkness.

Later, when copies of the aerial photos were delivered to him, along with brief analyses by the Air Force technicians, he took one of the photos and thumb-tacked it to the outside wall of the gate-keeper's cottage. He was not surprised by the attention it attracted, having guessed that the men shared his own uncertainty that their quarry was actually up there, that any man would deliberately seek and accept this kind of immolation.

Captain Delaney also noted a few other unusual characteristics of the men on duty: They were unaccountably quiet, with none of the loud talk, boasting, and bantering that usually accompanied a job of this type. And they were in no hurry, when relieved, to return to their warm dormitory in the high school gymnasium. Invariably, they hesitated, then wandered once again to the base of Devil's Needle, to stare upward, mouths open, at the unseen man who lay alone.

He discussed this with Thomas Handry. The reporter had gone out to the roadblocks to interview some of the people being turned back by the troopers.

"You wouldn't believe it," Handry said, shaking his head. "Hundreds and hundreds of cars. From all over the country. I talked to a family from Ohio and asked them why they drove so far, what they expected to see."

"What did they say?"

"The man said he had a week off, and it wasn't long enough to go to Disneyworld, so they decided to bring the kids here."

They were organized now: regular shifts with schedules mimeographed daily. There were enough men assigned to cover all the posts around the clock, and the big searchlights and generator truck were up from New York City so Devil's Needle was washed in light 24 hours a day.

Captain Delaney had a propane stove in his cottage now, and a heavy radio had been installed on the gate-keeper's counter. The radiomen had little to do and so, to occupy their time, had rigged up a loudspeaker, a timer, and a loop tape, so that every hour on the hour, the message went booming out mechanically: "Daniel Blank . . . Daniel Blank . . . come down . . . come down . . ." It did no good. By now no one expected it would.

Every morning Chief Forrest brought out bags of mail received at the Chilton Post Office, and Captain Delaney spent hours reading the letters. A few of them contained money sent to Daniel Blank, for what reason he could not guess. Blank also received a surprisingly large number of proposals of marriage from women; some included nude photos of the sender. But most of the letters, from all over the world, were suggestions on how to take Daniel Blank. Get four helicopters, each supporting the corner of a heavy cargo net, and drop the net over the top of Devil's Needle. Bring in a large group of "sincere religious people" and pray him down. Set up a giant electric fan and blow him off his rock. Most proposed a solution they had already rejected: send up a fighter plane or helicopter and kill him. One suggestion intrigued Captain Delaney: fire gas grenades onto the top of Devil's Needle and when Daniel Blank was unconscious, send up a climber in a gas mask to bring him down.

Captain Delaney wandered out that evening, telling himself he wanted to discuss the gas grenade proposal with one of the snipers. He walked down the worn path toward Devil's Needle, turned aside at the sniper's post. The three pale-faced men had improved their blind. They had dragged over a picnic table with attached benches. From somewhere, they had scrounged three burlap bags of sand—Chief Forrest had helped with that, Delaney guessed—and the bags were used as a bench rest for their rifles. The sniper could sit and be protected from the wind by canvas tarps tied to nearby trees.

The man on duty looked up as Delaney approached.

"Evening, Captain."

"Evening. How's it going?"

"Quiet."

Delaney knew that the three snipers didn't mix much with the other men. They were pariahs, as much as hangmen or executioners, but apparently it did not affect them, if they were aware of it. All three were tall, thin men, two from Kentucky, one from North Carolina. If Delaney felt any uneasiness with them, it was from their laconism rather than their chosen occupation.

"Happy New Year," the sniper said unexpectedly.

Delaney stared at him. "My God, is it?"

"Uh-huh. New Year's Eve."

"Well . . . Happy New Year to you. Forgot all about it."

The man was silent. The Captain glanced at the scope-fitted rifle resting on the sandbags.

"Springfield Oh-three," Delaney said. "Haven't seen one in years."

"Bought it from Army surplus," the man said, never taking his eyes from Devil's Needle.

"Sure," the Captain nodded. "Just like I bought my Colt Forty-five."

The man made a sound; the Captain hoped it was a laugh.

"Listen," Delaney said, "we got a suggestion, in the mail. You think there's any chance of putting a gas grenade up there?"

The sniper raised his eyes to the top of Devil's Needle. "Rifle or mortar?"

"Either."

"Not mortar. Rifle maybe. But it wouldn't stick. Skitter off or he'd kick it off."

"I guess so," Captain Delaney sighed. "We could clear the area and blanket it with gas, but the wind's too tricky."

"Uh-huh."

The Captain strolled away and only glanced once at that cathedral rock. Was he *really* up there? He had seen the day's photos—but could he trust them? The uneasiness returned.

He went back to the cottage, found a heavy envelope of reports a man coming on duty from Chilton had dropped off for him. They were from Sergeant MacDonald, copies of all the interrogations and statements of the people picked up in the continuing investigation. Delaney walked out to the van, got a paper cup of black coffee, brought it back. Then he sat down at his makeshift desk, pulled the gooseneck lamp closer, put on his heavy glasses, began reading the reports slowly.

He was looking for . . . what? Some explanation or lead or hint. What had turned Daniel G. Blank into a killer? Where and when did it begin? It was the motive he wanted, he needed. It wasn't good enough to use words like nut, crazy, insane, homosexual, psychopath. Just labels. There had to be more to it than that. There had to be something that could be comprehended, that might explain why this young man had deliberately murdered five people. And four of them strangers.

Because, Delaney thought angrily, if there was no explanation for it, then there was no explanation for anything.

It was almost two in the morning when he pulled on that crazy coat and wandered out again. The compound around the cottage was brilliantly lighted. So was the packed path through the black trees; so was the bleak column of Devil's Needle. As usual, there were men standing about, heads back, mouths gaping, eyes turned upward. Captain Delaney joined them without shame.

He opened himself to the crisp night, lightly moaning wind, stars that seemed holes punched in a black curtain beyond which shone a dazzling radiance. The shaft of Devil's Needle rose shimmering in light, smoothed by the glare. Was he up there? Was he *really* up there?

There came to Captain Edward X. Delaney such a compassion that he must close his mouth, bite his lower lip to keep from wailing aloud. Unbidden, unwanted even, he shared that man's passion, entered into him, knew his suffering. It was an unwelcome bond, but he could not deny it. The crime, the motive, the reason—all seemed unimportant now. What racked him was that lonely man, torn adrift. He wondered if that was why they all gathered here, at all hours, day and night. Was it to comfort the afflicted as best they might?

A few days later—was it three? It could have been four—

late in the afternoon, the daily envelope of aerial photos was delivered to Captain Delaney. Daniel G. Blank was lying naked on his rock, spread-eagled to the sky. The Captain looked, took a deep breath, turned his gaze away. Then, without looking again, he put the photos back into the envelope. He did not post one outside on the cottage wall.

Soon after, Major Samuel Barnes called.

"Delaney?"

"Yes."

"Barnes here. See the photos?"

"Yes."

"I don't think he can last much longer."

"No. Want to go up?"

"Not immediately. We'll check by air another day or so. Temperature's dropping."

"I know."

"No rush. We're getting a good press. Those bullhorn appeals are doing it. Everyone says we're doing all we can."

"Yes. All we can."

"Sure. But the weather's turning bad. A front moving in from the Great Lakes. Cloudy, windy, snow. Freezing. If we're socked in, we'll look like fools. I say January the sixth. In the morning. No matter what. How do you feel about it?"

"All right with me. The sooner the better. How do you want to do it: climber or 'copter?"

" 'Copter. Agreed?"

"Yes. That'll be best."

"All right. I'll start laying it on. I'll be over tomorrow and we'll talk. Shit, he's probably dead right now."

"Yes," Captain Delaney said. "Probably."

The world had become a song for Daniel Blank. A song. Soonnggg . . . Everything was singing. Not words, or even a tune. But an endless hum that filled his ears, vibrated so deep inside him that cells and particles of cells jiggled to that pleasing purr.

There was no thirst, no hunger and, best of all, there was no pain, none at all. For that he was thankful. He stared at a milky sky through filmed eyes almost closed by scratchy lids. The whiteness and the tuneless drone became one: a great oneness that went on forever, stretched him with a dreamy content.

He was happy he no longer heard his name shouted, happy he no longer saw a helicopter dipping and circling above his rock. But perhaps he had imagined those things; he had imagined so much: Celia Montfort was there once, wearing an African mask. Once he spoke to Tony. Once he saw a hunched, massive silhouette, lumbering away from him, dwindling. And once he embraced a man in a slow-motion dance that faded into milkiness before the ice ax struck, although he saw it raised.

But even these visions, all visions, disappeared; he was left only with an empty screen. Occasionally discs, whiter than white, floated into view, drifted, then went off, out of sight. They were nice to watch, but he was glad when they were gone.

He had a slowly diminishing apprehension of reality, but before weakness subdued his mind utterly, he felt his perception growing even as his senses faded. It seemed to him he had passed through the feel-taste-touch-smell-hear world and had emerged to this gentle purity with its celestial thrum, a world where everything was true and nothing was false.

There was, he now recognized with thanksgiving and delight, a logic to life, and this logic was beautiful. It was not the orderly logic of the computer, but was the unpredictable logic of birth, living, death. It was the mortality of one, and the immortality of all. It was all things, animate and inanimate, bound together in a humming whiteness.

It was an ecstasy to know that oneness, to understand, finally, that he was part of the slime and part of the stars. There was no Daniel Blank, no Devil's Needle, and never had been. There was only the continuum of life in which men and rocks, slime and stars, appear as seeds, grow a moment, and then are drawn back again into that timeless whole, continually beginning, continually ending.

He was saddened that he could not bring this final comprehension to others, describe to them the awful majesty of the certitude he had found: a universe of accident and possibility where a drop of water is no less than a moon, a passion no more than a grain of sand. All things are nothing, but all things are all. In his delirium, he could clutch that paradox to his heart, hug it, know it for truth.

He could feel life ebbing in him—*feel* it! It oozed away softly, no more than an invisible vapor rising from his wasted flesh, becoming part again of that oneness from whence it came. He died slowly, with love, for he was passing into another form; the process was so gentle that he could wonder why men cried out and fought.

Those discs of white on white appeared again to drift across his vision. He thought dimly there was a moisture on his face, a momentary tingle; he wondered if he might be weeping with joy.

It was only snow, but he did not know it. It covered him slowly, soothing the roughened skin, filling out the shrunken hollows of his body, hiding the seized joints and staring eyes.

Before the snow ended at dawn, he was a gently sculpted mound atop Devil's Needle. His shroud was white and without stain.

Late on the night of January 5th, Captain Delaney met with Major Samuel Barnes, Chief Forrest, Captain Sneed, the crew of the State Police helicopter, and the chief radioman. They all crowded into the gate-keeper's cottage; a uniformed guard was posted outside the door to keep curious reporters away.

Major Barnes had prepared a schedule, and handed around carbon copies.

"Before we get down to nuts-and-bolts," he said rapidly, "the latest weather advisory is this: Snow beginning at midnight, tapering off at dawn. Total accumulation about an inch and a half or two. Temperatures in the low thirties to upper twenties. Then, tomorrow morning, it should clear with temperatures rising to the middle thirties. Around noon, give or take an hour, the shit will really hit the fan, with a dropping barometer, temperature going way down, snow mixed with rain, hail, and sleet, and winds of twenty-five gusting to fifty.

"Beautiful," one of the pilots said. "I love it."

"So," Barnes went on, disregarding the interruption, "we have five or six hours to get him down. If we don't, the weather will murder us, maybe for days. This is a massive storm front moving in. All right, now look at your schedules. Take-off from the Newburgh field at nine ayem. I'll be aboard the 'copter. The flight down and final aerial reconnaissance completed by nine-thirty ayem, approximate. Lower a man to the top of Devil's Needle via cable and horse collar by ten ayem. Captain Delaney, you will be in command of ground operations here. This shack will be home base, radio coded Chilton One. The 'copter will be Chilton Two. The man going down will be Chilton Three. Everyone clear on that? Sneed, have your surgeon here at nine ayem. Forrest, can you bring out a local ambulance with attendants and a body bag?"

"Sure."

"I think Blank is dead, or at least unconscious. But if he's not, the man going down on the cable will be armed."

Captain Delaney looked up. "Who's Chilton Three?" he asked. "Who's going down on the cable?"

The three-man helicopter crew looked at each other. They were all young men, wearing sheepskin jackets over suntan uniforms, their feet in fleece-lined boots.

Finally the smallest man shrugged. "Shit, I'll go down," he said, rabbity face twisted into a tight grin. "I'm the lightest. I'll get the fucker."

"What's your name?" Delaney asked him.

"Farber, Robert H."

"You heard what the Major said, Farber. Blank is probably dead or unconscious. But there's no guarantee. He's already killed five people. If you get down there, and he makes any threatening movement—anything at all—grease him."

"Don't worry, Captain. If he as much as sneezes, he's a dead fucker."

"What will you carry?"

"What? Oh, you mean guns. My thirty-eight, I guess. Side holster. And I got a carbine."

Captain Delaney looked directly at Major Barnes. "I'd feel better if he carried more weight," he said. He turned back to Farber. "Can you handle a forty-five?" he asked.

"Sure, Captain. I was in the fuckin' Marine Corps."

"You can borrow mine, Bobby," one of the other pilots offered.

"And a shotgun rather than the carbine," Delaney said. "Loaded with buck."

"No problem," Major Barnes said.

"You really think I'll need all that fuckin' artillery?" Farber asked the Captain.

"No, I don't," Delaney said. "But the man was fast. So fast I can't tell you. Fast enough to take out one of my best men. But he's been up there a week now without food or water. If he's still alive, he won't be fast anymore. The heavy guns are just insurance. Don't hesitate to use them if you have to. Is that an order, Major Barnes?"

"Yes," Barnes nodded. "That's an order, Farber."

They discussed a few more details: briefing of the press, positioning of still and TV cameramen, parking of the ambulance, selection of men to stand by when Blank was brought down.

Finally, near midnight, the meeting broke up. Men shook hands, drifted away in silence. Only Delaney and the radioman were left in the cabin. The Captain wanted to call Barbara, but thought it too late; she'd probably be sleeping. He wanted very much to talk to her.

He spent a few minutes getting his gear together, stuffing reports, schedules, and memos into manila envelopes. If all went well in the morning, he'd be back in Manhattan by noon, leading his little squad of cops home again.

He hadn't realized how tired he was, how he longed for his own bed. Some of it was physical weariness: too many hours on his feet, muscles punished, nerves pulled and strained. But he also felt a spiritual exhaustion. This thing with Blank had gone on too long, had done too much to him.

Now, the last night, he pulled on cap and fur-lined greatcoat, plodded down to Devil's Needle for a final look. It was colder, no doubt of that, and the smell of snow was in the air. The sentries circling the base of the rock wore rubber ponchos over their sheepskin jackets; the sniper was huddled under a blanket, only the glowing end of a cigarette showing in black shadow. Captain Delaney stood a little apart from the few gawkers still there, still staring upward.

The gleaming pillar of Devil's Needle rose above him, probing the night sky, ghostly in the searchlight glare. About it, he thought he heard a faintly ululant wind, no louder than the cry of a distant child. He shivered inside his greatcoat: a chill of despair, a fear of something. It would have been easy, at that moment, to weep, but for what he could not have said.

It might, he thought dully, be despair for his own sins, for he suddenly knew he had sinned grievously, and the sin was pride. It was surely the most deadly; compared to pride, the other six seemed little more than physical excesses. But pride was a spiritual corruption and, worse, it had no boundaries, no limits, but could consume a man utterly.

In him, he knew, pride was not merely self-esteem, not just egotism. He knew his shortcomings better than anyone except, perhaps, his wife. His pride went beyond a satisfied self-respect; it was an arrogance, a presumption of moral superiority he brought to events, to people and, he supposed wryly, to God.

But now his pride was corroded by doubt. As usual, he had made a moral judgment—was that unforgivable for a cop?—and had brought Daniel G. Blank to this lonely death atop a cold rock. But what else could he have done?

There were, he now acknowledged sadly, several other courses that had been open to him if there had been a human softness in him, a sympathy for others, weaker than he, challenged by forces beyond their strength or control. He could have, for instance, sought a confrontation with Daniel Blank after he had discovered that damning evidence in the illegal search. Perhaps he could have convinced Blank to confess if he had, Celia Montfort would be alive tonight, and Blank would probably be in an asylum. The story this revealed would have meant the end of Captain Delaney's career, he supposed, but that no longer seemed of overwhelming importance.

Or he could have admitted the illegal search and at least attempted to obtain a search warrant. Or he could have resigned the job completely and left Blank's punishment to a younger, less introspective cop.

"Punishment." That was the key word. His damnable pride had driven him to making a moral judgment, and, having made it, he had to be cop, judge, jury. He had to play God; that's where his arrogance had led him.

Too many years as a cop. You started on the street, settling family squabbles, a Solomon in uniform; you ended hounding a man to his death because you knew him guilty and wanted him to suffer for his guilt. It was all pride, nothing but pride. Not the understandable, human pride of doing a difficult job well, but an overweening that led to judging, then to condemning, then to executing. Who would judge, condemn, and execute Captain Edward X. Delaney?

Something in his life had gone wrong, he now saw. He was not born with it. It did not come from genes, education, or environment, any more than Blank's homicidal mania had sprung from genes, education, or environment. But circumstances and chance had conspired to debase him, even as Daniel Blank had been perverted.

He did not know all things and would never know them; he saw that now. There were trends, currents, tides, accidents of such complexity that only an unthinking fool would say, "I am the master of my fate." Victim, Delaney thought. We are all victims, one way or another.

But, surprisingly, he did not feel this to be a gloomy concept, nor an excuse for licentious behavior. We are each dealt a hand at birth and play our cards as cleverly as we can, wasting no time lamenting that we received only one pair instead of a straight flush. The best man plays a successful game with a weak hand—bluffing, perhaps, when he has to—but staking everything, eventually, on what he's holding.

Captain Delaney thought now he had been playing a poor hand. His marriage had been a success, and so had his career. But he knew his failures . . . he knew. Somewhere along the way humanity had leaked out of him, compassion drained, pity became dry and withered. Whether it was too late to become something other than what he was, he did not know. He might try—but there were circumstance and chance to cope with and, as difficult, the habits and prejudices of more years than he cared to remember.

Uncertain, shaken, he stared upward at Devil's Needle, shaft toppling, world tilting beneath his tread. He was anxious and confused, sensing he had lost a certitude, wandered from a faith that, right or wrong, had supported him.

He felt something on his upturned face: a light, cold tingle of moisture. Tears? Just the first frail snowflakes. He could see them against the light: a fragile lacework. At that moment, almost hearing it, he knew the soul of Daniel Blank had escaped the flesh and gone winging away into the darkness, taking with it Captain Delaney's pride.

Shortly before dawn the snowfall dissolved into a freezing rain. Then that too ceased. When Captain Delaney came out on the porch at 8:30 a.m., the ground was a blinding diamond pavé; every black branch in sight was gloved with ice sparkling in the new sun.

He wore his greatcoat when he walked over to the van for black coffee and a doughnut. The air was clear, chill, almost unbearably sharp—like breathing ether. There was a chiselled quality to the day, and yet the world was not clear: a thin white scrim hung between sun and earth; the light was muted.

He went back to the shack and instructed the radioman to plug in an auxiliary microphone, a hand-held model with an extension cord so he could stand out on the porch, see the top of Devil's Needle above the skeleton trees, and communicate with Chilton Two and Chilton Three.

The ambulance rolled slowly into the compound. Chief Forrest climbed out, puffing, to direct its parking. A stretcher and body bag were removed; the two attendants went back into the warmth of the cab, smoking cigarettes. Captain Sneed showed a squad of ten men where they were to take up their positions, handling his duties with the solemnity of an officer arranging the defense of the Alamo. But Delaney didn't interfere; it made no difference. Finally Forrest and Sneed came up to join the Captain on the porch. They exchanged nods. Sneed looked at his watch. "Take-off about now," he said portentously.

Chief Forrest was the first to hear it. "Coming," he said, raised his old field glasses to his eyes, searched northward. A few minutes later Captain Delaney heard the fluttering throb of the helicopter and, shortly afterward, looking where Forrest was pointing, saw it descending slowly, beginning a tilted circle about Devil's Needle.

The radio crackled.

"Chilton One from Chilton Two. Do you read me?" It was Major Samuel Barnes' tight, rapid voice, partly muffled by the throb of rotors in the background.

"Loud and clear, Chilton Two," the radioman replied.

"Beginning descent and reconnaissance. Where is Captain Delaney?"

"Standing by with hand-held mike. On the porch. He can hear you."

"Top of rock covered with snow. Higher mound in the middle. I guess that's Blank. No movement. We're going down."

The men on the porch shielded their eyes from sun glare to stare upward. The 'copter, a noisy dragonfly, circled lower, then slowed, slipping sideways, hovered directly over the top of the rock.

"Chilton One from Chilton Two."

"We've got you, Chilton Two."

"No sign of life. No sign of anything. Our downdraft isn't moving the snow cover. Probably frozen over. We'll start the descent."

"Roger."

They watched the chopper hanging almost motionless in the air. They saw the wide cargo door open. It seemed a long time before a small figure appeared at the open door and stepped out into space, dangling from the cable, a padded leather horse collar around his chest, under his arms. The shotgun was held in his right hand; his left was on the radio strapped to his chest.

"Chilton One from Chilton Two. Chilton Three is now going down. We will stop at six feet for a radio check."

"Chilton Two from Chilton One. Delaney here. We can see you. Any movement on top of the rock?"

"None at all, Captain. Just an outline of a body. He's under the snow. Radio check now. Chilton Three from Chilton Two: How do you read?"

They watched the man dangling on the cable beneath the 'copter. He swung lazily in slow circles.

"Chilton Two from Chilton Three. I'm getting you loud and clear." Farber's voice was breathless, almost drowned in the rotor noise.

"Chilton Three from Chilton Two. Repeat, how do you read me?"

"Chilton Two, I said I was getting you loud and clear."

"Chilton Three from Chilton Two. Repeat, are you receiving me?"

Captain Delaney swore softly, moved his hand-held mike closer to his lips.

"Chilton Three from Chilton One. Do you read me?"

"Christ, yes, Chilton One. Loud and clear. What the hell's going on? Do you hear me?"

"Loud and clear, Chilton Three. I'll get right back to you. Chilton Two from Chilton One."

"Chilton Two here. Barnes speaking."

"Delaney here. Major, we're in communication with Chilton Three. He can read us and we're reading him. He can hear you, but apparently you're not getting him."

"Son of a bitch," Barnes said bitterly. "Let me try once more. Chilton Three from Chilton Two, do you read me? Acknowledge."

"Yes, I read you, Chilton Two, and I'm getting fuckin' cold."

"Chilton Two from Chilton One. We heard Chilton Three acknowledge. Did you get it?"

"Not a word," Barnes said grimly. "Well, we haven't got time to pull him back up and check out the goddamn radios. I'll relay all orders through you. Understood?"

"Understood," Delaney repeated. "Chilton Three from Chilton One. You are not being read by Chilton Two. But they read us. We'll relay all orders through Chilton One. Understood?"

"Understood, Chilton One. Who's this?"

"Captain Delaney."

"Captain, tell them to lower me down onto the fuckin' rock. I'm freezing my ass off up here."

"Chilton Two from Chilton One. Lower away."

They watched the swinging figure hanging from the cable. Suddenly it dropped almost three feet, then brought up with a jerk, Farber swinging wildly.

"Goddamn it!" he screamed. "Tell 'em to take it fuckin' easy up there. They almost jerked my fuckin' arms off."

Delaney didn't bother relaying that. He watched, and in a few minutes the cable began to run out slowly and smoothly. Farber came closer to the top of Devil's Needle.

"Chilton Three from Chilton One. Any movement?"

"No. Not a thing. Just snow. Mound in the middle. Snow drifted up along one side. I'm coming down. About ten feet. Tell them to slow. Slow the fuckin' winch, goddamn it!"

"Chilton Two from Chilton One. Farber is close. Slow the winch. Slow, slow."

"Roger, Chilton One. We see him. He's almost there. A little more. A little more . . ."

"Chilton Three here. I'm down. Feet are down."

"How much snow?"

"About an inch to three inches where it's drifted. I need more fuckin' cable slack to unshackle the horse collar."

"Chilton Two, Farber needs more cable slack."

"Roger."

"Okay, Chilton One. I've got it unsnapped. Tell them to get the fuck out of here; they're damn near blowing me off."

"Chilton Two, collar unshackled. You can take off."

The 'copter tilted and circled away, the cable slanting back beneath it. It began to make wide rings about Devil's Needle.

"Chilton Three, you there?" Delaney asked.

"I'm here. Where else?"

"Any sign of life?"

"Nothing. He's under the snow. Wait'll I get this fuckin' collar off."

"Is he breathing? Is the snow over his mouth melted? Is there a hole?"

"Don't see anything. He's covered completely with the fuckin' snow."

"Brush it off."

"What?"

"Brush the snow away. Brush all the snow off him."

"What with, Captain? I got no gloves."

"With your hands—what do you think? Use your hands. Scrape the snow and ice away."

They heard Farber's heavy breathing, the clang of shotgun on rock, some muffled curses.

"Chilton One from Chilton Two. What's going on?"

"He's brushing the snow away. Farber? Farber, how's it coming?"

"Captain, he's naked!"

Delaney took a deep breath and stared at Forrest and Sneed. But their eyes were on Devil's Needle.

"Yes, he's naked," he spoke into the mike as patiently as he could. "You knew that; you saw the photos. Now clean him off."

"Jesus, he's cold. And hard. So fuckin' hard. God, is he white."

"You got him cleaned off?"

"I—I'm—"

"What the hell's wrong?"

"I think I'm going to be sick."

"So be sick, you shithead!" Delaney roared. "Haven't you ever seen a dead man before?"

"Well . . . sure, Captain," the shaky voice came hesitantly, "but I never touched one."

"Well, touch him," Delaney shouted. "He's not going to bite you, for Chrissakes. Get his face cleaned off first."

"Yeah . . . face . . . sure . . . Jesus Christ."

"Now what?"

"His fuckin' eyes are open. He's looking right at me."

"You stupid sonofabitch," Delaney thundered into the mike. "Will you stop acting like an idiot slob and do your job like a man?"

"Chilton One from Chilton Two. Barnes here. What's the problem?"

"Farber's acting up," Delaney growled. "He doesn't enjoy touching the corpse."

"Do you have to rough him?"

"No, I don't," Delaney said. "I could sing lullabies to him. Do you want that stiff down or don't you?"

Silence.

"All right," Barnes said finally. "Do it your way. When I get down, you and I will have a talk."

"Any time, anywhere," Delaney said loudly, and saw that Forrest and Sneed were staring at him. "Now get off my back and let me talk to this infant. Farber, are you there? Farber?"

"Here," the voice came weakly.

"Have you got him brushed off?"

"Yes."

"Put your fingers on his chest. Lightly. See if you can pick up a heartbeat or feel any breathing. Well . . . ?"

After a moment: "No. Nothing, Captain."

"Put your cheek close to his lips."

"What?"

"Put. Your. Cheek. Close. To. His. Lips. Got that?"

"Well . . . sure . . ."

"See if you can feel any breath coming out."

"Jesus . . ."

"Well?"

"Nothing. Captain, this guy is dead, he's fuckin' *dead*."

"All right. Get the horse collar on him, up around his chest, under his arms. Make sure the shackle connection is upward."

They waited, all of them on the porch now straining their eyes to the top of Devil's Needle. So were all the men in the compound, sentries, snipers, reporters. Still and TV cameras were trained on the rock. There was remarkably little noise, Delaney noted, and little movement. Everyone was caught in the moment, waiting. . . .

"Farber?" Delaney called into his mike. "Farber, are you getting the collar on him?"

"I can't," the voice came wavering. "I just can't."

"What's wrong now?"

"Well . . . he's all spread out, Captain. His arms are out wide to his sides, and his legs are spread apart. Jesus, he's got no cock at all."

"Screw his cock!" Delaney shouted furiously. "Forget his cock. Forget his arms. Just get his feet together and slip the collar over them and up his body."

"I can't," the voice came back, and they caught the note of panic. "I just can't."

Delaney took a deep breath. "Listen, you shit-gutted bastard, you volunteered for this job. 'I'll bring the fucker down,' you said. All right, you're up there. Now bring the fucker down. Get his ankles together."

"Captain, he's cold and stiff as a board."

"Oh no," Captain Edward X. Delaney said. "Cold and stiff as a board, is he? Isn't it a shame this isn't the middle of July and you could pick him up with a shovel and a blotter. You're a cop, aren't you? What the hell do you think they pay you for? To clean up the world's garbage—right? Now listen, you milk-livered sonofabitch, you get working on those legs and get them together."

There was silence for a few moments. Delaney saw that Captain Bertram Sneed had turned away, walked to the other end of the porch He was gripping the railing tightly, staring off in the opposite direction.

"Captain?" Farber's voice came faintly.

"I'm here. How you coming with the legs?"

"Not so good, Captain. I can move the legs a little, but I think he's stuck. His skin is stuck to the fuckin' rock."

"Sure it is," Delaney said, his voice suddenly soft and encouraging now. "It's frozen to the rock. Of course it would be. Just pull the legs together slowly, son. Don't think about the skin. Work the legs back and forth."

"Well . . . all right . . . Oh God."

They waited. Delaney took advantage of the pause to pull off his coat. He looked around, then Chief Forrest took it from him. The Captain realized he was soaked with sweat; he could feel it running down his ribs.

"Captain?"

"I'm here, son."

"Some of the skin on his legs and ass came off. Patches stuck to the fuckin' rock."

"Don't worry about it. He didn't feel a thing. Got his ankles together?"

"Yes. Pretty good. Close enough to get through the collar."

"Fine. You're doing just fine. Now move his whole body back and forth, side to side. Rock him so his body comes free from the stone."

"Oh Jesus . . ." Farber gasped, and they knew he was weeping now. They didn't look at each other.

"He's all shrunk," Farber moaned. "All shrunk and his belly is puffed up."

"Don't look at him," Delaney said. "Just keep working. Keep moving him. Get him loose."

"Yes. All right. He's loose now. He didn't lose much skin."

"Good. You're doing great. Now get that horse collar on him. Can you lift his legs?"

"Oh sure. Christ, he don't weigh a thing. He's a skeleton. His arms are still out straight to the sides."

"That's all right. No problem there. Where's the collar?"

"Working it upward. Wait a minute . . . Okay. There. It's in position. Under his arms."

"He won't slip through?"

"No chance. His fuckin' arms go straight out."

"Ready for the 'copter?"

"Jesus, yes!"

"Chilton Two from Chilton One."

"Chilton Two. Loud and clear. Barnes here."

"The collar is on the body. You can pick up."

"Roger. Going in."

574

"Farber? Farber, are you there?"

"I'm still here, Captain."

"The 'copter is coming over for the pickup. Do me a favor, will you?"

"What's that, Captain?"

"Feel around under the snow and see if you can find an ice ax. It's about the size of a hammer, but it has a long pick on one side of the head. I'd like to have it."

"I'll take a look. And do me a favor, Captain."

"What?"

"After they pick him up and land him, make sure they come back for me. I don't like this fuckin' place."

"Don't worry," Delaney assured him. "They'll come back for you. I promise."

He watched until he saw the helicopter throttling down, moving slowly toward the top of Devil's Needle. He walked back inside to place his microphone on the radioman's counter. Then he took a deep breath, looked with wonder at his trembling hands. He went outside again, down the steps, into the compound. The photographers were busy now, lens turned to the 'copter hovering over Devil's Needle.

Delaney stood in the snow, his cap squarely atop his head, choker collar hooked up. Like the others, his head was tilted back, eyes turned upward, mouth agape. They waited. Then they heard the powered roar of the rotors as the 'copter rose swiftly, tilted, circled, came heading toward them.

At the end of the swinging cable, Daniel G. Blank hung in the horse collar. It was snug under his outstretched arms. His head was flung back in a position of agony. His ankles were close together. His shrunken body was water-white, all knobs and bruises.

The helicopter came lower. They saw the shaved skull, the purpled wounds where skin had torn away. The strange bird floated, dangling. Then, suddenly, caught against the low sun, there was a nimbus about the flesh, a luminous radiation that flared briefly and died as the body came back to earth.

Delaney turned, walked away. He felt a hand on his shoulder, stopped, turned to see Smokey the Bear.

"Well," Captain Sneed grinned, "we got him, didn't we?"

Delaney shrugged off that heavy hand and continued to walk, his back to the thunder of the descending 'copter.

"God help us all," Captain Edward X. Delaney said aloud. But no one heard him.

Epilogue

In the months after the events recounted here, the following occurred:

Christopher Langley and the Widow Zimmerman were wed, in a ceremony attended with great pleasure by Captain Delaney. The happy newlyweds moved to Sarasota, Florida.

Calvin Case, with the assistance of a professional writer, produced a book called "Basic Climbing Techniques." It had a modest but encouraging sale, and seems on its way to becoming a manual of Alpinism. Case is currently working on a second book: "The World's Ten Toughest Climbs."

Anthony (Tony) Montfort rejoined his parents in Europe. The whereabouts of Valenter is presently unknown.

Charles Lipsky became involved in a criminal ring forging welfare checks and is currently being held for trial.

Samuel and Florence Morton opened the first of a chain of "health clubs" featuring mixed nude swimming. They are under indictment for "maintaining a public nuisance," but are free on bail pending trial.

Former Deputy Commissioner Broughton was defeated in the primary to select his party's candidate for mayor of New York City. He is attempting to form a new political party based on the promise of "law and order."

Former Lt. Marty Dorfman passed the examination for captain, and was appointed Legal Officer of the Patrol Division.

Lt. Jeri Fernandez, Sergeant MacDonald, and Detective Blankenship received commendations.

Reporter Thomas Handry, apparently giving up hopes of becoming a poet, has been reassigned to his newspaper's Washington Bureau.

Dr. Sanford Ferguson was killed in an automobile accident early one morning when returning to his home from a visit to his mistress.

Deputy Mayor Herman Alinski is still Deputy Mayor. Former Inspector Johnson and former Deputy Inspector Thorsen have both been promoted one rank.

Captain Edward X. Delaney was jumped to Inspector and made Chief of the Detective Division. About a month after the death of Daniel Blank, Barbara Delaney died from Proteus infection. After a year's period of mourning, Inspector Delaney married the former Monica Gilbert. Mrs. Delaney is pregnant.

576